ACCLAIM FOR STEPHEN KING'S
DARK TOWER SERIES

THE GUNSLINGER

"An impressive work of mythic magnitude. May turn out to be
Stephen King's greatest literary achievement."
—*Atlanta Journal-Constitution*

"Brilliant, fresh and compelling . . . will leave you panting for more."
—*Booklist*

THE DRAWING OF THE THREE

"This quest is one of King's best . . . communication on a genuine
human level . . . but rich in symbolism and allegory."
—*Columbus Sunday Dispatch*

"Prime King . . . very suspenseful. An epic in the making."
—*Kirkus Reviews*

THE WASTE LANDS

"Gripping, compelling . . . King mesmerizing the reader."
—*Chicago Sun-Times*

"Splendidly tense—rip-roaring."
—*Publishers Weekly*

·STEPHEN KING·

THE WASTE LANDS

THE DARK TOWER III

ILLUSTRATED BY
NED DAMERON

Ⓟ

A PLUME BOOK

PLUME

Published by the Penguin Group
Penguin Putnam Inc., 375 Hudson Street, New York, New York 10014, U.S.A.
Penguin Books Ltd, 27 Wrights Lane, London W8 5TZ, England
Penguin Books Australia Ltd, Ringwood, Victoria, Australia
Penguin Books Canada Ltd, 10 Alcorn Avenue,
Toronto, Ontario, Canada M4V 3B2
Penguin Books (N.Z.) Ltd, 182-190 Wairau Road, Auckland 10, New Zealand

Penguin Books Ltd, Registered Offices: Harmondsworth, Middlesex, England

Published by Plume, an imprint of Dutton Signet, a member of Penguin Putnam Inc.
Originally published in a limited edition by Donald M. Grant, Publisher, Inc.,
West Kingston, Rhode Island.

First Plume Printing, January, 1992
3 5 7 9 11 13 14 12 10 8 6 4

"Velcro Fly" written by Billy Gibbons, Frank Beard and Dusty Hill copyright © 1985 by Hamstein Music Co.
All rights reserved. Used by permission.

Paint It Black written by Mick Jagger and Keith Richards copyright © 1966 by ABKCO Music, Inc.
All rights reserved. Used by permission.

Excerpts from "The Waste Land" in Collected Poems 1909–1962 by T. S. Eliot, copyright 1936 by Harcourt
Brace Jovanovich, Inc., copyright © 1964, 1963 by T. S. Eliot, reprinted by permission of the publisher.

Excerpt from "Hand in Glove" by Robert Aickman used by permission of the author's agent, the Kirby
McCauley Literary Agency.

 REGISTERED TRADEMARK—MARCA REGISTRADA

Library of Congress Cataloging-in-Publication Data:

King, Stephen.
    The waste lands / Stephen King : illustrated by Ned Dameron.
        p.   cm. — (The Dark tower : 3)
    ISBN 0-452-27962-3
    I. Title. II. Series: King, Stephen. Dark tower : 3.
PS3561.I483W37   1992
813'.54—dc20   91-32460
                                                         CIP

Printed in the United States of America
Designed by Steven N. Stathakis

This third volume of the tale
is gratefully dedicated to my son
OWEN PHILIP KING:
Khef, Ka, and *Ka-tet.*

CONTENTS

ILLUSTRATIONS

ARGUMENT

The Waste Lands is the third volume of a longer tale inspired by and to some degree dependent upon Robert Browning's narrative poem "Childe Roland to the Dark Tower Came."

The first volume, *The Gunslinger*, tells how Roland, the last gunslinger in a world which has "moved on," pursues and finally catches the man in black, a sorcerer named Walter who falsely claimed the friendship of Roland's father in the days when the unity of Mid-World still held. Catching this half-human spell-caster is not Roland's ultimate goal but only another landmark along the road to the powerful and mysterious Dark Tower, which stands at the nexus of time.

Who, exactly, is Roland? What was his world like before it moved on? What is the Tower and why does he pursue it? We have only fragmentary answers. Roland is clearly a kind of knight, one of those charged with holding (or possibly redeeming) a world Roland remembers as being "filled with love and light." Just how closely Roland's memory resembles the way that world actually was is very much open to question, however.

We *do* know that he was forced to an early trial of manhood after discovering that his mother had become the mistress of Marten, a much greater sorcerer than Walter; we know that Marten orchestrated Roland's discovery of his mother's affair, expecting Roland to fail his test of manhood and to be "sent West" into the wastes; we know that Roland laid Marten's plans at nines by passing the test.

We also know that the gunslinger's world is related to our own in some strange but fundamental way, and that passage between the worlds is sometimes possible.

At a way station on a long-deserted coach-road running through the desert, Roland meets a boy named Jake who died in our world, a boy who was, in fact, pushed from a mid-Manhattan street corner and into the path of an oncoming car. Jake Chambers died with the man in black—Walter—peering down at him, and awoke in Roland's world.

Before they reach the man in black, Jake dies again . . . this time because the gunslinger, faced with the second most agonizing choice of his life, elects to sacrifice this symbolic son. Given a choice between the Tower and the child, Roland chooses the Tower. Jake's last words to the gunslinger before plunging into the abyss are: "Go, then—there are other worlds than these."

The final confrontation between Roland and Walter occurs in a dusty golgotha of decaying bones. The man in black tells Roland's future with a deck of Tarot cards. Three *very* strange cards—The Prisoner, The Lady of the Shadows, and Death ("but not for you, gunslinger")—are called especially to Roland's attention.

The second volume, *The Drawing of the Three*, begins on the edge of the Western Sea not long after Roland's confrontation with Walter has ended. An exhausted gunslinger awakes in the middle of the night to discover that the incoming tide has brought a horde of crawling, carnivorous creatures—"lobstrosities"—with it. Before he can escape their limited range, Roland has been seriously wounded by these creatures, losing the first two fingers of his right hand to them. He is also poisoned by the venom of the lobstrosities, and as the gunslinger resumes his journey north along the edge of the Western Sea, he is sickening . . . perhaps dying.

He encounters three doors standing freely upon the beach. Each door opens—for Roland and Roland alone—upon our world; upon the city where Jake lived, in fact. Roland visits New York at three points along our time continuum, both in an effort to save his own life and to draw the three who must accompany him on his road to the Tower.

Eddie Dean is *The Prisoner*, a heroin addict from the New York of the late 1980s. Roland steps through the door on the beach of his world and into Eddie Dean's mind as Eddie, serving a man named Enrico Balazar as a cocaine mule, lands at JFK airport. In the course of their harrowing adventures together, Roland is able to obtain a limited quantity of penicillin and to bring Eddie Dean back to his own world. Eddie, a junkie who discovers he has been kidnapped to a world where there is no junk (or Popeye's fried chicken, for that matter), is less than overjoyed to be there.

The second door leads Roland to *The Lady of the Shadows*—actually *two* women in one body. This time Roland finds himself in the New York of the early 1960s and face to face with a young wheelchair-bound civil-rights activist named Odetta Holmes. The woman hidden inside Odetta is the crafty and hate-filled Detta Walker. When this double woman is pulled into Roland's world, the results are volatile for Eddie and the rapidly sickening gunslinger. Odetta believes that what's happening to her is either a dream or a delusion; Detta, a much more brutally direct intellect, simply dedicates herself to the task of killing Roland and Eddie whom she sees as torturing white devils.

Jack Mort, a serial killer hiding behind the third door (the New York of the mid-1970s), is *Death*. Mort has twice caused great changes in the life of Odetta Holmes/Detta Walker, although neither of them knows it. Mort, whose *modus operandi* is to either push his victims or drop something on them from above, has done both to Odetta during the course of his mad (but oh so careful) career. When Odetta was a child, he dropped a brick on her head, sending the little girl into a coma and also occasioning the birth of Detta Walker, Odetta's hidden sister. Years later, in 1959, Mort encounters Odetta again and pushes her into the path of an oncoming subway train in Greenwich Village. Odetta survives Mort again, but at a price: the oncoming train severed both legs at the knee. Only the presence of a heroic young doctor (and, perhaps, the ugly but indomitable spirit of Detta Walker) saves her life . . . or so it would seem. To Roland's eye, these interrelationships suggest a power greater than mere coincidence; he believes the titantic forces which surround the Dark Tower have begun to gather once again.

Roland learns that Mort may stand at the heart of another mystery as well, one which is also a potentially mind-destroying paradox. For the victim Mort is stalking at the time the gunslinger steps into his life is none other than Jake, the boy Roland met at the way station and lost under the mountains. Roland has never had any cause to doubt Jake's story of how he died in our world, or any cause to question who Jake's murderer was—Walter, of course. Jake saw him dressed as a priest as the crowd gathered around the spot where he lay dying, and Roland has never doubted the description.

Nor does he doubt it now; Walter was there, oh yes, no doubt about that. *But suppose it was Jack Mort, not Walter, who pushed Jake into the path of the oncoming Cadillac?* Is such a thing possible? Roland can't say, not for sure, but if that *is* the case, where is Jake now? Dead? Alive?

Caught somewhere in time? And if Jake Chambers is still alive and well in his own world of Manhattan in the mid-1970s, *how is it that Roland still remembers him?*

Despite this confusing and possibly dangerous development, the test of the doors—and the drawing of the three—ends in success for Roland. Eddie Dean accepts his place in Roland's world because he has fallen in love with The Lady of the Shadows. Detta Walker and Odetta Holmes, the other two of Roland's three, are driven together into one personality combining elements of both Detta and Odetta when the gunslinger is finally able to force the two personalities to acknowledge each other. This hybrid is able to accept and return Eddie's love. Odetta Susannah Holmes and Detta Susannah Walker thus become a new woman, a *third* woman: Susannah Dean.

Jack Mort dies beneath the wheels of the same subway—that fabled A-train—which took Odetta's legs fifteen or sixteen years before. No great loss there.

And for the first time in untold years, Roland of Gilead is no longer alone in his quest for the Dark Tower. Cuthbert and Alain, his lost companions of yore, have been replaced by Eddie and Susannah . . . but the gunslinger has a way of being bad medicine for his friends. Very bad medicine, indeed.

The Waste Lands takes up the story of these three pilgrims on the face of Mid-World some months after the confrontation by the final door on the beach. They have moved some fair way inland. The period of rest is ending, and a period of learning has begun. Susannah is learning to shoot . . . Eddie is learning to carve . . . and the gunslinger is learning how it feels to lose one's mind, a piece at a time.

(One further note: My New York readers will know that I have taken certain geographical liberties with the city. For these I hope I may be forgiven.)

A heap of broken images, where the sun beats,
And the dead tree gives no shelter, the cricket no relief,
And the dry stone no sound of water. Only
There is shadow under this red rock,
(Come in under the shadow of this red rock),
And I will show you something different from either
Your shadow in the morning striding behind you
Or your shadow at evening rising to meet you;
I will show you fear in a handful of dust.

—T. S. ELIOT
"The Waste Land"

If there pushed any ragged thistle-stalk
    Above its mates, the head was chopped; the bents
    Were jealous else. What made those holes and rents
In the dock's harsh swarth leaves, bruised as to balk
All hope of greenness? 'tis a brute must walk
    Pashing their life out, with a brute's intents.

—ROBERT BROWNING
"Childe Roland to the Dark Tower Came"

"What river is it?" enquired Millicent idly.
"It's only a stream. Well, perhaps a little more than that.
 It's called the Waste."
"Is it really?"
"Yes," said Winifred, "it is."

—ROBERT AICKMAN
"Hand in Glove"

■ BOOK ONE ■
JAKE

FEAR IN A HANDFUL OF DUST

I ▪ BEAR AND
BONE

▪ I ▪

BEAR AND BONE

1

IT WAS HER THIRD time with live ammunition . . . and her first time on the draw from the holster Roland had rigged for her.

They had plenty of live rounds; Roland had brought back better than three hundred from the world where Eddie and Susannah Dean had lived their lives up until the time of their drawing. But having ammunition in plenty did not mean it could be wasted; quite the contrary, in fact. The gods frowned upon wastrels. Roland had been raised, first by his father and then by Cort, his greatest teacher, to believe this, and so he still believed. Those gods might not punish at once, but sooner or later the penance would have to be paid . . . and the longer the wait, the greater the weight.

At first there had been no need for live ammunition, anyway. Roland had been shooting for more years than the beautiful brown-skinned woman in the wheelchair would believe. He had corrected her at first simply by watching her aim and dry-fire at the targets he had set up. She learned fast. Both she and Eddie learned fast.

As he had suspected, both were born gunslingers.

Today Roland and Susannah had come to a clearing less than a mile from the camp in the woods which had been home to them for almost two months now. The days had passed with their own sweet similarity. The gunslinger's body healed itself while Eddie and Susannah learned the things the gunslinger had to teach them: how to shoot, to hunt, to gut and clean what they had killed; how to first stretch, then tan and cure the hides of those kills; how to use as much as it was possible to use so that no part of the animal was wasted; how to find north by Old Star or south by Old Mother; how to listen to the forest in which they now found themselves, sixty miles or more northeast of the Western Sea. Today Eddie had stayed behind, and the gunslinger was not put out of countenance by this. The lessons which are remembered the longest, Roland knew, are always the ones that are self-taught.

But what had always been the most important lesson was still most important: how to shoot and how to hit what you shot at every time. How to kill.

The edges of this clearing had been formed by dark, sweet-smelling fir trees that curved around it in a ragged semicircle. To the south, the ground broke off and dropped three hundred feet in a series of crumbling shale ledges and fractured cliffs, like a giant's set of stairs. A clear stream ran out of the woods and across the center of the clearing, first bubbling through a deep channel in the spongy earth and friable stone, then pouring across the splintery rock floor which sloped down to the place where the land dropped away.

The water descended the steps in a series of waterfalls and made any number of pretty, wavering rainbows. Beyond the edge of the drop-off was a magnificent deep valley, choked with more firs and a few great old elm trees which refused to be crowded out. These latter towered green and lush, trees which might have been old when the land from which Roland had come was yet young; he could see no sign that the valley had ever burned, although he supposed it must have drawn lightning at some time or other. Nor would lightning have been the only danger. There had been people in this forest in some distant time; Roland had come across their leavings on several occasions over the past weeks. They were primitive artifacts, for the most part, but they included shards of pottery which could only have been cast in fire. And fire was evil stuff that delighted in escaping the hands which created it.

Above this picturebook scene arched a blameless blue sky in which a few crows circled some miles off, crying in their old, rusty voices. They seemed restless, as if a storm were on the way, but Roland had sniffed the air and there was no rain in it.

A boulder stood to the left of the stream. Roland had set up six chips of stone on top of it. Each one was heavily flecked with mica, and they glittered like lenses in the warm afternoon light.

"Last chance," the gunslinger said. "If that holster's uncomfortable—

even the slightest bit—tell me now. We didn't come here to waste ammunition."

She cocked a sardonic eye at him, and for a moment he could see Detta Walker in there. It was like hazy sunlight winking off a bar of steel. "What would you do if it *was* uncomfortable and I didn't tell you? If I missed all six of those itty bitty things? Whop me upside the head like that old teacher of yours used to do?"

The gunslinger smiled. He had done more smiling these last five weeks than he had done in the five years which had come before them. "I can't do that, and you know it. We were children, for one thing— children who hadn't been through our rites of manhood yet. You may slap a child to correct him, or her, but—"

"In my world, whoppin the kiddies is also frowned on by the better class of people," Susannah said dryly.

Roland shrugged. It was hard for him to imagine that sort of world— did not the Great Book say "Spare not the birch so you spoil not the child"?—but he didn't believe Susannah was lying. "Your world has not moved on," he said. "Many things are different there. Did I not see for myself that it is so?"

"I guess you did."

"In any case, you and Eddie are not children. It would be wrong for me to treat you as if you were. And if tests were needed, you both passed them."

Although he did not say so, he was thinking of how it had ended on the beach, when she had blown three of the lumbering lobstrosities to hell before they could peel him and Eddie to the bone. He saw her answering smile and thought she might be remembering the same thing.

"So what you goan do if I shoot fo' shit?"

"I'll look at you. I think that's all I'll need to do."

She thought this over, then nodded. "Might be."

She tested the gunbelt again. It was slung across her bosom almost like a shoulder-holster (an arrangement Roland thought of as a docker's clutch) and looked simple enough, but it had taken many weeks of trial and error—and a great deal of tailoring—to get it just right. The belt and the revolver which cocked its eroded sandalwood grip out of the ancient oiled holster had once been the gunslinger's; the holster had hung on his right hip. He had spent much of the last five weeks coming to realize it was never going to hang there again. Thanks to the lobstrosities, he was strictly a lefthanded gun now.

"So how is it?" he asked again.

This time she laughed up at him. "Roland, this ole gunbelt's as com'fable as it's ever gonna be. Now do you want me to shoot or are we just going to sit and listen to crowmusic from over yonder?"

He felt tension worming sharp little fingers under his skin now, and he supposed Cort had felt much the same at times like this under his gruff, bluff exterior. He wanted her to be good . . . *needed* her to be good. But to show how badly he wanted and needed—that could lead to disaster.

"Tell me your lesson again, Susannah."

She sighed in mock exasperation . . . but as she spoke her smile faded and her dark, beautiful face became solemn. And from her lips he heard the old catechism again, made new in her mouth. He had never expected to hear these words from a woman. How natural they sounded . . . yet how strange and dangerous, as well.

" 'I do not aim with my hand; she who aims with her hand has forgotten the face of her father.

" 'I aim with my eye.

" 'I do not shoot with my hand; she who shoots with her hand has forgotten the face of her father.

" 'I shoot with my mind.

" 'I do not kill with my gun—' "

She broke off and pointed at the mica-shiny stones on the boulder. "I'm not going to kill anything anyhow—they're just itty bitty *rocks*."

Her expression—a little haughty, a little naughty—suggested that she expected Roland to be exasperated with her, perhaps even angry. Roland, however, had been where she was now; he had not forgotten that apprentice gunslingers were fractious and high-spirited, nervy and apt to bite exactly at the wrong moment . . . and he had discovered an unexpected capacity in himself. He could teach. More, he *liked* to teach, and he found himself wondering, from time to time, if that had been true of Cort, as well. He guessed that it had been.

Now more crows began to call raucously, these from the forest behind them. Some part of Roland's mind registered the fact that the new cries were agitated rather than merely quarrelsome; these birds sounded as if they had been scared up and away from whatever they had been feeding on. He had more important things to think about than whatever it was that had scared a bunch of crows, however, so he simply filed the information away and refocused his concentration on Susannah. To do otherwise with a 'prentice was to ask for a second, less playful bite. And who would be to blame for that? Who but the teacher? For was he not training her to bite? Training *both* of them to bite? Wasn't that what a gunslinger was, when you stripped off the few stern lines of ritual and stilled the few iron grace-notes of catechism? Wasn't he (or she) only a human hawk, trained to bite on command?

"No," he said. "They're not rocks."

She raised her eyebrows a little and began to smile again. Now that she saw he wasn't going to explode at her as he sometimes did when she was slow or fractious (or at least not *yet*), her eyes again took on the mocking sun-on-steel glint he associated with Detta Walker. "They ain't?" The teasing in her voice was still good-natured, but he thought it would turn mean if he let it. She was tense, keyed up, her claws already halfway out of their sheaths.

"No, they *ain't*," he said, returning her mockery. His own smile began to return, but it was hard and humorless. "Susannah, do you remember the *honk mahfahs*?"

Her smile began to fade.

"The *honk mahfahs* in Oxford Town?"

Her smile was gone.

"Do you remember what the *honk mahfahs* did to you and your friends?"

"That wasn't *me*," she said. "That was another woman." Her eyes had taken on a dull, sullen cast. He hated that look, but he also liked it just fine. It was the *right* look, the one that said the kindling was burning well and soon the bigger logs would start to catch.

"Yes. It was. Like it or not, it was Odetta Susannah Holmes, daughter of Sarah Walker Holmes. Not you as you *are*, but you as you *were*. Remember the fire-hoses, Susannah? Remember the gold teeth, how you saw them when they used the hoses on you and your friends in Oxford? How you saw them twinkle when they laughed?"

She had told them these things, and many others, over many long nights as the campfire burned low. The gunslinger hadn't understood everything, but he had listened carefully, just the same. And remembered. Pain was a tool, after all. Sometimes it was the best tool.

"What's wrong with you, Roland? Why you want to go recallin that trash in my mind?"

Now the sullen eyes glinted at him dangerously; they reminded him of Alain's eyes when good-natured Alain was finally roused.

"Yonder stones are those men," Roland said softly. "The men who locked you in a cell and left you to foul yourself. The men with the clubs and the dogs. The men who called you a nigger cunt."

He pointed at them, moving his finger from left to right.

"There's the one who pinched your breast and laughed. There's the one who said he better check and see if you had something stuffed up your ass. There's the one who called you a chimpanzee in a five-hundred-dollar dress. That's the one that kept running his billyclub over the spokes of your wheelchair until you thought the sound would send you mad. There's the one who called your friend Leon *pinko-fag*. And the one on the end, Susannah, is Jack Mort.

"There. Those stones. *Those men*."

She was breathing rapidly now, her bosom rising and falling in swift little jerks beneath the gunslinger's gunbelt with its heavy freight of bullets. Her eyes had left him; they were looking at the mica-flecked chips of stone. Behind them and at some distance, a tree splintered and fell over. More crows called in the sky. Deep in the game which was no longer a game, neither of them noticed.

"Oh yeah?" she breathed. "That so?"

"It is. Now say your lesson, Susannah Dean, and be true."

This time the words fell from her lips like small chunks of ice. Her right hand trembled lightly on the arm of her wheelchair like an idling engine.

" 'I do not aim with my hand; she who aims with her hand has forgotten the face of her father.

" 'I aim with my eye.' "

"Good."

" 'I do not shoot with my hand; she who shoots with her hand has forgotten the face of her father.

" 'I shoot with my mind.' "

"So it has ever been, Susannah Dean."

" 'I do not kill with my gun; she who kills with her gun has forgotten the face of her father.

" 'I kill with my heart.' "

"Then KILL them, for your father's sake!" Roland shouted. *"KILL THEM ALL!"*

Her right hand was a blur between the arm of the chair and the butt of Roland's sixgun. It was out in a second, her left hand descending, fanning at the hammer in flutters almost as swift and delicate as the wing of a hummingbird. Six flat cracks pealed off across the valley, and five of the six chips of stone set atop the boulder blinked out of existence.

For a moment neither of them spoke—did not even breathe, it seemed—as the echoes rolled back and forth, dimming. Even the crows were silent, at least for the time being.

The gunslinger broke the silence with four toneless yet oddly emphatic words: "It is very well."

Susannah looked at the gun in her hand as if she had never seen it before. A tendril of smoke rose from the barrel, perfectly straight in the windless silence. Then, slowly, she returned it to the holster below her bosom.

"Good, but not perfect," she said at last. "I missed one."

"Did you?" He walked over to the boulder and picked up the remaining chip of stone. He glanced at it, then tossed it to her.

She caught it with her left; her right stayed near the holstered gun, he saw with approval. She shot better and more naturally than Eddie, but had not learned this particular lesson as swiftly as Eddie had done.

If she had been with them during the shootout at Balazar's nightclub,
she might have. Now, Roland saw, she was at last learning that, too. She
looked at the stone and saw the notch, barely a sixteenth of an inch deep,
in its upper corner.

"You only clipped it," Roland said, returning to her, "but in a
shooting scrape, sometimes that's all you need. If you clip a fellow,
throw his aim off . . ." He paused. "Why are you looking at me that
way?"

"You don't know, do you? You really don't?"

"No. Your mind is often closed to me, Susannah."

There was no defensiveness in his voice, and Susannah shook her
head in exasperation. The rapid turn-and-turn-about dance of her personality sometimes unnerved him; his seeming inability to say anything other
than exactly what was on his mind never failed to do the same to her.
He was the most *literal* man she had ever met.

"All right," she said, "I'll *tell* you why I'm looking at you that way,
Roland. Because what you did was a mean trick. You said you wouldn't
slap me, *couldn't* slap me, even if I cut up rough . . . but either you lied
or you're very stupid, and I *know* you ain't stupid. People don't always
slap with their hands, as every man and woman of my race could testify.
We have a little rhyme where I come from: 'Sticks and stones will break
my bones—' "

" '—yet taunts shall never wound me,' " Roland finished.

"Well, that's not exactly the way we say it, but I guess it's close
enough. It's bullshit no matter how you say it. They don't call what you
did a tongue-lashing for nothing. Your words *hurt* me, Roland—are you
gonna stand there and say you didn't know they would?"

She sat in her chair, looking up at him with bright, stern curiosity,
and Roland thought—not for the first time—that the *honk mahfahs* of
Susannah's land must have been either very brave or very stupid to cross
her, wheelchair or no wheelchair. And, having walked among them, he
didn't think bravery was the answer.

"I did not think or care about your hurt," he said patiently. "I saw
you show your teeth and knew you meant to bite, so I put a stick in your
jaws. And it worked . . . didn't it?"

Her expression was now one of hurt astonishment. "You *bastard!*"

Instead of replying, he took the gun from her holster, fumbled the
cylinder open with the remaining two fingers on his right hand, and
began to reload the chambers with his left hand.

"Of all the high-handed, arrogant—"

"You *needed* to bite," he said in that same patient tone. "Had you
not, you would have shot all wrong—with your hand and your gun instead
of your eye and mind and heart. Was that a trick? Was it arrogant? I

think not. I think, Susannah, that *you* were the one with arrogance in her heart. I think *you* were the one with a mind to get up to tricks. That doesn't distress me. Quite the opposite. A gunslinger without teeth is no gunslinger."

"Damn it, I'm *not* a gunslinger!"

He ignored that; he could afford to. If she was no gunslinger, then he was a billy-bumbler. "If we were playing a game, I might have behaved differently. But this is no game. It . . ."

His good hand went to his forehead for a moment and paused there, fingers tented just above the left temple. The tips of the fingers, she saw, were trembling minutely.

"Roland, what's ailing you?" she asked quietly.

The hand lowered slowly. He rolled the cylinder back into place and replaced the revolver in the holster she wore. "Nothing."

"Yes there is. I've seen it. Eddie has, too. It started almost as soon as we left the beach. It's something wrong, and it's getting worse."

"There is nothing wrong," he repeated.

She put her hands out and took his. Her anger was gone, at least for the time being. She looked earnestly up into his eyes. "Eddie and I . . . this isn't our world, Roland. Without you, we'd die here. We'd have your guns, and we can shoot them, you've taught us to do that well enough, but we'd die just the same. We . . . we depend on you. So tell me what's wrong. Let me try to help. Let *us* try to help."

He had never been a man who understood himself deeply or cared to; the concept of self-consciousness (let alone self-analysis) was alien to him. His way was to act—to quickly consult his own interior, utterly mysterious workings, and then act. Of them all, he had been the most perfectly made, a man whose deeply romantic core was encased in a brutally simple box which consisted of instinct and pragmatism. He took one of those quick looks inside now and decided to tell her everything. There was something wrong with him, oh yes. Yes indeed. Something wrong with his mind, something as simple as his nature and as strange as the weird, wandering life into which that nature had impelled him.

He opened his mouth to say *I'll tell you what's wrong, Susannah, and I'll do it in just three words. I'm going insane.* But before he could begin, another tree fell in the forest—it went with a huge, grinding crash. This treefall was closer, and this time they were not deeply engaged in a test of wills masquerading as a lesson. Both heard it, both heard the agitated cawing of the crows which followed it, and both registered the fact that the tree had fallen close to their camp.

Susannah had looked in the direction of the sound but now her eyes, wide and dismayed, returned to the gunslinger's face. "Eddie!" she said.

A cry rose from the deep green fastness of the woods in back of them—a vast cry of rage. Another tree went, and then another. They fell in what sounded like a hail of mortar-fire. *Dry wood*, the gunslinger thought. *Dead trees.*

"*Eddie!*" This time she screamed it. "Whatever it is, *it's near Eddie!*" Her hands flew to the wheels of her chair and began the laborious job of turning it around.

"No time for that." Roland seized her under her arms and pulled her free. He had carried her before when the going was too rough for her wheelchair—both men had—but she was still amazed by his uncanny, ruthless speed. At one moment she was in her wheelchair, an item which had been purchased in New York City's finest medical supply house in the fall of 1962. At the next she was balanced precariously on Roland's shoulders like a cheerleader, her muscular thighs gripping the sides of his neck, his palms over his head and pressing into the small of her back. He began to run with her, his sprung boots slapping the needle-strewn earth between the ruts left by her wheelchair.

"Odetta!" he cried, reverting in this moment of stress to the name by which he had first known her. "Don't lose the gun! For your father's sake!"

He was sprinting between the trees now. Shadow-lace and bright chains of sun-dapple ran across them in moving mosaics as Roland lengthened his stride. They were going downhill now. Susannah raised her left hand to ward off a branch that wanted to slap her from the gunslinger's shoulders. At the same moment she dropped her right hand to the butt of his ancient revolver, cradling it.

A mile, she thought. *How long to run a mile? How long with him going flat-out like this? Not long, if he can keep his feet on these slippery needles . . . but maybe too long. Let him be all right, Lord—let my Eddie be all right.*

As if in answer, she heard the unseen beast loose its cry again. That vast voice was like thunder. Like doom.

2

HE WAS THE LARGEST creature in the forest which had once been known as the Great West Woods, and he was the oldest. Many of the huge old elms which Roland had noticed in the valley below had been little more than twigs sprouting from the ground when the bear came out of the dim unknown reaches of Out-World like a brutal, wandering king.

Once, the Old People had lived in the West Woods (it was their leavings which Roland had found from time to time during the last weeks), and they had gone in fear of the colossal, undying bear. They had tried to kill him when they first discovered they were not alone in the new territory to which they had come, but although their arrows enraged him, they did no serious damage. And he was not confused about the *source* of his torment, as were the other beasts of the forest— even the predatory bushcats which denned and littered in the sandhills to the west. No; he knew where the arrows came from, this bear. *Knew.* And for every arrow which found its mark in the flesh below his shaggy pelt, he took three, four, perhaps as many as half a dozen of the Old People. Children if he could get them; women if he could not. Their warriors he disdained, and this was the final humiliation.

Eventually, as his real nature became clear to them, their efforts to kill him ceased. He was, of course, a demon incarnate—or the shadow of a god. They called him Mir, which to these people meant "the world beneath the world." He stood seventy feet high, and after eighteen or more centuries of undisputed rule in the West Woods, he was dying. Perhaps the instrument of his death had at first been a microscopic organism in something he had eaten or drunk; perhaps it was old age; more likely a combination of both. The cause didn't matter; the ultimate result—a rapidly multiplying colony of parasites foraging within his fabulous brain—did. After years of calculating, brutal sanity, Mir had run mad.

The bear had known men were in his woods again; he ruled the forest and although it was vast, nothing of importance which happened there escaped his attention for long. He had drawn away from the newcomers, not because he was afraid but because he had no business with them, nor they with him. Then the parasites had begun their work, and as his madness increased he became sure that it was the Old People again, that the trap-setters and forest-burners had returned and would soon set about their old, stupid mischief once more. Only as he lay in his final den some thirty miles from the place of the newcomers, sicker with each day's dawning than he had been at sunset the night before, had he come to believe that the Old People had finally found some mischief which worked: poison.

He came this time not to take revenge for some petty wound but to stamp them out entirely before their poison could finish having its way with him . . . and as he travelled, all thought ceased. What was left was red rage, the rusty buzz of the thing on top of his head—the turning thing between his ears which had once done its work in smooth silence— and an eerily enhanced sense of smell which led him unerringly toward the camp of the three pilgrims.

The bear, whose real name was not Mir but something else entirely, made his way through the forest like a moving building, a shaggy tower with reddish-brown eyes. Those eyes glowed with fever and madness.

His huge head, now wearing a garland of broken branches and fir-needles, swung ceaselessly from side to side. Every now and then he would sneeze in a muffled explosion of sound—*AH-CHOW!*—and clouds of squirming white parasites would be discharged from his dripping nostrils. His paws, armed with curved talons three feet in length, tore at the trees. He walked upright, sinking deep tracks in the soft black soil under the trees. He reeked of fresh balsam and old, sour shit.

The thing on top of his head whirred and squealed, squealed and whirred.

The course of the bear remained almost constant: a straight line which would lead him to the camp of those who had dared return to his forest, who had dared fill his head with dark green agony. Old People or New People, they would die. When he came to a dead tree, he sometimes left the straight path long enough to push it down. The dry, explosive roar of its fall pleased him; when the tree had finally collapsed its rotten length on the forest floor or come to rest against one of its mates, the bear would push on through slanting bars of sunlight turned misty with floating motes of sawdust.

3

TWO DAYS BEFORE, EDDIE Dean had begun carving again—the first time he'd tried to carve anything since the age of twelve. He remembered that he had enjoyed doing it, and he believed he must have been good at it, as well. He couldn't remember that part, not for sure, but there was at least one clear indication that it was so: Henry, his older brother, had hated to see him doing it.

Oh lookit the sissy, Henry would say. *Whatcha makin today, sissy? A dollhouse? A pisspot for your itty-bitty teeny peenie? Ohhh . . . ain't that CUTE?*

Henry would never come right out and tell Eddie not to do something; would never just walk up to him and say, *Would you mind quitting that, bro? See, it's pretty good, and when you do something that's pretty good, it makes me nervous. Because, you see,* I'm *the one that's supposed to be pretty good at stuff around here. Me. Henry Dean. So what I think I'll do, brother o' mine, is just sort of rag on you about certain things. I won't come right out and say "Don't do that, it's makin me nervous," because that might make me sound, you know, a little fucked up in the head. But I can rag on you, because that's part of what big brothers do, right? All part of the image. I'll rag on you and tease you and make fun of you until you just . . . fucking . . . QUIT IT! Okay?*

Well, it *wasn't* okay, not really, but in the Dean household, things usually went the way Henry wanted them to go. And until very recently, that had seemed right—not okay but *right*. There was a small but crucial difference there, if you could but dig it. There were two reasons why it seemed right. One was an on-top reason; the other was an underneath reason.

The on-top reason was because Henry had to Watch Out for Eddie when Mrs. Dean was at work. He had to Watch Out all the time, because once there had been a Dean *sister*, if you could but dig it. She would have been four years older than Eddie and four years younger than Henry if she had lived, but that was the thing, you see, because she *hadn't* lived. She had been run over by a drunk driver when Eddie was two. She had been watching a game of hopscotch on the sidewalk when it happened.

As a kid, Eddie had sometimes thought of his sister while listening to Mel Allen doing the play-by-play on The Yankee Baseball Network. Someone would really pound one and Mel would bellow, *"Holy cow, he got all of that one! SEEYA LATER!"* Well, the drunk had gotten all of Gloria Dean, holy cow, seeya later. Gloria was now in that great upper deck in the sky, and it had not happened because she was unlucky or because the State of New York had decided not to jerk the jerk's license after his third OUI or even because God had bent down to pick up a peanut; it had happened (as Mrs. Dean frequently told her sons) because there had been no one around to Watch Out for Gloria.

Henry's job was to make sure nothing like that ever happened to Eddie. That was his job and he did it, but it wasn't easy. Henry and Mrs. Dean agreed on that, if nothing else. Both of them frequently reminded Eddie of just how much Henry had sacrificed to keep Eddie safe from drunk drivers and muggers and junkies and possibly even malevolent aliens who might be cruising around in the general vicinity of the upper deck, aliens who might decide to come down from their UFOs on nuclear-powered jet-skis at any time in order to kidnap little kids like Eddie Dean. So it was wrong to make Henry more nervous than this terrible responsibility had already made him. If Eddie was doing something that *did* make Henry more nervous, Eddie ought to cease doing that thing immediately. It was a way of paying Henry back for all the time Henry had spent Watching Out for Eddie. When you thought about it that way, you saw that doing things better than Henry could do them was very unfair.

Then there was the underneath reason. That reason (the world beneath the world, one might say) was more powerful, because it could never be stated: Eddie could not allow himself to be better than Henry at much of anything, because Henry was, for the most part, good for nothing . . . except Watching Out for Eddie, of course.

Henry taught Eddie how to play basketball in the playground near the apartment building where they lived—this was in a cement suburb where the towers of Manhattan stood against the horizon like a dream and the welfare check was king. Eddie was eight years younger than Henry and much smaller, but he was also much faster. He had a natural feel for the game; once he got on the cracked, hilly cement of the court with the ball in his hands, the moves seemed to sizzle in his nerve-endings. He was faster, but that was no big deal. The big deal was this: he was *better* than Henry. If he hadn't known it from the results of the pick-up games in which they sometimes played, he would have known it from Henry's thunderous looks and the hard punches to the upper arm Henry often dealt out on their way home afterwards. These punches were supposedly Henry's little jokes—"Two for flinching!" Henry would cry cheerily, and then *whap-whap!* into Eddie's bicep with one knuckle extended—but they didn't *feel* like jokes. They felt like warnings. They felt like Henry's way of saying *You better not fake me out and make me look stupid when you drive for the basket, bro; you better remember that I'm Watching Out for You.*

The same was true with reading . . . baseball . . . Ring-a-Levio . . . math . . . even jump-rope, which was a girl's game. That he was better at these things, or *could* be better, was a secret that had to be kept at all costs. Because Eddie was the younger brother. Because Henry was Watching Out for him. But the most important part of the underneath reason was also the simplest: these things had to be kept secret because Henry was Eddie's big brother, and Eddie adored him.

4

TWO DAYS AGO, WHILE Susannah was skinning out a rabbit and Roland was starting supper, Eddie had been in the forest just south of camp. He had seen a funny spur of wood jutting out of a fresh stump. A weird feeling—he supposed it was the one people called *déjà vu*—swept over him, and he found himself staring fixedly at the spur, which looked like a badly shaped doorknob. He was distantly aware that his mouth had gone dry.

After several seconds, he realized he was *looking* at the spur sticking out of the stump but *thinking* about the courtyard behind the building where he and Henry had lived—thinking about the feel of the warm cement under his ass and the whopping smells of garbage from the dumpster around the corner in the alley. In this memory he had a chunk of wood in his left hand and a paring knife from the drawer by the sink in his right. The chunk of wood jutting from the stump had called up the memory of that brief period when he had fallen violently in love with wood-carving. It was just that the memory was buried so deep he hadn't realized, at first, what it was.

What he had loved most about carving was the *seeing* part, which happened even before you began. Sometimes you saw a car or a truck. Sometimes a dog or cat. Once, he remembered, it had been the face of an idol—one of the spooky Easter Island monoliths he had seen in an issue of *National Geographic* at school. That had turned out to be a good one. The game was to find out how much of that thing you could get out of the wood without breaking it. You could never get it all, but if you were very careful, you could sometimes get quite a lot.

There was something inside the boss on the side of the stump. He thought he might be able to release quite a lot of it with Roland's knife—it was the sharpest, handiest tool he had ever used.

Something inside the wood, waiting patiently for someone—someone like him!—to come along and let it out. To set it free.

Oh lookit the sissy! Whatcha makin today, sissy? A dollhouse? A pisspot for your itty-bitty teeny peenie? A slingshot, so you can pretend to hunt rabbits, just like the big boys? Awwww . . . ain't that CUTE?

He felt a burst of shame, a sense of wrongness; that strong sense of secrets that must be kept at any cost, and then he remembered—again—that Henry Dean, who had in his later years become the great sage and eminent junkie, was dead. This realization had still not lost its power to surprise; it kept hitting him in different ways, sometimes with sorrow, sometimes with guilt, sometimes with anger. On this day, two days before the great bear came charging out of the green corridors of the woods, it had hit him in the most surprising way of all. He had felt relief, and a soaring joy.

He was free.

Eddie had borrowed Roland's knife. He used it to cut carefully around the jutting boss of wood, then brought it back and sat beneath a tree with it, turning it this way and that. He was not looking *at* it; he was looking *into* it.

Susannah had finished with her rabbit. The meat went into the pot over the fire; the skin she stretched between two sticks, tying it with hanks of rawhide from Roland's purse. Later on, after the evening meal, Eddie would begin scraping it clean. She used her hands and arms, slipping effortlessly over to where Eddie was sitting with his back propped against the tall old pine. At the campfire, Roland was crumbling some arcane—and no doubt delicious—woods-herb into the pot. "What's doing, Eddie?"

Eddie had found himself restraining an absurd urge to hide the boss of wood behind his back. "Nothing," he said. "Thought I might, you know, carve something." He paused, then added: "I'm not very good, though." He sounded as if he might be trying to reassure her of this fact.

She had looked at him, puzzled. For a moment she seemed on the verge of saying something, then simply shrugged and left him alone. She had no idea why Eddie seemed ashamed to be passing a little time in whittling—her father had done it all the time—but if it was something that needed to be talked about, she supposed Eddie would get to it in his own time.

He knew the guilty feelings were stupid and pointless, but he also knew he felt more comfortable doing this work when Roland and Susannah were out of camp. Old habits, it seemed, sometimes died hard. Beating heroin was child's play compared to beating your childhood.

When they *were* away, hunting or shooting or keeping Roland's peculiar form of school, Eddie found himself able to turn to his piece of wood with surprising skill and increasing pleasure. The shape was in there, all right; he had been right about that. It was a simple one, and Roland's knife was setting it free with an eerie ease. Eddie thought he was going to get almost all of it, and that meant the slingshot might actually turn out to be a practical weapon. Not much compared to Roland's big revolvers, maybe, but something he had made himself, just the same. *His.* And this idea pleased him very much.

When the first crows rose in the air, cawing affrightedly, he did not hear. He was already thinking—hoping—that he might see a tree with a bow trapped in it before too long.

5

HE HEARD THE BEAR approaching before Roland and Susannah did, but not much before—he was lost in that high daze of concentration which accompanies the creative impulse at its sweetest and most powerful. He had suppressed these impulses for most of his life, and now this one held him wholly in its grip. Eddie was a willing prisoner.

He was pulled from his daze not by the sound of falling trees but by the rapid thunder of a .45 from the south. He looked up, smiling, and brushed hair from his forehead with a sawdusty hand. In that moment, sitting with his back against a tall pine in the clearing which had become home, his face crisscrossed with opposing beams of green-gold forest light, he looked handsome indeed—a young man with unruly dark hair which constantly tried to spill across his high forehead, a young man with a strong, mobile mouth and hazel eyes.

For a moment his eyes shifted to Roland's other gun, hanging by its belt from a nearby branch, and he found himself wondering how long it had been since Roland had gone anywhere without at least one of his fabulous weapons hanging by his side. That question led to two others.

How old *was* he, this man who had plucked Eddie and Susannah from their world and their *whens*? And, more important, what was wrong with him?

Susannah had promised to broach that subject . . . if she shot well and didn't get Roland's back hair up, that was. Eddie didn't think Roland would tell her—not at first—but it was time to let old long tall and ugly know that *they* knew *something* was wrong.

"There'll be water if God wills it," Eddie said. He turned back to his carving with a little smile playing on his lips. They had both begun to pick up Roland's little sayings . . . and he theirs. It was almost as if they were halves of the same—

Then a tree fell close by in the forest, and Eddie was on his feet in a second, the half-carved slingshot in one hand, Roland's knife in the other. He stared across the clearing in the direction of the sound, heart thumping, all his senses finally alert. Something was coming. Now he could hear it, trampling its heedless way through the underbrush, and he marvelled bitterly that this realization had come so late. Far back in his mind, a small voice told him this was what he got. This was what he got for doing something better than Henry, for making Henry nervous.

Another tree fell with a ratcheting, coughing crash. Looking down a ragged aisle between the tall firs, Eddie saw a cloud of sawdust rise in the still air. The creature responsible for that cloud suddenly bellowed— a raging, gut-freezing sound.

It was one huge motherfucker, whatever it was.

He dropped the chunk of wood, then flipped Roland's knife at a tree fifteen feet to his left. It somersaulted twice in the air and then stuck halfway to the hilt in the wood, quivering. He grabbed Roland's .45 from the place where it hung and cocked it.

Stand or run?

But he discovered he no longer had the luxury of that question. The thing was *fast* as well as huge, and it was now too late to run. A gigantic shape began to disclose itself in that aisle of trees north of the clearing, a shape which towered above all but the tallest trees. It was lumbering directly toward him, and as its eyes fixed upon Eddie Dean, it gave voice to another of those cries.

"Oh man, I'm *fucked*," Eddie whispered as another tree bent, cracked like a mortar, then crashed to the forest floor in a cloud of dust and dead needles. Now it was lumbering straight toward the clearing where he stood, a bear the size of King Kong. Its footfalls made the ground shake.

What will you do, Eddie? Roland suddenly asked. *Think! It's the only advantage you have over yon beast. What will you do?*

He didn't think he could kill it. Maybe with a bazooka, but probably not with the gunslinger's .45. He could run, but had an idea that the oncoming beast might be pretty fast when it wanted to be. He guessed the chances of ending up as jam between the great bear's toes might be as high as fifty-fifty.

So which one was it going to be? Stand here and start shooting or run like his hair was on fire and his ass was catching?

It occurred to him that there was a third choice. He could climb.

He turned toward the tree against which he had been leaning. It was a huge, hoary pine, easily the tallest tree in this part of the woods. The first branch spread out over the forest floor in a feathery green fan about eight feet up. Eddie dropped the revolver's hammer and then jammed the gun into the waistband of his pants. He leaped for the branch, grabbed it, and did a frantic chin-up. Behind him, the bear gave voice to another bellow as it burst into the clearing.

The bear would have had him just the same, would have left Eddie Dean's guts hanging in gaudy strings from the lowest branches of the pine, if another of those sneezing fits had not come on it at that moment. It kicked the ashy remains of the campfire into a black cloud and then stood almost doubled over, huge front paws on its huge thighs, looking for a moment like an old man in a fur coat, an old man with a cold. It sneezed again and again—*AH-CHOW! AH-CHOW! AH-CHOW!*—and clouds of parasites blew out of its muzzle. Hot urine flowed in a stream between its legs and hissed out the campfire's scattered embers.

Eddie did not waste the few crucial extra moments he had been given. He went up the tree like a monkey on a stick, pausing only once to make sure the gunslinger's revolver was still seated firmly in the waistband of his pants. He was in terror, already half convinced that he was going to die (what else could he expect, now that Henry wasn't around to Watch Out for him?), but a crazy laughter raved through his head just the same. *Been treed,* he thought. *How bout that, sports fans? Been treed by Bearzilla.*

The creature raised its head again, the thing turning between its ears catching winks and flashes of sunlight as it did so, then charged Eddie's tree. It reached high with one paw and slashed forward, meaning to knock Eddie loose like a pinecone. The paw tore through the branch he was standing on just as he lunged upward to the next. That paw tore through one of his shoes as well, pulling it from his foot and sending it flying in two ragged pieces.

That's okay, Eddie thought. *You can have em both, Br'er Bear, if you want. Goddam things were worn out, anyway.*

The bear roared and lashed at the tree, cutting deep wounds in its ancient bark, wounds which bled clear, resinous sap. Eddie kept on yanking himself up. The branches were thinning now, and when he risked a glance down he stared directly into the bear's muddy eyes. Below its cocked head, the clearing had become a target with the scattered smudge of campfire as its bullseye.

"Missed me, you hairy motherf—" Eddie began, and then the bear, its head still cocked back to look at him, sneezed. Eddie was immediately drenched in hot snot that was filled with thousands of small white worms. They wriggled frantically on his shirt, his forearms, his throat and face.

Eddie screamed in mingled surprise and revulsion. He began to brush at his eyes and mouth, lost his balance, and just managed to hook an arm around the branch beside him in time. He held on and raked at his skin, wiping off as much of the wormy phlegm as he could. The bear roared and hit the tree again. The pine rocked like a mast in a gale . . . but the fresh claw-marks which appeared were at least seven feet below the branch on which Eddie's feet were planted.

The worms were dying, he realized—must have begun dying as soon as they left the infected swamps inside the monster's body. It made him feel a little better, and he began to climb again. He stopped twelve feet further up, daring to go no higher. The trunk of the pine, easily eight feet in diameter at its base, was now no more than eighteen inches through the middle. He had distributed his weight on two branches, but he could feel both of them bending springily beneath him. He had a crow's nest view of the forest and foothills to the west now, spread out below him in an undulating carpet. Under other circumstances, it would have been a view to relish.

Top of the world, Ma, he thought. He looked down into the bear's upturned face again, and for a moment all coherent thought was driven from his mind by simple amazement.

There was something growing out of the bear's skull, and to Eddie it looked like a small radar-dish.

The gadget turned jerkily, kicking up flashes of sun as it did, and Eddie could hear it screaming thinly. He had owned a few old cars in his time—the kind that sat in the used-car lots with the words HANDYMAN'S SPECIAL soaped on the windshields—and he thought the sound coming from that gadget was the sound of bearings which will freeze up if they are not replaced soon.

The bear uttered a long, purring growl. Yellowish foam, thick with worms, squeezed between its paws in curdled gobbets. If he had never looked into the face of utter lunacy (and he supposed he had, having been eyeball to eyeball with that world-class bitch Detta Walker on more than one occasion), Eddie was looking into it now . . . but that face was, thankfully, a good thirty feet below him, and at their highest reach those killing talons were fifteen feet under the soles of his feet. And, unlike the trees upon which the bear had vented its spleen as it approached the clearing, this one was not dead.

"Mexican standoff, honey," Eddie panted. He wiped sweat from his forehead with one sap-sticky hand and flicked the mess down into the bugbear's face.

Then the creature the Old People had called Mir embraced the tree with its great forepaws and began to shake it. Eddie grabbed the trunk and held on for dear life, eyes squeezed into grim slits, as the pine began to sway back and forth like a pendulum.

6

ROLAND HALTED AT THE EDGE of the clearing. Susannah, perched on his shoulders, stared unbelievingly across the open space. The creature stood at the base of the tree where Eddie had been when the two of them left the clearing forty-five minutes ago. She could see only chunks and sections of its body through the screen of branches and dark green needles. Roland's other gunbelt lay beside one of the monster's feet. The holster, she saw, was empty.

"My God," she murmured.

The bear screamed like a distraught woman and began shaking the tree. The branches lashed as if in a high wind. Her eyes skated upward and she saw a dark form near the top. Eddie was hugging the trunk as the tree rocked and rolled. As she watched, one of his hands slipped and flailed wildly for purchase.

"*What do we do?*" she screamed down at Roland. "*It's goan shake him loose! What do we do?*"

Roland tried to think about it, but that queer sensation had returned again—it was always with him now, but stress seemed to make it worse. He felt like two men existing inside one skull. Each man had his own set of memories, and when they began to argue, each insisting that *his* memories were the true ones, the gunslinger felt as if he were being ripped in two. He made a desperate effort to reconcile these two halves and succeeded . . . at least for the moment.

"It's one of the Twelve!" he shouted. "One of the Guardians! *Must* be! But I thought they were—"

The bear bellowed up at Eddie again. Now it began to slap at the tree like a punchy fighter. Branches snapped and fell around its feet in a tangle.

"*What?*" Susannah screamed. "*What's the rest?*"

Roland closed his eyes. Inside his head, a voice shouted, *The boy's name was Jake!* Another voice shouted back, *There WAS no boy! There WAS no boy, and you know it!*

Get away, both of you! he snarled, and then called out aloud: "Shoot it! Shoot it in the ass, Susannah! It'll turn and charge! When it does, look for something on its head! It—"

The bear squalled again. It gave up slapping the tree and went back to shaking it. Ominous popping, grinding sounds were now coming from the upper part of the trunk.

When he could be heard again, Roland shouted: "I think it looks like a hat! A little steel hat! Shoot it, Susannah! And don't miss!"

Terror suddenly filled her—terror and another emotion, one she would never have expected: crushing loneliness.

"No! I'll miss! You do it, Roland!" She began to fumble his revolver out of the belt she wore, meaning to give it to him.

"Can't!" Roland shouted. "The angle's bad! *You* have to do it, Susannah! This is the real test, and you'd better pass it!"

"Roland—"

"*It means to snap the top of the tree off!*" he roared at her. "*Can't you see that?*"

She looked at the revolver in her hand. Looked across the clearing, at the gigantic bear obscured in the clouds and sprays of green needles. Looked at Eddie, swaying back and forth like a metronome. Eddie probably had Roland's other gun, but Susannah could see no way he could use it without being shaken from his perch like an over-ripe plum. Also, he might not shoot at the right thing.

She raised the revolver. Her stomach was thick with dread. "Hold me still, Roland," she said. "If you don't—"

"Don't worry about me!"

She fired twice, squeezing the shots as Roland had taught her. The heavy reports cut across the sound of the bear shaking the tree like the cracks of a bullwhip. She saw both bullets strike home in the left cheek of the bear's rump, less than two inches apart.

It shrieked in surprise, pain, and outrage. One of its huge front paws came out of the dense screen of branches and needles and slapped at the hurt place. The hand came away dripping scarlet and rose back out of sight. Susannah could imagine it up there, examining its bloody palm. Then there was a rushing, rustling, snapping sound as the bear turned, bending down at the same time, dropping to all fours in order to achieve maximum speed. For the first time she saw its face, and her heart quailed. Its muzzle was lathered with foam; its huge eyes glared like lamps. Its shaggy head swung to the left . . . back to the right . . . and centered upon Roland, who stood with his legs apart and Susannah Dean balanced on his shoulders.

With a shattering roar, the bear charged.

7

SAY YOUR LESSON, Susannah Dean, and be true.

The bear came at them in a rumbling lope; it was like watching a runaway factory machine over which someone had thrown a huge, moth-eaten rug.

It looks like a hat! A little steel hat!

She saw it . . . but it didn't look like a hat to her. It looked like a radar-dish—a much smaller version of the kind she had seen in MovieTone newsreel stories about how the DEW-line was keeping everyone safe from a Russian sneak attack. It was bigger than the pebbles she had shot off the boulder earlier, but the distance was greater. Sun and shadow ran across it in deceiving dapples.

I do not aim with my hand; she who aims with her hand has forgotten the face of her father.

I can't do it!

I do not shoot with my hand; she who shoots with her hand has forgotten the face of her father.

I'll miss! I know I'll miss!

I do not kill with my gun; she who kills with her gun—

"Shoot it!" Roland roared. "Susannah, *shoot it!*"

With the trigger as yet unpulled, she saw the bullet go home, guided from muzzle to target by nothing more or less than her heart's fierce desire that it should fly true. All fear fell away. What was left was a feeling of deep coldness and she had time to think: *This is what* he *feels. My God—how does he stand it?*

"I kill with my heart, motherfucker," she said, and the gunslinger's revolver roared in her hand.

8

THE SILVERY THING SPUN on a steel rod planted in the bear's skull. Susannah's bullet struck it dead center and the radar-dish blew into a hundred glittering fragments. The pole itself was suddenly engulfed in a burst of crackling blue fire which reached out in a net and seemed to grasp the sides of the bear's face for a moment.

It rose on its rear legs with a whistling howl of agony, its front paws boxing aimlessly at the air. It turned in a wide, staggering circle and began to flap its arms, as if it had decided to fly away. It tried to roar again but what came out instead was a weird warbling sound like an air-raid siren.

"It is very well." Roland sounded exhausted. "A good shot, fair and true."

"Should I shoot it again?" she asked uncertainly. The bear was still blundering around in its mad circle but now its body had begun to tilt sidewards and inwards. It struck a small tree, rebounded, almost fell over, and then began to circle again.

"No need," Roland said. She felt his hands grip her waist and lift her. A moment later she was sitting on the ground with her thighs folded beneath her. Eddie was slowly and shakily descending the pine, but she didn't see him. She could not take her eyes from the bear.

She had seen the whales at the Seaquarium near Mystic, Connecticut, and believed they had been bigger than this—much bigger, probably—but this was certainly the largest land creature she had ever seen. And it was clearly dying. Its roars had become liquid bubbling sounds, and although its eyes were open, it seemed blind. It flailed aimlessly about the camp, knocking over a rack of curing hides, stamping flat the little shelter she shared with Eddie, caroming off trees. She could see the steel post rising from its head. Tendrils of smoke were rising around it, as if her shot had ignited its brains.

Eddie reached the lowest branch of the tree which had saved his life and sat shakily astride it. "Holy Mary Mother of God," he said. "I'm looking right at it and I still don't beli—"

The bear wheeled back toward him. Eddie leaped nimbly from the tree and streaked toward Susannah and Roland. The bear took no notice, it marched drunkenly to the pine which had been Eddie's refuge, tried to grasp it, failed, and sank to its knees. Now they could hear other sounds coming from inside it, sounds that made Eddie think of some huge truck engine stripping its gears.

A spasm convulsed it, bowed its back. Its front claws rose and gored madly at its own face. Worm-infested blood flew and splattered. Then it fell over, making the ground tremble with its fall, and lay still. After all its strange centuries, the bear the Old People had called Mir—the world beneath the world—was dead.

9

EDDIE PICKED SUSANNAH UP, held her with his sticky hands locked together at the small of her back, and kissed her deeply. He reeked of sweat and pine-tar. She touched his cheeks, his neck; she ran her hands through his wet hair. She felt an insane urge to touch him everywhere until she was absolutely sure of his reality.

"It almost had me," he said. "It was like being on some crazy carnival ride. What a shot! Jesus, Suze—what a shot!"

"I hope I never have to do anything like that again," she said . . .

but a small voice at the center of her demurred. That voice suggested that she could not *wait* to do something like that again. And it was cold, that voice. Cold.

"What was—" he began, turning toward Roland, but Roland was no longer standing there. He was walking slowly toward the bear, which now lay on the ground with its shaggy knees up. From within it came a series of muffled gasps and gurgles as its strange guts continued to slowly run down.

Roland saw his knife planted deep in a tree near the scarred veteran that had saved Eddie's life. He pulled it free and wiped it clean on the soft deerskin shirt which had replaced the tatters he had been wearing when the three of them had left the beach. He stood by the bear, looking down at it with an expression of pity and wonder.

Hello, stranger, he thought. *Hello, old friend. I never believed in you, not really. I believe Alain did, and I know that Cuthbert did—Cuthbert believed in everything—but I was the hardheaded one. I thought you were only a tale for children . . . another wind which blew around in my old nurse's hollow head before finally escaping her jabbering mouth. But you were here all along, another refugee of the old times, like the pump at the way station and the old machines under the mountains. Are the Slow Mutants who worshipped those broken remnants the final descendents of the people who once lived in this forest and finally fled your wrath? I don't know, will never know . . . but it feels right. Yes. And then I came with my friends—my deadly new friends, who are becoming so much like my deadly old friends. We came, weaving our magic circle around us and around everything we touch, strand by poisonous strand, and now here you lie, at our feet. The world has moved on again, and this time, old friend, it's you who have been left behind.*

The monster's body still radiated a deep, sick heat. Parasites were leaving its mouth and tattered nostrils in hordes, but they died almost at once. Waxy-white piles of them were growing on either side of the bear's head.

Eddie approached slowly. He had shifted Susannah over to one hip, carrying her as a mother might carry a baby. "What was it, Roland? Do you know?"

"He called it a Guardian, I think," Susannah said.

"Yes." Roland's voice was slow with amazement. "I thought they were all gone, *must* all be gone . . . if they ever existed outside of the old wives' tales in the first place."

"Whatever it was, it was one crazy mother," Eddie said.

Roland smiled a little. "If you'd lived two or three thousand years, you'd be one crazy mother, too."

"Two or three thousand . . . Christ!"

Susannah said, "Is it a bear? Really? And what's that?" She was pointing at what appeared to be a square metal tag set high on one of the bear's thick rear legs. It was almost overgrown with tough tangles of hair, but the afternoon sun had pricked out a single starpoint of light on its stainless steel surface, revealing it.

Eddie knelt and reached hesitantly toward the tag, aware that strange muffled clicks and clacks were still coming from deep inside the fallen giant. He looked at Roland.

"Go ahead," the gunslinger told him. "It's finished."

Eddie pushed a clump of hair aside and leaned closer. Words had been stamped into the metal. They were quite badly eroded, but he found that with a little effort he could read them.

NORTH CENTRAL POSITRONICS, LTD.
Granite City
Northeast Corridor

Design 4 GUARDIAN
Serial # AA 24123 CX 755431297 L 14
Type/Species BEAR
SHARDIK

°°NR°°SUBNUCLEAR CELLS MUST NOT BE REPLACED°°NR°°

"Holy Jesus, this thing is a *robot*," Eddie said softly.

"It can't be," Susannah said. "When I shot it, it *bled.*"

"Maybe so, but your ordinary, garden-variety bear doesn't have a radar-dish growing out of its head. And, so far as I know, your ordinary, garden-variety bear doesn't live to be two or three th—" He broke off suddenly, looking at Roland. When he spoke again, his voice was revolted. "Roland, what are you doing?"

Roland did not reply; did not *need* to reply. What he was doing—gouging out one of the bear's eyes with his knife—was perfectly obvious. The surgery was quick, neat, and precise. When it was completed he balanced an oozing brown ball of jelly on the blade of his knife for a moment and then flicked it aside. A few more worms made their way out of the staring hole, tried to squirm their way down the bear's muzzle, and died.

The gunslinger leaned over the eyesocket of Shardik, the great Guardian bear, and peered inside. "Come and look, both of you," he said. "I'll show you a wonder of the latter days."

"Put me down, Eddie," Susannah said.

He did so, and she moved swiftly on her hands and upper

thighs to where the gunslinger was hunkered down over the bear's wide, slack face. Eddie joined them, looking between their shoulders. The three of them gazed in rapt silence for nearly a full minute; the only noise came from the crows which still circled and scolded in the sky.

Blood oozed from the socket in a few thick, dying trickles. Yet it was not *just* blood, Eddie saw. There was also a clear fluid which gave off an identifiable scent—bananas. And, embedded in the delicate crisscross of tendons which shaped the socket, he saw a webwork of what looked like strings. Beyond them, at the back of the socket, was a red spark, blinking on and off. It illuminated a tiny square board marked with silvery squiggles of what could only be solder.

"It isn't a bear, it's a fucking Sony Walkman," he muttered.

Susannah looked around at him. "What?"

"Nothing." Eddie glanced at Roland. "Do you think it's safe to reach in?"

Roland shrugged. "I think so. If there was a demon in this creature, it's fled."

Eddie reached in with his little finger, nerves set to draw back if he felt even a tickle of electricity. He touched the cooling meat inside the eyesocket, which was nearly the size of a baseball, and then one of those strings. Except it wasn't a string; it was a gossamer-thin strand of steel. He withdrew his finger and saw the tiny red spark blink once more before going out forever.

"Shardik," Eddie murmured. "I *know* that name, but I can't place it. Does it mean anything to you, Suze?"

She shook her head.

"The thing is . . ." Eddie laughed helplessly. "I associate it with rabbits. Isn't that nuts?"

Roland stood up. His knees popped like gunshots. "We'll have to move camp," he said. "The ground here is spoiled. The other clearing, the one where we go to shoot, will—"

He took two trembling steps and then collapsed to his knees, palms pressed to the sides of his sagging head.

10

EDDIE AND SUSANNAH EXCHANGED a single frightened glance and then Eddie leaped to Roland's side. "What is it? Roland, what's wrong?"

"There *was* a boy," the gunslinger said in a distant, muttering voice. And then, in the very next breath, "There *wasn't* a boy."

"Roland?" Susannah asked. She came to him, slipped an arm around his shoulders, felt him trembling. "Roland, what is it?"

"The boy," Roland said, looking at her with floating, dazed eyes. "It's the boy. *Always* the boy."

"*What* boy?" Eddie yelled frantically. "*What* boy?"

"Go then," Roland said, "there are other worlds than these." And fainted.

11

THAT NIGHT THE THREE of them sat around a huge bonfire Eddie and Susannah had built in the clearing Eddie called "the shooting gallery." It would have been a bad place to camp in the wintertime, open to the valley as it was, but for now it was fine. Eddie guessed that here in Roland's world it was still late summer.

The black vault of the sky arched overhead, speckled by what seemed to be whole galaxies. Almost straight ahead to the south, across the river of darkness that was the valley, Eddie could see Old Mother rising above the distant, unseen horizon. He glanced at Roland, who sat huddled by the fire with three skins wrapped around his shoulders despite the warmth of the night and the heat of the fire. There was an untouched plate of food by his side and a bone cradled in his hands. Eddie glanced back at the sky and thought of a story the gunslinger had told him and Susannah on one of the long days they had spent moving away from the beach, through the foothills, and finally into these deep woods where they had found a temporary refuge.

Before time began, Roland said, Old Star and Old Mother had been young and passionate newlyweds. Then one day there had been a terrible argument. Old Mother (who in those long-ago days had been known by her real name, which was Lydia) had caught Old Star (whose real name was Apon) hanging about a beautiful young woman named Cassiopeia. They'd had a real bang-up fight, those two, a hair-pulling, eye-gouging, crockery-throwing fight. One of those thrown bits of crockery had become the earth; a smaller shard the moon; a coal from their kitchen stove had become the sun. In the end, the gods had stepped in so Apon and Lydia might not, in their anger, destroy the universe before it was fairly begun. Cassiopeia, the saucy jade who caused the trouble in the first place ("Yeah, right—it's always the woman," Susannah had said at this point), had been banished to a rocking-chair made of stars forever and ever. Yet not even this had solved the problem. Lydia had been willing to try again, but Apon was stiffnecked and full of pride ("Yeah, always blame the man," Eddie had grunted at this point). So they had parted, and now they look at each other in mingled hatred and longing from across the star-strewn wreckage of their divorce. Apon and Lydia are three billion years gone, the gunslinger told them; they have become Old Star and Old Mother, the north and south, each pining for the other but both now too proud to beg for reconciliation . . . and Cassiopeia sits off to the side in her chair, rocking and laughing at them both.

Eddie was startled by a soft touch on his arm. It was Susannah. "Come on," she said. "We've got to make him talk."

Eddie carried her to the campfire and put her down carefully on Roland's right side. He sat on Roland's left. Roland looked first at Susannah, then at Eddie.

"How close you both sit to me," he remarked. "Like lovers . . . or warders in a gaol."

"It's time for you to do some talking." Susannah's voice was low, clear, and musical. "If we're your companions, Roland—and it seems like we are, like it or not—it's time you started *treating* us as companions. Tell us what's wrong . . ."

". . . and what we can do about it," Eddie finished.

Roland sighed deeply. "I don't know how to begin," he said. "It's been so long since I've had companions . . . or a tale to tell . . ."

"Start with the bear," Eddie said.

Susannah leaned forward and touched the jawbone Roland held in his hands. It frightened her, but she touched it anyway. "And finish with this."

"Yes." Roland lifted the bone to eye-level and looked at it for a moment before dropping it back into his lap. "We'll have to speak of this, won't we? It's the center of the thing."

But the bear came first.

12

"THIS IS THE STORY I was told when I was a child," Roland said. "When everything was new, the Great Old Ones—they weren't gods, but people who had almost the knowledge of gods—created Twelve Guardians to stand watch at the twelve portals which lead in and out of the world. Sometimes I heard that these portals were natural things, like the constellations we see in the sky or the bottomless crack in the earth we called Dragon's Grave, because of the great burst of steam they gave off every thirty or forty days. But other people—one I remember in particular, the head cook in my father's castle, a man named Hax—said they were *not* natural, that they had been created by the Great Old Ones themselves, in the days before they hanged themselves with pride like a noose and disappeared from the earth. Hax used to say that the creation of the Twelve Guardians was the last act of the Great Old Ones, their attempt to atone for the great wrongs they had done to each other, and to the earth itself."

"Portals," Eddie mused. "*Doors*, you mean. We're back to those again. Do these doors that lead in and out of the world open on the world Suze and I came from? Like the ones we found along the beach?"

"I don't know," Roland said. "For every thing I do know, there are a hundred things I don't. You—both of you—will have to reconcile yourselves to that fact. The world has moved on, we say. When it did, it went like a great receding wave, leaving only wreckage behind . . . wreckage that sometimes looks like a map."

"Well, make a *guess!*" Eddie exclaimed, and the raw eagerness in his voice told the gunslinger that Eddie had not given up the idea of returning to his own world—and Susannah's—even now. Not entirely.

"Leave him be, Eddie," Susannah said. "The man don't guess."

"Not true—sometimes the man *does*," Roland said, surprising them both. "When guessing's the only thing left, sometimes he does. The answer is no. I don't think—I don't *guess*—that these portals are much like the doors on the beach. I don't *guess* they go to a *where* or *when* that we would recognize. I think the doors on the beach—the ones that led into the world you both came from—were like the pivot at the center of a child's teeterboard. Do you know what that is?"

"Seesaw?" Susannah asked, and tipped her hand back and forth to demonstrate.

"Yes!" Roland agreed, looking pleased. "Just so. On one end of this sawsee—"

"Seesaw," Eddie said, smiling a little.

"Yes. On one end, my *ka*. On the other, that of the man in black—Walter. The doors were the center, creations of the tension between two opposing destinies. These other portals are things far greater than Walter, or me, or the little fellowship we three have made."

"Are you saying," Susannah asked hesitantly, "that the portals where these Guardians stand watch are *outside ka*? Beyond *ka*?"

"I'm saying that I believe so." He offered his own brief smile, a thin sickle in the firelight. "That I *guess* so."

He was silent a moment, then he picked up a stick of his own. He brushed away the carpet of pine needles and used the stick to draw in the dirt beneath:

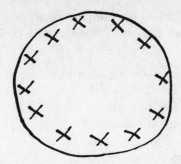

"Here is the world as I was told it existed when I was a child. The Xs are the portals standing in a ring at its eternal edge. If one drew six lines, connecting these portals in pairs—so—"

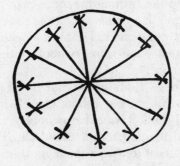

He looked up. "Do you see where the lines cross in the center?"

Eddie felt gooseflesh crawl up his back and down his arms. His mouth was suddenly dry. "Is that it, Roland? Is that—?"

Roland nodded. His long, lined face was grave. "At this nexus lies the Great Portal, the so-called Thirteenth Gate which rules not just this world but all worlds."

He tapped the center of the circle.

"Here is the Dark Tower for which I've searched my whole life."

13

THE GUNSLINGER RESUMED: "At each of the twelve lesser portals the Great Old Ones set a Guardian. In my childhood I could have named them all in the rimes my nursemaid—and Hax the cook—taught to me . . . but my childhood was long ago. There was the Bear, of course, and the Fish . . . the Lion . . . the Bat. And the Turtle—he was an important one . . ."

The gunslinger looked up into the starry sky, his brow creased in deep thought. Then an amazingly sunny smile broke across his features and he recited:

"See the TURTLE of enormous girth!
On his shell he holds the earth.
His thought is slow but always kind;
He holds us all within his mind.
On his back all vows are made;
He sees the truth but mayn't aid.
He loves the land and loves the sea,
And even loves a child like me."

Roland uttered a small, bemused laugh. "Hax taught that to me, singing it as he stirred the frosting for some cake and gave me little nips of the sweet from the edge of his spoon. Amazing what we remember, isn't it? Anyway, as I grew older, I came to believe that the Guardians didn't really exist—that they were symbols rather than substance. It seems that I was wrong."

"I called it a robot," Eddie said, "but that's not what it really was. Susannah's right—the only thing robots bleed when you shoot them is Quaker State 10-40. I think it was what people of my world call a cyborg, Roland—a creature that's part machine and part flesh and blood. There was a movie I saw . . . we told you about movies, didn't we?"

Smiling a little, Roland nodded.

"Well, this movie was called *Robocop*, and the guy in it wasn't a lot different from the bear Susannah killed. How did you know where she should shoot it?"

"That I remembered from the old tales as Hax told them," he said. "If it had been up to my nursemaid, Eddie, you'd be in the belly of the bear now. Do they sometimes tell puzzled children in your world to put on their thinking caps?"

"Yes," Susannah said. "They sure do."

"It's said here, as well, and the saying comes from the story of the Guardians. Each supposedly carried an extra brain on the outside of its head. In a hat." He looked at them with his dreadfully haunted eyes and smiled again. "It didn't look much like a hat, did it?"

"No," Eddie said, "but the story was close enough to save our bacon."

"I think now that I've been looking for one of the Guardians ever since I began my quest," Roland said. "When we find the portal this Shardik guarded—and that should only be a matter of following its back-trail—we will finally have a course to follow. We must set the portal to our backs and then simply move straight ahead. At the center of the circle . . . the Tower."

Eddie opened his mouth to say, *All right, let's talk about this Tower. Finally, once and for all, let's talk about it—what it is, what it means, and, most important of all, what happens to us when we get there.* But no sound came out, and after a moment he closed his mouth again. This wasn't the time—not now, with Roland in such obvious pain. Not now, with only the spark of their campfire to keep the night at bay.

"So now we come to the other part," Roland said heavily. "I have finally found my course—after all the long years I have found my course—but at the same time I seem to be losing my sanity. I can feel it crumbling away beneath my feet, like a steep embankment which has been loosened by rain. This is my punishment for letting a boy who never existed fall to his death. And that is also *ka*."

"Who is this boy, Roland?" Susannah asked.

Roland glanced at Eddie. "Do *you* know?"

Eddie shook his head.

"But I spoke of him," Roland said. "In fact, I *raved* of him, when the infection was at its worst and I was near dying." The gunslinger's voice suddenly rose half an octave, and his imitation of Eddie's voice was so good that Susannah felt a coil of superstitious fright. " 'If you don't shut up about that goddam kid, Roland, I'll gag you with your own shirt! I'm sick of hearing about him!' Do you remember saying that, Eddie?"

Eddie thought it over carefully. Roland had spoken of a thousand things as the two of them made their tortuous way up the beach from the door marked THE PRISONER to the one marked THE LADY OF THE SHADOWS, and he had mentioned what seemed like a thousand names in his fever-heated monologues—Alain, Cort, Jamie de Curry, Cuthbert (this one more often than all the others), Hax, Martin (or perhaps it was Marten, like the animal), Walter, Susan, even a guy with the unlikely name of Zoltan. Eddie had gotten very tired of hearing about these people he had never met (and didn't care to meet), but of course Eddie had had a few problems of his own at that time, heroin withdrawal and cosmic jet-lag being only two of them. And, if he was to be fair, he guessed Roland had gotten as tired of Eddie's own Fractured Fairy Tales—the ones about how he and Henry had grown up together and turned into junkies together—as Eddie had of Roland's.

But he couldn't remember ever telling Roland he would gag him with his own shirt if he didn't stop talking about some kid.

"Nothing comes to you?" Roland asked. "Nothing at all?"

Was there something? Some far-off tickle, like the feeling of *déjà vu* he'd gotten when he saw the slingshot hiding inside the chunk of wood jutting out of the stump? Eddie tried to find that tickle, but it was gone. He decided it had never been there in the first place; he only *wanted* it to be there, because Roland was hurting so badly.

"No," he said. "Sorry, man."

"But I *did* tell you." Roland's tone was calm, but urgency ran and pulsed beneath it like a scarlet thread. "The boy's name was Jake. I sacrificed him—killed him—in order that I might finally catch up with Walter and make him talk. I killed him under the mountains."

On this point Eddie could be more positive. "Well, maybe that's what happened, but it's not what you *said* happened. You said you went under the mountains alone, on some kind of crazy handcar. You talked about *that* a lot while we were coming up the beach, Roland. About how scary it was to be alone."

"I remember. But I also remember telling you about the boy, and how he fell from the trestle into the chasm. And it's the distance between those two memories that is pulling my mind apart."

"I don't understand any of this," Susannah said worriedly.

"I think," Roland said, "that I'm just beginning to."

He threw more wood on the fire, sending thick sheaves of red sparks spiralling up into the dark sky, and then settled back between them. "I'll tell you a story that's true," he said, "and then I'll tell you a story that isn't true . . . but *should* be.

"I bought a mule in Pricetown, and when I finally got to Tull, the last town before the desert, it was still fresh . . ."

14

SO THE GUNSLINGER EMBARKED on the most recent part of his long tale. Eddie had heard isolated fragments of the story, but he listened in utter fascination, as did Susannah, for whom it was completely new. He told them about the bar with the endless game of Watch Me going on in the corner, the piano player named Sheb, the woman named Allie with the scar on her forehead . . . and about Nort, the weed-eater who had died and then been brought back to some sort of tenebrous life by the man in black. He told them about Sylvia Pittston, that avatar of religious insanity, and about the final apocalyptic slaughter, in which he, Roland the Gunslinger, had killed every man, woman, and child in town.

"Holy crispy crap!" Eddie said in a low, shaky voice. "Now I know why you were so low on shells, Roland."

"Be quiet!" Susannah snapped. "Let him finish!"

Roland went on, telling his story as stolidly as he had crossed the desert after passing the hut of the last Dweller, a young man whose wild, strawberry-colored hair had reached almost to his waist. He told them about how his mule had finally died. He even told them about how the Dweller's pet bird, Zoltan, had eaten the mule's eyes.

He told them about the long desert days and the short desert nights which had come next, and how he had followed the cool remains of Walter's campfires, and how he had come at last, reeling and dying of dehydration, to the way station.

"It was empty. It had been empty, I think, since the days when yonder great bear was still a newly made thing. I stayed a night and pushed on. That's what happened . . . but now I'll tell you another story."

"The one that isn't true but should be?" Susannah asked.

Roland nodded. "In this made-up story—this fable—a gunslinger named Roland met a boy named Jake at the way station. This boy was from your world, from your city of New York, and from a *when* someplace between Eddie's 1987 and Odetta Holmes's 1963."

Eddie was leaning forward eagerly. "Is there a door in this story, Roland? A door marked THE BOY, or something like that?"

Roland shook his head. "The boy's doorway was death. He was on his way to school when a man—a man I believed to be Walter—pushed him into the street, where he was run over by a car. He heard this man say something like 'Get out of the way, let me through, I'm a priest.' Jake *saw* this man—just for an instant—and then he was in *my* world."

The gunslinger paused, looking into the fire.

"Now I want to leave this story of the boy who was never there and go back to what really happened for a minute. All right?"

Eddie and Susannah exchanged a puzzled glance and then Eddie made an "after you, my dear Alphonse" gesture with his hand.

"As I have said, the way station was deserted. There was, however, a pump that still worked. It was at the back of the stable where the coach-horses were kept. I followed my ears to it, but I would have found it even if it had been completely silent. I *smelled* the water, you see. After enough time in the desert, when you are on the edge of dying from thirst, you can really do that. I drank and then slept. When I woke, I drank again. I wanted to push on at once—the need to do that was like a fever. The medicine you brought me from your world—the *astin*—is wonderful stuff, Eddie, but there are fevers beyond the power of any medicine to cure, and this was one of them. I knew my body needed rest, but it still took every ounce of my willpower to stay there even one night. In the morning I felt rested, and so I refilled my waterskins and pushed on. *I took nothing from that place but water.* That's the most important part of what really happened."

Susannah spoke in her most reasonable, pleasant, and Odetta Holmes–like voice. "All right, that's what really happened. You refilled your waterskins and went on. Now tell us the rest of what *didn't* happen, Roland."

The gunslinger put the jawbone in his lap for a moment, curled his hands into fists, and rubbed his eyes with them—a curiously childlike gesture. Then he grasped the jawbone again, as if for courage, and went on.

"I hyptonized the boy who wasn't there," he said. "I did it with one of my shells. It's a trick I've known for years, and I learned it from a very unlikely source—Marten, my father's court magician. The boy was a good subject. While he was tranced, he told me the circumstances of his death, as I've told them to you. When I'd gotten as much of his story as I felt I could without upsetting or actually hurting him, I gave him a command that he should not remember anything about his dying when he woke up again."

"Who'd want to?" Eddie muttered.

Roland nodded. "Who, indeed? The boy passed from his trance directly into a natural sleep. I also slept. When we woke, I told the boy that I meant to catch the man in black. He knew who I meant; Walter had also stopped at the way station. Jake was afraid and hid from him. I'm sure Walter knew he was there, but it suited his purpose to pretend he didn't. He left the boy behind like a set trap.

"I asked him if there was anything to eat there. It seemed to me there must be. He looked healthy enough, and the desert climate is wonderful when it comes to preserving things. He had a little dried meat, and he said there was a cellar. He hadn't explored that, because he was afraid." The gunslinger looked at them grimly. "He was right to be afraid. I found food . . . and I also found a Speaking Demon."

Eddie looked down at the jawbone with widening eyes. Orange firelight danced on its ancient curves and hoodoo teeth. "Speaking Demon? Do you mean *that* thing?"

"No," he said. "Yes. Both. Listen and you shall understand."

He told them about the inhuman groans he'd heard coming from the earth beyond the cellar; how he had seen sand running from between two of the old blocks which made up the cellar walls. He told them of approaching the hole that was appearing there as Jake screamed for him to come up.

He had commanded the demon to speak . . . and so the demon had, in the voice of Allie, the woman with the scar on her forehead, the woman who had kept the bar in Tull. *Go slow past the Drawers, gunslinger. While you travel with the boy, the man in black travels with your soul in his pocket.*

"The Drawers?" Susannah asked, startled.

"Yes." Roland looked at her closely. "That means something to you, doesn't it?"

"Yes . . . and no."

She spoke with great hesitation. Some of it, Roland divined, was simple reluctance to speak of things which were painful to her. He thought most of it, however, was a desire not to confuse issues which were already confused by saying more than she actually knew. He admired that. He admired *her*.

"Say what you can be sure of," he said. "No more than that."

"All right. The Drawers was a place Detta Walker knew about. A place Detta *thought* about. It's a slang term, one she picked up from listening to the grownups when they sat out on the porch and drank beer and talked about the old days. It means a place that's spoiled, or useless, or both. There was something in the Drawers—in the *idea* of the Drawers—that called to Detta. Don't ask me what; I might have known once, but I don't anymore. And don't want to.

"Detta stole my Aunt Blue's china plate—the one my folks gave her for a wedding present—and took it to the Drawers—*her* Drawers—to break it. That place was a gravel-pit filled with trash. A dumping-ground. Later on, she sometimes picked up boys at roadhouses."

Susannah dropped her head for a moment, her lips pressed tightly together. Then she looked up again and went on.

"*White* boys. And when they took her back to their cars in the parking lot, she cock-teased them and then ran off. Those parking lots . . . they were the Drawers, too. It was a dangerous game, but she was young enough, quick enough, and mean enough to play it to the hilt and enjoy it. Later, in New York, she'd go on shoplifting expeditions . . . you know about that. Both of you. Always to the fancy stores—Macy's, Gimbel's, Bloomingdale's—and steal trinkets. And when she made up her mind to go on one of those sprees, she'd think: *I'm goan to the Drawers today. Goan steal me some shit fum de white folks. Goan steal me sumpin forspecial and den break dat sumbitch.*"

She paused, lips trembling, looking into the fire. When she looked around again, Roland and Eddie saw tears standing in her eyes.

"I'm crying, but don't let that fool you. I remember doing those things, and I remember *enjoying* them. I guess I'm crying because I know I'd do it all again, if the circumstances were right."

Roland seemed to have regained some of his old serenity, his weird equilibrium. "We have a proverb in my country, Susannah: 'The wise thief always prospers.'"

"I don't see nothing wise about stealing a bunch of paste jewelry," she said sharply.

"Were you ever caught?"

"No—"

He spread his hands as if to say, *There you have it.*

"So for Detta Walker, the Drawers were bad places?" Eddie asked. "Is that right? Because it doesn't exactly *feel* right."

"Bad and good at the same time. They were *powerful* places, places where she ... she *reinvented* herself, I suppose you could say ... but they were *lost* places, too. And this is all off the subject of Roland's ghost-boy, isn't it?"

"Maybe not," Roland said. "We had Drawers as well, you see, in my world. It was slang for us, too, and the meanings are very similar."

"What did it mean to you and your friends?" Eddie asked.

"That varied slightly from place to place and situation to situation. It might mean a trash-midden. It might mean a whorehouse or a place where men came to gamble or chew devil-weed. But the most common meaning that I know is also the simplest."

He looked at them both.

"The Drawers are places of desolation," he said. "The Drawers are the waste lands."

<h1 style="text-align:center">15</h1>

THIS TIME SUSANNAH THREW more wood on the fire. In the south, Old Mother blazed on brilliantly, not flickering. She knew from her school studies what that meant: it was a planet, not a star. *Venus?* she wondered. *Or is the solar system of which this world is a part as different as everything else?*

Again that feeling of unreality—the feeling that all this must surely be a dream—washed over her.

"Go on," she said. "What happened after the voice warned you about the Drawers and the little boy?"

"I punched my hand into the hole the sand had come from, as I was taught to do if such a thing ever happened to me. What I plucked forth was a jawbone ... but not this one. The jawbone I took from the wall of the way station was much larger; from one of the Great Old Ones, I have almost no doubt."

"What happened to it?" Susannah asked quietly.

"One night I gave it to the boy," Roland said. The fire painted his cheeks with hot orange highlights and dancing shadows. "As a protection—a kind of talisman. Later I felt it had served its purpose and threw it away."

"So whose jawbone you got there, Roland?" Eddie asked.

Roland held it up, looked at it long and thoughtfully, and let it drop back. "Later, after Jake ... after he died ... I caught up with the men I had been chasing."

"With Walter," Susannah said.

"Yes. We held palaver, he and I ... *long* palaver. I fell asleep at some point, and when I woke up, Walter was dead. A hundred years dead at least, and probably more. There was nothing left of him but bones, which was fitting enough, since we were in a place of bones."

"Yeah, it must have been a pretty long palaver, all right," Eddie said dryly.

Susannah frowned slightly at this, but Roland only nodded. "Long and long," he said, looking into the fire.

"You came to in the morning and reached the Western Sea that very evening," Eddie said. "That night the lobstrosities came, right?"

Roland nodded again. "Yes. But before I left the place where Walter and I had spoken . . . or dreamed . . . or whatever it was we did . . . I took this from the skull of his skeleton." He lifted the bone and the orange light again skated off the teeth.

Walter's jawbone, Eddie thought, and felt a little chill work through him. *The jawbone of the man in black. Remember this, Eddie my boy, the next time you get to thinking Roland's maybe just another one of the guys. He's been carrying it around with him all this time like some kind of a . . . a cannibal's trophy. Jee-sus.*

"I remember what I thought when I took it," Roland said. "I remember very well; it is the only memory I have of that time which hasn't doubled on me. I thought, 'It was bad luck to throw away what I found when I found the boy. This will replace it.' Only then I heard Walter's laughter—his mean, tittery laughter. I heard his voice, too."

"What did he say?" Susannah asked.

"'Too late, gunslinger,'" Roland said. "That's what he said. 'Too late—your luck will be bad from now until the end of eternity—that is your *ka*.'"

16

"ALL RIGHT," EDDIE SAID at last. "I understand the basic paradox. Your memory is divided—"

"*Not* divided. *Doubled.*"

"All right; it's almost the same thing, isn't it?" Eddie grasped a twig and made his own little drawing in the sand:

He tapped the line on the left. "This is your memory of the time before you got to the way station—a single track."

"Yes."

He tapped the line on the right. "And after you came out on the far side of the mountains in the place of bones ... the place where Walter was waiting for you. *Also* a single track."

"Yes."

Now Eddie first indicated the middle area and then drew a rough circle around it.

"That's what you've got to do, Roland—close this double track off. Build a stockade around it in your mind and then forget it. Because it doesn't *mean* anything, it doesn't *change* anything, it's *gone*, it's *done*—"

"But it isn't." Roland held up the bone. "If my memories of the boy Jake are false—and I know they are—*how can I have this?* I took it to replace the one I threw away ... but the one I threw away came from the cellar of the way station, and along the track I know is true, *I never went down cellar!* I never spoke with the demon! I moved on alone, with fresh water *and nothing else!*"

"Roland, listen to me," Eddie said earnestly. "If that jawbone you're holding was the one from the way station, that would be one thing. But isn't it possible that if you hallucinated that whole thing—the way station, the kid, the Speaking Demon—then maybe you took Walter's jawbone because—"

"It was no hallucination," Roland said. He looked at them both with his faded blue bombardier's eyes and then did something neither expected ... something Eddie would have sworn Roland did not know he meant to do himself.

He threw the jawbone into the fire.

17

FOR A MOMENT IT only lay there, a white relic bent in a ghostly half-grin. Then it suddenly blazed red, washing the clearing with dazzling scarlet light. Eddie and Susannah cried out and threw their hands up to shield their eyes from that burning shape.

The bone began to change. Not to melt, but to *change*. The teeth which leaned out of it like gravestones began to draw together in clumps.

The mild curve of the upper arc straightened, then snubbed down at the tip.

Eddie's hands fell into his lap and he stared at the bone which was no longer a bone with gape-jawed wonder. It was now the color of burning steel. The teeth had become three inverted V's, the middle one larger than those on the ends. And suddenly Eddie saw what it wanted to become, just as he had seen the slingshot in the wood of the stump.

He thought it was a key.

You must remember the shape, he thought feverishly. *You must, you must.*

His eyes traced it desperately—three V's, the one in the center larger and deeper than the two on the end. Three notches . . . and the one closest the end had a squiggle, the shallow shape of a lower-case *s* . . .

Then the shape in the flames changed again. The bone which had become something like a key drew inward, concentrating itself into bright, overlapping petals and folds as dark and velvety as a moonless summer midnight. For a moment Eddie saw a rose—a triumphant rose that might have bloomed in the dawn of this world's first day, a thing of depthless, timeless beauty. His eye saw, and his heart was opened. It was as if all love and life had suddenly risen from Roland's dead artifact; it was there in the fire, burning out in triumph and some wonderful, inchoate defiance, declaring that despair was a mirage and death a dream.

The rose! he thought incoherently. *First the key, then the rose! Behold! Behold the opening of the way to the Tower!*

There was a thick cough from the fire. A fan of sparks twisted outwards. Susannah screamed and rolled away, beating at the orange flecks on her dress as the flames gushed upward toward the starry sky. Eddie didn't move. He sat transfixed in his vision, held in a cradle of wonder which was both gorgeous and terrible, unmindful of the sparks which danced across his skin. Then the flames sank back.

The bone was gone.

The key was gone.

The rose was gone.

Remember, he thought. *Remember the rose . . . and remember the shape of the key.*

Susannah was sobbing with shock and terror, but he ignored her for the moment and found the stick with which he and Roland had both drawn. And in the dirt he made this shape with a shaking hand:

18

"WHY DID YOU DO it?" Susannah asked at last. "Why, for God's sake—and what was it?"

Fifteen minutes had gone by. The fire had been allowed to burn low; the scattered embers had either been stamped out or had gone out on their own. Eddie sat with his arms about his wife: Susannah sat before him, with her back against his chest. Roland was off to one side, knees hugged to his chest, looking moodily into the orange-red coals. So far as Eddie could tell, neither of them had seen the bone change. They had both seen it glowing superhot, and Roland had seen it explode (or had it imploded? to Eddie that seemed closer to what he had seen), but that was all. Or so he believed; Roland, however, sometimes kept his own counsel, and when he decided to play his cards close to the vest, he played them very close indeed, Eddie knew that from bitter experience. He thought of telling them what he had seen—or *thought* he had seen—and decided to play his own cards tight and close-up, at least for the time being.

Of the jawbone itself there was no sign—not even a splinter.

"I did it because a voice spoke in my mind and told me I must," Roland said. "It was the voice of my father; of *all* my fathers. When one hears such a voice, not to obey—and at once—is unthinkable. So I was taught. As to what it was, I can't say . . . not now, at least. I only know that the bone has spoken its final word. I have carried it all this way to hear it."

Or to see it, Eddie thought, and again: *Remember. Remember the rose. And remember the shape of the key.*

"It almost flash-fried us!" She sounded both tired and exasperated.

Roland shook his head. "I think it was more like the sort of firework the barons used to sometimes shoot into the sky at their year-end parties. Bright and startling, but not dangerous."

Eddie had an idea. "The doubling in your mind, Roland—is it gone? Did it leave when the bone exploded, or whatever it did?"

He was almost convinced that it had; in the movies he'd seen, such rough shock-therapy almost always worked. But Roland shook his head.

Susannah shifted in Eddie's arms. "You said you were beginning to understand."

Roland nodded. "I think so, yes. If I'm right, I fear for Jake. Wherever he is, *whenever* he is, I fear for him."

"What do you mean?" Eddie asked.

Roland got up, went to his roll of hides, and began to spread them out. "Enough stories and excitement for one night. It's time to sleep. In the morning we'll follow the bear's backtrail and see if we can find the portal he was set to guard. I'll tell you what I know and what I believe has happened—what I believe is happening still—along the way."

With that he wrapped himself in an old blanket and a new deerskin, rolled away from the fire, and would say no more.

Eddie and Susannah lay down together. When they were sure the gunslinger must be asleep, they made love. Roland heard them going about it as he lay wakeful and heard their quiet after-love talk. Most of it was about him. He lay quietly, open eyes looking into the darkness long after their talk had ceased and their breathing had evened out into a single easy note.

It was, he thought, fine to be young and in love. Even in the grave-yard which this world had become, it was fine.

Enjoy it while you can, he thought, *because there is more death ahead. We have come to a stream of blood. That it will lead us to a river of the same stuff I have no doubt. And, further along, to an ocean. In this world the graves yawn and none of the dead rest easy.*

As dawn began to come up in the east, he closed his eyes. Slept briefly. And dreamed of Jake.

19

EDDIE ALSO DREAMED—DREAMED he was back in New York, walking along Second Avenue with a book in his hand.

In this dream it was spring. The air was warm, the city was blooming, and homesickness sobbed within him like a muscle with a fishhook caught deep within it. *Enjoy this dream, and make it go on as long as you can,* he thought. *Savor it . . . because this is as close to New York as you're going to get. You can't go home, Eddie. That part's done.*

He looked down at the book and was utterly unsurprised to find it was *You Can't Go Home Again,* by Thomas Wolfe. Stamped into the dark red cover were three shapes; key, rose, and door. He stopped for a moment, flipped the book open, and read the first line. *The man in black fled across the desert,* Wolfe had written, *and the gunslinger followed.*

Eddie closed it and walked on. It was about nine in the morning, he judged, maybe nine-thirty, and traffic on Second Avenue was light. Taxis honked and wove their way from lane to lane with spring sunshine twinkling off their windshields and bright yellow paintjobs. A bum on the corner of Second and Fifty-second asked him for a handout and Eddie tossed the book with the red cover into his lap. He observed (also without surprise) that the bum was Enrico Balazar. He was sitting cross-legged in front of a magic shop. HOUSE OF CARDS, the sign in the window read, and the display inside showed a tower which had been built of

Tarot cards. Standing on top was a model of King Kong. There was a tiny radar-dish growing out of the great ape's head.

Eddie walked on, lazing his way downtown, the street-signs floating past him. He knew where he was going as soon as he saw it: a small shop on the corner of Second and Forty-sixth.

Yeah, he thought. A feeling of great relief swept through him. *This is the place. The very place.* The window was full of hanging meats and cheeses. TOM AND GERRY'S ARTISTIC DELI, the sign read. PARTY PLATTERS OUR SPECIALTY!

As he stood looking in, someone else he knew came around the corner. It was Jack Andolini, wearing a three-piece suit the color of vanilla ice cream and carrying a black cane in his left hand. Half of his face was gone, lopped off by the claws of the lobstrosities.

Go on in, Eddie, Jack said as he passed. *After all, there are other worlds than these and that fuckin train rolls through all of them.*

I can't, Eddie replied. *The door is locked.* He didn't know how he knew this, but he did; knew it beyond a shadow of a doubt.

Dad-a-chum, dud-a-chee, not to worry, you've got the key, Jack said, not looking back. Eddie looked down and saw he *did* have a key; a primitive-looking thing with three notches like inverted V's.

That little s-shape at the end of the last notch is the secret, he thought. He stepped under the awning of Tom and Gerry's Artistic Deli and inserted the key in the lock. It turned easily. He opened the door and stepped through into a huge open field. He looked back over his shoulder and saw the traffic on Second Avenue hurrying by, and then the door slammed shut and fell over. There was nothing behind it. Nothing at all. He turned back to survey his new surroundings, and what he saw filled him with terror at first. The field was a deep scarlet, as if some titanic battle had been fought here and the ground had been drenched with so much blood that it could not all be absorbed.

Then he realized that it was not blood he was looking at, but roses.

That feeling of mingled joy and triumph surged through him again, swelling his heart until he felt it might burst within him. He raised his clenched fists high over his head in a gesture of victory . . . and then froze that way.

The field stretched on for miles, climbing a gentle slope of land, and standing at the horizon was the Dark Tower. It was a pillar of dumb stone rising so high into the sky that he could barely discern its tip. Its base, surrounded by red, shouting roses, was formidable, titanic with weight and size, yet the Tower became oddly graceful as it rose and tapered. The stone of which it had been made was not black, as he had imagined it would be, but soot-colored. Narrow, slitted windows marched about it in a rising spiral; below the windows ran an almost endless flight of stone stairs, circling up and up. The Tower was a dark gray exclamation point planted in the earth and rising above the field of blood-red roses. The sky arched above it was blue, but filled with puffy white clouds like sailing ships. They flowed above and around the top of the Dark Tower in an endless stream.

How gorgeous it is! Eddie marvelled. *How gorgeous and strange!* But his feeling of joy and triumph had departed; he was left with a sense of deep malaise and impending doom. He looked about him and realized with sudden horror that he was standing in the shadow of the Tower. No, not just *standing* in it; buried alive in it.

He cried out but his cry was lost in the golden blast of some tremendous horn. It came from the top of the Tower, and seemed to fill the world. As that note of warning held and drew out over the field where he stood, blackness welled from the windows which girdled the Tower. It overspilled them and spread across the sky in flaggy streams which came together and formed a growing blotch of darkness. It did not look like a cloud; it looked like a tumor hanging over the earth. The sky was blotted out. And, he saw, it was not a cloud or a tumor but a *shape*, some tenebrous, cyclopean *shape* racing toward the place where he stood. It would do no good to run from that beast coalescing in the sky above the field of roses; it would catch him, clutch him, and bear him away. Into the Dark Tower it would bear him, and the world of light would see him no more.

Rents formed in the darkness and terrible inhuman eyes, each easily the size of the bear Shardik which lay dead in the forest, peered down at him. They were red—red as roses, red as blood.

Jack Andolini's dead voice hammered in his ears: *A thousand worlds, Eddie—ten thousand!—and that train rolls through every one. If you can get it started. And if you do get it started, your troubles are only beginning, because this device is a real bastard to shut down.*

Jack's voice had become mechanical, chanting. *A real bastard to shut down, Eddie boy, you better believe it, this bastard is—*

"—SHUTTING DOWN! SHUTDOWN WILL BE COMPLETE IN ONE HOUR AND SIX MINUTES!"

In his dream, Eddie threw his hands up to shield his eyes . . .

20

. . . AND WOKE, SITTING BOLT upright beside the dead campfire. He was looking at the world from between his own spread fingers. And still that voice rolled on and on, the voice of some heartless SWAT Squad commander bellowing through a bullhorn.

"THERE IS NO DANGER! REPEAT, THERE IS NO DANGER! FIVE SUBNUCLEAR CELLS ARE DORMANT, TWO SUBNUCLEAR CELLS ARE NOW IN SHUTDOWN PHASE, ONE SUBNUCLEAR CELL IS OPERATING AT TWO PER CENT CAPACITY. THESE CELLS ARE OF NO VALUE! REPEAT, THESE CELLS ARE OF NO VALUE! REPORT LOCATION TO NORTH CENTRAL POSITRONICS, LIMITED! CALL 1-900-44! THE CODE WORD FOR THIS DEVICE IS 'SHARDIK.' REWARD IS OFFERED! REPEAT, REWARD IS OFFERED!"

The voice fell silent. Eddie saw Roland standing at the edge of the clearing, holding Susannah in the crook of one arm. They were staring toward the sound of the voice, and as the recorded announcement began again, Eddie was finally able to shake off the chill remnants of his nightmare. He got up and joined Roland and Susannah, wondering how many centuries it had been since that announcement, pro- grammed to broadcast only in the event of a total system breakdown, had been recorded.

"THIS DEVICE IS SHUTTING DOWN! SHUTDOWN WILL BE COMPLETE IN ONE HOUR AND FIVE MINUTES! THERE IS NO DANGER! REPEAT—"

Eddie touched Susannah's arm and she looked around. "How long has this been going on?"

"About fifteen minutes. You were dead to the w—" She broke off. "Eddie, you look terrible! Are you sick?"

"No. I just had a bad dream."

Roland was studying him in a way that made Eddie feel uncomfort- able. "Sometimes there's truth in dreams, Eddie. What was yours?"

He thought for a moment, then shook his head. "I don't remember."

"You know, I doubt that."

Eddie shrugged and favored Roland with a thin smile. "Doubt away, then—be my guest. And how are *you* this morning, Roland?"

"The same," Roland said. His faded blue eyes still conned Eddie's face.

"Stop it," Susannah said. Her voice was brisk, but Eddie caught an undertone of nervousness. "Both of you. I got better things to do than watch you two dance around and kick each other's shins like a couple of little kids playin Two for Flinching. Specially this morning, with that dead bear trying to yell down the whole world."

The gunslinger nodded, but kept his eyes on Eddie. "All right . . . but are you sure there's nothing you want to tell me, Eddie?"

He thought about it then—really thought about telling. What he had seen in the fire, what he had seen in his dream. He decided against it. Perhaps it was only the memory of the rose in the fire, and the roses

which had blanketed that dream-field in such fabulous profusion. He knew he could not tell these things as his eyes had seen them and his heart had felt them; he could only cheapen them. And, at least for the time being, he wanted to ponder these things alone.

But remember, he told himself again ... except the voice in his mind didn't sound much like his own. It seemed deeper, older—the voice of a stranger. *Remember the rose ... and the shape of the key.*

"I will," he murmured.

"You will what?" Roland asked.

"Tell," Eddie said. "If anything comes up that seems, you know, really important, I'll tell you. Both of you. Right now there isn't. So if we're going somewhere, Shane, old buddy, let's saddle up."

"Shane? Who is this Shane?"

"I'll tell you that some other time, too. Meantime, let's go."

They packed the gear they had brought with them from the old campsite and headed back, Susannah riding in her wheelchair again. Eddie had an idea she wouldn't be riding in it for long.

21

ONCE, BEFORE EDDIE HAD become too interested in the subject of heroin to be interested in much else, he and a couple of friends had driven over to New Jersey to see a couple of speed-metal groups— Anthrax and Megadeth—in concert at the Meadowlands. He believed that Anthrax had been slightly louder than the repeating announcement coming from the fallen bear, but he wasn't a hundred per cent sure. Roland stopped them while they were still half a mile from the clearing in the woods and tore six small scaps of cloth from his old shirt. They stuffed them in their ears and then went on. Even the cloth didn't do much to deaden the steady blast of sound.

"THIS DEVICE IS SHUTTING DOWN!" the bear blared as they stepped into the clearing again. It lay as it had lain, at the foot of the tree Eddie had climbed, a fallen Colossus with its legs apart and its knees in the air, like a furry female giant who had died trying to give birth. *"SHUTDOWN WILL BE COMPLETE IN FORTY-SEVEN MINUTES! THERE IS NO DANGER—"*

Yes, there is, Eddie thought, picking up the scattered hides which had not been shredded in either the bear's attack or its flailing death-throes. *Plenty* of danger. To my fucking *ears*. He picked up Roland's gunbelt and silently handed it over. The chunk of wood he had been working on lay nearby; he grabbed it and tucked it into the pocket in the back of Susannah's wheelchair as the gunslinger slowly buckled the wide leather belt around his waist and cinched the rawhide tiedown.

"—*IN SHUTDOWN PHASE, ONE SUBNUCLEAR CELL OPERATING AT ONE PER CENT CAPACITY. THESE CELLS*—"

Susannah followed Eddie, holding in her lap a carry-all bag she had sewn herself. As Eddie handed her the hides, she stuffed them into the bag. When all of them were stored away, Roland tapped Eddie on the arm and handed him a shoulderpack. What it contained mostly was deer-meat, heavily salted from a natural lick Roland had found about three miles up the little creek. The gunslinger had already donned a similar pack. His purse—restocked and once again bulging with all sorts of odds and ends—hung from his other shoulder.

A strange, home-made harness with a seat of stitched deerskin dangled from a nearby branch. Roland plucked it off, studied it for a moment, and then draped it over his back and knotted the straps below his chest. Susannah made a sour face at this, and Roland saw it. He did not try to speak—this close to the bear, he couldn't have made himself heard even by shouting at the top of his voice—but he shrugged sympathetically and spread his hands: *You know we'll need it.*

She shrugged back. *I know . . . but that doesn't mean I like it.*

The gunslinger pointed across the clearing. A pair of leaning, splintered spruce trees marked the place where Shardik, who had once been known as Mir in these parts, had entered the clearing.

Eddie leaned toward Susannah, made a circle with his thumb and forefinger, then raised his eyebrows interrogatively. *Okay?*

She nodded, then pressed the heels of her palms against her ears. *Okay—but let's get out of here before I go deaf.*

The three of them moved across the clearing, Eddie pushing Susannah, who held the bag of hides in her lap. The pocket in the back of her wheelchair was stuffed with other items; the piece of wood with the slingshot still mostly hidden inside it was only one of them.

From behind them the bear continued to roar out its final communication to the world, telling them shutdown would be complete in forty minutes. Eddie couldn't wait. The broken spruces leaned in toward each other, forming a rude gate, and Eddie thought: *This is where the quest for Roland's Dark Tower really begins, at least for us.*

He thought of his dream again—the spiraling windows issuing their unfurling flags of darkness, flags which spread over the field of roses like a stain—and as they passed beneath the leaning trees, a deep shudder gripped him.

22

THEY WERE ABLE TO use the wheelchair longer than Roland had expected. The firs of this forest were very old, and their spreading branches had created a deep carpet of needles which discouraged most undergrowth. Susannah's arms were strong—stronger than Eddie's, although Roland did not think that would be true much longer—and she wheeled herself along easily over the level, shady forest floor. When they came to one of the trees the bear had pushed over, Roland lifted her out of the chair and Eddie boosted it over the obstacle.

From behind them, only a little deadened by distance, the bear told them, at the top of its mechanical voice, that the capacity of its last operating nuclear subcell was now negligible.

"I hope you keep that damn harness lying empty over your shoulders all day!" Susannah shouted at the gunslinger.

Roland agreed, but less than fifteen minutes later the land began to slope downward and this old section of the forest began to be invaded with smaller, younger trees: birch, alder, and a few stunted maples scrabbling grimly in the soil for purchase. The carpet of needles thinned and the wheels of Susannah's chair began to catch in the low, tough bushes which grew in the alleys between the trees. Their thin branches boinged and rattled in the stainless steel spokes. Eddie threw his weight against the handles and they were able to go on for another quarter of a mile that way. Then the slope began to grow more steep, and the ground underfoot became mushy.

"Time for a pig-back, lady," Roland said.

"Let's try the chair a little longer, what do you say? Going might get easier—"

Roland shook his head. "If you try that hill, you'll . . . what did you call it, Eddie? . . . do a dugout?"

Eddie shook his head, grinning. "It's called doing a doughnut, Roland. A term from my misspent sidewalk-surfing days."

"Whatever you call it, it means landing on your head. Come on, Susannah. Up you come."

"I hate being a cripple," Susannah said crossly, but allowed Eddie to hoist her out of the chair and worked with him to seat herself firmly in the harness Roland wore on his back. Once she was in place, she touched the butt of Roland's pistol. "Y'all want this baby?" she asked Eddie.

He shook his head. "You're faster. And you know it, too."

She grunted and adjusted the belt, settling the gunbutt so it was easily accessible to her right hand. "I'm slowing you boys down and I know *that* . . . but if we ever make it to some good old two-lane blacktop, I'll leave the both of you kneelin in the blocks."

"I don't doubt it," Roland said . . . and then cocked his head. The woods had fallen silent.

"Br'er Bear has finally given up," Susannah said. "Praise God."

"I thought it still had seven minutes to go," Eddie said.

Roland adjusted the straps of the harness. "Its clock must have started running a little slow during the last five or six hundred years."

"You really think it was that old, Roland?"

Roland nodded. "At least. And now it's passed . . . the last of the Twelve Guardians, for all we know."

"Yeah, ask me if I give a shit," Eddie replied, and Susannah laughed.

"Are you comfortable?" Roland asked her.

"No. My butt hurts already, but go on. Just try not to drop me."

Roland nodded and started down the slope. Eddie followed, pushing the empty chair and trying not to bang it too badly on the rocks which had begun to jut out of the ground like big white knuckles. Now that the bear had finally shut up, he thought the forest seemed much too quiet—it almost made him feel like a character in one of those hokey old jungle movies about cannibals and giant apes.

23

THE BEAR'S BACKTRAIL WAS easy to find but tougher to follow. Five miles or so out of the clearing, it led them through a low, boggy area that was not quite a swamp. By the time the ground began to rise and firm up a little again, Roland's faded jeans were soaked to the knees and he was breathing in long, steady rasps. Still, he was in slightly better shape than Eddie, who had found wrestling Susannah's wheelchair through the muck and standing water hard going.

"Time to rest and eat something," Roland said.

"Oh boy, gimme eats," Eddie puffed. He helped Susannah out of the harness and set her down on the bole of a fallen tree with claw-marks slashed into its trunk in long diagonal grooves. Then he half-sat, half-collapsed next to her.

"You got my wheelchair pretty muddy, white boy," Susannah said. "It's all goan be in my repote."

He cocked an eyebrow at her. "Next carwash we come to, I'll push you through myself. I'll even Turtle-wax the goddamn thing. Okay?"

She smiled. "You got a date, handsome."

Eddie had one of Roland's waterskins cinched around his waist. He tapped it. "Okay?"

"Yes," Roland said. "Not too much now; a little more for all of us before we set out again. That way no one takes a cramp."

"Roland, Eagle Scout of Oz," Eddie said, and giggled as he unslung the waterskin.

"What is this Oz?"

"A make-believe place in a movie," Susannah said.

"Oz was a lot more than that. My brother Henry used to read me the stories once in a while. I'll tell you one some night, Roland."

"That would be fine," the gunslinger replied seriously. "I am hungry to know more of your world."

"Oz isn't our world, though. Like Susannah said, it's a make-believe place—"

Roland handed them chunks of meat which had been wrapped in broad leaves of some sort. "The quickest way to learn about a new place is to know what it dreams of. I would hear of this Oz."

"Okay, that's a date, too. Suze can tell you the one about Dorothy and Toto and the Tin Woodman, and I'll tell you all the rest." He bit into his piece of meat and rolled his eyes approvingly. It had taken the flavor of the leaves in which it had been rolled, and was delicious. Eddie wolfed his ration, stomach gurgling busily all the while. Now that he was getting his breath back, he felt good—great, in fact. His body was growing a solid sheath of muscle, and every part of it felt at peace with every other part.

Don't worry, he thought. *Everything will be arguing again by tonight. I think he's gonna push on until I'm ready to drop in my tracks.*

Susannah ate more delicately, chasing every second or third bite with a little sip of water, turning the meat in her hands, eating from the outside in. "Finish what you started last night," she invited Roland. "You said you thought you understood these conflicting memories of yours."

Roland nodded. "Yes. I think both memories are true. One is a little truer than the other, but that does not *negate* the truth of that other."

"Makes no sense to me," Eddie said. "Either this boy Jake was at the way station or he wasn't, Roland."

"It is a paradox—something that is and isn't at the same time. Until it's resolved, I will continue divided. That's bad enough, but the basic split is widening. I can feel that happening. It is . . . unspeakable."

"What do you think caused it?" Susannah asked.

"I told you the boy was pushed in front of a car. *Pushed.* Now, who do we know who liked to push people in front of things?"

Understanding dawned in her face. "Jack Mort. Do you mean *he* was the one who pushed this boy into the street?"

"Yes."

"But you said the man in black did it," Eddie objected. "Your buddy

Walter. You said that the boy *saw* him—a man who looked like a priest. Didn't the kid even hear him *say* he was? 'Let me through, I'm a priest,' something like that?"

"Oh, Walter was there. They were *both* there, and they both pushed Jake."

"Somebody bring the Thorazine and the strait-jacket," Eddie called. "Roland just went over the high side."

Roland paid no attention to this; he was coming to understand that Eddie's jokes and clowning were his way of dealing with stress. Cuthbert had not been much different . . . as Susannah was, in her way, not so different from Alain. "What exasperates me about all of this," he said, "is that I should have *known*. I was *in* Jack Mort, after all, and I had access to his thoughts, just as I had access to yours, Eddie, and yours, Susannah. I *saw* Jake while I was in Mort. I saw him through Mort's eyes, *and I knew Mort planned to push him.* Not only that; I *stopped* him from doing it. All I had to do was enter his body. Not that he knew that was what it was; he was concentrating so hard on what he planned to do that he actually thought I was a fly landing on his neck."

Eddie began to understand. "If Jake wasn't pushed into the street, he never died. And if he never died, he never came into this world. And if he never came into this world, you never met him at the way station. Right?"

"Right. The thought even crossed my mind that if Jack Mort meant to kill the boy, I would have to stand aside and let him do it. To avoid creating the very paradox that is tearing me apart. But I couldn't do that. I . . . I . . ."

"You couldn't kill this kid twice, could you?" Eddie asked softly. "Every time I just about make up my mind that you're as mechanical as that bear, you surprise me with something that actually seems human. Goddam."

"Quit it, Eddie," Susannah said.

Eddie took a look at the gunslinger's slightly lowered face and grimaced. "Sorry, Roland. My mother used to say that my mouth had a bad habit of running away with my mind."

"It's all right. I had a friend who was the same way."

"Cuthbert?"

Roland nodded. He looked at his diminished right hand for a long moment, then clenched it into a painful fist, sighed, and looked up at them again. Somewhere, deeper in the forest, a lark sang sweetly.

"Here is what I believe. If I had not entered Jack Mort when I did, he *still* wouldn't have pushed Jake that day. Not then. Why not? *Ka-tet.* Simply that. For the first time since the last of the friends with whom I set forth on this quest died, I have found myself once again at the center of *ka-tet*."

"Quartet?" Eddie asked doubtfully.

The gunslinger shook his head. "*Ka*—the word you think of as 'destiny,' Eddie, although the actual meaning is much more complex and hard to define, as is almost always the case with words of the High Speech. And *tet*, which means a group of people with the same interests and goals. We three are a *tet*, for instance. *Ka-tet* is the place where many lives are joined by fate."

"Like in *The Bridge of San Luis Rey*," Susannah murmured.

"What's that?" Roland asked.

"A story about some people who die together when the bridge they're crossing collapses. It's famous in our world."

Roland nodded his understanding. "In this case, *ka-tet* bound Jake, Walter, Jack Mort, and me. There was no trap, as I first suspected when I realized who Jack Mort meant to be his next victim, because *ka-tet* cannot be changed or bent to the will of any one person. But *ka-tet* can be *seen, known,* and *understood.* Walter saw, and Walter knew." The gunslinger struck his thigh with his fist and exclaimed bitterly, "How he must have been laughing inside when I finally caught up to him!"

"Let's go back to what would have happened if you hadn't messed up Jack Mort's plans on the day he was following Jake," Eddie said. "You're saying that if *you* hadn't stopped Mort, someone or something else would have. Is that right?"

"Yes—because it wasn't the *right* day for Jake to die. It was *close* to the right day, but not *the* right day. I felt that, too. Perhaps, just before he did it, Mort would have seen someone watching him. Or a perfect stranger would have intervened. Or—"

"Or a cop," Susannah said. "He might have seen a cop in the wrong place and at the wrong time."

"Yes. The exact reason—the agent of *ka-tet*—doesn't matter. I know from firsthand experience that Mort was as wily as an old fox. If he sensed any slightest thing wrong, he would have called it off and waited for another day.

"I know something else, as well. He hunted in disguise. On the day he dropped the brick on Detta Holmes's head, he was wearing a knitted cap and an old sweater several sizes too big for him. He wanted to look like a wine-bibber, because he pushed the brick from a building where a large number of sots kept their dens. You see?"

They nodded.

"On the day, years later, when he pushed you in front of the train, Susannah, he was dressed as a construction worker. He was wearing a big yellow helmet he thought of as a 'hardhat' and a fake moustache. On the day when he actually *would* have pushed Jake into traffic, causing his death, *he would have been dressed as a priest.*"

"Jesus," Susannah nearly whispered. "The man who pushed him in New York was Jack Mort, and the man he saw at the way station was this fella you were chasing—Walter."

"Yes."

"And the little boy thought they were the same man because they were both wearing the same kind of black robe?"

Roland nodded. "There was even a physical resemblance between Walter and Jack Mort. Not as if they were brothers, I don't mean that, but both were tall men with dark hair and very pale complexions. And given the fact that Jake was dying when he got his only good look at Mort and was in a strange place and scared almost witless when he got his only good look at Walter, I think his mistake was both understandable and forgivable. If there's a horse's ass in this picture, it's me, for not realizing the truth sooner."

"Would Mort have known he was being used?" Eddie asked. Thinking back to his own experiences and wild thoughts when Roland had invaded his mind, he didn't see how Mort could *not* know . . . but Roland was shaking his head.

"Walter would have been extremely subtle. Mort would have thought the priest disguise his own idea . . . or so I believe. He would not have recognized the voice of an intruder—of Walter—whispering deep within his mind, telling him what to do."

"Jack Mort," Eddie marvelled. "It was Jack Mort all the time."

"Yes . . . with assistance from Walter. And so I ended up saving Jake's life after all. When I made Mort jump from the subway platform in front of the train, I changed everything."

Susannah asked, "If this Walter was able to enter our world—through his own private door, maybe—whenever he wanted, couldn't he have used someone else to push your little boy? If he could suggest to Mort that he dress up like a priest, then he could make somebody else do it . . . What, Eddie? Why are you shaking your head?"

"Because I don't think Walter would want that to happen. What Walter wanted is what *is* happening . . . for Roland to be losing his mind, bit by bit. Isn't that right?"

The gunslinger nodded.

"Walter couldn't have done it that way even if he *had* wanted to," Eddie added, "because he was dead long before Roland found the doors on the beach. When Roland went through that last one and into Jack Mort's head, ole Walt's messin-around days were done."

Susannah thought about this, then nodded her head. "I see ... I *think*. This time-travel business is some confusing shit, isn't it?"

Roland began to pick up his goods and strap them back into place. "Time we were moving on."

Eddie stood up and shrugged into his pack. "You can take comfort from one thing, at least," he told Roland. "You—or this *ka-tet* business— were able to save the kid after all."

Roland had been knotting the harness-strings at his chest. Now he looked up, and the blazing clarity of his eyes made Eddie flinch backward. "Have I?" he asked harshly. "Have I really? I'm going insane an inch at a time, trying to live with two versions of the same reality. I had hoped at first that one or the other would begin to fade away, but that's not happening. In fact, the exact opposite is happening: those two realities are growing louder and louder in my head, clamoring at each other like opposing factions which must soon go to war. So tell me this, Eddie: How do you suppose *Jake* feels? *How do you suppose it feels to know you are dead in one world and alive in another?*"

The lark sang again, but none of them noticed. Eddie stared into the faded blue eyes blazing out of Roland's pale face and could not think of a thing to say.

24

THEY CAMPED ABOUT FIFTEEN miles due east of the dead bear that night, slept the sleep of the completely exhausted (even Roland slept the night through, although his dreams were nightmare carnival-rides), and were up the next morning at sunrise. Eddie kindled a small fire without speaking, and glanced at Susannah as a pistol-shot rang out in the woods nearby.

"Breakfast," she said.

Roland returned three minutes later with a hide slung over one shoulder. On it lay the freshly gutted corpse of a rabbit. Susannah cooked it. They ate and moved on.

Eddie kept trying to imagine what it would be like to have a memory of your own death. On that one he kept coming up short.

25

SHORTLY AFTER NOON THEY entered an area where most of the trees had been pulled over and the bushes mashed flat—it looked as though a cyclone had touched down here many years before, creating a wide and dismal alley of destruction.

"We're close to the place we want to find," Roland said. "He pulled down everything to clear the sightlines. Our friend the bear wanted no surprises. He was big, but not complacent."

"Has it left *us* any surprises?" Eddie asked.

"He may have done so." Roland smiled a little and touched Eddie on the shoulder. "But there's this—they'll be *old* surprises."

Their progress through this zone of destruction was slow. Most of the fallen trees were very old—many had almost rejoined the soil from which they had sprung—but they still made enough of a tangle to create a formidable obstacle course. It would have been difficult enough if all three of them had been able-bodied; with Susannah strapped to the gunslinger's back in her harness, it became an exercise in aggravation and endurance.

The flattened trees and jumbles of underbrush served to obscure the bear's backtrail, and that also worked to slow their speed. Until midday they had followed claw-marks as clear as trail-blazes on the trees. Here, however, near its starting point, the bear's rage had not been full-blown, and these handy signs of its passage disappeared. Roland moved slowly, looking for droppings in the bushes and tufts of hair on the tree-trunks over which the bear had climbed. It took all afternoon to cross three miles of this decayed jumble.

Eddie had just decided they were going to lose the light and would have to camp in these creepy surroundings when they came to a thin skirt of alders. Beyond it, he could hear a stream babbling noisily over a bed of stones. Behind them, the setting sun was radiating spokes of sullen red light across the jumbled ground they had just crossed, turning the fallen trees into crisscrossing black shapes like Chinese ideograms.

Roland called a halt and eased Susannah down. He stretched his back, twisting it this way and that with his hands on his hips.

"That it for the night?" Eddie asked.

Roland shook his head. "Give Eddie your gun, Susannah."

She did as he said, looking at him questioningly.

"Come on, Eddie. The place we want is on the other side of those trees. We'll have a look. We might do a little work, as well."

"What makes you think—"

"Open your ears."

Eddie listened and realized he heard machinery. He further realized that he had been hearing it for some time now. "I don't want to leave Susannah."

"We're not going far and she has a good loud voice. Besides, if there's danger, it's ahead—we'll be between it and her."

Eddie looked down at Susannah.

"Go on—just make sure you're back soon." She looked back the way they had come with thoughtful eyes. "I don't know if there's ha'ants here or not, but it *feels* like there are."

"We'll be back before dark," Roland promised. He started toward the screen of alders, and after a moment, Eddie followed him.

26

FIFTEEN YARDS INTO THE trees, Eddie realized that they were following a path, one the bear had probably made for itself over the years. The alders bent above them in a tunnel. The sounds were louder now, and he began to sort them out. One was a low, deep, humming noise. He could feel it in his feet—a faint vibration, as if some large piece of machinery was running in the earth. Above it, closer and more urgent, were crisscrossing sounds like bright scratches—squeals, squeaks, chitterings.

Roland placed his mouth against Eddie's ear and said, "I think there's little danger if we're quiet."

They moved on another five yards and then Roland stopped again. He drew his gun and used the barrel to brush aside a branch which hung heavy with sunset-tinted leaves. Eddie looked through this small opening and into the clearing where the bear had lived for so long—the base of operations from which he had set forth on his many expeditions of pillage and terror.

There was no undergrowth here; the ground had been beaten bald long since. A stream emerged from the base of a rock wall about fifty feet high and ran through the arrowhead-shaped clearing. On their side of the stream, backed up against the wall, was a metal box about nine feet high. Its roof was curved, and it reminded Eddie of a subway entrance. The front was painted in diagonal yellow and black stripes. The earth which floored the clearing was not black, like the topsoil in the forest, but a strange powdery gray. It was littered with bones, and after a moment Eddie realized that what he had taken for gray soil was more bones, bones so old they were crumbling back to dust.

Things were moving in the dirt—the things making the squealing, chittering noises. Four . . . no, five of them. Small metal devices, the largest about the size of a Collie pup. They were robots, Eddie realized, or something *like* robots. They were similar to each other and to the bear they had undoubtedly served in one way only—atop each of them, a tiny radar-dish turned rapidly.

More thinking caps, Eddie thought. *My God, what kind of world is this, anyway?*

The largest of these devices looked a little like the Tonka tractor Eddie had gotten for his sixth or seventh birthday; its treads churned up tiny gray clouds of bone-dust as it rolled along. Another looked like a stainless steel rat. A third appeared to be a snake constructed of jointed steel segments—it writhed and humped its way along. They formed a rough circle on the far side of the stream, going around and around on a deep course they had carved in the ground. Looking at them made Eddie think of cartoons he had seen in the stacks of old *Saturday Evening Post* magazines his mother had for some reason saved and stored in the front hall of their apartment. In the cartoons, worried, cigarette-smoking men paced ruts in the carpet while they waited for their wives to give birth.

As his eyes grew used to the simple geography of the clearing, Eddie saw that there were a great many more than five of these assorted freaks. There were at least a dozen others that he could see and probably more hidden behind the bony remains of the bear's old kills. The difference was that the others weren't moving. The members of the bear's mechanical retinue had died, one by one, over the long years until just this little group of five were left . . . and they did not sound very healthy, with their squeaks and squalls and rusty chitterings. The snake in particular had a hesitant, crippled look as it followed the mechanical rat around and around the circle. Every now and then the device which followed the snake—a steel block that walked on stubby mechanical legs—would catch up with it and give the snake a nudge, as if telling it to hurry the fuck up.

Eddie wondered what their job had been. Surely not protection; the bear had been built to protect itself, and Eddie guessed that if old Shardik had come upon the three of them while still in its prime, it would have chewed them up and spat them out in short order. Perhaps these little robots had been its maintenance crew, or scouts, or messengers. He guessed that they could be dangerous, but only in their own defense . . . or their master's. They did not seem warlike.

There was, in fact, something pitiful about them. Most of the crew was now defunct, their master was gone, and Eddie believed they knew it somehow. It was not menace they projected but a strange, inhuman sadness. Old and almost worn out, they paced and rolled and wriggled their anxious way around the worry-track they had dug in this godforsaken clearing, and it almost seemed to Eddie that he could read the confused run of their thoughts; *Oh dear, oh dear, what now? What is our purpose, now that He is gone? And who will take care of us, now that He is gone? Oh dear, oh dear, oh dear . . .*

Eddie felt a tug on the back of his leg and came very close to screaming in fear and surprise. He wheeled, cocking Roland's gun, and saw Susannah looking up at him with wide eyes. Eddie let out a long breath and dropped the hammer carefully back to its resting position. He knelt, put his hands on Susannah's shoulders, kissed her cheek, then whispered in her ear: "I came really close to putting a bullet in your silly head—what are you doing here?"

"Wanted to see," she whispered back, looking not even slightly abashed. Her eyes shifted to Roland as he also hunkered beside her. "Besides, it was spooky back there by myself."

She had sustained a number of small scratches crawling after them through the brush, but Roland had to admit to himself that she could be as quiet as a ghost when she wanted to be; he hadn't heard a thing. He took a rag (the last remnant of his old shirt) from his back pocket and wiped the little trickles of blood from her arms. He examined his work for a moment and then dabbed at a small nick on her forehead as well. "Have your look, then," he said. His voice was hardly more than the movement of his lips. "I guess you earned it."

He used one hand to open a sightline at her level in the hock and greenberry bushes, then waited while she stared raptly into the clearing. At last she pulled back and Roland allowed the bushes to close again.

"I feel sorry for them," she whispered. "Isn't that crazy?"

"Not at all," Roland whispered back. "They are creatures of great sadness, I think, in their own strange way. Eddie is going to put them out of their misery."

Eddie began to shake his head at once.

"Yes, you are ... unless you want to hunker here in what you call 'the toolies' all night. Go for the hats. The little twirling things."

"What if I *miss*?" Eddie whispered at him furiously.

Roland shrugged.

Eddie stood up and reluctantly cocked the gunslinger's revolver again. He looked through the bushes at the circling servomechanisms, going around and around in their lonely, useless orbit. *It'll be like shooting puppies*, he thought glumly. Then he saw one of them—it was the thing that looked like a walking box—extrude an ugly-looking pincer device from its middle and clamp it for a moment on the snake. The snake made a surprised buzzing sound and leaped ahead. The walking box withdrew its pincer.

Well ... maybe not exactly *like shooting puppies*, Eddie decided. He glanced at Roland again. Roland looked back expressionlessly, arms folded across his chest.

You pick some goddam strange times to keep school, buddy.

Eddie thought of Susannah, first shooting the bear in the ass, then blowing its sensor device to smithereens as it bore down on her and Roland, and felt a little ashamed of himself. And there was more: part of him wanted to go for it, just as part of him had *wanted* to go up against Balazar and his crew of plug-uglies in The Leaning Tower. The compulsion was probably sick, but that didn't change its basic attraction: *Let's see who walks away .. let's just see.*

Yeah, that was pretty sick, all right.

Pretend it's just a shooting gallery, and you want to win your honey a stuffed dog, he thought. *Or a stuffed bear.* He drew a bead on the walking box and then looked around impatiently when Roland touched his shoulder.

"Say your lesson, Eddie. And be true."

Eddie hissed impatiently through his teeth, angry at the distraction, but Roland's eyes didn't flinch and so he drew a deep breath and tried to clear everything from his mind: the squeaks and squalls of equipment that had been running too long, the aches and pains in his body, the knowledge that Susannah was here, propped up on the heels of her hands, watching, the *further* knowledge that she was closest to the ground, and if he missed one of the gadgets out there, she would be the handiest target if it decided to retaliate.

" 'I do not shoot with my hand; he who shoots with his hand has forgotten the face of his father.' "

That was a joke, he thought; he wouldn't know his old man if he passed him on the street. But he could feel the words doing their work, clearing his mind and settling his nerves. He didn't know if he was the stuff of which gunslingers were made—the idea seemed fabulously unlikely to him, even though he knew he had managed to hold up his end pretty well during the shootout at Balazar's nightclub—but he *did* know that part of him liked the coldness that fell over him when he spoke the words of the old, old catechism the gunslinger had taught them; the coldness and the way things seemed to stand forth with their own breathless clarity. There was another part of him which understood that this was just another deadly drug, not much different from the heroin which had killed Henry and almost killed him, but that did not alter the thin, tight pleasure of the moment. It drummed in him like taut cables vibrating in a high wind.

" 'I do not aim with my hand; he who aims with his hand has forgotten the face of his father.

" 'I aim with my eye.

" 'I do not kill with my gun; he who kills with his gun has forgotten the face of his father.' "

Then, without knowing he meant to do it, he stepped out of the trees and spoke to the trundling robots on the far side of the clearing:

" 'I kill with my heart.' "

They stopped their endless circling. One of them let out a high buzz that might have been alarm or a warning. The radar-dishes, each no bigger than half a Hershey bar, turned toward the sound of his voice.

Eddie began to fire.

The sensors exploded like clay pigeons, one after the other. Pity was gone from Eddie's heart; there was only that coldness, and the knowledge that he would not stop, could not stop, until the job was done.

Thunder filled the twilit clearing and bounced back from the splintery rock wall at its wide end. The steel snake did two cartwheels and lay twitching in the dust. The biggest mechanism—the one that had reminded Eddie of his childhood Tonka tractor—tried to flee. Eddie blew its radar-dish to kingdom come as it made a herky-jerky run at the side of the rut. It fell on its squarish nose with thin blue flames squirting out of the steel sockets which held its glass eyes.

The only sensor he missed was the one on the stainless steel rat; that shot caromed off its metal back with a high mosquito whine. It surged out of the rut, made a half-circle around the box-shaped thing which had been following the snake, and charged across the clearing at surprising speed. It was making an angry clittering sound, and as it closed the distance, Eddie could see it had a mouth lined with long, sharp points. They did not look like teeth; they looked like sewing-machine needles, blurring up and down. No, he guessed these things were really not much like puppies, after all.

"Take it, Roland!" he shouted desperately, but when he snatched a quick look around he saw that Roland was still standing with his arms crossed on his chest, his expression serene and distant. He might have been thinking of chess problems or old love-letters.

The dish on the rat's back suddenly locked down. It changed direction slightly and buzzed straight toward Susannah Dean.

One bullet left, Eddie thought. *If I miss, it'll take her face off.*

Instead of shooting, he stepped forward and kicked the rat as hard as he could. He had replaced his shoes with a pair of deerskin moccasins, and he felt the jolt all the way up to his knee. The rat gave a rusty, ratcheting squeal, tumbled over and over in the dirt, and came to rest on its back. Eddie could see what looked like a dozen stubby mechanical legs pistoning up and down. Each was tipped with a sharp steel claw. These claws twirled around and around on gimbals the size of pencil-erasers.

A steel rod poked out of the robot's midsection and flipped the gadget upright again. Eddie brought Roland's revolver down, ignoring a momentary impulse to steady it with his free hand. That might be the way cops in his own world were taught to shoot, but it wasn't the way it was done here. *When you forget the gun is there, when it feels like you're shooting with your finger,* Roland had told them, *then you'll be somewhere near home.*

Eddie pulled the trigger. The tiny radar-dish, which had begun to turn again in an effort to find the enemies, disappeared in a blue flash. The rat made a choked noise—*Cloop!*—and fell dead on its side.

Eddie turned with his heart jackhammering in his chest. He couldn't remember being this furious since he realized that Roland meant to keep him in his world until his goddamned Tower was won or lost . . . probably until they were all worm-chow, in other words.

He levelled the empty gun at Roland's heart and spoke in a thick voice he hardly recognized as his own. "If there was a round left in this, you could stop worrying about your fucking Tower right now."

"Stop it, Eddie!" Susannah said sharply.

He looked at her. "It was going for *you*, Susannah, and it meant to turn you into ground chuck."

"But it didn't get me. *You* got *it*, Eddie. You got *it*."

"No thanks to him." Eddie made as if to re-holster the gun and then realized, to his further disgust, that he had nothing to put it in. Susannah was wearing the holster. "Him and his lessons. Him and his goddam *lessons*." He turned to Roland. "I tell you, for two cents—"

Roland's mildly interested expression suddenly changed. His eyes shifted to a point over Eddie's left shoulder. *"DOWN!"* he shouted.

Eddie didn't ask questions. His rage and confusion were wiped from his mind immediately. He dropped, and as he did, he saw the gunslinger's left hand blur down to his side. *My God*, he thought, still falling, *he CAN'T be that fast, no one can be that fast, I'm not bad but Susannah makes me look slow and he makes Susannah look like a turtle trying to walk uphill on a piece of glass—*

Something passed just over his head, something that squealed at him in mechanical rage and pulled out a tuft of his hair. Then the gunslinger was shooting from the hip, three fast shots like thunder-cracks, and the squealing stopped. A creature which looked to Eddie like a large mechanical bat thudded to earth between the place where Eddie now lay and the one where Susannah knelt beside Roland. One of its jointed, rust-speckled wings thumped the ground once, weakly, as if angry at the missed chance, and then became still.

Roland crossed to Eddie, walking easy in his old sprung boots. He extended a hand. Eddie took it and let Roland help him to his feet. The wind had been knocked out of him and he found he couldn't talk. *Probably just as well . . . seems like every time I open my mouth I stick my goddam foot into it.*

"Eddie! You all right?" Susannah was crossing the clearing to where he stood with his head bent and his hands planted on his upper thighs, trying to breathe.

"Yeah." The word came out in a croak. He straightened up with an effort. "Just got a little haircut."

"It was in a tree," Roland said mildly. "I didn't see it myself, at first. The light gets tricky this time of day." He paused and then went on in that same mild voice: "She was never in any danger, Eddie."

Eddie nodded his head. Roland, he now realized, could almost have eaten a hamburger and drunk a milkshake before beginning his draw. He was that fast.

"All right. Let's just say I disapprove of your teaching techniques, okay? I'm not going to apologize, though, so if you're waiting for one, you can stop now."

Roland bent, picked Susannah up, and began to brush her off. He did this with a kind of impartial affection, like a mother brushing off her toddler after she has taken one of her necessary tumbles in the dust of the back yard. "Your apology is not expected or necessary," he said. "Susannah and I had a conversation similar to this one two days ago. Didn't we, Susannah?"

She nodded. "Roland's of the opinion that apprentice gunslingers who won't bite the hand that feeds them from time to time need a good kick in the slats."

Eddie looked around at the wreckage and slowly began to beat the bone-dust out of his pants and shirt. "What if I told you I don't want to *be* a gunslinger, Roland old buddy?"

"I'd say that what you want doesn't much matter." Roland was looking at the metal kiosk which stood against the rock wall, and seemed to have lost interest in the conversation. Eddie had seen this before. When the conversation turned to questions of should-be, could-be, or oughtta-be, Roland almost always lost interest.

"*Ka?*" Eddie asked, with a trace of his old bitterness.

"That's right. *Ka.*" Roland walked over to the kiosk and passed a hand along the yellow and black stripes which ran down its front. "We have found one of the twelve portals which ring the edge of the world . . . one of the six paths to the Dark Tower.

"And that is also *ka.*"

27

EDDIE WENT BACK FOR Susannah's wheelchair. No one had to ask him to do this; he wanted some time alone, to get himself back under control. Now that the shooting was over, every muscle in his body seemed to have picked up its own little thrumming tremor. He did not want either of them to see him this way—not because they might misread it as fear, but because one or both might know it for what it really was: excitement overload. He had liked it. Even when you added in the bat which had almost scalped him, he had liked it.

That's bullshit, buddy. And you know it.

The trouble was, he *didn't* know it. He had come face to face with something Susannah had found out for herself after shooting the bear: he could *talk* about how he didn't want to be a gunslinger, how he didn't want to be tramping around this crazy world where the three of them seemed to be the only human life, that what he really wanted more than anything else was to be standing on the corner of Broadway and Forty-second Street, popping his fingers, munching a chili-dog, and listening to Creedence Clearwater Revival blast out of his Walkman earphones as he watched the girls go by, those ultimately sexy New York girls with their pouty go-to-hell mouths and their long legs in short skirts. He could talk about those things until he was blue in the face, but his heart knew other things. It knew that he had *enjoyed* blowing the electronic menagerie back to glory, at least while the game was on and Roland's gun was his own private hand-held thunderstorm. He had *enjoyed* kicking the robot rat, even though it had hurt his foot and even though he had been scared shitless. In some weird way, that part—the being scared part—actually seemed to add to the enjoyment.

All that was bad enough, but his heart knew something even worse: that if a door leading back to New York appeared in front of him right now, he might not walk through it. Not, at least, until he had seen the Dark Tower for himself. He was beginning to believe that Roland's illness was a communicable disease.

As he wrestled Susannah's chair through the tangle of junk-alders, cursing the branches that whipped at his face and tried to poke his eyes out, Eddie found himself able to admit at least some of these things, and the admission cooled his blood a little. *I want to see if it looks the way it did in my dream,* he thought. *To see something like that . . . that would be really fantastic.*

And another voice spoke up inside. *I'll bet his other friends—the ones with the names that sound like they came straight from the Round Table in King Arthur's court—I'll bet they felt the same way, Eddie. And they're all dead. Every one of them.*

He recognized that voice, like it or not. It belonged to Henry, and that made it a hard voice not to hear.

28

ROLAND, WITH SUSANNAH BALANCED on his right hip, was standing in front of the metal box that looked like a subway entrance closed for the night. Eddie left the wheelchair at the edge of the clearing and walked over. As he did, the steady humming noise and the vibration under his feet became louder. The machinery making the noise, he realized, was either inside the box or under it. It seemed that he heard it not with his ears but somewhere deep inside his head, and in the hollows of his gut.

"So this is one of the twelve portals. Where does it go, Roland? Disney World?"

Roland shook his head. "I don't know where it goes. Maybe nowhere . . . or everywhere. There's a lot about my world I don't know—surely you both have realized that. And there are things I used to know which have changed."

"Because the world has moved on?"

"Yes." Roland glanced at him. "Here, that is not a figure of speech. The world really *is* moving on, and it goes ever faster. At the same time, things are wearing out . . . falling apart . . ." He kicked the mechanical corpse of the walking box to illustrate his point.

Eddie thought of the rough diagram of the portals which Roland had drawn in the dirt. "*Is* this the edge of the world?" he asked, almost timidly. "I mean, it doesn't look much different than anyplace else." He laughed a little. "If there's a drop-off, I don't see it."

Roland shook his head. "It's not that kind of edge. It's the place where one of the Beams starts. Or so I was taught."

"Beams?" Susannah asked. "What Beams?"

"The Great Old Ones didn't make the world, but they did *re*-make it. Some tale-tellers say the Beams saved it; others say they are the seeds of the world's destruction. The Great Old Ones created the Beams. They are lines of some sort . . . lines which *bind* . . . and *hold* . . ."

"Are you talking about magnetism?" Susannah asked cautiously.

His whole face lit up, transforming its harsh planes and furrows into something new and amazing, and for a moment Eddie knew how Roland would look if he actually *did* reach his Tower.

"Yes! Not *just* magnetism, but that is a part of it . . . and gravity . . . and the proper alignment of space, size, and dimension. The Beams are the forces which bind these things together."

"Welcome to physics in the nuthouse," Eddie said in a low voice.

Susannah ignored this. "And the Dark Tower? Is it some kind of generator? A central power-source for these Beams?"

"I don't know."

"But you *do* know that this is point A," Eddie said. "If we walked long enough in a straight line, we'd come to another portal—call it point C—on the other edge of the world. But before we did, we'd come to point B. The center-point. The Dark Tower."

The gunslinger nodded.

"How long a trip is it? Do you know?"

"No. But I know it's very far, and that the distance grows with every day that passes."

Eddie had bent to examine the walking box. Now he straightened up and stared at Roland. "That can't be." He sounded like a man trying to explain to a small child that there really isn't a boogeyman living in his closet, that there *can't* be because there isn't any such thing as the boogeyman, not really. "Worlds don't *grow*, Roland."

"Don't they? When I was a boy, Eddie, there were maps. I remember one in particular. It was called The Greater Kingdoms of the Western Earth. It showed my land, which was called by the name Gilead. It showed the Downland Baronies, which were overrun by riot and civil war in the year after I won my guns, and the hills, and the desert, and the mountains, and the Western Sea. It was a long distance from Gilead to the Western Sea—a thousand miles or more—*but it had taken me over twenty years to cross that distance.*"

"That's impossible," Susannah said quickly, fearfully. "Even if you *walked* the whole distance it couldn't take twenty years."

"Well, you have to allow for stops to write postcards and drink beer," Eddie said, but they both ignored him.

"I didn't walk but rode most of the distance on horseback," Roland said. "I was—slowed up, shall we say?—every now and then, but for most of that time I was moving. Moving away from John Farson, who led the revolt which toppled the world I grew up in and who wanted my head on a pole in his courtyard—he had good reason to want that, I suppose, since I and my compatriots were responsible for the deaths of a great many of his followers—and because I stole something he held very dear."

"What, Roland?" Eddie asked curiously.

Roland shook his head. "That's a story for another day . . . or maybe never. For now, think not of that but of this: I've come *many* thousands of miles. Because the world is growing."

"A thing like that just can't happen," Eddie reiterated, but he was badly shaken, all the same. "There'd be earthquakes . . . floods . . . tidal waves . . . I don't know what all . . ."

"*Look!*" Roland said furiously. "Just look around you! What do you see? A world that is slowing down like a child's top even as it speeds up and moves on in some other way none of us understand. Look at your kills, Eddie! Look at your kills, for your father's sake!"

He took two strides toward the stream, picked up the steel snake, examined it briefly, and tossed it to Eddie, who caught it with his left hand. The snake broke in two pieces as he did so.

"You see? It's exhausted. *All* the creatures we found here were exhausted. If we hadn't come, they would have died before long, anyway. Just as the bear would have died."

"The bear had some sort of disease," Susannah said.

The gunslinger nodded. "Parasites which attacked the natural parts of its body. But why did they never attack it before?"

Susannah did not reply.

Eddie was examining the snake. Unlike the bear, it appeared to be a totally artificial construction, a thing of metal, circuits, and yards (or maybe *miles*) of gossamer-thin wire. Yet he could see flecks of rust, not just on the surface of the half-snake he still held, but in its guts as well. And there was a patch of wetness where either oil had leaked out or water had seeped in. This moisture had rotted away some of the wires, and a greenish stuff that looked like moss had grown over several of the thumbnail-sized circuit boards.

Eddie turned the snake over. A steel plate proclaimed it to be the work of North Central Positronics, Ltd. There was a serial number, but no name. *Probably too unimportant to name*, he thought. *Just a sophisticated mechanical Roto-Rooter designed to give old Br'er Bear an enema every once in a while, keep him regular, or something equally disgusting.*

He dropped the snake and wiped his hands on his pants.

Roland had picked up the tractor-gadget. He yanked at one of the treads. It came off easily, showering a cloud of rust down between his boots. He tossed it aside.

"Everything in the world is either coming to rest or falling to pieces," he said flatly. "At the same time, the forces which interlock and give the world its coherence—in time and size as well as in space—are weakening. We knew that even as children, but we had no idea what the time of the end would be like. How could we? Yet now I am living in those times, and I don't believe they affect my world alone. They affect yours, Eddie and Susannah; they may affect a billion others. The Beams are breaking down. I don't know if that's a cause or only another symptom, but I know it's true. Come! Draw close! Listen!"

As Eddie approached the metal box with its alternating diagonal slashes of yellow and black, a strong and unpleasant memory seized him—for the first time in years he found himself thinking of a crumbling Victorian wreck in Dutch Hill, about a mile away from the neighborhood he and Henry had grown up. This wreck, which was known as The Mansion to the neighborhood kids, occupied a plot of weedy, untended lawn on Rhinehold Street. Eddie guessed that practically all the kids in the borough had heard spooky stories about The Mansion. The house stood slumped beneath its steep roofs, seeming to glare at passersby from the deep shadows thrown by its eaves. The windows were gone, of course—kids can throw rocks through windows without getting too close to a place—but it had not been spray-painted, and it had not become a make-out spot or a shooting gallery. Oddest of all was the simple fact of its continued existence: no one had set it on fire to collect the insurance or just to see it burn. The kids said it was haunted, of course, and as Eddie stood on the sidewalk with Henry one day, looking at it (they had made the pilgrimage specifically to see this object of fabulous rumor, although Henry had told their mother they were only going for Hoodsie Rockets at Dahlberg's with some of his friends), it had seemed that it really *might* be haunted. Hadn't he felt some strong and unfriendly force seeping from that old Victorian's shadowy windows, windows that seemed to look at him with the fixed stare of a dangerous lunatic? Hadn't he felt some subtle wind stirring the hairs on his arms and the back of his neck? Hadn't he had the clear intuition that if he stepped inside that place, the door would slam and lock behind him and the walls would begin to close in, grinding the bones of dead mice to powder, wanting to crush *his* bones the same way?

Haunting. Haunted.

He felt that same old sense of mystery and danger now, as he approached the metal box. Gooseflesh began to ripple up his legs and down his arms; the hair on the back of his neck bushed out and became rough, overlapping hackles. He felt that same subtle wind blowing past him, although the leaves on the trees which ringed the clearing were perfectly still.

Yet he walked toward the door anyway (for that was what it was, of course, another door, although this one was locked and always would be against the likes of him), not stopping until his ear was pressed against it.

It was as if he had dropped a tab of really strong acid half an hour ago and it was just beginning to come on heavy. Strange colors flowed across the darkness behind his eyeballs. He seemed to hear voices murmuring up to him from long hallways like stone throats, halls which were lit with guttering electric torches. Once these flambeaux of the modern age had thrown a bright glare across everything, but now they were only sullen cores of blue light. He sensed emptiness . . . desertion . . . desolation . . . death.

The machinery rumbled on and on, but wasn't there a rough undertone to the sound? A kind of desperate thudding beneath the hum, like the arrhythmia of a diseased heart? A feeling that the machinery producing this sound, although far more sophisticated even than that within the bear had been, was somehow falling out of tune with itself?

"All is silent in the halls of the dead," Eddie heard himself whisper in a falling, fainting voice. "All is forgotten in the stone halls of the dead. Behold the stairways which stand in darkness; behold the rooms of ruin.

These are the halls of the dead where the spiders spin and the great circuits fall quiet, one by one."

Roland pulled him roughly back, and Eddie looked at him with dazed eyes.

"That's enough," Roland said.

"Whatever they put in there isn't doing so well, is it?" Eddie heard himself ask. His trembling voice seemed to come from far away. He could still feel the power coming out of that box. It called to him.

"No. Nothing in my world is doing so well these days."

"If you boys are planning to camp here for the night, you'll have to do without the pleasure of my company," Susannah said. Her face was a white blur in the ashy aftermath of twilight. "I'm going over yonder. I don't like the way that thing makes me feel."

"We'll *all* camp over yonder," Roland said. "Let's go."

"What a good idea," Eddie said. As they moved away from the box, the sound of the machinery began to dim. Eddie felt its hold on him weakening, although it still called to him, invited him to explore the half-lit hallways, the standing stairways, the rooms of ruin where the spiders spun and the control panels were going dark, one by one.

29

IN HIS DREAM THAT night, Eddie again went walking down Second Avenue toward Tom and Gerry's Artistic Deli on the corner of Second and Forty-sixth. He passed a record store and the Rolling Stones boomed from the speakers:

> *"I see a red door and I want to paint it black,*
> *No colours anymore, I want them to turn black,*
> *I see the girls walk by dressed in their summer clothes,*
> *I have to turn my head until my darkness goes . . ."*

He walked on, passing a store called Reflections of You between Forty-ninth and Forty-eighth. He saw himself in one of the mirrors hanging in the display window. He thought he looked better than he had in years—hair a little too long, but otherwise tanned and fit. The clothes, though . . . uh-uh, man. Square-bear shit all the way. Blue blazer, white shirt, dark red tie, gray dress pants . . . he had never owned a yuppie-from-hell outfit like that in his life.

Someone was shaking him.

Eddie tried to burrow deeper into the dream. He didn't want to wake up now. Not before he got to the deli and used his key to go through the door and into the field of roses. He wanted to see it all again—the endless blanket of red, the overarching blue sky where those great white cloud-ships sailed, and the Dark Tower. He was afraid of the darkness which lived within that eldritch column, waiting to eat anyone who got too close, but he wanted to see it again just the same. *Needed* to see it.

The hand, however, would not stop shaking. The dream began to darken, and the smells of car exhaust along Second Avenue became the smell of woodsmoke—thin now, because the fire was almost out.

It was Susannah. She looked scared. Eddie sat up and put an arm around her. They had camped on the far side of the alder grove, within earshot of the stream babbling through the bone-littered clearing. On the other side of the glowing embers which had been their campfire, Roland lay asleep. His sleep was not easy. He had cast aside his single blanket and lay with his knees drawn up almost to his chest. With his boots off, his feet looked white and narrow and defenseless. The great toe of the right foot was gone, victim of the lobster-thing which had also snatched away part of his right hand.

He was moaning some slurred phrase over and over again. After a few repetitions, Eddie realized it was the phrase he had spoken before keeling over in the clearing where Susannah had shot the bear: *Go, then—there are other worlds than these.* He would fall silent for a moment, then call out the boy's name: "Jake! Where are you? *Jake!*"

The desolation and despair in his voice filled Eddie with horror. His arms stole around Susannah and he pulled her tight against him. He could feel her shivering, although the night was warm.

The gunslinger rolled over. Starlight fell into his open eyes.

"*Jake, where are you?*" he called to the night. "*Come back!*"

"Oh Jesus—he's off again. What should we do, Suze?"

"I don't know. I just knew I couldn't listen to it anymore by myself. He sounds so far away. So far away from everything."

"Go, then," the gunslinger murmured, rolling back onto his side and drawing his knees up once more, "there are other worlds than these." He was silent for a moment. Then his chest hitched and he loosed the boy's name in a long, bloodcurdling cry. In the woods behind them, some large bird flew away in a dry whirr of wings toward some less exciting part of the world.

"Do you have any ideas?" Susannah asked. Her eyes were wide and wet with tears. "Maybe we should wake him up?"

"I don't know." Eddie saw the gunslinger's revolver, the one he wore on his left hip. It had been placed, in its holster, on a neatly folded square of hide within easy reach of the place where Roland lay. "I don't think I dare," he added at last.

"It's driving him crazy."

Eddie nodded.

"What do we do about it? Eddie, *what do we do?*"

Eddie didn't know. An antibiotic had stopped the infection caused by the bite of the lobster-thing; now Roland was burning with infection again, but Eddie didn't think there was an antibiotic in the world that would cure what was wrong with him this time.

"I don't know. Lie down with me, Suze."

Eddie threw a hide over both of them, and after a while her trembling quieted.

"If he goes insane, he may hurt us," she said.

"Don't I know it." This unpleasant idea had occurred to him in terms of the bear—its red, hate-filled eyes (and had there not been bewilderment as well, lurking deep in those red depths?) and its deadly slashing claws. Eddie's eyes moved to the revolver, lying so close to the gunslinger's good left hand, and he remembered again how fast Roland had been when he'd seen the mechanical bat swooping down toward them. So fast his hand had seemed to disappear. If the gunslinger went mad, and if he and Susannah became the focus of that madness, they would have no chance. No chance at all.

He pressed his face into the warm hollow of Susannah's neck and closed his eyes.

Not long after, Roland ceased his babbling. Eddie raised his head and looked over. The gunslinger appeared to be sleeping naturally again. Eddie looked at Susannah and saw that she had also gone to sleep. He lay down beside her, gently kissed the swell of her breast, and closed his own eyes.

Not you, buddy; you're gonna be awake a long, long time.

But they had been on the move for two days and Eddie was bone-tired. He drifted off . . . drifted down.

Back to the dream, he thought as he went. *I want to go back to Second Avenue . . . back to Tom and Gerry's. That's what I want.*

The dream did not return that night, however.

30

THEY ATE A QUICK breakfast as the sun came up, repacked and redistributed the gear, and then returned to the wedge-shaped clearing. It didn't look quite so spooky in the clear light of morning, but all three of them were still at pains to keep well away from the metal box with its warning slashes of black and yellow. If Roland had any recollection of the bad dreams which had haunted him in the night, he gave no sign. He had gone about the morning chores as he always did, in thoughtful, stolid silence.

"How do you plan to keep to a straight-line course from here?" Susannah asked the gunslinger.

"If the legends are right, that should be no problem. Do you remember when you asked about magnetism?"

She nodded.

He rummaged deep into his purse and at last emerged with a small square of old, supple leather. Threaded through it was a long silver needle.

"A compass!" Eddie said. "You really *are* an Eagle Scout!"

Roland shook his head. "Not a compass. I know what they are, of course, but these days I keep my directions by the sun and stars, and even now they serve me quite well."

"*Even now?*" Susannah asked, a trifle uneasily.

He nodded. "The directions of the world are also in drift."

"*Christ,*" Eddie said. He tried to imagine a world where true north was slipping slyly off to the east or west and gave up almost at once. It made him feel a little ill, the way looking down from the top of a high building had always made him feel a little ill.

"This is just a needle, but it *is* steel and it should serve our purpose as well as a compass. The Beam is our course now, and the needle will show it." He rummaged in his purse again and came out with a poorly made pottery cup. A crack ran down one side. Roland had mended this artifact, which he had found at the old campsite, with pine-gum. Now he went to the stream, dipped the cup into it, and brought it back to where Susannah sat in her wheelchair. He put the cup down carefully on the wheelchair's arm, and when the surface of the water inside was calm, he dropped the needle in. It sank to the bottom and rested there.

"Wow!" Eddie said. "Great! I'd fall at your feet in wonder, Roland, but I don't want to spoil the crease in my pants."

"I'm not finished. Hold the cup steady, Susannah."

She did, and Roland pushed her slowly across the clearing. When she was about twelve feet in front of the door, he turned the chair carefully so she was facing away from it.

"Eddie!" she cried. "Look at this!"

He bent over the pottery cup, marginally aware that water was already oozing through Roland's makeshift seal. The needle was rising slowly to the surface. It reached it and bobbed there as serenely as a cork would have done. Its direction lay in a straight line from the portal behind them and into the old, tangled forest ahead. "Holy shit—a floating needle. Now I really *have* seen everything."

"Hold the cup, Susannah."

She held it steady as Roland pushed the wheelchair further into the clearing, at right angles to the box. The needle lost its steady point, bobbed randomly for a moment, then sank to the bottom of the cup again. When Roland pulled the chair backward to its former spot, it rose once more and pointed the way.

"If we had iron filings and a sheet of paper," the gunslinger said, "we could scatter the filings on the paper's surface and watch them draw together into a line which would point that same course."

"Will that happen even when we leave the Portal?" Eddie asked.

Roland nodded. "Nor is that all. We can actually *see* the Beam."

Susannah looked over her shoulder. Her elbow bumped the cup a little as she did. The needle swung aimlessly as the water inside sloshed . . . and then settled firmly back in its original direction.

"Not that way," Roland said. "Look down, both of you—Eddie at your feet, Susannah into your lap."

They did as he asked.

"When I tell you to look up, look straight ahead, in the direction the needle points. Don't look at any one thing; let your eye see whatever it will. Now—look up!"

They did. For a moment Eddie saw nothing but the woods. He tried to make his eyes relax . . . and suddenly it was there, the way the shape of the slingshot had been there, inside the knob of wood, and he knew why Roland had told them not to look at any one thing. The effect of the Beam was everywhere along its course, but it was subtle. The needles of the pines and spruces pointed that way. The greenberry bushes grew slightly slanted, and the slant lay in the direction of the Beam. Not all the trees the bear had pushed down to clear its sightlines had fallen along that camouflaged path—which ran southeast, if Eddie had his directions right—but most had, as if the force coming out of the box had *pushed* them that way as they tottered. The clearest evidence was in the way the shadows lay on the ground. With the sun coming up in the east they all pointed west, of course, but as Eddie looked southeast, he saw a rough herringbone pattern that existed only along the line which the needle in the cup had pointed out.

"I might see *something*," Susannah said doubtfully, "but—"

"Look at the shadows! The *shadows*, Suze!"

Eddie saw her eyes widen as it all fell into place for her. "My God! It's there! *Right there!* It's like when someone has a natural part in their hair!"

Now that Eddie had seen it, he could not unsee it; a dim aisle driving through the untidy tangle which surrounded the clearing, a straight-edge course that was the way of the Beam. He was suddenly aware of how huge the force flowing around him (and probably right through him, like X-rays) must be, and had to control an urge to step away, either to the right or left. "Say, Roland, this won't make me sterile, will it?"

Roland shrugged, smiling faintly.

"It's like a riverbed," Susannah marvelled. "A riverbed so over-grown you can barely see it . . . but it's still there. The pattern of shadows will never change as long as we stay inside the path of the Beam, will it?"

"No," Roland said. "They'll change direction as the sun moves across the sky, of course, but we'll always be able to see the course of the Beam. You must remember that it has been flowing along this same path for thousands—perhaps *tens* of thousands—of years. Look up, you two, into the sky!"

They did, and saw that the thin cirrus clouds had also picked up that herringbone pattern along the course of the Beam . . . and those clouds within the alley of its power were flowing faster than those to either side. They were being pushed southeast. Being pushed in the direction of the Dark Tower.

"You see? Even the clouds must obey."

A small flock of birds coursed toward them. As they reached the path of the Beam, they were all deflected toward the southeast for a moment. Although Eddie clearly saw this happen, his eyes could hardly credit it. When the birds had crossed the narrow corridor of the Beam's influence, they resumed their former course.

"Well," Eddie said, "I suppose we ought to get going. A journey of a thousand miles begins with a single step, and all that shit."

"Wait a minute." Susannah was looking at Roland. "It *isn't* just a thousand miles, is it? Not anymore. How far *are* we talking about, Roland? Five thousand miles? Ten?"

"I can't say. It will be very far."

"Well, how in the hell we ever goan get there, with you two pushing me in this goddam wheelchair? We'll be lucky to make three miles a day through yonder Drawers, and you know it."

"The way has been opened," Roland said patiently, "and that's enough for now. The time may come, Susannah Dean, when we travel faster than you would like."

"Oh yeah?" She looked at him truculently, and both men could see Detta Walker dancing a dangerous hornpipe in her eyes again. "You got a race-car lined up? If you do, it might be nice if we had a damn road to run it on!"

"The land and the way we travel on it will change. It always does."

Susannah flapped a hand at the gunslinger; *go on with you*, it said. "You sound like my old mamma, sayin God will provide."

"Hasn't He?" Roland asked gravely.

She looked at him for a moment in silent surprise, then threw her head back and laughed at the sky. "Well, I guess that depends on how you look at it. All I can say is that if this is providin, Roland, I'd hate to see what'd happen if He decided to let us go hungry."

"Come on, let's do it," Eddie said. "I want to get out of this place. I don't like it." And that was true, but that wasn't all. He also felt a deep eagerness to set his feet upon that concealed path, that highway in hiding. Every step was a step closer to the field of roses and the Tower which dominated it. He realized—not without some wonder—that he meant to see that Tower . . . or die trying.

Congratulations, Roland, he thought. *You've done it. I'm one of the converted. Someone say hallelujah.*

"There's one other thing before we go." Roland bent and untied the rawhide lace around his left thigh. Then he slowly began to unbuckle his gunbelt.

"What's this jive?" Eddie asked.

Roland pulled the gunbelt free and held it out to him. "You know why I'm doing this," he said calmly.

"Put it back on, man!" Eddie felt a terrible stew of conflicting emotions roiling inside him; could feel his fingers trembling even inside his clenched fists. "What do you think you're *doing*?"

"Losing my mind an inch at a time. Until the wound inside me closes—if it ever does—I am not fit to wear this. And you know it."

"Take it, Eddie," Susannah said quietly.

"If you hadn't been wearing this goddamn thing last night, when that bat came at me, I'd be gone from the nose up this morning!"

The gunslinger replied by continuing to hold his remaining gun out to Eddie. The posture of his body said he was prepared to stand that way all day, if that was what it took.

"All right!" Eddie cried. "Goddammit, all *right*!"

He snatched the gunbelt from Roland's hand and buckled it about his own waist in a series of rough gestures. He should have been relieved, he supposed—hadn't he looked at this gun, lying so close to Roland's hand in the middle of the night, and thought about what might happen if Roland really *did* go over the high side? Hadn't he and Susannah both thought about it? But there was no relief. Only fear and guilt and a strange, aching sadness far too deep for tears.

He looked so strange without his guns.

So *wrong*.

"Okay? Now that the numb-fuck apprentices have the guns and the master's unarmed, can we please go? If something big comes out of the bush at us, Roland, you can always throw your knife at it."

"Oh, that," he murmured. "I almost forgot." He took the knife from his purse and held it out, hilt first, to Eddie.

"This is *ridiculous!*" Eddie shouted.

"*Life* is ridiculous."

"Yeah, put it on a postcard and send it to the fucking *Reader's Digest.*" Eddie jammed the knife into his belt and then looked defiantly at Roland. "*Now* can we go?"

"There *is* one more thing," Roland said.

"Weeping, creeping *Jesus!*"

The smile touched Roland's mouth again. "Just joking," he said.

Eddie's mouth dropped open. Beside him, Susannah began to laugh again. The sound rose, as musical as bells, in the morning stillness.

31

IT TOOK THEM MOST of the morning to clear the zone of destruction with which the great bear had protected itself, but the going was a little easier along the path of the Beam, and once they had put the deadfalls and tangles of underbrush behind them, deep forest took over again and they were able to move at better speed. The brook which had emerged from the rock wall in the clearing ran busily along to their right. It had been joined by several smaller streamlets, and its sound was deeper now. There were more animals here—they heard them moving through the woods, going about their daily round—and twice they saw small groups of deer. One of them, a buck with a noble rack of antlers on its upraised and questioning head, looked to be at least three hundred pounds. The brook bent away from their path as they began to climb again. And, as the afternoon began to slant down toward evening, Eddie saw something.

"Could we stop here? Rest a minute?"

"What is it?" Susannah asked.

"Yes," Roland said. "We can stop."

Suddenly Eddie felt Henry's presence again, like a weight settling on his shoulders. *Oh lookit the sissy. Does the sissy see something in the twee? Does the sissy want to carve something? Does he? Ohhhh, ain't that CUTE?*

"We don't *have* to stop. I mean, no big deal. I just—"

"—saw something," Roland finished for him. "Whatever it is, stop running your everlasting mouth and get it."

"It's really nothing." Eddie felt warm blood mount into his face. He tried to look away from the ash tree which had caught his eye.

"But it is. It's something you need, and that's a long way from nothing. If *you* need it, Eddie, *we* need it. What we don't need is a man who can't let go of the useless baggage of his memories."

The warm blood turned hot. Eddie stood with his flaming face pointed at his moccasins for a moment longer, feeling as if Roland had looked directly into his confused heart with his faded blue bombardier's eyes.

"Eddie?" Susannah asked curiously. "What is it, dear?"

Her voice gave him the courage he needed. He walked to the slim, straight ash, pulling Roland's knife from his belt.

"Maybe nothing," he muttered, and then forced himself to add: "Maybe a lot. If I don't fuck it up, maybe quite a lot."

"The ash is a noble tree, and full of power," Roland remarked from behind him, but Eddie barely heard. Henry's sneering, hectoring voice was gone; his shame was gone with it. He thought only of the one branch that had caught his eye. It thickened and bulged slightly as it ran into the trunk. It was this oddly shaped thickness that Eddie wanted.

He thought the shape of the key was buried within it—the key he had seen briefly in the fire before the burning remains of the jawbone had changed again and the rose had appeared. Three inverted V's, the center V both deeper and wider than the other two. And the little *s*-shape at the end. That was the secret.

A breath of his dream recurred: *Dad-a-chum, dud-a-chee, not to worry, you've got the key.*

Maybe, he thought. *But this time I'll have to get all of it. I think that this time ninety per cent just won't do.*

Working with great care, he cut the branch from the tree and then trimmed the narrow end. He was left with a fat chunk of ash about nine inches long. It felt heavy and vital in his hand, very much alive and willing enough to give up its secret shape . . . to a man skillful enough to tease it out, that was.

Was he that man? And did it matter?

Eddie Dean thought the answer to both questions was yes.

The gunslinger's good left hand closed over Eddie's right hand. "I think you know a secret."

"Maybe I do."

"Can you tell?"

He shook his head. "Better not to, I think. Not yet."

Roland thought this over, then nodded. "All right. I want to ask you one question, and then we'll drop the subject. Have you perhaps seen some way into the heart of my . . . my problem?"

Eddie thought: *And that's as close as he'll ever come to showing the desperation that's eating him alive.*

"I don't know. Right now I can't tell for sure. But I hope so, man. I really, really do."

Roland nodded again and released Eddie's hand. "I thank you. We still have two hours of good daylight—why don't we make use of them?"

"Fine by me."

They moved on. Roland pushed Susannah and Eddie walked ahead of them, holding the chunk of wood with the key buried in it. It seemed to throb with its own warmth, secret and powerful.

32

THAT NIGHT, AFTER SUPPER was eaten, Eddie took the gunslinger's knife from his belt and began to carve. The knife was amazingly sharp, and seemed never to lose its edge. Eddie worked slowly and carefully in the firelight, turning the chunk of ash this way and that in his hands, watching the curls of fine-grained wood rise ahead of his long, sure strokes.

Susannah lay down, laced her hands behind her head, and looked up at the stars wheeling slowly across the black sky.

At the edge of the campsite, Roland stood beyond the glow of the fire and listened as the voices of madness rose once more in his aching, confused mind.

There was a boy.

There was no boy.

Was.

Wasn't.

Was—

He closed his eyes, cupped his aching forehead in one cold hand, and wondered how long it would be until he simply snapped like an overwound bowstring.

Oh Jake, he thought. *Where are you? Where are you?*

And above the three of them, Old Star and Old Mother rose into their appointed places and stared at each other across the starry ruins of their ancient broken marriage.

II ▪ KEY AND ROSE

· II ·

KEY AND ROSE

1

FOR THREE WEEKS JOHN "Jake" Chambers fought bravely against the madness rising inside him. During that time he felt like the last man aboard a foundering ocean liner, working the bilge-pumps for dear life, trying to keep the ship afloat until the storm ended, the skies cleared, and help could arrive . . . help from somewhere. Help from *anywhere*. On May 31st, 1977, four days before school ended for the summer, he finally faced up to the fact that no help was going to come. It was time to give up; time to let the storm carry him away.

The straw that broke the camel's back was his Final Essay in English Comp.

John Chambers, who was Jake to the three or four boys who were almost his friends (if his father had known this little factoid, he undoubtedly would have hit the roof), was finishing his first year at The Piper School. Although he was eleven and in the sixth grade, he was small for his age, and people meeting him for the first time often thought he was much younger. In fact, he had sometimes been mistaken for a girl until a year or so ago, when he had made such a fuss about having his hair cut short that his mother had finally relented and allowed it. With his father, of course, there had been no problem about the haircut. His father had just grinned his hard, stainless steel grin and said, *The kid wants to look like a Marine, Laurie. Good for him.*

To his father, he was never Jake and rarely John. To his father, he was usually just "the kid."

The Piper School, his father had explained to him the summer before (the Bicentennial Summer, that had been—all bunting and flags and New York Harbor filled with Tall Ships), was, quite simply, The Best Damned School In The Country For A Boy Your Age. The fact that Jake had been accepted there had nothing to do with money, Elmer Chambers explained . . . almost *insisted.* He had been savagely proud of this fact, although, even at ten, Jake had suspected it might not be a *true* fact, that it might really be a bunch of bullshit his father had turned *into* a fact so he could casually drop it into the conversation at lunch or over cocktails: *My kid? Oh, he's going to Piper. Best Damned School In The Country For A Boy His Age. Money won't buy you into that school, you know; for Piper, it's brains or nothing.*

Jake was perfectly aware that in the fierce furnace of Elmer Chambers's mind, the gross carbon of wish and opinion was often blasted into the hard diamonds which he called facts . . . or, in more informal circumstances, "factoids." His favorite phrase, spoken often and with reverence, was *The fact is*, and he used it every chance he got.

The fact is, money doesn't get anyone *into The Piper School,* his father had told him during that Bicentennial Summer, the summer of blue skies and bunting and Tall Ships, a summer which seemed golden in Jake's memory because he had not yet begun to lose his mind and all he had to worry about was whether or not he could cut the mustard at The Piper School, which sounded like a nest for newly hatched geniuses. *The only thing that gets you into a place like Piper is what you've got up here.* Elmer Chambers had reached over his desk and tapped the center of his son's forehead with a hard, nicotine-stained finger. *Get me, kid?*

Jake had nodded. It wasn't necessary to talk to his father, because his father treated everyone—including his wife—the way he treated his underlings at the TV network where he was in charge of programming and an acknowledged master of The Kill. All you had to do was listen, nod in the right places, and after a while he let you go.

Good, his father said, lighting one of the eighty Camel cigarettes he smoked each and every day. *We understand each other, then. You're going to have to work your buttsky off, but you can cut it. They never would have sent us this if you couldn't.* He picked up the letter of acceptance from The Piper School and rattled it. There was a kind of savage triumph in the gesture, as if the letter was an animal he had killed in the jungle, an animal he would now skin and eat. *So work hard. Make your grades. Make your mother and me proud of you. If you end the year with an A average in your courses, there's a trip to Disney World in it for you. That's something to shoot for, right, kiddo?*

Jake had made his grades—A's in everything (until the last three weeks, that was). He had, presumably, made his mother and father proud of him, although they were around so little that it was hard to tell. Usually there was *nobody* around when he came home from school except for Greta Shaw—the housekeeper—and so he ended up showing his A papers to her. After that, they migrated to a dark corner of his room. Sometimes Jake looked through them and wondered if they meant anything. He *wanted* them to, but he had serious doubts.

Jake didn't think he would be going to Disney World this summer, A average or no A average.

He thought the nuthouse was a much better possibility.

As he walked in through the double doors of The Piper School at 8:45 on the morning of May 31st, a terrible vision came to him. He saw his father in his office at 70 Rockefeller Plaza, leaning over his desk with a Camel jutting from the corner of his mouth, talking to one of his underlings as blue smoke wreathed his head. All of New York was spread out behind and below his father, its thump and hustle silenced by two layers of Thermopane glass.

The fact is, money doesn't get anyone *into Sunnyvale Sanitarium,* his father was telling the underling in a tone of grim satisfaction. He reached out and tapped the underling's forehead. *The only thing that gets you into a place like that is when something big-time goes wrong up here in the attic. That's what happened to the kid. But he's working his goddam buttsky off. Makes the best fucking baskets in the place, they tell me. And when they let him out—if they ever do—there's a trip in it for him. A trip to—*

"—the way station," Jake muttered, then touched his forehead with a hand that wanted to tremble. The voices were coming back. The yelling, conflicting voices which were driving him mad.

You're dead, Jake. You were run over by a car and you're dead.

Don't be stupid! Look—see that poster? REMEMBER THE CLASS ONE PICNIC, it says. Do you think they have Class Picnics in the afterlife?

I don't know. But I know you were run over by a car.

No!

Yes. It happened on May 9th, at 8:25 A.M. You died less than a minute later.

No! No! No!

"John?"

He looked around, badly startled. Mr. Bissette, his French teacher, was standing there, looking a little concerned. Behind him, the rest of the student body was streaming into the Common Room for the morning assembly. There was very little skylarking, and no yelling at all. Presumably these other students, like Jake himself, had been told by their parents how lucky they were to be attending Piper, where money didn't matter (although tuition was $22,000 a year), only your brains. Presumably many of them had been promised trips this summer if their grades were good enough. Presumably the parents of the lucky trip-winners would even go along in some cases. Presumably—

"John, are you okay?" Mr. Bissette asked.

"Sure," Jake said. "Fine. I overslept a little this morning. Not awake yet, I guess."

Mr. Bissette's face relaxed and he smiled. "Happens to the best of us."

Not to my dad. The master of The Kill never oversleeps.

"Are you ready for your French final?" Mr. Bissette asked. *"Voulez-vous faire l'examen cet après-midi?"*

"I think so," Jake said. In truth he didn't know if he was ready for the exam or not. He couldn't even remember if he had *studied* for the French final or not. These days nothing seemed to matter much except for the voices in his head.

"I want to tell you again how much I enjoyed having you this year, John. I wanted to tell your folks, too, but they missed Parents' Night—"

"They're pretty busy," Jake said.

Mr. Bissette nodded. "Well, I have enjoyed you. I just wanted to say so . . . and that I'm looking forward to having you back for French II next year."

"Thanks," Jake said, and wondered what Mr. Bissette would say if he added, *But I don't think I'll be taking French II next year, unless I can get a correspondence course delivered to my postal box at good old Sunnyvale.*

Joanne Franks, the school secretary, appeared in the doorway of the Common Room with her small silver-plated bell in her hand. At The Piper School, *all* bells were rung by hand. Jake supposed that if you were a parent, that was one of its charms. Memories of the Little Red Schoolhouse and all that. He hated it himself. The sound of that bell seemed to go right through his head—

I can't hold on much longer, he thought despairingly. *I'm sorry, but I'm losing it. I'm really, really losing it.*

Mr. Bissette had caught sight of Ms. Franks. He turned away, then turned back again. *"Is* everything all right, John? You've seemed preoccupied these last few weeks. Troubled. Is something on your mind?"

Jake was almost undone by the kindness in Mr. Bissette's voice, but then he imagined how Mr. Bissette would look if he said: *Yes. Something is on my mind. One hell of a nasty little factoid. I died, you see, and I went into another world. And then I died again. You're going to say that stuff like that doesn't happen, and of course you're right, and part of my mind knows you're right, but most of my mind knows that you're wrong. It did happen. I did die.*

If he said something like that, Mr. Bissette would be on the phone to Elmer Chambers at once, and Jake thought that Sunnyvale Sanitarium would probably look like a rest-cure after all the stuff his father would have to say on the subject of kids who started having crazy notions just before Finals Week. Kids who did things that couldn't be discussed over lunch or cocktails. Kids Who Let Down The Side.

Jake forced himself to smile at Mr. Bissette. "I'm a little worried about exams, that's all."

Mr. Bissette winked. "You'll do fine."

Ms. Franks began to ring the Assembly Bell. Each peal stabbed into Jake's ears and then seemed to flash across his brain like a small rocket.

"Come on," Mr. Bissette said. "We'll be late. Can't be late on the first day of Finals Week, can we?"

They went in past Ms. Franks and her clashing bell. Mr. Bissette headed toward the row of seats called Faculty Choir. There were lots of cute names like that at Piper School; the auditorium was the Common Room, lunch-hour was Outs, seventh- and eighth-graders were Upper Boys and Girls, and, of course, the folding chairs over by the piano (which Ms. Franks would soon begin to pound as mercilessly as she rang her silver bell) was Faculty Choir. All part of the tradition, Jake supposed. If you were a parent who knew your kid had Outs in the Common Room at noon instead of just slopping up Tuna Surprise in the caff, you relaxed into the assurance that everything was A-OK in the education department.

He slipped into a seat at the rear of the room and let the morning's announcements wash over him. The terror ran endlessly on in his mind, making him feel like a rat trapped on an exercise wheel. And when he tried to look ahead to some better, brighter time, he could see only darkness.

The ship was his sanity, and it was sinking.

Mr. Harley, the headmaster, approached the podium and imparted a brief exordium about the importance of Finals Week, and how the grades they received would constitute another step upon The Great Road of Life. He told them that the school was depending on them, *he* was depending on them, and their parents were depending on them. He did not tell them that the entire free world was depending on them, but he strongly implied that this might be so. He finished by telling them that bells would be suspended during Finals Week (the first and only piece of good news Jake had received that morning).

Ms. Franks, who had assumed her seat at the piano, struck an invocatory chord. The student body, seventy boys and fifty girls, each turned out in a neat and sober way that bespoke their parents' taste and financial stability, rose as one and began to sing the school song. Jake mouthed the words and thought about the place where he had awakened after dying. At first he had believed himself to be in hell . . . and when the man in the black hooded robe came along, he had been sure of it.

Then, of course, the other man had come along. A man Jake had almost come to love.

But he let me fall. He killed me.

He could feel prickly sweat breaking out on the back of his neck and between his shoulderblades.

> *"So we hail the halls of Piper,*
> *Hold its banner high;*
> *Hail to thee, our alma mater,*
> *Piper, do or die!"*

God, what a shitty song, Jake thought, and it suddenly occurred to him that his father would love it.

2

PERIOD ONE WAS ENGLISH Comp, the only class where there was no final. Their assignment had been to write a Final Essay at home. This was to be a typed document between fifteen hundred and four thousand words long. The subject Ms. Avery had assigned was *My Understanding of Truth*. The Final Essay would count as twenty-five per cent of their final grade for the semester.

Jake came in and took his seat in the third row. There were only eleven pupils in all. Jake remembered Orientation Day last September, when Mr. Harley had told them that Piper had The Highest Teacher To Student Ratio Of Any Fine Private Middle School In The East. He had popped his fist repeatedly on the lectern at the front of the Common Room to emphasize this point. Jake hadn't been terribly impressed, but he had passed the information along to his father. He thought his father *would* be impressed, and he had not been wrong.

He unzipped his bookbag and carefully removed the blue folder which contained his Final Essay. He laid it on his desk, meaning to give it a final look-over, when his eye was caught by the door at the left side of the room. It led, he knew, to the cloakroom, and it was closed today because it was seventy degrees in New York and no one had a coat which needed storage. Nothing back there except a lot of brass coathooks in a line on the wall and a long rubber mat on the floor for boots. A few boxes of school supplies—chalk, blue-books and such—were stored in the far corner.

No big deal.

All the same, Jake rose from his seat, leaving the folder unopened on the desk, and walked across to the door. He could hear his classmates murmuring quietly together, and the riffle of pages as they checked their own Final Essays for that crucial misplaced modifier or fuzzy phrase, but these sounds seemed far away.

It was the door which held his attention.

In the last ten days or so, as the voices in his head grew louder and louder, Jake had become more and more fascinated with doors—all kinds of doors. He must have opened the one between his bedroom and the upstairs hallway five hundred times in just the last week, and the one between his bedroom and the bathroom a thousand. Each time he did it, he felt a tight ball of hope and anticipation in his chest, as if the answer to all of his problems lay somewhere behind this door or that one and he would surely find it . . . eventually. But each time it was only the hall, or the bathroom, or the front walk, or whatever.

Last Thursday he had come home from school, thrown himself on his bed, and had fallen asleep—sleep, it seemed, was the only refuge which remained to him. Except when he'd awakened forty-five minutes later, he had been standing in the bathroom doorway, peering dazedly in at nothing more exciting than the toilet and the basin. Luckily, no one had seen him.

Now, as he approached the cloakroom door, he felt that same dazzling burst of hope, a certainty that the door would not open on a shadowy closet containing only the persistent smells of winter—flannel, rubber, and wet wool—but on some other world where he could be *whole* again. Hot, dazzling light would fall across the classroom floor in a widening triangle, and he would see birds circling in a faded blue sky the color of

(*his eyes*)

old jeans. A desert wind would blow his hair back and dry the nervous sweat on his brow.

He would step through this door and be healed.

Jake turned the knob and opened the door. Inside was only darkness and a row of gleaming brass hooks. One long-forgotten mitten lay near the stacked piles of blue-books in the corner.

His heart sank, and suddenly Jake felt like simply creeping into that dark room with its bitter smells of winter and chalkdust. He could move the mitten and sit in the corner under the coathooks. He could sit on the rubber mat where you were supposed to put your boots in the winter-time. He could sit there, put his thumb in his mouth, pull his knees tight against his chest, close his eyes, and . . . and . . .

And just give up.

This idea—the *relief* of this idea—was incredibly attractive. It would be an end to the terror and confusion and dislocation. That last was somehow the worst; that persistent feeling that his whole life had turned into a funhouse mirror-maze.

Yet there was deep steel in Jake Chambers as surely as there was deep steel in Eddie and Susannah. Now it flashed out its dour blue lighthouse gleam in the darkness. There would be no giving up. What-ever was loose inside him might tear his sanity away from him in the end, but he would give it no quarter in the meantime. Be damned if he would.

Never! he thought fiercely. *Never! Nev*—

"When you've finished your inventory of the school-supplies in the cloakroom, John, perhaps you'd care to join us," Ms. Avery said from behind him in her dry, cultured voice.

There was a small gust of giggles as Jake turned away from the cloakroom. Ms. Avery was standing behind her desk with her long fingers tented lightly on the blotter, looking at him out of her calm, intelligent face. She was wearing her blue suit today, and her hair was pulled back in its usual bun. Nathaniel Hawthorne looked over her shoulder, frowning at Jake from his place on the wall.

"Sorry," Jake muttered, and closed the door. He was immediately seized by a strong impulse to open it again, to double-check, to see if *this* time that other world, with its hot sun and desert vistas, was there.

Instead he walked back to his seat. Petra Jesserling looked at him with merry, dancing eyes. "Take *me* in there with you next time," she whispered. "Then you'll have something to look at."

Jake smiled in a distracted way and slipped into his seat.

"Thank you, John," Ms. Avery said in her endlessly calm voice. "Now, before you pass in your Final Essays—which I am sure will all be very fine, very neat, very *specific*—I should like to pass out the English Department's Short List of recommended summer reading. I will have a word to say about several of these excellent books—"

As she spoke she gave a small stack of mimeographed sheets to David Surrey. David began to hand them out, and Jake opened his folder to take a final look at what he had written on the topic *My Understanding of Truth*. He was genuinely interested in this, because he could no more remember writing his Final Essay, than he could remember studying for his French final.

He looked at the title page with puzzlement and growing unease. MY UNDERSTANDING OF TRUTH, *By John Chambers*, was neatly typed and centered on the sheet, and that was all right, but he had for some reason pasted two photographs below it. One was of a door—he thought it might be the one at Number 10, Downing Street, in London—and the other was of an Amtrak train. They were color shots, undoubtedly culled from some magazine.

Why did I do that? And when *did I do it?*

He turned the page and stared down at the first page of his Final Essay, unable to believe or understand what he was seeing. Then, as understanding began to trickle through his shock, he felt an escalating sense of horror. It had finally happened; he had finally lost enough of his mind so that other people would be able to *tell*.

3

MY UNDERSTANDING OF TRUTH
By John Chambers

"I will show you fear in a handful of dust."
—T. S. "BUTCH" ELIOT

"My first thought was, he lied in every word."
—ROBERT "SUNDANCE" BROWNING

The gunslinger is the truth.
Roland is the truth.
The Prisoner is the truth.
The Lady of Shadows is the truth.
The Prisoner and the Lady are married. That is the truth.
The way station is the truth.
The Speaking Demon is the truth.
We went under the mountains and that is the truth.
There were monsters under the mountain. That is the truth.
One of them had an Amoco gas pump between his legs and was pretending it was his penis. That is the truth.

Roland let me die. That is the truth.
I still love him.
That is the truth.

"And it is so *very* important that you *all* read *The Lord of the Flies*," Ms. Avery was saying in her clear but somehow pale voice. "And when you do, you must ask yourselves certain questions. A good novel is often like a series of riddles within riddles, and this is a *very* good novel—one of the best written in the second half of the twentieth century. So ask yourselves first what the symbolic significance of the conch shell might be. Second—"

Far away. Far, far away. Jake turned to the second page of his Final Essay with a trembling hand, leaving a dark smear of sweat on the first page.

> *When is a door not a door? When it's a jar, and that is the*
>   *truth.*
> *Blaine is the truth.*
> *Blaine is the truth.*
> *What has four wheels and flies? A garbage truck, and that*
>   *is the truth.*
> *Blaine is the truth.*
> *You have to watch Blaine all the time, Blaine is a pain,*
>   *and that is the truth.*
> *I'm pretty sure that Blaine is dangerous, and that is the*
>   *truth.*
> *What is black and white and red all over? A blushing*
>   *zebra, and that is the truth.*
> *Blaine is the truth.*
> *I want to go back and that is the truth.*
> *I have to go back and that is the truth.*
> *I'll go crazy if I don't go back and that is the truth.*
> *I can't go home again unless I find a stone a rose a door*
>   *and that is the truth.*
> *Choo-choo, and that is the truth.*
> *Choo-choo. Choo-choo.*
> *Choo-choo. Choo-choo. Choo-choo.*
> *Choo-choo. Choo-choo. Choo-choo. Choo-choo.*
> *I am afraid. That is the truth.*
> *Choo-choo.*

Jake looked up slowly. His heart was beating so hard that he saw a bright light like the afterimage of a flashbulb dancing in front of his eyes, a light that pulsed in and out with each titanic thud of his heart.

He saw Ms. Avery handing his Final Essay to his mother and father. Mr. Bissette was standing beside Ms. Avery, looking grave. He heard Ms. Avery say in her clear, pale voice: *Your son is seriously ill. If you need proof, just look at this Final Essay.*

John hasn't been himself for the last three weeks or so, Mr. Bissette added. *He seems frightened some of the time and dazed all of the time . . . not quite there, if you see what I mean. Je pense que John est fou . . . comprenez-vous?*

Ms. Avery again: *Do you perhaps keep certain mood-altering prescription drugs in the house where John might have access to them?*

Jake didn't know about mood-altering drugs, but he knew his father kept several grams of cocaine in the bottom drawer of his study desk. His father would undoubtedly think he had been into it.

"Now let me say a word about *Catch-22,*" Ms. Avery said from the front of the room. "This is a very *challenging* book for sixth- and seventh-grade students, but you will nonetheless find it entirely enchanting, *if* you open your minds to its *special charm.* You may think of this novel, if you like, as a comedy of the surreal."

I don't need to read *something like that,* Jake thought. *I'm living something like that, and it's no comedy.*

He turned over to the last page of his Final Essay. There were no words on it. Instead he had pasted another picture to the paper. It was a photograph of the Leaning Tower of Pisa. He had used a crayon to scribble it black. The dark, waxy lines looped and swooped in lunatic coils.

He could remember doing none of this.

Absolutely *none* of it.

Now he heard his father saying to Mr. Bissette: Fou. *Yes, he's definitely* fou. *A kid who'd fuck up his chance at a school like Piper HAS to be* fou, *wouldn't you say? Well . . . I can handle this. Handling things is my job. Sunnyvale's the answer. He needs to spend some time in Sunnyvale, making baskets and getting his shit back together. Don't you worry about our kid, folks; he can run . . . but he can't hide.*

Would they actually send him away to the nuthatch if it started to seem that his elevator no longer went all the way to the top floor? Jake thought the answer to that was a big you bet. No way his father was going to put up with a loony around the house. The name of the place they put him in might not be Sunnyvale, but there would be bars on the windows and there would be young men in white coats and crepe-soled shoes prowling the halls. The young men would have big muscles and watchful eyes and access to hypodermic needles full of artificial sleep.

They'll tell everybody I went away, Jake thought. The arguing voices in his head were temporarily stilled by a rising tide of panic. *They'll say*

I'm spending the year with my aunt and uncle in Modesto . . . or in
Sweden as an exchange student . . . or repairing satellites in outer space.
My mother won't like it . . . she'll cry . . . but she'll go along. She has her
boyfriends, and besides, she always goes along with what he decides. She
. . . they . . . me . . .

He felt a shriek welling up his throat and pressed his lips tightly
together to hold it in. He looked down again at the wild black scribbles
snarled across the photograph of the Leaning Tower and thought: *I have*
to get out of here. I have to get out right now.

He raised his hand.

"Yes, John, what is it?" Ms. Avery was looking at him with the
expression of mild exasperation she reserved for students who interrupted
her in mid-lecture.

"I'd like to step out for a moment, if I may," Jake said.

This was another example of Piper-speak. Piper students did not
ever have to "take a leak" or "tap a kidney" or, God forbid, "drop a
load." The unspoken assumption was that Piper students were too perfect
to create waste byproducts in their tastefully silent glides through life.
Once in a while someone requested permission to "step out for a
moment," and that was all.

Ms. Avery sighed. "Must you, John?"

"Yes, ma'am."

"All right. Return as soon as possible."

"Yes, Ms. Avery."

He closed the folder as he got up, took hold of it, then reluctantly
let go again. No good. Ms. Avery would wonder why he was taking his
Final Essay to the toilet with him. He should have removed the damning
pages from the folder and stuffed them in his pocket before asking for
permission to step out. Too late now.

Jake walked down the aisle toward the door, leaving his folder on
the desk and his bookbag lying beneath it.

"Hope everything comes out all right, Chambers," David Surrey
whispered, and snickered into his hand.

"Still your restless lips, David," Ms. Avery said, clearly exasperated
now, and the whole class laughed.

Jake reached the door leading to the hall, and as he grasped the
knob, that feeling of hope and surety rose in him again: *This is it—really*
it. I'll open the door and the desert sun will shine in. I'll feel that dry
wind on my face. I'll step through and never see this classroom again.

He opened the door and it was only the hallway on the other side,
but he was right about one thing just the same: he never saw Ms. Avery's
classroom again.

4

HE WALKED SLOWLY DOWN the dim, wood-panelled corridor, sweating lightly. He walked past classroom doors he would have felt compelled to open if not for the clear glass windows set in each one. He looked into Mr. Bissette's French II class and Mr. Knopf's Introduction to Geometry class. In both rooms the pupils sat with pencils in hand and heads bowed over open blue-books. He looked into Mr. Harley's Spoken Arts class and saw Stan Dorfman—one of those acquaintances who were not quite friends—beginning his Final Speech. Stan looked scared to death, but Jake could have told Stan he didn't have the slightest idea what fear—*real* fear—was all about.

I died.

No. I didn't.

Did too.

Did not.

Did.

Didn't.

He came to a door marked GIRLS. He pushed it open, expecting to see a bright desert sky and a blue haze of mountains on the horizon. Instead he saw Belinda Stevens standing at one of the sinks, looking into the mirror above the basin and squeezing a pimple on her forehead.

"Jesus Christ, do you mind?" she asked.

"Sorry. Wrong door. I thought it was the desert."

"*What?*"

But he had already let the door go and it was swinging shut on its pneumatic elbow. He passed the drinking fountain and opened the door marked BOYS. *This* was it, he knew it, was sure of it, this was the door which would take him back—

Three urinals gleamed spotlessly under the fluorescent lights. A tap dripped solemnly into a sink. That was all.

Jake let the door close. He walked on down the hall, his heels making firm little clicks on the tiles. He glanced into the office before passing it and saw only Ms. Franks. She was talking on the telephone, swinging back and forth in her swivel chair and playing with a lock of her hair. The silver-plated bell stood on the desk beside her. Jake waited until she swivelled away from the door and then hurried past. Thirty seconds later he was emerging into the bright sunshine of a morning in late May.

I've gone truant, he thought. Even his distraction did not keep him from being amazed at this unexpected development. *When I don't come back from the bathroom in five minutes or so, Ms. Avery will send some-*

body to check . . . and then they'll know. They'll all know that I've left school, gone truant.

He thought of the folder lying on his desk.

They'll read it and they'll think I'm crazy. Fou. Sure they will. Of course. Because I am.

Then another voice spoke. It was, he thought, the voice of the man with the bombardier's eyes, the man who wore the two big guns slung low on his hips. The voice was cold . . . but not without comfort.

No, Jake, Roland said. *You're not crazy. You're lost and scared, but you're not crazy and need fear neither your shadow in the morning striding behind you nor your shadow at evening rising to meet you. You have to find your way back home, that's all.*

"But where do I go?" Jake whispered. He stood on the sidewalk of Fifty-sixth Street between Park and Madison, watching the traffic bolt past. A city bus snored by, laying a thin trail of acrid blue diesel smoke. "Where do I go? Where's the fucking *door*?"

But the voice of the gunslinger had fallen silent.

Jake turned left, in the direction of the East River, and began to walk blindly forward. He had no idea where he was going—no idea at all. He could only hope his feet would carry him to the right place . . . as they had carried him to the wrong one not long ago.

5

IT HAD HAPPENED THREE weeks earlier.

One could not say *It all began three weeks earlier,* because that gave the impression that there had been some sort of progression, and that wasn't right. There had been a progression to the *voices,* to the violence with which each insisted on its own particular version of reality, but the rest of it had happened all at once.

He left home at eight o'clock to walk to school—he always walked when the weather was good, and the weather this May had been absolutely fine. His father had left for the Network, his mother was still in bed, and Mrs. Greta Shaw was in the kitchen, drinking coffee and reading her *New York Post.*

"Goodbye, Greta," he said. "I'm going to school now."

She raised a hand to him without looking up from the paper. "Have a good day, Johnny."

All according to routine. Just another day in the life.

And so it had been for the next fifteen hundred seconds. Then everything had changed forever.

He idled along, bookbag in one hand, lunch sack in the other, looking in the windows. Seven hundred and twenty seconds from the end of his life as he had always known it, he paused to look in the window of Brendio's, where mannequins dressed in fur coats and Edwardian suits stood in stiff poses of conversation. He was thinking only of going bowling that afternoon after school. His average was 158, great for a kid who was only eleven. His ambition was to some day be a bowler on the pro tour (and if his father had known *this* little factoid, he *also* would have hit the roof).

Closing in now—closing in on the moment when his sanity would be suddenly eclipsed.

He crossed Thirty-ninth and there were four hundred seconds left. Had to wait for the WALK light at Forty-first and there were two hundred and seventy. Paused to look in the novelty shop on the corner of Fifth and Forty-second and there were a hundred and ninety. And now, with just over three minutes left in his ordinary life, Jake Chambers walked beneath the unseen umbrella of that force which Roland called *ka-tet*.

An odd, uneasy feeling began to creep over him. At first he thought it was a feeling of being watched, and then he realized it wasn't that at all . . . or not *precisely* that. He felt that he had been here before; that he was reliving a dream he had mostly forgotten. He waited for the feeling to pass, but it didn't. It grew stronger, and now began to mix with a sensation he reluctantly recognized as terror.

Up ahead, on the near corner of Fifth and Forty-third, a black man in a Panama hat was setting up a pretzel-and-soda cart.

He's the one that yells "Oh my God, he's kilt!" Jake thought.

Approaching the far corner was a fat lady with a Bloomingdale's bag in her hand.

She'll drop the bag. Drop the bag and put her hands to her mouth and scream. The bag will split open. There's a doll inside the bag. It's wrapped in a red towel. I'll see this from the street. From where I'll be lying in the street with my blood soaking into my pants and spreading around me in a pool.

Behind the fat woman was a tall man in a gray nailhead worsted suit. He was carrying a briefcase.

He's the one who vomits on his shoes. He's the one who drops his briefcase and throws up on his shoes. What's happening to me?

Yet his feet carried him numbly forward toward the intersection, where people were crossing in a brisk, steady stream. Somewhere behind him, closing in, was a killer priest. He *knew* this, just as he knew that the priest's hands would in a moment be outstretched to push . . . but he could not look around. It was like being locked in a nightmare where things simply had to take their course.

Fifty-three seconds left now. Ahead of him, the pretzel vendor was opening a hatch in the side of his cart.

He's going to take out a bottle of Yoo-Hoo, Jake thought. Not a can but a bottle. He'll shake it up and drink it all at once.

The pretzel vendor brought out a bottle of Yoo-Hoo, shook it vigorously, and spun off the cap.

Forty seconds left.

Now the light will change.

White WALK went out. Red DONT WALK began to flash rapidly on and off. And somewhere, less than half a block away, a big blue Cadillac was now rolling toward the intersection of Fifth and Forty-third. Jake *knew* this, just as he knew the driver was a fat man wearing a hat almost the exact same blue shade as his car.

I'm going to die!

He wanted to scream this aloud to the people walking heedlessly all around him, but his jaws were locked shut. His feet swept him serenely onward toward the intersection. The DONT WALK sign stopped flashing and shone out its solid red warning. The pretzel vendor tossed his empty Yoo-Hoo bottle into the wire trash basket on the corner. The fat lady stood on the corner across the street from Jake, holding her shopping bag by the handles. The man in the nailhead suit was directly behind her. Now there were eighteen seconds left.

Time for the toy truck to go by, Jake thought.

Ahead of him a van with a picture of a happy jumping-jack and the words TOOKER'S WHOLESALE TOYS printed on the side swept through the intersection, jolting up and down in the potholes. Behind him, Jake knew, the man in the black robe was beginning to move faster, closing the gap, now reaching out with his long hands. Yet he could not look around, as you couldn't look around in dreams when something awful was gaining on you.

Run! And if you can't run, sit down and grab hold of a No Parking sign! Don't just let it happen!

But he was powerless to *stop* it from happening. Ahead, on the edge of the curb, was a young woman in a white sweater and a black skirt. To her left was a young Chicano guy with a boombox. A Donna Summer disco tune was just ending. The next song, Jake knew, would be "Dr. Love," by Kiss.

They're going to move apart—

Even as the thought came, the woman moved a step to her right. The Chicano guy moved a step to his left, creating a gap between them. Jake's traitor feet swept him into the gap. Nine seconds now.

Down the street, bright May sunshine twinkled on a Cadillac hood ornament. It was, Jake knew, a 1976 Sedan de Ville. Six seconds. The

Caddy was speeding up. The light was getting ready to change and the man driving the de Ville, the fat man in the blue hat with the feather stuck jauntily in the brim, meant to scat through the intersection before it could. Three seconds. Behind Jake, the man in black was lunging forward. On the young man's boombox, "Love to Love You, Baby" ended and "Dr. Love" began.

Two.

The Cadillac changed to the lane nearest Jake's side of the street and charged down on the intersection, its killer grille snarling.

One.

Jake's breath stopped in his throat.

None.

"Uh!" Jake cried as the hands struck him firmly in the back, pushing him, pushing him into the street, pushing him out of his life—

Except there *were* no hands.

He reeled forward nevertheless, hands flailing at the air, his mouth a dark O of dismay. The Chicano guy with the boombox reached out, grabbed Jake's arm, and hauled him backward. "Look out, little hero," he said. "That traffic turn you into bratwurst."

The Cadillac floated by. Jake caught a glimpse of the fat man in the blue hat peering out through the windshield, and then it was gone.

That was when it happened; that was when he split down the middle and became two boys. One lay dying in the street. The other stood here on the corner, watching in dumb, stricken amazement as DONT WALK turned to WALK again and people began to cross around him just as if nothing had happened . . . as, indeed, nothing had.

I'm alive! half of his mind rejoiced, screaming with relief.

Dead! the other half screamed back. *Dead in the street! They're all gathering around me, and the man in black who pushed me is saying "I am a priest. Let me through."*

Waves of faintness rushed through him and turned his thoughts to billowing parachute silk. He saw the fat lady approaching, and as she passed, Jake looked into her bag. He saw the bright blue eyes of a doll peeping above the edge of a red towel, just as he had known he would. Then she was gone. The pretzel vendor was not yelling *Oh my God, he's kilt*; he was continuing to set up for the day's business while he whistled the Donna Summer tune that had been playing on the Chicano guy's radio.

Jake turned around, looking wildly for the priest who was not a priest. He wasn't there.

Jake moaned.

Snap out of it! What's wrong with you?

He didn't know. He only knew he was supposed to be lying in the street right now, getting ready to die while the fat woman screamed and the guy in the nailhead worsted suit threw up and the man in black pushed through the gathering crowd.

And in part of his mind, that did seem to be happening.

The faintness began to return. Jake suddenly dropped his lunch sack to the pavement and slapped himself across the face as hard as he could. A woman on her way to work gave him a queer look. Jake ignored her. He left his lunch lying on the sidewalk and plunged into the intersection, also ignoring the red DONT WALK light, which had begun to stutter on and off again. It didn't matter now. Death had approached . . . and then passed by without a second glance. It hadn't been meant to happen that way, and on the deepest level of his existence he knew that, but it had.

Maybe now he would live forever.

The thought made him feel like screaming all over again.

6

HIS HEAD HAD CLEARED a little by the time he got to school, and his mind had gone to work trying to convince him that nothing was wrong, really nothing at all. Maybe something a little weird *had* happened, some sort of psychic flash, a momentary peek into one possible future, but so what? No big deal, right? The idea was actually sort of cool—the kind of thing they were always printing in the weird supermarket newspapers Greta Shaw liked to read when she was sure Jake's mother wasn't around—papers like the *National Enquirer* and *Inside View*. Except, of course, in those papers the psychic flash was always a kind of tactical nuclear strike—a woman who dreamed of a plane crash and changed her reservations, or a guy who dreamed his brother was being held prisoner in a Chinese fortune cookie factory and it turned out to be true. When your psychic flash consisted of knowing that a Kiss song was going to play next on the radio, that a fat lady had a doll wrapped in a red towel in her Bloomingdale's bag, and that a pretzel vendor was going to drink a bottle of Yoo-Hoo instead of a can, how big a deal could it be?

Forget it, he advised himself. *It's over.*

A great idea, except by period three he knew it *wasn't* over; it was just beginning. He sat in pre-algebra, watching Mr. Knopf solving simple equations on the board, and realized with dawning horror that a whole new set of memories was surfacing in his mind. It was like watching strange objects float slowly toward the surface of a muddy lake.

I'm in a place I don't know, he thought. *I mean, I will know it—or* would *have known it if the Cadillac had hit me. It's the way station—*

but the part of me that's there doesn't know that yet. That part only knows it's in the desert someplace, and there are no people. I've been crying, because I'm scared. I'm scared that this might be hell.

By three o'clock, when he arrived at Mid-Town Lanes, he knew he had found the pump in the stables and had gotten a drink of water. The water was very cold and tasted strongly of minerals. Soon he would go inside and find a small supply of dried beef in a room which had once been a kitchen. He knew this as clearly and surely as he'd known the pretzel vendor would select a bottle of Yoo-Hoo, and that the doll peeking out of the Bloomingdale's bag had blue eyes.

It was like being able to remember forward in time.

He bowled only two strings—the first a 96, the second an 87. Timmy looked at his sheet when he turned it in at the counter and shook his head. "You're having an off-day today, champ," he said.

"You don't know the half of it," Jake said.

Timmy took a closer look. "You okay? You look really pale."

"I think I might be coming down with a bug." This didn't feel like a lie, either. He was sure as hell coming down with *something*.

"Go home and go to bed," Timmy advised. "Drink lots of clear liquids—gin, vodka, stuff like that."

Jake smiled dutifully. "Maybe I will."

He walked slowly home. All of New York was spread out around him, New York at its most seductive—a late-afternoon street serenade with a musician on every corner, all the trees in bloom, and everyone apparently in a good mood. Jake saw all this, but he also saw *behind* it: saw himself cowering in the shadows of the kitchen as the man in black drank like a grinning dog from the stable pump, saw himself sobbing with relief as he—or it—moved on without discovering him, saw himself falling deeply asleep as the sun went down and the stars began to come out like chips of ice in the harsh purple desert sky.

He let himself into the duplex apartment with his key and walked into the kitchen to get something to eat. He wasn't hungry, but it was habit. He was headed for the refrigerator when his eye happened on the pantry door and he stopped. He realized suddenly that the way station—and all the rest of that strange other world where he now belonged—was behind that door. All he had to do was push through it and rejoin the Jake that already existed there. The queer doubling in his mind would end; the voices, endlessly arguing the question of whether or not he had been dead since 8:25 that morning, would fall silent.

Jake pushed open the pantry door with both hands, his face already breaking into a sunny, relieved smile . . . and then froze as Mrs. Shaw, who was standing on a step-stool at the back of the pantry, screamed. The can of tomato paste she had been holding dropped out of her hand

and fell to the floor. She tottered on the stool and Jake rushed forward to steady her before she could join the tomato paste.

"Moses in the bullrushes!" she gasped, fluttering a hand rapidly against the front of her housedress. "You scared the bejabbers out of me, Johnny!"

"I'm sorry," he said. He really was, but he was also bitterly disappointed. It had only been the pantry, after all. He had been so *sure*—

"What are you doing, creeping around here, anyway? This is your bowling day! I didn't expect you for at least another hour! I haven't even made your snack yet, so don't be expecting it."

"That's okay. I'm not very hungry, anyway." He bent down and picked up the can she had dropped.

"Wouldn't know it from the way you came bustin in here," she grumbled.

"I thought I heard a mouse or something. I guess it was just you."

"I guess it was." She descended the step-stool and took the can from him. "You look like you're comin down with the flu or something, Johnny." She pressed her hand against his forehead. "You don't feel hot, but that doesn't always mean much."

"I think I'm just tired," Jake said, and thought: *If only that was all it was.* "Maybe I'll just have a soda and watch TV for a while."

She grunted. "You got any papers you want to show me? If you do, make it fast. I'm behind on supper."

"Nothing today," he said. He left the pantry, got a soda, then went into the living room. He turned on *Hollywood Squares* and watched vacantly as the voices argued and the new memories of that dusty other world continued to surface.

7

HIS MOTHER AND FATHER didn't notice anything was wrong with him— his father didn't even get in until 9:30—and that was fine by Jake. He went to bed at ten and lay awake in the darkness, listening to the city outside his window: brakes, horns, wailing sirens.

You died.

I didn't, though. I'm right here, safe in my own bed.

That doesn't matter. You died, and you know it.

The hell of it was, he knew both things.

I don't know which voice is true, but I know I can't go on like this. So just quit it, both of you. Stop arguing and leave me alone. Okay? Please?

But they wouldn't. *Couldn't*, apparently. And it came to Jake that he ought to get up—*right now*—and open the door to the bathroom. The other world would be there. The way station would be there and the rest of *him* would be there, too, huddled under an ancient blanket in the stable, trying to sleep and wondering what in hell had happened.

I can tell him, Jake thought excitedly. He threw back the covers, suddenly knowing that the door beside his bookcase no longer led into the bathroom but to a world that smelled of heat and purple sage and fear in a handful of dust, a world that now lay under the shadowing wing of night. *I can tell him, but I won't have to . . . because I'll be IN him . . . I'll BE him!*

He raced across his darkened room, almost laughing with relief, and shoved open the door. And—

And it was his bathroom. Just his bathroom, with the framed Marvin Gaye poster on the wall and the shapes of the venetian blinds lying on the tiled floor in bars of light and shadow.

He stood there for a long time, trying to swallow his disappointment. It wouldn't go. And it was bitter.

Bitter.

8

THE THREE WEEKS BETWEEN then and now stretched like a grim, blighted terrain in Jake's memory—a nightmare wasteland where there had been no peace, no rest, no respite from pain. He had watched, like a helpless prisoner watching the sack of a city he had once ruled, as his mind buckled under the steadily increasing pressure of the phantom voices and memories. He had hoped the memories would stop when he reached the point in them where the man named Roland had allowed him to drop into the chasm under the mountains, but they didn't. Instead they simply recycled and began to play themselves over again, like a tape set to repeat and repeat until it either breaks or someone comes along and shuts it off.

His perceptions of his more-or-less real life as a boy in New York City grew increasingly spotty as this terrible schism grew deeper. He could remember going to school, and to the movies on the weekend, and out to Sunday brunch with his parents a week ago (or had it been two?), but he remembered these things the way a man who has suffered malaria may remember the deepest, darkest phase of his illness: people became shadows, voices seemed to echo and overlap each other, and even such a simple act as eating a sandwich or obtaining a Coke from the machine in the gymnasium became a struggle. Jake had pushed through those days in a fugue of yelling voices and doubled memories. His obsession with doors—all kinds of doors—deepened; his hope that the gunslinger's world might lie behind one of them never quite died. Nor was that so strange, since it was the only hope he had.

But as of today the game was over. He'd never had a chance of winning anyway, not really. He had given up. He had gone truant. Jake walked blindly east along the gridwork of streets, head down, with no idea of where he was going or what he would do when he got there.

9

AFTER WALKING FOR A while, he began to come out of this unhappy daze and take some notice of his surroundings. He was standing on the corner of Lexington Avenue and Fifty-fourth Street with no memory at all of how he had come to be there. He noticed for the first time that it was an absolutely gorgeous morning. May 9th, the day this madness had started, had been pretty, but today was ten times better—that day, perhaps, when spring looks around herself and sees summer standing nearby, strong and handsome and with a cocky grin on his tanned face. The sun shone brightly off the glass walls of the midtown buildings; the shadow of each pedestrian was black and crisp. The sky overhead was a clear and blameless blue, dotted here and there with plump foul-weather clouds.

Down the street, two businessmen in expensive, well-cut suits were standing at a board wall which had been erected around a construction site. They were laughing and passing something back and forth. Jake walked in their direction, curious, and as he drew closer he saw that the two businessmen were playing tic-tac-toe on the wall, using an expensive Mark Cross pen to draw the grids and make the X's and O's. Jake thought this was a complete gas. As he approached, one of them made an O in the upper right-hand corner of the grid and then slashed a diagonal line through the middle.

"Skunked again!" his friend said. Then this man, who looked like a high-powered executive or lawyer or big-time stockbroker, took the Mark Cross pen and drew another grid.

The first businessman, the winner, glanced to his left and saw Jake. He smiled. "Some day, huh, kid?"

"It sure is," Jake said, delighted to find he meant every word.

"Too nice for school, huh?"

This time Jake actually laughed. Piper School, where you had Outs instead of lunch and where you sometimes stepped out but never had to take a crap, suddenly seemed far away and not at all important. "You know it."

"You want a game? Billy here couldn't beat me at this when we were in the fifth grade, and he still can't."

"Leave the kid alone," the second businessman said, holding out the Mark Cross pen. "This time you're history." He winked at Jake, and Jake amazed himself by winking back. He walked on, leaving the men to their game. The sense that something totally wonderful was going to happen—had perhaps already *begun* to happen—continued to grow, and his feet no longer seemed to be quite touching the pavement.

The WALK light on the corner came on, and he began to cross Lexington Avenue. He stopped in the middle of the street so suddenly that a messenger-boy on a ten-speed bike almost ran him down. It was a beautiful spring day—agreed. But that wasn't why he felt so good, so suddenly aware of everything that was going on around him, so sure that some great thing was about to occur.

The voices had stopped.

They weren't gone for good—he somehow knew this—but for the time being they had *stopped*. Why?

Jake suddenly thought of two men arguing in a room. They sit facing each other over a table, jawing at each other with increasing bitterness. After a while they begin to lean toward each other, thrusting their faces pugnaciously forward, bathing each other with a fine mist of outraged spittle. Soon they will come to blows. But before that can happen, they hear a steady thumping noise—the sound of a bass drum—and then a jaunty flourish of brass. The two men stop arguing and look at each other, puzzled.

What's that? one asks.

Dunno, the other replies. *Sounds like a parade.*

They rush to the window and it *is* a parade—a uniformed band marching in lock-step with the sun blazing off their horns, pretty majorettes twirling batons and strutting their long, tanned legs, convertibles decked with flowers and filled with waving celebrities.

The two men stare out the window, their quarrel forgotten. They will undoubtedly return to it, but for the time being they stand together like the best of friends, shoulder to shoulder, watching as the parade goes by—

10

A HORN BLARED, STARTLING Jake out of this story, which was as vivid as a powerful dream. He realized he was still standing in the middle of Lexington, and the light had changed. He looked around wildly, expecting to see the blue Cadillac bearing down on him, but the guy who had tooted his horn was sitting behind the wheel of a yellow Mustang convertible and grinning at him. It was as if everyone in New York had gotten a whiff of happy-gas today.

Jake waved at the guy and sprinted to the other side of the street. The guy in the Mustang twirled a finger around his ear to indicate that Jake was crazy, then waved back and drove on.

For a moment Jake simply stood on the far corner, face turned up to the May sunshine, smiling, digging the day. He supposed prisoners condemned to die in the electric chair must feel this way when they learn they have been granted a temporary reprieve.

The voices were still.

The question was, what was the parade which had temporarily diverted their attention? Was it just the uncommon beauty of this spring morning?

Jake didn't think that was all. He didn't think so because that sensation of *knowing* was creeping over him and through him again, the one which had taken possession of him three weeks ago, as he approached the corner of Fifth and Forty-sixth. But on May 9th, it had been a feeling of impending doom. Today it was a feeling of radiance, a sense of goodness and anticipation. It was as if . . . as if . . .

White. This was the word that came to him, and it clanged in his mind with clear and unquestionable rightness.

"It's the White!" he exclaimed aloud. "The coming of the White!"

He walked on down Fifty-fourth Street, and as he reached the corner of Second and Fifty-fourth, he once more passed under the umbrella of *ka-tet.*

11

HE TURNED RIGHT, THEN stopped, turned, and retraced his steps to the corner. He needed to walk down Second Avenue now, yes, that was unquestionably correct, but this was the wrong side again. When the light changed, he hurried across the street and turned right again. That feeling, that sense of

(Whiteness)

rightness, grew steadily stronger. He felt half-mad with joy and relief. He was going to be okay. This time there was no mistake. He felt sure that he would soon begin to see people he recognized, as he had recognized the fat lady and the pretzel vendor, and they would be doing things he remembered in advance.

Instead, he came to the bookstore.

12

THE MANHATTAN RESTAURANT OF THE MIND, the sign painted in the window read. Jake went to the door. There was a chalkboard hung there; it looked like the kind you saw on the wall in diners and lunchrooms.

TODAY'S SPECIALS

From Florida! Fresh-Broiled John D. MacDonald
   Hardcovers 3 for $2.50
   Paperbacks 9 for $5.00

From Mississippi! Pan-Fried William Faulkner
   Hardcovers Market Price
   Vintage Library Paperbacks 75¢ each

From California! Hard-Boiled Raymond Chandler
   Hardcovers Market Price
   Paperbacks 7 for $5.00

FEED YOUR NEED TO READ

Jake went in, aware that he had, for the first time in three weeks, opened a door without hoping madly to find another world on the other side. A bell jingled overhead. The mild, spicy smell of old books hit him, and the smell was somehow like coming home.

The restaurant motif continued inside. Although the walls were lined with shelves of books, a fountain-style counter bisected the room. On Jake's side of the counter were a number of small tables with wire-backed Malt Shoppe chairs. Each table had been arranged to display the day's specials: Travis McGee novels by John D. Mac-Donald, Philip Marlowe novels by Raymond Chandler, Snopes novels by William Faulkner. A small sign on the Faulkner table said: *Some rare 1st eds available—pls ask.* Another sign, this one on the counter, read simply: BROWSE! A couple of customers were doing just that. They sat at the counter, drinking coffee and reading. Jake thought this was without a doubt the best bookstore he'd ever been in.

The question was, why was he here? Was it luck, or was it part of that soft, insistent feeling that he was following a trail—a kind of force-beam—that had been left for him to find?

He glanced at the display on a small table to his left and knew the answer.

13

IT WAS A DISPLAY of children's books. There wasn't much room on the table, so there were only about a dozen of them—*Alice's Adventures in Wonderland, The Hobbit, Tom Sawyer,* things like that. Jake had been attracted by a story-book obviously meant for very young children. On the bright green cover was an anthropomorphic locomotive puffing its way up a hill. Its cowcatcher (which was bright pink) wore a happy grin and its headlight was a cheerful eye which seemed to invite Jake Chambers to come inside and read all about it. *Charlie the Choo-Choo,* the title proclaimed, Story and Pictures by Beryl Evans. Jake's mind flashed back to his Final Essay, with the picture of the Amtrak train on the title-page and the words *choo-choo* written over and over again inside.

He grabbed the book and clutched it tightly, as if it might fly away if he relaxed his grip. And as he looked down at the cover, Jake found that he did not trust the smile on Charlie the Choo-Choo's face. *You look happy, but I think that's just the mask you wear,* he thought. *I don't think you're happy at all. And I don't think Charlie's your real name, either.*

These were crazy thoughts to be having, undoubtedly crazy, but they did not *feel* crazy. They felt sane. They felt *true.*

Standing next to the place where *Charlie the Choo-Choo* had been was a tattered paperback. The cover was quite badly torn and had been mended with Scotch tape now yellow with age. The picture showed a puzzled-looking boy and girl with a forest of question-marks over their heads. The title of this book was *Riddle-De-Dum! Brain-Twisters and Puzzles for Everyone!* No author was credited.

Jake tucked *Charlie the Choo-Choo* under his arm and picked up the riddle book. He opened it at random and saw this:

When is a door not a door?

"When it's a jar," Jake muttered. He could feel sweat popping out on his forehead . . . his arms . . . all over his body.

"When it's a *jar!*"

"Find something, son?" a mild voice inquired.

Jake turned around and saw a fat guy in an open-throated white shirt standing at the end of the counter. His hands were stuffed in the pockets of his old gabardine slacks. A pair of half-glasses were pushed up on the bright dome of his bald head.

"Yes," Jake said feverishly. "These two. Are they for sale?"

"Everything you see is for sale," the fat guy said. "The building itself would be for sale, if I owned it. Alas, I only lease." He held out his hand for the books and for a moment Jake balked. Then, reluctantly, he handed them over. Part of him expected the fat guy to flee with them, and if he did—if he gave the slightest indication of trying it—Jake meant to tackle him, rip the books out of his hands, and boogie. He *needed* those books.

"Okay, let's see what you got," the fat man said. "By the way, I'm Tower. Calvin Tower." He stuck out his hand.

Jake's eyes widened, and he took an involuntary step backward. *"What?"*

The fat guy looked at him with some interest. "Calvin Tower. Which word is profanity in your language, O Hyperborean Wanderer?"

"Huh?"

"I just mean you look like someone goosed you, kid."

"Oh. Sorry." He clasped Mr. Tower's large, soft hand, hoping the man wouldn't pursue it. The name *had* given him a jump, but he didn't know why. "I'm Jake Chambers."

Calvin Tower shook his hand. "Good handle, pard. Sounds like the footloose hero in a Western novel—the guy who blows into Black Fork, Arizona, cleans up the town, and then travels on. Something by Wayne D. Overholser, maybe. Except you don't look footloose, Jake. You look like you decided the day was a little too nice to spend in school."

"Oh . . . no. We finished up last Friday."

Tower grinned. "Uh-huh. I bet. And you've gotta have these two items, huh? It's sort of funny, what people have to have. Now you—I would have pegged you as a Robert Howard kind of kid from the jump, looking for a good deal on one of those nice old Donald M. Grant editions—the ones with the Roy Krenkel paintings. Dripping swords, mighty thews, and Conan the Barbarian hacking his way through the Stygian hordes."

"That sounds pretty good, actually. These are for . . . uh, for my little brother. It's his birthday next week."

Calvin Tower used his thumb to flip his glasses down onto his nose and had a closer look at Jake. "Really? You look like an only child to me. An only child if I ever saw one, enjoying a day of French leave as Mistress May trembles in her green gown just outside the bosky dell of June."

"Come again?"

"Never mind. Spring always puts me in a William Cowper-ish mood. People are weird but interesting, Tex—am I right?"

"I guess so," Jake said cautiously. He couldn't decide if he liked this odd man or not.

One of the counter-browsers spun on his stool. He was holding a cup of coffee in one hand and a battered paperback copy of *The Plague* in the other. "Quit pulling the kid's chain and sell him the books, Cal," he said. "We've still got time to finish this game of chess before the end of the world, if you hurry up."

"Hurry is antithetical to my nature," Cal said, but he opened *Charlie the Choo-Choo* and peered at the price pencilled on the flyleaf. "A fairly common book, but this copy's in unusually fine condition. Little kids usually rack the hell out of the ones they like. I should get twelve dollars for it—"

"Goddam thief," the man who was reading *The Plague* said, and the other browser laughed. Calvin Tower paid no notice.

"—but I can't bear to dock you that much on a day like this. Seven bucks and it's yours. Plus tax, of course. The riddle book you can have for free. Consider it my gift to a boy wise enough to saddle up and light out for the territories on the last real day of spring."

Jake dug out his wallet and opened it anxiously, afraid he had left the house with only three or four dollars. He was in luck, however. He had a five and three ones. He held the money out to Tower, who folded the bills casually into one pocket and made change out of the other.

"Don't hurry off, Jake. Now that you're here, come on over to the counter and have a cup of coffee. Your eyes will widen with amazement as I cut Aaron Deepneau's spavined old Kiev Defense to ribbons."

"Don't you wish," said the man who was reading *The Plague*—Aaron Deepneau, presumably.

"I'd like to, but I can't. I . . . there's someplace I have to be."

"Okay. As long as it's not back to school."

Jake grinned. "No—not school. That way lies madness."

Tower laughed out loud and flipped his glasses up to the top of his head again. "Not bad! Not bad at all! Maybe the younger generation isn't going to hell after all, Aaron—what do you think?"

"Oh, they're going to hell, all right," Aaron said. "This boy's just an exception to the rule. Maybe."

"Don't mind that cynical old fart," Calvin Tower said. "Motor on, O Hyperborean Wanderer. I wish I were ten or eleven again, with a beautiful day like this ahead of me."

"Thanks for the books," Jake said.

"No problem. That's what we're here for. Come on back sometime."

"I'd like to."

"Well, you know where we are."

Yes, Jake thought. *Now if I only knew where I am.*

14

HE STOPPED JUST OUTSIDE the bookstore and flipped open the riddle book again, this time to page one, where there was a short uncredited introduction.

"Riddles are perhaps the oldest of all the games people still play today," it began. "The gods and goddesses of Greek myth teased each other with riddles, and they were employed as teaching tools in ancient Rome. The Bible contains several good riddles. One of the most famous of these was told by Samson on the day he was married to Delilah:

> 'Out of the eater came forth meat,
> and out of the strong came forth sweetness!'

"He asked this riddle of several young men who attended his wedding, confident that they wouldn't be able to guess the answer. The young men, however, got Delilah aside and she whispered the answer to them. Samson was furious, and had the young men put to death for cheating—in the old days, you see, riddles were taken much more seriously than they are today!

"By the way, the answer to Samson's riddle—and all the other riddles in this book—can be found in the section at the back. We only ask that you give each puzzler a fair chance before you peek!"

Jake turned to the back of the book, somehow knowing what he would find even before he got there. Beyond the page marked ANSWERS there was nothing but a few torn fragments and the back cover. The section had been ripped out.

He stood there for a moment, thinking. Then, on an impulse that didn't really feel like an impulse at all, Jake walked back inside The Manhattan Restaurant of the Mind.

Calvin Tower looked up from the chessboard. "Change your mind about that cup of coffee, O Hyperborean Wanderer?"

"No. I wanted to ask you if you know the answer to a riddle."

"Fire away," Tower invited, and moved a pawn.

"Samson told it. The strong guy in the Bible? It goes like this—"

" 'Out of the eater came forth meat,' " said Aaron Deepneau, swinging around again to look at Jake, " 'and out of the strong came forth sweetness.' That the one?"

"Yeah, it is," Jake said. "How'd you know—"

"Oh, I've been around the block a time or two. Listen to this." He threw his head back and sang in a full, melodious voice:

> " 'Samson and a lion got in attack,
> And Samson climbed up on the lion's back.
> Well, you've read about lion killin men with their paws,
> But Samson put his hands round the lion's jaws!
> He rode that lion 'til the beast fell dead,
> And the bees made honey in the lion's head.' "

Aaron winked and then laughed at Jake's surprised expression. "That answer your question, friend?"

Jake's eyes were wide. "Wow! Good song! Where'd you hear it?"

"Oh, Aaron knows them all," Tower said. "He was hanging around Bleecker Street back before Bob Dylan knew how to blow more than open G on his Hohner. At least, if you believe *him*."

"It's an old spiritual," Aaron said to Jake, and then to Tower: "By the way, you're in check, fatso."

"Not for long," Tower said. He moved his bishop. Aaron promptly bagged it. Tower muttered something under his breath. To Jake it sounded suspiciously like *fuckwad*.

"So the answer is a lion," Jake said.

Aaron shook his head. "Only *half* the answer. Samson's Riddle is a *double*, my friend. The other half of the answer is honey. Get it?"

"Yes, I think so."

"Okay, now try this one." Aaron closed his eyes for a moment and then recited,

> *What can run but never walks,*
> *Has a mouth but never talks,*
> *Has a bed but never sleeps,*
> *Has a head but never weeps?"*

"Smartass," Tower growled at Aaron.

Jake thought it over, then shook his head. He could have worried it longer—he found this business of riddles both fascinating and charming—but he had a strong feeling that he ought to be moving on from here, that he had other business on Second Avenue this morning.

"I give up."

"No, you don't," Aaron said. "That's what you do with *modern* riddles. But a *real* riddle isn't just a joke, kiddo—it's a puzzle. Turn it over in your head. If you still can't get it, make it an excuse to come back another day. If you need another excuse, fatso here *does* make a pretty good cup of joe."

"Okay," Jake said. "Thanks. I will."

But as he left, a certainty stole over him: he would never enter The Manhattan Restaurant of the Mind again.

15

JAKE WALKED SLOWLY DOWN Second Avenue, holding his new purchases in his left hand. At first he tried to think about the riddle—what *did* have a bed but never slept?—but little by little the question was driven from his mind by an increasing sense of anticipation. His senses seemed

more acute than ever before in his life; he saw billions of coruscating sparks in the pavement, smelled a thousand mixed aromas in every breath he took, and seemed to hear other sounds, secret sounds, within each of the sounds he heard. He wondered if this was the way dogs felt before thunderstorms or earthquakes, and felt almost sure that it was. Yet the sensation that the impending event was not bad but good, that it would balance out the terrible thing which had happened to him three weeks ago, continued to grow.

And now, as he drew close to the place where the course would be set, that knowing-in-advance fell upon him once again.

A bum is going to ask me for a handout, and I'll give him the change Mr. Tower gave me. And there's a record store. The door's open to let in the fresh air and I'll hear a Stones song playing when I pass. And I'm going to see my own reflection in a bunch of mirrors.

Traffic on Second Avenue was still light. Taxis honked and wove their way amid the slower-moving cars and trucks. Spring sunshine twinkled off their windshields and bright yellow hides. While he was waiting for a light to change, Jake saw the bum on the far corner of Second and Fifty-second. He was sitting against the brick wall of a small restaurant, and as Jake approached him, he saw that the name of the restaurant was Chew Chew Mama's.

Choo-choo, Jake thought. *And that's the truth.*

"Godda-quarder?" the bum asked tiredly, and Jake dropped his change from the bookstore into the bum's lap without even looking around. Now he could hear the Rolling Stones, right on schedule:

"I see a red door and I want to paint it black,
No colours anymore, I want them to turn black . . ."

As he passed, he saw—also without surprise—that the name of the store was Tower of Power Records.

Towers were selling cheap today, it seemed.

Jake walked on, the street-signs floating past in a kind of dream-daze. Between Forty-ninth and Forty-eighth he passed a store called Reflections of You. He turned his head and caught sight of a dozen Jakes in the mirrors, as he had known he would—a dozen boys who were small for their age, a dozen boys dressed in neat school clothes: blue blazers, white shirts, dark red ties, gray dress pants. Piper School didn't have an official uniform, but this was as close to the unofficial one as you could get.

Piper seemed long ago and far away now.

Suddenly Jake realized where he was going. This knowledge rose in his mind like sweet, refreshing water from an underground spring. *It's a delicatessen*, he thought. *That's what it looks like, anyway. It's really something else—a doorway to another world. The world. His world. The right world.*

He began to run, looking ahead eagerly. The light at Forty-seventh was against him but he ignored it, leaping from the curb and racing nimbly between the broad white lines of the crosswalk with just a perfunctory glance to the left. A plumbing van stopped short with a squeal of tires as Jake flashed in front of it.

"Hey! Whaddaya-whaddaya?" the driver yelled, but Jake ignored him.

Only one more block.

He began to sprint all-out now. His tie fluttered behind his left shoulder; his hair had blown back from his forehead; his school loafers hammered the sidewalk. He ignored the stares—some amused, some merely curious—of the passersby as he had ignored the van driver's outraged shout.

Up here—up here on the corner. Next to the stationery store.

Here came a UPS man in dark brown fatigues, pushing a dolly loaded with packages. Jake hurdled it like a long-jumper, arms up. The tail of his white shirt pulled free of his pants and flapped beneath his blazer like the hem of a slip. He came down and almost collided with a baby-carriage being pushed by a young Puerto Rican woman. Jake hooked around the pram like a halfback who has spotted a hole in the line and is bound for glory. "Where's the fire, handsome?" the young woman asked, but Jake ignored her, too. He dashed past The Paper Patch, with its window-display of pens and notebooks and desk calculators.

The door! he thought ecstatically. *I'm going to see it! And am I going to stop? No, way, José! I'm going to go straight through it, and if it's locked, I'll flatten it right in front of m—*

Then he saw what was at the corner of Second and Forty-sixth and stopped after all—skidded to a halt, in fact, on the heels of his loafers. He stood there in the middle of the sidewalk, hands clenched, his breath rasping harshly in and out of his lungs, his hair falling back onto his forehead in sweaty clumps.

"No," he almost whimpered. *"No!"* But his near-frantic negation did not change what he saw, which was nothing at all. There was nothing to see but a short board fence and a littered, weedy lot beyond it.

The building which had stood there had been demolished.

16

JAKE STOOD OUTSIDE THE fence without moving for almost two minutes, surveying the vacant lot with dull eyes. One corner of his mouth twitched randomly. He could feel his hope, his *absolute certainty*, draining out of him. The feeling which was replacing it was the deepest, bitterest despair he had ever known.

Just another false alarm, he thought when the shock had abated enough so he could think anything at all. *Another false alarm, blind alley, dry well. Now the voices will start up again, and when they do, I think I'm going to start screaming. And that's okay. Because I'm tired of toughing this thing out. I'm tired of going crazy. If this is what going crazy is like, then I just want to hurry up and get there so somebody will take me to the hospital and give me something that'll knock me out. I give up. This is the end of the line—I'm through.*

But the voices did not come back—at least, not yet. And as he began to think about what he was seeing, he realized that the lot wasn't completely empty, after all. Standing in the middle of the trash-littered, weedy waste ground was a sign.

MILLS CONSTRUCTION AND SOMBRA REAL ESTATE
ASSOCIATES
ARE CONTINUING TO REMAKE THE FACE OF
MANHATTAN!
COMING SOON TO THIS LOCATION:
TURTLE BAY LUXURY CONDOMINIUMS!
CALL 555-6712 FOR INFORMATION!
YOU WILL BE SO GLAD YOU DID!

Coming soon? Maybe ... but Jake had his doubts. The letters on the sign were faded and it was sagging a little. At least one graffiti artist, BANGO SKANK by name, had left his mark across the artist's drawing of the Turtle Bay Luxury Condominiums in bright blue spray-paint. Jake wondered if the project had been postponed or if it had maybe just gone belly-up. He remembered hearing his father talking on the telephone to his business advisor not two weeks ago, yelling at the man to stay away from any more condo investments. "I don't *care* how good the tax-picture looks!" he'd nearly screamed (this was, so far as Jake could tell, his father's normal tone of voice when discussing business matters—the coke in the desk drawer might have had something to do with that). "When they're offering a goddamn

TV set just so you'll come down and look at a *blueprint*, something's wrong!"

The board fence surrounding the lot was chin-high to Jake. It had been plastered with handbills—Olivia Newton-John at Radio City, a group called G. Gordon Liddy and the Grots at a club in the East Village, a film called *War of the Zombies* which had come and gone earlier that spring. NO TRESPASSING signs had also been nailed up at intervals along the fence, but most of them had been papered over by ambitious bill-posters. A little way farther along, another graffito had been spray-painted on the fence—this one in what had once undoubtedly been a bright red but which had now faded to the dusky pink of late-summer roses. Jake whispered the words aloud, his eyes wide and fascinated:

"See the TURTLE of enormous girth!
On his shell he holds the earth
If you want to run and play,
Come along the BEAM today."

Jake supposed the source of this strange little poem (if not its meaning) was clear enough. This part of Manhattan's East Side was known, after all, as Turtle Bay. But that didn't explain the gooseflesh which was now running up the center of his back in a rough stripe, or his clear sense that he had found another road-sign along some fabulous hidden highway.

Jake unbuttoned his shirt and stuck his two newly purchased books inside. Then he looked around, saw no one paying attention to him, and grabbed the top of the fence. He boosted himself up, swung a leg over, and dropped down on the other side. His left foot landed on a loose pile of bricks that promptly slid out from under him. His ankle buckled under his weight and bright pain lanced up his leg. He fell with a thud and cried out in mingled hurt and surprise as more bricks dug into his ribcage like thick, rude fists.

He simply lay where he was for a moment, waiting to get his breath back. He didn't think he was badly hurt, but he'd twisted his ankle and it would probably swell. He'd be walking with a limp by the time he got home. He'd just have to grin and bear it, though; he sure didn't have cab-fare.

You don't really plan to go home, do you? They'll eat you alive.

Well, maybe they would and maybe they wouldn't. So far as he could see, he didn't have much choice in the matter. And that was for later. Right now he was going to explore this lot which had drawn him as surely as a magnet draws steel shavings. That feeling of power was still all around him, he realized, and stronger than ever. He didn't think this was just a vacant lot. Something was going on here, something big. He could feel it thrumming in the air, like loose volts escaping from the biggest power-plant in the world.

As he got up, Jake saw that he had actually fallen lucky. Close by was a nasty jumble of broken glass. If he'd fallen into that, he might have cut himself very badly.

That used to be the show window, Jake thought. *When the deli was still here, you could stand on the sidewalk and look in at all the meats and cheeses. They used to hang them on strings.* He didn't know how he knew this, but he did—knew it beyond a shadow of a doubt.

He looked around thoughtfully and then walked a little farther into the lot. Near the middle, lying on the ground and half-buried in a lush growth of spring weeds, was another sign. Jake knelt beside it, pulled it upright, and brushed the dirt away. The letters were faded, but he could still make them out:

TOM AND GERRY'S ARTISTIC DELI
PARTY PLATTERS OUR SPECIALTY!

And below it, spray-painted in that same red-fading-to-pink, was this puzzling sentence: HE HOLDS US ALL WITHIN HIS MIND.

This is the place, Jake thought. *Oh yes.*

He let the sign fall back, stood up, and walked deeper into the lot, moving slowly, looking at everything. As he moved, that sensation of power grew. Everything he saw—the weeds, the broken glass, the clumps of bricks—seemed to stand forth with a kind of exclamatory force. Even the potato chip bags seemed beautiful, and the sun had turned a discarded beer-bottle into a cylinder of brown fire.

Jake was very aware of his own breathing, and of the sunlight falling upon everything like a weight of gold. He suddenly understood that he was standing on the edge of a great mystery, and he felt a shudder—half terror and half wonder—work through him.

It's all here. Everything. Everything is still here.

The weeds brushed at his pants; burdocks stuck to his socks. The breeze blew a Ring-Ding wrapper in front of him; the sun reflected off it and for a moment the wrapper was filled with a beautiful, terrible inner glow.

"Everything is still here," he repeated to himself, unaware that his face was filling with its own inner glow. *"Everything."*

He was hearing a sound—had been hearing it ever since he entered the lot, in fact. It was a wonderful high humming, inexpressibly lonely and inexpressibly lovely. It might have been the sound of a high wind on a deserted plain, except it was *alive*. It was, he thought, the sound of a thousand voices singing some great open chord. He looked down and realized there were *faces* in the tangled weeds and low bushes and heaps of bricks. *Faces*.

"What are you?" Jake whispered. "*Who* are you?" There was no answer, but he seemed to hear, beneath the choir, the sound of hoof-beats on the dusty earth, and gunfire, and angels calling hosannahs from the shadows. The faces in the wreckage seemed to turn as he passed. They seemed to follow his progress, but no evil intent did they bear. He could see Forty-sixth Street, and the edge of the U.N. Building on the other side of First Avenue, but the buildings did not matter—*New York* did not matter. It had become as pale as window-glass.

The humming grew. Now it was not a thousand voices but a million, an open funnel of voices rising from the deepest well of the universe. He caught names in that group voice, but could not have said what they were. One might have been Marten. One might have been Cuthbert. Another might have been Roland—Roland of Gilead.

There were names; there was a babble of conversation that might have been ten thousand entwined stories; but above all was that gorgeous, swelling hum, a vibration that wanted to fill his head with bright white light. It was, Jake realized with a joy so overwhelming that it threatened to burst him to pieces, the voice of *Yes*; the voice of *White*; the voice of *Always*. It was a great chorus of affirmation, and it sang in the empty lot. It sang for him.

Then, lying in a cluster of scrubby burdock plants, Jake saw the key . . . and beyond that, the rose.

17

HIS LEGS BETRAYED HIM and he fell to his knees. He was vaguely aware that he was weeping, even more vaguely aware that he had wet his pants a little. He crawled forward on his knees and reached toward the key lying in the snarl of burdocks. Its simple shape was one he seemed to have seen in his dreams:

He thought: *The little s-shape at the end—that's the secret.*
As he closed his hand around the key, the voices rose in a harmonic

shout of triumph. Jake's own cry was lost in the voice of that choir. He saw the key flash white within his fingers, and felt a tremendous jolt of power run up his arm. It was as if he had grasped a live high-tension wire, but there was no pain.

He opened *Charlie the Choo-Choo* and put the key inside. Then his eyes fixed upon the rose again, and he realized that it was the *real* key—the key to everything. He crawled toward it, his face a flaming corona of light, his eyes blazing wells of blue fire.

The rose was growing from a clump of alien purple grass.

As Jake neared this clump of alien grass, the rose began to open before his eyes. It disclosed a dark scarlet furnace, petal upon secret petal, each burning with its own secret fury. He had never seen anything so intensely and utterly alive in his whole life.

And now, as he stretched one grimy hand out toward this wonder, the voices began to sing his own name . . . and deadly fear began to steal in toward the center of his heart. It was as cold as ice and as heavy as stone.

There was something wrong. He could feel a pulsing discord, like a deep and ugly scratch across some priceless work of art or a deadly fever smouldering beneath the chilly skin of an invalid's brow.

It was something like a worm. An invading worm. And a shape. One which lurks just beyond the next turn of the road.

Then the heart of the rose opened for him, exposing a yellow dazzle of light, and all thought was swept away on a wave of wonder. Jake thought for a moment that what he was seeing was only pollen which had been invested with the supernatural glow which lived at the heart of every object in this deserted clearing—he thought it even though he had never heard of pollen within a rose. He leaned closer and saw that the concentrated circle of blazing yellow was not pollen at all. *It was a sun*: a vast forge burning at the center of this rose growing in the purple grass.

The fear returned, only now it had become outright terror. *It's right*, he thought, *everything here is right, but it could go wrong—has started going wrong already, I think. I'm being allowed to feel as much of that wrongness as I can bear . . . but what is it? And what can I do?*

It was something like a worm.

He could feel it beating like a sick and dirty heart, warring with the serene beauty of the rose, screaming harsh profanities against the choir of voices which had so soothed and lifted him.

He leaned closer to the rose and saw that its core was not just one sun but many . . . perhaps all suns contained within a ferocious yet fragile shell.

But it's wrong. It's all in danger.

Knowing it would almost surely mean his death to touch that glowing microcosm but helpless to stop himself, Jake reached forward. There was no curiosity or terror in this gesture; only a great, inarticulate need to protect the rose.

18

WHEN HE CAME BACK to himself, he was at first only aware that a great deal of time had passed and his head hurt like hell.

What happened? Was I mugged?

He rolled over and sat up. Another blast of pain went through his head. He raised a hand to his left temple, and his fingers came away sticky with blood. He looked down and saw a brick poking out of the weeds. Its rounded corner was too red.

If it had been sharp, I'd probably be dead or in a coma.

He looked at his wrist and was surprised to find he was still wearing his watch. It was a Seiko, not terribly expensive, but in this city you didn't snooze in vacant lots without losing your stuff. Expensive or not, someone would be more than happy to relieve you of it. This time he had been lucky, it seemed.

It was quarter past four in the afternoon. He had been lying here, dead to the world, for at least five hours. His father probably had the cops out looking for him by now, but that didn't seem to matter much. It seemed to Jake that he had walked out of Piper School about a thousand years ago.

Jake walked half the distance to the fence between the vacant lot and the Second Avenue sidewalk, then stopped.

What exactly *had* happened to him?

Little by little, the memories came back. Hopping the fence. Slipping and twisting his ankle. He reached down, touched it, and winced. Yes—that much had happened, all right. Then what?

Something magical.

He groped for that something like an old man groping his way across a shadowy room. Everything had been full of its own light. *Everything*—even the empty wrappers and discarded beer-bottles. There had been voices—they had been singing and telling thousands of overlapping stories.

"And *faces*," he muttered. This memory made him look around apprehensively. He saw no faces. The piles of bricks were just piles of bricks, and the tangles of weeds were just tangles of weeds. There were no faces, but—

—but they were here. It wasn't your imagination.

He believed that. He couldn't capture the essence of the memory, its quality of beauty and transcendence, but it seemed perfectly real. It was just that his memory of those moments before he had passed out seemed like photographs taken on the best day of your life. You can remember what that day was like—sort of, anyway—but the pictures are flat and almost powerless.

Jake looked around the desolate lot, now filling up with the violet shadows of late afternoon, and thought: *I want you back. God, I want you back the way you were.*

Then he saw the rose, growing in its clump of purple grass, very close to the place where he had fallen. His heart leaped into his throat. Jake blundered back toward it, unmindful of the beats of pain each step sent up from his ankle. He dropped to his knees in front of it like a worshipper at an altar. He leaned forward, eyes wide.

It's just a rose. Just a rose after all. And the grass—

The grass wasn't purple after all, he saw. There were *splatters* of purple on the blades, yes, but the color beneath was a perfectly normal green. He looked a little further and saw splashes of blue on another clump of weeds. To his right, a straggling burdock bush bore traces of both red and yellow. And beyond the burdocks was a little pile of discarded paint-cans. Glidden Spread Satin, the labels said.

That's all it was. Just splatters of paint. Only with your head all messed up the way it was, you thought you were seeing—

That was bullshit.

He knew what he had seen then, and what he was seeing now. "Camouflage," he whispered. "It was all right here. *Everything* was. And . . . it still is."

Now that his head was clearing, he could again feel the steady, harmonic power that this place held. The choir was still here, its voice just as musical, although now dim and distant. He looked at a pile of bricks and old broken chunks of plaster and saw a barely discernible face hiding within it. It was the face of a woman with a scar on her forehead.

"Allie?" Jake murmured. "Isn't your name Allie?"

There was no answer. The face was gone. He was only looking at an unlovely pile of bricks and plaster again.

He looked back at the rose. It was, he saw, not the dark red that lives at the heart of a blazing furnace, but a dusty, mottled pink. It was very beautiful, but not perfect. Some of the petals had curled back; the outer edges of these were brown and dead. It wasn't the sort of cultivated flower he had seen in florists' shops; he supposed it was a wild rose.

"You're very beautiful," he said, and once more stretched his hand out to touch it.

Although there was no breeze, the rose nodded toward him. For just a moment the pads of his fingers touched its surface, smooth and velvety and marvellously alive, and all around him the voice of the choir seemed to swell.

"Are you sick, rose?"

There was no answer, of course. When his fingers left the faded pink bowl of the flower, it nodded back to its original position, growing out of the paint-splattered weeds in its quiet, forgotten splendor.

Do roses bloom at this time of year? Jake wondered. *Wild ones? Why would a wild rose grow in a vacant lot, anyway? And if there's one, how come there aren't more?*

He remained on his hands and knees a little longer, then realized he could stay here looking at the rose for the rest of the afternoon (or maybe the rest of his life) and not come any closer to solving its mystery. He had seen it plain for a moment, as he had seen everything else in this forgotten, trash-littered corner of the city; he had seen it with its mask off and its camouflage tossed aside. He wanted to see that again, but wanting would not make it so.

It was time to go home.

He saw the two books he'd bought at The Manhattan Restaurant of the Mind lying nearby. As he picked them up, a bright silver object slipped from the pages of *Charlie the Choo-Choo* and fell into a scruffy patch of weeds. Jake bent, favoring his hurt ankle, and picked it up. As he did so, the choir seemed to sigh and swell, then fell back to its almost inaudible hum.

"So that part was real, too," he murmured. He ran the ball of his thumb over the blunt protruding points of the key and into those primitive V-shaped notches. He sent it skating over the mild *s*-curves at the end of the third notch. Then he tucked it deep into the right front pocket of his pants and began to limp back toward the fence.

He had reached it and was preparing to scramble over the top when a terrible thought suddenly seized his mind.

The rose! What if somebody comes in here and picks it?

A little moan of horror escaped him. He turned back and after a moment his eyes picked it out, although it was deep in the shadow of a neighboring building now—a tiny pink shape in the dimness, vulnerable, beautiful, and alone.

I can't leave it—I have to guard it!

But a voice spoke up in his mind, a voice that was surely that of the man he had met at the way station in that strange other life. *No one will pick it. Nor will any vandal crush it beneath his heel because his dull eyes cannot abide the sight of its beauty. That is not the danger. It can protect itself from such things as those.*

A sense of deep relief swept through Jake.

Can I come here again and look at it? he asked the phantom voice.

When I'm low, or if the voices come back and start their argument again?
Can I come back and look at it and have some peace?

The voice did not answer, and after a few moments of listening, Jake decided it was gone. He tucked *Charlie the Choo-Choo* and *Riddle-De-Dum!* into the waistband of his pants—which, he saw, were streaked with dirt and dotted with clinging burdocks—and then grabbed the board fence. He boosted himself up, swung over the top, and dropped onto the sidewalk of Second Avenue again, being careful to land on his good foot.

Traffic on the Avenue—both pedestrian and vehicular—was much heavier now as people made their way home for the night. A few passersby looked at the dirty boy in the torn blazer and untucked, flapping shirt as he jumped awkwardly down from the fence, but not many. New Yorkers are used to the sight of people doing peculiar things.

He stood there a moment, feeling a sense of loss and realizing something else, as well—the arguing voices were still absent. That, at least, was something.

He glanced at the board fence; and the verse of spray-painted doggerel seemed to leap out at him, perhaps because the paint was the same color as the rose.

"See the TURTLE of enormous girth" Jake muttered. "On his shell he holds the earth." He shivered. "What a day! Boy!"

He turned and began to limp slowly in the direction of home.

19

THE DOORMAN MUST HAVE buzzed up as soon as Jake entered the lobby, because his father was standing outside the elevator when it opened on the fifth floor. Elmer Chambers was wearing faded jeans and cowboy boots that improved his five-ten to a rootin, tootin six feet. His black, crewcut hair bolted up from his head; for as long as Jake could remember, his father had looked like a man who had just suffered some tremendous, galvanizing shock. As soon as Jake stepped out of the elevator, Chambers seized him by the arm.

"Look at you!" His father's eyes flicked up and down, taking in Jake's dirty face and hands, the blood drying on his cheek and temple, the dusty pants, the torn blazer, and the burdock that clung to his tie like some peculiar clip. "Get in here! Where the hell have you been? Your mother's just about off her fucking gourd!"

Without giving Jake a chance to answer, he dragged him through the apartment door. Jake saw Greta Shaw standing in the archway between the dining room and the kitchen. She gave him a look of guarded sympathy, then disappeared before the eyes of "the mister" could chance upon her.

Jake's mother was sitting in her rocker. She got to her feet when she saw Jake, but she did not *leap* to her feet; neither did she pelt across to the foyer so she could cover him with kisses and invective. As she came toward him, Jake assessed her eyes and guessed she'd had at least three Valium since noon. Maybe four. Both of his parents were firm believers in better living through chemistry.

"You're *bleeding*! Where have you been?" She made this inquiry in her cultured Vassar voice, pronouncing *been* so it rhymed with *seen*. She might have been greeting an acquaintance who had been involved in a minor traffic accident.

"Out," he said.

His father gave him a rough shake. Jake wasn't prepared for it. He stumbled and came down on his bad ankle. The pain flared again, and he was suddenly furious. Jake didn't think his father was pissed because he had disappeared from school, leaving only his mad composition behind; his father was pissed because Jake had had the temerity to fuck up his own precious schedule.

To this point in his life, Jake had been aware of only three feelings about his father: puzzlement, fear, and a species of weak, confused love. Now a fourth and fifth surfaced. One was anger; the other was disgust. Mixed in with these unpleasant feelings was that sense of homesickness. It was the largest thing inside him right now, weaving through everything else like smoke. He looked at his father's flushed cheeks and screaming haircut and wished he was back in the vacant lot, looking at the rose and listening to the choir. *This is not my place,* he thought. *Not anymore. I have work to do. If only I knew what it was.*

"Let go of me," he said.

"*What* did you say to me?" His father's blue eyes widened. They were very bloodshot tonight. Jake guessed he had been dipping heavily into his supply of magic powder, and that probably made this a bad time to cross him, but Jake realized he intended to cross him just the same. He would not be shaken like a mouse in the jaws of a sadistic tomcat. Not tonight. Maybe not ever again. He suddenly realized that a large part of his anger stemmed from one simple fact: he could not *talk* to them about what had happened—what was *still* happening. They had closed all the doors.

But I have a key, he thought, and touched its shape through the fabric of his pants. And the rest of that strange verse occurred to him: *If you want to run and play,/Come along the BEAM today.*

"I said let go of me," he repeated. "I've got a sprained ankle and you're hurting it."

"I'll hurt more than your ankle if you don't—"

Sudden strength seemed to flow into Jake. He seized the hand clamped on his arm just below the shoulder and shoved it violently away. His father's mouth dropped open.

"I don't *work* for you," Jake said. "I'm your *son*, remember? If you forgot, check the picture on your desk."

His father's upper lip pulled back from his perfectly capped teeth in a snarl that was two parts surprise and one part fury. "Don't you talk to me like that, mister—where in the hell is your respect?"

"I don't know. Maybe I lost it on the way home."

"You spend the whole goddamn day absent without leave and then you stand there running your fat, disrespectful mouth—"

"Stop it! Stop it, both of you!" Jake's mother cried. She sounded near tears in spite of the tranquilizers perking through her system.

Jake's father reached for Jake's arm again, then changed his mind. The surprising force with which his son had torn his hand away a moment ago might have had something to do with it. Or perhaps it was only the look in Jake's eyes. "I want to know where you've been."

"Out. I told you that. And that's *all* I'm going to tell you."

"Fuck that! Your headmaster called, your French teacher actually *came here*, and they both had *beaucoup* questions for you! So do I, and I want some *answers!*"

"Your clothes are dirty," his mother observed, and then added timidly: "Were you mugged, Johnny? Did you play hookey and get mugged?"

"Of course he wasn't mugged," Elmer Chambers snarled. "Still wearing his watch, isn't he?"

"But there's blood on his head."

"It's okay, Mom. I just bumped it."

"But—"

"I'm going to go to bed. I'm very, very tired. If you want to talk about this in the morning, okay. Maybe we'll all be able to make some sense then. But for now, I don't have a thing to say."

His father took a step after him, reaching out.

"*No, Elmer!*" Jake's mother almost screamed.

Chambers ignored her. He grabbed Jake by the back of the blazer. "Don't you just walk away from me—" he began, and then Jake whirled, tearing the blazer out of his hand. The seam under the right arm, already strained, let go with a rough purring sound.

His father saw those blazing eyes and stepped away. The rage on his face was doused by something that looked like terror. That blaze was not metaphorical; Jake's eyes actually seemed to be on fire. His mother gave voice to a strengthless little scream, clapped one hand to her mouth, took two large, stumbling steps backward, and dropped into her rocking chair with a small thud.

"Leave . . . me . . . alone," Jake said.

"What's *happened* to you?" his father asked, and now his tone was almost plaintive. "What in the *hell's* happened to you? You bug out of school without a word to anyone on the first day of exams, you come back filthy from head to toe . . . and you act as if you've gone crazy."

Well, there it was—*you act as if you've gone crazy.* What he'd been afraid of ever since the voices started three weeks ago. The Dread Accusation. Only now that it was out, Jake found it didn't frighten him much at all, perhaps because he had finally put the issue to rest in his own mind. Yes, something had happened to him. Was still happening. But no—he had *not* gone crazy. At least, not yet.

"We'll talk about it in the morning," he repeated. He walked across the dining room, and this time his father didn't try to stop him. He had almost reached the hall when his mother's voice, worried, stopped him: "Johnny . . . *are* you all right?"

And what should he answer? Yes? No? Both of the above? Neither of the above? But the voices had stopped, and that was something. That was, in fact, quite a lot.

"Better," he said at last. He went down to his room and closed the door firmly behind him. The sound of the door snicking firmly shut between him and all the rest of the round world filled him with tremendous relief.

20

HE STOOD BY THE door for a little while, listening. His mother's voice was only a murmur, his father's voice a little louder.

His mother said something about blood, and a doctor.

His father said the kid was fine; the only thing wrong with the kid was the junk coming out of his mouth, and he would fix that.

His mother said something about calming down.

His father said he *was* calm.

His mother said—

He said, she said, blah, blah, blah. Jake still loved them—he was pretty sure he did, anyway—but other stuff had happened now, and these things had made it necessary that still other things must occur.

Why? Because something was wrong with the rose. And maybe because he wanted to run and play . . . and see *his* eyes again, as blue as the sky above the way station had been.

Jake walked slowly over to his desk, removing his blazer as he went. It was pretty wasted—one sleeve torn almost completely off, the lining hanging like a limp sail. He slung it over the back of his chair, then sat down and put the books on his desk. He had been sleeping very badly over the last week and a half, but he thought tonight he would sleep well. He couldn't remember ever being so tired. When he woke up in the morning, perhaps he would know what to do.

There was a light knock at the door, and Jake turned warily in that direction.

"It's Mrs. Shaw, John. May I come in for a minute?"

He smiled. Mrs. Shaw—of course it was. His parents had drafted her as an intermediary. Or perhaps translator might be a better word.

You go see him, his mother would have said. *He'll tell you what's wrong with him. I'm his mother and this man with the bloodshot eyes and the runny nose is his father and you're only the housekeeper, but he'll tell you what he wouldn't tell us. Because you see more of him than either of us, and maybe you speak his language.*

She'll have a tray, Jake thought, and when he opened the door he was smiling.

Mrs. Shaw did indeed have a tray. There were two sandwiches on it, a wedge of apple pie, and a glass of chocolate milk. She was looking at Jake with mild anxiety, as if she thought he might lunge forward and try to bite her. Jake looked over her shoulder, but there was no sign of his parents. He imagined them sitting in the living room, listening anxiously.

"I thought you might like something to eat," Mrs. Shaw said.

"Yes, thanks." In fact, he was ravenously hungry; he hadn't eaten since breakfast. He stood aside and Mrs. Shaw came in (giving him another apprehensive look as she passed) and put the tray on the desk.

"Oh, look at this," she said, picking up *Charlie the Choo-Choo*. "I had this one when I was a little girl. Did you buy this today, Johnny?"

"Yes. Did my parents ask you to find out what I'd been up to?"

She nodded. No acting, no put-on. It was just a chore, like taking out the trash. *You can tell me if you want to*, her face said, *or you can keep still. I like you, Johnny, but it's really nothing to me, one way or the other. I just work here, and it's already an hour past my regular quitting time.*

He was not offended by what her face had to say; on the contrary, he was further calmed by it. Mrs. Shaw was another acquaintance who was not quite a friend . . . but he thought she might be a little closer to a friend than any of the kids at school were, and much closer than either his mother or father. Mrs. Shaw was honest, at least. She didn't dance. It all went on the bill at the end of the month, and she *always* cut the crusts off the sandwiches.

Jake picked up a sandwich and took a large bite. Bologna and cheese, his favorite. That was another thing in Mrs. Shaw's favor—she knew all his favorites. His mother was still under the impression that he liked corn on the cob and hated brussels sprouts.

"Please tell them I'm fine," he said, "and tell my father I'm sorry that I was rude to him."

He wasn't, but all his father really wanted was that apology. Once Mrs. Shaw conveyed it to him, he would relax and begin to tell himself the old lie—he had done his fatherly duty and all was well, all was well, and all manner of things were well.

"I've been studying very hard for my exams," he said, chewing as he talked, "and it all came down on me this morning, I guess. I sort of froze. It seemed like I had to get out or I'd suffocate." He touched the dried crust of blood on his forehead. "As for this, please tell my mother it's really nothing. I didn't get mugged or anything; it was just a stupid accident. There was a UPS guy pushing a hand-truck, and I walked right into it. The cut's no big deal. I'm not having double vision or anything, and even the headache's gone now."

She nodded. "I can see how it must have been—a high-powered school like that and all. You just got a little spooked. No shame in that, Johnny. But you really *haven't* seemed like yourself this last couple of weeks."

"I think I'll be okay now. I might have to re-do my Final Essay in English, but—"

"Oh!" Mrs. Shaw said. A startled looked crossed her face. She put *Charlie the Choo-Choo* back down on Jake's desk. "I almost forgot! Your French teacher left something for you. I'll just get it."

She left the room. Jake hoped he hadn't worried Mr. Bissette, who was a pretty good guy, but he supposed he must have, since Bissette had actually made a personal appearance. Jake had an idea that personal appearances were pretty rare for Piper School teachers. He wondered what Mr. Bissette had left. His best guess was an invitation to talk with Mr. Hotchkiss, the school shrink. That would have scared him this morning, but not tonight.

Tonight only the rose seemed to matter.

He tore into his second sandwich. Mrs. Shaw had left the door open, and he could hear her talking with his parents. They both sounded a little more cooled out now. Jake drank his milk, then grabbed the plate with the apple pie on it. A few moments later Mrs. Shaw came back. She was carrying a very familiar blue folder.

Jake found that not all of his dread had left him after all. They would all know by now, of course, students and faculty alike, and it was too late to do anything about it, but that didn't mean he liked all of them knowing he had flipped his lid. That they were talking about him.

A small envelope had been paper-clipped to the front of the folder.

Jake pulled it free and looked up at Mrs. Shaw as he opened it. "How are my folks doing now?" he asked.

She allowed herself a brief smile. "Your father wanted me to ask why you didn't just tell him you had Exam Fever. He said he had it himself once or twice when he was a boy."

Jake was struck by this; his father had never been the sort of man to indulge in reminiscences which began, *You know, when I was a kid* . . . Jake tried to imagine his father as a boy with a bad case of Exam Fever and found he couldn't quite do it—the best he could manage was the unpleasant image of a pugnacious dwarf in a Piper sweatshirt, a dwarf in custom-tooled cowboy boots, a dwarf with short black hair bolting up from his forehead.

The note was from Mr. Bissette.

Dear John,
  Bonnie Avery told me that you left early. She's very concerned about you, and so am I, although we have both seen this sort of thing before, especially during Exam Week. Please come and see me first thing tomorrow, okay? Any problems you have can be worked out. If you're feeling pressured by exams—and I want to repeat that it happens all the time—a postponement can be arranged. Our first concern is your welfare. Call me this evening, if you like; you can reach me at 555-7661. I'll be up until midnight.
  Remember that we all like you very much, and are on your side.

                                                        À votre santé

                                    Len Bissette

Jake felt like crying. The concern was stated, and that was wonderful, but there were other things, unstated things, in the note that were even more wonderful—warmth, caring, and an effort (however misconceived) to understand and console.

Mr. Bissette had drawn a small arrow at the bottom of the note. Jake turned it over and read this:

By the way, Bonnie asked me to send this along—congratulations!!
Congratulations? What in the hell did that mean?

He flipped open the folder. A sheet of paper had been clipped to the first page of his Final Essay. It was headed FROM THE DESK OF BONITA AVERY, and Jake read the spiky, fountain-penned lines with growing amazement.

John,

Leonard will undoubtedly voice the concern we all feel—he is awfully good at that—so let me confine myself to your Final Essay, which I read and graded during my free period. It is stunningly original, and superior to any student work I have read in the last few years. Your use of incremental repetition (". . . and that is the truth") is inspired, but of course incremental repetition is really just a trick. The real worth of the composition is in its symbolic quality, first stated by the images of the train and the door on the title page and carried through splendidly within. This reaches its logical conclusion with the picture of the "black tower," which I take as your statement that conventional ambitions are not only false but dangerous.

I do not pretend to understand all the symbolism (e.g., "Lady of Shadows," "gunslinger") but it seems clear that you yourself are "The Prisoner" (of school, society, etc.) and that the educational system is "The Speaking Demon." Is it possible that both "Roland" and "the gunslinger" are the same authority figure—your father, perhaps? I became so intrigued by this possibility that I looked up his name in your records. I note it is Elmer, but I further note that his middle initial is R.

I find this extremely provocative. Or is this name a double symbol, drawn both from your father and from Robert Browning's poem "Childe Roland to the Dark Tower Came"? This is not a question I would ask most students, but of course I know how omnivorously you read!

At any rate, I am extremely impressed. Younger students are often attracted to so-called "stream-of-consciousness" writing, but are rarely able to control it. You have done an outstanding job of merging s-of-c with symbolic language.

Bravo!

Drop by as soon as you're "back at it"—I want to discuss possible publication of this piece in the first issue of next year's student literary magazine.

B. Avery

P.S. If you left school today because you had sudden doubts about my ability to understand a Final Essay of such unexpected richness, I hope I have assuaged them.

Jake pulled the sheet off the clip, revealing the title page of his stunningly original and richly symbolic Final Essay. Written and circled there in the red ink of Ms. Avery's marking pen was the notation A+. Below this she had written *EXCELLENT JOB!!!*

Jake began to laugh.

The whole day—the long, scary, confusing, exhilarating, terrifying, mysterious day—was condensed in great, roaring sobs of laughter. He slumped in his chair, head thrown back, hands clutching his belly, tears streaming down his face. He laughed himself hoarse. He would almost stop and then some line from Ms. Avery's well-meaning critique would catch his eye and he would be off to the races again. He didn't see his father come to the door, look in at him with puzzled, wary eyes, and then leave again, shaking his head.

At last he *did* become aware that Mrs. Shaw was still sitting on his bed, looking at him with an expression of friendly detachment tinctured with faint curiosity. He tried to speak, but the laughter pealed out again before he could.

I gotta stop, he thought. *I gotta stop or it's gonna kill me. I'll have a stroke or a heart attack, or something.*

Then he thought, *I wonder what she made of "choo-choo, choo-choo?,"* and he began to laugh wildly again.

At last the spasms began to taper off to giggles. He wiped his arm across his streaming eyes and said, "I'm sorry, Mrs. Shaw—it's just that . . . well . . . I got an A-plus on my Final Essay. It was all very . . . very rich . . . and very sym . . . sym . . ."

But he couldn't finish. He doubled up with laughter again, holding his throbbing belly.

Mrs. Shaw got up, smiling. "That's very nice, John. I'm happy it's all turned out so well, and I'm sure your folks will be, too. I'm awfully late—I think I'll ask the doorman to call me a cab. Goodnight, and sleep well."

"Goodnight, Mrs. Shaw," Jake said, controlling himself with an effort. "And thanks."

As soon as she was gone, he began to laugh again.

21

DURING THE NEXT HALF hour he had separate visits from both parents. They had indeed calmed down, and the A+ grade on Jake's Final Essay seemed to calm them further. Jake received them with his French text open on the desk before him, but he hadn't really looked at it, nor did he have any intention of looking at it. He was only waiting for them to be gone so he could study the two books he had bought earlier that day. He had an idea that the *real* Final Exams were still waiting just over the horizon, and he wanted desperately to pass.

His father poked his head into Jake's room around quarter of ten, about twenty minutes after Jake's mother had concluded her own short, vague visit. Elmer Chambers was holding a cigarette in one hand and a glass of Scotch in the other. He seemed not only calmer but almost zonked. Jake wondered briefly and indifferently if he had been hitting his mother's Valium supply.

"Are you okay, kid?"

"Yes." He was once again the small, neat boy who was always completely in control of himself. The eyes he turned to his father were not blazing but opaque.

"I wanted to say I'm sorry about before." His father was not a man who made many apologies, and he did it badly. Jake found himself feeling a little sorry for him.

"It's all right."

"Hard day," his father said. He gestured with the empty glass. "Why don't we just forget it happened?" He spoke as if this great and logical idea had just come to him.

"I already have."

"Good." His father sounded relieved. "Time for you to get some sleep, isn't it? You'll have some explaining to do and some tests to take tomorrow."

"I guess so," Jake said. "Is Mom okay?"

"Fine. Fine. I'm going in the study. Got a lot of paperwork tonight."

"Dad?"

His father looked back at him warily.

"What's your middle name?"

Something in his father's face told Jake that he had looked at the Final Essay grade but hadn't bothered to read either the paper itself or Ms. Avery's critique.

"I don't have one," he said. "Just an initial, like Harry S Truman. Except mine's an R. What brought that on?"

"Just curious," Jake said.

He managed to hold onto his composure until his father was gone . . . but as soon as the door was closed, he ran to his bed and stuffed his face into his pillow to muffle another bout of wild laughter.

22

WHEN HE WAS SURE he was over the current fit (although an occasional snicker still rumbled up his throat like an aftershock) and his father would be safely locked away in his study with his cigarettes, his Scotch, his papers, and his little bottle of white powder, Jake went back to his desk, turned on the study lamp, and opened *Charlie the Choo-Choo*. He glanced briefly at the copyright page and saw it had originally been published in 1942; his copy was from the fourth printing. He looked at the back, but there was no information at all about Beryl Evans, the book's author.

Jake turned back to the beginning, looked at the picture of a grinning, blonde-haired man sitting in the cab of a steam locomotive, considered the proud grin on the man's face, and then began to read.

Bob Brooks was an engineer for the Mid-World Railway Company, on the St. Louis to Topeka run. Engineer Bob was the best trainman The Mid-World Railway Company ever had, and Charlie was the best train!

Charlie was a 402 Big Boy Steam Locomotive, and Engineer Bob was the only man who had ever been allowed to sit in his peak-seat and pull the whistle. Everyone knew the WHOOO-OOOO of Charlie's whistle, and whenever they heard it echoing across the flat Kansas countryside, they said, "There goes Charlie and Engineer Bob, the fastest team between St. Louis and Topeka!"

Boys and girls ran into their yards to watch Charlie and Engineer Bob go by. Engineer Bob would smile and wave. The children would smile and wave back.

Engineer Bob had a special secret. He was the only one who knew. Charlie the Choo-Choo was really, really alive. One day while they were making the run between Topeka and St. Louis, Engineer Bob heard singing, very soft and low.

"Who is in the cab with me?" Engineer Bob said sternly.

"You need to see a shrink, Engineer Bob," Jake murmured, and turned the page. Here was a picture of Bob bending over to look beneath Charlie the Choo-Choo's automatic firebox. Jake wondered who was driving the train and watching out for cows (not to mention boys and girls) on the tracks while Bob was checking for stowaways, and guessed that Beryl Evans hadn't known a lot about trains.

"Don't worry," said a small, gruff voice. "It is only I."

"Who's I?" Engineer Bob asked. He spoke in his biggest, sternest voice, because he still thought someone was playing a joke on him.

"Charlie," said the small, gruff voice.

"Hardy har-har!" said Engineer Bob. "Trains can't

talk! I may not know much, but I know that! If you're Charlie, I suppose you can blow your own whistle!"

"Of course," said the small, gruff voice, and just then the whistle made its big noise, rolling out across the Missouri plains: WHOOO-OOOO!

"Goodness!" said Engineer Bob. "It really *is* you!"

"I told you," said Charlie the Choo-Choo.

"How come I never knew you were alive before?" asked Engineer Bob. "Why didn't you ever talk to me before?"

Then Charlie sang this song to Engineer Bob in his small, gruff voice.

Don't ask me silly questions,
I won't play silly games.
I'm just a simple choo-choo train
And I'll always be the same.

I only want to race along
Beneath the bright blue sky,
And be a happy choo-choo train
Until the day I die.

"Will you talk to me some more when we're making our run?" asked Engineer Bob. "I'd like that."

"I would, too," said Charlie. "I love you, Engineer Bob."

"I love you too, Charlie," said Engineer Bob, and then he blew the whistle himself, just to show how happy he was.

WHOOO-OOO! It was the biggest and best Charlie had *ever* whistled, and everyone who heard it came out to see.

The picture which illustrated this last was similar to the one on the cover of the book. In the previous pictures (they were rough drawings which reminded Jake of the pictures in his favorite kindergarten book, *Mike Mulligan and His Steam Shovel*), the locomotive had been just a locomotive—cheery, undoubtedly interesting to the '40s-era boys who had been this book's intended audience, but still only a piece of machinery. In this picture, however, it had clearly human features, and this gave Jake a deep chill despite Charlie's smile and the rather heavy-handed cuteness of the story.

He didn't trust that smile.

He turned to his Final Essay and scanned down the lines. *I'm pretty sure Blaine is dangerous,* he read, *and that is the truth.*

He closed the folder, tapped his fingers on it thoughtfully for a few moments, then returned to *Charlie the Choo-Choo*.

Engineer Bob and Charlie spent many happy days together and talked of many things. Engineer Bob lived alone, and Charlie was the first real friend he'd had since his wife died, long ago, in New York.

Then one day, when Charlie and Engineer Bob returned to the roundhouse in St. Louis, they found a new diesel locomotive in Charlie's berth. And what a diesel locomotive it was! 5,000 horsepower! Stainless steel couplers! Traction motors from the Utica Engine Works in Utica, New York! And sitting on top, behind the generator, were three bright yellow radiator cooling fans.

"What is this?" Engineer Bob asked in a worried voice, but Charlie only sang his song in his smallest, gruffest voice:

Don't ask me silly questions,
I won't play silly games.
I'm just a simple choo-choo train
And I'll always be the same.

I only want to race along
Beneath the bright blue sky,
And be a happy choo-choo train
Until the day I die.

Mr. Briggs, the Roundhouse Manager, came over.

"That is a beautiful diesel locomotive," said Engineer Bob, "but you will have to move it out of Charlie's berth, Mr. Briggs. Charlie needs a lube job this very afternoon."

"Charlie won't be needing any more lube jobs, Engineer Bob," said Mr. Briggs sadly. "This is his replacement—a brand-new Burlington Zephyr diesel loco. Once, Charlie was the best locomotive in the world, but now he is old and his boiler leaks. I am afraid the time has come for Charlie to retire."

"Nonsense!" Engineer Bob was mad! "Charlie is still full of zip and zowie! I will telegraph the head office of The Mid-World Railway Company! I will telegraph the President, Mr. Raymond Martin, myself! I know him, because he once gave me a Good Service Award, and afterwards Charlie and I took his little daughter for a ride. I let her pull the lanyard, and Charlie whistled his loudest for her!"

"I am sorry, Bob," said Mr. Briggs, "but it was Mr. Martin himself who ordered the new diesel loco."

It was true. And so Charlie the Choo-Choo was shunted off to a siding in the furthest corner of Mid-World's St. Louis yard to rust in the weeds. Now the HONNNK! HONNNK! of the Burlington Zephyr was heard on the St. Louis to Topeka run, and Charlie's blew no more. A family of mice nested in the seat where Engineer Bob once sat so proudly, watching the countryside speed past; a family of swallows nested in his smoke-stack. Charlie was lonely and very sad. He missed the steel tracks and bright blue skies and wide open spaces. Sometimes, late at night, he thought of these things and cried dark, oily tears. This rusted his fine Stratham head-light, but he didn't care, because now the Stratham head-light was old, and it was always dark.

Mr. Martin, the President of The Mid-World Railway Company, wrote and offered to put Engineer Bob in the peak-seat of the new Burlington Zephyr. "It is a fine loco, Engineer Bob," said Mr. Martin, "chock-full of zip and zowie, and you should be the one to pilot it! Of all the Engineers who work for Mid-World, you are the best. And my daughter Susannah has never forgotten that you let her pull old Charlie's whistle."

But Engineer Bob said that if he couldn't pilot Char-lie, his days as a trainman were done. "I wouldn't under-stand such a fine new diesel loco," said Engineer Bob, "and it wouldn't understand me."

He was given a job cleaning the engines in the St. Louis yards, and Engineer Bob became Wiper Bob. Some-times the other engineers who drove the fine new diesels would laugh at him. "Look at that old fool!" they said. "He cannot understand that the world has moved on!"

Sometimes, late at night, Engineer Bob would go to the far side of the rail yard, where Charlie the Choo-Choo stood on the rusty rails of the lonely siding which had become his home. Weeds had twined in his wheels; his headlight was rusty and dark. Engineer Bob always talked to Charlie, but Charlie replied less and less. Many nights he would not talk at all.

One night, a terrible idea came into Engineer Bob's head. "Charlie, are you dying?" he asked, and in his smallest, gruffest voice, Charlie replied:

Don't ask me silly questions,
I won't play silly games,
I'm just a simple choo-choo train
And I'll always be the same.

Now that I can't race along
Beneath the bright blue sky
I guess that I'll just sit right here
Until I finally die.

Jake looked at the picture accompanying this not-exactly-unexpected turn of events for a long time. Rough drawing it might be, but it was still definitely a three-handkerchief job. Charlie looked old, beaten, and forgotten. Engineer Bob looked like he had lost his last friend . . . which, according to the story, he had. Jake could imagine children all over America blatting their heads off at this point, and it occurred to him that there were a *lot* of stories for kids with stuff like this in them, stuff that threw acid all over your emotions. Hansel and Gretel being turned out into the forest, Bambi's mother getting scragged by a hunter, the death of Old Yeller. It was easy to hurt little kids, easy to make them cry, and this seemed to bring out a strangely sadistic streak in many story-tellers . . . including, it seemed, Beryl Evans.

But, Jake found, *he* was not saddened by Charlie's relegation to the weedy wastelands at the outer edge of the Mid-World trainyards in St. Louis. Quite the opposite. *Good,* he thought. *That's the place for him. That's the place, because he's dangerous. Let him rot there, and don't trust that tear in his eye—they say crocodiles cry, too.*

He read the rest rapidly. It had a happy ending, of course, although it was undoubtedly that moment of despair on the edge of the trainyards which children remembered long after the happy ending had slipped their minds.

Mr. Martin, the President of The Mid-World Railway Company, came to St. Louis to check on the operation. His plan was to ride the Burlington Zephyr to Topeka, where his daughter was giving her first piano recital, that very afternoon. Only the Zephyr wouldn't start. There was water in the diesel fuel, it seemed.

(*Were you the one who watered the diesel, Engineer Bob?* Jake wondered. *I bet it was, you sly dog, you!*)

All the other trains were out on their runs! What to do?

Someone tugged Mr. Martin's arm. It was Wiper Bob, only he no longer looked like an engine-wiper. He had taken off his oil-stained dungarees and put on a clean pair of overalls. On his head was his old pillowtick engineer's cap.

"Charlie's is right over there, on that siding," he said. "Charlie will make the run to Topeka, Mr. Martin. Charlie will get you there in time for your daughter's piano recital."

"That old steamer?" scoffed Mr. Briggs. "Charlie would still be fifty miles out of Topeka at sundown!"

"Charlie can do it," Engineer Bob insisted. "Without a train to pull, I know he can! I have been cleaning his engine and his boiler in my spare time, you see."

"We'll give it a try," said Mr. Martin. "I would be sorry to miss Susannah's first recital!"

Charlie was all ready to go; Engineer Bob had filled his tender with fresh coal, and the firebox was so hot its sides were red. He helped Mr. Martin up into the cab and backed Charlie off the rusty, forgotten siding and onto the main track for the first time in years. Then, as he engaged Forward First, he pulled on the lanyard and Charlie gave his old brave cry: *WHOOO-OOOOO!*

All over St. Louis the children heard that cry, and ran out into their yards to watch the rusty old steam loco pass. "Look!" they cried. "It's Charlie! Charlie the Choo-Choo is back! Hurrah!" They all waved, and as Charlie steamed out of town, gathering speed, he blew his own whistle, just as he had in the old days: *WHOOOO-OOOOOOO!*

Clickety-clack went Charlie's wheels!

Chuffa-chuffa went the smoke from Charlie's stack!

Brump-brump went the conveyor as it fed coal into the firebox!

Talk about zip! Talk about zowie! Golly gee, gosh, and wowie! Charlie had never gone so fast before! The countryside went whizzing by in a blur! They passed the cars on Route 41 as if they were standing still!

"Hoptedoodle!" cried Mr. Martin, waving his hat in the air. "This is some locomotive, Bob! I don't know why we ever retired it! How do you keep the coal-conveyor loaded at this speed?"

Engineer Bob only smiled, because he knew Charlie was *feeding himself*. And, beneath the *clickety-clack* and the *chuffa-chuffa* and the *brump-brump*, he could hear Charlie singing his old song in his low, gruff voice:

> *Don't ask me silly questions,*
> *I won't play silly games,*
> *I'm just a simple choo-choo train*
> *And I'll always be the same.*
>
> *I only want to race along*
> *Beneath the bright blue sky,*
> *And be a happy choo-choo train*
> *Until the day I die.*

Charlie got Mr. Martin to his daughter's piano recital on time (of course), and Susannah was just tickled pink to see her old friend Charlie again (of course), and they all went back to St. Louis together with Susannah yanking hell out of the train-whistle the whole way. Mr. Martin got Charlie and Engineer Bob a gig pulling kids around the brand-new Mid-World Amusement Park and Fun Fair in California, and

> you will find them there to this day, pulling laughing children hither and thither in that world of lights and music and good, wholesome fun. Engineer Bob's hair is white, and Charlie doesn't talk as much as he once did, but both of them still have plenty of zip and zowie, and every now and then the children hear Charlie singing his old song in his soft, gruff voice.

THE END

"Don't ask me silly questions, I won't play silly games," Jake muttered, looking at the final picture. It showed Charlie the Choo-Choo pulling two bunting-decked passenger cars filled with happy children from the roller coaster to the Ferris wheel. Engineer Bob sat in the cab, pulling the whistle-cord and looking as happy as a pig in shit. Jake supposed Engineer Bob's smile was supposed to convey supreme happiness, but to him it looked like the grin of a lunatic. Charlie and Engineer Bob *both* looked like lunatics ... and the more Jake looked at the kids, the more he thought that their expressions looked like grimaces of terror. *Let us off this train*, those faces seemed to say. *Please, just let us off this train alive.*

And be a happy choo-choo train until the day I die.

Jake closed the book and looked at it thoughtfully. Then he opened it again and began to leaf through the pages, circling certain words and phrases that seemed to call out to him.

The Mid-World Railway Company ... Engineer Bob ... a small, gruff voice ... WHOO-OOOO ... the first real friend he'd had since his wife died, long ago, in New York ... Mr. Martin ... the world has moved on ... Susannah ...

He put his pen down. *Why* did these words and phrases call to him? The one about New York seemed obvious enough, but what about the others? For that matter, why this *book*? That he had been meant to buy it was beyond question. If he hadn't had the money in his pocket, he felt sure he would have simply grabbed it and bolted from the store. But *why*? He felt like a compass needle. The needle knows nothing about magnetic north; it only knows it must point in a certain direction, like it or not.

The only thing Jake knew for sure was that he was very, very tired, and if he didn't crawl into bed soon, he was going to fall asleep at his desk. He took off his shirt, then gazed down at the front of *Charlie the Choo-Choo* again.

That smile. He just didn't trust that smile.

Not a bit.

23

SLEEP DIDN'T COME AS soon as Jake had hoped. The voices began to argue again about whether he was alive or dead, and they kept him awake. At last he sat up in bed with his eyes closed and his fisted hands planted against his temples.

Quit! he screamed at them. *Just quit! You were gone all day, be gone again!*

I would if he'd just admit I'm dead, one of the voices said sulkily.

I would if he'd just take a for God's sake look around and admit I'm clearly alive, the other snapped back.

He was going to scream right out loud. There was no way to hold it back; he could feel it coming up his throat like vomit. He opened his eyes, saw his pants lying over the seat of his desk chair, and an idea occurred to him. He got out of bed, went to the chair, and felt in the right front pocket of the pants.

The silver key was still there, and the moment his fingers closed around it, the voices ceased.

Tell him, he thought, with no idea who the thought was for. *Tell him to grab the key. The key makes the voices go.*

He went back to bed and was asleep with the key clasped loosely in his hand three minutes after his head hit the pillow.

III ▪ DOOR AND DEMON

· III ·

DOOR AND DEMON

1

EDDIE WAS ALMOST ASLEEP when a voice spoke clearly in his ear: *Tell him to grab the key. The key makes the voices go.*

He sat bolt upright, looking around wildly. Susannah was sound asleep beside him; that voice had not been hers.

Nor anyone else's, it seemed. They had been moving through the woods and along the path of the Beam for eight days now, and this evening they had camped in the deep cleft of a pocket valley. Close by on the left, a large stream roared brashly past, headed in the same direction as they were: southeast. To the right, firs rose up a steep slope of land. There were no intruders here; only Susannah asleep and Roland awake. He sat huddled beneath his blanket at the edge of the stream's cut, staring out into the darkness.

Tell him to grab the key. The key makes the voices go.

Eddie hesitated for only a moment. Roland's sanity was in the balance now, the balance was tipping the wrong way, and the worst part of it was this: no one knew it better than the man himself. At this point, Eddie was prepared to clutch at any straw.

He had been using a folded square of deerskin as a pillow. He reached beneath it and removed a bundle wrapped in a piece of hide. He walked over to Roland, and was disturbed to see that the gunslinger did not notice him until he was less than four steps from his unprotected back. There had been a time—and it was not so long ago—when Roland would have known Eddie was awake even before Eddie sat up. He would have heard the change in his breathing.

He was more alert than this back on the beach, when he was half-dead from the lobster-thing's bite, Eddie thought grimly.

Roland at last turned his head and glanced at him. His eyes were bright with pain and weariness, but Eddie recognized these things as no more than a surface glitter. Beneath it, he sensed a growing confusion that would almost surely become madness if it continued to develop unchecked. Pity tugged at Eddie's heart.

"Can't sleep?" Roland asked. His voice was slow, almost drugged.

"I almost was, and then I woke up," Eddie said. "Listen—"

"I think I'm getting ready to die." Roland looked at Eddie. The bright shine left his eyes, and now looking into them was like staring into a pair of deep, dark wells that seemed to have no bottom. Eddie shuddered, more because of that empty stare than because of what Roland had said. "And do you know what I hope lies in the clearing where the path ends, Eddie?"

"Roland—"

"Silence," Roland said. He exhaled a dusty sigh. "Just silence. That will be enough. An end to . . . this."

He planted his fists against his temples, and Eddie thought: *I've seen someone else do that, and not long ago. But who? Where?*

It was ridiculous of course; he had seen no one but Roland and Susannah for almost two months now. But it *felt* true, all the same.

"Roland, I've been making something," Eddie said.

Roland nodded. A ghost of a smile touched his lips. "I know. What is it? Are you finally ready to tell?"

"I think it might be part of this *ka-tet* thing."

The vacant look left Roland's eyes. He gazed at Eddie thoughtfully but said nothing.

"Look." Eddie began to unfold the piece of hide.

That won't do any good! Henry's voice suddenly brayed. It was so loud that Eddie actually flinched a little. *It's just a stupid piece of wood-carving! He'll take one look and laugh at it! He'll laugh at you!* "Oh, lookit this!" *he'll say.* "Did the sissy carve something?"

"Shut up," Eddie muttered.

The gunslinger raised his eyebrows.

"Not you."

"...And be a happy
choo-choo train
Until the day I die."

Roland nodded, unsurprised. "Your brother comes to you often, doesn't he, Eddie?"

For a moment Eddie only stared at him, his carving still hidden in the hide square. Then he smiled. It was not a very pleasant smile. "Not as often as he used to, Roland. Thank Christ for small favors."

"Yes," Roland said. "Too many voices weigh heavy on a man's heart . . . What is it, Eddie? Show me, please."

Eddie held up the chunk of ash. The key, almost complete, emerged from it like the head of a woman from the prow of a sailing ship . . . or the hilt of a sword from a chunk of stone. Eddie didn't know how close he had come to duplicating the key-shape he had seen in the fire (and never would, he supposed, unless he found the right lock in which to try it), but he thought it was close. Of one thing he was quite sure: it was the best carving he had ever done. By far.

"By the gods, Eddie, it's beautiful!" Roland said. The apathy was gone from his voice; he spoke in a tone of surprised reverence Eddie had never heard before. "Is it done? It's not, is it?"

"No—not quite." He ran his thumb into the third notch, and then over the s-shape at the end of the last notch. "There's a little more to do on this notch, and the curve at the end isn't right yet. I don't know how I know that, but I do."

"This is your secret." It wasn't a question.

"Yes. Now if only I knew what it meant."

Roland looked around. Eddie followed his gaze and saw Susannah. He found some relief in the fact that Roland had heard her first.

"What you boys doin up so late? Chewin the fat?" She saw the wooden key in Eddie's hand and nodded. "I wondered when you were going to get around to showing that off. It's good, you know. I don't know what it's for, but it's damned good."

"You don't have any idea what door it might open?" Roland asked Eddie. "That was not part of your *khef*?"

"No—but it might be good for something even though it isn't done." He held the key out to Roland. "I want you to keep it for me."

Roland didn't move to take it. He regarded Eddie closely. "Why?"

"Because . . . well . . . because I think someone told me you should."

"Who?"

Your boy, Eddie thought suddenly, and as soon as the thought came he knew it was true. *It was your goddamned boy*. But he didn't want to say so. He didn't want to mention the boy's name at all. It might just set Roland off again.

"I don't know. But I think you ought to give it a try."

Roland reached slowly for the key. As his fingers touched it, a bright glimmer seemed to flash down its barrel, but it was gone so quickly that Eddie could not be sure he had seen it. It might have been only starlight.

Roland's hand closed over the key growing out of the branch. For a moment his face showed nothing. Then his brow furrowed and his head cocked in a listening gesture.

"What is it?" Susannah asked. "Do you hear—"

"*Shhhh!*" The puzzlement on Roland's face was slowly being replaced with wonder. He looked from Eddie to Susannah and then back to Eddie. His eyes were filling with some great emotion, as a pitcher fills with water when it is dipped in a spring.

"Roland?" Eddie asked uneasily. "Are you all right?"

Roland whispered something. Eddie couldn't hear what it was.

Susannah looked scared. She glanced frantically at Eddie, as if to ask, *What did you do to him?*

Eddie took one of her hands in both of his own. "I think it's all right."

Roland's hand was clamped so tightly on the chunk of wood that Eddie was momentarily afraid he might snap it in two, but the wood was strong and Eddie had carved thick. The gunslinger's throat bulged; his Adam's apple rose and fell as he struggled with speech. And suddenly he yelled at the sky in a fair, strong voice:

"GONE! THE VOICES ARE GONE!"

He looked back at them, and Eddie saw something he had never expected to see in his life—not even if that life stretched over a thousand years.

Roland of Gilead was weeping.

2

THE GUNSLINGER SLEPT SOUNDLY and dreamlessly that night for the first time in months, and he slept with the not-quite finished key clenched tightly in his hand.

3

IN ANOTHER WORLD, BUT beneath the shadow of the same *ka-tet*, Jake Chambers was having the most vivid dream of his life.

He was walking through the tangled remains of an ancient forest— a dead zone of fallen trees and scruffy, aggravating bushes that bit his ankles and tried to steal his sneakers. He came to a thin belt of younger trees (alders, he thought, or perhaps beeches—he was a city boy, and the only thing he knew for sure about trees was that some had leaves and some had needles) and discovered a path through them. He made his way along this, moving a little faster. There was a clearing of some sort up ahead.

He stopped once before reaching it, when he spied some sort of stone marker to his right. He left the path to look at it. There were letters carved into it, but they were so eroded he couldn't make them out. At last he closed his eyes (he had never done this in a dream before) and let his fingers trace each letter, like a blind boy reading Braille. Each formed in the darkness behind his lids until they made a sentence which stood forth in an outline of blue light:

TRAVELLER, BEYOND LIES MID-WORLD.

Sleeping in his bed, Jake drew his knees up against his chest. The hand holding the key was under his pillow, and now his fingers tightened their grip on it.

Mid-World, he thought, *of course. St. Louis and Topeka and Oz and the World's Fair and Charlie the Choo-Choo.*

He opened his dreaming eyes and pressed on. The clearing behind the trees was paved with old cracked asphalt. A faded yellow circle had been painted in the middle. Jake realized it was a playground basketball court even before he saw the boy at the far end, standing at the foul line and shooting baskets with a dusty old Wilson ball. They popped in one after another, falling neatly through the netless hole. The basket jutted out from something that looked like a subway kiosk which had been shut up for the night. Its closed door was painted in alternating diagonal stripes of yellow and black. From behind it—or perhaps from below it—Jake could hear the steady rumble of powerful machinery. The sound was somehow disturbing. Scary.

Don't step on the robots, the boy shooting the baskets said without turning around. *I guess they're all dead, but I wouldn't take any chances, if I were you.*

Jake looked around and saw a number of shattered mechanical devices lying around. One looked like a rat or mouse, another like a bat. A mechanical snake lay in two rusty pieces almost at his feet.

ARE you me? Jake asked, taking a step closer to the boy at the basket, but even before he turned around, Jake knew that wasn't the case. The boy was bigger than Jake, and at least thirteen. His hair was darker, and when he looked at Jake, he saw that the stranger's eyes were hazel. His own were blue.

What do you think? the strange boy asked, and bounce-passed the ball to Jake.

No, of course not, Jake said. He spoke apologetically. *It's just that I've been cut in two for the last three weeks or so.* He dipped and shot from mid-court. The ball arched high and dropped silently through the hoop. He was delighted . . . but he discovered he was also afraid of what this strange boy might have to tell him.

I know, the boy said. *It's been a bitch for you, hasn't it?* He was wearing faded madras shorts and a yellow t-shirt that said NEVER A DULL MOMENT IN MID-WORLD. He had tied a green bandanna around his forehead to keep his hair out of his eyes. *And things are going to get worse before they get better.*

What is this place? Jake asked. *And who are you?*

It's the Portal of the Bear . . . but it's also Brooklyn.

That didn't seem to make sense, and yet somehow it did. Jake told himself that things always seemed that way in dreams, but this didn't really *feel* like a dream.

As for me, I don't matter much, the boy said. He hooked the basket-ball over his shoulder. It rose, then dropped smoothly through the hoop. *I'm supposed to guide you, that's all. I'll take you where you need to go, and I'll show you what you need to see, but you have to be careful because I won't know you. And strangers make Henry nervous. He can get mean when he's nervous, and he's bigger than you.*

Who's Henry? Jake asked.

Never mind. Just don't let him notice you. All you have to do is hang out . . . and follow us. Then, when we leave . . .

The boy looked at Jake. There was both pity and fear in his eyes. Jake suddenly realized that the boy was starting to *fade*—he could see the yellow and black slashes on the box right through the boy's yellow t-shirt.

How will I find you? Jake was suddenly terrified that the boy would melt away completely before he could say everything Jake needed to hear.

No problem, the boy said. His voice had taken on a queer, chiming echo. *Just take the subway to Co-Op City. You'll find me.*

No, I won't! Jake cried. *Co-Op City's huge! There must be a hundred thousand people living there!*

Now the boy was just a milky outline. Only his hazel eyes were still completely there, like the Cheshire cat's grin in *Alice*. They regarded Jake with compassion and anxiety. *No problem-o*, he said. *You found the key and the rose, didn't you? You'll find me the same way. This afternoon, Jake. Around three o'clock should be good. You'll have to be careful, and you'll have to be quick.* He paused, a ghostly boy with an old basketball lying near one transparent foot. *I have to go now . . . but it was good to meet you. You seem like a nice kid, and I'm not surprised he loves you. Remember, there's danger, though. Be careful . . . and be quick.*

Wait! Jake yelled, and ran across the basketball court toward the disappearing boy. One of his feet struck a shattered robot that looked like a child's toy tractor. He stumbled and fell to his knees, shredding his pants. He ignored the thin burn of pain. *Wait! You have to tell me what all this is about! You have to tell me why these things are happening to me!*

Because of the Beam, the boy who was now only a pair of floating eyes replied, *and because of the Tower. In the end, all things, even the Beams, serve the Dark Tower. Did you think you would be any different?*

Jake flailed and stumbled to his feet. *Will I find him? Will I find the gunslinger?*

I don't know, the boy answered. His voice now seemed to come from a million miles away. *I only know you must try. About that you have no choice.*

The boy was gone. The basketball court in the woods was empty. The only sound was that faint rumble of machinery, and Jake didn't like it. There was something wrong with that sound, and he thought that what was wrong with the machinery was affecting the rose, or vice-versa. It was all hooked together somehow.

He picked up the old, scuffed-up basketball and shot. It went neatly through the hoop . . . and disappeared.

A river, the strange boy's voice sighed. It was like a puff of breeze. It came from nowhere and everywhere. *The answer is a river.*

4

JAKE WOKE IN THE first milky light of dawn, looking up at the ceiling of his room. He was thinking of the guy in The Manhattan Restaurant of the Mind—Aaron Deepneau, who'd been hanging around on Bleecker Street back when Bob Dylan only knew how to blow open G on his Hohner. Aaron Deepneau had given Jake a riddle.

What can run but never walks,
Has a mouth but never talks,
Has a bed but never sleeps,
Has a head but never weeps?

Now he knew the answer. A river ran; a river had a mouth; a river had a bed; a river had a head. The boy had told him the answer. The boy in the dream.

And suddenly he thought of something else Deepneau had said: *That's only half the answer. Samson's riddle is a double, my friend.*

Jake glanced at his bedside clock and saw it was twenty past six. It was time to get moving if he wanted to be out of here before his parents woke up. There would be no school for him today; Jake thought that maybe, as far as he was concerned, school had been cancelled forever.

He threw back the bedclothes, swung his feet out onto the floor, and saw that there were scrapes on both knees. Fresh scrapes. He had bruised his left side yesterday when he slipped on the bricks and fell, and he had banged his head when he fainted near the rose, but nothing had happened to his knees.

"That happened in the dream," Jake whispered, and found he wasn't surprised at all. He began to dress swiftly.

5

IN THE BACK OF his closet, under a jumble of old laceless sneakers and a heap of *Spiderman* comic books, he found the packsack he had worn to grammar school. No one would be caught dead with a packsack at Piper—how too, too common, my deah—and as Jake grabbed it, he felt a wave of powerful nostalgia for those old days when life had seemed so simple.

He stuffed a clean shirt, a clean pair of jeans, some underwear and socks into it, then added *Riddle-De-Dum!* and *Charlie the Choo-Choo*. He had put the key on his desk before foraging in the closet for his old pack, and the voices came back at once, but they were distant and muted. Besides, he felt sure he could make them go away completely by holding the key again, and that eased his mind.

Okay, he thought, looking into the pack. Even with the books added, there was plenty of room left. *What else?*

For a moment he thought there was nothing else . . . and then he knew.

6

HIS FATHER'S STUDY SMELLED of cigarettes and ambition.

It was dominated by a huge teakwood desk. Across the room, set into a wall otherwise lined with books, were three Mitsubishi television monitors. Each was tuned to one of the rival networks, and at night, when his father was in here, each played out its progression of prime-time images with the sound off.

The curtains were drawn, and Jake had to turn on the desk lamp in order to see. He felt nervous just being in here, even wearing sneakers. If his father should wake up and come in (and it was possible; no matter how late he went to bed or how much he drank, Elmer Chambers was a light sleeper and an early riser), he would be angry. At the very least it would make a clean getaway much tougher. The sooner he was out of here, the better Jake would feel.

The desk was locked, but his father had never made any secret of where he kept the key. Jake slid his fingers under the blotter and hooked it out. He opened the third drawer, reached past the hanging files, and touched cold metal.

A board creaked in the hall and he froze. Several seconds passed. When the creak didn't come again, Jake pulled out the weapon his father kept for "home defense"—a .44 Ruger automatic. His father had shown this weapon to Jake with great pride on the day he had bought it—two years ago, that had been. He had been totally deaf to his wife's nervous demands that he put it away before someone got hurt.

Jake found the button on the side that released the clip. It fell out into his hand with a metallic *snak!* sound that seemed very loud in the quiet apartment. He glanced nervously toward the door again, then turned his attention to the clip. It was fully loaded. He started to slide it back into the gun, and then took it out again. Keeping a loaded gun in a locked desk drawer was one thing; carrying one around New York City was quite another.

He stuffed the automatic down to the bottom of his pack, then felt behind the hanging files again. This time he brought out a box of shells, about half-full. He remembered his father had done some target shooting at the police range on First Avenue before losing interest.

The board creaked again. Jake wanted to get out of here.

He removed one of the shirts he'd packed, laid it on his father's desk, and rolled up the clip and the box of .44 slugs in it. Then he replaced it in the pack and used the buckles to snug down the flap. He was about to leave when his eye fixed on the little pile of stationery sitting beside his father's In/Out tray. The reflectorized Ray-Ban sunglasses his father liked to wear were folded on top of the stationery. He took a sheet of paper, and, after a moment's thought, the sunglasses as well. He slipped the shades into his breast pocket. Then he removed the slim gold pen from its stand, and wrote *Dear Dad and Mom* beneath the letterhead.

He stopped, frowning at the salutation. What went below it? What, exactly, did he have to say? That he loved them? It was true, but it wasn't enough—there were all sorts of other unpleasant truths stuck through that central one, like steel needles jabbed into a ball of yarn.

That he would miss them? He didn't know if that was true or not, which was sort of horrible. That he hoped *they* would miss *him*?

He suddenly realized what the problem was. If he were planning to be gone just today, he would be able to write something. But he felt a near-certainty that it *wasn't* just today, or this week, or this month, or this summer. He had an idea that when he walked out of the apartment this time, it would be for good.

He almost crumpled the sheet of paper, then changed his mind. He wrote: *Please take care of yourselves. Love, J.* That was pretty limp, but at least it was something.

Fine. Now will you stop pressing your luck and get out of here?

He did.

The apartment was almost dead still. He tiptoed across the living room, hearing only the sounds of his parents' breathing: his mother's soft little snores, his father's more nasal respiration, where every indrawn breath ended in a slim high whistle. The refrigerator kicked on as he reached the entryway and he froze for a moment, his heart thumping hard in his chest. Then he was at the door. He unlocked it as quietly as he could, then stepped out and pulled it gently shut behind him.

A stone seemed to roll off his heart as the latch snicked, and a strong sense of anticipation seized him. He didn't know what lay ahead, and he had reason to believe it would be dangerous, but he was eleven years old—too young to deny the exotic delight which suddenly filled him. There was a highway ahead—a hidden highway leading deep into some unknown land. There were secrets which might disclose themselves to him if he was clever . . . and if he was lucky. He had left his home in the long light of dawn, and what lay ahead was some great adventure.

If I stand, if I can be true, I'll see the rose, he thought as he pushed the button for the elevator. *I know it . . . and I'll see* him, *too.*

This thought filled him with an eagerness so great it was almost ecstasy.

Three minutes later he stepped out from beneath the awning which shaded the entrance to the building where he had lived all his life. He paused for a moment, then turned left. This decision did not feel random, and it wasn't. He was moving southeast, along the path of the Beam, resuming his own interrupted quest for the Dark Tower.

7

TWO DAYS AFTER EDDIE had given Roland his unfinished key, the three travellers—hot, sweaty, tired, and out of sorts—pushed through a particularly tenacious tangle of bushes and second-growth trees and discovered what first appeared to be two faint paths, running in tandem beneath the interlacing branches of the old trees crowding close on either side. After a few moments of study, Eddie decided they weren't just paths but the remains of a long-abandoned road. Bushes and stunted trees grew like untidy quills along what had been its crown. The grassy indentations were wheelruts, and either of them was wide enough to accommodate Susannah's wheelchair.

"Hallelujah!" he cried. "Let's drink to it!"

Roland nodded and unslung the waterskin he wore around his waist. He first handed it up to Susannah, who was riding in her sling on his back. Eddie's key, now looped around Roland's neck on a piece of rawhide, shifted beneath his shirt with each movement. She took a swallow and passed the skin to Eddie. He drank and then began to unfold her chair. Eddie had come to hate this bulky, balky contraption; it was like an iron anchor, always holding them back. Except for a broken spoke or two, it was still in fine condition. Eddie had days when he thought the goddam thing would outlast all of them. Now, however, it might be useful . . . for a while, at least.

Eddie helped Susannah out of the harness and placed her in the chair. She put her hands against the small of her back, stretched, and grimaced with pleasure. Both Eddie and Roland heard the small crackle her spine made as it stretched.

Up ahead, a large creature that looked like a badger crossed with a raccoon ambled out of the woods. It looked at them with its large, gold-rimmed eyes, twitched its sharp, whiskery snout as if to say *Huh! Big deal!*, then strolled the rest of the way across the road and disappeared again. Before it did, Eddie noted its tail—long and closely coiled, it looked like a fur-covered bedspring.

"What was that, Roland?"

"A billy-bumbler."

"No good to eat?"

Roland shook his head. "Tough. Sour. I'd rather eat dog."

"Have you?" Susannah asked. "Eaten dog, I mean?"

Roland nodded, but did not elaborate. Eddie found himself thinking of a line from an old Paul Newman movie: *That's right, lady—eaten em and lived like one.*

Birds sang cheerily in the trees. A light breeze blew along the road. Eddie and Susannah turned their faces up to it gratefully, then looked at each other and smiled. Eddie was struck again by his gratitude for her—it was scary to have someone to love, but it was also very fine.

"Who made this road?" Eddie asked.

"People who have been gone a long time," Roland said.

"The same ones who made the cups and dishes we found?" Susannah asked.

"No—not them. This used to be a coach-road, I imagine, and if it's still here, after all these years of neglect, it must have been a great one indeed . . . perhaps *the* Great Road. If we dug down, I imagine we'd find the gravel undersurface, and maybe the drainage system, as well. As long as we're here, let's have a bite to eat."

"Food!" Eddie cried. "Bring it on! Chicken Florentine! Polynesian shrimp! Veal lightly sautéed with mushrooms and—"

Susannah elbowed him. "Quit it, white boy."

"I can't help it if I've got a vivid imagination," Eddie said cheerfully.

Roland slipped his purse off his shoulder, hunkered down, and began to put together a small noon meal of dried meat wrapped in olive-colored leaves. Eddie and Susannah had discovered that these leaves tasted a little like spinach, only much stronger.

Eddie wheeled Susannah over to him and Roland handed her three of what Eddie called "gunslinger burritos." She began to eat.

When Eddie turned back, Roland was holding out three of the wrapped pieces of meat to him—and something else, as well. It was the chunk of ash with the key growing out of it. Roland had taken it off the rawhide string, which now lay in an open loop around his neck.

"Hey, you need that, don't you?" Eddie asked.

"When I take it off, the voices return, but they're very distant," Roland said. "I can deal with them. Actually, I hear them even when I'm wearing it—like the voices of men who are speaking low over the next hill. I think that's because the key is yet unfinished. You haven't worked on it since you gave it to me."

"Well . . . you were wearing it, and I didn't want to . . ."

Roland said nothing, but his faded blue eyes regarded Eddie with their patient teacher's look.

"All right," Eddie said, "I'm afraid of fucking it up. Satisfied?"

"According to your brother, you fucked everything up . . . isn't that right?" Susannah asked.

"Susannah Dean, Girl Psychologist. You missed your calling, sweetheart."

Susannah wasn't offended by the sarcasm. She lifted the waterskin with her elbow, like a redneck tipping a jug, and drank deeply. "It's true, though, isn't it?"

Eddie, who realized he hadn't finished the slingshot, either—not yet, at least—shrugged.

"You have to finish it," Roland said mildly. "I think the time is coming when you'll have to put it to use."

Eddie started to speak, then closed his mouth. It sounded easy when you said it right out like that, but neither of them really understood the bottom line. The bottom line was this: seventy per cent or eighty or even ninety-eight and a half just wouldn't do. Not this time. And if he *did* screw up, he couldn't just toss the thing over his shoulder and walk away. For one thing, he hadn't seen another ash-tree since the day he had cut this particular piece of wood. But mostly the thing that was fucking him up was just this: it was all or nothing. If he messed up even a little, the key wouldn't turn when they needed it to turn. And he was increasingly nervous about that little squiggle at the end. It looked simple, but if the curves weren't exactly right . . .

It won't work the way it is now, though; that much you do know.

He sighed, looking at the key. Yes, that much he did know. He would have to try to finish it. His fear of failure would make it even harder than it maybe had to be, but he would have to swallow the fear and try anyway. Maybe he could even bring it off. God knew he had brought off a lot in the weeks since Roland had entered his mind on a Delta jet bound into JFK Airport. That he was still alive and sane was an accomplishment in itself.

Eddie handed the key back to Roland. "Wear it for now," he said. "I'll go back to work when we stop for the night."

"Promise?"

"Yeah."

Roland nodded, took the key, and began to re-knot the rawhide string. He worked slowly, but Eddie did not fail to notice how dextrously the remaining fingers on his right hand moved. The man was nothing if not adaptable.

"Something *is* going to happen, isn't it?" Susannah asked suddenly.

Eddie glanced up at her. "What makes you say so?"

"I sleep with you, Eddie, and I know you dream every night now. Sometimes you talk, too. They don't seem like nightmares, exactly, but it's pretty clear that *something* is going on inside your head."

"Yes. Something is. I just don't know what."

"Dreams are powerful," Roland remarked. "You don't remember the ones you're having at all?"

Eddie hesitated. "A little, but they're confused. I'm a kid again, I know that much. It's after school. Henry and I are shooting hoops at the old Markey Avenue playground, where the Juvenile Court Building is now. I want Henry to take me to see a place over in Dutch Hill. An old house. The kids used to call it The Mansion, and everyone said it was haunted. Maybe it even was. It was creepy, I know that much. *Real* creepy."

Eddie shook his head, remembering.

"I thought of The Mansion for the first time in years when we were in the bear's clearing, and I put my head close to that weird box. I dunno—maybe that's why I'm having the dream."

"But you don't think so," Susannah said.

"No. I think whatever's happening is a lot more complicated than just remembering stuff."

"Did you and your brother actually go to this place?" Roland asked.

"Yeah—I talked him into it."

"And did something happen?"

"No. But it was scary. We stood there and looked at it for a little while, and Henry teased me—saying he was going to make me go in and pick up a souvenir, stuff like that—but I knew he didn't really mean it. He was as scared of the place as I was."

"And that's it?" Susannah asked. "You just dream of going to this place? The Mansion?"

"There's a little more than that. Someone comes . . . and then just kind of hangs out. I notice him in the dream, but just a little . . . like out of the corner of my eye, you know? Only I know we're supposed to pretend we don't know each other."

"Was this someone really there that day?" Roland asked. He was watching Eddie intently. "Or is he only a player in this dream?"

"That was a long time ago. I couldn't have been more than thirteen. How could I remember a thing like that for sure?"

Roland said nothing.

"Okay," Eddie said at last. "Yeah. I think he *was* there that day. A kid who was either carrying a gym-bag or wearing a backpack, I can't remember which. And sunglasses that were too big for his face. The ones with the mirror lenses."

"Who was this person?" Roland asked.

Eddie was silent for a long time. He was holding the last of his *burritos à la Roland* in one hand, but he had lost his appetite. "I think it's the kid you met at the way station," he said at last. "I think your old friend Jake was hanging around, watching me and Henry on the afternoon we went over to Dutch Hill. I think he followed us. Because he hears the voices, just like you, Roland. And because he's sharing my dreams, and I'm sharing his. I think that what I remember is what's happening now, in Jake's when. The kid is trying to come back here. And if the key isn't done when he makes his move—or if it's done wrong—he's probably going to die."

Roland said, "Maybe he has a key of his own. Is that possible?"

"Yeah, I think it is," Eddie said, "but it isn't enough." He sighed and stuck the last burrito in his pocket for later. *"And I don't think he knows that."*

8

THEY MOVED ALONG, ROLAND and Eddie trading off on Susannah's wheelchair. They picked the left-hand wheelrut. The chair bumped and pitched, and every now and then Eddie and Roland had to lift it over the cobbles which stuck out of the dirt here and there like old teeth. They were still making faster, easier time than they had in a week, however. The ground was rising, and when Eddie looked over his shoulder he could see the forest sloping away in what looked like a series of gentle steps. Far to the northwest, he could see a ribbon of water spilling over a fractured rock face. It was, he realized with wonder, the place they had dubbed "the shooting gallery." Now it was almost lost behind them in the haze of this dreaming summer afternoon.

"Whoa down, boy!" Susannah called sharply. Eddie faced forward again just in time to keep from pushing the wheelchair into Roland. The gunslinger had stopped and was peering into the tangled bushes at the left of the road.

"You keep that up, I'm gonna revoke your driver's license," Susannah said waspily.

Eddie ignored her. He was following Roland's gaze. "What is it?"

"One way to find out." He turned, hoisted Susannah from her chair, and planted her on his hip. "Let's all take a look."

"Put me down, big boy—I can make my way. Easier'n you boys, if you really want to know."

As Roland gently lowered her to the grassy wheelrut, Eddie peered into the woods. The late light threw overlapping crosses of shadow, but he thought he saw what had caught Roland's eye. It was a tall gray stone, almost completely hidden in a shag of vines and creepers.

Susannah slipped into the woods at the side of the road with eely sinuousness. Roland and Eddie followed.

"It's a marker, isn't it?" Susannah was propped on her hands studying the rectangular chunk of rock. It had once been straight, but now it leaned drunkenly to the right, like an old gravestone.

"Yes. Give me my knife, Eddie."

Eddie handed it over, then hunkered next to Susannah as the gunslinger cut away the vines. As they fell, he could see eroded letters carved into the stone, and he knew what they said before Roland had uncovered even half of the inscription:

TRAVELLER, BEYOND LIES MID-WORLD.

9

"WHAT DOES IT MEAN?" Susannah asked at last. Her voice was soft and awestruck; her eyes ceaselessly measured the gray stone plinth.

"It means that we're nearing the end of this first stage." Roland's face was solemn and thoughtful as he handed his knife back to Eddie. "I think that we'll keep to this old coach-road now—or rather, it will keep to us. It has taken up the path of the Beam. The woods will end soon. I expect a great change."

"What is Mid-World?" Eddie asked.

"One of the large kingdoms which dominated the earth in the times before these. A kingdom of hope and knowledge and light—the sort of things we were trying to hold onto in my land before the darkness overtook us, as well. Some day if there's time, I'll tell you all the old stories . . . the ones I know, at least. They form a large tapestry, one which is beautiful but very sad.

"According to the old tales, a great city once stood at the edge of Mid-World—perhaps as great as your city of New York. It will be in ruins now, if it still exists at all. But there may be people . . . or monsters . . . or both. We'll have to be on our guard."

He reached out his two-fingered right hand and touched the inscription. "Mid-World," he said in a low, meditative voice. "Who would have thought . . ." He trailed off.

"Well, there's no help for it, is there?" Eddie asked.

The gunslinger shook his head. "No help."

"*Ka*," Susannah said suddenly, and they both looked at her.

10

THERE WERE TWO HOURS of daylight left, and so they moved on. The road continued southeast, along the path of the Beam, and two other overgrown roads—smaller ones—joined the one they were following. Along one side of the second were the mossy, tumbled remains of what must have once been an immense rock wall. Nearby, a dozen fat billy-bumblers sat upon the ruins, watching the pilgrims with their odd gold-ringed eyes. To Eddie they looked like a jury with hanging on its mind.

The road continued to grow wider and more clearly defined. Twice they passed the shells of long-deserted buildings. The second one, Roland said, might have been a windmill. Susannah said it looked haunted. "I wouldn't be surprised," the gunslinger replied. His matter-of-fact tone chilled both of them.

When darkness forced a halt, the trees were thinning and the breeze which had chased around them all day became a light, warm wind. Ahead, the land continued to rise.

"We'll come to the top of the ridge in a day or two," Roland said. "Then we'll see."

"See what?" Susannah asked, but Roland only shrugged.

That night Eddie began to carve again, but with no real feeling of inspiration. The confidence and happiness he'd felt as the key first began to take shape had left him. His fingers felt clumsy and stupid. For the first time in months he thought longingly of how good it would be to have some heroin. Not a lot; he felt sure that a nickel bag and a rolled-up dollar bill would send him flying through this little carving project in no time flat.

"What are you smiling about, Eddie?" Roland asked. He was sitting on the other side of the campfire; the low, wind-driven flames danced capriciously between them.

"Was I smiling?"

"Yes."

"I was just thinking about how stupid some people can be—you put them in a room with six doors, they'll still walk into the walls. And then have the nerve to bitch about it."

"If you're afraid of what might be on the other side of the doors, maybe bouncing off the walls seems safer," Susannah said.

Eddie nodded. "Maybe so."

He worked slowly, trying to see the shapes in the wood—that little s-shape in particular. He discovered it had become very dim.

Please, God, help me not to fuck this up, he thought, but he was terribly afraid that he had already begun to do just that. At last he gave up, returned the key (which he had barely changed at all) to the gunslinger, and curled up beneath one of the hides. Five minutes later, the dream about the boy and the old Markey Avenue playground had begun to unspool again.

11

JAKE STEPPED OUT OF his apartment building at about quarter of seven, which left him with over eight hours to kill. He considered taking the train out to Brooklyn right away, then decided it was a bad idea. A kid out of school was apt to attract more attention in the hinterlands than in the heart of a big city, and if he really had to *search* for the place and the boy he was supposed to meet there, he was cooked already.

No problem-o, the boy in the yellow T-shirt and green bandanna had said. *You found the key and the rose, didn't you? You'll find me the same way.*

Except Jake could no longer remember just how he *had* found the key and the rose. He could only remember the joy and the sense of surety which had filled his heart and head. He would just have to hope that would happen again. In the meantime, he'd keep moving. That was the best way to keep from being noticed in New York.

He walked most of the way to First Avenue, then headed back the way he had come, only sliding uptown little by little as he followed the pattern of the WALK lights (perhaps knowing, on some deep level, that even they served the Beam). Around ten o'clock he found himself in front of the Metropolitan Museum of Art on Fifth Avenue. He was hot, tired, and depressed. He wanted a soda, but he thought he ought to hold onto what little money he had for as long as he could. He'd taken every cent out of the box he kept by his bed, but it only amounted to eight dollars, give or take a few cents.

A group of school-kids were lining up for a tour. Public school, Jake was almost sure—they were dressed as casually as he was. No blazers from Paul Stuart, no ties, no jumpers, no simple little skirts that cost a hundred and twenty-five bucks at places like Miss So Pretty or Tweenity. This crowd was Kmart all the way. On impulse, Jake stood at the end of the line and followed them into the museum.

The tour took an hour and fifteen minutes. Jake enjoyed it. The museum was quiet. Even better, it was air-conditioned. And the pictures were nice. He was particularly fascinated by a small group of Frederick Remington's Old West paintings and a large picture by Thomas Hart Benton that showed a steam locomotive charging across the great plains toward Chicago while beefy farmers in bib overalls and straw hats stood in their fields and watched. He wasn't noticed by either of the teachers with the group until the very end. Then a pretty black woman in a severe blue suit tapped him on the shoulder and asked who he was.

Jake hadn't seen her coming, and for a moment his mind froze. Without thinking about what he was doing, he reached into his pocket and closed his hand around the silver key. His mind cleared immediately, and he felt calm again.

"My group is upstairs," he said, smiling guiltily. "We're supposed to be looking at a bunch of modern art, but I like the stuff down here a lot better, because they're real pictures. So I sort of . . . you know . . ."

"Snuck away?" the teacher suggested. The corners of her lips twitched in a suppressed smile.

"Well, I'd rather think of it as French leave." These words simply popped out of his mouth.

The students now staring at Jake only looked puzzled, but this time the teacher actually laughed. "Either you don't know or have forgotten," she said, "but in the French Foreign Legion they used to shoot deserters. I suggest you rejoin your class at once, young man."

"Yes, ma'am. Thank you. They'll be almost done now, anyway."

"What school is it?"

"Markey Academy," Jake said. This also just popped out.

He went upstairs, listening to the disembodied echo of foot-falls and low voices in the great space of the rotunda and wondering why he had said that. He had never heard of a place called Markey Academy in his life.

12

HE WAITED AWHILE IN the upstairs lobby, then noticed a guard looking at him with growing curiosity and decided it wouldn't be wise to wait any longer—he would just have to hope the class he had joined briefly was gone.

He looked at his wristwatch, put an expression on his face that he hoped looked like *Gosh! Look how late it's getting!*, and trotted back downstairs. The class—and the pretty black teacher who had laughed at the idea of French leave—was gone, and Jake decided it might be a good idea to get gone himself. He would walk awhile longer—slowly, in deference to the heat—and catch a subway.

He stopped at a hot-dog stand on the corner of Broadway and Forty-second, trading in a little of his meager cash supply for a sweet sausage and a Nehi. He sat on the steps of a bank building to eat his lunch, and that turned out to be a bad mistake.

A cop came walking toward him, twirling his nightstick in a complex series of maneuvers. He seemed to be paying attention to nothing but this, but when he came abreast of Jake he abruptly shoved his stick back into his loop and turned to him.

"Say-hey, big guy," he said. "No school today?"

Jake had been wolfing his sausage, but the last bite abruptly stuck in his throat. This was a lousy piece of luck . . . if luck was all it was. They were in Times Square, sleaze capital of America; there were pushers, junkies, whores, and chicken-chasers everywhere . . . but this cop was ignoring *them* in favor of *him*.

Jake swallowed with an effort, then said, "It's finals week at my school. I only had one test today. Then I could leave." He paused, not liking the bright, searching look in the cop's eyes. "I had permission," he concluded uneasily.

"Uh-huh. Can I see some ID?"

Jake's heart sank. Had his mother and father already called the cops? He supposed that, after yesterday's adventure, that was pretty likely. Under ordinary circumstances, the NYPD wouldn't take much notice of another missing kid, especially one that had been gone only half a day, but his father was a big deal at the Network, and he prided himself on the number of strings he could pull. Jake doubted if this cop had his picture . . . but he might very well have his name.

"Well," Jake said reluctantly, "I've got my student discount card from Mid-World Lanes, but that's about all."

"Mid-World Lanes? Never heard of it. Where's that? Queens?"

"Mid-*Town*, I mean," Jake thought. God, this was going north instead of south . . . and fast. "You know? On Thirty-third?"

"Uh-huh. That'll do fine." The cop held out his hand.

A black man with dreadlocks spilling over the shoulders of his canary-yellow suit glanced over. "Bussim, ossifer!" this apparition said cheerfully. "Bussiz lil whitebread ass! Do yo duty, now!"

"Shut up and get in the wind, Eli," the cop said without looking around.

Eli laughed, exposing several gold teeth, and moved along.

"Why don't you ask *him* for some ID?" Jake asked.

"Because right now I'm asking you. Snap it up, son."

The cop either had his name or had sensed something wrong about him—which wasn't so surprising, maybe, since he was the only white in the area who wasn't obviously trolling. Either way, it came to the same: sitting down here to eat his lunch had been dumb. But his feet had hurt, and he'd been hungry, dammit—*hungry.*

You're not going to stop me, Jake thought. *I can't* let *you stop me. There's someone I'm supposed to meet this afternoon in Brooklyn . . . and I'm going to be there.*

Instead of reaching for his wallet, he reached into his front pocket and brought out the key. He held it up to the policeman; the late-morning sunshine bounced little coins of reflected light onto the man's cheeks and forehead. His eyes widened.

"Heyy!" he breathed. "What you got there, kid?"

He reached for it, and Jake pulled the key back a little. The reflected circles of light danced hypnotically on the cop's face. "You don't need to take it," Jake said. "You can read my name without doing that, can't you?"

"Yes, sure."

The curiosity had left the cop's face. He looked only at the key. His gaze was wide and fixed, but not quite empty. Jake read both amazement and unexpected happiness in his look. *That's me,* Jake thought, *just spreading joy and goodwill wherever I go. The question is, what do I do now?*

A young woman (probably not a librarian, judging from the green silk hotpants and see-through blouse she was wearing) came wiggle-wobbling up the sidewalk on a pair of purple fuck-me shoes with three-inch heels. She glanced first at the cop, then at Jake to see what the cop was looking at. When she got a good look, she stopped cold. One of her hands drifted up and touched her throat. A man bumped into her and told her to watch where the damn-hell she was going. The young woman who was probably not a librarian took no notice whatever. Now Jake saw that four or five other people had stopped as well. All were staring at the key. They were gathering as people sometimes will around a very good three-card-monte dealer plying his trade on a streetcorner.

You're doing a great job of being inconspicious, he thought. *Oh yeah.* He glanced over the cop's shoulder, and his eye caught a sign on the far side of the street. Denby's Discount Drug, it said.

"My name's Tom Denby," he told the cop. "It says so right here on my discount bowling card—right?"

"Right, right," the cop breathed. He had lost all interest in Jake; he was only interested in the key. The little coins of reflected light bounced and spun on his face.

"And you're not looking for anybody named Tom Denby, are you?"

"No," the cop said. "Never heard of him."

Now there were at least half a dozen people gathered around the cop, all of them staring with silent wonder at the silver key in Jake's hand.

"So I can go, can't I?"

"Huh? Oh! Oh, sure—go, for your father's sake!"

"Thanks," Jake said, but for a moment he wasn't sure *how* to go. He was hemmed in by a silent crowd of zombies, and more were joining it all the time. They were only coming to see what the deal was, he realized, but the ones who saw the key just stopped dead and stared.

He got to his feet and backed slowly up the wide bank steps, holding the key out in front of him like a lion-tamer with a chair. When he got to the wide concrete plaza at the top, he stuffed it back into his pants pockets, turned, and fled.

He stopped just once on the far side of the plaza, and looked back. The small group of people around the place where he had been standing was coming slowly back to life. They looked around at each other with dazed expressions, then walked on. The cop glanced vacantly to his left, to his right, and then straight up at the sky, as if trying to remember how he had gotten here and what he had been meaning to do. Jake had seen enough. It was time to find a subway station and get his ass over to Brooklyn before anything else weird could happen.

13

AT QUARTER OF TWO that afternoon he walked slowly up the steps of the subway station and stood on the corner of Castle and Brooklyn Avenues, looking at the sandstone towers of Co-Op City. He waited for that feeling of sureness and direction—that feeling that was like being able to remember forward in time—to overtake him. It didn't come. *Nothing* came. He was just a kid standing on a hot Brooklyn streetcorner with his short shadow lying at his feet like a tired pet.

Well, I'm here . . . now what do I do?

Jake discovered he didn't have the slightest idea.

14

ROLAND'S SMALL BAND OF travellers reached the crest of the long, gentle hill they had been climbing and stood looking southeast. For a long time none of them spoke. Susannah opened her mouth twice, then closed it again. For the first time in her life as a woman, she was completely speechless.

Before them, an almost endless plain dozed in the long golden light of a summer's afternoon. The grass was lush, emerald green, and very high. Groves of trees with long, slender trunks and wide, spreading tops dotted the plain. Susannah had once seen similar trees, she thought, in a travelogue film about Australia.

The road they had been following swooped down the far side of the hill and then ran straight as a string into the southeast, a bright white lane cutting through the grass. To the west, some miles off, she could see a herd of large animals grazing peacefully. They looked like buffalo. To the east, the last of the forest made a curved peninsula into the grassland. This incursion was a dark, tangled shape that looked like a forearm with a cocked fist at the end.

That was the direction, she realized, in which all the creeks and streams they had encountered had been flowing. They were tributaries of the vast river that emerged from that jutting arm of forest and flowed, placid and dreaming under the summer sun, toward the eastern edge of the world. It was wide, that river—perhaps two miles from bank to bank.

And she could see the city.

It lay dead ahead, a misty collection of spires and towers rising above the far edge of the horizon. Those airy ramparts might have been a hundred miles away, or two hundred, or four hundred. The air of this world seemed to be totally clear, and that made judging distances a fool's game. All she knew for sure was that the sight of those dim towers filled her with silent wonder . . . and a deep, aching homesickness for New York. She thought, *I believe I'd do most anything just to see the Manhattan skyline from the Triborough Bridge again.*

Then she had to smile, because that wasn't the truth. The truth was that she wouldn't trade Roland's world for anything. Its silent mystery and empty spaces were intoxicating. And her lover was here. In New York—the New York of her own time, at least—they would have been objects of scorn and anger, the butt of every idiot's crude, cruel jokes: a black woman of twenty-six and her whitebread lover who was three years younger and who had a tendency to talk like dis and dat when he got excited. Her whitebread lover who had been carrying a heavy monkey on his back only eight months before. Here, there was no one to jeer or laugh. Here, no one was pointing a finger. Here, there were only Roland, Eddie, and herself, the world's last three gunslingers.

She took Eddie's hand and felt it close over hers, warm and reassuring.

Roland pointed. "That must be the Send River," he said in a low voice. "I never thought to see it in my life . . . wasn't even sure it was real, like the Guardians."

"It's so lovely," Susannah murmured. She was unable to take her eyes from the vast landscape before her, dreaming richly in the cradle of summer. She found her eyes tracing the shadows of the trees, which trailed across the plain for what seemed miles as the sun sank toward the horizon. "It's the way our Great Plains must have looked before they were settled—even before the Indians came." She raised her free hand and pointed toward the place where the Great Road narrowed to a point. "There's your city," she said. "Isn't it?"

"Yes."

"It looks okay," Eddie said. "Is that possible, Roland? Could it still be pretty much intact. Did the old-timers build that well?"

"Anything is possible in these times," Roland said, but he sounded doubtful. "You shouldn't get your hopes up, though, Eddie."

"Huh? No." But Eddie's hopes *were* up. That dimly sketched skyline had awakened homesickness in Susannah's heart; in Eddie's it kindled a sudden blaze of supposition. If the city was still there—and it clearly was—it might still be populated, and maybe not just by the subhuman things Roland had met under the mountains, either. The city-dwellers might be

(*Americans*, Eddie's subconscious whispered)

intelligent and helpful; they might, in fact, spell the difference between success and failure for the quest of the pilgrims . . . or even between life and death. In Eddie's mind a vision (partly cribbed from movies like *The Last Starfighter* and *The Dark Crystal*) gleamed brightly:

a council of gnarled but dignified City Elders who would serve them a whopping meal drawn from the unspoiled stores of the city (or perhaps from special gardens cradled within environmental bubbles) and who would, as he and Roland and Susannah ate themselves silly, explain exactly what lay ahead and what it all meant. Their parting gift to the wayfarers would be an AAA-approved TourGuide map with the best route to the Dark Tower marked in red.

Eddie did not know the phrase *deus ex machina*, but he knew—had now grown up enough to know—that such wise and kindly folk lived mostly in comic books and B-movies. The idea was intoxicating, all the same: an enclave of civilization in this dangerous, mostly empty world; wise old elf-men who would tell them just what the fuck it was they were supposed to be doing. And the fabulous shapes of the city disclosed in that hazy skyline made the idea seem at least possible. Even if the city was totally deserted, the population wiped out by some long-ago plague or outbreak of chemical warfare, it might still serve them as a kind of giant toolbox—a huge Army-Navy Surplus Store where they could outfit themselves for the hard passages Eddie was sure must lie ahead. Besides, he was a city boy, born and bred, and the sight of all those tall towers just naturally got him up.

"All *right!*" he said, almost laughing out loud in his excitement. "Hey-ho, let's go! Bring on those wise fuckin elves!"

Susannah looked at him, puzzled but smiling. "What you ravin about, white boy?"

"Nothing. Never mind. I just want to get moving. What do you say, Roland? Want to—"

But something on Roland's face or just beneath it—some lost, dreaming thing—caused him to fall silent and put one arm around Susannah's shoulders, as if to protect her.

15

AFTER ONE BRIEF, DISMISSIVE glance at the city skyline, Roland's gaze had been caught by something a good deal closer to their current position, something that filled him with disquiet and foreboding. He had seen such things before, and the last time he'd come across one, Jake had been with him. He remembered how they had finally come out of the desert, the trail of the man in black leading them through the foothills and toward the mountains. Hard going, it had been, but at least there had been water again. And grass.

One night he had awakened to find Jake gone. He had heard strangled, desperate cries coming from a willow-grove hard by a narrow trickle of stream. By the time he had fought his way through to the clearing at the center of the grove, the boy's cries had ceased. Roland had found him standing in a place exactly like the one which lay below and ahead. A place of stones; a place of sacrifice; a place where an Oracle lived . . . and spoke when it was forced to . . . and killed whenever it could.

"Roland?" Eddie asked. "What is it? What's wrong?"

"Do you see that?" Roland pointed. "It's a speaking ring. The shapes you see are tall standing stones." He found himself staring at Eddie, whom he had first met in the frightening but wonderful air-carriage of that strange other world where the gunslingers wore blue uniforms and there was an endless supply of sugar, paper, and wonderful drugs like *astin*. Some strange expression—some foreknowledge—was dawning on Eddie's face. The bright hope which had lit his eyes as he surveyed the city whiffed out, leaving him with a look both gray and bleak. It was the expression of a man studying the gallows on which he will soon be hanged.

First Jake, and now Eddie, the gunslinger thought. *The wheel which turns our lives is remorseless; always it comes around to the same place again.*

"Oh shit," Eddie said. His voice was dry and scared. "I think that's the place where the kid is going to try and come through."

The gunslinger nodded. "Very likely. They're thin places, and they're also *attractive* places. I followed him to such a place once before. The Oracle that kept there came very close to killing him."

"How do you *know* this?" Susannah asked Eddie. "Was it a dream?"

He only shook his head. "I don't know. But the minute Roland pointed that goddamn place out . . ." He broke off and looked at the gunslinger. "We have to get there, just as fast as we can." Eddie sounded both frantic and fearful.

"Is it going to happen today?" Roland asked. "Tonight?"

Eddie shook his head again, and licked his lips. "I don't know that, either. Not for sure. Tonight? I don't think so. Time . . . it isn't the same over here as it is where the kid is. It goes slower in his where and when. Maybe tomorrow." He had been battling panic, but now it broke free. He turned and grabbed Roland's shirt with his cold, sweating fingers. "But I'm supposed to finish the key, and I haven't, and I'm supposed to do something else, and I don't have a clue about what it is. And if the kid dies, it'll be *my fault!*"

The gunslinger locked his own hands over Eddie's and pulled them away from his shirt. "Get control of yourself."

"Roland, don't you understand—"

"I understand that whining and puling won't solve your problem. I understand that you have forgotten the face of your father."

"Quit that bullshit! I don't care *dick* about my father!" Eddie shouted hysterically, and Roland hit him across the face. His hand made a sound like a breaking branch.

Eddie's head rocked back; his eyes widened with shock. He stared at the gunslinger, then slowly raised his hand to touch the reddening handprint on his cheek. "You *bastard!*" he whispered. His hand dropped to the butt of the revolver he still wore on his left hip. Susannah tried to put her own hands over it; Eddie pushed them away.

And now I must teach again, Roland thought, *only this time I teach for my own life, I think, as well as for his.*

Somewhere in the distance a crow hailed its harsh cry into the stillness, and Roland thought for a moment of his hawk, David. Now *Eddie* was his hawk . . . and like David, he would not scruple to tear out his eye if he gave so much as a single inch.

Or his throat.

"Will you shoot me? Is that how you'd have it end, Eddie?"

"Man, I'm so fucking tired of your jive," Eddie said. His eyes were blurred with tears and fury.

"You haven't finished the key, but not because you are afraid to finish. You're afraid of finding you *can't* finish. You're afraid to go down to where the stones stand, but not because you're afraid of what may come once you enter the circle. You're afraid of what may *not* come. You're not afraid of the great world, Eddie, but of the small one inside yourself. You haven't forgotten the face of your father. So do it. Shoot me if you dare. I'm tired of watching you blubber."

"Stop it!" Susannah screamed at him. "Can't you see he'll do it? Can't you see you're *forcing* him to do it?"

Roland cut his eyes toward her. "I'm forcing him to *decide.*" He looked back at Eddie, and his deeply lined face was stern. "You have come from the shadow of the heroin and the shadow of your brother, my friend. Come from the shadow of yourself, if you dare. Come now. Come out or shoot me *and have done with it.*"

For a moment he thought Eddie was going to do just that, and it would all end right here, on this high ridge, beneath a cloudless summer sky with the spires of the city glimmering on the horizon like blue ghosts. Then Eddie's cheek began to twitch. The firm line of his lips softened and began to tremble. His hand fell from the sandalwood butt of Roland's gun. His chest hitched once . . . twice . . . three times. His mouth opened and all his despair and terror came out in one groaning cry as he blundered toward the gunslinger.

"*I'm* afraid, *you numb fuck! Don't you understand that? Roland*, I'm afraid!"

His feet tangled together. He fell forward. Roland caught him and held him close, smelling the sweat and dirt on his skin, smelling his tears and terror.

The gunslinger embraced him for a moment, then turned him toward Susannah. Eddie dropped to his knees beside her chair, his head hanging wearily. She put a hand on the back of his neck, pressing his head against her thigh, and said bitterly to Roland, "Sometimes I hate you, big white man."

Roland placed the heels of his hands against his forehead and pressed hard. "Sometimes I hate myself."

"Don't ever stop you, though, do it?"

Roland didn't reply. He looked at Eddie, who lay with his cheek pressed against Susannah's thigh and his eyes tightly shut. His face was a study in misery. Roland fought away the dragging weariness that made him want to leave the rest of this charming discussion for another day. If Eddie was right, there *was* no other day. Jake was almost ready to make his move. Eddie had been chosen to midwife the boy into this world. If he wasn't prepared to do that, Jake would die at the point of entry, as surely as an infant must strangle if the mother-root is tangled about its neck when the contractions begin.

"Stand up, Eddie."

For a moment he thought Eddie would simply go on crouching there and hiding his face against the woman's leg. If so, everything was lost . . . and that was *ka*, too. Then, slowly, Eddie got to his feet. He stood there with everything—hands, shoulders, head, hair—hanging, not good, but he was up, and that was a start.

"Look at me."

Susannah stirred uneasily, but this time she said nothing.

Slowly, Eddie raised his head and brushed the hair out of his eyes with a trembling hand.

"This is for you. I was wrong to take it at all, no matter how deep my pain." Roland curled his hand around the rawhide strip and yanked, snapping it. He held the key out to Eddie. Eddie reached for it like a man in a dream, but Roland did not immediately open his hand. "Will you try to do what needs to be done?"

"Yes." His voice was almost inaudible.

"Do you have something to tell me?"

"I'm sorry I'm afraid." There was something terrible in Eddie's voice, something which hurt Roland's heart, and he supposed, he knew what it was: here was the last of Eddie's childhood, expiring painfully among the three of them. It could not be seen, but Roland could hear its weakening cries. He tried to make himself deaf to them.

Something else I've done in the name of the Tower. My score grows ever longer, and the day when it will all have to be totted up, like a long-time drunkard's bill in an alehouse, draws ever nearer. How will I ever pay?

"I don't want your apology, least of all for being afraid," he said. "Without fear, what would we be? Mad dogs with foam on our muzzles and shit drying on our hocks."

"What *do* you want, then?" Eddie cried. "You've taken everything else—everything I have to give! No, not even that, because in the end, I gave it to you! So *what else do you want from me?*"

Roland held the key which was their half of Jake Chambers's salvation locked in his fist and said nothing. His eyes held Eddie's, and the sun shone on the green expanse of plain and the blue-gray reach of the Send River, and somewhere in the distance the crow hailed again across the golden leagues of this fading summer afternoon.

After a while, understanding began to dawn in Eddie Dean's eyes. Roland nodded.

"I have forgotten the face ..." Eddie paused. Dipped his head. Swallowed. Looked up at the gunslinger once more. The thing which had been dying among them had moved on now—Roland knew it. That thing was gone. Just like that. Here, on this sunny wind-swept ridge at the edge of everything, it had gone forever. "I have forgotten the face of my father, gunslinger ... and I cry your pardon."

Roland opened his hand and returned the small burden of the key to him who *ka* had decreed must carry it. "Speak not so, gunslinger," he said in the High Speech. "Your father sees you very well ... loves you very well ... and so do I."

Eddie closed his own hand over the key and turned away with his tears still drying on his face. "Let's go," he said, and they began to move down the long hill toward the plain which stretched beyond.

16

JAKE WALKED SLOWLY ALONG Castle Avenue, past pizza shops and bars and bodegas where old women with suspicious faces poked the potatoes and squeezed the tomatoes. The straps of his pack had chafed the skin beneath his arms, and his feet hurt. He passed beneath a digital thermometer which announced it was eighty-five. It felt more like a hundred and five to Jake.

Up ahead, a police car turned onto the Avenue. Jake at once became extremely interested in a display of gardening supplies in the window of a hardware store. He watched the reflection of the blue-and-white pass in the window and didn't move until it was gone.

Hey, Jake, old buddy—where, exactly, are you going?

He hadn't the slightest idea. He felt positive that the boy he was looking for—the boy in the green bandanna and the yellow T-shirt that said NEVER A DULL MOMENT IN MID-WORLD—was somewhere close by, but so what? To Jake he was still nothing but a needle hiding in the haystack which was Brooklyn.

He passed an alley which had been decorated with a tangle of spray-painted graffiti. Mostly they were names—EL TIANTE 91, SPEEDY GONZALES, MOTORVAN MIKE—but a few mottos and words to the wise had been dropped in here and there, and Jake's eyes fixed on two of these.

A ROSE IS A ROSE IS A ROSE

had been written across the bricks in spray-paint which had weathered to the same dusky-pink shade of the rose which grew in the vacant lot where Tom and Gerry's Artistic Deli had once stood. Below it, in a blue so dark it was almost black, someone had spray-painted this oddity:

I CRY YOUR PARDON.

What does that *mean?* Jake wondered. He didn't know—something from the Bible, maybe—but it held like the eye of a snake is reputed to hold a bird. At last he walked on, slowly and thoughtfully. It was almost two-thirty, and his shadow was beginning to grow longer.

Just ahead, he saw an old man walking down the street, keeping to the shade as much as possible and leaning on a gnarled cane. Behind the thick glasses he wore, his brown eyes swam like oversized eggs.

"I cry your pardon, sir," Jake said without thinking or even really hearing himself.

The old man turned to look at him, blinking in surprise and fear. "Liff me alone, boy," he said. He raised his walking-stick and brandished it clumsily in Jake's direction.

"Would you know if there's a place called Markey Academy anyplace around here, sir?" This was utter desperation, but it was the only thing he could think to ask.

The old man slowly lowered his stick—it was the *sir* that had done it. He looked at Jake with the slightly lunatic interest of the old and almost senile. "How come you not in school, boy?"

Jake smiled wearily. This one was getting very old. "Finals Week. I came down here to look up an old friend of mine who goes to Markey Academy, that's all. Sorry to have bothered you."

He stepped around the old man (hoping he wouldn't decide to whop him one across the ass with his cane just for good luck) and was almost down to the corner when the old man yelled: "Boy! Bo*yyyyy*!"

Jake turned around.

"There is no Markey Akidimy down here," the old man said. "Twenty-two years I'm living here, so I should know. Markey *Avenue*, yes, but no Markey Akidimy."

Jake's stomach cramped with sudden excitement. He took a step back toward the old man, who at once raised his cane into a defensive position again. Jake stopped at once, leaving a twenty-foot safety zone between them. "Where's Markey Avenue, sir? Can you tell me that?"

"Of *gorse*," the old man said. "Didn't I just say I'm livink here twenty-two years? Two blogs down. Turn left at the Majestic Theatre. But I'm tellink you now, there iss no Markey Akidimy."

"Thank you, sir! Thank you!"

Jake turned around and looked up Castle Avenue. Yes—he could see the unmistakable shape of a movie marquee jutting out over the sidewalk a couple of blocks up. He started to run toward it, then decided that might attract attention and slowed down to a fast walk.

The old man watched him go. "*Sir!*" he said to himself in a tone of mild amazement. "*Sir*, yet!"

He chuckled rustily and moved on.

17

ROLAND'S BAND STOPPED AT dusk. The gunslinger dug a shallow pit and lit a fire. They didn't need it for cooking purposes, but they needed it, nonetheless. *Eddie* needed it. If he was going to finish his carving, he would need light to work by.

The gunslinger looked around and saw Susannah, a dark silhouette against the fading aquamarine sky, but he didn't see Eddie.

"Where is he?" he asked.

"Down the road apiece. You leave him alone now, Roland—you've done enough."

Roland nodded, bent over the firepit, and struck at a piece of flint with a worn steel bar. Soon the kindling he had gathered was blazing. He added small sticks, one by one, and waited for Eddie to return.

18

HALF A MILE BACK the way they had come, Eddie sat cross-legged in the middle of the Great Road with his unfinished key in one hand, watching the sky. He glanced down the road, saw the spark of the fire, and knew exactly what Roland was doing . . . and why. Then he turned his gaze to the sky again. He had never felt so lonely or so afraid.

The sky was *huge*—he could not remember ever seeing so much uninterrupted space, so much pure emptiness. It made him feel very small, and he supposed there was nothing at all wrong with that. In the scheme of things, he *was* very small.

The boy was close now. He thought he knew where Jake was and what he was about to do, and it filled him with silent wonder. Susannah had come from 1963. Eddie had come from 1987. Between them . . . Jake. Trying to come over. Trying to be born.

I met him, Eddie thought. *I must have met him, and I think I remember . . . sort of. It was just before Henry went into the Army, right? He was taking courses at Brooklyn Vocational Institute, and he was heavily into black—black jeans, black motorcycle boots with steel caps, black T-shirts with the sleeves rolled up. Henry's James Dean look. Smoking Area Chic. I used to think that, but I never said it out loud, because I didn't want him pissed at me.*

He realized that what he had been waiting for had happened while he was thinking: Old Star had come out. In fifteen minutes, maybe less, it would be joined by a whole galaxy of alien jewelry, but for now it gleamed alone in the ungathered darkness.

Eddie slowly held up the key until Old Star gleamed within its wide central notch. And then he recited the old formula of his world, the one his mother had taught him as she knelt beside him at the bedroom window, both of them looking out at the evening star which rode the oncoming darkness above the rooftops and fire-escapes of Brooklyn: "Star light, star bright, first star I see tonight; wish I may, wish I might, have the wish I wish tonight."

Old Star glowed in the notch of the key, a diamond caught in ash.

"Help me find some guts," Eddie said. "That's my wish. Help me find the guts to try and finish this damned thing."

He sat there a moment longer, then got to his feet and walked slowly back to camp. He sat down as close to the fire as he could get, took the gunslinger's knife without a word to either him or Susannah, and began to work. Tiny, curling slivers of wood rolled up from the *s*-shape at the end of the key. Eddie worked fast, turning the key this way and that, occasionally closing his eyes and letting his thumb slip along the mild curves. He tried not to think about what might happen if the shape were to go wrong—that would freeze him for sure.

Roland and Susannah sat behind him, watching silently. At last Eddie put the knife aside. His face was running with sweat. "This kid of yours," he said. "This Jake. He must be a gutty brat."

"He was brave under the mountains," Roland said. "He was afraid, but never gave an inch."

"I wish I could be that way."

Roland shrugged. "At Balazar's you fought well even though they had taken your clothes. It's very hard for a man to fight naked, but you did it."

Eddie tried to remember the shootout in the nightclub, but it was just a blur in his mind—smoke, noise, and light shining through one wall in confused, intersecting rays. He thought that wall had been torn apart by automatic-weapons fire, but couldn't remember for sure.

He held the key up so its notches were sharply outlined against the flames. He held it that way for a long time, looking mostly at the s-shape. It looked exactly as he remembered it from his dream and from the momentary vision he had seen in the fire . . . but it didn't *feel* exactly right. Almost, but not quite.

That's just Henry again. That's just all those years of never being quite good enough. You did it, buddy—it's just that the Henry inside doesn't want to admit it.

He dropped the key onto the square of hide and folded the edges carefully around it. "I'm done. I don't know if it's right or not, but I guess it's as right as I can make it." He felt oddly empty now that he no longer had the key to work on—purposeless and directionless.

"Do you want something to eat, Eddie?" Susannah asked quietly.

There's your purpose, he thought. *There's your direction. Sitting right over there, with her hands folded in her lap. All the purpose and direction you'll ever—*

But now something else rose in his mind—it came all at once. Not a dream . . . not a vision . . .

No, not either of those. It's a memory. It's happening again—you're remembering forward in time.

"I have to do something else first," he said, and got up.

On the far side of the fire, Roland had stacked some odd lots of scavenged wood. Eddie hunted through them and found a dry stick about two feet long and four inches or so through the middle. He took it, returning to his place by the fire, and picked up Roland's knife again. This time he worked faster because he was simply sharpening the stick, turning it into something that looked like a small tent-peg.

"Can we get moving before daybreak?" he asked the gunslinger. "I think we should get to that circle as soon as we can."

"Yes. Sooner, if we must. I don't want to move in the dark—a speaking ring is an unsafe place to be at night—but if we have to, we have to."

"From the look on your face, big boy, I doubt if those stone circles are very safe *any* time," Susannah said.

Eddie put the knife aside again. The dirt Roland had taken out of the shallow hole he'd made for the campfire was piled up by Eddie's right foot. Now he used the sharp end of the stick to carve a question-mark shape in the dirt. The shape was crisp and clear.

"Okay," he said, brushing it away. "All done."

"Have something to eat, then," Susannah said.

Eddie tried, but he wasn't very hungry. When he finally went to sleep, nestled against Susannah's warmth, his rest was dreamless but very thin. Until the gunslinger shook him awake at four in the morning, he heard the wind racing endlessly over the plain below them, and it seemed to him that he went with it, flying high into the night, away from these cares, while Old Star and Old Mother rode serenely above him, painting his cheeks with frost.

19

"It's time," Roland said.

Eddie sat up. Susannah sat up beside him, rubbing her palms over her face. As Eddie's head cleared, his mind was filled with urgency. "Yes. Let's go, and fast."

"He's getting close, isn't he?"

"Very close." Eddie got to his feet, grasped Susannah around the waist, and boosted her into her chair.

She was looking at him anxiously. "Do we still have enough time to get there?"

Eddie nodded. "Barely."

Three minutes later they were headed down the Great Road again. It glimmered ahead of them like a ghost. And an hour after that, as the first light of dawn began to touch the sky in the east, a rhythmic sound began far ahead of them.

The sound of drums, Roland thought.

Machinery, Eddie thought. Some huge piece of machinery.

It's a heart, Susannah thought. *Some huge, diseased, beating heart . . . and it's in that city, where we have to go.*

Two hours later, the sound stopped as suddenly as it had begun. White, featureless clouds had begun to fill the sky above them, first veiling the early sun, then blotting it out. The circle of standing stones lay less than five miles ahead now, gleaming in the shadowless light like the teeth of a fallen monster.

20

SPAGHETTI WEEK AT THE MAJESTIC!

the battered, dispirited marquee jutting over the corner of Brooklyn and Markey Avenues proclaimed.

2 SERGIO LEONE CLASSIX!
A FISTFUL OF $$ PLUS GOOD BAD & UGLY!
99¢ ALL SHOWS

A gum-chewing cutie with rollers in her blonde hair sat in the box office listening to Led Zep on her transistor and reading one of the tabloids of which Mrs. Shaw was so fond. To her left, in the theater's remaining display case, there was a poster showing Clint Eastwood.

Jake knew he should get moving—three o'clock was almost here— but he paused a moment anyway, staring at the poster behind the dirty, cracked glass. Eastwood was wearing a Mexican serape. A cigar was clamped in his teeth. He had thrown one side of the serape back over his shoulder to free his gun. His eyes were a pale, faded blue. Bombardier's eyes.

It's not him, Jake thought, *but it's* almost *him. It's the eyes, mostly . . . the eyes are almost the same.*

"You let me drop," he said to the man in the old poster, the man who was not Roland. "You let me die. What happens this time?"

"Hey, kid," the blonde ticket-seller called, making Jake start. "You gonna come in or just stand there and talk to yourself?"

"Not me," Jake said. "I've already seen those two."

He got moving again, turning left on Markey Avenue.

Once again he waited for the feeling of *remembering forward* to seize him, but it didn't come. This was just a hot, sunny street lined with sandstone-colored apartment buildings that looked like prison cellblocks to Jake. A few young women were walking along, pushing baby-carriages in pairs and talking desultorily, but the street was otherwise deserted. It was unseasonably hot for May—too hot to stroll.

What am I looking for? What?

From behind him came a burst of raucous male laughter. It was followed by an outraged female shriek: "You give that *back!*"

Jake jumped, thinking the owner of the voice must mean him.

"Give it *back*, Henry! I'm not kidding!"

Jake turned and saw two boys, one at least eighteen and the other a lot younger . . . twelve or thirteen. At the sight of this second boy, Jake's heart did something that felt like a loop-the-loop in his chest. The kid was wearing green corduroys instead of madras shorts, but the yellow T-shirt was the same, and he had a battered old basketball under one arm. Although his back was to Jake, Jake knew he had found the boy from last night's dream.

21

THE GIRL WAS THE gum-chewing cutie from the ticket-booth. The older of the two boys—who looked almost old enough to be called a man— had her newspaper in his hands. She grabbed for it. The newspaper-grabber—he was wearing denims and a black T-shirt with the sleeves rolled up—held it over his head and grinned.

"Jump for it, Maryanne! Jump, girl, jump!"

She stared at him with angry eyes, her cheeks flushed. "Give it to me!" she said. "Quit fooling around and give it back! *Bastard!*"

"Oooo wisten to *dat*, Eddie!" the old kid said. "Bad wang-gwidge! Naughty, naughty!" He waved the newspaper just out of the blonde ticket-seller's grasp, grinning, and Jake suddenly understood. These two were walking home from school together—although they probably didn't go to the same one, if he was right about the difference in their ages—and the bigger boy had gone over to the box office, pretending he had something interesting to tell the blonde. Then he had reached through the slot at the bottom and snatched her paper.

The big boy's face was one that Jake had seen before; it was the face of a kid who would think it the height of hilarity to douse a cat's tail with lighter fluid or feed a bread-ball with a fishhook planted in the middle to a hungry dog. The sort of kid who sat in the back of the room and snapped bra-straps and then said "Who me?" with a big, dumb look of surprise on his face when someone finally complained. There weren't many kids like him at Piper, but there were a few. Jake supposed there were a few in every school. They dressed better at Piper, but the face was the same. He guessed that in the old days, people would have said it was the face of a boy who was born to be hung.

Maryanne jumped for her newspaper, which the old boy in the black pants had rolled into a tube. He pulled it out of her reach just before she could grab it, then whacked her on the head with it, the way you might whack a dog for piddling on the carpet. She was beginning to cry now—mostly from humiliation, Jake guessed. Her face was now so red it was almost glowing. "Keep it, then!" she yelled at him. "I know you can't read, but you can look at the pictures, at least!"

She began to turn away.

"Give it back, why don't you?" the younger boy—Jake's boy—said softly.

The old boy held out the newspaper tube. The girl snatched it from him, and even from his place thirty feet farther down the street, Jake heard it rip. "You're a turd, Henry Dean!" she cried. "A real *turd!*"

"Hey, what's the big deal?" Henry sounded genuinely injured. "It was just a joke. Besides, it only ripped in one place—you can still read it, for Chrissake. Lighten up a little, why don'tcha?"

And that was right, too, Jake thought. Guys like this Henry always pushed even the most unfunny joke two steps too far . . . then looked wounded and misunderstood when someone yelled at them. And it was always *Wassa matter?* and it was *Can'tcha take a joke?* and it was *Why don'tcha lighten up a little?*

What are you doing with him, kid? Jake wondered. *If you're on my side, what are you doing with a jerk like that?*

But as the younger kid turned around and they started to walk down the street again, Jake knew. The old boy's features were heavier, and his complexion was badly pitted with acne, but otherwise the resemblance was striking. The two boys were brothers.

22

JAKE TURNED AWAY AND began to idle up the sidewalk ahead of the two boys. He reached into his breast pocket with a shaky hand, pulled out his father's sunglasses, and managed to fumble them onto his face.

Voices swelled behind him, as if someone was gradually turning up the volume on a radio.

"You shouldn't have ranked on her that bad, Henry. It was mean."

"She loves it, Eddie." Henry's voice was complacent, worldly-wise. "When you get a little older, you'll understand."

"She was *cryin.*"

"Prob'ly got the rag on," Henry said in a philosophical tone.

They were very close now. Jake shrank against the side of the building. His head was down, his hands stuffed deep into the pockets of his jeans. He didn't know why it seemed so vitally important that he not be noticed, but it did. Henry didn't matter, one way or the other, but—

The younger one isn't supposed to remember me, he thought. *I don't know why, exactly, but he's not.*

They passed him without so much as a glance, the one Henry had called Eddie walking on the outside, dribbling the basketball along the gutter.

"You gotta admit she looked funny," Henry was saying. "Ole Be-Bop Maryanne, jumpin for her newspaper. Woof! Woof!"

Eddie looked up at his brother with an expression that wanted to be reproachful . . . and then he gave up and dissolved into laughter. Jake saw the unconditional love in that upturned face and guessed that Eddie would forgive a lot in his big brother before giving it up as a bad job.

"So are we going?" Eddie asked now. "You said we could. After school."

"I said *maybe.* I dunno if I wanna walk all the way over there. Mom'll be home by now, too. Maybe we just oughtta forget it. Go upstairs and watch some tube."

They were now ten feet ahead of Jake and pulling away.

"Ah, come on! You *said!*"

Beyond the building the two boys were currently passing was a chainlink fence with an open gate in it. Beyond it, Jake saw, was the playground of which he had dreamed last night . . . a version of it, anyway. It wasn't surrounded by trees, and there was no odd subway kiosk with diagonal slashes of yellow and black across the front, but the cracked concrete was the same. So were the faded yellow foul lines.

"Well . . . maybe. I dunno." Jake realized Henry was teasing again. Eddie didn't, though; he was too anxious about wherever it was he wanted to go. "Let's shoot some hoops while I think it over."

He stole the ball from his younger brother, dribbled clumsily onto the playground, and went for a lay-up that hit high on the backboard and bounced back without even touching the rim of the hoop. Henry was good at stealing newspapers from teenage girls, Jake thought, but on the basketball court he sucked the big one.

Eddie walked in through the gate, unbuttoned his corduroy pants, and slipped them down. Beneath them were the faded madras shorts he had been wearing in Jake's dream.

"Oh, is he wearing his shortie panties?" Henry said. "Ain't they *cuuute*?" He waited until his brother balanced himself on one leg to pull off his cords, then flung the basketball at him. Eddie managed to bat it away, probably saving himself a bloody nose, but he lost his balance and fell clumsily to the concrete. He didn't cut himself, but he could have done so, Jake saw; a great deal of broken glass glittered in the sun along the chainlink.

"Come on, Henry, quit it," he said, but with no real reproach. Jake guessed Henry had been pulling shit like this on him so long that Eddie only noticed it when Henry pulled it on someone else—someone like the blonde ticket-seller.

"Tum on, Henwy, twit it."

Eddie got to his feet and trotted out onto the court. The ball had struck the chainlink fence and bounced back to Henry. Henry now tried to dribble past his younger brother. Eddie's hand went out, lightning-quick but oddly delicate, and stole the ball. He easily ducked under Henry's outstretched, flailing arm and went for the basket. Henry dogged him, frowning thunderously, but he might as well have been taking a nap. Eddie went up, knees bent, feet neatly cocked, and laid the ball in. Henry grabbed it and dribbled out to the stripe.

Shouldn't have done that, Eddie, Jake thought. He was standing just beyond the place where the fence ended, watching the two boys. This seemed safe enough, at least for the moment. He was wearing his dad's sunglasses, and the two boys were so involved in what they were doing that they wouldn't have noticed if President Carter had strolled up to watch. Jake doubted if Henry knew who President Carter was, anyway.

He expected Henry to foul his brother, perhaps heavily, as a payback for the steal, but he had underestimated Eddie's guile. Henry offered a head-fake that wouldn't have fooled Jake's mother, but Eddie appeared to fall for it. Henry broke past him and drove for the basket, gaily travel-ling the ball most of the way. Jake was quite sure Eddie could have caught him easily and stolen the ball again, but instead of doing so, the kid hung back. Henry laid it up—clumsily—and the ball bounced off the rim again. Eddie grabbed it . . . and then let it squirt through his fingers. Henry snatched it, turned, and put it through the netless hoop.

"One-up," Henry panted. "Play to twelve?"

"Sure."

Jake had seen enough. It would be close, but in the end Henry would win. Eddie would see to it. It would do more than save him from getting lumped up; it would put Henry in a good mood, making him more agreeable to whatever it was Eddie wanted to do.

Hey Moose—I think your little brother has been playing you like a violin for a long time now, and you don't have the slightest idea, do you?

He drew back until the apartment building which stood at the north end of the court cut off his view of the Dean brothers, and their view of him. He leaned against the wall and listened to the thump of the ball on the court. Soon Henry was puffing like Charlie the Choo-Choo going up a steep hill. He would be a smoker, of course; guys like Henry were always smokers.

The game took almost ten minutes, and by the time Henry claimed victory, the street was filled up with other home-going kids. A few gave Jake curious glances as they passed by.

"Good game, Henry," Eddie said.

"Not bad," Henry panted. "You're still falling for the old head-fake."

Sure he is, Jake thought. *I think he'll go on falling for it until he's gained about eighty pounds. Then you might get a surprise.*

"I guess I am. Hey, Henry, can't we *please* go look at the place?"

"Yeah, why not? Let's do it."

"All *right!*" Eddie yelled. There was the smacking sound of flesh on flesh; probably Eddie giving his brother a high-five. "Boss!"

"You go on up to the apartment. Tell Mom we'll be in by four-thirty, quarter of five. But don't say anything about The Mansion. She'd have a shit-fit. She thinks it's haunted, too."

"You want me to tell her we're going over Dewey's?"

Silence as Henry considered this. "Naw. She might call Mrs. Bunkowski. Tell her . . . tell her we're goin down to Dahlie's to get Hoodsie Rockets. She'll believe that. Ask her for a coupla bucks, too."

"She won't give me any money. Not two days before payday."

"Bullshit. You can get it out of her. Go on, now."

"Okay." But Jake didn't hear Eddie moving. "Henry?"

"*What?*" Impatiently.

"*Is* The Mansion haunted, do you think?"

Jake sidled a little closer to the playground. He didn't want to be noticed, but he strongly felt that he needed to hear this.

"Naw. There ain't no *real* haunted houses—just in the fuckin movies."

"Oh." There was unmistakable relief in Eddie's voice.

"But if there ever *was* one," Henry resumed (perhaps he didn't want his little brother feeling *too* relieved, Jake thought), "it'd be The Mansion. I heard that a couple of years ago, two kids from Norwood Street went in there to bump uglies and the cops found em with their throats cut and all the blood drained out of their bodies. But there wasn't any blood on em or around em. Get it? The blood was *all gone.*"

"You shittin me?" Eddie breathed.

"Nope. But that wasn't the worst thing."

"What was?"

"Their hair was dead white," Henry said. The voice that drifted to Jake was solemn. He had an idea that Henry wasn't teasing this time, that this time he believed every word he was saying. (He also doubted that Henry had brains enough to make such a story up.) "Both of em. And their eyes were wide open and staring, like they saw the most gross-awful thing in the world."

"Aw, gimme a break," Eddie said, but his voice was soft, awed.

"You still wanna go?"

"Sure. As long as we don't . . . you know, hafta get too close."

"Then go see Mom. And try to get a couple of bucks out of her. I need cigarettes. Take the fuckin ball up, too."

Jake drifted backward and stepped into the nearest apartment building entryway just as Eddie came out through the playground gate.

To his horror, the boy in the yellow T-shirt turned in Jake's direction. *Holy crow!* he thought, dismayed. *What if this is his building?*

It was. Jake just had time to turn around and began to scan the names beside the rank of buzzers before Eddie Dean brushed past him, so close that Jake could smell the sweat he had worked up on the basketball court. He half-sensed, half-saw the curious glance the boy tossed in his direction. Then Eddie was in the lobby and headed for the elevators with his school-pants bundled under one arm and the scuffed basketball under the other.

Jake's heart was thudding heavily in his chest. Shadowing people was a lot harder in real life than it was in the detective novels he sometimes read. He crossed the street and stood between two apartment buildings half a block up. From here he could see both the entrance to the Dean brothers' building and the playground. The playground was filling up now, mostly with little kids. Henry leaned against the chainlink, smoking a cigarette and trying to look full of teenage angst. Every now and then he would stick out a foot as one of the little kids bolted toward him at an all-out run, and before Eddie returned, he had succeeded in tripping three of them. The last of these went sprawling full-length, smacking his face on the concrete, and ran wailing up the street with a bloody forehead. Henry flicked his cigarette butt after him and laughed cheerfully.

Just an all-around fun guy, Jake thought.

After that, the little kids wised up and began giving him a wide berth. Henry strolled out of the playground and down the street to the apartment building Eddie had entered five minutes before. As he reached it, the door opened and Eddie came out. He had changed into a pair of jeans and a fresh T-shirt; he had also tied a green bandanna, the same one he had been wearing in Jake's dream, around his forehead. He was waving a couple of dollar bills triumphantly. Henry snatched them, then asked Eddie something. Eddie nodded, and the two boys set off.

Keeping half a block between himself and them, Jake followed.

23

THEY STOOD IN THE high grass at the edge of the Great Road, looking at the speaking ring.

Stonehenge, Susannah thought, and shuddered. *That's what it looks like. Stonehenge.*

Although the thick grass which covered the plain grew around the bases of the tall gray monoliths, the circle they enclosed was bare earth, littered here and there with white things.

"What are those?" she asked in a low voice. "Chips of stone?"

"Look again," Roland said.

She did, and saw that they were bones. The bones of small animals, maybe. She hoped.

Eddie switched the sharpened stick to his left hand, dried the palm of his right against his shirt, and then switched it back again. He opened his mouth, but no sound came from his dry throat. He cleared it and tried again. "I think I'm supposed to go in and draw something in the dirt."

Roland nodded. "Now?"

"Soon." He looked into Roland's face. "There's something here, isn't there? Something we can't see."

"It's not here right now," Roland said. "At least, I don't *think* it is. But it will come. Our *khef*—our life-force—will draw it. And, of course, it will be jealous of its place. Give me my gun back, Eddie."

Eddie unbuckled the belt and handed it over. Then he turned back to the circle of twenty-foot-high stones. Something lived in there, all right. He could smell it, a stench that made him think of damp plaster and moldering sofas and ancient mattresses rotting beneath half-liquid coats of mildew. It was familiar, that smell.

The Mansion—I smelled it there. The day I talked Henry into taking me over to see The Mansion on Rhinehold Street, in Dutch Hill.

Roland buckled his gunbelt, then bent to knot the tiedown. He looked up at Susannah as he did it. "We may need Detta Walker," he said. "Is she around?"

"That bitch always around." Susannah wrinkled her nose.

"Good. One of us is going to have to protect Eddie while he does what he's supposed to do. The other is going to be so much useless baggage. This is a demon's place. Demons are not human, but they are male and female, just the same. Sex is both their weapon and their weakness. No matter what the sex of the demon may be, it will go for Eddie. To protect its place. To keep its place from being used by an outsider. Do you understand?"

Susannah nodded. Eddie appeared not to be listening. He had tucked the square of hide containing the key into his shirt and now he was staring into the speaking ring as if hypnotized.

"There's no time to say this in a gentle or refined way," Roland told her. "One of us will—"

"One of us gonna have to fuck it to keep it off Eddie," Susannah interrupted. "This the sort of thing can't *ever* turn down a free fuck. That's what you're gettin at, isn't it?"

Roland nodded.

Her eyes gleamed. They were the eyes of Detta Walker now, both wise and unkind, shining with hard amusement, and her voice slid steadily deeper into the bogus Southern plantation drawl which was Delta's trademark. "If it's a girl demon, you git it. But if it's a boy demon, it's mine. That about it?"

Roland nodded.

"What about if it swings both ways? What about *that*, big boy?"

Roland's lips twitched in the barest suggestion of a smile. "Then we'll take it together. Just remember—"

Beside them, in a fainting, distant voice, Eddie murmured: "Not all is silent in the halls of the dead. Behold, the sleeper wakes." He turned his haunted, terrified eyes on Roland. "There's a monster."

"The demon—"

"No. A *monster*. Something between the doors—between the *worlds*. Something that waits. *And it's opening its eyes.*"

Susannah cast a frightened glance at Roland.

"Stand, Eddie," Roland said. "Be true."

Eddie drew a deep breath. "I'll stand until it knocks me down," he said. "I have to go in now. It's starting to happen."

"We all goin in," Susannah said. She arched her back and slipped out of her wheelchair. "Any demon want to fuck wit' me he goan find out he's fuckin wit' the finest. I th'ow him a fuck he ain't *never* goan f'git."

As they passed between two of the tall stones and into the speaking circle, it began to rain.

24

AS SOON AS JAKE saw the place, he understood two things: first, that he had seen it before, in dreams so terrible his conscious mind would not let him remember them; second, that it was a place of death and murder and madness. He was standing on the far corner of Rhinehold Street and Brooklyn Avenue, seventy yards from Henry and Eddie Dean, but even from where he was he could feel The Mansion ignoring them and reaching for him with its eager invisible hands. He thought there were talons at the ends of those hands. Sharp ones.

It wants me, and I can't run away. It's death to go in . . . but it's madness not to. Because somewhere inside that place is a locked door. I have the key that will open it, and the only salvation I can hope for is on the other side.

He stared at The Mansion, a house that almost screamed abnormality, with a sinking heart. It stood in the center of its weedy, rioting yard like a tumor.

The Dean brothers had walked across nine blocks of Brooklyn, moving slowly under the hot afternoon sun, and had finally entered a section of town which had to be Dutch Hill, given the names on the shops and stores. Now they stood halfway down the block, in front of The Mansion. It looked as if it had been deserted for years, yet it had suffered remarkably little vandalism. And once, Jake thought, it really *had* been a mansion—the home, perhaps, of a wealthy merchant and his large family. In those long-gone days it must have been white, but now it was a dirty gray no-color. The windows had been knocked out and the peeling picket fence which surrounded it had been spray-painted, but the house itself was still intact.

It slumped in the hot light, a ramshackle slate-roofed revenant growing out of a hummocky trash-littered yard, somehow making Jake think of a dangerous dog which pretended to be asleep. Its steep roof overhung the front porch like a beetling brow. The boards of the porch were splintery and warped. Shutters which might once have been green leaned askew beside the glassless windows; ancient curtains still hung in some of these, dangling like strips of dead skin. To the left, an elderly trellis leaned away from the building, now held up not by nails but only by the nameless and somehow filthy clusters of vine which crawled over it. There was a sign on the lawn and another on the door. From where Jake stood, he could read neither of them.

The house was *alive*. He knew this, could feel its awareness reaching out from the boards and the slumping roof, could feel it pouring in rivers from the black sockets of its windows. The idea of approaching that terrible place filled him with dismay; the idea of actually going inside filled him with inarticulate horror. Yet he would have to. He could hear a low, slumbrous buzzing in his ears—the sound of a beehive on a hot summer day—and for a moment he was afraid he might faint. He closed his eyes . . . and *his* voice filled his head.

You must *come, Jake. This is the path of the Beam, the way of the Tower, and the time of your Drawing. Be true; stand; come to me.*

The fear didn't pass, but that terrible sense of impending panic did. He opened his eyes again and saw that he was not the only one who had sensed the power and awakening sentience of the place. Eddie was trying to pull away from the fence. He turned toward Jake, who could see Eddie's eyes, wide and uneasy beneath his green head-band. His big brother grabbed him and pushed him toward the rusty gate, but the gesture was too half-hearted to be much of a tease; however thick-headed he might be, Henry liked The Mansion no better than Eddie did.

They drew away a little and stood looking at the place for a while. Jake could not make out what they were saying to each other, but the tone of their voices was awed and uneasy. Jake suddenly remembered Eddie speaking in his dream: *Remember there's danger, though. Be careful . . . and be quick.*

Suddenly the real Eddie, the one across the street, raised his voice enough so that Jake could make out the words. "Can we go home now, Henry? Please? I don't like it." His tone was pleading.

"Fuckin little sissy," Henry said, but Jake thought he heard relief as well as indulgence in Henry's voice. "Come on."

They turned away from the ruined house crouching high-shouldered behind its sagging fence and approached the street. Jake backed up, then turned and looked into the window of the dispirited little hole-in-the-wall shop called Dutch Hill Used Appliances. He watched Henry and Eddie, dim and ghostly reflections superimposed on an ancient Hoover vacuum cleaner, cross Rhinehold Street.

"Are you *sure* it's not really haunted?" Eddie asked as they stepped onto the sidewalk on Jake's side.

"Well, I tell you what," Henry said. "Now that I been out here again, I'm really not so sure."

They passed directly behind Jake without looking at him. "Would you go in there?" Eddie asked.

"Not for a million dollars," Henry replied promptly.

They rounded the corner. Jake stepped away from the window and peeped after them. They were headed back the way they had come, close together on the sidewalk, Henry hulking along in his steel-toed shit-kickers, his shoulders already slumped like those of a much older man, Eddie walking beside him with neat, unconscious grace. Their shadows, long and trailing out into the street now, mingled amicably together.

They're going home, Jake thought, and felt a wave of loneliness so strong that he felt it would crush him. *Going to eat supper and do homework and argue over which TV shows to watch and then go to bed. Henry may be a bullying shit, but they've got a life, those two, one that makes sense . . . and they're going back to it. I wonder if they have any idea of how lucky they are. Eddie might, I suppose.*

Jake turned, adjusted the straps of his pack, and crossed Rhinehold Street.

25

SUSANNAH SENSED MOVEMENT IN the empty grassland beyond the circle of standing stones: a sighing, whispering rush.

"Something comin," she said tautly. "Comin fast."

"Be careful," Eddie said, "but keep it off me. You understand? Keep it off me."

"I hear you, Eddie. You just do your own thing."

Eddie nodded. He knelt in the center of the ring, holding the sharpened stick out in front of him as if assessing its point. Then he lowered it and drew a dark straight line in the dirt. "Roland, watch out for her . . ."

"I will if I can, Eddie."

". . . but keep it off me. Jake's coming. Crazy little mother's really coming."

Susannah could now see the grasses due north of the speaking ring parting in a long dark line, creating a furrow that lanced straight at the circle of stones.

"Get ready," Roland said. "It'll go for Eddie. One of us will have to ambush it."

Susannah reared up on her haunches like a snake coming out of a Hindu fakir's basket. Her hands, rolled into hard brown fists, were held at the sides of her face. Her eyes blazed. "I'm ready," she said and then shouted: *"Come on, big boy! You come on right now! Run like it's yo birfday!"*

The rain began to fall harder as the demon which lived here re-entered its circle in a booming rush. Susannah had just time to sense thick and merciless masculinity—it came to her as an eyewatering smell of gin and juniper—and then it shot toward the center of the circle. She closed her eyes and reached for it, not with her arms or her mind but with all the female force which lived at the core of her: *Hey, big boy! Where you goan? D'pussy be ovah heah!*

It whirled. She felt its surprise . . . and then its raw hunger, as full and urgent as a pulsing artery. It leaped upon her like a rapist springing from the mouth of an alley.

Susannah howled and rocked backward, cords standing out on her neck. The dress she wore first flattened against her breasts and belly, and then began to tear itself to shreds. She could hear a pointless, directionless panting, as if the air itself had decided to rut with her.

"Suze!" Eddie shouted, and began to get to his feet.

"No!" she screamed back. *"Do it! I got this sumbitch right where . . . right where I want him! Go on, Eddie! Bring the kid! Bring—"*
Coldness battered at the tender flesh between her legs. She grunted, fell

backward . . then supported herself with one hand and thrust defiantly forward and upward. *"Bring him through!"*

Eddie looked uncertainly at Roland, who nodded. Eddie glanced at Susannah again, his eyes full of dark pain and darker fear, and then deliberately turned his back on both of them and fell to his knees again. He reached forward with the sharpened stick which had become a make-shift pencil, ignoring the cold rain falling on his arms and the back of his neck. The stick began to move, making lines and angles, creating a shape Roland knew at once.

It was a door.

26

JAKE REACHED OUT, PUT his hands on the splintery gate, and pushed. It swung slowly open on screaming, rust-clotted hinges. Ahead of him was an uneven brick path. Beyond the path was the porch. Beyond the porch was the door. It had been boarded shut.

He walked slowly toward the house, heart telegraphing fast dots and dashes in his throat. Weeds had grown up between the buckled bricks. He could hear them rustling against his bluejeans. All his senses seemed to have been turned up two notches. *You're not really going in there, are you?* a panic-stricken voice in his head asked.

And the answer that occurred to him seemed both totally nuts and perfectly reasonable: *All things serve the Beam.*

The sign on the lawn read

ABSOLUTELY *NO TRESPASSING* UNDER PENALTY OF LAW!

The yellowing, rust-stained square of paper nailed to one of the boards crisscrossing the front door was more succinct:

BY ORDER OF NYC HOUSING AUTHORITY
THIS PROPERTY CONDEMNED

Jake paused at the foot of the steps, looking up at the door. He had heard voices in the vacant lot and now he could hear them again . . . but this was a choir of the damned, a babble of insane threats and equally insane promises. Yet he thought it was all one voice. The voice of the house; the voice of some monstrous doorkeeper, roused from its long unpeaceful sleep.

He thought briefly of his father's Ruger, even considered pulling it out of his pack, but what good would it do? Behind him, traffic passed back and forth on Rhinehold Street and a woman was yelling for her daughter to stop holding hands with that boy and bring in the wash, but here was another world, one ruled by some bleak being over whom guns could have no power.

Be true, Jake—stand.

"Okay," he said in a low, shaky voice. "Okay, I'll try. But you better not drop me again."

Slowly, he began to mount the porch steps.

27

THE BOARDS WHICH BARRED the door were old and rotten, the nails rusty. Jake grabbed hold of the top set at the point where they crossed each other and yanked. They came free with a squall that was the gate all over again. He tossed them over the porch rail and into an ancient flowerbed where only witchgrass and dogweed grew. He bent, grasped the lower crossing . . . and paused for a moment.

A hollow sound came through the door; the sound of some animal slobbering hungrily from deep inside a concrete pipe. Jake felt a sick sheen of sweat begin to break out on his cheeks and forehead. He was so frightened that he no longer felt precisely real; he seemed to have become a character in someone else's bad dream.

The evil choir, the evil presence, was behind this door. The sound of it seeped out like syrup.

He yanked at the lower boards. They came free easily.

Of course. It wants me to come in. It's hungry, and I'm supposed to be the main course.

A snatch of poetry occurred to him suddenly, something Ms. Avery had read to them. It was supposed to be about the plight of modern man, who was cut off from all his roots and traditions, but to Jake it suddenly seemed that the man who had written that poem must have seen this house: *I will show you something different from either/Your shadow in the morning striding behind you/Or your shadow at evening rising to meet you;/I will show you . . .*

"I'll show you fear in a handful of dust," Jake muttered, and put his hand on the doorknob. And as he did, that clear sense of relief and surety flooded him again, the feeling that this was it, this time the door would open on that other world, he would see a sky untouched by smog and industrial smoke, and, on the far horizon, not the mountains but the hazy blue spires of some gorgeous unknown city.

He closed his fingers around the silver key in his pocket, hoping the door was locked so he could use it. It wasn't. The hinges screamed and flakes of rust sifted down from their slowly revolving cylinders as the door opened. The smell of decay struck Jake like a physical blow: wet wood, spongy plaster, rotting laths, ancient stuffing. Below these smells was another—the smell of some beast's lair. Ahead was a dank, shadowy hallway. To the left, a staircase pitched and yawed its crazy way into the upper shadows. Its collapsed bannister lay splintered on the hallway floor, but Jake was not foolish enough to think it was *just* splinters he was looking at. There were bones in that litter, as well—the bones of small animals. Some did not look precisely like animal bones, and these Jake would not look at overlong; he knew he would never summon the courage to go further if he did. He paused on the threshold, screwing himself up to take the first step. He heard a faint, muffled sound, very hard and very rapid, and realized it was his own teeth chattering in his head.

Why doesn't someone stop me? he thought wildly. *Why doesn't somebody passing on the sidewalk shout "Hey, you! You're not supposed to be in there—can'tcha read?"*

But he knew why. Pedestrians stuck mostly to the other side of this street, and those who came near this house did not linger.

Even if someone did happen to look, they wouldn't see me, because I'm not really here. For better or worse, I've already left my world behind. I've started to cross over. His *world is somewhere ahead. This* . . .

This was the hell between.

Jake stepped into the corridor, and although he screamed when the door swung shut behind him with the sound of a mausoleum door being slammed, he wasn't surprised.

Down deep, he wasn't surprised at all.

28

ONCE UPON A TIME there had been a young woman named Detta Walker who liked to frequent the honky-tonks and roadhouses along Ridgeline Road outside of Nutley and on Route 88 down by the power-lines, out-side of Amhigh. She had had legs in those days, and, as the song says, she knew how to use them. She would wear some tight cheap dress that looked like silk but wasn't and dance with the white boys while the band played all those ofay party tunes like "Double Shot of My Baby's Love" and "The Hippy-Hippy Shake." Eventually she would cut one of the honkeys out of the pack and let him lead her back to his car in the parking lot. There she would make out with him (one of the world's great soul-kissers was Detta Walker, and no slouch with the old fingernails, either) until he was just about insane . . . and then she'd shut him down. What happened next? Well, that was the question, wasn't it? That was the game. Some of them wept and begged—all right, but not great. Some of them raved and roared, which was better.

And although she had been slapped upside the head, punched in the eye, spat upon, and once kicked in the ass so hard she had gone sprawling in the gravel parking lot of The Red Windmill, she had never been raped. They had all gone home with the blue balls, every damned ofay one of them. Which meant, in Detta Walker's book, that she was the reigning champion, the undefeated queen. Of what? Of *them.* Of all those crewcut, button-down, tightass honkey motherfuckers.

Until now.

There was no way to withstand the demon who lived in the speaking ring. No doorhandles to grab, no car to tumble out of, no building to run back into, no cheek to slap, no face to claw, no balls to kick if the ofay sumbitch was slow getting the message.

The demon was on her . . . and then, in a flash, it—*he*—was in her.

She could feel it—*him*—pressing her backward, even though she could not see it—*him.* She could not see its—*his*—hands, but she could see their work as her dress tore violently open in several places. Then, suddenly, pain. It felt as though she were being ripped open down there, and in her agony and surprise she screamed. Eddie looked around, his eyes narrowing.

"I'm all right!" she yelled. "Go on, Eddie, forget about me! I'm all right!"

But she wasn't. For the first time since Detta had strode onto the sexual battlefield at the age of thirteen, she was losing. A horrid, engorged coldness plunged into her; it was like being fucked with an icicle.

Dimly, she saw Eddie turn away and begin drawing in the dirt again, his expression of warm concern fading back into the terrible, concentrated coldness she sometimes felt in him and saw on his face. Well, that was all right, wasn't it? She had told him to go on, to forget her, to do what he needed to do in order to bring the boy over. This was her part of Jake's drawing and she had no right to hate either of the men, who had not twisted her arm—or anything else—to make her do it, but as the coldness froze her and Eddie turned away from her, she hated them both; could, in fact, have torn their honkey balls off.

Then Roland was with her, his strong hands were on her shoulders and although he didn't speak, she heard him: *Don't fight. You can't win if you fight—you can only die. Sex is its weapon, Susannah, but it's also its weakness.*

Yes. It was *always* their weakness. The only difference was that this time she was going to have to give a little more—but maybe that was all right. Maybe in the end, she would be able to make this invisible honkey demon *pay* a little more.

She forced herself to relax her thighs. Immediately they spread apart, pushing long, curved fans in the dirt. She threw her head back into the rain which was now pelting down and sensed its face lolling just over hers, eager eyes drinking in every contorted grimace which passed over her face.

She reached up with one hand, as if to slap . . . and instead, slid it around the nape of her demon rapist's neck. It was like cupping a palmful of solid smoke. And did she feel it twitch backward, surprised at her caress? She tilted her pelvis upward, using her grip on the invisible neck to create the leverage. At the same time she spread her legs even wider, splitting what remained of her dress up the side-seams. God, it was huge!

"Come on," she panted. "You ain't gonna rape me. You *ain't*. You want t'fuck me? *I* fuck *you*. I give you a fuckin like you ain't *nevah* had! Fuck you to *death*!"

She felt the engorgement within her tremble; felt the demon try, at least momentarily, to draw back and regroup.

"Unh-unh, honey," she croaked. She squeezed her thighs inward, pinning it. "De fun jus' *startin*." She began to flex her butt, humping at the invisible presence. She reached up with her free hand, interlaced all ten fingers, and allowed herself to fall backward with her hips cocked, her straining arms seeming to hold nothing. She tossed her sweat-damp hair out of her eyes; her lips split in a sharklike grin.

Let me go! a voice cried out in her mind. But at the same time she could feel the owner of the voice responding in spite of itself.

"No way, sugar. You wanted it . . . now you goan get it." She thrust upward, holding on, concentrating fiercely on the freezing cold inside her. "I'm goan melt that icicle, sugar, and when it's gone, what you goan do then?" Her lips rose and fell, rose and fell. She squeezed her thighs mercilessly together, closed her eyes, clawed more deeply into the unseen neck, and prayed that Eddie would be quick.

She didn't know how long she could do this.

29

THE PROBLEM, JAKE THOUGHT, was simple: somewhere in this dank, terrible place was a locked door. The *right* door. All he had to do was find it. But it was hard, because he could feel the presence in the house gathering. The sound of those dissonant, gabbling voices was beginning to merge into one sound—a low, grating whisper.

And it was approaching.

A door stood open to the right. Beside it, thumbtacked to the wall, was a faded daguerreotype which showed a hanged man dangling like a piece of rotten fruit from a dead tree. Beyond it was a room that had once been a kitchen. The stove was gone, but an ancient icebox—the kind with the circular refrigeration drum on top—stood on the far side of the hilly, faded linoleum. Its door gaped open. Black, smelly stuff was caked inside and had trickled down to form a long-congealed puddle on the floor. The kitchen cabinets stood open. In one he saw what was probably the world's oldest can of Snow's Clam Fry-Ettes. Poking out of another was the head of a dead rat. Its eyes were white and seemingly in motion, and after a moment Jake realized that the empty sockets were filled with squirming maggots.

Something fell into his hair with a flabby thump. Jake screamed in surprise, reached for it, and grasped something that felt like a soft, bristle-covered rubber ball. He pulled it free and saw it was a spider, its bloated body the color of a fresh bruise. Its eyes regarded him with stupid malevolence. Jake threw it against the wall. It broke open and splattered there, legs twitching feebly.

Another one dropped onto his neck. Jake felt a sudden painful bite just below the place where his hair stopped. He ran backward into the hall, tripped over the fallen bannister, fell heavily, and felt the spider pop. Its innards—wet, feverish, and slippery—slid between his shoulder-blades like warm egg-yoke. Now he could see other spiders in the kitchen doorway. Some hung on almost invisible silken threads like obscene plumb-bobs; others simply dropped on the floor in a series of muddy plops and scuttered eagerly over to greet him.

Jake flailed to his feet, still screaming. He felt something in his mind, something that felt like a frayed rope, starting to give way. He supposed it was his sanity, and at that realization, Jake's considerable courage finally broke. He could bear this no longer, no matter what the stake. He bolted, meaning to flee if he still could, and realized too late that he had turned the wrong way and was running deeper into The Mansion instead of back toward the porch.

He lunged into a space too big to be a parlor or living room; it seemed to be a ballroom. Elves with strange, sly smiles on their faces capered on the wallpaper, peering at Jake from beneath peaked green caps. A mouldy couch was pushed against one wall. In the center of the warped wooden floor was a splintered chandelier, its rusty chain lying in snarls among the spilled glass beads and dusty teardrop pendants. Jake skirted the wreck, snatching one terrified glance back over his shoulder. He saw no spiders; if not for the nastiness still trickling down his back, he might have believed he had imagined them.

He looked forward again and came to a sudden, skidding halt. Ahead, a pair of french doors stood half-open on their recessed tracks. Another hallway stretched beyond. At the end of this second corridor stood a closed door with a golden knob. Written across the door—or perhaps carved into it—were two words:

THE BOY

Below the doorknob was a filigreed silver plate and a keyhole.

I found it! Jake thought fiercely. *I finally found it! That's it! That's the door!*

From behind him a low groaning noise began, as if the house was beginning to tear itself apart. Jake turned and looked back across the ballroom. The wall on the far side of the room had begun to swell outward, pushing the ancient couch ahead of it. The old wallpaper shuddered; the elves began to ripple and dance. In places the paper simply snapped upward in long curls, like windowshades which have been released too suddenly. The plaster bulged forward in a pregnant curve. From beneath it, Jake could hear dry snapping sounds as the lathing broke, rearranging itself into some new, as-yet-hidden shape. And still the sound increased. Only it was no longer precisely a groan; now it sounded like a snarl.

He stared, hypnotized, unable to pull his eyes away.

The plaster didn't crack and then vomit outward in chunks; it seemed to have become plastic, and as the wall continued to bulge, making an irregular white bubble-shape from which scraps and draggles of wallpaper still hung, the surface began to mold itself into hills and curves and valleys. Suddenly Jake realized he was looking at a huge plastic face that was pushing itself out of the wall. It was like looking at someone who has walked headfirst into a wet sheet.

There was a loud snap as a chunk of broken lath tore free of the rippling wall. It became the jagged pupil of one eye. Below it, the wall writhed into a snarling mouth filled with jagged teeth. Jake could see fragments of wallpaper clinging to its lips and gums.

One plaster hand tore free of the wall, trailing an unravelling bracelet of rotted electrical wire. It grasped the sofa and threw it aside, leaving ghostly white fingermarks on its dark surface. More lathing burst free as the plaster fingers flexed. They created sharp, splintery claws. Now the face was all the way out of the wall and staring at Jake with its one wooden eye. Above it, in the center of its forehead, one wallpaper elf still danced. It looked like a weird tattoo. There was a wrenching sound as the thing began to slide forward. The hall doorway tore out and became a hunched shoulder. The thing's one free hand clawed across the floor, spraying glass droplets from the fallen chandelier.

Jake's paralysis broke. He turned, lunged through the french doors, and pelted down the second length of hallway with his pack bouncing and his right hand groping for the key in his pocket. His heart was a runaway factory machine in his chest. Behind him, the thing which was crawling out of The Mansion's woodwork bellowed at him, and although there were no words, Jake knew what it was saying; it was telling him to stand still, telling him that it was useless to run, telling him there was no escape. The whole house now seemed alive; the air resounded with splintering wood and squalling beams. The humming, insane voice of the doorkeeper was everywhere.

Jake's hand closed on the key. As he brought it out, one of the notches caught in the pocket. His fingers, wet with sweat, slipped. The key fell to the floor, bounced, dropped through a crack between two warped boards, and disappeared.

30

"HE'S IN TROUBLE!" SUSANNAH heard Eddie shout, but the sound of his voice was distant. She had plenty of trouble herself . . . but she thought she might be doing okay, just the same.

I'm goan melt that icicle, sugar, she had told the demon. *I'm goan melt it, and when it's gone, what you goan do then?*

She hadn't melted it, exactly, but she had *changed* it. The thing inside her was certainly giving her no pleasure, but at least the terrible pain had subsided and it was no longer cold. It was trapped, unable to disengage. Nor was she holding it in with her body, exactly. Roland had said sex was its weakness as well as its weapon, and he had been right, as usual. It had taken her, but *she* had also taken *it,* and now it was as if each of them had a finger stuck in one of those fiendish Chinese tubes, where yanking only sticks you tighter.

She hung onto one idea for dear life; *had* to, because all other conscious thought had vanished. She had to hold this sobbing, frightened, vicious thing in the snare of its own helpless lust. It wriggled and thrust and convulsed within her, screaming to be let go at the same time it used her body with greedy, helpless intensity, but she would not let it go free.

And what's gonna happen when I finally do let go? she wondered desperately. *What's it gonna do to pay me back?*

She didn't know.

31

THE RAIN WAS FALLING in sheets, threatening to turn the circle within the stones into a sea of mud. *"Hold something over the door!"* Eddie shouted. *"Don't let the rain wash it out!"*

Roland snatched a glance at Susannah and saw she was still struggling with the demon. Her eyes were half-shut, her mouth pulled down in a harsh grimace. He could not see or hear the demon, but he could sense its angry, frightened thrashings.

Eddie turned his streaming face toward him. *"Did you hear me?"* he shouted. *"Get something over the goddam door, and do it NOW!"*

Roland yanked one of their hides from his pack and held a corner in each hand. Then he stretched his arms out and leaned over Eddie, creating a makeshift tent. The tip of Eddie's homemade pencil was caked with mud. He wiped it across his arm, leaving a smear the color of bitter chocolate, then wrapped his fist around the stick again and bent over his drawing. It was not exactly the same size as the door on Jake's side of the barrier—the ratio was perhaps .75:1—but it would be big enough for Jake to come through . . . *if* the keys worked.

If he even has a key, isn't that what you mean? he asked himself. *Suppose he's dropped it . . . or that house made him drop it?*

He drew a plate under the circle which represented the doorknob, hesitated, and then squiggled the familiar shape of a keyhole within it:

He hesitated. There was one more thing, but what? It was hard to think of, because it felt as if there were a tornado roaring through his head, a tornado with random thoughts flipping around inside it instead of uprooted barns and privies and chicken-houses.

"Come on, sugah!" Susannah cried from behind him. "You weakenin on me! Wassa matta? I thought you was some kind of hot-shit studboy!"

Boy. That was it.

Carefully, he wrote THE BOY across the top panel of the door with the tip of his stick. At the instant he finished the Y, the drawing changed. The circle of rain-darkened earth he had drawn suddenly darkened even more . . . and pushed up from the ground, becoming a dark, gleaming knob. And instead of brown, wet earth within the shape of the keyhole, he could see dim light.

Behind him, Susannah shrieked at the demon again, urging it on, but now she sounded as if she were tiring. This had to end, and soon.

Eddie bent forward from the waist like a Muslim saluting Allah, and put his eye to the keyhole he had drawn. He looked through it into his own world, into that house which he and Henry had gone to see in May of 1977, unaware (except he, Eddie, had not been unaware; no, not totally unaware, even then) that a boy from another part of the city was following them.

He saw a hallway. Jake was down on his hands and knees, tugging frantically at a board. Something was coming for him. Eddie could see it, but at the same time he could not—it was as if part of his brain *refused* to see it, as if seeing would lead to comprehension and comprehension to madness.

"Hurry up, Jake!" he screamed into the keyhole. *"For Christ's sake, move it!"*

Above the speaking ring, thunder ripped the sky like cannon-fire and the rain turned to hail.

32

FOR A MOMENT AFTER the key fell, Jake only stood where he was, staring down at the narrow crack between the boards.

Incredibly, he felt sleepy.

That shouldn't have happened, he thought. *It's one thing too much. I can't go on with this, not one minute, not one single second longer. I'm going to curl up against that door instead. I'm going to go to sleep, right away, all at once, and when it grabs me and pulls me toward its mouth, I'll never wake up.*

Then the thing coming out of the wall grunted, and when Jake looked up, his urge to give in vanished in a single stroke of terror. Now it was all the way out of the wall, a giant plaster head with one broken wooden eye and one reaching plaster hand. Chunks of lathing stood out on its skull in random hackles, like a child's drawing of hair. It saw Jake and opened its mouth, revealing jagged wooden teeth. It grunted again. Plaster-dust drifted out of its yawning mouth like cigar smoke.

Jake fell to his knees and peered into the crack. The key was a small brave shimmer of silvery light down there in the dark, but the crack was far too narrow to admit his fingers. He seized one of the boards and yanked with all his might. The nails which held it groaned . . . but held.

There was a jangling crash. He looked down the hallway and saw the hand, which was bigger than his whole body, seize the fallen chandelier and throw it aside. The rusty chain which had once held it suspended rose like a bullwhip and then came down with a heavy crump. A dead lamp on a rusty chain rattled above Jake, dirty glass chattering against ancient brass.

The doorkeeper's head, attached only to its single hunched shoulder and reaching arm, slid forward above the floor. Behind it, the remains of the wall collapsed in a cloud of dust. A moment later the fragments humped up and became the creature's twisted, bony back.

The doorkeeper saw Jake looking and seemed to grin. As it did, splinters of wood poked out of its wrinkling cheeks. It dragged itself forward through the dust-hazed ballroom, mouth opening and closing. Its great hand groped amid the ruins, feeling for purchase, and ripped one of the french doors at the end of the hall from its track.

Jake screamed breathlessly and began to wrench at the board again. It wouldn't come, but the gunslinger's voice did:

"The other one, Jake! Try the other one!"

He let go of the board he had been yanking at and grabbed the one on the other side of the crack. As he did, another voice spoke. He heard this one not in his head but with his ears, and understood it was coming from the other side of the door—the door he had been looking for ever since the day he hadn't been run over in the street.

"Hurry up, Jake! For Christ's sake, hurry up!"

When he yanked this other board, it came free so easily that he almost tumbled over backward.

33

TWO WOMEN WERE STANDING in the doorway of the used appliance shop across the street from The Mansion. The older was the proprietor; the younger had been her only customer when the sounds of crashing walls and breaking beams began. Now, without knowing they were doing it, they linked arms about each other's waists and stood that way, trembling like children who hear a noise in the dark.

Up the street, a trio of boys on their way to the Dutch Hill Little League field stood gaping at the house, their Red Ball Flyer wagon filled with baseball equipment forgotten behind them. A delivery driver nosed his van into the curb and got out to look. The patrons of Henry's Corner Market and the Dutch Hill Pub came straggling up the street, looking around wildly.

Now the ground began to tremble, and a fan of fine cracks started to spread across Rhinehold Street.

"Is it an earthquake?" the delivery van driver shouted at the women standing outside the appliance shop, but instead of waiting for an answer he jumped back behind the wheel of his van and drove away rapidly, swerving to the wrong side of the street to keep away from the ruined house which was the epicenter of this convulsion.

The entire house seemed to be bowing inward. Boards splintered, jumped off its face, and rained down into the yard. Dirty gray-black waterfalls of slate shingles poured down from the eaves. There was an earsplitting bang and a long, zigzagging crack shot down the center of The Mansion. The door disappeared into it and then the whole house began to swallow itself from the outside in.

The younger woman suddenly broke the older one's grip. "I'm getting out of here," she said, and began to run up the street without looking back.

34

A HOT, STRANGE WIND began to sigh down the hallway, blowing Jake's sweaty hair back from his brow as his fingers closed over the silver key. He now understood on some instinctive level what this place was, and what was happening. The doorkeeper was not just *in* the house, it *was* the house: every board, every shingle, every windowsill, every eave. And now it was pushing forward, becoming some crazily jumbled representation of its true shape as it did. It meant to catch him before he could use the key. Beyond the giant white head and the crooked, hulking shoulder, he could see boards and shingles and wire and bits of glass—even the front door and the broken bannister—flying up the main hall and into the ballroom, joining the form which bulked there, creating more and more of the misshapen plaster-man that was even now groping toward him with its freakish hand.

Jake yanked his own hand out of the hole in the floor and saw it was covered with huge trundling beetles. He slapped it against the wall to knock them off, and cried out as the wall first opened and then tried to close around his wrist. He yanked his hand free just in time, whirled, and jammed the silver key into the hole in the plate.

The plaster-man roared again, but its voice was momentarily drowned out by a harmonic shout which Jake recognized: he had heard it in the vacant lot, but it had been quiet then, perhaps dreaming. Now it was an unequivocal cry of triumph. That sense of certainty—overwhelming, inarguable—filled him again, and this time he felt sure there would be no disappointment. He heard all the affirmation he needed in that voice. It was the voice of the rose.

The dim light in the hallway was blotted out as the plaster hand tore away the other french door and squeezed into the corridor. The face socked itself into the opening above the hand, peering at Jake. The plaster fingers crawled toward him like the legs of a huge spider.

Jake turned the key and felt a sudden surge of power rush up his arm. He heard a heavy, muffled thump as the locked bolt inside withdrew. He seized the knob, turned it, and yanked the door open. It swung wide. Jake cried out in confused horror as he saw what lay behind.

The doorway was blocked with earth, from top to bottom and side to side. Roots poked out like bunches of wire. Worms, seeming as confused as Jake was himself, crawled hither and thither on the door-shaped pack of dirt. Some dived back into it; others only went on crawling about, as if wondering where the earth which had been below them a moment ago had gone. One dropped onto Jake's sneaker.

The keyhole shape remained for a moment, shedding a spot of misty white light on Jake's shirt. Beyond it—so close, so out of reach—he could hear rain and a muffled boom of thunder across an open sky. Then the keyhole shape was also blotted out, and gigantic plaster fingers curled around Jake's lower leg.

35

EDDIE DID NOT FEEL the sting of the hail as Roland dropped the hide, got to his feet, and ran to where Susannah lay.

The gunslinger grabbed her beneath the arms and dragged her—as gently and carefully as he could—across to where Eddie crouched. "Let it go when I tell you, Susannah!" Roland shouted. "Do you understand? *When I tell you!*"

Eddie saw and heard none of this. He heard only Jake, screaming faintly on the other side of the door.

The time had come to use the key.

He pulled it out of his shirt and slid it into the keyhole he had drawn. He tried to turn it. The key would not turn. Not so much as a milllimeter. Eddie lifted his face to the pelting hail, oblivious to the iceballs which struck his forehead and cheeks and lips, leaving welts and red blotches.

"NO!" he howled. "*OH GOD, PLEASE! NO!*"

But there was no answer from God; only another crash of thunder and a streak of lightning across a sky now filled with racing clouds.

36

JAKE LUNGED UPWARD, GRABBED the chain of the lamp which hung above him, and ripped free of the doorkeeper's clutching fingers. He swung backward, used the packed earth in the doorway to push off, and then swung forward again like Tarzan on a vine. He raised his legs and kicked out at the clutching fingers as he closed on them. Plaster exploded in chunks, revealing a crudely jointed skeleton of lathing beneath. The plaster-man roared, a sound of intermingled hunger and rage. Beneath that cry, Jake could hear the whole house collapsing, like the one in that story of Edgar Allan Poe.

He pendulumed back on the chain, struck the wall of packed earth which blocked the doorway, then swung forward again. The hand reached up for him and he kicked at it wildly, legs scissoring. He felt a stab of pain in his foot as those wooden fingers clutched. When he swung back again, he was minus a sneaker.

He tried for a higher grip on the chain, found it, and began to shinny up toward the ceiling. There was a muffled, creaking thud above him. Fine plaster dust had begun to sift down on his upturned, sweating face. The ceiling had begun to sag; the lamp-chain was pulling out of it a link at a time. There was a thick crunching sound from the end of the hallway as the plaster-man finally pushed its hungry face through the opening.

Jake swung helplessly back toward that face, screaming.

37

EDDIE'S TERROR AND PANIC suddenly fell away. The cloak of coldness dropped over him—a cloak Roland of Gilead had worn many times. It was the only armor the true gunslinger possessed . . . and all such a one needed. At the same moment, a voice spoke in his mind. He had been haunted by such voices over the last three months; his mother's voice, Roland's voice, and, of course, Henry's. But this one, he recognized with relief, was his own, and it was at last calm and rational and courageous.

You saw the shape of the key in the fire, you saw it again in the wood, and both times you saw it perfectly. Later on, you put a blindfold of fear over your eyes. Take it off. Take it off and look again. It may not be too late, even now.

He was faintly aware that the gunslinger was staring at him grimly; faintly aware that Susannah was shrieking at the demon in a fading but still defiant voice; faintly aware that, on the other side of the door, Jake was screaming in terror—or was it now agony?

Eddie ignored them all. He pulled the wooden key out of the key-hole he had drawn, out of the door which was now real, and looked at it fixedly, trying to recapture the innocent delight he had sometimes known as a child—the delight of seeing a coherent shape hidden in senselessness. And there it was, the place he'd gone wrong, so clearly visible he couldn't understand how he'd missed it in the first place. *I really* must *have been wearing a blindfold,* he thought. It was the *s*-shape at the end of the key, of course. The second curve was a bit too fat. Just a tiny bit.

"Knife," he said, and held out his hand like a surgeon in an operating room. Roland slapped it into his palm without a word.

Eddie gripped the top of the blade between the thumb and first finger of his right hand. He bent over the key, unmindful of the hail which pelted his unprotected neck, and the shape in the wood stood out more clearly—stood out with its own lovely and undeniable reality.

He scraped.

Once.

Delicately.

A single sliver of ash, so thin it was almost transparent, curled up from the belly of the *s*-shape at the end of the key.

On the other side of the door, Jake Chambers shrieked again.

38

THE CHAIN LET GO with a rattling crash and Jake fell heavily, landing on his knees. The doorkeeper roared in triumph. The plaster hand seized Jake about his hips and began to drag him down the hall. He stuck his legs out in front of him and planted his feet, but it did no good. He felt splinters and rust-blunted nails digging into his skin as the hand tightened its grip and continued to drag him forward.

The face appeared to be stuck just inside the entrance to the hallway like a cork in a bottle. The pressure it had exerted to get in that far had squeezed the rudimentary features into a new shape, that of some monstrous, malformed troll. The mouth yawned open to receive him. Jake groped madly for the key, wanting to use it as some last-ditch talisman, but of course he had left it in the door.

"You son of a bitch!" he screamed, and threw himself backward with all his strength, bowing his back like an Olympic diver, unmindful of the broken boards which dug into him like a belt of nails. He felt his jeans slide down on his hips, and the grip of the hand slipped momentarily.

Jake lunged again. The hand clenched brutally, but Jake's jeans slid down to his knees and his back slammed to the floor, with the pack to cushion the blow. The hand loosened, perhaps wanting to secure a firmer grip upon its prey. Jake was able to draw his knees up a little, and when the hand tightened again, Jake drove his legs forward. The hand yanked backward at the same time, and what Jake had hoped for happened: his jeans (and his remaining sneaker) were peeled from his body, leaving him free again, at least for the moment. He saw the hand rotate on his wrist of boards and disintegrating plaster and jam his dungarees into his mouth. Then he was crawling back toward the blocked doorway on his hands and knees, oblivious of the glass fragments from the fallen lamp, wanting only to get his key again.

He had almost reached the door when the hand closed over his naked legs and began to pull him back once more.

39

THE SHAPE WAS THERE now, finally all there.

Eddie put the key back into the keyhole and applied pressure. For a moment there was resistance . . . and then it revolved beneath his hand. He heard the locking mechanism turn, heard the bar pull back, felt the key crack in two the moment it had served its purpose. He grasped the dark, polished knob with both hands and pulled. There was a sense of great weight wheeling on an unseen pivot. A feeling that his arm had been gifted with boundless strength. And a clear knowledge that two worlds had suddenly come in contact, and a way had been opened between them.

He felt a moment of dizziness and disorientation, and as he looked through the doorway he realized why: although he was looking down—vertically—he was seeing *horizontally*. It was like a strange optical illusion created with prisms and mirrors. Then he saw Jake being pulled backward down the glass- and plaster-littered hallway, elbows dragging, calves pinned together by a giant hand. And he saw the monstrous mouth which awaited him, fuming some white fog that might have been either smoke or dust.

"*Roland!*" Eddie shouted. "*Roland, it's got h—*"

Then he was knocked aside.

40

SUSANNAH WAS AWARE OF being hauled up and whirled around. The world was a carousel blur: standing stones, gray sky, hailstone-littered ground . . . and a rectangular hole that looked like a trapdoor in the ground. Screams drifted up from it. Within her, the demon raved and struggled, wanting only to escape but helpless to do so until she allowed it.

"*Now!*" Roland was shouting. "*Let it go now, Susannah! For your father's sake, let it go NOW!*"

And she did.

She had (with Detta's help) constructed a trap for it in her mind, something like a net of woven rushes, and now she cut them. She felt the demon fly back from her at once, and there was an instant of terrible hollowness, terrible emptiness. These feelings were at once overshadowed by relief and a grim sense of nastiness and defilement.

As its invisible weight fell away, she glimpsed it—an inhuman shape like a manta-ray with huge, curling wings and something that looked like a cruel baling hook curving out and up from beneath. She saw/sensed the thing flash above the open hole in the ground. Saw Eddie looking up with wide eyes. Saw Roland spread his arms wide to catch the demon.

The gunslinger staggered back, almost knocked off his feet by the unseen weight of the demon. Then he rocked forward again with an armload of nothing.

Clutching it, he jumped through the doorway and was gone.

41

SUDDEN WHITE LIGHT FLOODED the hallway of The Mansion; hailstones struck the walls and bounced up from the broken boards of the floor. Jake heard confused shouts, then saw the gunslinger come through. He seemed to *leap* through, as if he had come from above. His arms were held far out in front of him, the tips of the fingers locked.

Jake felt his feet slide into the doorkeeper's mouth.

"*Roland!*" he shrieked. "*Roland, help me!*"

The gunslinger's hands parted and his arms were immediately thrown wide. He staggered backward. Jake felt serrated teeth touch his skin, ready to tear flesh and grind bone, and then something huge rushed over his head like a gust of wind. A moment later the teeth were gone. The hand which had pinned his legs together relaxed. He heard an unearthly shriek of pain and surprise begin to issue from the doorkeeper's dusty throat, and then it was muffled, crammed back.

Roland grabbed Jake and hauled him to his feet.

"You came!" Jake shouted. "You really came!"

"I came, yes. By the grace of the gods and the courage of my friends, I came."

As the doorkeeper roared again, Jake burst into tears of relief and terror. Now the house sounded like a ship foundering in a heavy sea. Chunks of wood and plaster fell all around them. Roland swept Jake into his arms and ran for the door. The plaster hand, groping wildly, struck one of his booted feet and spun him into the wall, which again tried to bite. Roland pushed forward, turned, and drew his gun. He fired twice into the aimlessly thrashing hand, vaporizing one of the crude plaster fingers. Behind them, the face of the doorkeeper had gone from white to a dingy purplish-black, as if it were choking on something—something which had been fleeing so rapidly that it had entered the monster's mouth and jammed in its gullet before it realized what it was doing.

Roland turned again and ran through the doorway. Although there was now no visible barrier, he was stopped cold for a moment, as if an unseen meshwork had been drawn across the chair.

Then he felt Eddie's hands in his hair and he was yanked not forward but upward.

42

THEY EMERGED INTO WET air and slackening hail like babies being born. Eddie was the midwife, as the gunslinger had told him he must be. He was sprawled forward on his chest and belly, his arms out of sight in the doorway, his hands clutching fistfuls of Roland's hair.

"Suze! Help me!"

She wriggled forward, reached through, and groped a hand under Roland's chin. He came up to her with his head cocked backward and his lips parted in a snarl of pain and effort.

Eddie felt a tearing sensation and one of his hands came free holding a thick lock of the gunslinger's gray-streaked hair. "He's slipping!"

"This motherfucker . . . ain't . . . *nowhere!*" Susannah gasped, and gave a terrific wrench, as if she meant to snap Roland's neck.

Two small hands shot out of the doorway in the center of the circle and clutched one of the edges. Freed of Jake's weight, Roland got an elbow up, and a moment later he was boosting himself out. As he did it, Eddie grabbed Jake's wrists and hauled him up.

Jake rolled onto his back and lay there, panting.

Eddie turned to Susannah, took her in his arms, and began to rain kisses on her forehead, cheeks, and neck. He was laughing and crying at the same time. She clung to him, breathing hard . . . but there was a small, satisfied smile on her lips and one hand slipped over Eddie's wet hair in slow, contented strokes.

From below them came a cauldron of black sounds: squeals, grunts, thuds, crashes.

Roland crawled away from the hole with his head down. His hair stood up in a wild wad. Threads of blood trickled down his cheeks. "Shut it!" he gasped at Eddie. "Shut it, for your father's sake!"

Eddie got the door moving, and those vast, unseen hinges did the rest. The door fell with a gigantic, toneless bang, cutting off all sound from below. As Eddie watched, the lines that had marked its edges faded back to smudged marks in the dirt. The doorknob lost its dimension and was once more only a circle he'd drawn with a stick. Where the keyhole had been there was only a crude shape with a chunk of wood sticking out of it, like the hilt of a sword from a stone.

Susannah went to Jake and pulled him gently to a sitting position. "You all right, sugar?"

He looked at her dazedly. "Yes, I think so. Where is he? The gun-slinger? There's something I have to ask him."

"I'm here, Jake," Roland said. He got to his feet, drunk-walked over to Jake, and hunkered beside him. He touched the boy's smooth cheek almost unbelievingly.

"You won't let me drop this time?"

"No," Roland said. "Not this time, not ever again." But in the deep-est darkness of his heart, he thought of the Tower and wondered.

43

THE HAIL CHANGED TO a hard, driving rain, but Eddie could see gleams of blue sky behind the unravelling clouds in the north. The storm was going to end soon, but in the meantime, they were going to get drenched.

He found he didn't mind. He could not remember when he had felt so calm, so at peace with himself, so utterly drained. This mad adven-ture wasn't over yet—he suspected, in fact, that it had barely begun—but today they had won a big one.

"Suze?" He pushed her hair away from her face and looked into her dark eyes. "Are you okay? Did it hurt you?"

"Hurt me a little, but I'm okay. I think that bitch Detta Walker is still the undefeated Roadhouse Champeen, demon or no demon."

"What's that mean?"

She grinned impishly. "Not much, not anymore . . . thank God. How about you, Eddie? All right?"

Eddie listened for Henry's voice and didn't hear it. He had an idea that Henry's voice might be gone for good. "Even better than that," he said, and, laughing, folded her into his arms again. Over her shoulder he could see what was left of the door: only a few faint lines and angles. Soon the rain would wash those away, too.

44

"WHAT'S YOUR NAME?" JAKE asked the woman whose legs stopped just above the knee. He was suddenly aware that he had lost his pants in his struggle to escape the doorkeeper, and he pulled the tail of his shirt down over his underwear. There wasn't very much left of her dress, either, as far as that went.

"Susannah Dean," she said. "I already know your name."

"Susannah," Jake said thoughtfully. "I don't suppose your father owns a railroad company, does he?"

She looked astonished for a moment, then threw her head back and laughed. "Why, no, sugar! He was a dentist who went and invented a few things and got rich. What makes you ask a thing like that?"

Jake didn't answer. He had turned his attention to Eddie. The terror had already left his face, and his eyes had regained that cool, assessing look which Roland remembered so well from the way station.

"Hi, Jake," Eddie said. "Good to see you, man."

"Hi," Jake said. "I met you earlier today, but you were a lot younger then."

"I was a lot younger ten minutes ago. Are you okay?"

"Yes," Jake said. "Some scratches, that's all." He looked around. "You haven't found the train yet." This was not a question.

Eddie and Susannah exchanged puzzled looks, but Roland only shook his head. "No train."

"Are your voices gone?"

Roland nodded. "All gone. Yours?"

"Gone. I'm all together again. We both are."

They looked at the same instant, with the same impulse. As Roland swept Jake into his arms, the boy's unnatural self-possession broke and he began to cry—it was the exhausted, relieved weeping of a child who has been lost long, suffered much, and is finally safe again. As Roland's arms closed about his waist, Jake's own arms slipped about the gunslinger's neck and gripped like hoops of steel.

"I'll never leave you again," Roland said, and now his own tears came. "I swear to you on the names of all my fathers: *I'll never leave you again.*"

Yet his heart, that silent, watchful, lifelong prisoner of *ka*, received the words of this promise not just with wonder but with doubt.

• BOOK TWO •
LUD

A HEAP OF BROKEN IMAGES

IV ▪ TOWN AND *KA-TET*

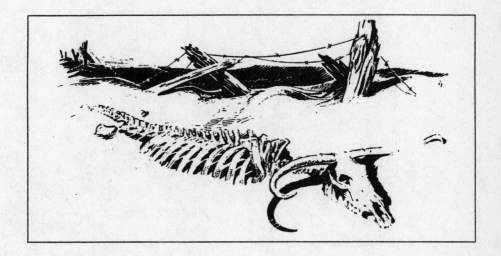

· IV ·

TOWN AND
KA-TET

1

FOUR DAYS AFTER EDDIE had yanked him through the doorway between worlds, minus his original pair of pants and his sneakers but still in possession of his pack and his life, Jake awoke with something warm and wet nuzzling at his face.

If he had come around to such a sensation on any of the three previous mornings, he undoubtedly would have wakened his companions with his screams, for he had been feverish and his sleep had been haunted by nightmares of the plaster-man. In these dreams his pants did not slide free, the doorkeeper kept its grip, and it tucked him into its unspeakable mouth, where its teeth came down like the bars guarding a castle keep. Jake awoke from these dreams shuddering and moaning helplessly.

The fever had been caused by the spider-bite on the back of his neck. When Roland examined it on the second day and found it worse instead of better, he had conferred briefly with Eddie and had then given Jake a pink pill. "You'll want to take four of these every day for at least a week," he said.

Jake had gazed at it doubtfully. "What is it?"

"*Cheflet*," Roland said, then looked disgustedly at Eddie. "You tell him. I *still* can't say it."

"Keflex. You can trust it, Jake; it came from a government-approved pharmacy in good old New York. Roland swallowed a bunch of it, and he's as healthy as a horse. Looks a little like one, too, as you can see."

Jake was astonished. "How did you get medicine in New York?"

"That's a long story," the gunslinger said. "You'll hear all of it in time, but for now just take the pill."

Jake did. The response was both quick and satisfying. The angry red swelling around the bite began to fade in twenty-four hours, and now the fever was gone as well.

The warm thing nuzzled again and Jake sat up with a jerk, his eyes flying open.

The creature which had been licking his cheek took two hasty steps backward. It was a billy-bumbler, but Jake didn't know that; he had never seen one before now. It was skinnier than the ones Roland's party had seen earlier, and its black- and gray-striped fur was matted and mangy. There was a clot of old dried blood on one flank. Its gold-ringed black eyes looked at Jake anxiously; its hindquarters switched hopefully back and forth. Jake relaxed. He supposed there were exceptions to the rule, but he had an idea that something wagging its tail—or trying to—was probably not too dangerous.

It was just past first light, probably around five-thirty in the morning. Jake could peg it no closer than that because his digital Seiko no longer worked . . . or rather, was working in an extremely eccentric way. When he had first glanced at it after coming through, the Seiko claimed it was 98:71:65, a time which did not, so far as Jake knew, exist. A longer look showed him that the watch was now running backward. If it had been doing this at a steady rate, he supposed it might still have been of some use, but it wasn't. It would unwind its numbers at what seemed like the right speed for awhile (Jake verified this by saying the word "Mississippi" between each number), and then the readout would either stop entirely for ten or twenty seconds—making him think the watch had finally given up the ghost—or a bunch of numbers would blur by all at once.

He had mentioned this odd behavior to Roland and had shown him the watch, thinking it would amaze him, but Roland examined it closely for only a moment or two before nodding in a dismissive way and telling Jake it was an interesting clock, but as a rule no timepiece did very good work these days. So the Seiko was useless, but Jake still found himself loath to throw it away . . . because, he supposed, it was a piece of his old life, and there were only a few of those left.

Right now the Seiko claimed it was sixty-two minutes past forty on a Wednesday, Thursday, and Saturday in both December and March.

The morning was extremely foggy; beyond a radius of fifty or sixty feet, the world simply disappeared. If this day was like the previous three, the sun would show up as a faint white circle in another two hours or so, and by nine-thirty the day would be clear and hot. Jake looked around and saw his travelling companions (he didn't quite dare call them friends, at least not yet) asleep beneath their hide blankets—Roland close by, Eddie and Susannah a larger hump on the far side of the dead campfire.

He once more turned his attention to the animal which had awakened him. It looked like a combination raccoon and woodchuck, with a dash of dachshund thrown in for good measure.

"How you doin, boy?" he asked softly.

"*Oy!*" the billy-bumbler replied at once, still looking at him anxiously. Its voice was low and deep, almost a bark; the voice of an English footballer with a bad cold in his throat.

Jake recoiled, surprised. The billy-bumbler, startled by the quick movement, took several further steps backward, seemed about to flee, and then held its ground. Its hindquarters wagged back and forth more strenuously than ever, and its gold-black eyes continued to regard Jake nervously. The whiskers on its snout trembled.

"This one remembers men," a voice remarked at Jake's shoulder. He looked around and saw Roland squatting just behind him with his forearms resting on his thighs and his long hands dangling between his knees. He was looking at the animal with a great deal more interest than he had shown in Jake's watch.

"What is it?" Jake asked softly. He did not want to startle it away; he was enchanted. "Its eyes are beautiful!"

"Billy-bumbler," Roland said.

"*Umber!*" the creature ejaculated, and retreated another step.

"It talks!"

"Not really. Bumblers just repeat what they hear—or used to. I haven't heard one do it in years. This fellow looks almost starved. Probably came to forage."

"He was licking my face. Can I feed it?"

"We'll never get rid of it if you do," Roland said, then smiled a little and snapped his fingers. "Hey! Billy!"

The creature mimicked the sound of the snapping fingers somehow; it sounded as if it were clucking its tongue against the roof of its mouth. "Ay!" it called in its hoarse voice. "Ay, Illy!" Now its ragged hindquarters were positively *flagging* back and forth.

"Go ahead and give it a bite. I knew an old groom once who said a good bumbler is good luck. This looks like a good one."

"Yes," Jake agreed. "It does."

"Once they were tame, and every barony had half a dozen roaming around the castle or manor-house. They weren't good for much except amusing the children and keeping the rat population down. They can be quite faithful—or were in the old days—although I never heard of one that would remain as loyal as a good dog. The wild ones are scavengers. Not dangerous, but a pain in the ass."

"Ass!" cried the bumbler. Its anxious eyes continued to flick back and forth between Jake and the gunslinger.

Jake reached into his pack, slowly, afraid to startle the creature, and drew out the remains of a gunslinger burrito. He tossed it toward the billy-bumbler. The bumbler flinched back and then turned with a small, childlike cry, exposing its furry corkscrew tail. Jake felt sure it would run, but it stopped, looking doubtfully back over its shoulder.

"Come on," Jake said. "Eat it, boy."

"Oy," the bumbler muttered, but it didn't move.

"Give it time," Roland said. "It'll come, I think."

The bumbler stretched forward, revealing a long and surprisingly graceful neck. Its slender black nose twitched as it sniffed the food. At last it trotted forward, and Jake noticed it was limping a little. The bumbler sniffed the burrito, then used one paw to separate the chunk of deermeat from the leaf. It carried out this operation with a delicacy that was oddly solemn. Once the meat was clear of the leaf, the bumbler wolfed it in a single bite, then looked up at Jake. "Oy!" it said, and when Jake laughed, it shrank away again.

"That's a skinny one," Eddie said sleepily from behind them. At the sound of his voice, the bumbler immediately turned and was gone into the mist.

"You scared it away!" Jake accused.

"Jeez, I'm sorry," Eddie said. He ran a hand through his sleep-corkscrewed hair. "If I'd known it was one of your close personal friends, Jake, I would have dragged out the goddam coffee-cake."

Roland clapped Jake briefly on the shoulder. "It'll be back."

"Are you sure?"

"If something doesn't kill it, yes. We fed it, didn't we?"

Before Jake could reply, the sound of the drums began again. This was the third morning they had heard them, and twice the sound had come to them as afternoon slipped down toward evening: a faint, toneless thudding from the direction of the city. The sound was clearer this morning, if no more comprehensible. Jake hated it. It was as if, somewhere out in that thick and featureless blanket of morning mist, the heart of some big animal was beating.

"You still don't have any idea what that is, Roland?" Susannah asked. She had slipped on her shift, tied back her hair, and was now folding the blankets beneath which she and Eddie had slept.

"No. But I'm sure we'll find out."

"How reassuring," Eddie said sourly.

Roland got to his feet. "Come on. Let's not waste the day."

2

THE FOG BEGAN TO unravel after they had been on the road for an hour or so. They took turns pushing Susannah's chair, and it jolted unhappily along, for the road was now mined with large, rough cobblestones. By midmorning the day was fair, hot, and cloudless; the city skyline stood out clearly on the southeastern horizon. To Jake it didn't look much different from the skyline of New York, although he thought these buildings might not be as high. If the place had fallen apart, as most things in Roland's world apparently had, you certainly couldn't tell it from here. Like Eddie, Jake had begun to entertain the unspoken hope that they might find help there . . . or at least a good hot meal.

To their left, thirty or forty miles away, they could see the broad sweep of the Send River. Birds circled above it in large flocks. Every now and then one would fold its wings and drop like a stone, probably on a fishing expedition. The road and the river were moving slowly toward one another, although the junction point could not yet be seen.

They could see more buildings ahead. Most looked like farms, and all appeared deserted. Some of them had fallen down, but these wrecks seemed to be the work of time rather than violence, furthering Eddie's and Jake's hopes of what they might find in the city—hopes each had kept strictly within himself, lest the others scoff. Small herds of shaggy beasts grazed their way across the plains. They kept well away from the road except to cross, and this they did quickly, at a gallop, like packs of small children afraid of traffic. They looked like bison to Jake . . . except he saw several which had two heads. He mentioned this to the gunslinger and Roland nodded.

"Muties."

"Like under the mountains?" Jake heard the fear in his own voice and knew the gunslinger must, also, but he was helpless to keep it out. He remembered that endless nightmare journey on the handcart very well.

"I think that here the mutant strains are being bred out. The things we found under the mountains were still getting worse."

"What about up there?" Jake pointed toward the city. "Will there be mutants there, or—" He found it was as close as he could come to voicing his hope.

Roland shrugged. "I don't know, Jake. I'd tell you if I did."

They were passing an empty building—almost surely a farmhouse—that had been partially burnt. *But that could have been lightning,* Jake thought, and wondered which it was he was trying to do—explain to himself or fool himself.

Roland, perhaps reading his mind, put an arm around Jake's shoulders. "No use even trying to guess, Jake," he said. "Whatever happened here happened long ago." He pointed. "That over there was probably a corral. Now it's just a few sticks poking out of the grass."

"The world has moved on, right?"

Roland nodded.

"What about the people? Did they go to the city, do you think?"

"Some may have," Roland said. "Some are still around."

"What?" Susannah jerked around to look at him, startled.

Roland nodded. "We've been watched the last couple of days. There aren't a lot of folk denning in these old buildings, but there are some. There'll be more as we get closer to civilization." He paused. "Or what *used* to be civilization."

"How do you know they're there?" Jake asked.

"Smelled them. Seen a few gardens hidden behind banks of weeds grown purposely to hide the crops. And at least one working windmill way back in a grove of trees. Mostly, though, it's just a feeling . . . like shade on your face instead of sunshine. It'll come to you three in time, I imagine."

"Do you think they're dangerous?" Susannah asked. They were approaching a large, ramshackle building that might once have been a storage shed or an abandoned country market, and she eyed it uneasily, her hand dropping to the butt of the gun she wore on her chest.

"Will a strange dog bite?" the gunslinger countered.

"What's that mean?" Eddie asked. "I hate it when you start up with your Zen Buddhist shit, Roland."

"It means I don't know," Roland said. "Who is this man Zen Buddhist? Is he wise like me?"

Eddie looked at Roland for a long, long time before deciding the gunslinger was making one of his rare jokes. "Ah, get outta here," he said. He saw one corner of Roland's mouth twitch before he turned away. As Eddie started to push Susannah's chair again, something else caught his eye. "Hey, Jake!" he called. "I think you made a friend!"

Jake looked around, and a big grin overspread his face. Forty yards to the rear, the scrawny billy-bumbler was limping industriously after them, sniffing at the weeds which grew between the crumbling cobbles of the Great Road.

3

SOME HOURS LATER ROLAND called a halt and told them to be ready.

"For what?" Eddie asked.

Roland glanced at him. "Anything."

It was perhaps three o'clock in the afternoon. They were standing at a point where the Great Road crested a long, rolling drumlin which ran diagonally across the plain like a wrinkle in the world's biggest bedspread. Below and beyond, the road ran through the first real town they had seen. It looked deserted, but Eddie had not forgotten the conversation that morning. Roland's question—*Will a strange dog bite?*—no longer seemed quite so Zenny.

"Jake?"

"What?"

Eddie nodded to the butt of the Ruger, which protruded from the waistband of Jake's bluejeans—the extra pair he had tucked into his pack before leaving home. "Do you want me to carry that?"

Jake glanced at Roland. The gunslinger only shrugged, as if to say *It's your choice.*

"Okay." Jake handed it over. He unshouldered his pack, rummaged through it, and brought out the loaded clip. He could remember reaching behind the hanging files in one of his father's desk drawers to get it, but all that seemed to have occurred a long, long time ago. These days, thinking about his life in New York and his career as a student at Piper was like looking into the wrong end of a telescope.

Eddie took the clip, examined it, rammed it home, checked the safety, then stuck the Ruger in his own belt.

"Listen closely and heed me well," Roland said. "If there *are* people, they'll likely be old and much more frightened of us than we are of them. The younger folk will be long gone. It's unlikely that those left will have firearms—in fact, ours may be the first guns many of them have ever seen, except maybe for a picture or two in the old books. Make no threatening gestures. And the childhood rule is a good one: speak only when spoken to."

"What about bows and arrows?" Susannah asked.

"Yes, they may have those. Spears and clubs, as well."

"Don't forget rocks," Eddie said bleakly, looking down at the cluster of wooden buildings. The place looked like a ghost-town, but who knew for sure? "And if they're hard up for rocks, there's always the cobbles from the road."

"Yes, there's always something," Roland agreed. *"But we'll start no trouble ourselves*—is that clear?"

They nodded.

"Maybe it would be easier to detour around," Susannah said.

Roland nodded, eyes never leaving the simple geography ahead. Another road crossed the Great Road at the center of the town, making the dilapidated buildings look like a target centered in the telescopic sight of a high-powered rifle. "It would, but we won't. Detouring's a bad habit that's easy to get into. It's always better to go straight on, unless there's a good visible reason not to. I see no reason not to here. And if there *are* people, well, that might be a good thing. We could do with a little palaver."

Susannah reflected that Roland seemed different now, and she didn't think it was simply because the voices in his mind had ceased. *This is the way he was when he still had wars to fight and men to lead and his old friends around him,* she thought. *How he was before the world moved on and he moved on with it, chasing that man Walter. This is how he was before the Big Empty turned him inward on himself and made him strange.*

"They might know what those drum sounds are," Jake suggested.

Roland nodded again. "*Anything* they know—particularly about the city—would come in handy, but there's no need to think ahead too much about people who may not even be there."

"Tell you what," Susannah said, "*I* wouldn't come out if I saw us. Four people, three of them armed? We probably look like a gang of those old-time outlaws in your stories, Roland—what do you call them?"

"Harriers." His left hand dropped to the sandalwood grip of his remaining revolver and he pulled it a little way out of the holster. "But no harrier ever born carried one of these, and if there are old-timers in yon village, they'll know it. Let's go."

Jake glanced behind them and saw the bumbler lying in the road with his muzzle between his short front paws, watching them closely. "Oy!" Jake called.

"Oy!" the bumbler echoed, and scrambled to its feet at once.

They started down the shallow knoll toward the town with Oy trotting along behind them.

4

Two BUILDINGS ON THE outskirts had been burned; the rest of the town appeared dusty but intact. They passed an abandoned livery stable on the left, a building that might have been a market on the right, and then they were in the town proper—such as it was. There were perhaps a dozen rickety buildings standing on either side of the road. Alleys ran between some of them. The other road, this one a dirt track mostly overgrown with plains grass, ran northeast to southwest.

Susannah looked at its northeast arm and thought: *Once there were barges on the river, and somewhere down that road there was a landing, and probably another shacky little town, mostly saloons and cribs, built up around it. That was the last point of trade before the barges went on down to the city. The wagons came through this place going to that place and then back again. How long ago was that?*

She didn't know—but a long time, from the look of this place.

Somewhere a rusty hinge squalled monotonously. Somewhere else one shutter clapped lonesomely to and fro in the plains wind.

There were hitching rails, most of them broken, in front of the buildings. Once there had been board sidewalks, but now most of the boards were gone and grass grew up through the holes where they had been. The signs on the buildings were faded, but some were still readable, written in a bastardized form of English which was, she supposed, what Roland called the low speech. FOOD AND GRAIN, one said, and she guessed that might mean *feed* and grain. On the false front next to it, below a crude drawing of a plains-buffalo lying in the grass, were the words REST EAT DRINK. Under the sign, batwing doors hung crookedly, moving a little in the wind.

"Is that a saloon?" She didn't know exactly why she was whispering, only that she couldn't have spoken in a normal tone of voice. It would have been like playing "Clinch Mountain Breakdown" on the banjo at a funeral.

"It was," Roland said. He didn't whisper, but his voice was low-pitched and thoughtful. Jake was walking close by his side, looking around nervously. Behind them, Oy had closed up his distance to ten yards. He trotted quickly, head swinging from side to side like a pendulum as he examined the buildings.

Now Susannah began to feel it: that sensation of being watched. It was exactly as Roland had said it would be, a feeling sunshine had been replaced by shade.

"There *are* people, aren't there?" she whispered.

Roland nodded.

Standing on the northeast corner of the crossroads was a building with another sign she recognized: HOSTEL, it said, and COTTS. Except for a church with a tilted steeple up ahead, it was the tallest building in town—three stories. She glanced up in time to see a white blur, surely a face, draw away from one of the glassless windows. Suddenly she wanted to get out of here. Roland was setting a slow, deliberate pace, however, and she supposed she knew why. Hurrying might give the watchers the impression that they were scared . . . and that they could be taken. All the same—

At the crossroads the intersecting streets widened out, creating a town square which had been overrun by grass and weeds. In the center was an eroded stone marker. Above it, a metal box hung on a sagging length of rusty cable.

Roland, with Jake by his side, walked toward the marker. Eddie pushed Susannah's chair after. Grass whispered in its spokes and the wind tickled a lock of hair against her cheek. Further along the street, the shutter banged and the hinge squealed. She shivered and brushed the hair away.

"I wish he'd hurry up," Eddie said in a low voice. "This place gives me the creeps."

Susannah nodded. She looked around the square and again she could almost see how it must have been on market-day—the sidewalks thronged with people, a few of them town ladies with their baskets over their arms, most of them waggoners and roughly-dressed bargemen (she did not know why she was so sure of the barges and bargemen, but she was); the wagons passing through the town square, the ones on the unpaved road raising choking clouds of yellow dust as the drivers flogged their carthorses

(oxen they were oxen)

along. She could *see* those carts, dusty swatches of canvas tied down over bales of cloth on some and pyramids of tarred barrels on others; could see the oxen, double-yoked and straining patiently, flicking their ears at the flies buzzing around their huge heads; could hear voices, and laughter, and the piano in the saloon pounding out a lively tune like "Buffalo Gals" or "Darlin' Katy."

It's as if I lived here in another life, she thought.

The gunslinger bent over the inscription on the marker. "Great Road," he read. "Lud, one hundred and sixty wheels."

"Wheels?" Jake asked.

"An old form of measurement."

"Have you heard of Lud?" Eddie asked.

"Perhaps," the gunslinger said. "When I was very small."

"It rhymes with crud," Eddie said. "Maybe not such a good sign."

Jake was examining the east side of the stone. "River Road. It's written funny, but that's what it says."

Eddie looked at the west side of the marker. "It says Jimtown, forty wheels. Isn't that the birthplace of Wayne Newton, Roland?"

Roland looked at him blankly.

"Shet ma mouf," Eddie said, and rolled his eyes.

On the southwest corner of the square was the town's only stone building—a squat, dusty cube with rusty bars on the windows. Combination county jail and courthouse, Susannah thought. She had seen similar ones down south; add a few slant parking spaces in front and you wouldn't be able to tell the difference. Something had been daubed across the facade of the building in fading yellow paint. She could read it, and although she couldn't understand it, it made her more anxious than ever to get out of this town. PUBES DIE, it said.

"Roland!" When she had his attention, she pointed at the graffito. "What does that mean?"

He read it, then shook his head. "Don't know."

She looked around again. The square now seemed smaller, and the buildings seemed to be leaning over them. "Can we get out of here?"

"Soon." He bent down and pried a small chunk of cobble out of the roadbed. He bounced it thoughtfully in his left hand as he looked up at the metal box which hung over the marker. He cocked his arm and Susannah realized, an instant too late, what he meant to do.

"No, Roland!" she cried, then cringed back at the sound of her own horrified voice.

He took no notice of her but fired the stone upward. His aim was as true as ever, and it struck the box dead center with a hollow, metallic bang. There was a whir of clockwork from within, and a rusty green flag unfolded from a slot in the side. When it locked in place, a bell rang briskly. Written in large black letters on the side of the flag was the word GO.

"I'll be damned," Eddie said. "It's a Keystone Kops traffic-light. If you hit it again, does it say STOP?"

"We have company," Roland said quietly, and pointed toward the building Susannah thought of as the county courthouse. A man and a woman had emerged from it and were descending the stone steps. *You win the kewpie doll, Roland*, Susannah thought. *They're older'n God, the both of em.*

The man was wearing bib overalls and a huge straw sombrero. The woman walked with one hand clamped on his naked sunburned shoulder. She wore homespun and a poke bonnet, and as they drew closer to the marker, Susannah saw she was blind, and that the accident which had taken her sight must have been exceedingly horrible. Where her eyes had been there were now only two shallow sockets filled with scar-tissue. She looked both terrified and confused.

"Be they harriers, Si?" she cried in a cracked, quavering voice. "You'll have us killed yet, I'll warrant!"

"Shut up, Mercy," he replied. Like the woman, he spoke with a thick accent Susannah could barely understand. "They ain't harriers, not these. There's a Pube with em, I told you that—ain't no harrier ever been travellin with a Pube."

Blind or not, she tried to pull away from him. He cursed and caught her arm. "Quit it, Mercy! Quit it, I say! You'll fall down and do y'self evil, dammit!"

"We mean you no harm," the gunslinger called. He used the High Speech, and at the sound of it the man's eyes lit up with incredulity. The woman turned back, swinging her blind face in their direction.

"A gunslinger!" the man cried. His voice cracked and wavered with excitement. " 'Fore God! I knew it were! I knew!"

He began to run across the square toward them, pulling the woman after. She stumbled along helplessly, and Susannah waited for the inevitable moment when she must fall. But the man fell first, going heavily to his knees, and she sprawled painfully beside him on the cobbles of the Great Road.

5

JAKE FELT SOMETHING FURRY against his ankle and looked down. Oy was crouched beside him, looking more anxious than ever. Jake reached down and cautiously stroked his head, as much to receive comfort as to give it. Its fur was silky, incredibly soft. For a moment he thought the bumbler was going to run, but it only looked up at him, licked his hand, and then looked back at the two new people. The man was trying to help the woman to her feet and not succeeding very well. Her head craned this way and that in avid confusion.

The man named Si had cut his palms on the cobblestones, but he took no notice. He gave up trying to help the woman, swept off his sombrero, and held it over his chest. To Jake the hat looked as big as a bushel basket. "We bid ye welcome, gunslinger!" he cried. "Welcome indeed! I thought all your kind had perished from the earth, so I did!"

"I thank you for your welcome," Roland said in the High Speech. He put his hands gently on the blind woman's upper arms. She cringed for a moment, then relaxed and allowed him to help her up. "Put on your hat, old-timer. The sun is hot."

He did, then just stood there, looking at Roland with shining eyes. After a moment or two, Jake realized what that shine was. Si was crying.

"A gunslinger! I told you, Mercy! I seen the shooting-iron and *told* you!"

"No harriers?" she asked, as if unable to believe it. "Are you sure they ain't harriers, Si?"

Roland turned to Eddie. "Make sure of the safety and then give her Jake's gun."

Eddie pulled the Ruger from his waistband, checked the safety, and then put it gingerly in the blind woman's hands. She gasped, almost dropped it, then ran her hands over it wonderingly. She turned the empty sockets where her eyes had been up to the man. "A gun!" she whispered. "My sainted hat!"

"Ay, some kind," the old man replied dismissively, taking it from her and giving it back to Eddie, "but the gunslinger's got a *real* one, and there's a woman got another. She's got a brown skin, too, like my da' said the people of Garlan had."

Oy gave his shrill, whistling bark. Jake turned and saw more people coming up the street—five or six in all. Like Si and Mercy, they were all old, and one of them, a woman hobbling over a cane like a witch in a fairy-tale, looked positively ancient. As they neared, Jake realized that two of the men were identical twins. Long white hair spilled over the shoulders of their patched homespun shirts. Their skin was as white as fine linen, and their eyes were pink. *Albinos*, he thought.

The crone appeared to be their leader. She hobbled toward Roland's party on her cane, staring at them with gimlet eyes as green as emeralds. Her toothless mouth was tucked deeply into itself. The hem of the old shawl she wore fluttered in the prairie breeze. Her eyes settled upon Roland.

"Hail, gunslinger! Well met!" She spoke the High Speech herself, and, like Eddie and Susannah, Jake understood the words perfectly, although he guessed they would have been gibberish to him in his own world. "Welcome to River Crossing!"

The gunslinger had removed his own hat, and now he bowed to her, tapping his throat three times, rapidly, with his diminished right hand. "Thankee-sai, Old Mother."

She cackled freely at this and Eddie suddenly realized Roland had at the same time made a joke and paid a compliment. The thought which had already occurred to Susannah now came to him: *This is how he was . . . and this is what he did. Part of it, anyway.*

"Gunslinger ye may be, but below your clothes you're but another foolish man," she said, lapsing into low speech.

Roland bowed again. "Beauty has always made me foolish, mother."

This time she positively *cawed* laughter. Oy shrank against Jake's leg. One of the albino twins rushed forward to catch the ancient as she rocked backward within her dusty cracked shoes. She caught her balance on her own, however, and made an imperious shooing gesture with one hand. The albino retreated.

"Be ye on a quest, gunslinger?" Her green eyes gleamed shrewdly at him; the puckered pocket of her mouth worked in and out.

"Ay," Roland said. "We go in search of the Dark Tower."

The others only looked puzzled, but the old woman recoiled and forked the sign of the evil eye—not at them, Jake realized, but to the southeast, along the path of the Beam.

"I'm sorry to hear it!" she cried. "For no one who ever went in search of that black dog ever came back! So said my grandfather, and his grandfather before him! Not ary one!"

"*Ka*," the gunslinger said patiently, as if this explained everything . . . and, Jake was coming to realize, to Roland it did.

"Ay," she agreed, "black dog *ka*! Well-a-well; ye'll do as ye're called, and live along your path, and die when it comes to the clearing in the trees. Will ye break bread with us before you push on, gunslinger? You and your band of knights?"

Roland bowed again. "It has been long and long since we have broken bread in company other than our own, Old Mother. We cannot stay long, but yes—we'll eat your food with thanks and pleasure."

The old woman turned to the others. She spoke in a cracked and ringing voice—yet it was the words she spoke and not the tone in which they were spoken that sent chills racing down Jake's back: "Behold ye, the return of the White! After evil ways and evil days, the White comes again! Be of good heart and hold up your heads, for ye have lived to see the wheel of *ka* begin to turn once more!"

6

THE OLD WOMAN, WHOSE name was Aunt Talitha, led them through the town square and to the church with the leaning spire—it was The Church of the Blood Everlasting, according to the faded board on the run-to-riot lawn. Written over the words, in green paint that had faded to a ghost, was another message: DEATH TO GRAYS.

She led them through the ruined church, hobbling rapidly along the center aisle past the splintered and overturned pews, down a short flight of stairs, and into a kitchen so different from the ruin above that Susannah blinked in surprise. Here everything was neat as a pin. The wooden floor was very old, but it had been faithfully oiled and glowed with its own serene inner light. The black cookstove took up one whole corner. It was immaculate, and the wood stacked in the brick alcove next to it looked both well-chosen and well-seasoned.

Their party had been joined by three more senior citizens, two women and a man who limped along on a crutch and a wooden leg. Two of the women went to the cupboards and began to make themselves busy; a third opened the belly of the stove and struck a long sulphur match to the wood already laid neatly within; a fourth opened another door and went down a short set of narrow steps into what looked like a cold-pantry. Aunt Talitha, meanwhile, led the rest of them into a spacious entry at the rear of the church building. She waved her cane at two trestle tables which had been stored there under a clean but ragged dropcoth, and the two elderly albinos immediately went over and began to wrestle with one of them.

"Come on, Jake," Eddie said. "Let's lend a hand."

"Nawp!" Aunt Talitha said briskly. "We may be old, but we don't need comp'ny to lend a hand! Not yet, youngster!"

"Leave them be," Roland said.

"Old fools'll rupture themselves," Eddie muttered, but he followed the others, leaving the old men to their chosen table.

Susannah gasped as Eddie lifted her from her chair and carried her through the back door. This wasn't a lawn but a showplace, with beds of flowers blazing like torches in the soft green grass. She saw some she recognized—marigolds and zinnias and phlox—but many others were strange to her. As she watched, a horsefly landed on a bright blue petal . . . which at once folded over it and rolled up tight.

"Wow!" Eddie said, staring around. "Busch Gardens!"

Si said, "This is the one place we keep the way it was in the old days, before the world moved on. And we keep it hidden from those who ride through—Pubes, Grays, harriers. They'd burn it if they knew . . . and kill us for keeping such a place. They hate anything nice—all of em. It's the one thing all those bastards have in common."

The blind woman tugged his arm to shush him.

"No riders these days," the old man with the wooden leg said. "Not for a long time now. They keep closer in to the city. Guess they find all they need to keep em well right there."

The albino twins struggled out with the table. One of the old women followed them, urging them to hurry up and get the hell out of her way. She held a stoneware pitcher in each hand.

"Sit ye down, gunslinger!" Aunt Talitha cried, sweeping her hand at the grass. "Sit ye down, all!"

Susannah could smell a hundred conflicting perfumes. They made her feel dazed and unreal, as if this was a dream she was having. She could hardly believe this strange little pocket of Eden, carefully hidden behind the crumbling facade of the dead town.

Another woman came out with a tray of glasses. They were mismatched but spotless, twinkling in the sun like fine crystal. She held the tray out first to Roland, then to Aunt Talitha, Eddie, Susannah, and Jake at the last. As each took a glass, the first woman poured a dark golden liquid into it.

Roland leaned over to Jake, who was sitting tailor-fashion near an oval bed of bright green flowers with Oy at his side. He murmured: "Drink only enough to be polite, Jake, or we'll be carrying you out of town—this is *graf*—strong apple-beer."

Jake nodded.

Talitha held up her glass, and when Roland followed suit, Eddie, Susannah, and Jake did the same.

"What about the others?" Eddie whispered to Roland.

"They'll be served after the voluntary. Now be quiet."

"Will ye set us on with a word, gunslinger?" Aunt Talitha asked.

The gunslinger got to his feet, his glass upraised in his hand. He lowered his head, as if in thought. The few remaining residents of River Crossing watched him respectfully and, Jake thought, a little fearfully. At last he raised his head again. "Will you drink to the earth, and to the days which have passed upon it?" he asked. His voice was hoarse, trembling with emotion. "Will you drink to the fullness which was, and to friends who have passed on? Will you drink to good company, well met? Will these things set us on, Old Mother?"

She was weeping, Jake saw, but her face broke into a smile of radiant happiness all the same . . . and for a moment she was almost young. Jake looked at her with wonder and sudden, dawning happiness. For the first time since Eddie had hauled him through the door, he felt the shadow of the doorkeeper truly leave his heart.

"Ay, gunslinger!" she said. "Fair spoken! They'll set us on by the league, so they shall!" She tilted her glass up and drank it at a draught. When the glass was empty, Roland emptied his own. Eddie and Susannah also drank, although less deeply.

Jake tasted his own drink, and was surprised to find he liked it— the brew was not bitter, as he had expected, but both sweet and tart, like cider. He could feel the effects almost at once, however, and he put the glass carefully aside. Oy sniffed at it, then drew back, and dropped his muzzle on Jake's ankle.

Around them, the little company of old people—the last residents of River Crossing—were applauding. Most, like Aunt Talitha, were weeping openly. And now other glasses—not so fine but wholly serviceable—were passed around. The party began, and a fine party it was on that long summer's afternoon beneath the wide prairie sky.

7

EDDIE THOUGHT THE MEAL he ate that day was the best he had had
since the mythic birthday feasts of his childhood, when his mother had
made it her business to serve everything he liked—meatloaf and roasted
potatoes and corn on the cob and devil's food cake with vanilla ice cream
on the side.

The sheer variety of the edibles put before them—especially after
the months they had spent eating nothing but lobster meat, deer meat,
and the few bitter greens which Roland pronounced safe—undoubtedly
had something to do with the pleasure he took in the food, but Eddie
didn't think that was the sole answer; he noticed that the kid was packing
it away by the plateful (and feeding a chunk of something to the bumbler
crouched at his feet every couple of minutes), and Jake hadn't been here
a week yet.

There were bowls of stew (chunks of buffalo meat floating in a rich
brown gravy loaded with vegetables), platters of fresh biscuits, crocks of
sweet white butter, and bowls of leaves that looked like spinach but
weren't . . . exactly. Eddie had never been crazy about greens, but at the
first taste of these, some deprived part of him awoke and cried for them.
He ate well of everything, but his need for the green stuff approached
greed, and he saw Susannah was also helping herself to them again and
again. Among the four of them, the travellers emptied three bowls of the
leaves.

The dinner dishes were swept away by the old women and the albino
twins. They returned with chunks of cake piled high on two thick white
plates and a bowl of whipped cream. The cake gave off a sweetly fragrant
smell that made Eddie feel as if he had died and gone to heaven.

"Only buffaler cream," Aunt Talitha said dismissively. "No more
cows—last one croaked thirty year ago. Buffaler cream ain't no prize-
winner, but better'n nothin, by Daisy!"

The cake turned out to be loaded with blueberries. Eddie thought
it beat by a country mile any cake he'd ever had. He finished three
pieces, leaned back, and belched ringingly before he could clap a hand
over his mouth. He looked around guiltily.

Mercy, the blind woman, cackled. "I heard that! Someone be thankin
the cook, Auntie!"

"Ay," Aunt Talitha said, laughing herself. "So he do."

The two women who had served the food were returning yet again.
One carried a steaming jug; the other had a number of thick ceramic
cups balanced precariously on her tray.

Aunt Talitha was sitting at the head of the table with Roland by her right hand. Now he leaned over and murmured something in her ear. She listened, her smile fading a little, then nodded.

"Si, Bill, and Till," she said. "You three stay. We are going to have us a little palaver with this gunslinger and his friends, on account of they mean to move along this very afternoon. The rest of you take your coffee in the kitchen and so cut down the babble. Mind you make your manners before you go!"

Bill and Till, the albino twins, remained sitting at the foot of the table. The others formed a line and moved slowly past the travellers. Each of them shook hands with Eddie and Susannah, then kissed Jake on the cheek. The boy accepted this with good grace, but Eddie could see he was both surprised and embarrassed.

When they reached Roland, they knelt before him and touched the sandalwood butt of the revolver which jutted from the holster he wore on his left hip. He put his hands on their shoulders and kissed their old brows. Mercy was the last; she flung her arms around Roland's waist and baptized his cheek with a wet, ringing kiss.

"Gods bless and keep ye, gunslinger! If only I could see ye!"

"Mind your manners, Mercy!" Aunt Talitha said sharply, but Roland ignored her and bent over the blind woman.

He took her hands gently but firmly in his own, and raised them to his face. "See me with these, beauty," he said, and closed his eyes as her fingers, wrinkled and misshapen with arthritis, patted gently over his brow, his cheeks, his lips and chin.

"Ay, gunslinger!" she breathed, lifting the sightless sockets of her eyes to his faded blue ones. "I see you very well! 'Tis a good face, but full of sadness and care. I fear for you and yours."

"Yet we are well met, are we not?" he asked, and planted a gentle kiss on the smooth, worn skin of her forehead.

"Ay—so we are. So we are. Thank'ee for your kiss, gunslinger. From my heart I thank'ee."

"Go on, Mercy," Aunt Talitha said in a gentler voice. "Get your coffee."

Mercy rose to her feet. The old man with the crutch and peg leg guided her hand to the waistband of his pants. She seized it and, with a final salute to Roland and his band, allowed him to lead her away.

Eddie wiped at his eyes, which were wet. "Who blinded her?" he asked hoarsely.

"Harriers," Aunt Talitha said. "Did it with a branding-iron, they did. Said it was because she was looking at em pert. Twenty-five years agone, that was. Drink your coffee, now, all of you! It's nasty when it's hot, but it ain't nothin but roadmud once it's cold."

Eddie lifted the cup to his mouth and sipped experimentally. He wouldn't have gone so far as to call it roadmud, but it wasn't exactly Blue Mountain Blend, either.

Susannah tasted hers and looked amazed. "Why, this is chicory!"

Talitha glanced at her. "I know it not. Dockey is all I know, and dockey-coffee's all we've had since I had the woman's curse—and that curse was lifted from me long, long ago."

"How old *are* you, ma'am?" Jake asked suddenly.

Aunt Talitha looked at him, surprised, then cackled. "In truth, lad, I disremember. I recall sitting in this same place and having a party to celebrate my eighty, but there were over fifty people settin out on this lawn that day, and Mercy still had her eyes." Her own eyes dropped to the bumbler lying at Jake's feet. Oy didn't remove his muzzle from Jake's ankle, but he raised his gold-ringed eyes to gaze at her. "A billy-bumbler, by Daisy! It's been long and long since I've seen a bumbler in company with people . . . seems they have lost the memory of the days when they walked with men."

One of the albino twins bent down to pat Oy. Oy pulled away from him.

"Once they used to herd sheep," Bill (or perhaps it was Till) said to Jake. "Did ye know that, youngster?"

Jake shook his head.

"Do he talk?" the albino asked. "Some did, in the old days."

"Yes, he does." He looked down at the bumbler, who had returned his head to Jake's ankle as soon as the strange hand left his general area. "Say your name, Oy."

Oy only looked up at him.

"Oy!" Jake urged, but Oy was silent. Jake looked at Aunt Talitha and the twins, mildly chagrined. "Well, he does . . . but I guess he only does it when he wants to."

"That boy doesn't look as if he belongs here," Aunt Talitha said to Roland. "His clothes are strange . . . and his *eyes* are strange, as well."

"He hasn't been here long." Roland smiled at Jake, and Jake smiled uncertainly back. "In a month or two, no one will be able to see his strangeness."

"Ay? I wonder, so I do. And where does he come from?"

"Far from here," the gunslinger said. "Very far."

She nodded. "And when will he go back?"

"Never," Jake said. "This is my home now."

"Gods pity you, then," she said, "for the sun is going down on the world. It's going down forever."

At that Susannah stirred uneasily; one hand went to her belly, as if her stomach was upset.

"Suze?" Eddie asked. "You all right?"

She tried to smile, but it was a weak effort; her normal confidence and self-possession seemed to have temporarily deserted her. "Yes, of course. A goose walked over my grave, that's all."

Aunt Talitha gave her a long, assessing look that seemed to make Susannah uncomfortable . . . and then smiled. "'A goose on my grave'— ha! I haven't heard that one in donkey's years."

"My dad used to say it all the time." Susannah smiled at Eddie—a stronger smile this time. "And anyway, whatever it was is gone now. I'm fine."

"What do you know about the city, and the lands between here and there?" Roland asked, picking up his coffee cup and sipping. "Are there harriers? And who are these others? These Grays and Pubes?"

Aunt Talitha sighed deeply.

8

"YE'D HEAR MUCH, GUNSLINGER, and we know but little. One thing I do know is this: the city's an evil place, especially for this youngster. *Any* youngster. Is there any way you can steer around it as you go your course?"

Roland looked up and observed the now familiar shape of the clouds as they flowed along the path of the Beam. In this wide plains sky, that shape, like a river in the sky, was impossible to miss.

"Perhaps," he said at last, but his voice was oddly reluctant. "I suppose we could skirt around Lud to the southwest and pick up the Beam on the far side."

"It's the Beam ye follow," she said. "Ay, I thought so."

Eddie found his own consideration of the city colored by the steadily strengthening hope that when and if they got there, they would find help—abandoned goodies which would aid them in their quest, or maybe even some people who could tell them a little more about the Dark Tower and what they were supposed to do when they got there. The ones called the Grays, for instance—they sounded like the sort of wise old elves he kept imagining.

The drums were creepy, true enough, reminding him of a hundred low-budget jungle epics (mostly watched on TV with Henry by his side and a bowl of popcorn between them) where the fabulous lost cities the explorers had come looking for were in ruins and the natives had degenerated into tribes of blood-thirsty cannibals, but Eddie found it impossible to believe something like that could have happened in a city that looked, at least from a distance, so much like New York. If there were not wise old elves or abandoned goodies, there would surely be *books*, at least;

he had listened to Roland talk about how rare paper was here, but every city Eddie had ever been in was absolutely drowning in books. They might even find some working transportation; the equivalent of a Land Rover would be nice. That was probably just a silly dream, but when you had thousands of miles of unknown territory to cover, a few silly dreams were undoubtedly in order, if only to keep your spirits up. And weren't those things at least *possible*, damn it?

He opened his mouth to say some of these things, but Jake spoke before he could.

"I don't think we can go around," he said, then blushed a little when they all turned to look at him. Oy shifted at his feet.

"No?" Aunt Talitha said. "And why do ye think that, pray tell?"

"Do you know about trains?" Jake asked.

There was a long silence. Bill and Till exchanged an uneasy glance. Aunt Talitha only looked at Jake steadily. Jake did not drop his eyes.

"I heard of one," she said. "Mayhap even saw it. Over there." She pointed in the direction of the Send. "Long ago, when I was but a child and the world hadn't moved on . . . or at least not s'far's it has now. Is it Blaine ye speak of, boy?"

Jake's eyes flashed in surprise and recognition. "Yes! Blaine!" Roland was studying Jake closely.

"And how would ye know of Blaine the Mono?" Aunt Talitha asked.

"Mono?" Jake looked blank.

"Ay, so it was called. How would you know of that old lay?"

Jake looked helplessly at Roland, then back at Aunt Talitha. "I don't know *how* I know."

And that's the truth, Eddie thought suddenly, *but it's not all the truth. He knows more than he wants to tell here . . . and I think he's scared.*

"This is our business, I think," Roland said in a dry, brisk administrator's voice. "You must let us work it out for ourselves, Old Mother."

"Ay," she agreed quickly. "You'll keep your own counsel. Best that such as us not know."

"What of the city?" Roland prompted. "What do you know of Lud?"

"Little now, but what we know, ye shall hear." And she poured herself another cup of coffee.

9

IT WAS THE TWINS, Bill and Till, who actually did most of the talking, one taking up the tale smoothly whenever the other left off. Every now and then Aunt Talitha would add something or correct something, and the twins would wait respectfully until they were sure she was done. Si didn't speak at all—merely sat with his untouched coffee in front of him, plucking at the pieces of straw which bristled up from the wide brim of his sombrero.

They knew little, indeed, Roland realized quickly, even about the history of their own town (nor did this surprise him; in these latter days, memories faded rapidly and all but the most recent past seemed not to exist), but what they did know was disturbing. Roland was not surprised by this, either.

In the days of their great-great-grandparents, River Crossing had been much the town Susannah had imagined: a trade-stop at the Great Road, modestly prosperous, a place where goods were sometimes sold but more often exchanged. It had been at least nominally part of River Barony, although even then such things as Baronies and Estates o' Land had been passing.

There had been buffalo-hunters in those days, although the trade had been dying out; the herds were small and badly mutated. The meat of these mutant beasts was not poison, but it had been rank and bitter. Yet River Crossing, located between a place they simply called The Landing and the village of Jimtown, had been a place of some note. It was on the Great Road and only six days travel from the city by land and three by barge. "Unless the river were low," one of the twins said. "Then it took longer, and my gran'da said there was times when there was barges grounded all the way upriver to Tom's Neck."

The old people knew nothing of the city's original residents, of course, or the technologies they had used to build the towers and turrets; these were the Great Old Ones, and their history had been lost in the furthest reaches of the past even when Aunt Talitha's great-great-grandfather had been a boy.

"The buildings are still standing," Eddie said. "I wonder if the machines the Great Golden Oldies used to build them still run."

"Mayhap," one of the twins said. "If so, young fella, there don't be ary man or woman that lives there now who'd still know how to run em . . . or so I believe, so I do."

"Nay," his brother said argumentatively, "I doubt the old ways are entirely lost to the Grays 'n Pubes, even now." He looked at Eddie. "Our da' said there was once electric candles in the city. There are those who say they mought still burn."

"Imagine that," Eddie replied wonderingly, and Susannah pinched his leg, hard, under the table.

"Yes," the other twin said. He spoke seriously, unaware of Eddie's sarcasm. "You pushed a button and they came on—bright, heatless candles with ary wicks or reservoirs for oil. And I've heard it said that once, in the old days, Quick, the outlaw prince, actually flew up into the sky in a mechanical bird. But one of its wings broke and he died in a great fall, like Icarus."

Susannah's mouth dropped open. "You know the story of Icarus?"

"Ay, lady," he said, clearly surprised she should find this strange. "He of the beeswax wings."

"Children's stories, both of them," Aunt Talitha said with a sniff. "I know the story of the endless lights is true, for I saw them with my own eyes when I was but a green girl, and they may still glow from time to time, ay; there are those I trust who say they've seen them on clear nights, although it's been long years since I have myself. But no man ever flew, not even the Great Old Ones."

Nonetheless, there *were* strange machines in the city, built to do peculiar and sometimes dangerous things. Many of them might still run, but the elderly twins reckoned that none now in the city knew how to start them up, for they hadn't been heard in years.

Maybe that could change, though, Eddie thought, his eyes gleaming. *If, that is, an enterprising, travel-minded young man with a little knowledge of strange machinery and endless lights came along. It could be just a matter of finding the ON switches. I mean, it really could be that simple. Or maybe they just blew a bunch of fuses—think of that, friends and neighbors! Just replace half a dozen 400-amp Busses and light the whole place up like a Reno Saturday night!*

Susannah elbowed him and asked, in a low voice, what was so funny. Eddie shook his head and put a finger to his lips, earning an irritated look from the love of his life. The albinos, meanwhile, were continuing their story, handing its thread back and forth with the unconscious ease which probably nothing but lifetime twinship can provide.

Four or five generations ago, they said, the city had still been quite heavily populated and reasonably civilized, although the residents drove wagons and buckboards along the wide boulevards the Great Old Ones had constructed for their fabulous horseless vehicles. The city-dwellers were artisans and what the twins called "manufactories," and trade both on the river and over it had been brisk.

"Over it?" Roland asked.

"The bridge over the Send still stands," Aunt Talitha said, "or did twenty year ago."

"Ay, old Bill Muffin and his boy saw it not ten year agone," Si agreed, making his first contribution to the conversation.

"What sort of bridge?" the gunslinger asked.

"A great thing of steel cables," one of the twins said. "It stands in the sky like the web of some great spider." He added shyly: "I should like to see it again before I die."

"Probably fallen in by now," Aunt Talitha said dismissively, "and good riddance. Devil's work." She turned to the twins. "Tell them what's happened since, and why the city's so dangerous now—apart from any haunts that may den there, that is, and I'll warrant there's a power of em. These folks want to get on, and the sun's on the wester."

10

THE REST OF THE story was but another version of a tale Roland of Gilead had heard many times and had, in some measure, lived through himself. It was fragmentary and incomplete, undoubtedly shot through with myth and misinformation, its linear progress distorted by the odd changes—both temporal and directional—which were now taking place in the world, and it could be summed up in a single compound sentence: *Once there was a world we knew, but that world has moved on.*

These old people of River Crossing knew of Gilead no more than Roland knew of the River Barony, and the name of John Farson, the man who had brought ruin and anarchy on Roland's land, meant nothing to them, but all stories of the old world's passing were similar . . . too similar, Roland thought, to be coincidence.

A great civil war—perhaps in Garlan, perhaps in a more distant land called Porla—had erupted three, perhaps even four hundred years ago. Its ripples had spread slowly outward, pushing anarchy and dissension ahead of them. Few if any kingdoms had been able to stand against those slow waves, and anarchy had come to this part of the world as surely as night follows sunset. At one time, whole armies had been on the roads, sometimes in advance, sometimes in retreat, always confused and without long-term goals. As time passed, they crumbled into smaller groups, and these degenerated into roving bands of harriers. Trade faltered, then broke down entirely. Travel went from a matter of inconvenience to one of danger. In the end, it became almost impossible. Communication with the city thinned steadily and had all but ceased a hundred and twenty years ago.

Like a hundred other towns Roland had ridden through—first with Cuthbert and the other gunslingers cast out of Gilead, then alone, in pursuit of the man in black—River Crossing had been cut off and thrown on its own resources.

At this point Si roused himself, and his voice captured the travellers at once. He spoke in the hoarse, cadenced tones of a lifelong teller of tales—one of those divine fools born to merge memory and mendacity into dreams as airily gorgeous as cobwebs strung with drops of dew.

"We last sent tribute to the Barony castle in the time of my great-gran'da," he said. "Twenty-six men went with a wagon of hides—there was no hard coin anymore by then; o' course, and 'twas the best they could do. It was a long and dangerous journey of almost eighty wheels, and six died on the way. Half fell to harriers bound for the war in the city; the other half died either of disease or devilgrass.

"When they finally arrived, they found the castle deserted but for the rooks and black-birds. The walls had been broken; weeds o'ergrew the Court o' State. There had been a great slaughter on the fields to the west; it were white with bones and red with rusty armor, so my da's gran'da said, and the voices of demons cried out like the east wind from the jawbones o' those who'd fallen there. The village beyond the castle had been burned to the ground and a thousand or more skulls were posted along the walls of the keep. Our folk left their bounty o' hides without the shattered barbican gate—for none would venture inside that place of ghosts and moaning voices—and began the homeward way again. Ten more fell on that journey, so that of the six-and-twenty who left only ten returned, my great-gran'da one of them . . . but he picked up a ringworm on his neck and bosom that never left until the day he died. It were the radiation sickness, or so they said. After that, gunslinger, none left the town. We were on our own."

They grew used to the depredations of the harriers, Si continued in his cracked but melodious voice. Watches were posted; when bands of riders were seen approaching—almost always moving southeast along the Great Road and the path of the Beam, going to the war which raged endlessly in Lud—the townspeople hid in a large shelter they had dug beneath the church. Casual damages to the town were not repaired, lest they make those roving bands curious. Most were beyond curiosity; they only rode through at a gallop, bows or battle-axes slung over their shoulders, bound for the killing-zones.

"What war is it that you speak of?" Roland asked.

"Yes," Eddie said, "and what about that drumming sound?"

The twins again exchanged a quick, almost superstitious glance.

"We know not of the god-drums," Si told them. "Ary word or watch. The war of the city, now . . ."

The war had originally been the harriers and outlaws against a loose confederation of artisans and "manufactories" who lived in the city. The residents had decided to fight instead of allowing the harriers to loot them, burn their shops, and then turn the survivors out into the Big Empty, where they would almost certainly die. And for some years they had successfully defended Lud against the vicious but badly organized groups of raiders which tried to storm across the bridge or invade by boat and barge.

"The city-folk used the old weapons," one of the twins said, "and though their numbers were small, the harriers could not stand against such things with their bows and maces and battle-axes."

"Do you mean the city-people used guns?" Eddie asked.

One of the albinos nodded. "Ay, guns, but not *just* guns. There were things that hurled the firebangs over a mile or more. Explosions like dynamite, only more powerful. The outlaws—who are now the Grays, as you must ken—could do nothing but lay siege beyond the river, and that was what they did."

Lud became, in effect, the last fortress-refuge of the latter world. The brightest and most able travelled there from the surrounding countryside by ones and twos. When it came to intelligence tests, sneaking through the tangled encampments and front lines of the besiegers was the newcomers' final exam. Most came unarmed across the no-man's-land of the bridge, and those who made it that far were let through. Some were found wanting and sent packing again, of course, but those who had a trade or a skill (or brains enough to learn one) were allowed to stay. Farming skills were particularly prized; according to the stories, every large park in Lud had been turned into a vegetable garden. With the countryside cut off, it was grow food in the city or starve amid the glass towers and metal alleys. The Great Old Ones were gone, their machines were a mystery, and the silent wonders which remained were inedible.

Little by little, the character of the war began to change. The balance of power had shifted to the besieging Grays—so called because they were, on average, much older than the city-dwellers. Those latter were also growing older, of course. They were still known as Pubes, but in most cases their puberty was long behind them. And they eventually either forgot how the old weapons worked or used them up.

"Probably both," Roland grunted.

Some ninety years ago—within the lifetimes of Si and Aunt Talitha—a final band of outlaws had appeared, one so large that the outriders had gone galloping through River Crossing at dawn and the drogues did not pass until almost sundown. It was the last army these parts had ever seen, and it was led by a warrior prince named David Quick—the same fellow who supposedly later fell to his death from the sky. He had organized the raggle-taggle remnants of the outlaw bands which still hung about the city, killing anyone who showed opposition to his plans. Quick's army of Grays used neither boat nor bridge to attempt entry into the city, but instead built a pontoon bridge twelve miles below it and attacked on the flank.

"Since then the war has guttered like a chimney-fire," Aunt Talitha finished. "We hear reports every now and then from someone who has managed to leave, ay, so we do. These come a little more often now, for the bridge, they say, is undefended and I think the fire is almost out. Within the city, the Pubes and Grays squabble over the remaining spoils, only I reckon that the descendents of the harriers who followed Quick over the pontoon bridge are the real Pubes now, although they are still called Grays. The descendents of the original city-dwellers must now be almost as old as we are, although there are still some younkers who go to be among them, drawn by the old stories and the lure of the knowledge which may still remain there.

"These two sides still keep up their old enmity, gunslinger, and both would desire this young man you call Eddie. If the dark-skinned woman is fertile, they would not kill her even though her legs are short-ended; they would keep her to bear children, for children are fewer now, and although the old sicknesses are passing, some are still born strange."

At this, Susannah stirred, seemed about to say something, then only drank the last of her coffee and settled back into her former listening position.

"But if they would desire the young man and woman, gunslinger, I think they would lust for the boy."

Jake bent and began to stroke Oy's fur again. Roland saw his face and knew what he was thinking: it was the passage under the mountains all over again, just another version of the Slow Mutants.

"You they'd just as soon kill," Aunt Talitha said, "for you are a gunslinger, a man out of his own time and place, neither fish nor fowl, and no use to either side. But a boy can be taken, used, schooled to remember some things and to forget all the others. *They've* all forgotten whatever it was they had to fight about in the first place; the world has moved on since then. Now they just fight to the sound of them awful drumbeats, some few still young, most of them old enough for the rocking chair, like us here, all of them stupid grots who only live to kill and kill to live." She paused. "Now that you've heard us old cullies to the end, are ye sure it would not be best to go around, and leave them to their business?"

Before Roland could reply, Jake spoke up in a clear, firm voice. "Tell what you know about Blaine the Mono," he said. "Tell about Blaine and Engineer Bob."

11

"ENGINEER *WHO*?" EDDIE ASKED, but Jake only went on looking at the old people.

"Track lies over yonder," Si answered at last. He pointed toward the river. "One track only, set up high on a colyum of man-made stone, such as the Old Ones used to make their streets and walls."

"A monorail!" Susannah exclaimed. "Blaine the Monorail!"

"Blaine is a pain," Jake muttered.

Roland glanced at him but said nothing.

"Does this train run now?" Eddie asked Si.

Si shook his head slowly. His face was troubled and uneasy. "No, young sir—but in my lifetime and Auntie's, it did. When we were green and the war of the city still went forrad briskly. We'd hear it before we saw it—a low humming noise, a sound like ye sometimes hear when a bad summer storm's on the way—one that's full of lightning."

"Ay," Aunt Talitha said. Her face was lost and dreaming.

"Then it'd come—Blaine the Mono, twinkling in the sun, with a nose like one of the bullets in your revolver, gunslinger. Maybe two wheels long. I know that sounds like it couldn't be, and maybe it wasn't (we were green, ye must remember, and that makes a difference), but I still think it *was*, for when it came, it seemed to run along the whole horizon. Fast, low, and gone before you could even see it proper!

"Sometimes, on days when the weather were foul and the air low, it'd shriek like a harpy as it came out of the west. Sometimes it'd come in the night with a long white light spread out before it, and that shriek would wake all of us. It were like the trumpet they say will raise the dead from their graves at the end of the world, so it was."

"Tell em about the bang, Si!" Bill or Till said in a voice which trembled with awe. "Tell em about the godless bang what always came after!"

"Ay, I was just getting to that," Si answered with a touch of annoyance. "After it passed by, there would be quiet for a few seconds . . . sometimes as long as a minute, maybe . . . and then there'd come an explosion that rattled the boards and knocked cups off the shelves and sometimes even broke the glass in the window-panes. But never did anyone see ary flash nor fire. It was like an explosion in the world of spirits."

Eddie tapped Susannah on the shoulder, and when she turned to him he mouthed two words: *Sonic boom.* It was nuts—no train he had ever heard of travelled faster than the speed of sound—but it was also the only thing that made sense.

She nodded and turned back to Si.

"It's the only one of the machines the Great Old Ones made that I've ever seen running with my own eyes," he said in a soft voice, "and if it weren't the devil's work, there be no devil. The last time I saw it was the spring I married Mercy, and that must have been sixty year agone."

"Seventy," Aunt Talitha said with authority.

"And this train went *into* the city," Roland said. "From back the way we came . . . from the west . . . from the forest."

"Ay," a new voice said unexpectedly, "but there was another . . . one that went *out from* the city . . . and mayhap that one still runs."

12

THEY TURNED. MERCY STOOD by a bed of flowers between the back of the church and the table where they sat. She was walking slowly toward the sound of their voices, with her hands spread out before her.

Si got clumsily to his feet, hurried to her as best he could, and took her hand. She slipped an arm about his waist and they stood there looking like the world's oldest wedding couple.

"Auntie told you to take your coffee inside!" he said.

"Finished my coffee long ago," Mercy said. "It's a bitter brew and I hate it. Besides—I wanted to hear the palaver." She raised a trembling finger and pointed it in Roland's direction. "I wanted to hear *his* voice. It's fair and light, so it is."

"I cry your pardon, Auntie," Si said, looking at the ancient woman a little fearfully. "She was never one to mind, and the years have made her no better."

Aunt Talitha glanced at Roland. He nodded, almost imperceptibly. "Let her come forward and join us," she said.

Si led her over to the table, scolding all the while. Mercy only looked over his shoulder with her sightless eyes, her mouth set in an intractable line.

When Si had gotten her seated, Aunt Talitha leaned forward on her forearms and said, "Now do you have something to say, old sister-sai, or were you just beating your gums?"

"I hear what I hear. My ears are as sharp as they ever were, Talitha—sharper!"

Roland's hand dropped to his belt for a moment. When he brought it back to the table, he was holding a cartridge in his fingers. He tossed it to Susannah, who caught it. "Do you, sai?" he asked.

"Well enough," she said, turning in his direction, "to know that you just threw something. To your woman, I think—the one with the brown skin. Something small. What was it, gunslinger? A biscuit?"

"Close enough," he said, smiling. "You hear as well as you say. Now tell us what you meant."

"There is another mono," she said, "unless 'tis the same one, running a different course. Either way, a different course was run by *some* mono . . . until seven or eight year ago, anyways. I used to hear it leaving the city and going out into the waste lands beyond."

"Dungheap!" one of the albino twins ejaculated. "*Nothing* goes to the waste lands! Nothing can live there!"

She turned her face to him. "Is a train alive, Till Tudbury?" she asked. "Does a machine fall sick with sores and puking?"

Well, Eddie thought of saying, *there* was *this bear* . . .

He thought it over a little more and decided it might be better to keep his silence.

"We would have heard it," the other twin was insisting hotly. "A noise like the one Si always tells of—"

"This one didn't make no bang," she admitted, "but I heard that other sound, that humming noise like the one you hear sometimes after lightning has struck somewhere close. When the wind was strong, blowing out from the city, I heard it." She thrust out her chin and added: "I *did* hear the bang once, too. From far, far out. The night Big Charlie Wind came and almost blew the steeple off the church. Must have been two hundred wheels from here. Maybe two hundred and fifty."

"Bulldink!" the twin cried. "You been chewing the weed!"

"I'll chew on *you*, Bill Tudbury, if you don't shut up your honkin. You've no business sayin bulldink to a lady, either. Why—"

"Stop it, Mercy!" Si hissed, but Eddie was barely listening to this exchange of rural pleasantries. What the blind woman had said made sense to him. Of *course* there would be no sonic boom, not from a train which *started* its run in Lud; he couldn't remember exactly what the speed of sound was, but he thought it was somewhere in the neighborhood of six hundred and fifty miles an hour. A train starting from a dead stop would take some time getting up to that speed, and by the time it reached it, it would be out of earshot . . . unless the listening conditions happened to be just right, as Mercy claimed they had been on the night when the Big Charlie Wind—whatever that was—had come.

And there were possibilities here. Blaine the Mono was no Land Rover, but maybe . . . maybe . . .

"You haven't heard the sound of this other train for seven or eight years, sai?" Roland asked. "Are you sure it wasn't much longer?"

"Couldn't have been," she said, "for the last time was the year old Bill Muffin took blood-sick. Poor Bill!"

"That's almost ten year agone," Aunt Talitha said, and her voice was queerly gentle.

"Why did you never say you heard such a thing?" Si asked. He looked at the gunslinger. "You can't believe everything she says, lord—always longing to be in the middle of the stage is my Mercy."

"Why, you old slumgullion!" she cried, and slapped his arm. "I didn't say because I didn't want to o'ertop the story you're so proud of, but now that it matters what I heard, I'm bound to tell!"

"I believe you, sai," Roland said, "but are you sure you haven't heard the sounds of the mono since then?"

"Nay, not since then. I imagine it's finally reached the end of its path."

"I wonder," Roland said. "Indeed, I wonder very much." He looked down at the table, brooding, suddenly far away from all of them.

Choo-choo, Jake thought, and shivered.

13

HALF AN HOUR LATER they were in the town square again, Susannah in her wheelchair, Jake adjusting the straps of his pack while Oy sat at his heel, watching him attentively. Only the town elders had attended the dinner-party in the little Eden behind the Church of the Blood Everlasting, it seemed, because when they returned to the square, another dozen people were waiting. They glanced at Susannah and looked a bit longer at Jake (his youth apparently more interesting to them than her dark skin), but it was clearly Roland they had come to see; their wondering eyes were full of ancient awe.

He's a living remnant of a past they only know from stories, Susannah thought. *They look at him the way religious people would look at one of the saints—Peter or Paul or Matthew—if he decided to drop by the Saturday night bean supper and tell them stories of how it was, traipsing around the Sea of Galilee with Jesus the Carpenter.*

The ritual which had ended the meal was now repeated, only this time everyone left in River Crossing participated. They shuffled forward in a line, shaking hands with Eddie and Susannah, kissing Jake on the cheek or forehead, then kneeling in front of Roland for his touch and his blessing. Mercy threw her arms about him and pressed her blind face against his stomach. Roland hugged her back and thanked her for her news.

"Will ye not stay the night with us, gunslinger? Sunset comes on apace, and it's been long since you and yours spent the night beneath a roof, I'll warrant."

"It has been, but it's best we go on. Thankee-sai."

"Will ye come again if ye may, gunslinger?"

"Yes," Roland said, but Eddie did not need to look into his strange friend's face to know the chances were small. "If we can."

"Ay." She hugged him a final time, then passed on with her hand resting on Si's sunburned shoulder. "Fare ye well."

Aunt Talitha came last. When she began to kneel, Roland caught her by the shoulders. "No, sai. You shall not do." And before Eddie's amazed eyes, Roland knelt before her in the dust of the town square. "Will you bless me, Old Mother? Will you bless all of us as we go our course?"

"Ay," she said. There was no surprise in her voice, no tears in her eyes, but her voice throbbed with deep feeling, all the same. "I see your heart is true, gunslinger, and that you hold to the old ways of your kind; ay, you hold to them very well. I bless you and yours and will pray that no harm will come to you. Now take this, if you will." She reached into the bodice of her faded dress and removed a silver cross at the end of a fine-link silver chain. She took it off.

Now it was Roland's turn to be surprised. "Are you sure? I did not come to take what belongs to you and yours, Old Mother."

"I'm sure as sure can be. I've worn this day and night for over a hundred years, gunslinger. Now you shall wear it, and lay it at the foot of the Dark Tower, and speak the name of Talitha Unwin at the far end of the earth." She slipped the chain over his head. The cross dropped into the open neck of his deerskin shirt as if it belonged there. "Go now. We have broken bread, we have held palaver, we have your blessing, and you have ours. Go your course in safety. Stand and be true." Her voice trembled and broke on the last word.

Roland rose to his feet, then bowed and tapped his throat three times. "Thankee-sai."

She bowed back, but did not speak. Now there were tears coursing down her cheeks.

"Ready?" Roland asked.

Eddie nodded. He did not trust himself to speak.

"All right," Roland said. "Let's go."

They walked down what remained of the town's high street, Jake pushing Susannah's wheelchair. As they passed the last building (TRADE & CHANGE, the faded sign read), he looked back. The old people were still gathered about the stone marker, a forlorn cluster of humanity in the middle of this wide, empty plain. Jake raised his hand. Up to this point he had managed to hold himself in, but when several of the old folks—Si, Bill, and Till among them—raised their own hands in return, Jake burst into tears himself.

Eddie put an arm around his shoulders. "Just keep walking, sport," he said in an uneasy voice. "That's the only way to do it."

"They're so *old*!" Jake sobbed. "How can we just leave them like this? It's not right!"

"It's *ka*," Eddie said without thinking.

"Is it? Well *ka* suh-suh-*sucks*!"

"Yeah, *hard*," Eddie agreed . . . but he kept walking. So did Jake, and he didn't look back again. He was afraid they would still be there, standing at the center of their forgotten town, watching until Roland and his friends were out of view. And he would have been right.

14

THEY HAD MADE LESS than seven miles before the sky began to darken and sunset colored the western horizon blaze orange. There was a grove of Susannah's eucalyptus trees nearby; Jake and Eddie foraged there for wood.

"I just don't see why we didn't stay," Jake said. "The blind lady invited us, and we didn't get very far, anyway. I'm still so full I'm practically waddling."

Eddie smiled. "Me, too. And I can tell you something else: your good friend Edward Cantor Dean is looking forward to a long and leisurely squat in this grove of trees first thing tomorrow morning. You wouldn't believe how tired I am of eating deermeat and crapping rabbit-turds. If you'd told me a year ago that a good dump would be the high point of my day, I would have laughed in your face."

"Is your middle name really Cantor?"

"Yes, but I'd appreciate it if you didn't spread it around."

"I won't. Why *didn't* we stay, Eddie?"

Eddie sighed. "Because we would have found out they needed firewood."

"Huh?"

"And after we got the firewood, we would've found they *also* needed fresh meat, because they served us the last of what they had. And we'd be real creeps not to replace what we ate, right? Especially when we're packing guns and the best they can probably do is a bunch of bows and arrows fifty or a hundred years old. So we would have gone hunting for them. By then it would be night again, and when we got up the next day, Susannah would be saying we ought to at least make a few repairs before we moved on—oh, not to the *front* of the town, that'd be dangerous, but maybe in the hotel or wherever it is they live. Only a few days, and what's a few days, right?"

Roland materialized out of the gloom. He moved as quietly as ever, but he looked tired and preoccupied. "I thought maybe you two fell into a quickpit," he said.

"Nope. I've just been telling Jake the facts as I see them."

"So what *would* have been wrong with that?" Jake asked. "This Dark Tower thingy has been wherever it is for a long time, right? It's not going anywhere, is it?"

"A few days, then a few more, then a few more." Eddie looked at the branch he had just picked up and threw it aside disgustedly. *I'm starting to sound just like him*, he thought. And yet he knew that he was only speaking the truth. "Maybe we'd see that their spring is getting silted up, and it wouldn't be polite to go until we'd dug it out for them. But why stop there when we could take another couple of weeks and build a jackleg waterwheel, right? They're old, and have no more foot." He glanced at Roland, and his voice was tinged with reproach. "I tell you what—when I think of Bill and Till there stalking a herd of wild buffalo, I get the shivers."

"They've been doing it a long time," Roland said, "and I imagine they could show us a thing or two. They'll manage. Meantime, let's get that wood—it's going to be a chilly night."

But Jake wasn't done with it yet. He was looking closely—almost sternly—at Eddie. "You're saying we could never do enough for them, aren't you?"

Eddie stuck out his lower lip and blew hair off his forehead. "Not exactly. I'm saying it would never be any easier to leave than it was today. Harder, maybe, but no easier."

"It *still* doesn't seem right."

They reached the place that would become, once the fire was lit, just another campsite on the road to the Dark Tower. Susannah had eased herself out of her chair and was lying on her back with her hands behind her head, looking up at the stars. Now she sat up and began to arrange the wood in the way Roland had shown her months ago.

"Right is what all this is about," Roland said. "But if you look too long at the small rights, Jake—the ones that lie close at hand—it's easy to lose sight of the big ones that stand farther off. Things are out of joint—going wrong and getting worse. We see it all around us, but the answers are still ahead. While we were helping the twenty or thirty people left in River Crossing, twenty or thirty thousand more might be suffering or dying somewhere else. And if there is any place in the universe where these things can be set right, it's at the Dark Tower."

"Why? How?" Jake asked. "What *is* this Tower, anyway?"

Roland squatted beside the fire Susannah had built, produced his flint and steel, and began to flash sparks into the kindling. Soon small flames were growing amid the twigs and dried handfuls of grass. "I can't answer those questions," he said. "I wish I could."

That, Eddie thought, was an exceedingly clever reply. Roland had said *I can't answer* . . . but that wasn't the same thing as *I don't know*. Far from it.

15

SUPPER CONSISTED OF WATER and greens. They were all still recovering from the heavy meal they'd eaten in River Crossing; even Oy refused the scraps Jake offered him after the first one or two.

"How come you wouldn't talk back there?" Jake scolded the bumbler. "You made me look like an idiot!"

"Id-yit!" Oy said, and put his muzzle on Jake's ankle.

"He's talking better all the time," Roland remarked. "He's even starting to sound like you, Jake."

"Ake," Oy agreed, not lifting his muzzle. Jake was fascinated by the gold rings in Oy's eyes; in the flickering light of the fire, they seemed to revolve slowly.

"But he wouldn't talk to the old people."

"Bumblers are choosy about that sort of thing," Roland said. "They're odd creatures. If I had to guess, I'd say this one was driven away by its own pack."

"Why do you think so?"

Roland pointed at Oy's flank. Jake had cleaned off the blood (Oy hadn't enjoyed this, but had stood for it) and the bite was healing, although the bumbler still limped a little. "I'd bet an eagle that's the bite of another bumbler."

"But why would his own pack—"

"Maybe they got tired of his chatter," Eddie said. He had lain down beside Susannah and put an arm about her shoulders.

"Maybe they did," Roland said, "especially if he was the only one of them who was still trying to talk. The others might have decided he was too bright—or too uppity—for their taste. Animals don't know as much about jealousy as people, but they're not ignorant of it, either."

The object of this discussion closed his eyes and appeared to go to sleep . . . but Jake noticed his ears began twitching when the talk resumed.

"How bright *are* they?" Jake asked.

Roland shrugged. "The old groom I told you about—the one who said a good bumbler is good luck—swore he had one in his youth that could add. He said it told sums either by scratching on the stable floor or pushing stones together with its muzzle." He grinned. It lit his whole face, chasing away the gloomy shadows which had lain there ever since they left River Crossing. "Of course, grooms and fishermen are born to lie."

A companionable silence fell among them, and Jake could feel drowsiness stealing over him. He thought he would sleep soon, and that was fine by him. Then the drums began, coming out of the southeast in rhythmic pulses, and he sat back up. They listened without speaking.

"That's a rock and roll backbeat," Eddie said suddenly. "I know it is. Take away the guitars and that's what you've got left. In fact, it sounds quite a lot like Z.Z. Top."

"Z.Z. *who*?" Susannah asked.

Eddie grinned. "They didn't exist in your when," he said. "I mean, they probably did, but in '63 they would have been just a bunch of kids going to school down in Texas." He listened. "I'll be goddamned if that doesn't sound just like the backbeat to something like 'Sharp-Dressed Man' or 'Velcro Fly.' "

" 'Velcro Fly'?" Jake said. "That's a stupid name for a song."

"Pretty funny, though," Eddie said. "You missed it by ten years or so, sport."

"We'd better roll over," Roland said. "Morning comes early."

"I can't sleep with that shit going on," Eddie said. He hesitated, then said something which had been on his mind ever since the morning when they had pulled Jake, whitefaced and shrieking, through the doorway and into this world. "Don't you think it's about time we exchanged stories, Roland? We might find out we know more than we think."

"Yes, it's almost time for that. But not in the dark." Roland rolled onto his side, pulled up a blanket, and appeared to go to sleep.

"Jesus," Eddie said. "Just like that." He blew a disgusted little whistle between his teeth.

"He's right," Susannah said. "Come on, Eddie—go to sleep."

He grinned and kissed the tip of her nose. "Yes, Mummy."

Five minutes later he and Susannah were dead to the world, drums or no drums. Jake found that his own sleepiness had stolen away, however. He lay looking up at the strange stars and listening to that steady, rhythmic throbbing coming out of the darkness. Maybe it was the Pubes, boogying madly to a song called "Velcro Fly" while they worked themselves into a sacrificial killing frenzy.

He thought of Blaine the Mono, a train so fast that it travelled across the huge, haunted world trailing a sonic boom behind it, and that led him naturally enough to thoughts of Charlie the Choo-Choo, who had been retired to a forgotten siding when the new Burlington Zephyr arrived, rendering him obsolete. He thought of the expression on Charlie's face, the one that was supposed to be cheery and pleasant but somehow wasn't. He thought about The Mid-World Railway Company, and the empty lands between St. Louis and Topeka. He thought about how Charlie had been all ready to go when Mr. Martin needed him, and how Charlie could blow his own whistle and feed his own firebox. He wondered again if Engineer Bob had sabotaged the Burlington Zephyr in order to give his beloved Charlie a second chance.

At last—and as suddenly as it had begun—the rhythmic drumming stopped, and Jake drifted off to sleep.

16

HE DREAMED, BUT NOT of the plaster-man.

He dreamed instead that he was standing on a stretch of blacktop highway somewhere in the Big Empty of western Missouri. Oy was with him. Railroad warning signals—white X-shapes with red lights in their centers—flanked the road. The lights were flashing and bells were ringing.

Now a humming noise began to rise out of the southeast getting steadily louder. It sounded like lightning in a bottle.

Here it comes, he told Oy.

Ums! Oy agreed.

And suddenly a vast pink shape two wheels long was slicing across the plain toward them. It was low and bullet-shaped, and when Jake saw it, a terrible fear filled his heart. The two big windows flashing in the sun at the front of the train looked like eyes.

Don't ask it silly questions, Jake told Oy. *It won't play silly games. It's just an awful choo-choo train, and its name is Blaine the Pain.*

Suddenly Oy leaped onto the tracks and crouched there with his ears flattened back. His golden eyes were blazing. His teeth were bared in a desperate snarl.

No! Jake screamed. *No, Oy!*

But Oy paid no attention. The pink bullet was bearing down on the tiny, defiant shape of the billy-bumbler now, and that humming seemed to be crawling all over Jake's skin, making his nose bleed and shattering the fillings in his teeth.

He leaped for Oy, Blaine the Mono (or was it Charlie the Choo-Choo?) bore down on them, and he woke up suddenly, shivering, bathed in sweat. The night seemed to be pressing down upon him like a physical weight. He rolled over and felt frantically for Oy. For a terrible moment he thought the bumbler was gone, and then his fingers found the silky fur. Oy uttered a squeak and looked at him with sleepy curiosity.

"That's all right," Jake whispered in a dry voice. "There's no train. It was just a dream. Go back to sleep, boy."

"Oy," the bumbler agreed, and closed his eyes again.

Jake rolled over on his back and lay looking up at the stars. *Blaine is more than a pain,* he thought. *It's dangerous. Very dangerous.*

Yes, perhaps.

No perhaps about it! his mind insisted frantically.

All right, Blaine was a pain—given. But his Final Essay had had something else to say on the subject of Blaine, hadn't it?

Blaine is the truth. Blaine is the truth. Blaine is the truth.

"Oh Jeez, what a mess," Jake whispered. He closed his eyes and was asleep again in seconds. This time his sleep was dreamless.

17

AROUND NOON THE NEXT day they reached the top of another drumlin and saw the bridge for the first time. It crossed the Send at a point where the river narrowed, bent due south, and passed in front of the city.

"Holy Jesus," Eddie said softly. "Does that look familiar to you, Suze?"

"Yes."

"Jake?"

"Yes—it looks like the George Washington Bridge."

"It sure does," Eddie agreed.

"But what's the GWB doing in Missouri?" Jake asked.

Eddie looked at him. "Say *what*, sport?"

Jake looked confused. "Mid-World, I mean. You know."

Eddie was looking at him harder than ever. "How do *you* know this is Mid-World? You weren't with us when we came to that marker."

Jake stuffed his hands in his pockets and looked down at his moccasins. "Dreamed it," he said briefly. "You don't think I booked this trip with my dad's travel-agent, do you?"

Roland touched Eddie's shoulder. "Let it alone for now." Eddie glanced briefly at Roland and nodded.

They stood looking at the bridge a little longer. They'd had time to get used to the city skyline, but this was something new. It dreamed in the distance, a faint shape sketched against the blue midmorning sky. Roland could make out four sets of impossibly tall metal towers—one set at each end of the bridge and two in the middle. Between them, gigantic cables swooped through the air in long arcs. Between these arcs and the base of the bridge were many vertical lines—either more cables or metal beams, he could not tell which. But he also saw gaps, and realized after a long time that the bridge was no longer perfectly level.

"Yonder bridge is going to be in the river soon, I think," Roland said.

"Well, maybe," Eddie said reluctantly, "but it doesn't really look that bad to me."

Roland sighed. "Don't hope for too much, Eddie."

"What's that supposed to mean?" Eddie heard the touchiness in his voice, but it was too late to do anything about it now.

"It means that I want you to believe your eyes, Eddie—that's all. There was a saying when I was growing up: 'Only a fool believes he's dreaming before he wakes up.' Do you understand?"

Eddie felt a sarcastic reply on his tongue and banished it after a brief struggle. It was just that Roland had a way—it was unintentional, he was sure, but that didn't make it any easier to deal with—of making him feel like such a *kid*.

"I guess I do," he said at last. "It means the same thing as my mother's favorite saying."

"And what was that?"

"Hope for the best and expect the worst," Eddie said sourly.

Roland's face lightened in a smile. "I think I like your mother's saying better."

"But it *is* still standing!" Eddie burst out. "I agree it's not in such fantastic shape—probably nobody's done a really thorough maintenance check on it for a thousand years or so—but it *is* still there. The whole city is! Is it so wrong to hope we might find some things that'll help us there? Or some people that'll feed us and talk to us, like the old folks back in River Crossing, instead of shooting at us? Is it so wrong to hope our luck might be turning?"

In the silence which followed, Eddie realized with embarrassment that he had been making a speech.

"No." There was a kindness in Roland's voice—that kindness which always surprised Eddie when it came. "It's never wrong to hope." He looked around at Eddie and the others like a man coming out of a deep dream. "We're done travelling for today. It's time we had our own pala-ver, I think, and it's going to take awhile."

The gunslinger left the road and walked into the high grass without looking back. After a moment, the other three followed.

18

UNTIL THEY MET THE old people in River Crossing, Susannah had seen Roland strictly in terms of television shows she rarely watched: *Cheyenne*, *The Rifleman*, and, of course, the archetype of them all, *Gunsmoke*. That was one she had sometimes listened to on the radio with her father before it came on TV (she thought of how foreign the idea of radio drama would be to Eddie and Jake and smiled—Roland's was not the only world which had moved on). She could still remember what the narrator said at the beginning of every one of those radio playlets: "It makes a man watchful . . . and a little lonely."

Until River Crossing, that had summed Roland up perfectly for her. He was not broad-shouldered, as Marshal Dillon had been, nor anywhere near as tall, and his face seemed to her more that of a tired poet than a wild-west lawman, but she had still seen him as an existential version of that make-believe Kansas peace officer, whose only mission in life (other than an occasional drink in The Longbranch with his friends Doc and Kitty) had been to Clean Up Dodge.

Now she understood that Roland had once been much more than a cop riding a Dalíesque range at the end of the world. He had been a diplomat; a mediator; perhaps even a teacher. Most of all, he had been a soldier of what these people called "the white," by which she guessed they meant the civilizing forces that kept people from killing each other enough of the time to allow some sort of progress. In his time he had been more wandering knight-errant than bounty hunter. And in many ways, this still *was* his time; the people of River Crossing had certainly thought so. Why else would they have knelt in the dust to receive his blessing?

In light of this new perception, Susannah could see how cleverly the gunslinger had managed them since that awful morning in the speaking ring. Each time they had begun a line of conversation which would lead to the comparing of notes—and what could be more natural, given the cataclysmic and inexplicable "drawing" each of them had experienced?— Roland had been there, stepping in quickly and turning the conversation into other channels so smoothly that none of them (even she, who had spent almost four years up to her neck in the civil-rights movement) had noticed what he was doing.

Susannah thought she understood why—he had done it in order to give Jake time to heal. But understanding his motives didn't change her own feelings—astonishment, amusement, chagrin—about how neatly he had handled them. She remembered something Andrew, her chauffeur, had said shortly before Roland had drawn her into this world. Something about President Kennedy being the last gunslinger of the western world. She had scoffed then, but now she thought she understood. There was a lot more JFK than Matt Dillon in Roland. She suspected that Roland possessed little of Kennedy's imagination, but when it came to romance . . . dedication . . . charisma . . .

And guile, she thought. *Don't forget guile.*

She surprised herself by suddenly bursting into laughter.

Roland had seated himself cross-legged. Now he turned toward her, raising his eyebrows. "Something funny?"

"Very. Tell me something—how many languages can you speak?"

The gunslinger thought it over. "Five," he said at last. "I used to speak the Sellian dialects fairly well, but I believe I've forgotten everything but the curses."

Susannah laughed again. It was a cheerful, delighted sound. "You a fox, Roland," she said. "Indeed you are."

Jake looked interested. "Say a swear in Strelleran," he said.

"*Sellian,*" Roland corrected. He thought a minute, then said something very fast and greasy—to Eddie it sounded a little as if he was gargling with some very thick liquid. Week-old coffee, say. Roland grinned as he said it.

Jake grinned back. "What does it mean?"

Roland put an arm around the boy's shoulders for a moment. "That we have a lot of things to talk about."

19

"WE ARE KA-TET," ROLAND began, "which means a group of people bound together by fate. The philosophers of my land said a *ka-tet* could only be broken by death or treachery. My great teacher, Cort, said that since death and treachery are also spokes on the wheel of *ka*, such a binding can never be broken. As the years pass and I see more, I come more and more to Cort's way of looking at it.

"Each member of a *ka-tet* is like a piece in a puzzle. Taken by itself, each piece is a mystery, but when they are put together, they make a picture . . . or *part* of a picture. It may take a great many *ka-tets* to finish one picture. You mustn't be surprised if you discover your lives have been touching in ways you haven't seen until now. For one thing, each of you three is capable of knowing each other's thoughts—"

"What?" Eddie cried.

"It's true. You share your thoughts so naturally that you haven't even been aware it's happening, but it has been. It's easier for me to see, no doubt, because I am not a full member of this *ka-tet*—possibly because I am not from your world—and so cannot take part completely in the thought-sharing ability. But I *can* send. Susannah . . . do you remember when we were in the circle?"

"Yes. You told me to let the demon go when you told me. But you didn't say that out loud."

"Eddie . . . do you remember when we were in the bear's clearing, and the mechanical bat came at you?"

"Yes. You told me to get down."

"He never opened his mouth, Eddie," Susannah said.

"Yes, you did! You *yelled!* I *heard* you, man!"

"I yelled, all right, but I did it with my *mind.*" The gunslinger turned to Jake. "Do you remember? In the house?"

"When the board I was pulling on wouldn't come up, you told me to pull on the other one. But if you can't read my mind, Roland, how did you know what kind of trouble I was in?"

"I *saw*. I heard nothing, but I *saw*—just a little, as if through a dirty window." His eyes surveyed them. "This closeness and sharing of minds is called *khef*, a word that means many other things in the original tongue of the Old World—water, birth, and life-force are only three of them. Be aware of it. For now, that's all I want."

"Can you be aware of something you don't believe in?" Eddie asked.

Roland smiled. "Just keep an open mind."

"That I can do."

"Roland?" It was Jake. "Do you think Oy might be part of our *ka-tet*?"

Susannah smiled. Roland didn't. "I'm not prepared to even guess right now, but I'll tell you this, Jake—I've been thinking about your furry friend a good deal. *Ka* does not rule all, and coincidences still happen . . . but the sudden appearance of a billy-bumbler that still remembers people doesn't seem completely coincidental to me."

He glanced around at them.

"I'll begin. Eddie will speak next, taking up from the place where I leave off. Then Susannah. Jake, you'll speak last. All right?"

They nodded.

"Fine," Roland said. "We are *ka-tet*—one from many. Let the palaver begin."

20

THE TALK WENT ON until sundown, stopping only long enough for them to eat a cold meal, and by the time it was over, Eddie felt as if he had gone twelve hard rounds with Sugar Ray Leonard. He no longer doubted that they had been "sharing *khef*," as Roland put it; he and Jake actually seemed to have been living each other's life in their dreams, as if they were two halves of the same whole.

Roland began with what had happened under the mountains, where Jake's first life in this world had ended. He told of his own palaver with the man in black, and Walter's veiled words about a Beast and someone he called the Ageless Stranger. He told of the strange, daunting dream which had come to him, a dream in which the whole universe had been swallowed in a beam of fantastic white light. And how, at the end of that dream, there had been a single blade of purple grass.

Eddie glanced sideways at Jake and was stunned by the knowledge— the *recognition*—in the boy's eyes.

21

ROLAND HAD BABBLED PARTS of this story to Eddie in his time of delirium, but it was entirely new to Susannah, and she listened with wide eyes. As Roland repeated the things Walter had told him, she caught glints of her own world, like reflections in a smashed mirror: automobiles, cancer, rockets to the moon, artificial insemination. She had no idea who the Beast might be, but she recognized the name of the Ageless Stranger as a variation upon the name of Merlin, the magician who had supposedly orchestrated the career of King Arthur. Curiouser and curiouser.

Roland told of how he had awakened to find Walter long years dead—time had somehow slipped forward, perhaps a hundred years, perhaps five hundred. Jake listened in fascinated silence as the gunslinger told of reaching the edge of the Western Sea, of how he had lost two of the fingers on his right hand, and how he had drawn Eddie and Susannah before encountering Jack Mort, the dark third.

The gunslinger motioned to Eddie, who took up the tale with the coming of the great bear.

"Shardik?" Jake interjected. "But that's the name of a *book*! A book in *our* world! It was written by the man who wrote that famous book about the rabbits—"

"Richard Adams!" Eddie shouted. "And the book about the bunnies was *Watership Down*! I *knew* I knew that name! But how can that be, Roland? How is it that the people in your world know about things in ours?"

"There are doors, aren't there?" Roland responded. "Haven't we seen four of them already? Do you think they never existed before, or never will again?"

"But—"

"All of us have seen the leavings of your world in mine, and when I was in your city of New York, I saw the marks of my world in yours. I saw *gunslingers*. Most were lax and slow, but they were gunslingers all the same, clearly members of their own ancient *ka-tet*."

"Roland, they were just cops. You ran rings around them."

"Not the last one. When Jack Mort and I were in the underground railway station, that one almost took me down. Except for blind luck—Mort's flint-and-steel—he would have done. That one . . . I saw his eyes. He knew the face of his father. I believe he knew it very well. And then . . . do you remember the name of Balazar's nightclub?"

"Sure," Eddie said uneasily. "The Leaning Tower. But it could have been coincidence; you yourself said *ka* doesn't rule everything."

Roland nodded. "You really are like Cuthbert—I remember something he said when we were boys. We were planning a midnight lark in the cemetery, but Alain wouldn't go. He said he was afraid of offending the shades of his fathers and mothers. Cuthbert laughed at him. He said he wouldn't believe in ghosts until he caught one in his teeth."

"Good for him!" Eddie exclaimed. "Bravo!"

Roland smiled. "I thought you'd like that. At any rate, let's leave this ghost for now. Go on with your story."

Eddie told of the vision which had come to him when Roland threw the jawbone into the fire—the vision of the key and the rose. He told of his dream, and how he had walked through the door of Tom and Gerry's Artistic Deli and into the field of roses which was dominated by the tall, soot-colored Tower. He told of the blackness which had issued from its windows, forming a shape in the sky overhead, speaking directly to Jake now, because Jake was listening with hungry concentration and growing wonder. He tried to convey some sense of the exaltation and terror which had permeated the dream, and saw from their eyes—Jake's most of all—that he was either doing a better job of that than he could have hoped for . . . or that they'd had dreams of their own.

He told of following Shardik's backtrail to the Portal of the Bear, and how, when he put his head against it, he'd found himself remembering the day he had talked his brother into taking him to Dutch Hill, so he could see The Mansion. He told about the cup and the needle, and how the pointing needle had become unnecessary once they realized they could see the Beam at work in everything it touched, even the birds in the sky.

Susannah took up the tale at this point. As she spoke, telling of how Eddie had begun to carve his own version of the key, Jake lay back, laced his hands together behind his head, and watched the clouds run slowly toward the city on their straight southeasterly course. The orderly shape they made showed the presence of the Beam as clearly as smoke leaving a chimney shows the direction of the wind.

She finished with the story of how they had finally hauled Jake into this world, closing the split track of his and Roland's memories as suddenly and as completely as Eddie had closed the door in the speaking ring. The only fact she left out was really not a fact at all—at least, not yet. She'd had no morning sickness, after all, and a single missed period meant nothing by itself. As Roland himself might have said, that was a tale best left for another day.

Yet as she finished, she found herself wishing she could forget what Aunt Talitha had said when Jake told her this was his home now: *Gods pity you, then, for the sun is going down on this world. It's going down forever.*

"And now it's your turn, Jake," Roland said.

Jake sat up and looked toward Lud, where the windows of the western towers reflected back the late afternoon light in golden sheets. "It's all crazy," he murmured, "but it almost makes sense. Like a dream when you wake up."

"Maybe we can help you make sense of it," Susannah said.

"Maybe you can. At least you can help me think about the train. I'm tired of trying to make sense of Blaine by myself." He sighed. "You know what Roland went through, living two lives at the same time, so I can skip that part. I'm not sure I could ever explain how it felt, anyway, and I don't want to. It was gross. I guess I better start with my Final Essay, because that's when I finally stopped thinking that the whole thing might just go away." He looked around at them somberly. "That was when I gave up."

22

JAKE TALKED THE SUN down.

He told them everything he could remember, beginning with *My Understanding of Truth* and ending with the monstrous doorkeeper which had literally come out of the woodwork to attack him. The other three listened without a single interruption.

When he was finished, Roland turned to Eddie, his eyes bright with a mixture of emotions Eddie initially took for wonder. Then he realized he was looking at powerful excitement . . . and deep fear. His mouth went dry. Because if *Roland* was afraid—

"Do you still doubt that our worlds overlap each other, Eddie?"

He shook his head. "Of course not. I walked down the same street, *and I did it in his clothes!* But . . . Jake, can I see that book? *Charlie the Choo-Choo?*"

Jake reached for his pack, but Roland stayed his hand. "Not yet," he said. "Go back to the vacant lot, Jake. Tell that part once more. Try to remember everything."

"Maybe you should hypnotize me," Jake said hesitantly. "Like you did before, at the way station."

Roland shook his head. "There's no need. What happened to you in that lot was the most important thing ever to happen in your life, Jake. In all our lives. You can remember everything."

So Jake went through it again. It was clear to all of them that his experience in the vacant lot where Tom and Gerry's once had stood was the secret heart of the *ka-tet* they shared. In Eddie's dream, the Artistic Deli had still been standing; in Jake's reality it had been torn down, but in both cases it was a place of enormous, talismanic power. Nor did Roland doubt that the vacant lot with its broken bricks and shattered glass was another version of what Susannah knew as the Drawers and the place he had seen at the end of his vision in the place of bones.

As he told this part of his story for the second time, speaking very slowly now, Jake found that what the gunslinger had said was true: he *could* remember everything. His recall improved until he almost seemed to be reliving the experience. He told them of the sign which said that a building called Turtle Bay Condominiums was slated to stand on the spot where Tom and Gerry's had once stood. He even remembered the little poem which had been spray-painted on the fence, and recited it for them:

"See the TURTLE of enormous girth!
On his shell he holds the earth.
If you want to run and play,
Come along the BEAM today."

Susannah murmured, "His thought is slow but always kind; He holds us all within his mind . . . isn't that how it went, Roland?"

"What?" Jake asked. "How what went?"

"A poem I learned as a child," Roland said. "It's another connection, one that really tells us something, although I'm not sure it's anything we need to know . . . still, one never knows when a little understanding may come in handy."

"Twelve portals connected by six Beams," Eddie said. "We started at the Bear. We're only going as far as the middle—to the Tower—but if we went all the way to the other end, we'd come to the Portal of the Turtle, wouldn't we?"

Roland nodded. "I'm sure we would."

"Portal of the Turtle," Jake said thoughtfully, rolling the words in his mouth, seeming to taste them. Then he finished by telling them again about the gorgeous voice of the choir, his realization that there were faces and stories and histories everywhere, and his growing belief that he had stumbled on something very like the core of all existence. Last of all, he told them again about finding the key and seeing the rose. In the totality of his recall, Jake began to weep, although he seemed unaware of it.

"When it opened," he said, "I saw the middle was the brightest yellow you ever saw in your life. At first I thought it was pollen and it only looked bright because *everything* in that lot looked bright. Even looking at the old candy-wrappers and beer-bottles was like looking at the greatest paintings you ever saw. Only then I realized it was a sun. I know it sounds crazy, but that's what it was. Only it was more than one. It was—"

"It was *all* suns," Roland murmured. "It was everything *real*."

"Yes! And it was *right*—but it was *wrong*, too. I can't explain *how* it was wrong, but it was. It was like two heartbeats, one inside of the other, and the one inside had a disease. Or an infection. And then I fainted."

23

"YOU SAW THE SAME thing at the end of your dream, Roland, didn't you?" Susannah asked. Her voice was soft with awe. "The blade of grass you saw near the end of it . . . you thought that blade was purple because it was splattered with paint."

"You don't understand," Jake said. "It really *was* purple. When I was seeing it the way it really was, it was *purple*. Like no grass I ever saw before. The paint was just camouflage. The way the doorkeeper camouflaged itself to look like an old deserted house."

The sun had reached the horizon. Roland asked Jake if he would now show them *Charlie the Choo-Choo* and then read it to them. Jake handed the book around. Both Eddie and Susannah looked at the cover for a long time.

"I had this book when I was a little kid," Eddie said at last. He spoke in the flat tones of utter surety. "Then we moved from Queens to Brooklyn—I wasn't even four years old—and I lost it. But I remember the picture on the cover. And I felt the same way you do, Jake. I didn't like it. I didn't trust it."

Susannah raised her eyes to look at Eddie. "I had it, too—how could I ever forget the little girl with my name . . . although of course it was my middle name back in those days. And I felt the same way about the train. I didn't like it and I didn't trust it." She tapped the front of the book with her finger before passing it on to Roland. "I thought that smile was a great big fake."

Roland gave it only a cursory glance before returning his eyes to Susannah. "Did you lose yours, too?"

"Yes."

"And I'll bet I know when," Eddie said.

Susannah nodded. "I'll bet you do. It was after that man dropped the brick on my head. I had it when we went north to my Aunt Blue's wedding. I had it on the train. I remember, because I kept asking my dad if Charlie the Choo-Choo was pulling us. I didn't *want* it to be Charlie, because we were supposed to go to Elizabeth, New Jersey, and I thought Charlie might take us anywhere. Didn't he end up pulling folks around a toy village or something like that, Jake?"

"An amusement park."

"Yes, of course it was. There's a picture of him hauling kids around that place at the end, isn't there? They're all smiling and laughing, except I always thought they looked like they were screaming to be let off."

"Yes!" Jake cried. "Yes, that's right! That's *just* right!"

"I thought Charlie might take us to *his* place—wherever he lived—instead of to my Aunt's wedding, and never let us go home again."

"You can't go home again," Eddie muttered, and ran his hands nervously through his hair.

"All the time we were on that train I wouldn't let go of the book. I even remember thinking, 'If he tries to steal us, I'll rip out his pages until he quits.' But of course we arrived right where we were supposed to, and on time, too. Daddy even took me up front, so I could see the engine. It was a diesel, not a steam engine, and I remember that made me happy. Then, after the wedding, that man Mort dropped the brick on me and I was in a coma for a long time. I never saw *Charlie the Choo-Choo* after that. Not until now." She hesitated, then added: "This could be my copy, for all I know—or Eddie's."

"Yeah, and probably is," Eddie said. His face was pale and solemn ... and then he grinned like a kid. " 'See the TURTLE, ain't he keen? All things serve the fuckin Beam.' "

Roland glanced west. "The sun's going down. Read the story before we lose the light, Jake."

Jake turned to the first page, showed them the picture of Engineer Bob in Charlie's cab, and began: " 'Bob Brooks was an engineer for The Mid-World Railway Company, on the St. Louis to Topeka run ...' "

24

" '... AND EVERY NOW AND then the children hear him singing his old song in his soft, gruff voice,' " Jake finished. He showed them the last picture—the happy children who might actually have been screaming—and then closed the book. The sun had gone down; the sky was purple.

"Well, it's not a *perfect* fit," Eddie said, "more like a dream where the water sometimes runs uphill—but it fits well enough to scare *me* silly. This is Mid-World—Charlie's territory. Only his name over here isn't Charlie at all. Over here it's Blaine the Mono."

Roland was looking at Jake. "What do you think?" he asked. "Should we go around the city? Stay away from this train?"

Jake thought it over, head down, hands working distractedly through Oy's thick, silky fur. "I'd like to," he said at last, "but if I've got this stuff about *ka* right, I don't think we're supposed to."

Roland nodded. "If it's *ka*, questions of what we're supposed to or not supposed to do aren't even in it; if we tried to go around, we'd find circumstances forcing us back. In such cases it's better to give in to the inevitable promptly instead of putting it off. What do you think, Eddie?"

Eddie thought as long and as carefully as Jake had done. He didn't want anything to do with a talking train that ran by itself, and whether you called it Charlie the Choo-Choo or Blaine the Mono, everything Jake had told them and read them suggested that it might be a very nasty piece of work. But they had a tremendous distance to cross, and somewhere, at the end of it, was the thing they had come to find. And with that thought, Eddie was amazed to discover he knew exactly what he thought, and what he wanted. He raised his head and for almost the first time since he had come to this world, he fixed Roland's faded blue eyes firmly with his hazel ones.

"I want to stand in that field of roses, and I want to see the Tower that stands there. I don't know what comes next. Mourners please omit flowers, probably, and for all of us. But I don't care. I want to stand there. I guess I don't care if Blaine's the devil and the train runs through hell itself on the way to the Tower. I vote we go."

Roland nodded and turned to Susannah.

"Well, I didn't have any dreams about the Dark Tower," she said, "so I can deal with the question on that level—the level of desire, I suppose you'd say. But I've come to believe in *ka*, and I'm not so numb that I can't feel it when someone starts rapping on my head with his knuckles and saying, 'That way, idiot.' What about you, Roland? What do you think?"

"I think there's been enough talk for one day, and it's time to let it go until tomorrow."

"What about *Riddle-De-Dum!*—" Jake asked, "do you want to look at that?"

"There'll be time enough for that another day," Roland said. "Let's get some sleep."

25

BUT THE GUNSLINGER LAY long awake, and when the rhythmic drumming began again, he got up and walked back to the road. He stood looking toward the bridge and the city. He was every inch the diplomat Susannah had suspected, and he had known the train was the next step on the road they must travel almost from the moment he had heard of it . . . but he'd felt it would be unwise to say so. Eddie in particular hated to feel pushed; when he sensed that was being done, he simply lowered his head, planted his feet, made his silly jokes, and balked like a mule. This time he wanted what Roland wanted, but he was still apt to say day if Roland said night, and night if Roland said day. It was safer to walk softly, and surer to ask instead of telling.

He turned to go back . . . and his hand dropped to his gun as he saw a dark shape standing on the edge of the road, looking at him. He didn't draw, but it was a near thing.

"I wondered if you'd be able to sleep after that little performance," Eddie said. "Guess the answer's no."

"I didn't hear you at all, Eddie. You're learning . . . only this time you almost got a bullet in the gut for your pains."

"You didn't hear me because you have a lot on your mind." Eddie joined him, and even by starlight, Roland saw he hadn't fooled Eddie a bit. His respect for Eddie continued to grow. It was Cuthbert Eddie reminded him of, but in many ways he had already surpassed Cuthbert.

If I underestimate him, Roland thought, *I'm apt to come away with a bloody paw. And if I let him down, or do something that looks to him like a double-cross, he'll probably try to kill me.*

"What's on *your* mind, Eddie?"

"You. Us. I want you to know something. I guess until tonight I just assumed that you knew already. Now I'm not so sure."

"Tell me, then." He thought again: *How like Cuthbert he is!*

"We're with you because we have to be—that's your goddamned *ka.* But we're also with you because we *want* to be. I know that's true of me and Susannah, and I'm pretty sure it's true of Jake, too. You've got a good brain, me old *khef*-mate, but I think you must keep it in a bomb-shelter, because it's bitchin hard to get through sometimes. I want to see it, Roland. Can you dig what I'm telling you? *I want to see the Tower.*" He looked closely into Roland's face, apparently did not see what he'd hoped to find there, and raised his hands in exasperation. "What I mean is I want you to let go of my ears."

"Let go of your ears?"

"Yeah. Because you don't have to drag me anymore. I'm coming of my own accord. *We're* coming of our own accord. If you died in your sleep tonight, we'd bury you and then go on. We probably wouldn't last long, but we'd die in the path of the Beam. *Now* do you understand?"

"Yes. Now I do."

"You say you understand me, and I think you do . . . but do you believe me, as well?"

Of course, he thought. *Where else do you have to go, Eddie, in this world that's so strange to you? And what else could you do? You'd make a piss-poor farmer.*

But that was mean and unfair, and he knew it. Denigrating free will by confusing it with *ka* was worse than blasphemy; it was tiresome and stupid. "Yes," he said. "I believe you. Upon my soul, I do."

"Then stop behaving like we're a bunch of sheep and you're the shepherd walking along behind us, waving a crook to make sure we don't trot our stupid selves off the road and into a quicksand bog. Open your mind to us. If we're going to die in the city or on that train, I want to die knowing I was more than a marker on your game-board."

Roland felt anger heat his cheeks, but he had never been much good at self-deception. He wasn't angry because Eddie was wrong but because Eddie had seen through him. Roland had watched him come steadily forward, leaving his prison further and further behind—and Susannah, too, for she had also been imprisoned—and yet his heart had never quite accepted the evidence of his senses. His heart apparently wanted to go on seeing them as different, lesser creatures.

Roland drew in deep air. "Gunslinger, I cry your pardon."

Eddie nodded. "We're running into a whole hurricane of trouble here . . . I feel it, and I'm scared to death. But it's not *your* trouble, it's *our* trouble. Okay?"

"Yes."

"How bad do you think it can get in the city?"

"I don't know. I only know that we have to try and protect Jake, because the old auntie said both sides would want him. Some of it depends on how long it takes us to find this train. A lot more depends on what happens when we find it. If we had two more in our party, I'd put Jake in a moving box with guns on every side of him. Since we don't, we'll move in column—me first, Jake pushing Susannah behind, and you on drogue."

"How much trouble, Roland? Make a guess."

"I can't."

"I think you can. You don't know the city, but you know how the people in your world have been behaving since things started to fall apart. How much trouble?"

Roland turned toward the steady sound of the drumbeats and thought it over. "Maybe not too much. I'd guess the fighting men who are still there are old and demoralized. It may be that you have the straight of it, and some will even offer to help us on our way, as the River Crossing *ka-tet* did. Mayhap we won't see them at all—they'll see *us*, see we're packing iron, and just put their heads down and let us go our way. If that fails, I'm hoping that they'll scatter like rats if we gun a few."

"And if they decide to make a fight of it?"

Roland smiled grimly. "Then, Eddie, we'll *all* remember the faces of our fathers."

Eddie's eyes gleamed in the darkness, and Roland was once more reminded forcibly of Cuthbert—Cuthbert who had once said he would believe in ghosts when he could catch one in his teeth, Cuthbert with whom he had once scattered breadcrumbs beneath the hangman's gibbet.

"Have I answered all your questions?"

"Nope—but I think you played straight with me this time."

"Then goodnight, Eddie."

"Goodnight."

Eddie turned and walked away. Roland watched him go. Now that he was listening, he could hear him . . . but just barely. He started back himself, then turned toward the darkness where the city of Lud was.

He's what the old woman called a Pube. She said both sides would want him.

You won't let me drop this time?

No. Not this time, not ever again.

But he knew something none of the others did. Perhaps, after the talk he'd just had with Eddie, he should tell them . . . yet he thought he would keep the knowledge to himself a little while longer.

In the old tongue which had once been his world's *lingua franca*, most words, like *khef* and *ka*, had many meanings. The word *char*, however—*char* as in Charlie the Choo-Choo—had only one.

Char meant death.

V ∎ BRIDGE AND CITY

·V·

BRIDGE AND CITY

1

THEY CAME UPON THE downed airplane three days later.

Jake pointed it out first at midmorning—a flash of light about ten miles away, as if a mirror lay in the grass. As they drew closer, they saw a large dark object at the side of the Great Road.

"It looks like a dead bird," Roland said. "A big one."

"That's no bird," Eddie said. "That's an airplane. I'm pretty sure the glare is sunlight bouncing off the canopy."

An hour later they stood silently at the edge of the road, looking at the ancient wreck. Three plump crows stood on the tattered skin of the fuselage, staring insolently at the newcomers. Jake pried a cobble from the edge of the road and shied it at them. The crows lumbered into the air, cawing indignantly.

One wing had broken off in the crash and lay thirty yards away, a shadow like a diving board in the tall grass. The rest of the plane was pretty much intact. The canopy had cracked in a starburst pattern where the pilot's head had struck it. There was a large, rust-colored stain there.

Oy trotted over to where three rusty propeller blades rose from the grass, sniffed at them, then returned hastily to Jake.

The man in the cockpit was a dust-dry mummy wearing a padded leather vest and a helmet with a spike on top. His lips were gone, his teeth exposed in a final desperate grimace. Fingers which had once been as large as sausages but were now only skin-covered bones clutched the wheel. His skull was caved in where it had hit the canopy, and Roland guessed that the greenish-gray scales which coated the left side of his face were all that remained of his brains. The dead man's head was tilted back, as if he had been sure, even at the moment of his death, that he could regain the sky again. The plane's remaining wing still jutted from the encroaching grass. On it was a fading insignia which depicted a fist holding a thunderbolt.

"Looks like Aunt Talitha was wrong and the old albino man had the right of it, after all," Susannah said in an awed voice. "That must be David Quick, the outlaw prince. Look at the size of him, Roland—they must have had to grease him to get him into the cockpit!"

Roland nodded. The heat and the years had wasted the man in the mechanical bird to no more than a skeleton wrapped in dry hide, but he could still see how broad the shoulders had been, and the misshapen head was massive. "So fell Lord Perth," he said, "and the countryside did shake with that thunder."

Jake looked at him questioningly.

"It's from an old poem. Lord Perth was a giant who went forth to war with a thousand men, but he was still in his own country when a little boy threw a stone at him and hit him in the knee. He stumbled, the weight of his armor bore him down, and he broke his neck in the fall."

Jake said, "Like our story of David and Goliath."

"There was no fire," Eddie said. "I bet he just ran out of gas and tried a dead-stick landing on the road. He might have been an outlaw and a barbarian, but he had a yard of guts."

Roland nodded, and looked at Jake. "You all right with this?"

"Yes. If the guy was still, you know, runny, I might not be." Jake looked from the dead man in the airplane to the city. Lud was much closer and clearer now, and although they could see many broken windows in the towers, he, like Eddie, had not entirely given up hope of finding some sort of help there. "I bet things sort of fell apart in the city once he was gone."

"I think you'd win that bet," Roland said.

"You know something?" Jake was studying the plane again. "The people who built that city might have made their own airplanes, but I'm pretty sure this is one of ours. I did a school paper on air combat when I was in the fifth grade, and I think I recognize it. Roland, can I take a closer look?"

Roland nodded. "I'll go with you."

Together they walked over to the plane with the high grass swishing at their pants. "Look," Jake said. "See the machine-gun under the wing? That's an air-cooled German model, and this is a Focke-Wulf from just before World War II. I'm sure it is. So what's it doing here?"

"Lots of planes disappear," Eddie said. "Take the Bermuda Triangle, for instance. That's a place over one of our oceans, Roland. It's supposed to be jinxed. Maybe it's a great big doorway between our worlds—one that's almost always open." Eddie hunched his shoulders and essayed a bad Rod Serling imitation. "Fasten your seatbelts and prepare for turbulence: you're flying into . . . the Roland Zone!"

Jake and Roland, who were now standing beneath the plane's remaining wing, ignored him.

"Boost me up, Roland."

Roland shook his head. "That wing looks solid, but it's not—this thing has been here a long time, Jake. You'd fall."

"Make a step, then."

Eddie said, "I'll do it, Roland."

Roland studied his diminished right hand for a moment, shrugged, then laced his hands together. "This'll do. He's light."

Jake shook off his moccasin and then stepped lightly into the stirrup Roland had made. Oy began to bark shrilly, though whether in excitement or alarm, Roland couldn't tell.

Jake's chest was now pressing against one of the airplane's rusty flaps, and he was looking right at the fist-and-thunderbolt design. It had peeled up a little from the surface of the wing along one edge. He seized this flap and pulled. It came off the wing so easily that he would have fallen backward if Eddie, standing directly behind him, hadn't steadied him with a hand on the butt.

"I *knew* it," Jake said. There was another symbol beneath the fist-and-thunderbolt, and now it was almost totally revealed. It was a swastika. "I just wanted to see it. You can put me down now."

They started out again, but they could see the tail of the plane every time they looked back that afternoon, looming out of the high grass like Lord Perth's burial monument.

2

IT WAS JAKE'S TURN to make the fire that night. When the wood was laid to the gunslinger's satisfaction, he handed Jake his flint and steel. "Let's see how you do."

Eddie and Susannah were sitting off to one side, their arms linked companionably about each other's waist. Toward the end of the day, Eddie had found a bright yellow flower beside the road and had picked it for her. Tonight Susannah was wearing it in her hair, and every time she looked at Eddie, her lips curved in a small smile and her eyes filled with light. Roland had noted these things, and they pleased him. Their love was deepening, strengthening. That was good. It would have to be deep and strong indeed if it was to survive the months and years ahead.

Jake struck a spark, but it flashed inches away from the kindling.

"Move your flint in closer," Roland said, "and hold it steady. And don't *hit* it with the steel, Jake; *scrape* it."

Jake tried again, and this time the spark flashed directly into the kindling. There was a little tendril of smoke but no fire.

"I don't think I'm very good at this."

"You'll get it. Meantime, think on this. What's dressed when night falls and undressed when day breaks?"

"Huh?"

Roland moved Jake's hands even closer to the little pile of kindling. "I guess that one's not in your book."

"Oh, it's a riddle!" Jake struck another spark. This time a small flame glowed in the kindling before dying out. "You know some of those, too?"

Roland nodded. "Not just some—a lot. As a boy, I must have known a thousand. They were part of my studies."

"Really? Why would anyone study riddles?"

"Vannay, my tutor, said a boy who could answer a riddle was a boy who could think around corners. We had riddling contests every Friday noon, and the boy or girl who won could leave school early."

"Did you get to leave early often, Roland?" Susannah asked.

He shook his head, smiling a little himself. "I enjoyed riddling, but I was never very good at it. Vannay said it was because I thought too deeply. My father said it was because I had too little imagination. I think they were both right . . . but I think my father had a little more of the truth. I could always haul a gun faster than any of my mates, and shoot straighter, but I've never been much good at thinking around corners."

Susannah, who had watched closely as Roland dealt with the old people of River Crossing, thought the gunslinger was underrating himself, but she said nothing.

"Sometimes, on winter nights, there would be riddling competitions in the great hall. When it was just the younkers, Alain always won. When the grownups played as well, it was always Cort. He'd forgotten more riddles than the rest of us ever knew, and after the Fair-Day Riddling, Cort always carried home the goose. Riddles have great power, and everyone knows one or two."

"Even me," Eddie said. "For instance, why did the dead baby cross the road?"

"That's dumb, Eddie," Susannah said, but she was smiling.

"Because it was stapled to the chicken!" Eddie yelled, and grinned when Jake burst into laughter, knocking his little pile of kindling apart. "Hyuk, hyuk, hyuk, I got a million of em, folks!"

Roland, however, didn't laugh. He looked, in fact, a trifle offended. "Pardon me for saying so, Eddie, but that *is* rather silly."

"Jesus, Roland, I'm sorry," Eddie said. He was still smiling, but he sounded slightly peeved. "I keep forgetting you got your sense of humor shot off in the Children's Crusade, or whatever it was."

"It's just that I take riddling seriously. I was taught that the ability to solve them indicates a sane and rational mind."

"Well, they're never going to replace the works of Shakespeare or the Quadratic Equation," Eddie said. "I mean, let's not get carried away."

Jake was looking at Roland thoughtfully. "My book said riddling is the oldest game people still play. In our world, I mean. And riddles used to be really serious business, not just jokes. People used to get killed over them."

Roland was looking out into the growing darkness. "Yes. I've seen it happen." He was remembering a Fair-Day Riddling which had ended not with the giving of the prize goose but with a cross-eyed man in a cap of bells dying in the dirt with a dagger in his chest. Cort's dagger. The man had been a wandering singer and acrobat who had attempted to cheat Cort by stealing the judge's pocket-book, in which the answers were kept on small scraps of bark.

"Well, excyoooose *me*," Eddie said.

Susannah was looking at Jake. "I forgot all about the book of riddles you carried over. May I look at it now?"

"Sure. It's in my pack. The answers are gone, though. Maybe that's why Mr. Tower gave it to me for fr—"

His shoulder was suddenly seized, and with painful force.

"*What* was his name?" Roland asked.

"Mr. Tower," Jake said. "Calvin Tower. Didn't I tell you that?"

"No." Roland slowly relaxed his grip on Jake's shoulder. "But now that I hear it, I suppose I'm not surprised."

Eddie had opened Jake's pack and found *Riddle-De-Dum!* He tossed it to Susannah. "You know," he said, "I always thought that dead-baby joke was pretty good. Tasteless, maybe, but pretty good."

"I don't care about taste," Roland said. "It's senseless and unsolvable, and that's what makes it silly. A good riddle is neither."

"Jesus! You guys *did* take this stuff seriously, didn't you?"

"Yes."

Jake, meanwhile, had been restacking the kindling and mulling over the riddle which had started the discussion. Now he suddenly smiled. "A fire. That's the answer, right? Dress it at night, undress it in the morning. If you change 'dress' to 'build,' it's simple."

"That's it." Roland returned Jake's smile, but his eyes were on Susannah, watching as she thumbed through the small, tattered book. He thought, looking at her studious frown and the absent way she read-justed the yellow flower in her hair when it tried to slip free, that she alone might sense that the tattered book of riddles could be as important as *Charlie the Choo-Choo* . . . maybe more important. He looked from her to Eddie and felt a recurrence of his irritation at Eddie's foolish riddle. The young man bore another resemblance to Cuthbert, this one rather unfortunate: Roland sometimes felt like shaking him until his nose bled and his teeth fell out.

Soft, gunslinger—soft! Cort's voice, not quite laughing, spoke up in his head, and Roland resolutely put his emotions at arm's length. It was easier to do that when he remembered that Eddie couldn't help his occasional forays into nonsense; character was also at least partly formed by *ka,* and Roland knew well that there was more to Eddie than non-sense. Anytime he started to make the mistake of thinking that wasn't so, he would do well to remember their conversation by the side of the road three nights before, when Eddie had accused him of using them as markers on his own private game-board. That had angered him . . . but it had been close enough to the truth to shame him, as well.

Blissfully unaware of these long thoughts, Eddie now inquired: "What's green, weighs a hundred tons, and lives at the bottom of the ocean?"

"I know," Jake said. "Moby Snot, the Great Green Whale."

"Idiocy," Roland muttered.

"Yeah—but that's what's supposed to make it funny," Eddie said. "*Jokes* are supposed to make you think around corners, too. You see . . ." He looked at Roland's face, laughed, and threw up his hands. "Never mind. I give up. You wouldn't understand. Not in a million years. Let's look at the damned book. I'll even try to take it seriously . . . if we can eat a little supper first, that is."

"Watch Me," the gunslinger said with a flicker of a smile.

"Huh?"

"That means you have a deal."

Jake scraped the steel across the flint. A spark jumped, and this time the kindling caught fire. He sat back contentedly and watched the flames spread, one arm slung around Oy's neck. He felt well pleased with him-self. He had started the evening fire . . . and he had guessed the answer to Roland's riddle.

3

"I'VE GOT ONE," JAKE said as they ate their evening burritos.

"Is it a foolish one?" Roland asked.

"Nah. It's a real one."

"Then try me with it."

"Okay. What can run but never walks, has a mouth but never talks, has a bed but never sleeps, has a head but never weeps?"

"A good one," Roland said kindly, "but an old one. A river."

Jake was a little crestfallen. "You really *are* hard to stump."

Roland tossed the last bite of his burrito to Oy, who accepted it eagerly. "Not me. I'm what Eddie calls an overpush. You should have seen Alain. He collected riddles the way a lady collects fans."

"That's pushover, Roland, old buddy," Eddie said.

"Thank you. Try this one: What lies in bed, and stands in bed?/ First white, then red/ The plumper it gets/ The better the old woman likes it?"

Eddie burst out laughing. "A dork!" he yelled. "Crude, Roland! But I like it! I *liyyyke* it!"

Roland shook his head. "Your answer is wrong. A good riddle is sometimes a puzzle in words, like Jake's about the river, but sometimes it's more like a magician's trick, making you look in one direction while it's going somewhere else."

"It's a double," Jake said. He explained what Aaron Deepneau had said about the Riddle of Samson. Roland nodded.

"Is it a strawberry?" Susannah asked, then answered her own question. "Of course it is. It's like the fire-riddle. There's a metaphor hidden inside it. Once you understand the metaphor, you can solve the riddle."

"I metaphor sex, but she slapped my face and walked away when I asked," Eddie told them sadly. They all ignored him.

"If you change 'gets' to 'grows,' " Susannah went on, "it's easy. First white, then red. Plumper it grows, the better the old woman likes it." She looked pleased with herself.

Roland nodded. "The answer I always heard was a wenberry, but I'm sure both answers mean the same thing."

Eddie picked up *Riddle-De-Dum!* and began flipping through it. "How about this one, Roland? When is a door not a door?"

Roland frowned. "Is it another piece of your stupidity? Because my patience—"

"No. I promised to take it seriously, and I am—I'm *trying*, at least. It's in this book, and I just happen to know the answer. I heard it when I was a kid."

Jake, who also knew the answer, winked at Eddie. Eddie winked back, and was amused to see Oy also trying to wink. The bumbler kept shutting both eyes, and eventually gave up.

Roland and Susannah, meanwhile, were puzzling over the question. "It must have something to do with love," Roland said. "A door, adore. When is adore not adore . . . hmmm . . ."

"Hmmm," Oy said. His imitation of Roland's thoughtful tone was perfect. Eddie winked at Jake again. Jake covered his mouth to hide a smile.

"Is the answer false love?" Roland asked at last.

"Nope."

"Window," Susannah said suddenly and decisively. "When is a door not a door? When it's a window."

"Nope." Eddie was grinning broadly now, but Jake was struck by how far from the real answer both of them had wandered. There was magic at work here, he thought. Pretty common stuff, as magic went, no flying carpets or disappearing elephants, but magic, all the same. He suddenly saw what they were doing—a simple game of riddles around a campfire—in an entirely new light. It was like playing blind-man's bluff, only in this game the blindfold was made of words.

"I give up," Susannah said.

"Yes," Roland said. "Tell if you know."

"The answer is a jar. A door is not a door when it's ajar. Get it?" Eddie watched as comprehension dawned on Roland's face and asked, a little apprehensively, "*Is* it a bad one? I was trying to be serious this time, Roland—really."

"Not bad at all. On the contrary, it's quite good. Cort would have gotten it, I'm sure . . . probably Alain, too, it's still very clever. I did what I always used to do in the schoolroom: made it more complicated than it really was and shot right past the answer."

"There really is something to it, isn't there?" Eddie mused. Roland nodded, but Eddie didn't see; he was looking into the depths of the fire, where dozens of roses bloomed and faded in the coals.

Roland said, "One more, and we'll turn in. Only from tonight on, we'll stand a watch. You first, Eddie, then Susannah. I'll take the last one."

"What about me?" Jake asked.

"Later on you may have to take a turn. Right now it's more important for you to get your sleep."

"Do you really think sentry-duty is necessary?" Susannah asked.

"I don't know. And that's the best reason of all to do it. Jake, choose us a riddle from your book."

Eddie handed *Riddle-De-Dum!* to Jake, who thumbed through the pages and finally stopped near the back. "Whoa! This one's a killer."

"Let's hear it," Eddie said. "If I don't get it, Suze will. We're known at Fair-Days all across the land as Eddie Dean and His Riddling Queen."

"We're witty tonight, ain't we?" Susannah said. "Let's see how witty you are after settin by the side o' the road until midnight or so, honeychild."

Jake read: " 'There is a thing that nothing is, and yet it has a name. It's sometimes tall and sometimes short, joins our talks, joins our sport, and plays at every game.' "

They discussed this riddle for almost fifteen minutes, but none of them could even hazard an answer.

"Maybe it'll come to one of us while we're asleep," Jake said. "That's how I got the one about the river."

"Cheap book, with the answers torn out," Eddie said. He stood up and wrapped a hide blanket around his shoulders like a cloak.

"Well, it *was* cheap. Mr. Tower gave it to me for free."

"What am I looking for, Roland?" Eddie asked.

Roland shrugged as he lay down. "I don't know, but I think you'll know it if you see it or hear it."

"Wake me up when you start feeling sleepy," Susannah said.

"You better believe it."

4

A GRASSY DITCH RAN along the side of the road and Eddie sat on the far side of it with his blanket around his shoulders. A thin scud of clouds had veiled the sky tonight, dimming the starshow. A strong west wind was blowing. When Eddie turned his face in that direction, he could clearly smell the buffalo which now owned these plains—a mixed perfume of hot fur and fresh dung. The clarity which had returned to his senses in these last few months was amazing . . . and, at times like these, a little spooky, as well.

Very faintly, he could hear a buffalo calf bawling.

He turned toward the city, and after a while he began to think he might be seeing distant sparks of light there—the electric candles of the twins' story—but he was well aware that he might be seeing nothing more than his own wishful thinking.

You're a long way from Forty-second Street, sweetheart—hope is a great thing, no matter what anyone says, but don't hope so hard you lose sight of that one thought: you're a long way from Forty-second Street. That's not New York up ahead, no matter how much you might wish it was. That's Lud, and it'll be whatever it is. And if you keep that in mind, maybe you'll be okay.

He passed his time on watch trying to think of an answer to the last riddle of the evening. The scolding Roland had given him about his dead-baby joke had left him feeling disgruntled, and it would please him to be able to start off the morning by giving them a good answer. Of course they wouldn't be able to check *any* answer against the back of the book, but he had an idea that with good riddles a good answer was usually self-evident.

Sometimes tall and sometimes short. He thought that was the key and all the rest was probably just misdirection. What *was* sometimes tall and sometimes short? Pants? No. Pants were sometimes short and sometimes long, but he had never heard of tall pants. Tales? Like pants, it only fit snugly one way. *Drinks* were sometimes both tall and short—

"Order," he murmured, and thought for a moment that he must have stumbled across the solution—both adjectives fit the noun glove-tight. A tall order was a big job; a short order was something you got on the quick in a restaurant—a hamburger or a tuna melt. Except that tall orders and tuna melts didn't *join our talk* or *play at every game.*

He felt a rush of frustration and had to smile at himself, getting all wound up about a harmless word-game in a kid's book. All the same, he found it a little easier to believe that people might really kill each other over riddles . . . if the stakes were high enough and cheating was involved.

Let it go—you're doing exactly what Roland said, thinking right past it.

Still, what else did he have to think about?

Then the drumming from the city began again, and he did have something else. There was no build-up; at one moment it wasn't there, and at the next it was going full force, as if a switch had been turned. Eddie walked to the edge of the road, turned toward the city, and listened. After a few moments he looked around to see if the drums had awakened the others, but he was still alone. He turned toward Lud again and cupped his ears forward with the sides of his hands.

Bump . . . ba-bump . . . ba-bump-bumpbump-bump.

Bump . . . ba-bump . . . ba-bump-bumpbump-bump.

Eddie became more and more sure that he had been right about what it was; that he had, at least, solved this riddle.

Bump . . . ba-bump . . . ba-bump-bumpbump-bump.

The idea that he was standing by a deserted road in an almost empty world, standing some one hundred and seventy miles from a city which had been built by some fabulous lost civilization and listening to a rock-and-roll drum-line . . . that was crazy, but was it any crazier than a traffic-light that dinged and dropped a rusty green flag with the word GO printed on it? Any crazier than discovering the wreck of a German plane from the 1930s?

Eddie sang the words to the Z.Z. Top song in a whisper:

"You need just enough of that sticky stuff
To hold the seam on your fine blue-jeans
I say yeah, yeah . . ."

They fit the beat perfectly. It was the disco-pulse percussion of "Velcro Fly." Eddie was sure of it.

A short time later the sound ceased as suddenly as it had begun, and he could hear only the wind, and, more faintly, the Send River, which had a bed but never slept.

5

THE NEXT FOUR DAYS were uneventful. They walked; they watched the bridge and the city grow larger and define themselves more clearly; they camped; they ate; they riddled; they kept watch turn and turn about (Jake had pestered Roland into letting him keep a short watch in the two hours just before dawn); they slept. The only remarkable incident had to do with the bees.

Around noon on the third day after the discovery of the downed plane, a buzzing sound came to them, growing louder and louder until it dominated the day. At last Roland stopped. "There," he said, and pointed toward a grove of eucalyptus trees.

"It sounds like bees," Susannah said.

Roland's faded blue eyes gleamed. "Could be we'll have a little dessert tonight."

"I don't know how to tell you this, Roland," Eddie said, "but I have this aversion to being stung."

"Don't we all," Roland agreed, "but the day is windless. I think we can smoke them to sleep and steal their comb right out from under them without setting half the world on fire. Let's have a look."

He carried Susannah, who was as eager for the adventure as the gunslinger himself, toward the grove. Eddie and Jake lagged behind, and Oy, apparently having decided that discretion was the better part of valor, remained sitting at the edge of the Great Road, panting like a dog and watching them carefully.

Roland paused at the edge of the trees. "Stay where you are," he told Eddie and Jake, speaking softly. "We're going to have a look. I'll give you a come-on if all's well." He carried Susannah into the dappled shadows of the grove while Eddie and Jake remained in the sunshine, peering after them.

It was cooler in the shade. The buzzing of the bees was a steady, hypnotic drone. "There are too many," Roland murmured. "This is late summer; they should be out working. I don't—"

He caught sight of the hive, bulging tumorously from the hollow of a tree in the center of the clearing, and broke off.

"What's the matter with them?" Susannah asked in a soft, horrified voice. "Roland, what's the *matter* with them?"

A bee, as plump and slow-moving as a horsefly in October, droned past her head. Susannah flinched away from it.

Roland motioned for the others to join them. They did, and stood looking at the hive without speaking. The chambers weren't neat hexagons but random holes of all shapes and sizes; the beehive itself looked queerly melted, as if someone had turned a blowtorch on it. The bees which crawled sluggishly over it were as white as snow.

"No honey tonight," Roland said. "What we took from yonder comb might taste sweet, but it would poison us as surely as night follows day."

One of the grotesque white bees lumbered heavily past Jake's head. He ducked away with an expression of loathing.

"What did it?" Eddie asked. "What did it to them, Roland?"

"The same thing that has emptied this whole land; the thing that's still causing many of the buffalo to be born as sterile freaks. I've heard it called the Old War, the Great Fire, the Cataclysm, and the Great Poisoning. Whatever it was, it was the start of all our troubles and it happened long ago, a thousand years before the great-great-grandfathers of the River Crossing folk were born. The physical effects—the two-headed buffalo and the white bees and such—have grown less as time passes. I have seen this for myself. The other changes are greater, if harder to see, and they are still going on."

They watched the white bees crawl, dazed and almost completely helpless, about their hive. Some were apparently trying to work; most simply wandered about, butting heads and crawling over one another. Eddie found himself remembering a newsclip he'd seen once. It had shown a crowd of survivors leaving the area where a gas-main had exploded, flattening almost a whole city block in some California town. These bees reminded him of those dazed, shellshocked survivors.

"You had a nuclear war, didn't you?" he asked—almost accused. "These Great Old Ones you like to talk about . . . they blew their great old asses straight to hell. Didn't they?"

"I don't *know* what happened. No one knows. The records of those times are lost, and the few stories are confused and conflicting."

"Let's get out of here," Jake said in a trembling voice. "Looking at those things makes me sick."

"I'm with you, sugar," Susannah said.

So they left the bees to their aimless, shattered life in the grove of ancient trees, and there was no honey that night.

6

"WHEN ARE YOU GOING to tell us what you *do* know?" Eddie asked the next morning. The day was bright and blue, but there was a bite in the air; their first autumn in this world was almost upon them.

Roland glanced at him. "What do you mean?"

"I'd like to hear your whole story, from beginning to end, starting with Gilead. How you grew up there and what happened to end it all. I want to know how you found out about the Dark Tower and why you started chasing after it in the first place. I want to know about your first bunch of friends, too. And what happened to them."

Roland removed his hat, armed sweat from his brow, then replaced it. "You have the right to know all those things, I suppose, and I'll tell them to you . . . but not now. It's a very long story. I never expected to tell it to anyone, and I'll only tell it once."

"When?" Eddie persisted.

"When the time is right," Roland said, and with that they had to be content.

7

ROLAND CAME AWAKE THE moment before Jake began to shake him. He sat up and looked around, but Eddie and Susannah were still fast asleep and in the first faint light of morning, he could see nothing amiss.

"What is it?" he asked Jake in a low voice.

"I don't know. Fighting, maybe. Come and listen."

Roland threw his blanket aside and followed Jake out to the road. He reckoned they were now only three days' walk from the place where the Send passed in front of the city, and the bridge—built squarely along the path of the Beam—dominated the horizon. Its pronounced tilt was more clearly visible than ever, and he could see at least a dozen gaps where over-stressed cables had snapped like the strings of a lyre.

Tonight the wind blew directly into their faces as they looked toward the city, and the sounds it carried to them were faint but clear.

"*Is* it fighting?" Jake asked.

Roland nodded and held a finger to his lips.

He heard faint shouts, a crash that sounded like some huge object falling, and—of course—the drums. Now there was another crash, this one more musical: the sound of breaking glass.

"Jeepers," Jake whispered, and moved closer to the gunslinger.

Then came the sounds which Roland had hoped not to hear: a fast, sandy rattle of small-arms fire followed by a loud hollow bang—clearly an explosion of some kind. It rolled across the flatlands toward them like an invisible bowling ball. After that, the shouts, thuds, and sounds of breakage quickly sank below the level of the drums, and when the drums quit a few minutes later with their usual unsettling suddenness, the city was silent again. But now that silence had an unpleasant waiting quality.

Roland put an arm around Jake's shoulders. "Still not too late to detour around," he said.

Jake glanced up at him. "We can't."

"Because of the train?"

Jake nodded and singsonged: "Blaine is a pain, but we *have* to take the train. And the city's the only place where we can get on."

Roland looked thoughtfully at Jake. "Why do you say we *have* to? Is it *ka*? Because, Jake, you have to understand that you don't know much about *ka* yet—it's the sort of subject men study all their lives."

"I don't know if it's *ka* or not, but I do know that we can't go into the waste lands unless we're protected, and that means Blaine. Without him we'll die, like those bees we saw are going to die when winter comes. We have to be protected. Because the waste lands are poison."

"How do you know these things?"

"I don't *know!*" Jake said, almost angrily. "I just *do*."

"All right," Roland said mildly. He looked toward Lud again. "But we'll have to be damned careful. It's unlucky that they still have gunpowder. If they have that, they may have things that are even more powerful. I doubt if they know how to use them, but that only increases the danger. They could get excited and blow us all to hell."

"Ell," a grave voice said from behind them. They glanced around and saw Oy sitting by the side of the road, watching them.

8

LATER THAT DAY THEY came to a new road which swept toward them out of the west and joined their own way. Beyond this point, the Great Road—now much wider and split down the middle by a median divider of some polished dark stone—began to sink, and the crumbling concrete embankments which rose on either side of them gave the pilgrims a claustrophobic trapped feeling. They stopped at a point where one of these concrete dikes had been broken open, affording a comforting line of sight to the open land beyond, and ate a light, unsatisfying meal.

"Why do you think they dropped the road down like this, Eddie?" Jake asked. "I mean, someone *did* do it this way on purpose, didn't they?"

Eddie looked through the break in the concrete, where the flatlands stretched on as smoothly as ever, and nodded.

"Then why?"

"Dunno, champ," Eddie said, but he thought he did. He glanced at Roland and guessed that he knew, too. The sunken road leading to the bridge had been a defensive measure. Troops placed atop the concrete slopes were in control of two carefully engineered redoubts. If the defenders didn't like the look of the folks approaching Lud along the Great Road, they could rain destruction down on them.

"You *sure* you don't know?" Jake asked.

Eddie smiled at Jake and tried to stop imagining that there was some nut up there right now, getting ready to roll a large, rusty bomb down one of those decayed concrete ramps. "No idea," he said.

Susannah whistled disgustedly between her teeth. "This road's goin to hell, Roland. I was hoping we were done with that damn harness, but you better get it out again." He nodded and rummaged in his purse for it without a word.

The condition of the Great Road deteriorated as other, smaller roads joined it like tributaries joining a great river. As they neared the bridge, the cobbles were replaced with a surface Roland thought of as metal and the rest of them thought of as asphalt or hot-top. It had not held up as well as the cobbles. Time had done some damage; the passage of count-less horses and wagons since the last repairs were made had done more. The surface had been chewed into a treacherous rubble. Foot travel would be difficult, and the idea of pushing Susannah's wheelchair over that crumbled surface was ridiculous.

The banks on either side had grown steadily steeper, and now, at their tops, they could see slim, pointed shapes looming against the sky. Roland thought of arrowheads—huge ones, weapons made by a tribe of giants. To his companions, they looked like rockets or guided missiles. Susannah thought of Redstones fired from Cape Canaveral; Eddie thought about SAMs, some built to be fired from the backs of flatbed trucks, stored all over Europe; Jake thought of ICBMs hiding in rein-forced concrete silos under the plains of Kansas and the unpopulated mountains of Nevada, programmed to hit back at China or the USSR in the event of nuclear armageddon. All of them felt as if they had passed into a dark and woeful zone of shadow, or into a countryside laboring under some old but still powerful curse.

Some hours after they entered this area—Jake called it The Gaunt-let—the concrete embankments ended at a place where half a dozen access roads drew together, like the strands of a spiderweb, and here the land opened out again . . . a fact which relieved all of them, although none of them said so out loud. Another traffic-light swung over the junc-tion. This one was more familiar to Eddie, Susannah, and Jake; it had once had lenses on its four faces, although the glass had been broken out long ago.

"I'll bet this road was the eighth wonder of the world, once upon a time," Susannah said, "and look at it now. It's a minefield."

"Old ways are sometimes the best ways," Roland agreed.

Eddie was pointing west. "Look."

Now that the high concrete barriers were gone, they could see exactly what old Si had described to them over cups of bitter coffee in River Crossing. "One track only," he had said, "set up high on a colyum of man-made stone, such as the Old Ones used to make their streets and walls." The track raced toward them out of the west in a slim, straight line, then flowed across the Send and into the city on a narrow golden trestle. It was a simple, elegant construction—and the only one they had seen so far which was totally without rust—but it was badly marred, all the same. Halfway across, a large piece of the trestle had fallen into the rushing river below. What remained were two long, jutting piers that pointed at each other like accusing fingers. Jutting out of the water below the hole was a streamlined tube of metal. Once it had been bright blue, but now the color had been dimmed by spreading scales of rust. It looked very small from this distance.

"So much for Blaine," Eddie said. "No wonder they stopped hearing it. The supports finally gave way while it was crossing the river and it fell in the drink. It must have been decelerating when it happened, or it would have carried straight across and all we'd see would be a big hole like a bomb-crater in the far bank. Well, it was a great idea while it lasted."

"Mercy said there was another one," Susannah reminded him.

"Yeah. She also said she hadn't heard it in seven or eight years, and Aunt Talitha said it was more like ten. What do you think, Jake . . . Jake? Earth to Jake, Earth to Jake, come in, little buddy."

Jake, who had been staring intently at the remains of the train in the river, only shrugged.

"You're a big help, Jake," Eddie said. "Valuable input—that's why I love you. Why we *all* love you."

Jake paid no attention. He knew what he was seeing, and it wasn't Blaine. The remains of the mono sticking out of the river were blue. In his dream, Blaine had been the dusty, sugary pink of the bubblegum you got with baseball trading cards.

Roland, meanwhile, had cinched the straps of Susannah's carry-harness across his chest. "Eddie, boost your lady into this contraption. It's time we moved on and saw for ourselves."

Jake now shifted his gaze, looking nervously toward the bridge looming ahead. He could hear a high, ghostly humming noise in the distance—the sound of the wind playing in the decayed steel hangers which connected the overhead cables to the concrete deck below.

"Do you think it'll be safe to cross?" Jake asked.

"We'll find out tomorrow," Roland replied.

9

THE NEXT MORNING, ROLAND'S band of travellers stood at the end of the long, rusty bridge, gazing across at Lud. Eddie's dreams of wise old elves who had preserved a working technology on which the pilgrims could draw were disappearing. Now that they were this close, he could see holes in the city-scape where whole blocks of buildings appeared to have been either burned or blasted. The skyline reminded him of a diseased jaw from which many teeth have already fallen.

It was true that most of the buildings were still standing, but they had a dreary, disused look that filled Eddie with an uncharacteristic gloom, and the bridge between the travellers and that shuttered maze of steel and concrete looked anything but solid and eternal. The vertical hangers on the left sagged slackly; the ones remaining on the right almost screamed with tension. The deck had been constructed of hollow concrete boxes shaped like trapezoids. Some of these had buckled upward, displaying empty black interiors; others had slipped askew. Many of these latter had merely cracked, but others were badly broken, leaving gaps big enough to drop trucks—*big* trucks—into. In places where the bottoms of the box-sections as well as the tops had shattered, they could see the muddy riverbank and the gray-green water of the Send beyond it. Eddie put the distance between the deck and the water as three hundred feet at the center of the bridge. And that was probably a conservative estimate.

Eddie peered at the huge concrete caissons to which the main cables were anchored and thought the one on the right side of the bridge looked as if it had been pulled partway out of the earth. He decided he might do well not to mention this fact to the others; it was bad enough that the bridge was swaying slowly but perceptibly back and forth. Just looking at it made him feel seasick. "Well?" he asked Roland. "What do you think?"

Roland pointed to the right side of the bridge. Here was a canted walkway about five feet wide. It had been constructed atop a series of smaller concrete boxes and was, in effect, a separate deck. This segmented deck appeared to be supported by an undercable—or perhaps it was a thick steel rod—anchored to the main support cables by huge bow-clamps. Eddie inspected the closest one with the avid interest of a man who may soon be entrusting his life to the object he is studying. The bow-clamp appeared rusty but still sound. The words LaMERK FOUNDRY had been stamped into its metal. Eddie was fascinated to realize he no longer knew if the words were in the High Speech or in English.

"I think we can use that," Roland said. "There's only one bad place. Do you see it?"

"Yeah—it's kind of hard to miss."

The bridge, which had to be at least three quarters of a mile long, might not have had any proper maintenance for over a thousand years, but Roland guessed that the real destruction might have been going on for only the last fifty or so. As the hangers on the right snapped, the bridge had listed farther and farther to the left. The greatest twist had occurred in the center of the bridge, between the two four-hundred-foot cable-towers. At the place where the pressure of the twist was the greatest, a gaping, eye-shaped hole ran across the deck. The break in the walkway was narrower, but even so, at least two adjoining concrete box-sections had fallen into the Send, leaving a gap at least twenty or thirty feet wide. Where these boxes had been, they could clearly see the rusty steel rod or cable which supported the walkway. They would have to use it to get across the gap.

"I think we can cross," Roland said, calmly pointing. "The gap is inconvenient, but the side-rail is still there, so we'll have something to hold onto."

Eddie nodded, but he could feel his heart pounding hard. The exposed walkway support looked like a big pipe made of jointed steel, and was probably four feet across at the top. In his mind's eye he could see how they would have to edge across, feet on the broad, slightly curved back of the support, hands clutching the rail, while the bridge swayed slowly like a ship in a mild swell.

"Jesus," he said. He tried to spit, but nothing came out. His mouth was too dry. "You sure, Roland?"

"So far as I can see, it's the only way." Roland pointed downriver and Eddie saw a second bridge. This one had fallen into the Send long ago. The remains stuck out of the water in a rusted tangle of ancient steel.

"What about you, Jake?" Susannah asked.

"Hey, no problem," Jake said at once. He was actually smiling.

"I hate you, kid," Eddie said.

Roland was looking at Eddie with some concern. "If you feel you can't do it, say so now. Don't get halfway across and then freeze up."

Eddie looked along the twisted surface of the bridge for a long time, then nodded. "I guess I can handle it. Heights have never been my favorite thing, but I'll manage."

"Good." Roland surveyed them. "Soonest begun, soonest done. I'll go first, with Susannah. Then Jake, and Eddie's drogue. Can you handle the wheelchair?"

"Hey, no problem," Eddie said giddily.

"Let's go, then."

10

AS SOON AS HE stepped onto the walkway, fear filled up Eddie's hollow places like cold water and he began to wonder if he hadn't made a very dangerous mistake. From solid ground, the bridge seemed to be swaying only a little, but once he was actually on it, he felt as if he were standing on the pendulum of the world's biggest grandfather clock. The movement was very slow, but it was regular, and the length of the swings was much longer than he had anticipated. The walkway's surface was badly cracked and canted at least ten degrees to the left. His feet gritted in loose piles of powdery concrete, and the low squealing sound of the box-segments grinding together was constant. Beyond the bridge, the city skyline tilted slowly back and forth like the artificial horizon of the world's slowest-moving video game.

Overhead, the wind hummed constantly in the taut hangers. Below, the ground fell away sharply to the muddy northwest bank of the river. He was thirty feet up . . . then sixty . . . then a hundred and ten. Soon he would be over the water. The wheelchair banged against his left leg with every step.

Something furry brushed between his feet and he clutched madly for the rusty handrail with his right hand, barely holding in a scream. Oy went trotting past him with a brief upward glance, as if to say *Excuse me—just passing.*

"Fucking dumb animal," Eddie said through gritted teeth.

He discovered that, although he didn't like looking down, he had an even greater aversion to looking at the hangers which were still managing to hold the deck and the overhead cables together. They were sleeved with rust and Eddie could see snarls of metal thread poking out of most—

these snarls looked like metallic puffs of cotton. He knew from his Uncle Reg, who had worked on both the George Washington and Triborough bridges as a painter, that the hangers and overhead cables were "spun" from thousands of steel threads. On this bridge, the spin was finally letting go. The hangers were quite literally becoming unravelled, and as they did, the threads were snapping, one interwoven strand at a time.

It's held this long, it'll hold a little longer. You think this thing's going to fall into the river just because you're crossing it? Don't flatter yourself.

He wasn't comforted, however. For all Eddie knew, they might be the first people to attempt the crossing in *decades*. And the bridge, after all, would have to collapse *sometime*, and from the look of things, it was going to be soon. Their combined weight might be the straw that broke the camel's back.

His moccasin struck a chunk of concrete and Eddie watched, sickened but helpless to look away, as the chunk fell down and down and down, turning over as it went. There was a small—*very* small—splash when it hit the river. The freshening wind gusted and stuck his shirt against his sweaty skin. The bridge groaned and swayed. Eddie tried to remove his hands from the side-rail, but they seemed frozen to the pitted metal in a deathgrip.

He closed his eyes for a moment. *You're not going to freeze. You're not. I . . . I forbid it. If you need something to look at, make it long tall and ugly.* Eddie opened his eyes again, fixed them on the gunslinger, forced his hands to open, and began to move forward again.

11

ROLAND REACHED THE GAP and looked back. Jake was five feet behind him. Oy was at his heels. The bumbler was crouched down with his neck stretched forward. The wind was much stronger over the river-cut, and Roland could see it rippling Oy's silky fur. Eddie was about twenty-five feet behind Jake. His face was tightly drawn, but he was still shuffling grimly along with Susannah's collapsed wheelchair in his left hand. His right was clutching the rail like grim death.

"Susannah?"

"Yes," she responded at once. "Fine."

"Jake?"

Jake looked up. He was still grinning, and the gunslinger saw there was going to be no problem there. The boy was having the time of his life. His hair blew back from his finely made brow in waves, and his eyes sparkled. He jerked one thumb up. Roland smiled and returned the gesture.

"Eddie?"

"Don't worry about me."

Eddie appeared to be looking at Roland, but the gunslinger decided he was really looking past him, at the windowless brick buildings which crowded the riverbank at the far end of the bridge. That was all right; given his obvious fear of heights, it was probably the best thing he could do to keep his head.

"All right, I won't," Roland murmured. "We're going to cross the hole now, Susannah. Sit easy. No quick movements. Understand?"

"Yes."

"If you want to adjust your position, do it now."

"I'm fine, Roland," she said calmly. "I just hope Eddie will be all right."

"Eddie's a gunslinger now. He'll behave like one."

Roland turned to the right, so he was facing directly downriver, and grasped the handrail. Then he began to edge out across the hole, shuffling his boots along the rusty cable.

12

JAKE WAITED UNTIL ROLAND and Susannah were part of the way across the gap and then started himself. The wind gusted and the bridge swayed back and forth, but he felt no alarm at all. He was, in fact, totally buzzed. Unlike Eddie, he'd never had any fear of heights; he liked being up here where he could see the river spread out like a steel ribbon under a sky which was beginning to cloud over.

Halfway across the hole in the bridge (Roland and Susannah had reached the place where the uneven walkway resumed and were watching the others), Jake looked back and his heart sank. They had forgotten one member of the party when they were discussing how to cross. Oy was crouched, frozen and clearly terrified, on the far side of the hole in the walkway. He was sniffing at the place where the concrete ended and the rusty, curved support took over.

"Come on, Oy!" Jake called.

"Oy!" the bumbler called back, and the tremble in his hoarse voice was almost human. He stretched his long neck forward toward Jake but didn't move. His gold-ringed eyes were huge and dismayed.

Another gust of wind struck the bridge, making it sway and squall. Something twanged beside Jake's head—the sound of a guitar string which has been tightened until it snaps. A steel thread had popped out of the nearest vertical hanger, almost scratching his cheek. Ten feet away, Oy crouched miserably with his eyes fixed on Jake.

"Come on!" Roland shouted. "Wind's freshening! Come on, Jake!"

"Not without Oy!"

Jake began to shuffle back the way he had come. Before he had gone more than two steps, Oy stepped gingerly onto the support rod. The claws at the ends of his stiffly braced legs scratched at the rounded metal surface. Eddie stood behind the bumbler now, feeling helpless and scared to death.

"That's it, Oy!" Jake encouraged. "Come to me!"

"Oy-Oy! Ake-Ake!" the bumbler cried, and trotted rapidly along the rod. He had almost reached Jake when the traitorous wind gusted again. The bridge swung. Oy's claws scratched madly at the support rod for purchase, but there was none. His hindquarters slued off the edge and into space. He tried to cling with his forepaws, but there was nothing to cling to. His rear legs ran wildly in midair.

Jake let go of the rail and dived for him, aware of nothing but Oy's gold-ringed eyes.

"*No, Jake!*" Roland and Eddie bellowed together, each from his own side of the gap, each too far away to do anything but watch.

Jake hit the cable on his chest and belly. His pack bounced against his shoulderblades and he heard his teeth click together in his head with the sound of a cueball breaking a tight rack. The wind gusted again. He went with it, looping his right hand around the support rod and reaching for Oy with his left as he swayed out into space. The bumbler began to fall, and clamped his jaws on Jake's reaching hand as he did. The pain was immediate and excruciating. Jake screamed but held on, head down, right arm clasping the rod, knees pressing hard against its wretchedly smooth surface. Oy dangled from his left hand like a circus acrobat, staring up with his gold-ringed eyes, and Jake could now see his own blood flowing along the sides of the bumbler's head in thin streams.

Then the wind gusted again and Jake began to slip outward.

13

EDDIE'S FEAR LEFT HIM In its place came that strange yet welcome coldness. He dropped Susannah's wheelchair to the cracked cement with a clatter and raced nimbly out along the support cable, not even bothering with the handrail. Jake hung head-down over the gap with Oy swinging at the end of his left hand like a furry pendulum. And the boy's right hand was slipping.

Eddie opened his legs and seat-dropped to a sitting position. His undefended balls smashed painfully up into his crotch, but for the moment even this exquisite pain was news from a distant country. He seized Jake by the hair with one hand and one strap of his pack with the other. He felt himself beginning to tilt outward, and for a nightmarish moment he thought all three of them were going to go over in a daisy-chain.

He let go of Jake's hair and tightened his grip on the packstrap, praying the kid hadn't bought the pack at one of the cheap discount outlets. He flailed above his head for the handrail with his free hand. After an interminable moment in which their combined outward slide continued, he found it and seized it.

"ROLAND!" he bawled. *"I COULD USE A LITTLE HELP HERE!"*

But Roland was already there, with Susannah still perched on his back. When he bent, she locked her arms around his neck so she wouldn't drop headfirst from the sling. The gunslinger wrapped an arm around Jake's chest and pulled him up. When his feet were on the support rod again, Jake put his right arm around Oy's trembling body. His left hand was an agony of fire and ice.

"Let go, Oy," he gasped. "You can let go now we're—safe."

For a terrible moment he didn't think the billy-bumbler would. Then, slowly, Oy's jaws relaxed and Jake was able to pull his hand free. It was covered with blood and dotted with a ring of dark holes.

"Oy," the bumbler said feebly, and Eddie saw with wonder that the animal's strange eyes were full of tears. He stretched his neck and licked Jake's face with his bloody tongue.

"That's okay," Jake said, pressing his face into the warm fur. He was crying himself, his face a mask of shock and pain. "Don't worry, that's okay. You couldn't help it and I don't mind."

Eddie was getting slowly to his feet. His face was dirty gray, and he felt as if someone had driven a bowling ball into his guts. His left hand stole slowly to his crotch and investigated the damage there.

"Cheap fucking vasectomy," he said hoarsely.

"Are you going to faint, Eddie?" Roland asked. A fresh gust of wind flipped his hat from his head and into Susannah's face. She grabbed it and jammed it down all the way to his ears, giving Roland the look of a half-crazed hillbilly.

"No," Eddie said. "I almost wish I could, but—"

"Take a look at Jake," Susannah said. "He's really bleeding."

"I'm fine," Jake said, and tried to hide his hand. Roland took it gently in his own hands before he could. Jake had sustained at least a dozen puncture-wounds in the back of his hand, his palm, and his fingers.

Most of them were deep. It would be impossible to tell if bones had been broken or tendons severed until Jake tried to flex the hand, and this wasn't the time or place for such experiments.

Roland looked at Oy. The billy-bumbler looked back, his expressive eyes sad and frightened. He had made no effort to lick Jake's blood from his chops, although it would have been the most natural thing in the world for him to have done so.

"Leave him alone," Jake said, and wrapped the encircling arm more tightly about Oy's body. "It wasn't his fault. It was my fault for forgetting him. The wind blew him off."

"I'm not going to hurt him," Roland said. He was positive the billy-bumbler wasn't rabid, but he still did not intend for Oy to taste any more of Jake's blood than he already had. As for any other diseases Oy might be carrying in his blood . . . well, *ka* would decide, as, in the end, it always did. Roland pulled his neckerchief free and wiped Oy's lips and muzzle. "There," he said. "Good fellow. Good boy."

"Oy," the billy-bumbler said feebly, and Susannah, who was watching over Roland's shoulder, could have sworn she heard gratitude in that voice.

Another gust of wind struck them. The weather was turning dirty, and fast. "Eddie, we have to get off the bridge. Can you walk?"

"No, massa; I'sa gwinter shuffle." The pain in his groin and the pit of his stomach was still bad, but not quite so bad as it had been a minute ago.

"All right. Let's move. Fast as we can."

Roland turned, began to take a step, and stopped. A man was now standing on the far side of the gap, watching them expressionlessly.

The newcomer had approached while their attention was focused on Jake and Oy. A crossbow was slung across his back. He wore a bright yellow scarf around his head; the ends streamed out like banners in the freshening wind. Gold hoops with crosses in their centers dangled from his ears. One eye was covered with a white silk patch. His face was blotched with purple sores, some of them open and festering. He might have been thirty, forty, or sixty. He held one hand high over his head. In it was something Roland could not make out, except that its shape was too regular to be a stone.

Behind this apparition, the city loomed with a kind of weird clarity in the darkening day. As Eddie looked past the huddles of brick buildings on the other shore—warehouses long since scooped empty by looters, he had no doubt—and into those shadowy canyons and stone mazes, he understood for the first time how terribly mistaken, how terribly foolish, his dreams of hope and help had been. Now he saw the shattered facades and broken roofs; now he saw the shaggy birds' nests on cornices and in glassless, gaping windows; now he allowed himself to actually *smell* the city, and that odor was not of fabulous spices and savory foods of the sort his mother had sometimes brought home from Zabar's but rather the stink of a mattress that has caught fire, smouldered awhile, and then been put out with sewer-water. He suddenly understood Lud, understood it completely. The grinning pirate who had appeared while their attention was elsewhere was probably as close to a wise old elf as this broken, dying place could provide.

Roland pulled his revolver.

"Put it away, my cully," the man in the yellow scarf said in an accent so thick that the sense of his words was almost lost. "Put it away, my dear heart. Ye're a fierce trim, ay, that's clear, but this time you're outmatched."

14

THE NEWCOMER'S PANTS WERE patched green velvet, and as he stood on the edge of the hole in the bridge, he looked like a buccaneer at the end of his days of plunder: sick, ragged, and still dangerous.

"Suppose I choose not to?" Roland asked. "Suppose I choose to simply put a bullet through your scrofulous head?"

"Then I'll get to hell just enough ahead of ye to hold the door," the man in the yellow scarf said, and chuckled chummily. He wiggled the hand he held in the air. "It's all the same jolly fakement to me, one way or t'other."

Roland guessed that was the truth. The man looked as if he might have a year to live at most . . . and the last few months of that year would probably be very unpleasant. The oozing sores on his face had nothing to do with radiation; unless Roland was badly deceived, this man was in the late stages of what the doctors called mandrus and everyone else called whore's blossoms. Facing a dangerous man was always a bad business, but at least one could calculate the odds in such an encounter. When you were facing the dead, however, everything changed.

"Do yer know what I've got here, my dear ones?" the pirate asked. "Do yer ken whatcher old friend Gasher just happens to have laid his hands on? It's a grenado, something pretty the Old Folks left behind, and I've already tipped its cap—for to wear one's cap before the introductin' is complete would be wery bad manners, so it would!"

He cackled happily for a moment, and then his face grew still and grave once more. All humor left it, as if a switch had been turned somewhere in his degenerating brains.

"My finger is all that's holdin the pin now, dearie. If you shoot me, there's going to be a wery big bang. You and the cunt-monkey on yer back will be vaporized. The squint, too, I reckon. The young buck stand-ing behind you and pointing that toy pistol in my face might live, but only until he hits the water . . . and hit it he would, because this bridge has been hangin by a thread these last forty year, and all it'd take to finish it is one little push. So do ye want to put away your iron, or shall we all toddle off to hell on the same handcart?"

Roland briefly considered trying to shoot the object Gasher called a grenado out of his hand, saw how tightly the man was gripping it, and holstered his gun.

"Ah, good!" Gasher cried, cheerful once more. "I knew ye was a trig cove, just lookin at yer! Oh yes! So I did!"

"What do you want?" Roland asked, although he thought he already knew this, too.

Gasher raised his free hand and pointed a dirty finger at Jake. "The squint. Gimme the squint and the rest of you go free."

"Go fuck yourself," Susannah said at once.

"Why not?" the pirate cackled. "Gimme a chunk of mirror and I'll rip it right off and stick it right in—why not, for all the good it's a-doin me these days? Why, I can't even run water through it without it burns me all the way to the top of my gullywash!" His eyes, which were a strange calm shade of gray, never left Roland's face. "What do *you* say, my good old mate?"

"What happens to the rest of us if I hand over the boy?"

"Why, you go on yer way without no trouble from us!" the man in the yellow headscarf returned promptly. "You have the Tick-Tock Man's word on that. It comes from his lips to my lips to your ears, so it does, and Tick-Tock's a trig cove, too, what don't break his word once it's been given. I can't say ary word nor watch about any Pubies you might run into, but you'll have no trouble with the Tick-Tock Man's Grays."

"What the fuck are you *saying*, Roland?" Eddie roared. "You're not really thinking about doing it, are you?"

Roland didn't look down at Jake, and his lips didn't move as he murmured: "I'll keep my promise."

"Yes—I know you will." Then Jake raised his voice and said: "Put the gun away, Eddie. I'll decide."

"Jake, you're out of your *mind*!"

The pirate cackled cheerily. "Not at all, cully! *You're* the one who's lost his mind if you disbelieve me. At the wery least, he'll be safe from the drums with us, won't he? And just think—if I didn't mean what I say, I would have told you to toss your guns overside first thing! Easiest thing in the world! But did I? Nay!"

Susannah had heard the exchange between Jake and Roland. She had also had a chance to realize how bleak their options were as things now stood. "Put it away, Eddie."

"How do we know you won't toss the grenade at us once you have the kid?" Eddie called.

"I'll shoot it out of the air if he tries," Roland said. "I can do it, and he *knows* I can do it."

"Mayhap I do. You've got a cosy look about you, indeed ye do."

"If he's telling the truth," Roland went on, "he'd be burned even if I missed his toy, because the bridge would collapse and we'd all go down together."

"Wery clever, my dear old son!" Gasher said. "You *are* a cosy one, ain't you?" He cawed laughter, then grew serious and confiding. "The talking's done, old mate of mine. Decide. Will you give me the boy, or do we all march to the end of the path together?"

Before Roland could say a word, Jake had slipped past him on the support rod. He still held Oy curled in his right arm. He held his bloody left hand stiffly out in front of him.

"Jake, *no!*" Eddie shouted desperately.

"I'll come for you," Roland said in the same low voice.

"I know," Jake repeated. The wind gusted again. The bridge swayed and groaned. The Send was now speckled with whitecaps, and water boiled whitely around the wreck of the blue mono jutting from the river on the upstream side.

"Ay, my cully!" Gasher crooned. His lips spread wide, revealing a few remaining teeth that jutted from his white gums like decayed tombstones. "Ay, my fine young squint! Just keep coming."

"Roland, he could be bluffing!" Eddie yelled. "That thing could be a dud!"

The gunslinger made no reply.

As Jake neared the other side of the hole in the walkway, Oy bared his own teeth and began to snarl at Gasher.

"Toss that talking bag of guts overside," Gasher said.

"Fuck you," Jake replied in the same calm voice.

The pirate looked surprised for a moment, then nodded. "Tender of him, are you? Wery well." He took two steps backward. "Put him down the second you reach the concrete, then. And if he runs at me, I promise to kick his brains right out his tender little asshole."

"Asshole," Oy said through his bared teeth.

"Shut up, Oy," Jake muttered. He reached the concrete just as the strongest gust of wind yet struck the bridge. This time the twanging sound of parting cable-strands seemed to come from everywhere. Jake glanced back and saw Roland and Eddie clinging to the rail. Susannah was watching him from over Roland's shoulder, her tight cap of curls rippling and shaking in the wind. Jake raised his hand to them. Roland raised his in return.

You won't let me drop this time? he had asked. *No—not ever again,* Roland had replied. Jake believed him . . . but he was very much afraid of what might happen before Roland arrived. He put Oy down. Gasher rushed forward the moment he did, kicking out at the small animal. Oy skittered aside, avoiding the booted foot.

"Run!" Jake shouted. Oy did, shooting past them and loping toward the Lud end of the bridge with his head down, swerving to avoid the holes and leaping across the cracks in the pavement. He didn't look back. A moment later Gasher had his arm around Jake's neck. He stank of dirt and decaying flesh, the two odors combining to create a single deep stench, crusty and thick. It made Jake's gorge rise.

He bumped his crotch into Jake's buttocks. "Maybe I ain't quite s'far gone's I thought. Don't they say youth's the wine what makes old men drunk? We'll have us a time, won't we, my sweet little squint? Ay, we'll have a time such as will make the angels sing."

Oh Jesus, Jake thought.

Gasher raised his voice again. "We're leaving now, my hardcase friend—we have grand things to do and grand people to see, so we do, but I keep my word. As for you, you'll stand right where you are for a good fifteen minutes, if you're wise. If I see you start to move, we're all going to ride the handsome. Do you understand me?"

"Yes," Roland said.

"Do you believe me when I say I have nothing to lose?"

"Yes."

"That's wery well, then. Move, boy! Hup!"

Gasher's hold tightened on Jake's throat until he could hardly breathe. At the same time he was pulled backward. They retreated that way, facing the gap where Roland stood with Susannah on his back and Eddie just behind him, still holding the Ruger which Gasher had called a toy pistol. Jake could feel Gasher's breath puffing against his ear in hot little blurts. Worse, he could smell it.

"Don't try a thing," Gasher whispered, "or I'll rip off yer sweetmeats and stuff em up your bung. And it would be sad to lose em before you ever got a chance to use em, wouldn't it? Wery sad indeed."

They reached the end of the bridge. Jake stiffened, believing Gasher would throw the grenade anyway, but he didn't . . . at least not immediately. He backed Jake through a narrow alley between two small cubicles which had probably served as tollbooths, once upon a time. Beyond them, the brick warehouses loomed like prison cellblocks.

"Now, cully, I'm going to let go of your neck, or how would'je ever have wind to run with? But I'll be holdin yer arm, and if ye don't run like the wind, I promise I'll rip it right off and use it for a club to beat you with. Do you understand?"

Jake nodded, and suddenly the terrible, stifling pressure was gone from his windpipe. As soon as it was, he became aware of his hand again—it felt hot and swollen and full of fire. Then Gasher seized his bicep with fingers like bands of iron, and he forgot all about his hand.

"Toodle-doo!" Gasher called in a grotesquely cheery falsetto. He waggled the grenado at the others. "Bye-bye, dears!" Then he growled to Jake: "Now *run*, you whoring little squint! *Run!*"

Jake was first whirled and then yanked into a run. The two of them went flying down a curved ramp to street level. Jake's first confused thought was that this was what the East River Drive would look like two or three hundred years after some weird brain-plague had killed all the sane people in the world.

The ancient, rusty hulks of what had once surely been automobiles stood at intervals along both curbs. Most were bubble-shaped roadsters that looked like no cars Jake had ever seen before (except, maybe, for the ones the white-gloved creations of Walt Disney drove in the comic books), but among them he saw an old Volkswagen Beetle, a car that might have been a Chevrolet Corvair, and something he believed was a Model A Ford. There were no tires on any of these eerie hulks; they either had been stolen or had rotted away to dust long since. And all the glass had been broken, as if the remaining denizens of this city abhorred anything which might show them their own reflections, even accidentally.

Beneath and between the abandoned cars, the gutters were filled with drifts of unidentifiable metal junk and bright glints of glass. Trees had been planted at intervals along the sidewalks in some long-gone, happier time, but they were now so emphatically dead that they looked like stark metal sculptures against the cloudy sky. Some of the warehouses had either been bombed or had collapsed on their own, and beyond the jumbled heaps of bricks which was all that remained of them Jake could see the river and the rusty, sagging underpinnings of the Send Bridge. That smell of wet decay—a smell that seemed almost to snarl in the nose—was stronger than ever.

The street headed due east, diverging from the path of the Beam, and Jake could see it became more and more choked with rubble and rickrack as it went. Six or seven blocks down it appeared to be entirely plugged, but it was in this direction that Gasher pulled him. At first he kept up, but Gasher was setting a fearsome pace. Jake began to pant and fell a step behind. Gasher almost jerked him off his feet as he dragged Jake toward the barrier of junk and concrete and rusty steel beams which lay ahead. The plug—which looked like a deliberate construction to Jake—lay between two broad buildings with dusty marble facades. In front of the one on the left was a statue Jake recognized at once: it was the woman called Blind Justice, and that almost surely made the building she guarded a courthouse. But he only had a moment to look; Gasher was dragging him relentlessly toward the barricade, and he wasn't slowing down.

He'll kill us if he tries to take us through there! Jake thought, but Gasher—who ran like the wind in spite of the disease which advertised itself on his face—simply buried his fingers deeper in Jake's upper arm and swept him along. And now Jake saw a narrow alley in the not-quite-haphazard pile of concrete, splintered furniture, rusted plumbing fixtures, and chunks of trucks and automobiles. He suddenly understood. This maze would hold Roland up for hours . . . but it was Gasher's back yard, and he knew *exactly* where he was going.

The small dark opening to the alley was on the left side of the tottery pile of junk. As they reached it, Gasher tossed the green object back over his shoulder. "Better duck, dearie!" he cried, and voiced a series of shrill, hysterical giggles. A moment later a huge, crumping explosion shook the street. One of the bubble-shaped cars jumped twenty feet into the air and then came down on its roof. A hail of bricks whistled over Jake's head, and something thumped him hard on the left shoulderblade. He stumbled and would have fallen if Gasher hadn't yanked him upright and pulled him into the narrow opening in the rubble. Once they were in the passageway which lay beyond, gloomy shadows reached out eagerly and enfolded them.

When they were gone, a small, furry shape crept out from behind a concrete boulder. It was Oy. He stood at the mouth of the passage for a moment, neck stretched forward, eyes gleaming. Then he followed after, nose low to the ground and sniffing carefully.

15

"COME ON," ROLAND SAID as soon as Gasher had turned tail.

"How could you do it?" Eddie asked. "How could you let that freak have him?"

"Because I had no choice. Bring the wheelchair. We're going to need it."

They had reached the concrete on the far side of the gap when an explosion shook the bridge, spraying rubble into the darkening sky.

"Christ!" Eddie said, and turned his white, dismayed face to Roland.

"Don't worry yet," Roland said calmly. "Fellows like Gasher rarely get careless with their high-explosive toys." They reached the tollbooths at the end of the bridge. Roland stopped just beyond, at the top of the curving ramp.

"You knew the guy wasn't just bluffing, didn't you?" Eddie said. "I mean, you weren't guessing—you *knew*."

"He's a walking dead man, and such men don't need to bluff." Roland's voice was calm enough, but there was a deep undertone of bitterness and pain in it. "I knew something like this could happen, and if we'd seen the fellow earlier, while we were still beyond the range of his exploding egg, we could have stood him off. But then Jake fell and he got too close. I imagine he thinks our real reason for bringing a boy in the first place was to pay for safe conduct through the city. Damn! Damn the luck!" Roland struck his fist against his leg.

"Well, let's go get him!"

Roland shook his head. "This is where we split up. We can't take Susannah where the bastard's gone, and we can't leave her alone."

"But—"

"Listen and don't argue—not if you want to save Jake. The longer we stand here, the colder his trail gets. Cold trails are hard to follow. You've got your own job to do. If there's another Blaine, and I am sure Jake believes there is, then you and Susannah must find it. There must be a station, or what was once called a cradle in the far lands. Do you understand?"

For once, blessedly, Eddie didn't argue. "Yeah. We'll find it. What then?"

"Fire a shot every half hour or so. When I get Jake, I'll come."

"Shots may attract other people as well," Susannah said. Eddie had helped her out of the sling and she was seated in her chair again.

Roland surveyed them coldly. "Handle them."

"Okay." Eddie stuck out his hand and Roland took it briefly. "Find him, Roland."

"Oh, I'll find him. Just pray to your gods that I find him soon enough. And remember the faces of your fathers, both of you."

Susannah nodded. "We'll try."

Roland turned and ran light-footed down the ramp. When he was out of sight, Eddie looked at Susannah and was not very surprised to see she was crying. He felt like crying himself. Half an hour ago they had been a tight little band of friends. Their comfortable fellowship had been smashed to bits in the space of just a few minutes—Jake abducted, Roland gone after him. Even Oy had run away. Eddie had never felt so lonely in his life.

"I have a feeling we're never going to see either of them again," Susannah said.

"Of course we will!" Eddie said roughly, but he knew what she meant, because he felt the same way. The premonition that their quest was all over before it was fairly begun lay heavy on his heart. "In a fight with Attila the Hun, I'd give you three-to-two odds on Roland the Barbarian. Come on, Suze—we've got a train to catch."

"But where?" she asked forlornly.

"I don't know. Maybe we should just find the nearest wise old elf and ask him, huh?"

"What are you talking about, Edward Dean?"

"Nothing," he said, and because that was so goddam true he thought he might burst into tears, he grasped the handles of her wheelchair and began to push it down the cracked and glass-littered ramp that led into the city of Lud.

16

JAKE QUICKLY DESCENDED INTO a foggy world where the only landmarks were pain: his throbbing hand, the place on his upper arm where Gasher's fingers dug in like steel pegs, his burning lungs. Before they had gone far, these pains were first joined and then overmatched by a deep, burning stitch in his left side. He wondered if Roland was following after them yet. He also wondered how long Oy would be able to live in this world which was so unlike the plains and forest which were all he had known until now. Then Gasher clouted him across the face, bloodying his nose, and thought was lost in a red wash of pain.

"Come on, yer little bastard! Move yer sweet cheeks!"

"Running . . . as fast as I can," Jake gasped, and just managed to dodge a thick shard of glass which jutted like a long transparent tooth from the wall of junk to his left.

"You better not be, because I'll knock yer cold and drag yer along by the hair o' yer head if y'are! Now *hup*, you little barstard!"

Jake somehow forced himself to run faster. He'd gone into the alley with the idea that they must shortly re-emerge onto the avenue, but he now reluctantly realized that wasn't going to happen. This was more than an alley; it was a camouflaged and fortified road leading ever deeper into the country of the Grays. The tall, tottery walls which pressed in on them had been built from an exotic array of materials: cars which had been partially or completely flattened by the chunks of granite and steel placed on top of them; marble pillars; unknown factory machines which were dull red with rust wherever they weren't still black with grease; a chrome-and-crystal fish as big as a private plane with one cryptic word of the High Speech—DELIGHT—carefully incised into its scaly gleaming side; crisscrossing chains, each link as big as Jake's head, wrapped around mad jumbles of furniture that appeared to balance above them as precariously as circus elephants do on their tiny steel platforms.

They came to a place where this lunatic path branched, and Gasher chose the left fork without hesitation. A little further along, three more alleyways, these so narrow they were almost tunnels, spoked off in various directions. This time Gasher chose the right-hand branching. The new path, which seemed to be formed by banks of rotting boxes and huge blocks of old paper—paper that might once have been books or magazines—was too narrow for them to run in side by side. Gasher shoved Jake into the lead and began beating him relentlessly on the back to make him go faster. *This is how a steer must feel when it's driven down the chute to the slaughtering pen*, Jake thought, and vowed that if he got out of this alive, he would never eat steak again.

"Run, my sweet little boycunt! *Run!*"

Jake soon lost all track of the twistings and turnings they made, and as Gasher drove him deeper and deeper into this jumble of torn steel, broken furniture, and castoff machinery, he began to give up hope of rescue. Not even Roland would be able to find him now. If the gunslinger tried, he would become lost himself, and wander the choked paths of this nightmare world until he died.

Now they were going downhill, and the walls of tightly packed paper had given way to ramparts of filing cabinets, jumbles of adding machines, and piles of computer gear. It was like running through some nightmarish Radio Shack warehouse. For almost a full minute the wall flowing past on Jake's left appeared to be constructed solely of either TV sets or carelessly stacked video display terminals. They stared at him like the glazed eyes of dead men. And as the pavement beneath their feet continued to descend, Jake realized that they *were* in a tunnel. The strip of cloudy sky overhead narrowed to a band, the band narrowed to a ribbon, and the ribbon became a thread. They were in a gloomy netherworld, scurrying like rats through a gigantic trash-midden.

What if it all comes down on us? Jake wondered, but in his current state of aching exhaustion, this possibility did not frighten him much. If the roof fell in, he would at least be able to rest.

Gasher drove him as a farmer would a mule, striking his left shoulder to indicate a left turn and his right to indicate a right turn. When the course was straight on, he thumped Jake on the back of the head. Jake tried to dodge a jutting pipe and didn't quite succeed. It whacked into one hip and sent him flailing across the narrow passage toward a snarl of glass and jagged boards. Gasher caught him and shoved him forward again. "Run, you clumsy squint! Can't you run? If it wasn't for the Tick-Tock Man, I'd bugger you right here and cut yer throat while I did it, ay, so I would!"

Jake ran in a red daze where there was only pain and the frequent thud of Gasher's fists coming down on his shoulders or the back of his head. At last, when he was sure he could run no longer, Gasher grabbed him by the neck and yanked him to a stop so fiercely that Jake crashed into him with a strangled squawk.

"*Here's* a tricky little bit!" Gasher panted jovially. "Look straight ahead and you'll see two wires what cross in an X low to the ground. Do yer see em?"

At first Jake didn't. It was very gloomy here; heaps of huge copper kettles were piled up to the left, and to the right were stacks of steel tanks that looked like scuba-diving gear. Jake thought he could turn these latter into an avalanche with one strong breath. He swiped his forearm across his eyes, brushing away tangles of hair, and tried not to think about how he'd look with about sixteen tons of those tanks piled on top of him. He squinted in the direction Gasher was pointing. Yes, he could make out—barely—two thin, silvery lines that looked like guitar or banjo strings. They came down from opposite sides of the passageway and crossed about two feet above the pavement.

"Crawl under, dear heart. And be ever so careful, for if you so much as twang one of those wires, harf the steel and cement puke in the city'll come down on your dear little head. Mine, too, although I doubt if that'd disturb you much, would it? Now crawl!"

Jake shrugged out of his pack, lay down, and pushed it through the gap ahead of him. And as he eased his way under the thin, taut wires, he discovered that he wanted to live a little longer after all. It seemed that he could actually feel all those tons of carefully balanced junk waiting to come down on him. *These wires are probably holding a couple of carefully chosen keystones in place,* he thought. *If one of them breaks . . . ashes, ashes, we all fall down.* His back brushed one of the wires, and high overhead, something creaked.

"Careful, cully!" Gasher almost moaned. "Be oh so careful!"

Jake pushed himself beneath the crisscrossing wires, using his feet and his elbows. His stinking, sweat-clogged hair fell in his eyes again, but he did not dare brush it away.

"You're clear," Gasher grunted at last, and slipped beneath the tripwires himself with the ease of long practice. He stood up and snatched Jake's pack before Jake could reshoulder it. "What's in here, cully?" he asked, undoing the straps and peering in. "Got any treats for yer old pal? For the Gasherman loves his treaties, so he does!"

"There's nothing in there but—"

Gasher's hand flashed out and rocked Jake's head back with a hard slap that sent a fresh spray of bloody froth flying from the boy's nose.

"What did you do that for?" Jake cried, hurt and outraged.

"For tellin me what my own beshitted eyes can see!" Gasher yelled, and cast Jake's pack aside. He bared his remaining teeth at the boy in a dangerous, terrible grin. "And fer almost bringin the whole beshitted works down on us!" He paused, then added in a quieter voice: "*And* because I felt like it—I must admit that. Your stupid sheep's face puts me wery much in a slappin temper, so it does." The grin widened, revealing his oozing whitish gums, a sight Jake could have done without. "If your hardcase friend follows us this far, he'll have a surprise when he runs into those wires, won't he?" Gasher looked up, still grinning. "There's a city bus balanced up there someplace, as I remember."

Jake began to weep—tired, hopeless tears that cut through the dirt on his cheeks in narrow channels.

Gasher raised an open, threatening hand. "Get moving, cully, before I start cryin myself . . . for a wery sentermental fellow is yer old pal, so he is, and when he starts to grieve and mourn, a little slappin is the only thing to put a smile on his face again. *Run!*"

They ran. Gasher chose pathways leading deeper into the smelly, creaking maze seemingly at random, indicating his choices with hard whacks to the shoulders. At some point the sound of the drums began. It seemed to come from everywhere and nowhere, and for Jake it was the final straw. He gave up hope and thought alike, and allowed himself to descend wholly into the nightmare.

17

ROLAND HALTED IN FRONT of the barricade which choked the street from side to side and top to bottom. Unlike Jake, he had no hopes of emerging into the open on the other side. The buildings lying east of this point would be sentry-occupied islands emerging from an inland sea of trash, tools, artifacts . . . and booby-traps, he had no doubt. Some of these leavings undoubtedly still remained where they had fallen five hundred or seven hundred or a thousand years ago, but Roland thought most of it had been dragged here by the Grays a piece at a time. The eastern portion of Lud had become, in effect, the castle of the Grays, and Roland was now standing outside its wall.

He walked forward slowly and saw the mouth of a passageway half-hidden behind a ragged cement boulder. There were footprints in the powdery dust—two sets, one big, one small. Roland started to get up, looked again, and squatted on his hunkers once more. Not two sets but three, the third marking the paws of a small animal.

"Oy?" Roland called softly. For a moment there was no response, and then a single soft bark came from the shadows. Roland stepped into the passageway and saw gold-ringed eyes peering at him from around the first crooked corner. Roland trotted down to the bumbler. Oy, who still didn't like to come really close to anyone but Jake, backed up a step and then held his ground, looking anxiously up at the gunslinger.

"Do you want to help me?" Roland asked. He could feel the dry red curtain that was battle fever at the edge of his consciousness, but this was not the time for it. The time would come, but for now he must not allow himself that inexpressible relief. "Help me find Jake?"

"Ake!" Oy barked, still watching Roland with his anxious eyes.

"Go on, then. Find him."

Oy turned away at once and ran rapidly down the alley, nose skimming the ground. Roland followed, his eyes only occasionally flicking up to glance at Oy. Mostly he kept his gaze fixed on the ancient pavement, looking for sign.

18

"JESUS," EDDIE SAID. "WHAT kind of people *are* these guys?"

They had followed the avenue at the base of the ramp for a couple of blocks, had seen the barricade (missing Roland's entry into the partially hidden passageway by less than a minute) which lay ahead, and had turned north onto a broad thoroughfare which reminded Eddie of Fifth Avenue. He hadn't dared to tell Susannah that; he was still too bitterly disappointed with this stinking, littered ruin of a city to articulate anything hopeful.

"Fifth Avenue" led them into an area of large white stone buildings that reminded Eddie of the way Rome looked in the gladiator movies he'd watched on TV as a kid. They were austere and, for the most part, still in good shape. He was pretty sure they had been public buildings of some sort—galleries, libraries, maybe museums. One, with a big domed roof that had cracked like a granite egg, might have been an observatory, although Eddie had read someplace that astronomers liked to be *away* from big cities, because all the electric lights fucked up their star-gazing.

There were open areas between these imposing edifices, and although the grass and flowers which had once grown there had been choked off by weeds and tangles of underbrush, the area still had a stately feel, and Eddie wondered if it had once been the center of Lud's cultural life. Those days were long gone, of course; Eddie doubted if Gasher and his pals were very interested in ballet or chamber music.

He and Susannah had come to a major intersection from which four more broad avenues radiated outward like spokes on a wheel. At the hub of the wheel was a large paved square. Ringing it were loudspeakers on forty-foot steel posts. In the center of the square was a pedestal with the remains of a statue upon it—a mighty copper war-horse, green with verdigris, pawing its forelegs at the air. The warrior who had once ridden this charger lay off to the side on one corroded shoulder, waving what looked like a machine-gun in one hand and a sword in the other. His legs were still bowed around the shape of the horse he had once ridden, but his boots remained welded to the sides of his metal mount. GRAYS DIE! was written across the pedestal in fading orange letters.

Glancing down the radiating streets, Eddie saw more of the speaker-poles. A few had fallen over, but most still stood, and each of these had been festooned with a grisly garland of corpses. As a result, the square into which "Fifth Avenue" emptied and the streets which led away were guarded by a small army of the dead.

"What kind of people *are* they?" Eddie asked again.

He didn't expect an answer and Susannah didn't give one . . . but she could have. She'd had insights into the past of Roland's world before, but never one as clear and sure as this. All of her earlier insights, like those which had come to her in River Crossing, had had a haunting visionary quality, like dreams, but what came now arrived in a single flash, and it was like seeing the twisted face of a dangerous maniac illuminated by a stroke of lightning.

The speakers . . . the hanging bodies . . . the drums. She suddenly understood how they went together as clearly as she had understood that the heavy-laden wagons passing through River Crossing on their way to Jimtown had been pulled by oxen rather than mules or horses.

"Never mind this trash," she said, and her voice only quivered a little. "It's the train we want—which way is it, d'you think?"

Eddie glanced up at the darkening sky and easily picked out the path of the Beam in the rushing clouds. He looked back down and wasn't much surprised to see that the entrance to the street corresponding most closely to the path of the Beam was guarded by a large stone turtle. Its reptilian head peered out from beneath the granite lip of its shell; its deepset eyes seemed to stare curiously at them. Eddie nodded toward it and managed a small dry smile. "See the turtle of enormous girth?"

Susannah took a brief look of her own and nodded. He pushed her across the city square and into The Street of the Turtle. The corpses which lined it gave off a dry, cinnamony smell that made Eddie's stomach clench . . . not because it was bad but because it was actually rather pleasant—the sugar-spicy aroma of something a kid would enjoy shaking onto his morning toast.

The Street of the Turtle was mercifully broad, and most of the corpses hanging from the speaker-poles were little more than mummies, but Susannah saw a few which were relatively fresh, with flies still crawling busily across the blackening skin of their swollen faces and maggots still squirming out of their decaying eyes.

And below each speaker was a little drift of bones.

"There must be thousands," Eddie said. "Men, women, and kids."

"Yes." Susannah's calm voice sounded distant and strange to her own ears. "They've had a lot of time to kill. And they've used it to kill each other."

"Bring on those wise fuckin elves!" Eddie said, and the laugh that followed sounded suspiciously like a sob. He thought he was at last beginning to fully understand what that innocuous phrase—*the world has moved on*—really meant. What a breadth of ignorance and evil it covered. And what a depth.

The speakers were a wartime measure, Susannah thought. *Of course they were. God only knows which war, or how long ago, but it must have been a doozy. The rulers of Lud used the speakers to make city-wide announcements from some central, bomb-proof location—a bunker like the one Hitler and his high command retreated to at the end of World War II.*

And in her ears she could hear the voice of authority which had come rolling out of those speakers—could hear it as clearly as she had heard the creak of the wagons passing through River Crossing, as clearly as she had heard the crack of the whip above the backs of the straining oxen.

Ration centers A and D will be closed today; please proceed to centers B, C, E, and F with proper coupons.

Militia squads Nine, Ten, and Twelve report to Sendside.

Aerial bombardment is likely between the hours of eight and ten of the clock. All noncombatant residents should report to their designated shelters. Bring your gas masks. Repeat, bring your gas masks.

Announcements, yes . . . and some garbled version of the news—a propagandized, militant version George Orwell would have called double-speak. And in between the news bulletins and the announcements, squalling military music and exhortations to respect the fallen by sending more men and women into the red throat of the abattoir.

Then the war had ended and silence had fallen . . . for a while. But at some point, the speakers had begun broadcasting again. How long ago? A hundred years? Fifty? Did it matter? Susannah thought not. What mattered was that when the speakers were reactivated, the only thing they broadcast was a single tape-loop . . . the loop with the drum-track on it. And the descendents of the city's original residents had taken it for . . . what? The Voice of the Turtle? The Will of the Beam?

Susannah found herself remembering the time she had asked her

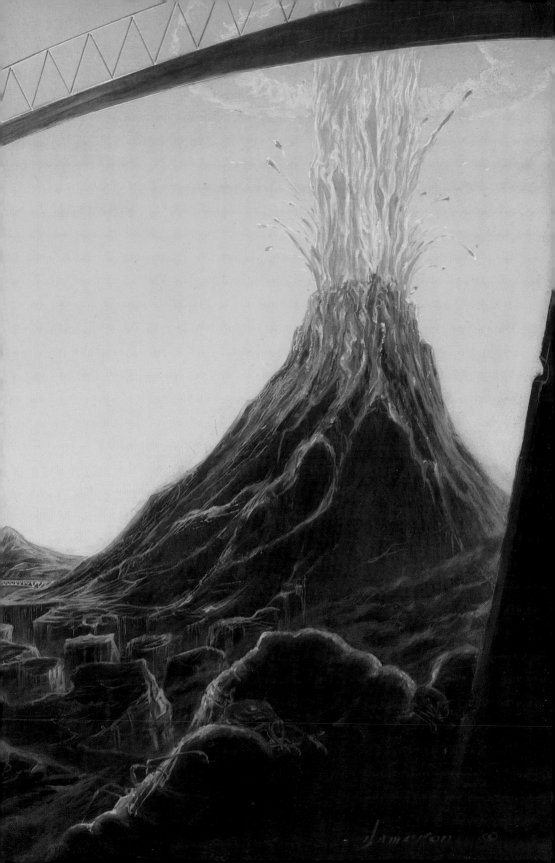

Jameron

father, a quiet but deeply cynical man, if he believed there was a God in heaven who guided the course of human events. *Well*, he had said, *I think it's sort of half 'n half, Odetta. I'm sure there's a God, but I don't think He has much if anything to do with us these days; I believe that after we killed His son, He finally got it through His head that there wasn't nothing to be done with the sons of Adam or the daughters of Eve, and He washed His hands of us. Wise fella.*

She had responded to this (which she had fully expected; she was eleven at the time, and knew the turn of her father's mind quite well) by showing him a squib on the Community Churches page of the local newspaper. It said that Rev. Murdock of the Grace Methodist Church would that Sunday elucidate on the topic "God Speaks to Each of Us Every Day"—with a text from First Corinthians. Her father had laughed over that so hard that tears had squirted from the corners of his eyes. *Well, I guess each of us hears someone talking,* he had said at last, *and you can bet your bottom dollar on one thing, sweetie: each of us—including this here Reverend Murdock—hears that voice say just exactly what he wants to hear. It's so convenient that way.*

What *these* people had apparently wanted to hear in the recorded drum-track was an invitation to commit ritual murder. And now, when the drums began to throb through these hundreds or thousands of speakers—a hammering back-beat which was only the percussion to a Z.Z. Top song called "Velcro Fly," if Eddie was right—it became their signal to unlimber the hangropes and run a few folks up the nearest speaker-posts.

How many? she wondered as Eddie rolled her along in her wheelchair, its nicked and dented hard rubber tires crackling over broken glass and whispering through drifts of discarded paper. *How many have been killed over the years because some electronic circuit under the city got the hiccups? Did it start because they recognized the essential alienness of the music, which came somehow—like us, and the airplane, and some of the cars along these streets—from another world?*

She didn't know, but she knew she had come around to her father's cynical point of view on the subject of God and the chats He might or might not have with the sons of Adam and the daughters of Eve. These people had been looking for a reason to slaughter each other, that was all, and the drums had been as good a reason as any.

She found herself thinking of the hive they had found—the misshapen hive of white bees whose honey would have poisoned them if they had been foolish enough to eat of it. Here, on this side of the Send, was another dying hive; more mutated white bees whose sting would be no less deadly for their confusion, loss, and perplexity.

And how many more will have to die before the tape finally breaks?

As if her thoughts had caused it to happen, the speakers suddenly began to transmit the relentless, syncopated heartbeat of the drums. Eddie yelled in surprise. Susannah screamed and clapped both hands to her ears—but before she did, she could faintly hear the rest of the music: the track or tracks which had been muted decades ago when someone (probably quite by accident) had bumped the balance control, knocking it all the way to one side and burying both the guitars and the vocal.

Eddie continued to push her along The Street of the Turtle and the Path of the Beam, trying to look in all directions at once and trying not to smell the odor of putrefaction. *Thank God for the wind*, he thought.

He began to push the wheelchair faster, scanning the weedy gaps between the big white buildings for the graceful sweep of an overhead monorail track. He wanted to get out of this endless aisle of the dead. As he took yet another deep breath of that speciously sweet cinnamon smell, it seemed to him that he had never wanted anything so badly in his whole life.

19

JAKE'S DAZE WAS BROKEN abruptly when Gasher grabbed him by the collar and yanked with all the force of a cruel rider braking a galloping horse. He stuck one leg out at the same time and Jake went crashing backward over it. His head connected with the pavement and for a moment all the lights went out. Gasher, no humanitarian, brought him around quickly by seizing Jake's lower lip and yanking it upward and outward.

Jake screamed and bolted to a sitting position, striking out blindly with his fists. Gasher dodged the blows easily, hooked his other hand into Jake's armpit, and yanked him to his feet. Jake stood there, rocking drunkenly back and forth. He was beyond protest now; almost beyond understanding. All he knew for sure was that every muscle in his body felt sprung and his wounded hand was howling like an animal caught in a trap.

Gasher apparently needed a breather, and this time he was slower getting his wind back. He stood bent over with his hands planted on the knees of his green trousers, panting in fast little whistling breaths. His yellow headscarf had slipped askew. His good eye glittered like a trumpery diamond. The white silk eyepatch was now wrinkled, and curds of evil-looking yellow muck oozed onto his cheek from beneath it.

"Take a look over your head, cully, and you'll see why I brung you up short. Get an eyeful!"

Jake tilted his head upward, and in the depths of his shock he was not at all surprised to see a marble fountain as big as a house-trailer dangling eighty feet above them. He and Gasher were almost below it. The fountain was held suspended by two rusty cables which were mostly hidden within huge, unsteady stacks of church pews. Even in his less-than-acute state, Jake saw that these cables were more seriously frayed than the remaining hangers on the bridge had been.

"See it?" Gasher asked, grinning. He raised his left hand to his covered eye, scooped a mass of the pussy material from beneath it, and flicked it indifferently aside. "Beauty, ain't it? Oh, the Tick-Tock Man's a trig cove, all right, and no mistake. (Where's those goat-fucking drums? They should have started by now—if Copperhead's forgot em, I'll ram a stick so far up his arse he'll taste bark.) Now look ahead of you, my delicious little squint."

Jake did, and Gasher immediately clouted him so hard that he staggered backward and almost fell.

"Not *across*, idiot child! *Down!* See them two dark cobblestones?"

After a moment, Jake did. He nodded apathetically.

"Yer don't wanter step on em, for that'd bring the whole works down on your head, cully, and anybody who wanted yer after that'd have to pick yer up with a blotter. Understand?"

Jake nodded again.

"Good." Gasher took a final deep breath and slapped Jake's shoulder. "Go on, then, whatcher waitin for? *Hup!*"

Jake stepped over the first of the discolored stones and saw it wasn't really a cobblestone at all but a metal plate which had been rounded to look like one. The second was just ahead of it, cunningly placed so that if an unaware intruder happened to miss the first one, he or she would almost certainly step on the second.

Go ahead and do it, then, he thought. *Why not? The gunslinger's never going to find you in this maze, so go ahead and bring it down. It's got to be cleaner than what Gasher and his friends have got planned for you. Quicker, too.*

His dusty moccasin wavered in the air above the booby-trap.

Gasher hit him with a fist in the middle of the back, but not hard. "Thinkin about takin a ride on the handsome, are you, my little cull?" he asked. The laughing cruelty in his voice had been replaced by simple curiosity. If it was tinged with any other emotion, it wasn't fear but amusement. "Well, go ahead, if it's what yer mean to do, for I have my ticket already. Only be quick about it, gods blast your eyes."

Jake's foot came down beyond the trigger of the booby-trap. His decision to live a little longer was not based on any hope that Roland would find him; it was just that this was what Roland would do—go on until someone made him stop, and then a few yards farther still if he could.

If he did it now, he could take Gasher with him, but Gasher alone wasn't sufficient—one look was enough to make it clear that he was telling the truth when he said he was dying already. If he went on, he might have a chance to take some of the Gasherman's friends, too— maybe even the one he called the Tick-Tock Man.

If I'm going to ride what he calls the handsome, Jake thought, *I'd just as soon go with plenty of company.*

Roland would have understood.

20

JAKE WAS WRONG IN his assessment of the gunslinger's ability to follow their path through the maze; Jake's pack was only the most obvious bit of sign they left behind them, but Roland quickly realized he did not have to pause to look for sign. He only had to follow Oy.

He paused at several intersecting passages nevertheless, wanting to make sure, and each time he did, Oy looked back and uttered his low, impatient bark that seemed to say, *Hurry up! Do you want to lose them?* After the signs he saw—a track, a thread from Jake's shirt, a scrap of bright yellow cloth from Gasher's scarf—had three times confirmed the bumbler's choices, Roland simply followed Oy. He did not give up looking for sign, but he quit making stops to hunt for it. Then the drums started up, and it was the drums—plus Gasher's nosiness about what Jake might be carrying—that saved Roland's life that afternoon.

He skidded to a halt in his dusty boots, and his gun was in his hand before he realized what the sound was. When he did realize, he dropped the revolver back into its holster with an impatient grunt. He was about to go on again when his eye happened first on Jake's pack . . . and then on a pair of faint, gleaming streaks in midair just to the left of it. Roland narrowed his eyes and made out two thin wires which crisscrossed at knee level not three feet in front of him. Oy, who was built low to the ground, had scurried neatly through the inverted V formed by the wires, but if not for the drums and spotting Jake's castoff pack, Roland would have run right into them. As his eyes moved upward, tracing the not-quite-random piles of junk poised on either side of the passageway at this point, Roland's mouth tightened. It had been a close call, and only *ka* had saved him.

Oy barked impatiently.

Roland dropped to his belly and crawled beneath the wires, moving slowly and carefully—he was bigger than either Jake or Gasher, and he realized a really big man wouldn't be able to get under here at all without triggering the carefully prepared avalanche. The drums pumped and thumped in his ears. *I wonder if they've all gone mad*, he thought. *If I had to listen to that every day, I think I would have.*

He got to the far side of the wires, picked up the pack, and looked inside. Jake's books and a few items of clothing were still in there, so were the treasures he had picked up along the way—a rock which gleamed with yellow flecks that looked like gold but weren't; an arrowhead, probably the leaving of the old forest folk, which Jake had found in a grove of trees the day after his drawing; some coins from his own world; his father's sunglasses; a few other things which only a boy not yet in his teens could really love and understand. Things he would want back again . . . if, that was, Roland got to him before Gasher and his friends could change him, hurt him in ways that would cause him to lose interest in the innocent pursuits and curiosities of pre-adolescent boyhood.

Gasher's grinning face swam into Roland's mind like the face of a demon or a djinni from a bottle: the snaggle teeth, the vacant eyes, the mandrus crawling over the cheeks and spreading beneath the stubbly lines of the jaws. *If you hurt him* . . . he thought, and then forced his mind away, because that line of thought was a blind alley. If Gasher hurt the boy (*Jake!* his mind insisted fiercely—*Not just the boy but Jake! Jake!*), Roland would kill him, yes. But the act would mean nothing, for Gasher was a dead man already.

The gunslinger lengthened the straps of the pack, marvelling at the clever buckles which made this possible, slipped it onto his own back, and stood up again. Oy turned to be off, but Roland called his name and the bumbler looked back.

"To me, Oy." Roland didn't know if the bumbler could understand (or if he would obey even if he did), but it would be better—safer—if he stayed close. Where there was one booby-trap, there were apt to be more. Next time Oy might not be so lucky.

"Ake!" Oy barked, not moving. The bark was assertive, but Roland thought he saw more of the truth about how Oy felt in his eyes: they were dark with fear.

"Yes, but it's dangerous," Roland said. "To me, Oy."

Back the way they had come, there was a thud as something heavy fell, probably dislodged by the punishing vibration of the drums. Roland could now see speaker-poles here and there, poking out of the wreckage like strange long-necked animals.

Oy trotted back to him and looked up, panting.

"Stay close."

"Ake! Ake-Ake!"

"Yes. Jake." He began to run again, and Oy ran beside him, heeling as neatly as any dog Roland had ever seen.

21

FOR EDDIE, IT WAS, as some wise man had once said, *déjà vu* all over again: he was running with the wheelchair, racing time. The beach had been replaced by The Street of the Turtle, but somehow everything else was the same. Oh, there *was* one other relevant difference: now it was a railway station (or a cradle) he was looking for, not a free-standing door.

Susannah was sitting bolt upright with her hair blowing out behind her and Roland's revolver in her right hand, its barrel pointed up at the cloudy, troubled sky. The drums thudded and pounded, bludgeoning them with sound. A gigantic, dish-shaped object lay in the street just ahead, and Eddie's overstrained mind, perhaps cued by the classical buildings on either side of them, produced an image of Jove and Thor playing Frisbee. Jove throws one wide and Thor lets it fall through a cloud—what the hell, it's Miller Time on Olympus, anyway.

Frisbees of the gods, he thought, swerving Susannah between two crumbling, rusty cars, *what a concept.*

He bumped the chair up on the sidewalk to get around the artifact, which looked like some sort of telecommunications dish now that he was really close to it. He was easing the wheelchair over the curb and back into the street again—the sidewalk was too littered with crap to make any real time—when the drums suddenly cut out. The echoes rolled away into a new silence, except it wasn't really silent at all, Eddie realized. Up ahead, the arched entrance to a marble building stood at the intersection of The Street of the Turtle and another avenue. This building had been overgrown by vines and some straggly green stuff that looked like cypress beards, but it was still magnificent and somehow dignified. Beyond it, around the corner, a crowd was babbling excitedly.

"Don't stop!" Susannah snapped. "We haven't got time to—"

A hysterical shriek drilled through the babble. It was accompanied by yells of approval, and, incredibly, the sort of applause Eddie had heard in Atlantic City hotel-casinos after some lounge act had finished doing its thing. The shriek was choked into a long, dying gargle that sounded like the buzz of a cicada. Eddie felt the hair on the nape of his neck coming to attention. He glanced at the corpses hanging from the nearest speaker-pole and understood that the fun-loving Pubes of Lud were holding another public execution.

Marvellous, he thought. *Now if they only had Tony Orlando and Dawn to sing "Knock Three Times," they could all die happy.*

Eddie looked curiously at the stone pile on the corner. This close, the vines which overgrew it had a powerful herbal smell. That smell was eye-wateringly bitter, but he still liked it better than the cinnamon-sweet odor of the mummified corpses. The beards of greenery growing from the vines drooped in ratty sheaves, creating waterfalls of vegetation where once there had been a series of arched entrances. A figure suddenly barrelled out through one of these waterfalls and hurried toward them. It was a kid, Eddie realized, and not that many years out of diapers, judging by the size. He was wearing a weird little Lord Fauntleroy outfit, complete with ruffled white shirt and velveteen short pants. There were ribbons in his hair. Eddie felt a sudden mad urge to wave his hands above his head and scream *But-wheat say, "Lud is o-tay!"*

"Come on!" the kid cried in a high, piping voice. Several sprays of the green stuff had gotten caught in his hair; he brushed absently at these with his left hand as he ran. "They're gonna do Spankers! It's the Spankerman's turn to go to the land of the drums! Come on or you'll miss the whole fakement, gods cuss it!"

Susannah was equally stunned by the child's appearance, but as he got closer, it struck her that there was something extremely odd and awkward about the way he was brushing at the crumbles and strands of greenery which had gotten caught in his beribboned hair: he kept using just that one hand. His other had been behind his back when he ran out through the weedy waterfall, and there it remained.

How awkward that must be! she thought, and then a tape-player turned on in her mind and she heard Roland speaking at the end of the bridge. *I knew something like this could happen . . . if we'd seen the fellow earlier, while we were still beyond the range of his exploding egg . . . Damn the luck!*

She levelled Roland's gun at the child, who had leaped from the curb and was running straight for them. *"Hold it!"* she screamed. *"Stand still, you!"*

"Suze, what are you *doing*?" Eddie yelled.

Susannah ignored him. In a very real sense, Susannah Dean was no longer even here; it was Detta Walker in the chair now, and her eyes were glittering with feverish suspicion. *"Stop or I'll shoot!"*

Little Lord Fauntleroy might have been deaf for all the effect her warning had. "Hoss it!" he shouted jubilantly. "Yer gointer miss the whole show! Spanker's gointer—"

His right hand finally began to come out from behind his back. As it did, Eddie realized they weren't looking at a kid but at a misshapen dwarf whose childhood was many years past. The expression Eddie had at first taken for childish glee was actually a chilly mixture of hate and rage. The dwarf's cheeks and brow were covered with the oozing, discolored patches Roland called whore's blossoms.

Susannah never saw his face. Her attention was fixed on the emerging right hand, and the dull green sphere it held. That was all she needed to see. Roland's gun crashed. The dwarf was hammered backward. A shrill cry of pain and rage rose from his tiny mouth as he landed on the sidewalk. The grenade bounced out of his hand and rolled back into the same arch through which he had emerged.

Detta was gone like a dream, and Susannah looked from the smoking gun to the tiny, sprawled figure on the sidewalk with surprise, horror, and dismay. "Oh, my Jesus! I shot him! Eddie, I shot him!"

"Grays . . . *die!*"

Little Lord Fauntleroy tried to scream these words defiantly, but they came out in a bubbling choke of blood that drenched the few remaining white patches on his frilly shirt. There was a muffled explosion from inside the overgrown plaza of the corner building, and the shaggy carpets of green stuff hanging in front of the arches billowed outward like flags in a brisk gale. With them came clouds of choking, acrid smoke. Eddie flung himself on top of Susannah to shield her, and felt a gritty shower of concrete fragments—all small ones, luckily—patter down on his back, his neck, and the crown of his head. There was a series of unpleasantly wet smacking sounds to his left. He opened his eyes a crack, looked in that direction, and saw Little Lord Fauntleroy's head just coming to a stop in the gutter. The dwarf's eyes were still open, his mouth still fixed in its final snarl.

Now there were other voices, some shrieking, some yelling, all furious. Eddie rolled off Susannah's chair—it tottered on one wheel before deciding to stay up—and stared in the direction from which the dwarf had come. A ragged mob of about twenty men and women had appeared, some coming from around the corner, others pushing through the mats of foliage which obscured the corner building's arches, materializing from the smoke of the dwarf's grenade like evil spirits. Most were wearing blue headscarves and all were carrying weapons—a varied (and somehow pitiful) assortment of them which included rusty swords, dull knives, and splintery clubs. Eddie saw one man defiantly waving a hammer. *Pubes,* Eddie thought. *We interrupted their necktie party, and they're pissed as hell about it.*

A tangle of shouts—*Kill the Grays! Kill them both! They've done for Luster, God kill their eyes!*—arose from this charming group as they caught sight of Susannah in her wheelchair and Eddie, who was now crouched on one knee before it. The man in the forefront was wearing a kilt-like wrap and waving a cutlass. He brandished this wildly (he would have decapitated the heavyset woman standing close behind him, had she not ducked) and then charged. The others followed, yelling happily.

Roland's gun pounded its bright thunder into the windy, overcast day, and the top of the kilt-wearing Pube's head lifted off. The sallow skin of the woman who had almost been decapitated by his cutlass was suddenly stippled with red rain and she voiced a sound of barking dismay. The others came on past the woman and the dead man, raving and wild-eyed.

"Eddie!" Susannah screamed, and fired again. A man wearing a silk-lined cape and knee-boots collapsed into the street.

Eddie groped for the Ruger and had one panicky moment when he thought he had lost it. The butt of the gun had somehow slipped down inside the waistband of his pants. He wrapped his hand around it and yanked hard. The fucking thing wouldn't come. The sight at the end of the barrel had somehow gotten stuck in his underwear.

Susannah fired three closely spaced shots. Each found a target, but the oncoming Pubes didn't slow.

"Eddie, help me!"

Eddie tore his pants open, feeling like some cut-rate version of Superman, and finally managed to free the Ruger. He hit the safety with the heel of his left palm, placed his elbow on his leg just above the knee, and began to fire. There was no need to think—no need to even aim. Roland had told them that in battle a gunslinger's hands worked on their own, and Eddie now discovered it was true. It would have been hard for a blind man to miss at this range, anyway. Susannah had cut the numbers of the charging Pubes to no more than fifteen; Eddie went through the remainder like a storm wind in a wheatfield, dropping four in less than two seconds.

Now the single face of the mob, that look of glazed and mindless eagerness, began to break apart. The man with the hammer abruptly tossed his weapon aside and ran for it, limping extravagantly on a pair of arthritis-twisted legs. He was followed by two others. The rest of them milled uncertainly in the street.

"Come on, you deucies!" a relatively young man snarled. He wore his blue scarf around his throat like a rally-racer's ascot. He was bald except for two fluffs of frizzy red hair, one on each side of his head. To Susannah, this fellow looked like Clarabell the Clown; to Eddie he looked like Ronald McDonald; to both of them he looked like trouble. He threw a home-made spear that might have started life as a steel tableleg. It clattered harmlessly into the street to Eddie and Susannah's right. "Come on, I say! We can get em if we all stick togeth—"

"Sorry, guy," Eddie murmured, and shot him in the chest.

Clarabell/Ronald staggered backward, one hand going to his shirt.

He stared at Eddie with huge eyes that told his tale with heartbreaking clarity: this wasn't supposed to happen. The hand dropped heavily to the young man's side. A single runlet of blood, incredibly bright in the gray day, slipped from the corner of his mouth. The few remaining Pubes stared at him mutely as he slipped to his knees, and one of them turned to run.

"Not at all," Eddie said. "Stay put, my retarded friend, or you're going to get a good look at the clearing where your path ends." He raised his voice. "Drop em, boys and girls! All of em! Now!"

"You . . ." the dying man whispered. "You . . . gunslinger?"

"That's right," Eddie said. His eyes surveyed the remaining Pubes grimly.

"Cry your . . . pardon," the man with the frizzy red hair gasped, and then he fell forward onto his face.

"*Gunslingers?*" one of the others asked. His tone was one of dawning horror and realization.

"Well, you're stupid, but you ain't deaf," Susannah said, "and that's somethin, anyway." She waggled the barrel of the gun, which Eddie was quite sure was empty. For that matter, how many rounds could be left in the Ruger? He realized he didn't have any idea how many rounds the clip held, and cursed himself for a fool . . . but had he really believed it could come to something like this? He didn't think so. "You heard him, folks. Drop em. Recess is over."

One by one, they complied. The woman who was wearing a pint or so of Mr. Sword-and-Kilt's blood on her face said, "You shouldn't've killed Winston, missus—'twas his birthday, so it was."

"Well, I guess he should have stayed home and eaten some more birthday cake," Eddie said. Given the overall quality of this experience, he didn't find either the woman's comment or his own response at all surreal.

There was one other woman among the remaining Pubes, a scrawny thing whose long blonde hair was coming out in big patches, as if she had the mange. Eddie observed her sidling toward the dead dwarf—and the potential safety of the overgrown arches beyond him—and put a bullet into the cracked cement close by her foot. He had no idea what he wanted with her, but what he didn't want was one of them giving the rest of them ideas. For one thing, he was afraid of what his hands might do if the sickly, sullen people before him tried to run. Whatever his head thought about this gunslinging business, his hands had discovered they liked it just fine.

"Stand where you are, beautiful. Officer Friendly says play it safe." He glanced at Susannah and was disturbed by the grayish quality of her complexion. "Suze, you all right?" he asked in a lower voice.

"Yes."

"You're not going to faint or anything, are you? Because—"

"No." She looked at him with eyes so dark they were like caves. "It's just that I never shot anyone before . . . okay?"

Well, you better get used to it rose to his lips. He bit it back and returned his gaze to the five people who remained before them. They were looking at him and Susannah with a species of sullen fear which nevertheless stopped well short of terror.

Shit, most of them have forgotten what terror is, he thought. *Joy, sadness, love . . . same thing. I don't think they feel much of anything, anymore. They've been living in this purgatory too long.*

Then he remembered the laughter, the excited cries, the lounge-act applause, and revised his thinking. There was at least one thing that still got their motors running, one thing that still pushed their buttons. Spanker could have testified to that.

"Who's in charge here?" Eddie asked. He was watching the intersection behind the little group very carefully in case the others should get their courage back. So far he saw and heard nothing alarming from that direction. He thought that the others had probably left this ragged crew to its fate.

They looked at each other uncertainly, and finally the woman with the blood-spattered face spoke up. "Spanker was, but when the god-drums started up this time, it was Spanker's stone what come out of the hat and we set him to dance. I guess Winston would have come next, but you did for him with your god-rotted guns, so you did." She wiped blood deliberately from her cheek, looked at it, and then returned her sullen glance to Eddie.

"Well, what do you think Winston was trying to do to me with his god-rotted spear?" Eddie asked. He was disgusted to find the woman had actually made him feel guilty about what he had done. "Trim my sideburns?"

"Killed Frank 'n Luster, too," she went on doggedly, "and what are you? Either Grays, which is bad, or a couple of god-rotted outlanders, which is worse. Who's left for the Pubes in City North? Topsy, I suppose—Topsy the Sailor—but he ain't here, is he? Took his boat and went off downriver, ay, so he did, and god rot him, too, says I!"

Susannah had ceased listening; her mind had fixed with horrified fascination on something the woman had said earlier. *It was Spanker's stone what come out of the hat and we set him to dance.* She remembered reading Shirley Jackson's story "The Lottery" in college and understood that these people, the degenerate descendents of the original Pubes, were living Jackson's nightmare. No wonder they weren't capable of any strong emotion when they knew they would have to participate in such a grisly drawing not once a year, as in the story, but two or three times each day.

"Why?" she asked the bloody woman in a harsh, horrified voice. "Why do you do it?"

The woman looked at Susannah as if she was the world's biggest fool. "Why? So the ghosts what live in the machines won't take over the bodies of those who have died here—Pubes and Grays alike—and send them up through the holes in the streets to eat us. Any fool knows that."

"There are no such things as ghosts," Susannah said, and her voice sounded like so much meaningless quacking to her own ears. Of course there were. In this world, there were ghosts everywhere. Nevertheless, she pushed ahead. "What you call the god-drums is only a tape stuck in a machine. That's really all it is." Sudden inspiration struck her and she added: "Or maybe the Grays are doing it on purpose—did you ever think of that? They live in the other part of the city, don't they? And under it, as well? They've always wanted you out. Maybe they've just hit on a really efficient way of getting you guys to do their work for them."

The bloody woman was standing next to an elderly gent wearing what looked like the world's oldest bowler hat and a pair of frayed khaki shorts. Now he stepped forward and spoke to her with a patina of good manners that turned his underlying contempt into a dagger with razor-sharp edges. "You are quite wrong, Madam Gunslinger. There are a great many machines under Lud, and there are ghosts in all of them— demonous spirits which bear only ill will to mortal men and women. These demon-ghosts are *very* capable of raising the dead . . . and in Lud, there are a great many dead to raise."

"Listen," Eddie said. "Have you ever seen one of these zombies with your own eyes, Jeeves? Have *any* of you?"

Jeeves curled his lip and said nothing—but that lip-curl really said it all. What else could one expect, it asked, from outlanders who used guns as a substitute for understanding?

Eddie decided it would be best to close off the whole line of discussion. He had never been cut out for missionary work, anyway. He waggled the Ruger at the bloodstained woman. "You and your friend there— the one who looks like an English butler on his day off—are going to take us to the railroad station. After that, we can all say goodbye, and I'll tell you the truth: that's going to make my fuckin day."

"Railroad station?" the guy who looked like Jeeves the Butler asked. "What is a railroad station?"

"Take us to the cradle," Susannah said. "Take us to Blaine."

This finally rattled Jeeves; an expression of shocked horror replaced the world-weary contempt with which he had thus far treated them. "You can't go there!" he cried. "The cradle is forbidden ground, and Blaine is the most dangerous of all Lud's ghosts!"

Forbidden ground? Eddie thought. *Great. If it's the truth, at least we'll be able to stop worrying about you assholes.* It was also nice to hear that there still *was* a Blaine . . . or that these people thought there was, anyway.

The others were staring at Eddie and Susannah with expressions of uncomprehending amazement; it was as if the interlopers had suggested to a bunch of born-again Christians that they hunt up the Ark of the Covenant and turn it into a pay toilet.

Eddie raised the Ruger until the center of Jeeves's forehead lay in the sight. "We're going," he said, "and if you don't want to join your ancestors right here and now, I suggest you stop pissing and moaning and take us there."

Jeeves and the bloodstained woman exchanged an uncertain glance, but when the man in the bowler hat looked back at Eddie and Susannah, his face was firm and set. "Shoot us if you like," he said. "We'd sooner die here than there."

"You folks are a bunch of sick motherfuckers with dying on the brain!" Susannah cried at them. "*Nobody* has to die! Just take us where we want to go, for the love of God!"

The woman said somberly, "But it *is* death to enter Blaine's cradle, mum, so it is. For Blaine sleeps, and he who disturbs his rest must pay a high price."

"Come on, beautiful," Eddie snapped. "You can't smell the coffee with your head up your ass."

"I don't know what that means," she said with an odd and perplexing dignity.

"It means you can take us to the cradle and risk the Wrath of Blaine, or you can stand your ground here and experience the Wrath of Eddie. It doesn't have to be a nice clean head-shot, you know. I can take you a piece at a time, and I'm feeling just mean enough to do it. I'm having a very bad day in your city—the music sucks, everybody has a bad case of b.o., and the first guy we saw threw a grenade at us and kidnapped our friend. So what do you say?"

"Why would you go to Blaine in any case?" one of the others asked. "He stirs no more from his berth in the cradle—not for years now. He has even stopped speaking in his many voices and laughing."

Speaking in his many voices and laughing? Eddie thought. He looked at Susannah. She looked back and shrugged.

"Ardis was the last to go nigh Blaine," the bloodstained woman said.

Jeeves nodded somberly. "Ardis always was a fool when he were in drink. Blaine asked him some question. I heard it, but it made no sense to me—something about the mother of ravens, I think—and when Ardis couldn't answer what was asked, Blaine slew him with blue fire."

"Electricity?" Eddie asked.

Jeeves and the bloodstained woman both nodded. "Ay," the woman said. "Electricity, so it were called in the old days, so it were."

"You don't have to go in with us," Susannah proposed suddenly. "Just get us within sight of the place. We'll go the rest of the way on our own."

The woman looked at her mistrustfully, and then Jeeves pulled her head close to his lips and mumbled in her ear for a while. The other Pubes stood behind them in a ragged line, looking at Eddie and Susannah with the dazed eyes of people who have survived a bad air-raid.

At last the woman looked around. "Ay," she said. "We'll take you nigh the cradle, and then it's good riddance to bad swill."

"My idea exactly," Eddie said. "You and Jeeves. The rest of you, scatter." He swept them with his eyes. "But remember this—one spear thrown from ambush, one arrow, one brick, and these two die." This threat came out sounding so weak and pointless that Eddie wished he hadn't made it. How could they possibly care for these two, or for any of the individual members of their clan, when they dusted two or more of them each and every day? Well, he thought, watching the others trot off without so much as a backward glance, it was too late to worry about that now.

"Come on," the woman said. "I want to be done with you."

"The feeling's mutual," Eddie replied.

But before she and Jeeves led them away, the woman did something which made Eddie repent a little of his hard thoughts: knelt, brushed back the hair of the man in the kilt, and placed a kiss on his dirty cheek. "Goodbye, Winston," she said. "Wait for me where the trees clear and the water's sweet. I'll come to ye, ay, as sure as dawn makes shadows run west."

"I didn't want to kill him," Susannah said. "I want you to know that. But I wanted to die even less."

"Ay." The face that turned toward Susannah was stern and tearless. "But if ye mean to enter Blaine's cradle, ye'll die anyway. And the chances are that ye'll die envying poor old Winston. He's cruel, is Blaine. The cruelest of all demons in this cruel, cruel place."

"Come on, Maud," Jeeves said, and helped her up.

"Ay. Let's finish with them." She surveyed Susannah and Eddie again, her eyes stern but somehow confused, as well. "Gods curse my eyes that they should ever have happened on you two in the first place.

And gods curse the guns ye carry, as well, for they were always the springhead of our troubles."

And with that attitude, Susannah thought, *your troubles are going to last at least a thousand years, sugar.*

Maud set a rapid pace along The Street of the Turtle. Jeeves trotted beside her. Eddie, who was pushing Susannah in the wheelchair, was soon panting and struggling to keep up. The palatial buildings which lined their way spread out until they resembled ivy-covered country houses on huge, run-to-riot lawns, and Eddie realized they had entered what had once been a very ritzy neighborhood indeed. Ahead of them, one building loomed above all others. It was a deceptively simple square construction of white stone blocks, its overhanging roof supported by many pillars. Eddie thought again of the gladiator movies he'd so enjoyed as a kid. Susannah, educated in more formal schools, was reminded of the Parthenon. Both saw and marvelled at the gorgeously sculpted bestiary—Bear and Turtle, Fish and Rat, Horse and Dog—which ringed the top of the building in two-by-two parade, and understood it was the place they had come to find.

That uneasy sensation that they were being watched by many eyes—eyes filled equally with hate and wonder—never left them. Thunder boomed as they came in sight of the monorail track; like the storm, the track came sweeping in from the south, joined The Street of the Turtle, and ran straight on toward the Cradle of Lud. And as they neared it, ancient bodies began to twist and dance in the strengthening wind on either side of them.

22

AFTER THEY HAD RUN for God knew how long (all Jake knew for sure was that the drums had stopped again), Gasher once more yanked him to a stop. This time Jake managed to keep his feet. He had gotten his second wind. Gasher, who would never see eleven again, had not.

"Hoo! My old pump's doing nip-ups, sweetie."

"Too bad," Jake said unfeelingly, then stumbled backward as Gasher's gnarled hand connected with the side of his face.

"Yar, you'd cry a bitter tear if I dropped dead right here, woontcher? Too likely! But no such luck, my fine young squint—old Gasher's seen em come and seen em go, and I wasn't born to drop dead at the feet of any little sweetcheeks berry like you."

Jake listened to these incoherencies impassively. He meant to see Gasher dead before the day was over. Gasher might take Jake with him, but Jake no longer cared about that. He dabbed blood from his freshly split lip and looked at it thoughtfully, wondering at how quickly the desire to do murder could invade and conquer the human heart.

Gasher observed Jake looking at his bloody fingers and grinned. "Sap's runnin, ennet? Nor will it be the last your old pal Gasher beats out of your young tree, unless you look sharp; unless you look *wery* sharp indeed." He pointed down at the cobbled surface of the narrow alley they were currently negotiating. There was a rusty manhole cover there, and Jake realized he had seen the words stamped into the steel not long ago: LaMERK FOUNDRY, they said.

"There's a grip on the side," Gasher said. "Yer see? Get your hands into that and pull away. Step lively, now, and maybe ye'll still have all your teeth when ye meet up with Tick-Tock."

Jake grasped the steel cover and pulled. He pulled hard, but not quite as hard as he could have done. The maze of streets and alleys through which Gasher had run him was bad, but at least he could see. He couldn't imagine what it might be like in the underworld below the city, where the blackness would preclude even dreams of escape, and he didn't intend to find out unless he absolutely had to.

Gasher quickly made it clear to him that he did.

"It's too heavy for—" Jake began, and then the pirate seized him by the throat and yanked him upward until they were face to face. The long run through the alleys had brought a thin, sweaty flush to his cheeks and turned the sores eating into his flesh an ugly yellow-purple color. Those which were open exuded thick infected matter and threads of blood in steady pulses. Jake caught just a whiff of Gasher's thick stench before his wind was cut off by the hand which had encircled his throat.

"Listen, you stupid cull, and listen well, for this is your last warning. You yank that fucking streethead off right now or I'll reach into your mouth and rip the living tongue right out of it. And feel free to bite all you want while I do it, for what I have runs in the blood and you'll see the first blossoms on yer own face before the week's out—if yer lives that long. Now, do you see?"

Jake nodded frantically. Gasher's face was disappearing into deepening folds of gray, and his voice seemed to be coming from a great distance.

"All right." Gasher shoved him backward. Jake fell in a heap beside the manhole cover, gagging and retching. He finally managed to draw in a deep, whooping breath that burned like liquid fire. He spat out a blood-flecked wad of stuff and almost threw up at the sight of it.

"Now yank back that cover, my heart's delight, and let's have no more natter about it.

Jake crawled over to it, slid his hands into the grip, and this time pulled with all his might. For one terrible moment he thought he was still not going to be able to budge it. Then he imagined Gasher's fingers reaching into his mouth and seizing his tongue, and found a little extra. There was a dull, spreading agony in his lower back as something gave there, but the circular lid slipped slowly aside, grinding on the cobbles and exposing a grinning crescent of darkness.

"Good, cully, good!" Gasher cried cheerfully. "What a little mule y'are! Keep pulling—don't give up now!"

When the crescent had become a half-moon and the pain in Jake's lower back was a white-hot fire, Gasher booted him in the ass, knocking him asprawl.

"Wery good!" Gasher said, peering in. "Now, cully, go smartly down the ladder on the side. Mind you don't lose your grip and tumble all the way to the bottom, for those rungs are fearsome slick and greezy. There's twenty or so, as I remember. And when you get to the bottom, stand stock-still and wait for me. You might feel like runnin from yer old pal, but do you think that would be a good idea?"

"No," Jake said. "I suppose not."

"Wery intelligent, old son!" Gasher's lips spread in his hideous smile, once more revealing his few surviving teeth. "It's dark down there, and there are a thousand tunnels going every which-a-way. Yer old pal Gasher knows em like the back of his hand, so he does, but you'd be lost in no time. Then there's the rats—wery big and wery hungry they are. So you just wait."

"I will."

Gasher regarded him narrowly. "You speak just like a little triggie, you do, but you're no Pube—I'll set my watch and warrant to that. Where are you from, squint?"

Jake said nothing.

"Bumbler got your tongue, do he? Well, that's all right; Tick-Tock'll get it all out of you, so he will. He's got a way about him, Ticky does; just naturally wants to make people conwerse. Once he gets em goin, they sometimes talks so fast and screams so loud someone has to hit em over the head to slow em down. Bumblers ain't allowed to hold no one's tongue around the Tick-Tock Man, not even fine young triggers like you. Now get the fuck down that ladder. *Hup!*"

He lashed out with his foot. This time Jake managed to tuck in and dodge the blow. He looked into the half-open manhole, saw the ladder, and started down. He was still chest-high to the alley when a tremendous stonelike crash hammered the air. It came from a mile or more away, but Jake knew what it was without having to be told. A cry of pure misery burst from his lips.

A grim smile tugged at the corners of Gasher's mouth. "Your hard-case friend trailed ye a little better than ye thought he would, didn't he?

Not better than *I* thought, though, cully, for I got a look at his eyes—wery pert and cunning they were. I thought he'd come arter his juicy little night-nudge a right smart, if he was to come at all, and so he did. He spied the tripwires, but the fountain's got him, so *that's* all right. Get on, sweetcheeks."

He aimed a kick at Jake's protruding head. Jake ducked it, but one foot slipped on the ladder bolted to the side of the sewer shaft and he only saved himself from falling by clutching Gasher's scab-raddled ankle. He looked up, pleading, and saw no softening on that dying, infected face.

"Please," he said, and heard the word trying to break into a sob. He kept seeing Roland lying crushed beneath the huge fountain. What had Gasher said? If anyone wanted him, they would have to pick him up with a blotter.

"Beg if you want, dear heart. Just don't expect no good to come of it, for mercy stops on this side of the bridge, so it does. Now go down, or I'll kick your bleedin brains right outcher bleedin ears."

So Jake went down, and by the time he reached the standing water at the bottom, the urge to cry had passed. He waited, shoulders slumped and head down, for Gasher to descend and lead him to his fate.

23

ROLAND HAD COME CLOSE to tripping the crossed wires which held back the avalanche of junk, but the dangling fountain was absurd—a trap which might have been set by a stupid child. Cort had taught them to constantly check all visual quadrants as they moved in enemy territory, and that included above as well as behind and below.

"Stop," he told Oy, raising his voice to be heard over the drums.

"Op!" Oy agreed, then looked ahead and immediately added, "Ake!"

"Yes." The gunslinger took another look up at the suspended marble fountain, then examined the street, looking for the trigger. There were two, he saw. Perhaps their camouflage as cobblestones had once been effective, but that time was long past. Roland bent down, hands on his knees, and spoke into Oy's upturned face. "Going to pick you up for a minute now. Don't fuss, Oy."

"Oy!"

Roland put his arms around the bumbler. At first Oy stiffened and attempted to pull away, and then Roland felt the small animal give in. He wasn't happy about being this close to someone who wasn't Jake, but he clearly intended to put up with it. Roland found himself wondering again just how intelligent Oy was.

He carried him up the narrow passage and beneath The Hanging Fountain of Lud, stepping carefully over the mock cobbles. Once they were safely past, he bent to let Oy go. As he did, the drums stopped.

"Ake!" Oy said impatiently. "Ake-Ake!"

"Yes—but there's a little piece of business to attend to first."

He led Oy fifteen yards farther down the alley, then bent and picked up a chunk of concrete. He tossed it thoughtfully from hand to hand, and as he did, he heard the sound of a pistol-shot from the east. The amplified thump of the drums had buried the sound of Eddie and Susannah's battle with the ragged band of Pubes, but he heard this gunshot clearly and smiled—it almost surely meant that the Deans had reached the cradle, and that was the first good news of this day, which already seemed at least a week long.

Roland turned and threw the piece of concrete. His aim was as true as it had been when he had thrown at the ancient traffic signal in River Crossing; the missile struck one of the discolored triggers dead center, and one of the rusty cables snapped with a harsh twang. The marble fountain dropped, rolling over as the other cable snubbed it for a moment longer—long enough so that a man with fast reflexes could have cleared the drop-zone anyway, Roland reckoned. Then it too let go, and the fountain fell like a pink, misshapen stone.

Roland dropped behind a pile of rusty steel beams and Oy jumped nimbly into his lap as the fountain hit the street with a vast, shattery thump. Chunks of pink marble, some as big as carts, flew through the air. Several small chips stung Roland's face. He brushed others out of Oy's fur. He looked over the makeshift barricade. The fountain had cracked in two like a vast plate. *We won't be coming back this way*, Roland thought. The passageway, narrow to begin with, was now completely blocked.

He wondered if Jake had heard the fall of the fountain, and what he had made of it if he had. He didn't waste such speculation on Gasher; Gasher would think he had been crushed to paste, which was exactly what Roland wanted him to think. Would Jake think the same thing? The boy should know better than to believe a gunslinger could be killed by such a simple device, but if Gasher had terrorized him enough, Jake might not be thinking that clearly. Well, it was too late to worry about it now, and if he had it to do over again, he would do exactly the same thing. Dying or not, Gasher had displayed both courage and animal cunning. If he was off his guard now, the trick was worth it.

Roland got to his feet. "Oy—find Jake."

"Ake!" Oy stretched his head forward on his long neck, sniffed around in a semicircle, picked up Jake's scent, and was off again with Roland running after. Ten minutes later he came to a stop at a manhole cover in the street, sniffed all the way around it, then looked up at Roland and barked shrilly.

The gunslinger dropped to one knee and observed both the confusion of tracks and a wide path of scratches on the cobbles. He thought this particular manhole cover had been moved quite often. His eyes narrowed as he saw the wad of bloody phlegm in a crease between two nearby cobbles.

"The bastard keeps hitting him," he murmured.

He pulled the manhole cover back, looked down, then untied the rawhide lacings which held his shirt closed. He picked the bumbler up and tucked him into his shirt. Oy bared his teeth, and for a moment Roland felt his claws splayed against the flesh of his chest and belly like small sharp knives. Then they withdrew and Oy only peered out of Roland's shirt with his bright eyes, panting like a steam engine. The gunslinger could feel the rapid beat of Oy's heart against his own. He pulled the rawhide lace from the eyelets in his shirt and found another, longer, lace in his purse.

"I'm going to leash you. I don't like it and you're going to like it even less, but it's going to be very dark down there."

He tied the two lengths of rawhide together and formed one end into a wide loop which he slipped over Oy's head. He expected Oy to bare his teeth again, perhaps even to nip him, but Oy didn't. He only looked up at Roland with his gold-ringed eyes and barked "Ake!" again in his impatient voice.

Roland put the loose end of his makeshift leash in his mouth, then sat down on the edge of the sewer shaft . . . if that was what it was. He felt for the top rung of the ladder and found it. He descended slowly and carefully, more aware than ever that he was missing half a hand and that the steel rungs were slimy with oil and some thicker stuff that was probably moss. Oy was a heavy, warm weight between his shirt and belly, panting steadily and harshly. The gold rings in his eyes gleamed like medallions in the dim light.

At last, the gunslinger's groping foot splashed into the water at the bottom of the shaft. He glanced up briefly at the coin of white light far above him. *This is where it starts getting hard,* he thought. The tunnel was warm and dank and smelled like an ancient charnel house. Somewhere nearby, water was dripping hollowly and monotonously. Farther off, Roland could hear the rumble of machinery. He lifted a very grateful Oy out of his shirt and set him down in the shallow water running sluggishly along the sewer tunnel.

"Now it's all up to you," he murmured in the bumbler's ear. "To Jake, Oy. To Jake!"

"Ake!" the bumbler barked, and splashed rapidly off into the darkness, swinging his head from side to side at the end of his long neck like a pendulum. Roland followed with the end of the rawhide leash wrapped around his diminished right hand.

24

THE CRADLE—IT WAS easily big enough to have acquired proper-noun status in their minds—stood in the center of a square five times larger than the one where they had come upon the blasted statue, and when she got a really good look at it, Susannah realized how old and gray and fundamentally grungy the rest of Lud really was. The Cradle was so clean it almost hurt her eyes. No vines overgrew its sides; no graffiti daubed its blinding white walls and steps and columns. The yellow plains dust which had coated everything else was absent here. As they drew closer, Susannah saw why: streams of water coursed endlessly down the sides of the Cradle, issuing from nozzles hidden in the shadows of the copper-sheathed eaves. Interval sprays created by other hidden nozzles washed the steps, turning them into off-and-on waterfalls.

"Wow," Eddie said. "It makes Grand Central look like a Greyhound station in Buttfuck, Nebraska."

"What a poet you are, dear," Susannah said dryly.

The steps surrounded the entire building and rose to a great open lobby. There were no obscuring mats of vegetation here, but Eddie and Susannah found they still couldn't get a good look inside; the shadows thrown by the overhanging roof were too deep. The Totems of the Beam marched all the way around the building, two by two, but the corners were reserved for creatures Susannah fervently hoped never to meet outside of the occasional nightmare—hideous stone dragons with scaly bodies, clutching, claw-tipped hands, and nasty peering eyes.

Eddie touched her shoulder and pointed higher. Susannah looked . . . and felt her breath come to a stop in her throat. Standing astride the peak of the roof, far above The Totems of the Beam and the dragonish gargoyles, as if given dominion over them, was a golden warrior at least sixty feet high. A battered cowboy hat was shoved back to reveal his lined and careworn brow; a bandanna hung askew on his upper chest, as if it had just been pulled down after serving long, hard duty as a dust-muffle. In one upraised fist he held a revolver; in the other, what appeared to be an olive branch.

Roland of Gilead stood atop the Cradle of Lud, dressed in gold.

No, she thought, at last remembering to breathe again. *It's not him . . . but in another way, it is. That man was a gunslinger, and the resem-*

blance between him, who's probably been dead a thousand years or more, and Roland is all the truth of ka-tet you'll ever need to know.

Thunder slammed out of the south. Lightning harried racing clouds across the sky. She wished she had more time to study both the golden statue which stood atop the Cradle and the animals which surrounded it; each of these latter appeared to have words carved upon them, and she had an idea that what was written there might be knowledge worth having. Under these circumstances, however, there was no time to spare.

A wide red strip had been painted across the pavement at the point where The Street of the Turtle emptied into The Plaza of the Cradle. Maud and the fellow Eddie called Jeeves the Butler stopped a prudent distance from the red mark.

"This far and no farther," Maud told them flatly. "You may take us to our deaths, but each man and woman owes one to the gods anyway, and I'll die on this side of the dead-line no matter what. I'll not dare Blaine for outlanders."

"Nor will I," Jeeves said. He had taken off his dusty bowler and was holding it against his naked chest. On his face was an expression of fearful reverence.

"Fine," Susannah said. "Now scat on out of here, both of you."

"Ye'll backshoot us the second we turn from ye," Jeeves said in a trembling voice. "I'll take my watch and warrant on it, so I will."

Maud shook her head. The blood on her face had dried to a grotesque maroon stippling. "There never were a backshooting gunslinger—that much I *will* say."

"We only have *their* word for it that that's what they are."

Maud pointed to the big revolver with the worn sandalwood grip which Susannah held in her hand. Jeeves looked . . . and after a moment he stretched out his hand to the woman. When Maud took it, Susannah's image of them as dangerous killers collapsed. They looked more like Hansel and Gretel than Bonnie and Clyde; tired, frightened, confused, and lost so long in the woods that they had grown old there. Her hate and fear of them departed. What replaced it was pity and a deep, aching sadness.

"Fare you well, both of you," she said softly. "Walk as you will, and with no fear of harm from me or my man here."

Maud nodded. "I believe you mean us no harm, and I forgive you for shooting Winston. But listen to me, and listen well: *stay out of the Cradle.* Whatever reasons you think you have for going in, they're not good enough. To enter Blaine's Cradle is death."

"We don't have any choice," Eddie said, and thunder banged overhead again, as if in agreement. "Now let me tell *you* something. I don't know what's underneath Lud and what isn't, but I do know those drums you're so whacked out about are part of a recording—a *song*—that was made in the world my wife and I came from." He looked at their uncomprehending faces and raised his arms in frustration. "Jesus Pumpkin-Pie Christ, don't you get it? You're killing each other over a piece of music that was never even released as a single!"

Susannah put her hand on his shoulder and murmured his name. He ignored her for the moment, his eyes flicking from Jeeves to Maud and then back to Jeeves again.

"You want to see monsters? Take a good look at each other, then. And when you get back to whatever funhouse it is you call home, take a good look at your friends and relatives."

"You don't understand," Maud said. Her eyes were dark and somber. "But you will. Ay—you will."

"Go on, now," Susannah said quietly. "Talk between us is no good; the words only drop dead. Just go your way and try to remember the faces of your fathers, for I think you lost sight of those faces long ago."

The two of them walked back in the direction from which they had come without another word. They did look back over their shoulders from time to time, however, and they were still holding hands: Hansel and Gretel lost in the deep dark forest.

"Lemme outta here," Eddie said heavily. He made the Ruger safe, stuck it back in the waistband of his pants, and then rubbed his red eyes with the heels of his hands. "Just lemme out, that's all I ask."

"I know what you mean, handsome." She was clearly scared, but her head had that defiant tilt he had come to recognize and love. He put his hands on her shoulders, bent down, and kissed her. He did not let either their surroundings or the oncoming storm keep him from doing a thorough job. When he pulled back at last, she was studying him with wide, dancing eyes. "Wow! What was that about?"

"About how I'm in love with you," he said, "and I guess that's about all. Is it enough?"

Her eyes softened. For a moment she thought about telling him the secret she might or might not be keeping, but of course the time and place were wrong—she could no more tell him she might be pregnant now than she could pause to read the words written on the sculpted Portal Totems.

"It's enough, Eddie," she said.

"You're the best thing that ever happened to me." His hazel eyes were totally focused on her. "It's hard for me to say stuff like that— living with Henry made it hard, I guess—but it's true. I think I started loving you because you were everything Roland took me away from—in

New York, I mean—but it's a lot more than that now, because I don't want to go back anymore. Do you?"

She looked at the Cradle. She was terrified of what they might find in there, but all the same . . . she looked back at him. "No, I don't want to go back. I want to spend the rest of my life going forward. As long as you're with me, that is. It's funny, you know, you saying you started loving me because of all the things he took you away from."

"Funny how?"

"I started loving you because you set me free of Detta Walker." She paused, thought, then shook her head slightly. "No—it goes further than that. I started loving you because you set me free of *both* those bitches. One was a foul-mouthed, cock-teasing thief, and the other was a self-righteous, pompous prig. Comes down to six of one and half a dozen of the other, as far as I'm concerned. I like Susannah Dean better than either one . . . and you were the one who set me free."

This time it was she who did the reaching, pressing her palm to his stubbly cheeks, drawing him down, kissing him gently. When he put a light hand on her breast, she sighed and covered it with her own.

"I think we better get going," she said, "or we're apt to be laying right here in the street . . . and getting wet, from the look."

Eddie stared around at the silent towers, the broken windows, the vine-encrusted walls a final time. Then he nodded. "Yeah. I don't think there's any future in this town, anyway."

He pushed her forward, and they both stiffened as the wheels of the chair passed over what Maud had called the dead-line, fearful that they would trip some ancient protective device and die together. But nothing happened. Eddie pushed her into the plaza, and as they approached the steps leading up to the Cradle, a cold, wind-driven rain began to fall.

Although neither of them knew it, the first of the great autumn storms of Mid-World had arrived.

25

ONCE THEY WERE IN the smelly darkness of the sewers, Gasher slowed the killing pace he'd maintained aboveground. Jake didn't think it was because of the darkness; Gasher seemed to know every twist and turn of the route he was following, just as advertised. Jake believed it was because his captor was satisfied that Roland had been squashed to jelly by the deadfall trap.

Jake himself had begun to wonder.

If Roland had spotted the tripwires—a far more subtle trap than the one which followed—was it really likely that he had missed seeing the fountain? Jake supposed it was possible, but it didn't make much sense. Jake thought it more likely that Roland had tripped the fountain on purpose, to lull Gasher and perhaps slow him down. He didn't believe Roland could follow them through this maze under the streets—the total darkness would defeat even the gunslinger's tracking abilities—but it cheered his heart to think that Roland might not have died in an attempt to keep his promise.

They turned right, left, then left again. As Jake's other senses sharpened in an attempt to compensate for his lack of sight, he had a vague perception of other tunnels around him. The muffled sounds of ancient, laboring machinery would grow loud for a moment, then fade as the stone foundations of the city drew close around them again. Drafts blew intermittently against his skin, sometimes warm, sometimes chilly. Their splashing footfalls echoed briefly as they passed the intersecting tunnels from which these stenchy breaths blew, and once Jake nearly brained himself on some metal object jutting down from the ceiling. He slapped at it with one hand and felt something that might have been a large valve-wheel. After that he waved his hands as he trotted along in an attempt to read the air ahead of him.

Gasher guided him with taps to the shoulders, as a waggoner might have guided his oxen. They moved at a good clip, trotting but not running. Gasher got enough of his breath back to first hum and then begin singing in a low, surprisingly tuneful tenor voice.

> "Ribble-ti-tibble-ti-ting-ting-ting,
> I'll get a job and buy yer a ring,
> When I get my -mitts
> On yer jiggly tits,
> Ribble-ti-tibble-ti-ting-ting-ting!
>
> O ribble-ti-tibble,
> I just wanter fiddle,
> Fiddle around with your ting-ting-ting!"

There were five or six more verses along this line before Gasher quit. "Now *you* sing somethin, squint."

"I don't know anything," Jake puffed. He hoped he sounded more out of breath than he actually was. He didn't know if it would do him any good or not, but down here in the dark any edge seemed worth trying for.

Gasher brought his elbow down in the center of Jake's back, almost hard enough to send him sprawling into the ankle-high water running sluggishly through the tunnel they were traversing. "You *better* know sommat, 'less you want me to rip your ever-lovin spine right outcher back." He paused, then added: "There's haunts down here, boy. They live inside the fuckin machines, so they do. Singin keeps em off . . . don't you know that? Now *sing!*"

Jake thought hard, not wanting to earn another love-tap from Gasher, and came up with a song he'd learned in summer day camp at the age of seven or eight. He opened his mouth and began to bawl it into the darkness, listening to the echoes bounce back amid the sounds of running water, falling water, and ancient thudding machinery.

> *"My girl's a corker, she's a New Yorker,*
> *I buy her everything to keep her in style,*
> *She got a pair of hips*
> *Just like two battleships,*
> *Oh boy, that's how my money goes.*
>
> *My girl's a dilly, she comes from Philly,*
> *I buy her everything to keep her in style,*
> *She's got a pair of eyes*
> *Just like two pizza pies,*
> *Oh boy, that's how—"*

Gasher reached out, seized Jake's ears as if they were jug-handles, and yanked him to a stop. "There's a hole right ahead of yer," he said. "With a voice like yours, squint, it'd be doin the world a mercy to letcher fall in, so it would, but Tick-Tock wouldn't approve at all, so I reckon ye're safe for a little longer." Gasher's hands left Jake's ears, which burned like fire, and fastened on the back of his shirt. "Now lean forward until you feel the ladder on the t'other side. And mind you don't slip and drag us both down!"

Jake leaned cautiously forward, hands outstretched, terrified of falling into a pit he couldn't see. As he groped for the ladder, he became aware of warm air—clean and almost fragrant—whooshing past his face, and a faint blush of rose-colored light from beneath him. His fingers touched a steel rung and closed over it. The bite-wounds on his left hand broke open again, and he felt warm blood running across his palm.

"Got it?" Gasher asked.

"Yes."

"Then climb down! What are you waitin for, gods damn it!" Gasher let go of his shirt, and Jake could imagine him drawing his foot back, meaning to hurry him along with a kick in the ass. Jake stepped across the faintly glimmering gap and began to descend the ladder, using his hurt hand as little as possible. This time the rungs were clear of moss and oil, and hardly rusted at all. The shaft was very long and as Jake went down, hurrying to keep Gasher from stepping on his hands with his thick-soled boots, he found himself remembering a movie he'd once seen on TV—*Journey to the Center of the Earth.*

The throb of machinery grew louder and the rosy glow grew stronger. The machines still didn't sound right, but his ears told him these were in better shape than the ones above. And when he finally reached the bottom, he found the floor was dry. The new horizontal shaft was square, about six feet high, and sleeved with riveted stainless steel. It stretched away for as far as Jake could see in both directions, straight as a string. He knew instinctively, without even thinking about it, that this tunnel (which had to be at least seventy feet under Lud) also followed the path of the Beam. And somewhere up ahead—Jake was sure of this, although he couldn't have said why—the train they had come looking for lay directly above it.

Narrow ventilation grilles ran along the sides of the walls just below the shaft's ceiling; it was from these that the clean, dry air was flowing. Moss dangled from some of them in blue-gray beards, but most were still clear. Below every other grille was a yellow arrow with a symbol that looked a bit like a lower-case *t*. The arrows pointed in the direction Jake and Gasher were heading.

The rose-colored light was coming from glass tubes which ran along the ceiling of the shaft in parallel rows. Some—about one in every three—were dark, and others sputtered fitfully, but at least half of them were still working. *Neon tubing,* Jake thought, amazed. *How about that?*

Gasher dropped down beside him. He saw Jake's expression of surprise and grinned. "Nice, ennet? Cool in the summer, warm in the winter, and so much food that five hunnert men couldn't eat it in five hunnert years. And do yer know the best part, squint? The very best part of the whole coozy fakement?"

Jake shook his head.

"Farkin Pubies don't have the leastest idear the place even exists. They think there's monsters down here. Catch a Pubie goin within twenty feet of a sewer-cap, less'n he has to!"

He threw his head back and laughed heartily. Jake didn't join in, even though a cold voice in the back of his mind told him it might be politic to do so. He didn't join in because he knew exactly how the Pubes felt. There *were* monsters under the city—trolls and boggerts and orcs. Hadn't he been captured by just such a one?

Gasher shoved him to the left. "Garn—almost there now. *Hup!*"

They jogged on, their footfalls chasing them in a pack of echoes. After ten or fifteen minutes of this, Jake saw a watertight hatchway about two hundred yards ahead. As they drew closer, he could see a big valve-wheel sticking out of it. A communicator box was mounted on the wall to the right.

"I'm blown out," Gasher gasped as they reached the door at the end of the tunnel. "Doin's like this are too much for an inwalid like yer old pal, so they are!" He thumbed the button on the intercom and bawled: "I got im, Tick-Tock—got him as dandy as you please! Didn't even muss 'is hair! Didn't I tell yer I would? Trust the Gasherman, I said, for he'll leadjer straight and true! Now open up and let us in!"

He let go of the button and looked impatiently at the door. The valve-wheel didn't turn. Instead a flat, drawling voice came out of the intercom speaker: "What's the password?"

Gasher frowned horribly, scratched his chin with his long, dirty nails, then lifted his eyepatch and swabbed out another clot of yellow-green goo. "Tick-Tock and his passwords!" he said to Jake. He sounded worried as well as irritated. "He's a trig cove, but that's takin it a deal too far if you ask me, so it is."

He pushed the button and yelled, "Come on, Tick-Tock! If you don't reckergnize the sound of my voice, you need a heary-aid!"

"Oh, I recognize it," the drawling voice returned. To Jake it sounded like Jerry Reed, who played Burt Reynolds's sidekick in *Smokey and the Bandit*. "But I don't know who's with you, do I? Or have you forgotten that the camera out there went tits-up last year? You give the password, Gasher, or you can rot out there!"

Gasher stuck a finger up his nose, extracted a chunk of snot the color of mint jelly, and squashed it into the grille of the speaker. Jake watched this childish display of ill temper in silent fascination, feeling unwelcome, hysterical laughter bubbling around inside him. Had they come all this way, through the boobytrapped mazes and lightless tunnels, to be balked here at this watertight door simply because Gasher couldn't remember the Tick-Tock Man's password?

Gasher looked at him balefully, then slid his hand across his skull, peeling off his sweat-soaked yellow scarf. The skull beneath was bald, except for a few straggling tufts of black hair like porcupine quills, and deeply dented above the left temple. Gasher peered into the scarf and plucked forth a scrap of paper. "Gods bless Hoots," he muttered. "Hoots takes care of me a right proper, he does."

He peered at the scrap, turning it this way and that, and then held it out to Jake. He kept his voice pitched low, as if the Tick-Tock Man could hear him even though the TALK button on the intercom wasn't depressed.

"You're a proper little gennelman, ain't you? And the very first thing they teach a gennelman to do after he's been larned not to eat the paste and piss in the corners is read. So read me the word on this paper, cully, for it's gone right out of my head—so it has."

Jake took the paper, looked at it, then looked up at Gasher again. "What if I won't?" he asked coolly.

Gasher was momentarily taken aback at this response . . . and then he began to grin with dangerous good humor. "Why, I'll grab yer by the throat and use yer head for a doorknocker," he said. "I doubt if it'll conwince old Ticky to let me in—for he's still nervous of your hardcase friend, so he is—but it'll do my heart a world of good to see your brains drippin off that wheel."

Jake considered this, the dark laughter still bubbling away inside him. The Tick-Tock Man was a trig enough cove, all right—he had known that it would be difficult to persuade Gasher, who was dying anyway, to speak the password even if Roland had taken him prisoner. What Tick-Tock hadn't taken into account was Gasher's defective memory.

Don't laugh. If you do, he really will beat your brains out.

In spite of his brave words, Gasher was watching Jake with real anxiety, and Jake realized a potentially powerful fact: Gasher might not be afraid of dying . . . but he *was* afraid of being humiliated.

"All right, Gasher," he said calmly. "The word on this piece of paper is *bountiful*."

"Gimme that." Gasher snatched the paper back, returned it to his scarf, and quickly wrapped the yellow cloth around his head again. He thumbed the intercom button. "Tick-Tock? Yer still there?"

"Where else would I be? The West End of the World?" The drawling voice now sounded mildly amused.

Gasher stuck his whitish tongue out at the speaker, but his voice was ingratiating, almost servile. "The password's bountyful, and a fine word it is, too! Now let me in, gods cuss it!"

"Of course," the Tick-Tock Man said. A machine started up somewhere nearby, making Jake jump. The valve-wheel in the center of the door spun. When it stopped, Gasher seized it, yanked it outward, grabbed Jake's arm, and propelled him over the raised lip of the door and into the strangest room he had ever seen in his life.

26

ROLAND DESCENDED INTO DUSKY pink light. Oy's bright eyes peered out from the open V of his shirt; his neck stretched to the limit of its considerable length as he sniffed at the warm air that blew through the ventilator grilles. Roland had had to depend completely on the bumbler's nose in the dark passages above, and he had been terribly afraid the animal would lose Jake's scent in the running water . . . but when he had heard the sound of singing—first Gasher, then Jake—echoing back through the pipes, he had relaxed a little. Oy had not led them wrong.

Oy had heard it, too. Up until then he had been moving slowly and cautiously, even backtracking every now and again to be sure of himself, but when he heard Jake's voice he began to run, straining the rawhide leash. Roland was afraid he might call after Jake in his harsh voice—*Ake! Ake!*—but he hadn't done so. And, just as they reached the shaft which led to the lower levels of this Dycian Maze, Roland had heard the sound of some new machine—a pump of some sort, perhaps—followed by the metallic, echoing crash of a door being slammed shut.

He reached the foot of the square tunnel and glanced briefly at the double line of lighted tubes which led off in either direction. They were lit with swamp-fire, he saw, like the sign outside the place which had belonged to Balazar in the city of New York. He looked more closely at the narrow chrome ventilation strips running along the top of each wall, and the arrows below them, then slipped the rawhide loop off Oy's neck. Oy shook his head impatiently, clearly glad to be rid of it.

"We're close," he murmured into the bumbler's cocked ear, "and so we have to be quiet. Do you understand, Oy? Very quiet."

"I-yet," Oy replied in a hoarse whisper that would have been funny under other circumstances.

Roland put him down and Oy was immediately off down the tunnel, neck out, muzzle to the steel floor. Roland could hear him muttering *Ake-Ake! Ake-Ake!* under his breath. Roland unholstered his gun and followed him.

27

EDDIE AND SUSANNAH LOOKED up at the vastness of Blaine's Cradle as the skies opened and the rain began to fall in torrents.

"It's a hell of a building, but they forgot the handicap ramps!" Eddie yelled, raising his voice to be heard over the rain and thunder.

"Never mind that," Susannah said impatiently, slipping out of the wheelchair. "Let's get up there and out of the rain."

Eddie looked dubiously up the incline of steps. The risers were shallow . . . but there were a lot of them. "You sure, Suze?"

"Race you, white boy," she said, and began to wriggle upward with uncanny ease, using hands, muscular forearms, and the stumps of her legs.

And she almost *did* beat him; Eddie had the ironmongery to contend with, and it slowed him down. Both of them were panting when they reached the top, and tendrils of steam were rising from their wet clothes. Eddie grabbed her under the arms, swung her up, and then just held her with his hands locked together in the small of her back instead of dropping her back into the chair, as he had meant to do. He felt randy and half-crazy without the slightest idea why.

Oh, give me a break, he thought. *You've gotten this far alive; that's what's got your glands pumped up and ready to party.*

Susannah licked her full lower lip and wound her strong fingers into his hair. She pulled. It hurt . . . and at the same time it felt wonderful. "Told you I'd beat you, white boy," she said in a low, husky voice.

"Get outta here—I had you . . . by half a step." He tried to sound less out of breath than he was and found it was impossible.

"Maybe . . . but it blew you out, didn't it?" One hand left his hair, slid downward, and squeezed gently. A smile gleamed in her eyes. "*Somethin* ain't blown out, though."

Thunder rumbled across the sky. They flinched, then laughed together.

"Come on," he said. "This is nuts. The time's all wrong."

She didn't contradict him, but she squeezed him again before returning her hand to his shoulder. Eddie felt a pang of regret as he swung her back into her chair and ran her across vast flagstones and under cover of the roof. He thought he saw the same regret in Susannah's eyes.

When they were out of the downpour, Eddie paused and they looked back. The Plaza of the Cradle, The Street of the Turtle, and all the city beyond was rapidly disappearing into a shifting gray curtain. Eddie wasn't a bit sorry. Lud hadn't earned itself a place in his mental scrapbook of fond memories.

"Look," Susannah murmured. She was pointing at a nearby downspout. It ended in a large, scaly fish-head that looked like a close relation to the dragon-gargoyles which decorated the corners of the Cradle. Water ran from its mouth in a silver torrent.

"This isn't just a passing shower, is it?" Eddie asked.

"Nope. It's gonna rain until it gets tired of it, and then it's gonna rain some more, just for spite. Maybe a week; maybe a month. Not that it's gonna matter to us, if Blaine decides he doesn't like our looks and fries us. Fire a shot to let Roland know we got here, sugar, and then we'll have us a look around. See what we can see."

Eddie pointed the Ruger into the gray sky, pulled the trigger, and fired the shot which Roland heard a mile or more away, as he followed Jake and Gasher through the booby-trapped maze. Eddie stood where he was a moment longer, trying to persuade himself that things might still turn out all right, that his heart was wrong in its stubborn insistence that they had seen the last of the gunslinger and the boy Jake. Then he made the automatic safe again, returned it to the waistband of his pants, and went back to Susannah. He turned her chair away from the steps and rolled her along an aisle of columns which led deeper into the building. She popped the cylinder of Roland's gun and reloaded it as they went.

Under the roof the rain had a secret, ghostly sound and even the harsh thundercracks were muted. The columns which supported the structure were at least ten feet in diameter, and their tops were lost in the gloom. From up there in the shadows, Eddie heard the cooing conversation of pigeons.

Now a sign hanging on thick chrome-silver chains swam out of the shadows:

NORTH CENTRAL POSITRONICS WELCOMES YOU
TO THE CRADLE OF LUD
← SOUTHEAST TRAVEL (BLAINE)
NORTHWEST TRAVEL (PATRICIA) →

"Now we know the name of the one that fell in the river," Eddie said. "Patricia. They got their colors wrong, though. It's supposed to be pink for girls and blue for boys, not the other way around."

"Maybe they're *both* blue."

"They're not. Blaine's pink."

"How would you know that?"

Eddie looked confused. "I don't know how . . . but I do."

They followed the arrow pointing toward Blaine's berth, entering what had to be a grand concourse. Eddie didn't have Susannah's ability to see the past in clear, visionary flashes, but his imagination nonetheless filled this vast, pillared space with a thousand hurrying people; he heard clicking heels and murmuring voices, saw embraces of homecoming and farewell. And over everything, the speakers chanting news of a dozen different destinations.

Patricia is now boarding for Northwest Baronies . . .

Will Passenger Killington, passenger Killington, please report to the information booth on the lower level?

Blaine is now arriving at Berth #2, and will be debarking shortly . . .

Now there was only the pigeons.

Eddie shivered.

"Look at the faces," Susannah murmured. "I don't know if they give you the willies, but they sure do me." She was pointing to the right.

High up on the wall, a series of sculpted heads seemed to push out of the marble, peering down at them from the shadows—stern men with the harsh faces of executioners who are happy in their work. Some of the faces had fallen from their places and lay in granite shards and splinters seventy or eighty feet below their peers. Those remaining were spider-webbed with cracks and splattered with pigeon dung.

"They must have been the Supreme Court, or something," Eddie said, uneasily scanning all those thin lips and cracked, empty eyes. "Only judges can look so smart and so completely pissed off at the same time—you're talking to a guy who knows. There isn't one of them who looks like he'd give a crippled crab a crutch."

" 'A heap of broken images, where the sun beats and the dead tree gives no shelter,' " Susannah murmured, and at these words Eddie felt gooseflesh waltz across the skin of his arms and chest and legs.

"What's that, Suze?"

"A poem by a man who must have seen Lud in his dreams," she said. "Come on, Eddie. Forget them."

"Easier said than done." But he began to push her again.

Ahead, a vast grilled barrier like a castle barbican swam out of the gloom . . . and beyond it, they caught their first glimpse of Blaine the Mono. It was pink, just as Eddie had said it would be, a delicate shade which matched the veins running through the marble pillars. Blaine flowed above the wide loading platform in a smooth, streamlined bullet shape which looked more like flesh than metal. Its surface was broken only once—by a triangular window equipped with a huge wiper. Eddie knew there would be another triangular window with another big wiper on the other side of the mono's nose, so that if you looked at Blaine head-on, it would seem to have a face, just like Charlie the Choo-Choo. The wipers would look like slyly drooping eyelids.

White light from the southeastern slot in the Cradle fell across Blaine in a long, distorted rectangle. To Eddie, the body of the train looked like the breaching back of some fabulous pink whale—one that was utterly silent.

"Wow." His voice had fallen to a whisper. "We found it."

"Yes. Blaine the Mono."

"Is it dead, do you think? It *looks* dead."

"It's not. Sleeping, maybe, but a long way from dead."

"You sure?"

"Were you sure it would be pink?" It wasn't a question he had to answer, and he didn't. The face she turned up to him was strained and badly frightened. "It's sleeping, and you know what? I'm scared to wake it up."

"Well, we'll wait for the others, then."

She shook her head. "I think we better try to be ready for when they get here . . . because I've got an idea that they're going to come on the run. Push me over to that box mounted on the bars. It looks like an intercom. See it?"

He did, and pushed her slowly toward it. It was mounted on one side of a closed gate in the center of the barrier which ran the length of the Cradle. The vertical bars of the barrier were made of what looked like stainless steel; those of the gate appeared to be ornamental iron, and their lower ends disappeared into steel-ringed holes in the floor. There was no way either of them was going to wriggle through those bars, either, Eddie saw. The gap between each set was no more than four inches. It would have been a tight squeeze even for Oy.

Pigeons ruffled and cooed overhead. The left wheel of Susannah's chair squawked monotonously. *My kingdom for an oilcan*, Eddie thought, and realized he was a lot more than just scared. The last time he had felt this level of terror had been on the day when he and Henry had stood on the sidewalk of Rhinehold Street in Dutch Hill, looking at the slumped ruin of The Mansion. They hadn't gone in on that day in 1977; they had turned their backs on the haunted house and walked away, and he remembered vowing to himself that he would never, never, *ever* go back to that place. It was a promise he'd kept, but here he was, in another haunted house, and there was the haunter, right over there—Blaine the Mono, a long low pink shape with one window peering at him like the eye of a dangerous animal who is shamming sleep.

He stirs no more from his berth in the Cradle. . . . He has even stopped speaking in his many voices and laughing. . . . Ardis was the last to go nigh Blaine . . . and when Ardis couldn't answer what was asked, Blaine slew him with blue fire.

If it speaks to me, I'll probably go crazy, Eddie thought.

The wind gusted outside, and a fine spray of rain flew in through the tall egress slot cut in the side of the building. He saw it strike Blaine's window and bead up there.

Eddie shuddered suddenly and looked sharply around. "We're being watched—I can feel it."

"I wouldn't be at all surprised. Push me closer to the gate, Eddie. I want to get a better look at that box."

"Okay, but don't touch it. If it's electrified—"

"If Blaine wants to cook us, he will," Susannah said, looking through the bars at Blaine's back. "You know it, and I do, too."

And because Eddie knew that was only the truth, he said nothing.

The box looked like a combination intercom and burglar alarm. There was a speaker set into the top half, with what looked like a TALK/

LISTEN button next to it. Below this were numbers arranged in a shape which made a diamond:

```
                    1
                   2 3
                  4 5 6
                 7 8 9 10
               11 12 13 14 15
              16 17 18 19 20 21
            22 23 24 25 26 27 28
           29 30 31 32 33 34 35 36
         37 38 39 40 41 42 43 44 45
       46 47 48 49 50 51 52 53 54 55
         56 57 58 59 60 61 62 63 64
           65 66 67 68 69 70 71 72
            73 74 75 76 77 78 79
              80 81 82 83 84 85
               86 87 88 89 90
                91 92 93 94
                 95 96 97
                  98 99
                   100
```

Under the diamond were two other buttons with words of the High Speech printed on them: COMMAND and ENTER.

Susannah looked bewildered and doubtful. "What *is* this thing, do you think? It looks like a gadget in a science fiction movie."

Of course it did, Eddie realized. Susannah had probably seen a home security system or two in her time—she had, after all, lived among the Manhattan rich, even if she had not been very enthusiastically accepted by them—but there was a world of difference between the electronics gear available in her when, 1963, and his own, which was 1987. *We've never talked much about the differences, either,* he thought. *I wonder what she'd think if I told her Ronald Reagan was President of the United States when Roland snatched me? Probably that I was crazy.*

"It's a security system," he said. Then, although his nerves and instincts screamed out against it, he forced himself to reach out with his right hand and thumb the TALK/LISTEN switch.

There was no crackle of electricity; no deadly blue fire went racing up his arm. No sign that the thing was even still connected.

Maybe Blaine is dead. Maybe he's dead, after all.

But he didn't really believe that.

"Hello?" he said, and in his mind's eye saw the unfortunate Ardis, screaming as he was microwaved by the blue fire dancing all over his face and body, melting his eyes and setting his hair ablaze. "Hello . . . Blaine? *Anybody?*"

He let go of the button and waited, stiff with tension. Susannah's hand crept into his, cold and small. There was still no answer, and Eddie—now more reluctant than ever—pushed the button again.

"Blaine?"

He let go of the button. Waited. And when there was still no answer, a dangerous giddiness overcame him, as it often did in moments of stress and fear. When that giddiness took him, counting the cost no longer seemed to matter. *Nothing* mattered. It had been like that when he had outfaced Balazar's sallow-faced contact man in Nassau, and it was like that now. And if Roland had seen him in the moment this lunatic impatience overtook him, he would have seen more than just a resemblance between Eddie and Cuthbert; he would have sworn Eddie *was* Cuthbert.

He jammed the button in with his thumb and began to bellow into the speaker, adopting a plummy (and completely bogus) British accent. "Hullo, Blaine! Cheerio, old fellow! This is Robin Leach, host of *Lifestyles of the Rich and Brainless*, here to tell you that *you* have won six billion dollars and a new Ford Escort in the Publishers Clearing House Sweepstakes!"

Pigeons took flight above them in soft, startled explosions of wings. Susannah gasped. Her face wore the dismayed expression of a devout woman who has just heard her husband blaspheme in a cathedral. "Eddie, stop it! *Stop it!*"

Eddie couldn't stop it. His mouth was smiling, but his eyes glittered with a mixture of fear, hysteria, and frustrated anger. "You and your monorail girlfriend, Patricia, will spend a lux-*yoo*-rious month in scenic Jimtown, where you'll drink only the finest wine and eat only the finest virgins! You—"

"*. . . shhhh . . .*"

Eddie broke off, looking at Susannah. He was at once sure that it had been she who had shushed him—not only because she had already tried but because she was the only other person here—and yet at the same time he knew it *hadn't* been Susannah. That had been *another* voice: the voice of a very young and very frightened child.

"Suze? Did you—"

Susannah was shaking her head and raising her hand at the same time. She pointed at the intercom box, and Eddie saw the button marked COMMAND was glowing a very faint shell-pink. It was the same color as the mono sleeping in its berth on the other side of the barrier.

"Shhh . . . don't wake him up," the child's voice mourned. It drifted from the speaker, soft as an evening breeze.

"What . . ." Eddie began. Then he shook his head, reached toward the TALK/LISTEN switch and pressed it gently. When he spoke again, it was not in the blaring Robin Leach bellow but in the almost-whisper of a conspirator. "What are you? Who are you?"

He released the button. He and Susannah regarded each other with the big eyes of children who now know they are sharing the house with a dangerous—perhaps psychotic—adult. How have they come by the knowledge? Why, because another child has told them, a child who has lived with the psychotic adult for a long time, hiding in corners and stealing out only when it knows the adult is asleep; a frightened child who happens to be almost invisible.

There was no answer. Eddie let the seconds spin out. Each one seemed long enough to read a whole novel in. He was reaching for the button again when the faint pink glow reappeared.

"I'm Little Blaine," the child's voice whispered. *"The one he doesn't see. The one he forgot. The one he thinks he left behind in the rooms of ruin and the halls of the dead."*

Eddie pushed the button again with a hand that had picked up an uncontrollable shake. He could hear that shake in his voice, as well. *"Who? Who* is the one who doesn't see? Is it the Bear?"

No—not the bear; not he. Shardik lay dead in the forest, many miles behind them; the world had moved on even since then. Eddie suddenly remembered what it had been like to lay his ear against that strange unfound door in the clearing where the bear had lived its violent half-life, that door with its somehow terrible stripes of yellow and black. It was all of a piece, he realized now; all part of some awful, decaying whole, a tattered web with the Dark Tower at its center like an incomprehensible stone spider. All of Mid-World had become one vast haunted mansion in these strange latter days; all of Mid-World had become The Drawers; all of Mid-World had become a waste land, haunting and haunted.

He saw Susannah's lips form the words of the real answer before the voice from the intercom could speak them, and those words were as obvious as the solution to a riddle once the answer is spoken.

"Big Blaine," the unseen voice whispered. *"Big Blaine is the ghost in the machine—the ghost in* all *the machines."*

Susannah's hand had gone to her throat and was clutching it, as if she intended to strangle herself. Her eyes were full of terror, but they were not glassy, not stunned; they were sharp with understanding. Perhaps she knew a voice like this one from her own when—the when where the integrated whole that was Susannah had been shunted aside by the warring personalities of Detta and Odetta. The childish voice had surprised her as well as him, but her agonized eyes said she was no stranger to the concept being expressed.

Susannah knew all about the madness of duality.

"Eddie we have to go," she said. Her terror turned the words into an unpunctuated auditory smear. He could hear air whistling in her windpipe like a cold wind around a chimney. "Eddie we have to get away Eddie we have to get away Eddie—"

"Too late," the tiny, mourning voice said. "He's awake. Big Blaine is awake. He knows you are here. And he's coming."

Suddenly lights—bright orange arc-sodiums—began to flash on in pairs above them, bathing the pillared vastness of the Cradle in a harsh glare that banished all shadows. Hundreds of pigeons darted and swooped in frightened, aimless flight, startled from their complex of interlocked nests high above.

"Wait!" Eddie shouted. "Please, wait!"

In his agitation he forgot to push the button, but it made no difference; Little Blaine responded anyway. "No! I can't let him catch me! I can't let him kill me, too!"

The light on the intercom box went dark again, but only for a moment. This time both COMMAND and ENTER lit up, and their color was not pink but the lurid dark red of a blacksmith's forge.

"WHO ARE YOU?" a voice roared, and it came not just from the box but from every speaker in the city which still operated. The rotting bodies hanging from the poles shivered with the vibrations of that mighty voice; it seemed that even the dead would run from Blaine, if they could.

Susannah shrank back in her chair, the heels of her hands pressed to her ears, her face long with dismay, her mouth distorted in a silent scream. Eddie felt himself shrinking toward all the fantastic, hallucinatory terrors of eleven. Had it been this voice he had feared when he and Henry stood outside The Mansion? That he had perhaps even *anticipated*? He didn't know ... but he *did* know how Jack in that old story must have felt when he realized that he had tried the beanstalk once too often, and awakened the giant.

"HOW DARE YOU DISTURB MY SLEEP? TELL ME NOW, OR DIE WHERE YOU STAND."

He might have frozen right there, leaving Blaine—Big Blaine—to do to them whatever it was he had done to Ardis (or something even worse); perhaps *should* have frozen, locked in that down-the-rabbit-hole, fairy-tale terror. It was the memory of the small voice which had spoken first that enabled him to move. It had been the voice of a terrified child, but it had tried to help them, terrified or not.

So now you have to help yourself, he thought. *You woke it up; deal with it, for Christ's sake!*

Eddie reached out and pushed the button again. "My name is Eddie Dean. The woman with me is my wife, Susannah. We're . . ."

He looked at Susannah, who nodded and made frantic motions for him to go on.

"We're on a quest. We seek the Dark Tower which lies in the Path of the Beam. We're in the company of two others, Roland of Gilead and . . . and Jake of New York. We're from New York too. If you're—" He paused for a moment, biting back the words *Big Blaine*. If he used them, he might make the intelligence behind the voice aware that they had heard another voice; a ghost inside the ghost, so to speak.

Susannah gestured again for him to go on, using both hands.

"If you're Blaine the Mono . . . well . . . we want you to take us."

He released the button. There was no response for what seemed like a very long time, only the agitated flutter of the disturbed pigeons from overhead. When Blaine spoke again, his voice came only from the speaker-box mounted on the gate and sounded almost human.

"DO NOT TRY MY PATIENCE. ALL THE DOORS TO THAT WHERE ARE CLOSED. GILEAD IS NO MORE, AND THOSE KNOWN AS GUNSLINGERS ARE ALL DEAD. NOW ANSWER MY QUESTION: WHO ARE YOU? THIS IS YOUR LAST CHANCE."

There was a sizzling sound. A ray of brilliant blue-white light lanced down from the ceiling and seared a hole the size of a golf-ball in the marble floor less than five feet to the left of Susannah's wheelchair. Smoke that smelled like the aftermath of a lightning-bolt rose lazily from it. Susannah and Eddie stared at each other in mute terror for a moment, and then Eddie lunged for the communicator-box and thumbed the button.

"You're wrong! We *did* come from New York! We came through the doors, on the beach, only a few weeks ago!"

"It's true!" Susannah called. "I swear it is!"

Silence. Beyond the long barrier, Blaine's pink back humped smoothly. The window at the front seemed to regard them like a vapid glass eye. The wiper could have been a lid half-closed in a sly wink.

"PROVE IT," Blaine said at last.

"Christ, how do I do that?" Eddie asked Susannah.

"I don't know."

Eddie pushed the button again. "The Statue of Liberty! Does that ring a bell?"

"GO ON," Blaine said. Now the voice sounded almost thoughtful.

"The Empire State Building! The Stock Exchange! The World Trade Center! Coney Island Red-Hots! Radio City Music Hall! The East Vil—"

Blaine cut him off . . . and now, incredibly, the voice which came from the speaker was the drawling voice of John Wayne.

"OKAY, PILGRIM. I BELIEVE YOU."

Eddie and Susannah shared another glance, this one of confusion and relief. But when Blaine spoke again, the voice was again cold and emotionless.

"ASK ME A QUESTION, EDDIE DEAN OF NEW YORK. AND IT BETTER BE A GOOD ONE." There was a pause, and then Blaine added: "BECAUSE IF IT'S NOT, YOU AND YOUR WOMAN ARE GOING TO DIE, NO MATTER WHERE YOU CAME FROM."

Susannah looked from the box on the gate to Eddie. "What's it *talking* about?" she hissed.

Eddie shook his head. "I don't have the slightest idea."

28

To JAKE, THE ROOM Gasher dragged him into looked like a Minuteman missile silo which had been decorated by the inmates of a lunatic asylum: part museum, part living room, part hippie crash pad. Above him, empty space vaulted up to a rounded ceiling and below him it dropped seventy-five or a hundred feet to a similarly rounded base. Running all around the single curved wall in vertical lines were tubes of neon in alternating strokes of color: red, blue, green, yellow, orange, peach, pink. These long tubes came together in roaring rainbow knots at the bottom and top of the silo . . . if that was what it had been.

The room was about three-quarters of the way up the vast capsule-shaped space and floored with rusty iron grillework. Rugs that looked Turkish (he later learned that such rugs were actually from a barony called Kashmin) lay on the grilled floor here and there. Their corners were held down with brass-bound trunks or standing lamps or the squat legs of over-stuffed chairs. If not, they would have flapped like strips of paper tied to an electric fan, because a steady warm draft rushed up from below. Another draft, this one issuing from a circular band of ventilators like the ones in the tunnel they had followed here, swirled about four or five feet above Jake's head. On the far side of the room was a door identical to the one through which he and Gasher had entered, and Jake assumed it was a continuation of the subterranean corridor following the Path of the Beam.

There were half a dozen people in the room, four men and two women. Jake guessed that he was looking at the Gray high command—if, that was, there were enough Grays left to warrant a high command. None of them were young, but all were still in the prime of their lives. They looked at Jake as curiously as he looked at them.

Sitting in the center of the room, with one massive leg thrown casually over the arm of a chair big enough to be a throne, was a man who looked like a cross between a Viking warrior and a giant from a child's fairy-tale. His heavily muscled upper body was naked except for a silver band around one bicep, a knife-scabbard looped over one shoulder, and a strange charm about his neck. His lower body was clad in soft, tight-fitting leather breeches which were tucked into high boots. He wore a yellow scarf tied around one of these. His hair, a dirty gray-blonde, cascaded almost to the middle of his broad back; his eyes were as green and curious as the eyes of a tomcat who is old enough to be wise but not old enough to have lost that refined sense of cruelty which passes for fun in feline circles. Hung by its strap from the back of the chair was what looked like a very old machine-gun.

Jake looked more closely at the ornament on the Viking's chest and saw that it was a coffin-shaped glass box hung on a silver chain. Inside it, a tiny gold clock-face marked the time at five minutes past three. Below the face, a tiny gold pendulum went back and forth, and despite the soft whoosh of circulating air from above and below, he could hear the tick-tock sound it made. The hands of the clock were moving faster than they should have done, and Jake was not very surprised to see that they were moving backward.

He thought of the crocodile in *Peter Pan*, the one that was always chasing after Captain Hook, and a little smile touched his lips. Gasher saw it, and raised his hand. Jake cringed away, putting his own hands to his face.

The Tick-Tock Man shook his finger at Gasher in an amusing school-marmish gesture. "Now, now . . . no need of that, Gasher," he said.

Gasher lowered his hand at once. His face had changed completely. Before, it had alternated between stupid rage and a species of cunning, almost existential humor. Now he only looked servile and adoring. Like the others in the room (and Jake himself), the Gasherman could not look away from Tick-Tock for long; his eyes were drawn inexorably back. And Jake could understand why. The Tick-Tock Man was the only person here who seemed wholly vital, wholly healthy, and wholly alive.

"If you say there's no need, there ain't," Gasher said, but he favored Jake with a dark look before shifting his eyes back to the blonde giant on the throne. "Still, he's wery pert, Ticky. Wery pert, Ticky. Wery pert indeed, so he is, and if you want my opinion, he'll take a deal of training!"

"When I want your opinion, I'll ask for it," the Tick-Tock Man said. "Now close the door, Gash—was you bore in a barn?"

A dark-haired woman laughed shrilly, a sound like the caw of a crow. Tick-Tock flicked his eyes toward her; she quieted at once and cast her eyes down to the grilled floor.

The door through which Gasher had dragged him was actually two doors. The arrangement reminded Jake of the way spaceship airlocks looked in the more intelligent science fiction movies. Gasher shut them both and turned to Tick-Tock, giving him a thumbs-up gesture. The Tick-Tock Man nodded and reached languidly up to press a button set into a piece of furniture that looked like a speaker's podium. A pump began to cycle wheezily within the wall, and the neon tubes dimmed perceptibly. There was a faint hiss of air and the valve-wheel of the inside door spun shut. Jake supposed the one in the outer door was doing the same. This was some sort of bomb-shelter, all right; no doubt of that. When the pump died, the long neon tubes resumed their former muted brilliance.

"There," Tick-Tock said pleasantly. His eyes began to look Jake up and down. Jake had a clear and very uncomfortable sense of being expertly catalogued and filed. "All safe and sound, we are. Snug as bugs in a rug. Right, Hoots?"

"Yar!" a tall, skinny man in a black suit replied promptly. His face was covered with some sort of rash which he scratched obsessively.

"I brung him," Gasher said. "I told yer you could trust me to do it, and didn't I?"

"You did," Tick-Tock said. "Bang on. I had some doubts about your ability to remember the password at the end, there, but—"

The dark-haired woman uttered another shrill caw. The Tick-Tock Man half-turned in her direction, that lazy smile dimpling the corners of his mouth, and before Jake was able to grasp what was happening—what had *already* happened—she was staggering backward, her eyes bulging in surprise and pain, her hands groping at some strange tumor in the middle of her chest which hadn't been there a second before.

Jake realized the Tick-Tock Man had made some sort of move as he was turning, a move so quick it had been no more than a flicker. The slim white hilt which had protruded from the scabbard looped over the Tick-Tock Man's shoulder was gone. The knife was now on the other side of the room, sticking out of the dark-haired woman's chest. Tick-Tock had drawn and thrown with an uncanny speed Jake wasn't sure even Roland could match. It had been like some malign magic trick.

The others watched silently as the woman staggered toward Tick-Tock, gagging harshly, her hands wrapped loosely around the hilt of the knife. Her hip bumped one of the standing lamps and the one called Hoots darted forward to catch it before it could fall. Tick-Tock himself never moved; he only went on sitting with his leg tossed over the arm of his throne, watching the woman with his lazy smile.

Her foot caught beneath one of the rugs and she tumbled forward. Once more the Tick-Tock Man moved with that spooky speed, pulling back the foot which had been dangling over the arm of the chair and then driving it forward again like a piston. It buried itself in the pit of the dark-haired woman's stomach and she went flying backward. Blood spewed from her mouth and splattered the furniture. She struck the wall, slid down it, and ended up sitting with her chin on her breastbone. To Jake she looked like a movie Mexican taking a siesta against an adobe wall. It was hard for him to believe she had gone from living to dead with such terrible speed. Neon tubes turned her hair into a haze that was half red and half blue. Her glazing eyes stared at the Tick-Tock Man with terminal amazement.

"I *told* her about that laugh," Tick-Tock said. His eyes shifted to the other woman, a heavyset redhead who looked like a long-haul trucker. "Didn't I, Tilly?"

"Ay," Tilly said at once. Her eyes were lustrous with fear and excitement, and she licked her lips obsessively. "So you did, many and many a time. I'll set my watch and warrant on it."

"So you might, if you could reach up your fat ass far enough to find them," Tick-Tock said. "Bring me my knife, Brandon, and mind you wipe that slut's stink off it before you put it in my hand."

A short, bandy-legged man hopped to do as he had been bidden. The knife wouldn't come free at first; it seemed caught on the unfortunate dark-haired woman's breastbone. Brandon threw a terrified glance over his shoulder at the Tick-Tock Man and then tugged harder.

Tick-Tock, however, appeared to have forgotten all about both Brandon and the woman who had literally laughed herself to death. His brilliant green eyes had fixed on something which interested him much more than the dead woman.

"Come here, cully," he said. "I want a better look at you."

Gasher gave him a shove. Jake stumbled forward. He would have fallen if Tick-Tock's strong hands hadn't caught him by the shoulders. Then, when he was sure Jake had his balance again, Tick-Tock grasped the boy's left wrist and raised it. It was Jake's Seiko which had drawn his interest.

"If this here's what I think it is, it's an omen for sure and true," Tick-Tock said. "Talk to me, boy—what's this *sigul* you wear?"

Jake, who hadn't the slightest idea what a *sigul* was, could only hope for the best. "It's a watch. But it doesn't work, Mr. Tick-Tock."

Hoots chuckled at that, then clapped both hands over his mouth when the Tick-Tock Man turned to look at him. After a moment, Tick-

Tock looked back at Jake, and a sunny smile replaced the frown. Looking at that smile almost made you forget that it was a dead woman and not a movie Mexican taking a siesta over there against the wall. Looking at it almost made you forget that these people were crazy, and the Tick-Tock Man was likely the craziest inmate in the whole asylum.

"*Watch,*" Tick-Tock said, nodding. "Ay, a likely enough name for such; after all, what does a person want with a timepiece but to watch it once in a while? Ay, Brandon? Ay, Tilly? Ay, Gasher?"

They responded with eager affirmatives. The Tick-Tock Man favored them with his winning smile, then turned back to Jake again. Now Jake noticed that the smile, winning or not, stopped well short of the Tick-Tock Man's green eyes. They were as they had been throughout: cool, cruel, and curious.

He reached a finger toward the Seiko, which now proclaimed the time to be ninety-one minutes past seven—A.M. *and* P.M.—and pulled it back just before touching the glass above the liquid crystal display. "Tell me, dear boy—is this 'watch' of yours boobyrigged?"

"Huh? Oh! No. No, it's not boobyrigged." Jake touched his own finger to the face of the watch.

"That means nothing, if it's set to the frequency of your own body," the Tick-Tock Man said. He spoke in the sharp, scornful tone Jake's father used when he didn't want people to figure out that he didn't have the slightest idea what he was talking about. Tick-Tock glanced briefly at Brandon, and Jake saw him weigh the pros and cons of making the bowlegged man his designated toucher. Then he dismissed the notion and looked back into Jake's eyes. "If this thing gives me a shock, my little friend, you're going to be choking to death on your own sweetmeats in thirty seconds."

Jake swallowed hard but said nothing. The Tick-Tock Man reached out his finger again, and this time allowed it to settle on the face of the Seiko. The moment that it did, all the numbers went to zeros and then began to count upward again.

Tick-Tock's eyes had narrowed in a grimace of potential pain as he touched the face of the watch. Now their corners crinkled in the first genuine smile Jake had seen from him. He thought it was partly pleasure at his own courage but mostly simple wonder and interest.

"May I have it?" he asked Jake silkily. "As a gesture of your goodwill, shall we say? I am something of a clock fancier, my dear young cully—so I am."

"Be my guest." Jake stripped the watch off his arm at once and dropped in onto the Tick-Tock Man's large waiting palm.

"Talks just like a little silk-arse gennelman, don't he?" Gasher said happily. "In the old days someone would have paid a wery high price for the return o' such as him, Ticky, ay, so they would. Why, my father—"

"Your father died so blowed-out-rotten with the mandrus that not even the dogs would eat him," the Tick-Tock Man interrupted. "Now shut up, you idiot."

At first Gasher looked furious . . . and then only abashed. He sank into a nearby chair and closed his mouth.

Tick-Tock, meanwhile, was examining the Seiko's expansion band with an expression of awe. He pulled it wide, let it snap back, pulled it wide again, let it snap back again. He dropped a lock of his hair into the open links, then laughed when they closed on it. At last he slipped the watch over his hand and pushed it halfway up his forearm. Jake thought this souvenir of New York looked very strange there, but said nothing.

"Wonderful!" Tick-Tock exclaimed. "Where did you get it, cully?"

"It was a birthday present from my father and mother," Jake said. Gasher leaned forward at this, perhaps wanting to mention the idea of ransom again. If so, the intent look on the Tick-Tock Man's face changed his mind and he sat back without saying anything.

"*Was* it?" Tick-Tock marvelled, raising his eyebrows. He had discovered the small button which lit the face of the watch and kept pushing it, watching the light go off and on. Then he looked back at Jake, and his eyes were narrowed to bright green slits again. "Tell me something, cully—does this run on a dipolar or unipolar circuit?"

"Neither one," Jake said, not knowing that his failure to say he did not know what either of these terms meant was buying him a great deal of future trouble. "It runs on a nickel-cadmium battery. At least I'm pretty sure it does. I've never had to replace it, and I lost the instruction folder a long time ago."

The Tick-Tock Man looked at him for a long time without speaking, and Jake realized with dismay that the blonde man was trying to decide if Jake had been making fun of him. If he decided Jake *had* been making fun, Jake had an idea that the abuse he had suffered on the way here would seem like tickling compared to what the Tick-Tock Man might do. He suddenly wanted to divert Tick-Tock's train of thought—wanted that more than anything in the world. He said the first thing he thought might turn the trick.

"He was your grandfather, wasn't he?"

The Tick-Tock Man raised his brows interrogatively. His hands returned to Jake's shoulders, and although his grip was not tight, Jake could feel the phenomenal strength there. If Tick-Tock chose to tighten his grip and pull sharply forward, he would snap Jake's collarbones like pencils. If he shoved, he would probably break his back.

"*Who* was my grandfather, cully?"

Jake's eyes once more took in the Tick-Tock Man's massive, nobly shaped head and broad shoulders. He remembered what Susannah had said: *Look at the size of him, Roland—they must have had to grease him to get him into the cockpit!*

"The man in the airplane. David Quick."

The Tick-Tock Man's eyes widened in surprise and amazement. Then he threw back his head and roared out a gust of laughter that echoed off the domed ceiling high above. The others smiled nervously. None, however, dared to laugh right out loud . . . not after what had happened to the woman with the dark hair.

"Whoever you are and wherever you come from, boy, you're the triggest cove old Tick-Tock's run into for many a year. Quick was my great-grandfather, not my grandfather, but you're close enough—wouldn't you say so, Gasher, my dear?"

"Ay," Gasher said. "He's trig, right enough, I could've toldjer that. But wery pert, all the same."

"Yes," the Tick-Tock Man said thoughtfully. His hands tightened on the boy's shoulders and drew Jake closer to that smiling, handsome, lunatic face. "I can see he's pert. It's in his eyes. But we'll take care of that, won't we, Gasher?"

It's not Gasher he's talking to, Jake thought. *It's me. He thinks he's hypnotizing me . . . and maybe he is.*

"Ay," Gasher breathed.

Jake felt he was drowning in those wide green eyes. Although the Tick-Tock Man's grip was still not really tight, he couldn't get enough breath into his lungs. He summoned all of his own force in an effort to break the blonde man's hold over him, and again spoke the first words which came to mind:

"So fell Lord Perth, and the countryside did shake with that thunder."

It acted upon Tick-Tock like a hard open-handed blow to the face. He recoiled, green eyes narrowing, his grip on Jake's shoulders tightening painfully. "*What* do you say? Where did you hear that?"

"A little bird told me," Jake replied with calculated insolence, and the next instant he was flying across the room.

If he had struck the curved wall headfirst, he would have been knocked cold or killed. As it happened, he struck on one hip, rebounded, and landed in a heap on the iron grillework. He shook his head groggily, looked around, and found himself face to face with the woman who was not taking a siesta. He uttered a shocked cry and crawled away on his hands and knees. Hoots kicked him in the chest, flipping him onto his back. Jake lay there gasping, looking up at the knot of rainbow colors where the neon tubes came together. A moment later, Tick-Tock's face filled his field of vision. The man's lips were pressed together in a hard, straight line, his cheeks flared with color, and there was fear in his eyes. The coffin-shaped glass ornament he wore around his neck dangled directly in front of Jake's eyes, swinging gently back and forth on its silver chain, as if imitating the pendulum of the tiny grandfather clock inside.

"Gasher's right," he said. He gathered a handful of Jake's shirt into one fist and pulled him up. "You're pert. But you don't want to be pert with me, cully. You don't *ever* want to be pert with me. Have you heard of people with short fuses? Well, I have no fuse at all, and there's a thousand could testify to it if I hadn't stilled their tongues for good. If you ever speak to me of Lord Perth again ... ever, ever, *ever* ... I'll tear off the top of your skull and eat your brains. I'll have none of that bad-luck story in the Cradle of the Grays. *Do you understand me?*"

He shook Jake back and forth like a rag, and the boy burst into tears.

"Do you?"

"Y-Y-Yes!"

"Good." He set Jake upon his feet, where he swayed woozily back and forth, wiping at his streaming eyes and leaving smudges of dirt on his cheeks so dark they looked like mascara. "Now, my little cull, we're going to have a question and answer session here. I'll ask the questions and you'll give the answers. Do you understand?"

Jake didn't reply. He was looking at a panel of the ventilator grille which circled the chamber.

The Tick-Tock Man grabbed his nose between two of his fingers and squeezed it viciously. *"Do you understand me?"*

"Yes!" Jake cried. His eyes, now watering with pain as well as terror, returned to Tick-Tock's face. He wanted to look back at the ventilator grille, wanted desperately to verify that what he had seen there was not simply a trick of his frightened, overloaded mind, but he didn't dare. He was afraid someone else—Tick-Tock himself, most likely—would follow his gaze and see what he had seen.

"Good." Tick-Tock pulled Jake back over to the chair by his nose, sat down, and cocked his leg over the arm again. "Let's have a nice little chin, then. We'll begin with your name, shall we? Just what might that be, cully?"

"Jake Chambers." With his nose pinched shut, his voice sounded nasal and foggy.

"And are you a Not-See, Jake Chambers?"

For a moment Jake wondered if this was a peculiar way of asking him if he was blind . . . but of course they could all see he wasn't. "I don't understand what—"

Tick-Tock shook him back and forth by the nose. "Not-See! Not-See! You just want to stop playing with me, boy!"

"*I don't understand—*" Jake began, and then he looked at the old machine-gun hanging from the chair and thought once more of the crashed Focke-Wulf. The pieces fell together in his mind. "No—I'm not a Nazi. I'm an American. All that ended long before I was born!"

The Tick-Tock Man released his hold on Jake's nose, which immediately began to gush blood. "You could have told me that in the first place and saved yourself all sorts of pain, Jake Chambers . . . but at least now you understand how we do things around here, don't you?"

Jake nodded.

"Ay. Well enough! We'll start with the simple questions."

Jake's eyes drifted back to the ventilator grille. What he had seen before was still there; it hadn't been just his imagination. Two gold-ringed eyes floated in the dark behind the chrome louvers.

Oy.

Tick-Tock slapped his face, knocking him back into Gasher, who immediately pushed him forward again. "It's school-time, dear heart," Gasher whispered. "Mind yer lessons, now! Mind em wery sharp!"

"Look at me when I'm talking to you," Tick-Tock said. "I'll have some respect, Jake Chambers, or I'll have your balls."

"All right."

Tick-Tock's green eyes gleamed dangerously. "All right *what*?"

Jake groped for the right answer, pushing away the tangle of questions and the sudden hope which had dawned in his mind. And what came was what would have served at his own Cradle of the Pubes . . . otherwise known as The Piper School. "All right, *sir*?"

Tick-Tock smiled. "That's a start, boy," he said, and leaned forward, forearms on his thighs. "Now . . . what's an American?"

Jake began to talk, trying with all his might not to look toward the ventilator grille as he did so.

29

ROLAND HOLSTERED HIS GUN, laid both hands on the valve-wheel, and tried to turn it. It wouldn't budge. That didn't much surprise him, but it presented serious problems.

Oy stood by his left boot, looking up anxiously, waiting for Roland to open the door so they could continue the journey to Jake. The gunslinger only wished it was that easy. It wouldn't do to simply stand out here and wait for someone to leave; it might be hours or even days before one of the Grays decided to use this particular exit again. Gasher and his friends might take it into their heads to flay Jake alive while the gunslinger was waiting for it to happen.

He leaned his head against the steel but heard nothing. That didn't surprise him, either. He had seen doors like this a long time ago—you couldn't shoot out the locks, and you certainly couldn't hear through them. There might be one; there might be two, facing each other, with some dead airspace in between. Somewhere, though, there would be a button which would spin the wheel in the middle of the door and release the locks. If Jake could reach that button, all might still be well.

Roland understood that he was not a full member of this *ka-tet*; he guessed that even Oy was more fully aware than he of the secret life which existed at its heart (he very much doubted that the bumbler had tracked Jake with his nose alone through those tunnels where water ran in polluted streamlets). Nevertheless, he had been able to help Jake when the boy had been trying to cross from his world to this one. He had been able to *see* . . . and when Jake had been trying to regain the key he had dropped, he had been able to send a message.

He had to be very careful about sending messages this time. At best, the Grays would realize something was up. At worst, Jake might misinterpret what Roland tried to tell him and do something foolish.

But if he could *see* . . .

Roland closed his eyes and bent all his concentration toward Jake. He thought of the boy's eyes and sent his *ka* out to find them.

At first there was nothing, but at last an image began to form. It was a face framed by long, gray-blonde hair. Green eyes gleamed in deep sockets like firedims in a cave. Roland quickly understood that this was the Tick-Tock Man, and that he was a descendent of the man who had died in the air-carriage—interesting, but of no practical value in this situation. He tried to look beyond the Tick-Tock Man, to see the rest of the room in which Jake was being held, and the people in it.

"Ake," Oy whispered, as if reminding Roland that this was neither the time nor the place to take a nap.

"Shhh," the gunslinger said, not opening his eyes.

But it was no good. He caught only blurs, probably because Jake's concentration was focused so tightly on the Tick-Tock Man; everyone and everything else was little more than a series of gray-shrouded shapes on the edges of Jake's perception.

Roland opened his eyes again and pounded his left fist lightly into the open palm of his right hand. He had an idea that he could push harder and see more . . . but that might make the boy aware of his presence. That would be dangerous. Gasher might smell a rat, and if he didn't the Tick-Tock Man would.

He looked up at the narrow ventilator grilles, then down at Oy. He had wondered several times just how smart he was; now it looked as though he was going to find out.

Roland reached up with his good left hand, slipped his fingers between the horizontal slats of the ventilator grille closest to the hatchway through which Jake had been taken, and pulled. The grille popped out in a shower of rust and dried moss. The hole behind it was far too small for a man . . . but not for a billy-bumbler. He put the grille down, picked Oy up, and spoke softly into his ear.

"Go . . . see . . . come back. Do you understand? Don't let them see you. Just go and see and come back."

Oy gazed up into his face, saying nothing, not even Jake's name. Roland had no idea if he had understood or not, but wasting time in ponderation would not help matters. He placed Oy in the ventilator shaft. The bumbler sniffed at the crumbles of dried moss, sneezed delicately, then only crouched there with the draft rippling through his long, silky fur, looking doubtfully at Roland with his strange eyes.

"Go and see and come back," Roland repeated in a whisper, and Oy disappeared into the shadows, walking silently, claws retracted, on the pads of his paws.

Roland drew his gun again and did the hardest thing. He waited.

Oy returned less than three minutes later. Roland lifted him out of the shaft and put him on the floor. Oy looked up at him with his long neck extended. "How many, Oy?" Roland asked. "How many did you see?"

For a long moment he thought the bumbler wouldn't do anything except go on staring in his anxious way. Then he lifted his right paw tentatively in the air, extended the claws, and looked at it, as if trying to remember something very difficult. At last he began to tap on the steel floor.

One . . . two . . . three . . . four. A pause. Then two more, quick and delicate, the extended claws clicking lightly on the steel: five, six. Oy paused a second time, head down, looking like a child lost in the throes of some titanic mental struggle. Then he tapped his claws one final time on the steel, looking up at Roland as he did it. "Ake!"

Six Grays . . . and Jake.

Roland picked Oy up and stroked him. "Good!" he murmured into Oy's ear. In truth, he was almost overwhelmed with surprise and gratitude. He had hoped for something, but this careful response was amazing. And he had few doubts about the accuracy of the count. "Good boy!"

"Oy! Ake!"

Yes, Jake. Jake was the problem. Jake, to whom he had made a promise he intended to keep.

The gunslinger thought deeply in his strange fashion—that combination of dry pragmatism and wild intuition which had probably come from his strange grandmother, Deidre the Mad, and had kept him alive all these years after his old companions had passed. Now he was depending on it to keep Jake alive, too.

He picked Oy up again, knowing Jake might live—*might*—but the bumbler was almost certainly going to die. He whispered several simple words into Oy's cocked ear, repeating them over and over. At last he ceased speaking and returned him to the ventilator shaft. "Good boy," he whispered. "Go on, now. Get it done. My heart goes with you."

"Oy! Art! Ake!" the bumbler whispered, and then scurried off into the darkness again.

Roland waited for all hell to break loose.

30

ASK ME A QUESTION, *Eddie Dean of New York. And it better be a good one . . . if it's not, you and your woman are going to die, no matter where you came from.*

And, dear *God*, how did you respond to something like that?

The dark red light had gone out; now the pink one reappeared. "Hurry," the faint voice of Little Blaine urged them. *"He's worse than ever before . . . hurry or he'll kill you!"*

Eddie was vaguely aware that flocks of disturbed pigeons were still swooping aimlessly through the Cradle, and that some of them had smashed headfirst into the pillars and dropped dead on the floor.

"What does it want?" Susannah hissed at the speaker and the voice of Little Blaine somewhere behind it. "For God's sake, *what does it want?*"

No reply. And Eddie could feel any period of grace they might have started with slipping away. He thumbed the TALK/LISTEN and spoke with frantic vivacity as the sweat trickled down his cheeks and neck.

Ask me a question.

"So—Blaine! What have you been up to these last few years? I guess you haven't been doing the old southeast run, huh? Any reason why not? Haven't been feeling up to snuff?"

No sound but the rustle and flap of the pigeons. In his mind he saw Ardis trying to scream as his cheeks melted and his tongue caught fire.

He felt the hair on the nape of his neck stirring and clumping together. Fear? Or gathering electricity?

Hurry ... he's worse than ever before.

"Who built you, anyway?" Eddie asked frantically, thinking: *If I only knew what the fucking thing* wanted! "Want to talk about that? Was it the Grays? Nah ... probably the Great Old Ones, right? Or ..."

He trailed off. Now he could feel Blaine's silence as a physical weight on his skin, like fleshy, groping hands.

"What do you *want*?" he shouted. "Just what in hell do you want to *hear*?"

No answer—but the buttons on the box were glowing an angry dark red again, and Eddie knew their time was almost up. He could hear a low buzzing sound nearby—a sound like an electrical generator—and he didn't believe that sound was just his imagination, no matter how much he wanted to think so.

"Blaine!" Susannah shouted suddenly. "Blaine, do you hear me?"

No answer ... and Eddie felt the air was filling up with electricity as a bowl under a tap fills up with water. He could feel it crackling bitterly in his nose with every breath he took; could feel his fillings buzzing like angry insects.

"Blaine, *I've* got a question, and it *is* a pretty good one! Listen!" She closed her eyes for a moment, fingers rubbing frantically at her temples, and then opened her eyes again. "'There is a thing that ... uh ... that nothing is, and yet it has a name; 'tis sometimes tall and ... and sometimes short ...'" She broke off and stared at Eddie with wide, agonized eyes. "Help me! I can't remember how the rest of it goes!"

Eddie only stared at her as if she had gone mad. What in the name of God was she talking about? Then it came to him, and it made a weirdly perfect sense, and the rest of the riddle clicked into his mind as neatly as the last two pieces of a jigsaw puzzle. He swung toward the speaker again.

"'It joins our talks, it joins our sport, and plays at every game.' What is it? That's our question, Blaine—what is it?"

The red light illuminating the COMMAND and ENTER buttons below the diamond of numbers blinked out. There was an endless moment of silence before Blaine spoke again ... but Eddie was aware that the feeling of electricity crawling all over his skin was diminishing.

"A SHADOW, OF COURSE," the voice of Blaine responded. "AN EASY ONE ... BUT NOT BAD. NOT BAD AT ALL."

The voice coming out of the speaker was animated by a thoughtful quality ... and something else, as well. Pleasure? Longing? Eddie couldn't quite decide, but he *did* know there was something in that voice that reminded him of Little Blaine. He knew something else, as well: Susannah had saved their bacon, at least for the time being. He bent down and kissed her cold, sweaty brow.

"DO YOU KNOW ANY MORE RIDDLES?" Blaine asked.

"Yes, lots," Susannah said at once. "Our companion, Jake, has a whole book of them."

"FROM THE NEW YORK PLACE OF WHERE?" Blaine asked, and now the tone of his voice was perfectly clear, at least to Eddie. Blaine might be a machine, but Eddie had been a heroin junkie for six years, and he knew stone greed when he heard it.

"From New York, right," he said. "But Jake has been taken prisoner. A man named Gasher took him."

No answer . . . and then the buttons glowed that faint, rosy pink again. *"Good so far,"* the voice of Little Blaine whispered. *"But you must be careful . . . he's tricky. . . ."*

The red lights reappeared at once.

"DID ONE OF YOU SPEAK?" Blaine's voice was cold and—Eddie could have sworn it was so—suspicious.

He looked at Susannah. Susannah looked back with the wide, frightened eyes of a little girl who has heard something unnameable moving slyly beneath the bed.

"I cleared my throat, Blaine," Eddie said. He swallowed and armed sweat from his forehead. "I'm . . . shit, tell the truth and shame the devil. I'm scared to death."

"THAT IS VERY WISE OF YOU. THESE RIDDLES OF WHICH YOU SPEAK—ARE THEY STUPID? I WON'T HAVE MY PATIENCE TRIED WITH STUPID RIDDLES."

"Most are smart," Susannah said, but she looked anxiously at Eddie as she said it.

"YOU LIE. YOU DON'T KNOW THE QUALITY OF THESE RIDDLES AT ALL."

"How can you say—"

"VOICE ANALYSIS. FRICTIVE PATTERNS AND DIPH-THONG STRESS-EMPHASIS PROVIDE A RELIABLE QUOTIENT OF TRUTH/UNTRUTH. PREDICTIVE RELIABILITY IS 97 PER CENT, PLUS OR MINUS .5 PER CENT." The voice fell silent for a moment, and when it spoke again, it did so in a menacing drawl that Eddie found very familiar. It was the voice of Humphrey Bogart. "I SHUGGEST YOU SHTICK TO WHAT YOU KNOW, SHWEET-HEART. THE LAST GUY THAT TRIED SHADING THE TRUTH WITH ME WOUND UP AT THE BOTTOM OF THE SEND IN A PAIR OF SHEMENT COWBOY BOOTS."

"Christ," Eddie said. "We walked four hundred miles or so to meet the computer version of Rich Little. How can you imitate guys like John Wayne and Humphrey Bogart, Blaine? Guys from our world?"

Nothing.

"Okay, you don't want to answer that one. How about this one—if a riddle was what you wanted, why didn't you just say so?"

Again there was no answer, but Eddie discovered that he didn't really need one. Blaine liked riddles, so he had asked *them* one. Susannah had solved it. Eddie guessed that if she had failed to do so, the two of them would now look like a couple of giant-economy-size charcoal briquets lying on the floor of the Cradle of Lud.

"Blaine?" Susannah asked uneasily. There was no answer. "Blaine, are you still there?"

"YES. TELL ME ANOTHER ONE."

"When is a door not a door?" Eddie asked.

"WHEN IT'S AJAR. YOU'LL HAVE TO DO BETTER THAN THAT IF YOU REALLY EXPECT ME TO TAKE YOU SOMEWHERE. *CAN* YOU DO BETTER THAN THAT?"

"If Roland gets here, I'm sure we can," Susannah said. "Regardless of how good the riddles in Jake's book may be, Roland knows hundreds— he actually studied them as a child." Having said this, she realized she could not conceive of Roland as a child. "*Will* you take us, Blaine?"

"I MIGHT," Blaine said, and Eddie was quite sure he heard a dim thread of cruelty running through that voice. "BUT YOU'LL HAVE TO PRIME THE PUMP TO GET ME GOING, AND MY PUMP PRIMES BACKWARD."

"Meaning what?" Eddie asked, looking through the bars at the smooth pink line of Blaine's back. But Blaine did not reply to this or any of the other questions they asked. The bright orange lights stayed on, but both Big Blaine and Little Blaine seemed to have gone into hibernation. Eddie, however, knew better. Blaine was awake. Blaine was watching them. Blaine was listening to their frictive patterns and diphthong stress-emphasis.

He looked at Susannah.

" 'You'll have to prime the pump, but my pump primes backward,' " he said bleakly. "It's a riddle, isn't it?"

"Yes, of course." She looked at the triangular window, so like a half-lidded, mocking eye, and then pulled him close so she could whisper in his ear. "It's totally insane, Eddie—schizophrenic, paranoid, probably delusional as well."

"Tell me about it," he breathed back. "What we've got here is a lunatic genius ghost-in-the-computer monorail that likes riddles and goes faster than the speed of sound. Welcome to the fantasy version of *One Flew Over the Cuckoo's Nest.*"

"Do you have any idea what the answer is?"

Eddie shook his head. "You?"

"A little tickle, way back in my mind. False light, probably. I keep thinking about what Roland said: a good riddle is always sensible and always solvable. It's like a magician's trick."

"Misdirection."

She nodded. "Go fire another shot, Eddie—let em know we're still here."

"Yeah. Now if we could only be sure that they're still there."

"Do you think they are, Eddie?"

Eddie had started away, and he spoke without stopping or looking back. "I don't know—that's a riddle not even Blaine could answer."

31

"COULD I HAVE SOMETHING to drink?" Jake asked. His voice came out sounding furry and nasal. Both his mouth and the tissues in his abused nose were swelling up. He looked like someone who has gotten the worst of it in a nasty street-fight.

"Oh, yes," Tick-Tock replied judiciously. "You *could.* I'd say you certainly *could.* We have lots to drink, don't we, Copperhead?"

"Ay," said a tall, bespectacled man in a white silk shirt and a pair of black silk trousers. He looked like a college professor in a turn-of-the-century *Punch* cartoon. "No shortage of po-ter-bulls here."

The Tick-Tock Man, once more seated at ease in his throne-like chair, looked humorously at Jake. "We have wine, beer, ale, and, of course, good old water. Sometimes that's all a body wants, isn't it? Cool, clear, sparkling water. How does that sound, cully?"

Jake's throat, which was also swollen and as dry as sandpaper, prickled painfully. "Sounds good," he whispered.

"It's woke *my* thirsty up, I know that," Tick-Tock said. His lips spread in a smile. His green eyes sparkled. "Bring me a dipper of water, Tilly—I'll be damned if I know what's happened to my manners."

Tilly stepped through the hatchway on the far side of the room—it was opposite the one through which Jake and Gasher had entered. Jake watched her go and licked his swollen lips.

"Now," Tick-Tock said, returning his gaze to Jake, "you say the American city you came from—this New York—is much like Lud."

"Well . . . not exactly . . ."

"But you *do* recognize some of the machinery," Tick-Tock pressed. "Valves and pumps and such. Not to mention the firedim tubes."

"Yes. We call it neon, but it's the same."

Tick-Tock reached out toward him. Jake cringed, but Tick-Tock only patted him on the shoulder. "Yes, yes; close enough." His eyes gleamed. "*And* you've heard of computers?"

"Sure, but—"

Tilly returned with the dipper and timidly approached the Tick-Tock Man's throne. He took it and held it out to Jake. When Jake reached for it, Tick-Tock pulled it back and drank himself. As Jake watched the water trickle from Tick-Tock's mouth and roll down his naked chest, he began to shake. He couldn't help it.

The Tick-Tock Man looked over the dipper at him, as if just remembering that Jake was still there. Behind him, Gasher, Copperhead, Brandon, and Hoots were grinning like schoolyard kids who have just heard an amusing dirty joke.

"Why, I got thinking about how thirsty *I* was and forgot all about *you!*" Tick-Tock cried. "That's mean as hell, gods damn my eyes! But, of course, it looked so good . . . and it *is* good . . . cold . . . clear . . ."

He held the dipper out to Jake. When Jake reached for it, Tick-Tock pulled it back.

"First, cully, tell me what you know about dipolar computers and transitive circuits," he said coldly.

"What . . ." Jake looked toward the ventilator grille, but the golden eyes were still gone. He was beginning to think he had imagined them after all. He shifted his gaze back to the Tick-Tock Man, understanding one thing clearly: he wasn't going to get any water. He had been stupid to even dream he might. "What are dipolar computers?"

The Tick-Tock Man's face contorted with rage; he threw the remainder of the water into Jake's bruised, puffy face. "*Don't you play it light with me!*" he shrieked. He stripped off the Seiko watch and shook it in front of Jake. "*When I asked you if this ran on a dipolar circuit, you said it didn't! So don't tell me you don't know what I'm talking about when you already made it clear that you do!*"

"But . . . but . . ." Jake couldn't go on. His head was whirling with fear and confusion. He was aware, in some far-off fashion, that he was licking as much water as he could off his lips.

"*There's a thousand of those ever-fucking dipolar computers right under the ever-fucking city, maybe a HUNDRED thousand, and the only one that still works don't do a thing except play Watch Me and run those drums! I want those computers! I want them working for ME!*"

The Tick-Tock Man bolted forward on his throne, seized Jake, shook him back and forth, and then threw him to the floor. Jake struck one of the lamps, knocking it over, and the bulb blew with a hollow coughing sound. Tilly gave a little shriek and stepped backward, her eyes wide and frightened. Copperhead and Brandon looked at each other uneasily.

Tick-Tock leaned forward, elbows on his thighs, and screamed into Jake's face: *"I want them AND I MEAN TO HAVE THEM!"*

Silence fell in the room, broken only by the soft whoosh of warm air pouring from the ventilators. Then the twisted rage on the Tick-Tock Man's face disappeared so suddenly it might never have existed at all. It was replaced by another charming smile. He leaned further forward and helped Jake to his feet.

"Sorry. I get thinking about the potential of this place and sometimes I get carried away. Please accept my apology, cully." He picked up the overturned dipper and threw it at Tilly. "Fill this up, you useless bitch! What's the matter with you?"

He turned his attention back to Jake, still smiling his TV game-show host smile.

"All right; you've had your little joke and I've had mine. Now tell me everything you know about dipolar computers and transitive circuits. Then you can have a drink."

Jake opened his mouth to say something—he had no idea what— and then, incredibly, Roland's voice was in his mind, filling it.

Distract them, Jake—and if there's a button that opens the door, get close to it.

The Tick-Tock Man was watching him closely. "Something just came into your mind, didn't it, cully? I always know. So don't keep it a secret; tell your old friend Ticky."

Jake caught movement in the corner of his eye. Although he did not dare glance up at the ventilator panel—not with all the Tick-Tock Man's notice bent upon him—he knew that Oy was back, peering down through the louvers.

Distract them . . . and suddenly Jake knew just how to do that.

"I *did* think of something," he said, "but it wasn't about computers. It was about my old pal Gasher. And *his* old pal, Hoots."

"Here! Here!" Gasher cried. "What are you talking about, boy?"

"Why don't you tell Tick-Tock who *really* gave you the password, Gasher? Then *I* can tell Tick-Tock where you keep it."

The Tick-Tock Man's puzzled gaze shifted from Jake to Gasher. "What's he talking about?"

"Nothin!" Gasher said, but he could not forbear a quick glance at Hoots. "He's just runnin his gob, tryin to get off the hot-seat by puttin me on it, Ticky. I told you he was pert! Didn't I say—"

"Take a look in his scarf, why don't you?" Jake asked. "He's got a scrap of paper with the word written on it. I had to read it to him because he couldn't even do that."

There was no sudden rage on Tick-Tock's part this time; his face darkened gradually instead, like a summer sky before a terrible thunderstorm.

"Let me see your scarf, Gasher," he said in a soft, thick voice. "Let your old pal sneak a peek."

"He's lyin, I tell you!" Gasher cried, putting his hands on his scarf and taking two steps backward toward the wall. Directly above him, Oy's gold-ringed eyes gleamed. "All you got to do is look in his face to see lyin's what a pert little cull like him does best!"

The Tick-Tock Man shifted his gaze to Hoots, who looked sick with fear. "What about it?" Tick-Tock asked in his soft, terrible voice. "What about it, Hooterman? I know you and Gasher was butt-buddies of old, and I know you've the brains of a hung goose, but surely not even you could be stupid enough to write down a password to the inner chamber . . . could you? *Could* you?"

"I . . . I oney thought . . ." Hoots began.

"Shut up!" Gasher shouted. He shot Jake a look of pure, sick hate. "I'll kill you for this, dearie—see if I don't."

"Take off your scarf, Gasher," the Tick-Tock Man said. "I want a look inside it."

Jake sidled a step closer to the podium with the buttons on it.

"No!" Gasher's hands returned to the scarf and pressed against it as if it might fly away of its own accord. "Be damned if I will!"

"Brandon, grab him," Tick-Tock said.

Brandon lunged for Gasher. Gasher's move wasn't as quick as Tick-Tock's had been, but it was quick enough; he bent, yanked a knife from the top of his boot, and buried it in Brandon's arm.

"*Oh, you barstard!*" Brandon shouted in surprise and pain as blood began to pour out of his arm.

"*Lookit what you did!*" Tilly screamed.

"Do I have to do *everything* around here myself?" Tick-Tock shouted, more exasperated than angry, it seemed, and rose to his feet. Gasher retreated from him, weaving the bloody knife back and forth in front of his face in mystic patterns. He kept his other hand planted firmly on top of his head.

"Draw back," he panted. "I loves you like a brother, Ticky, but if you don't draw back, I'll hide this blade in your guts—so I will."

"*You?* Not likely," the Tick-Tock Man said with a laugh. He removed his own knife from its scabbard and held it delicately by the bone hilt. All eyes were on the two of them. Jake took two quick steps to the podium with its little cluster of buttons and reached for the one he thought the Tick-Tock man had pushed.

Gasher was backing along the curved wall, the tubes of light painting his mandrus-riddled face in a succession of sick colors: bile-green, fever-red, jaundice-yellow. Now it was the Tick-Tock Man standing below the ventilator grille where Oy was watching.

"Put it down, Gasher," Tick-Tock said in a reasonable tone of voice. "You brought the boy as I asked; if anyone else gets pricked over this, it'll be Hoots, not you. Just show me—"

Jake saw Oy crouching to spring and understood two things: what the bumbler meant to do and who had put him up to it.

"*Oy, no!*" he screamed.

All of them turned to look at him. At that moment Oy leaped, hitting the flimsy ventilator grille and knocking it free. The Tick-Tock Man wheeled toward the sound, and Oy fell onto his upturned face, biting and slashing.

32

ROLAND HEARD IT FAINTLY even through the twin doors—*Oy, no!*—and his heart sank. He waited for the valve-wheel to turn, but it did not. He closed his eyes and sent with all his might: *The door, Jake! Open the door!*

He sensed no response, and the pictures were gone. His communication line with Jake, flimsy to begin with, had now been severed.

33

THE TICK-TOCK MAN blundered backward, cursing and screaming and grabbing at the writhing, biting, digging thing on his face. He felt Oy's claws punch into his left eye, popping it, and a horrible red pain sank into his head like a flaming torch thrown down a deep well. At that point, rage overwhelmed pain. He seized Oy, tore him off his face, and held him over his head, meaning to twist him like a rag.

"*No!*" Jake wailed. He forgot about the button which unlocked the doors and seized the gun hanging from the back of the chair.

Tilly shrieked. The others scattered. Jake levelled the old German machine-gun at the Tick-Tock Man. Oy, upside down in those huge, strong hands and bent almost to the snapping point, writhed madly and slashed his teeth into the air. He shrieked in agony—a horribly human sound.

"Leave him alone, you bastard!" Jake screamed, and pressed the trigger.

He had enough presence of mind left to aim low. The roar of the Schmeisser .40 was ear-splitting in the enclosed space, although it fired only five or six rounds. One of the lighted tubes popped in a burst of cold orange fire. A hole appeared an inch above the left knee of the Tick-Tock Man's tight-fitting trousers, and a dark red stain began to spread at once. Tick-Tock's mouth opened in a shocked O of surprise, an expression which said more clearly than words could have done that, for all his intelligence, Tick-Tock had expected to live a long, happy life where he shot people but was never shot himself. Shot *at*, perhaps, but actually hit? That surprised expression said that just wasn't supposed to be in the cards.

Welcome to the real world, you fuck, Jake thought.

Tick-Tock dropped Oy to the iron grillework floor to grab at his wounded leg. Copperhead lunged at Jake, got an arm around his throat, and then Oy was on him, barking shrilly and chewing at Copperhead's ankle through the black silk pants. Copperhead screamed and danced away, shaking Oy back and forth at the end of his leg. Oy clung like a limpet. Jake turned to see the Tick-Tock Man crawling toward him. He had retrieved his knife and the blade was now clamped between his teeth.

"Goodbye, Ticky," Jake said, and pressed the Schmeisser's trigger again. Nothing happened. Jake didn't know if it was empty or jammed, and this was hardly the time to speculate. He took two steps backward before finding further retreat blocked by the big chair which had served the Tick-Tock Man as a throne. Before he could slip around, putting the chair between them, Tick-Tock had grabbed his ankle. His other hand went to the hilt of his knife. The ruins of his left eye lay on his cheek like a glob of mint jelly; the right eye glared up at Jake with insane hatred.

Jake tried to pull away from the clutching hand and went sprawling on the Tick-Tock man's throne. His eye fell on a pocket which had been sewn into the right-hand arm-rest. Jutting from the elasticized top was the cracked pearl handle of a revolver.

"Oh, cully, how you'll suffer!" the Tick-Tock Man whispered ecstatically. The O of surprise had been replaced by a wide, trembling grin. "Oh how you'll suffer! And how happy I'll be to . . . *What—?*"

The grin slackened and the surprised O began to reappear as Jake pointed the cheesy nickel-plated revolver at him and thumbed back the hammer. The grip on Jake's ankle tightened until it seemed to him that the bones there must snap.

"You *dasn't!*" Tick-Tock said in a screamy whisper.

"Yes I *do*," Jake said grimly, and pulled the trigger of the Tick-Tock Man's runout gun. There was a flat crack, much less dramatic than the Schmeisser's Teutonic roar. A small black hole appeared high up on the right side of Tick-Tock's forehead. The Tick-Tock Man went on staring up at Jake, disbelief in his remaining eye.

Jake tried to make himself shoot him again and couldn't do it.

Suddenly a flap of the Tick-Tock Man's scalp peeled away like old wallpaper and dropped on his right cheek. Roland would have known what this meant; Jake, however, was now almost beyond coherent thought. A dark, panicky horror was spinning across his mind like a tornado funnel. He cringed back in the big chair as the hand on his ankle fell away and the Tick-Tock Man collapsed forward on his face.

The door. He had to open the door and let the gunslinger in.

Focusing on that and nothing but, Jake let the pearl-handled revolver clatter to the iron grating and pushed himself out of the chair. He was reaching again for the button he thought he had seen Tick-Tock push when a pair of hands settled around his throat and dragged him backward, away from the podium.

"I said I'd kill you for it, my narsty little pal," a voice whispered in his ear, "and the Gasherman always keeps his promises."

Jake flailed behind him with both hands and found nothing but thin air. Gasher's fingers sank into his throat, choking relentlessly. The world started to turn gray in front of his eyes. Gray quickly deepened to purple, and purple to black.

34

A PUMP STARTED UP, and the valve-wheel in the center of the hatch spun rapidly. *Gods be thanked!* Roland thought. He seized the wheel with his right hand almost before it had stopped moving and yanked it open. The other door was ajar; from beyond it came the sounds of men fighting and Oy's bark, now shrill with pain and fury.

Roland kicked the door open with his boot and saw Gasher throttling Jake. Oy had left Copperhead and was now trying to make Gasher let go of Jake, but Gasher's boot was doing double duty: protecting its owner from the bumbler's teeth, and protecting Oy from the virulent infection which ran in Gasher's blood. Brandon stabbed Oy in the flank again in an effort to make him stop worrying Gasher's ankle, but Oy paid no heed. Jake hung from his captor's dirty hands like a puppet whose strings have been cut. His face was bluish-white, his swollen lips a delicate shade of lavender.

Gasher looked up. "*You*," he snarled.

"Me," Roland agreed. He fired once and the left side of Gasher's head disintegrated. The man went flying backward, bloodstained yellow scarf unravelling, and landed on top of the Tick-Tock Man. His feet drummed spastically on the iron grillework for a moment and then fell still.

The gunslinger shot Brandon twice, fanning the hammer of his revolver with the flat of his right hand. Brandon, who had been bent over Oy for another stroke, spun around, struck the wall, and slid slowly down it, clutching at one of the tubes. Green swamplight spilled out from between his loosening fingers.

Oy limped to where Jake lay and began licking his pale, still face.

Copperhead and Hoots had seen enough. They ran side by side for the small door through which Tilly had gone to get the dipper of water. It was the wrong time for chivalry; Roland shot them both in the back. He would have to move fast now, very fast indeed, and he would not risk being waylaid by these two if they should chance to rediscover their guts.

A cluster of bright orange lights came on at the top of the capsule-shaped enclosure, and an alarm began to go off: in broad, hoarse blats that battered the walls. After a moment or two, the emergency lights began to pulse in sync with the alarm.

35

EDDIE WAS RETURNING TO Susannah when the alarm began to wail. He yelled in surprise and raised the Ruger, pointing it at nothing. *"What's happening?"*

Susannah shook her head—she had no idea. The alarm was scary, but that was only part of the problem; it was also loud enough to be physically painful. Those amplified jags of sound made Eddie think of a tractor-trailer horn raised to the tenth power.

At that moment, the orange arc-sodiums began to pulse. When he reached Susannah's chair, Eddie saw that the COMMAND and ENTER buttons were also pulsing in bright red beats. They looked like winking eyes.

"Blaine, what's happening?" he shouted. He looked around but saw only wildly jumping shadows. "Are you doing this?"

Blaine's only response was laughter—terrible mechanical laughter that made Eddie think of the clockwork clown that had stood outside the House of Horrors at Coney Island when he was a little kid.

"Blaine, stop it!" Susannah shrieked. *"How can we think of an answer to your riddle with that air-raid siren going off?"*

The laughter stopped as suddenly as it began, but Blaine made no reply. Or perhaps he did; from beyond the bars that separated them from the platform, huge engines powered by frictionless slo-trans turbines awoke at the command of the dipolar computers the Tick-Tock Man had so lusted after. For the first time in a decade, Blaine the Mono was awake and cycling up toward running speed.

36

THE ALARM, WHICH HAD indeed been built to warn Lud's long-dead residents of an impending air attack (and which had not even been tested in almost a thousand years), blanketed the city with sound. All the lights which still operated came on and began to pulse in sync. Pubes above the streets and Grays below them were alike convinced that the end they had always feared was finally upon them. The Grays suspected some cataclysmic mechanical breakdown was occurring. The Pubes, who had always believed that the ghosts lurking in the machines below the city would some day rise up to take their long-delayed vengeance on the still living, were probably closer to the actual truth of what was happening.

Certainly there had been an intelligence left in the ancient computers below the city, a single living organism which had long ago ceased to exist sanely under conditions that, within its merciless dipolar circuits, could only be absolute reality. It had held its increasingly alien logic within its banks of memory for eight hundred years and might have held them so for eight hundred more, if not for the arrival of Roland and his friends; yet this *mens non corpus* had brooded and grown ever more insane with each passing year; even in its increasing periods of sleep it could be said to dream, and these dreams grew steadily more abnormal as the world moved on. Now, although the unthinkable machinery which maintained the Beams had weakened, this insane and inhuman intelligence had awakened in the rooms of ruin and had begun once more, although as bodiless as any ghost, to stumble through the halls of the dead.

In other words, Blaine the Mono was preparing to get out of Dodge.

37

ROLAND HEARD A FOOTSTEP behind him as he knelt by Jake and turned, raising his gun. Tilly, her dough-colored face a mask of confusion and superstitious fear, raised her hands and shrieked: *"Don't kill me, sai! Please! Don't kill me!"*

"Run, then," Roland said curtly, and as Tilly began to move, he struck her calf with the barrel of his revolver. "Not that way—through the door I came in. And if you ever see me again, I'll be the last thing you ever see. Now *go!*"

She disappeared into the leaping, circling shadows.

Roland dropped his head to Jake's chest, slamming his palm against his other ear to deaden the pulse of the alarm. He heard the boy's heartbeat, slow but strong. He slipped his arms around the boy, and as he did, Jakes's eyes fluttered open. "You didn't let me fall this time." His voice was no more than a hoarse whisper.

"No. Not this time, and not ever again. Don't try your voice."

"Where's Oy?"

"Oy!" the bumbler barked. *"Oy!"*

Brandon had slashed Oy several times, but none of the wounds seemed mortal or even serious. It was clear that he was in some pain, but it was equally clear he was transported with joy. He regarded Jake with sparkling eyes, his pink tongue lolling out. "Ake, Ake, *Ake!*"

Jake burst into tears and reached for him; Oy limped into the circle of his arms and allowed himself to be hugged for a moment.

Roland got up and looked around. His gaze fixed on the door on the far side of the room. The two men he'd backshot had been heading in that direction, and the woman had also wanted to go that way. The gunslinger went toward the door with Jake in his arms and Oy at his heel. He kicked one of the dead Grays aside, and ducked through. The room beyond was a kitchen. It managed to look like a hog-wallow in spite of the built-in appliances and the stainless steel walls; the Grays were apparently not much interested in housekeeping.

"Drink," Jake whispered. "Please . . . so thirsty."

Roland felt a queer doubling, as if time had folded backward on itself. He remembered lurching out of the desert, crazy with the heat and the emptiness. He remembered passing out in the stable of the way station, half-dead from thirst, and waking at the taste of cool water trickling down his throat. The boy had taken off his shirt, soaked it under the flow from the pump, and given him to drink. Now it was his turn to do for Jake what Jake had already done for him.

Roland glanced around and saw a sink. He went over to it and turned on the faucet. Cold, clear water rushed out. Over them, around them, under them, the alarm roared on and on.

"Can you stand?"

Jake nodded. "I think so."

Roland set the boy on his feet, ready to catch him if he looked too wobbly, but Jake hung onto the sink, then ducked his head beneath the flowing water. Roland picked Oy up and looked at his wounds. They

were already clotting. *You got off very lucky, my furry friend,* Roland thought, then reached past Jake to cup a palmful of water for the animal. Oy drank it eagerly.

Jake drew back from the faucet with his hair plastered to the sides of his face. His skin was still too pale and the signs that he had been badly beaten were clearly visible, but he looked better than he had when Roland had first bent over him. For one terrible moment, the gunslinger had been positive Jake was dead.

He found himself wishing he could go back and kill Gasher again, and that led him to another thought.

"What about the one Gasher called the Tick-Tock Man? Did you see him, Jake?"

"Yes. Oy ambushed him. Tore up his face. Then I shot him."

"Dead?"

Jake's lips began to tremble. He pressed them firmly together. "Yes. In his . . ." He tapped his forehead high above his right eyebrow. "I was l-l- . . . I was lucky."

Roland looked at him appraisingly, then slowly shook his head. "You know, I doubt that. But never mind now. Come on."

"Where are we going?" Jake's voice was still little more than a husky murmur, and he kept looking past Roland's shoulder toward the room where he had almost died.

Roland pointed across the kitchen. Beyond another hatchway, the corridor continued. "That'll do for a start."

"GUNSLINGER," a voice boomed from everywhere.

Roland wheeled around, one arm cradling Oy and the other around Jake's shoulders, but there was no one to see.

"Who speaks to me?" he shouted.

"NAME YOURSELF, GUNSLINGER."

"Roland of Gilead, son of Steven. Who speaks to me?"

"GILEAD IS NO MORE," the voice mused, ignoring the question.

Roland looked up and saw patterns of concentric rings in the ceiling. The voice was coming from those.

"NO GUNSLINGER HAS WALKED IN-WORLD OR MID-WORLD FOR ALMOST THREE HUNDRED YEARS."

"I and my friends are the last."

Jake took Oy from Roland. The bumbler at once began to lick the boy's swollen face; his gold-ringed eyes were full of adoration and happiness.

"It's Blaine," Jake whispered to Roland. "Isn't it?"

Roland nodded. Of course it was—but he had an idea that there was a great deal more to Blaine than just a monorail train.

"BOY! ARE YOU JAKE OF NEW YORK?"

Jake pressed closer to Roland and looked up at the speakers. "Yes," he said. "That's me. Jake of New York. Uh . . . son of Elmer."

"DO YOU STILL HAVE THE BOOK OF RIDDLES? THE ONE OF WHICH I HAVE BEEN TOLD?"

Jake reached over his shoulder, and an expression of dismayed recollection filled his face as his fingers touched nothing but his own back. When he looked at Roland again, the gunslinger was holding his pack out toward him, and although the man's narrow, finely carved face was as expressionless as ever, Jake sensed the ghost of a smile lurking at the corners of his mouth.

"You'll have to fix the straps," Roland said as Jake took the pack. "I made them longer."

"But *Riddle-De-Dum!*—?"

Roland nodded. "Both books are still in there."

"WHAT YOU GOT, LITTLE PILGRIM?" the voice inquired in a leisurely drawl.

"Cripes!" Jake said.

It can see us as well as hear us, Roland thought, and a moment later he spotted a small glass eye in one corner, far above a man's normal line of sight. He felt a chill slip over his skin, and knew from both the troubled look on Jake's face and the way the boy's arms had tightened around Oy that he wasn't alone in his unease. That voice belonged to a machine, an incredibly *smart* machine, a *playful* machine, but there was something very wrong with it, all the same.

"The book," Jake said. "I've got the riddle book."

"GOOD." There was an almost human satisfaction in the voice. "REALLY EXCELLENT."

A scruffy, bearded fellow suddenly appeared in the doorway on the far side of the kitchen. A bloodstained, dirt-streaked yellow scarf flapped from the newcomer's upper arm. "Fires in the walls!" he screamed. In his panic, he seemed not to realize that Roland and Jake were not part of his miserable subterranean *ka-tet*. "Smoke on the lower levels! People killin theirselves! Somepin's gone wrong! Hell, *everythin's* gone wrong! We gotta—"

The door of the oven suddenly dropped open like an unhinged jaw. A thick beam of blue-white fire shot out and engulfed the scruffy man's head. He was driven backward with his clothes in flames and his skin boiling on his face.

Jake stared up at Roland, stunned and horrified. Roland put an arm about the boy's shoulders.

"HE INTERRUPTED ME," the voice said. "THAT WAS RUDE, WASN'T IT?"

"Yes," Roland said calmly. "Extremely rude."

"SUSANNAH OF NEW YORK SAYS YOU HAVE A GREAT MANY RIDDLES BY HEART, ROLAND OF GILEAD. IS THIS TRUE?"

"Yes."

There was an explosion in one of the rooms opening off this arm of the corridor; the floor shuddered beneath their feet and voices screamed in a jagged chorus. The pulsing lights and the endless, blatting siren faded momentarily, then came back strong. A little skein of bitter, acrid smoke drifted from the ventilators. Oy got a whiff and sneezed.

"TELL ME ONE OF YOUR RIDDLES, GUNSLINGER," the voice invited. It was serene and untroubled, as if they were all sitting together in a peaceful village square somewhere instead of beneath a city that seemed on the verge of ripping itself apart.

Roland thought for a moment, and what came to mind was Cuthbert's favorite riddle. "All right, Blaine," he said, "I will. What's better than all the gods and worse than Old Man Splitfoot? Dead people eat it always; live people who eat it die slow."

There was a long pause. Jake put his face in Oy's fur to try to get away from the stink of the roasted Gray.

"Be careful, gunslinger." The voice was as small as a cool puff of breeze on summer's hottest day. The voice of the machine had come from all the speakers, but this one came only from the speaker directly overhead. *"Be careful, Jake of New York. Remember that these are The Drawers. Go slow and be very careful."*

Jake looked at the gunslinger with widening eyes. Roland gave his head a small, faint shake and raised one finger. He looked as if he was scratching the side of his nose, but that finger also lay across his lips, and Jake had an idea Roland was actually telling him to keep his mouth shut.

"A CLEVER RIDDLE," Blaine said at last. There seemed to be real admiration in its voice. "THE ANSWER IS NOTHING, IS IT NOT?"

"That's right," Roland said. "You're pretty clever yourself, Blaine."

When the voice spoke again, Roland heard what Eddie had heard already: a deep and ungovernable greed. "ASK ME ANOTHER."

Roland drew a deep breath. "Not just now."

"I HOPE YOU ARE NOT REFUSING ME, ROLAND, SON OF STEVEN, FOR THAT IS ALSO RUDE. *EXTREMELY* RUDE."

"Take us to our friends and help us get out of Lud," Roland said. "Then there may be time for riddling."

"I COULD KILL YOU WHERE YOU STAND," the voice said, and now it was as cold as winter's darkest day.

"Yes," Roland said. "I'm sure you could. But the riddles would die with us."

"I COULD TAKE THE BOY'S BOOK."

"Thieving is ruder than either refusal or interruption," Roland remarked. He spoke as if merely passing the time of day, but the remaining fingers of his right hand were tight on Jake's shoulder.

"Besides," Jake said, looking up at the speaker in the ceiling, "the answers aren't in the book. Those pages were torn out." In a flash of inspiration, he tapped his temple. "They're up here, though."

"YOU FELLOWS WANT TO REMEMBER THAT NOBODY LOVES A SMARTASS," Blaine said. There was another explosion, this one louder and closer. One of the ventilator grilles blew off and shot across the kitchen like a projectile. A moment later two men and a woman emerged through the door which led to the rest of the Grays' warren. The gunslinger levelled his revolver at them, then lowered it as they stumbled across the kitchen and into the silo beyond without so much as a look at Roland and Jake. To Roland they looked like animals fleeing before a forest fire.

A stainless steel panel in the ceiling slid open, revealing a square of darkness. Something silvery flashed within it, and a few moments later a steel sphere, perhaps a foot in diameter, dropped from the hole and hung in the air of the kitchen.

"FOLLOW," Blaine said flatly.

"Will it take us to Eddie and Susannah?" Jake asked hopefully.

Blaine replied only with silence . . . but when the sphere began floating down the corridor, Roland and Jake followed it.

38

JAKE HAD NO CLEAR memory of the time which followed, and that was probably merciful. He had left his world over a year before nine hundred people would commit suicide together in a small South American country called Gyana, but he knew about the periodic death-rushes of the lemmings, and what was happening in the disintegrating undercity of the Grays was like that.

There were explosions, some on their level but most far below them; acrid smoke occasionally drifted from the ventilator grilles, but most of the air-purifiers were still working and they whipped the worst of it away before it could gather in choking clouds. They saw no fires. Yet the Grays were reacting as if the time of the apocalypse had come. Most only fled, their faces blank O's of panic, but many had committed suicide in the halls and interconnected rooms through which the steel sphere led Roland and Jake. Some had shot themselves; many more had slashed their throats or wrists; a few appeared to have swallowed poison. On all the faces of the dead was the same expression of overmastering terror. Jake could only vaguely understand what had driven them to this. Roland had a better idea of what had happened to them—to their *minds*—when the long-dead city first came to life around them and then seemed to commence tearing itself apart. And it was Roland who understood that Blaine was doing it on purpose. That Blaine was driving them to it.

They ducked around a man hanging from an overhead heating-duct and pounded down a flight of steel stairs behind the floating steel ball.

"Jake!" Roland shouted. "You never let me in at all, did you?"

Jake shook his head.

"I didn't think so. It was Blaine."

They reached the bottom of the stairs and hurried along a narrow corridor toward a hatch with the words ABSOLUTELY NO ADMITTANCE printed on it in the spiked letters of the High Speech.

"*Is* it Blaine?" Jake asked.

"Yes—that's as good a name as any."

"What about the other v—"

"Hush!" Roland said grimly.

The steel ball paused in front of the hatchway. The wheel spun and the hatch popped ajar. Roland pulled it open, and they stepped into a huge underground room which stretched away in three directions as far as they could see. It was filled with seemingly endless aisles of control panels and electronic equipment. Most of the panels were still dark and dead, but as Jake and Roland stood inside the door, looking about with wide eyes, they could see pilot-lights coming on and hear machinery cycling up.

"The Tick-Tock Man said there were thousands of computers," Jake said. "I guess he was right. My God, look!"

Roland did not understand the word Jake had used and so said nothing. He only watched as row after row of panels lit up. A cloud of sparks and a momentary tongue of green fire jumped from one of the consoles as some ancient piece of equipment malfunctioned.

Most of the machinery, however, appeared to be up and running just fine. Needles which hadn't moved in centuries suddenly jumped into the green. Huge aluminum cylinders spun, spilling data stored on silicon chips into memory banks which were once more wide awake and ready for input. Digital displays, indicating everything from the mean aquifer water-pressure in the West River Barony to available power amperage in the hibernating Send Basin Nuclear Plant, lit up in brilliant dot-matrices of red and green. Overhead, banks of hanging globes began to flash on, radiating outward in spokes of light. And from below, above, and around them—from everywhere—came the deep bass hum of generators and slo-trans engines awakening from their long sleep.

Jake had begun to flag badly. Roland swept him into his arms again and chased the steel ball past machines at whose function and intent he could not even guess. Oy ran at his heels. The ball banked left, and the aisle in which they now found themselves ran between banks of TV monitors, thousands of them, stacked in rows like a child's building blocks.

My dad would love it, Jake thought.

Some sections of this vast video arcade were still dark, but many of the screens were on. They showed a city in chaos, both above and below. Clumps of Pubes surged pointlessly through the streets, eyes wide, mouths moving soundlessly. Many were leaping from the tall buildings. Jake observed with horror that hundreds more had congregated at the Send Bridge and were throwing themselves into the river. Other screens showed large, cot-filled rooms like dormitories. Some of these rooms were on fire, but the panic-stricken Grays seemed to be setting the fires themselves—torching their own mattresses and furniture for God alone knew what reason.

One screen showed a barrel-chested giant tossing men and women into what looked like a blood-spattered stamping press. This was bad enough, but there was something worse: the victims were standing in an unguarded line, docilely waiting their turns. The executioner, his yellow scarf pulled tight over his skull and the knotted ends swinging below his ears like pigtails, seized an old woman and held her up, waiting patiently for the stainless steel block of metal to clear the killing floor so he could toss her in. The old woman did not struggle; seemed, in fact, to be *smiling*.

"IN THE ROOMS THE PEOPLE COME AND GO," Blaine said, "BUT I DON'T THINK ANY OF THEM ARE TALKING OF MICHELANGELO." He suddenly laughed—strange, tittery laughter that sounded like rats scampering over broken glass. The sound sent chills chasing up Jake's neck. He wanted nothing at all to do with an intelligence that laughed like that . . . but what choice did they have?

He turned his gaze helplessly back to the monitors . . . and Roland at once turned his head away. He did this gently but firmly. "There's nothing there you need to look at, Jake," he said.

"But why are they doing it?" Jake asked. He had eaten nothing all day, but he still felt like vomiting. *"Why?"*

"Because they're frightened, and Blaine is feeding their fear. But mostly, I think, because they've lived too long in the graveyard of their grandfathers and they're tired of it. And before you pity them, remember how happy they would have been to take you along with them into the clearing where the path ends."

The steel ball zipped around another corner, leaving the TV screens and electronic monitoring equipment behind. Ahead, a wide ribbon of some synthetic stuff was set into the floor. It gleamed like fresh tar between two narrow strips of chrome steel that dwindled to a point on what was not the far side of this room, but its horizon.

The ball bounced impatiently above the dark strip, and suddenly the belt—for that was what it was—swept into silent motion, trundling along between its steel facings at jogging speed. The ball made small arcs in the air, urging them to climb on.

Roland trotted beside the moving strip until he was roughly matching its speed, then did just that. He set Jake down and the three of them—gunslinger, boy, and golden-eyed bumbler—were carried rapidly across this shadowy underground plain where the ancient machines were awakening. The moving strip carried them into an area of what looked like filing cabinets—row after endless row of them. They were dark . . . but not dead. A low, sleepy humming sound came from within them, and Jake could see hairline cracks of bright yellow light shining between the steel panels.

He suddenly found himself thinking of the Tick-Tock Man.

There's maybe a hundred thousand of those ever-fucking dipolar computers under the ever-fucking city! I want those computers!

Well, Jake thought, *they're waking up, so I guess you're getting what you wanted, Ticky . . . but if you were here, I'm not sure you'd still want it.*

Then he remembered Tick-Tock's great-grandfather, who'd been brave enough to climb into an airplane from another world and take it into the sky. With that kind of blood running in his veins, Jake supposed, Tick-Tock, far from being frightened to the point of suicide, would have been delighted by this turn of events . . . and the more people who killed themselves in terror, the happier he would have been.

Too late now, Ticky, he thought. *Thank God.*

Roland spoke in a soft, wondering voice. "All these boxes . . . I think we're riding through the mind of the thing that calls itself Blaine, Jake. *I think we're riding through its mind.*"

Jake nodded, and found himself thinking of his Final Essay. "Blaine the Brain is a hell of a pain."

"Yes."

Jake looked closely at Roland. "Are we going to come out where I think we're going to come out?"

"Yes," Roland said. "If we're still following the Path of the Beam, we'll come out in the Cradle."

Jake nodded. "Roland?"

"What?"

"Thanks for coming after me."

Roland nodded and put an arm around Jake's shoulders.

Far ahead of them, huge motors rumbled to life. A moment later a heavy grinding sound began and new light—the harsh glow of orange arc-sodiums—flooded down on them. Jake could now see the place where the moving belt stopped. Beyond it was a steep, narrow escalator, leading up into that orange light.

39

EDDIE AND SUSANNAH HEARD heavy motors start up almost directly beneath them. A moment later, a wide strip of the marble floor began to pull slowly back, revealing a long lighted slot below. The floor was disappearing in their direction. Eddie seized the handles of Susannah's chair and rolled it rapidly backward along the steel barrier between the monorail platform and the rest of the Cradle. There were several pillars along the course of the growing rectangle of light, and Eddie waited for them to tumble into the hole as the floor upon which they stood disappeared from beneath their bases. It didn't happen. The pillars went on serenely standing, seeming to float on nothing.

"I see an escalator!" Susannah shouted over the endless, pulsing alarm. She was leaning forward, peering into the hole.

"Uh-huh," Eddie shouted back. "We got the el station up here, so it must be notions, perfume, and ladies' lingerie down there."

"What?"

"Never mind!"

"Eddie!" Susannah screamed. Delighted surprise burst over her face like a Fourth of July firework. She leaned even further forward, pointing, and Eddie had to grab her to keep her from tumbling out of the chair. "It's Roland! It's both of them!"

There was a shuddery thump as the slot in the floor opened to its maximum length and stopped. The motors which had driven it along its hidden tracks cut out in a long, dying whine. Eddie ran to the edge of the hole and saw Roland riding on one of the escalator steps. Jake— white-faced, bruised, bloody, but clearly Jake and clearly alive—was standing next to him and leaning on the gunslinger's shoulder. And sitting on the step right behind them, looking up with his bright eyes, was Oy.

"Roland! Jake!" Eddie shouted. He leaped up, waving his hands over his head, and came down dancing on the edge of the slot. If he had been wearing a hat, he would have thrown it in the air.

They looked up and waved. Jake was grinning, Eddie saw, and even old long tall and ugly looked as if he might break down and crack a smile before long. Wonders, Eddie thought, would never cease. His heart suddenly felt too big for his chest and he danced faster, waving his arms and whooping, afraid that if he didn't keep moving, his joy and relief might actually cause him to burst. Until this moment he had not realized how positive his heart had become that they would never see Roland and Jake again.

"Hey, guys! All RIGHT! Far fucking out! Get your asses up here!"

"Eddie, help me!

He turned. Susannah was trying to struggle out of her chair, but a fold of the deerskin trousers she was wearing had gotten caught in the brake mechanism. She was laughing and weeping at the same time, her dark eyes blazing with happiness. Eddie lifted her from the chair so violently that it crashed over on its side. He danced her around in a circle. She clung to his neck with one hand and waved strenuously with the other.

"Roland! Jake! Get on up here! Shuck your butts, you hear me?"

When they reached the top, Eddie embraced Roland, pounding him on the back while Susannah covered Jake's upturned, laughing face with kisses. Oy ran around in tight figure eights, barking shrilly.

"Sugar!" Susannah said. "You all right?"

"Yes," Jake said. He was still grinning, but tears stood in his eyes. "And glad to be here. You'll never know how glad."

"I can guess, sugar. You c'n bet on *that*." She turned to look at Roland. "What'd they do to him? His face look like somebody run over it with a bulldozer."

"That was mostly Gasher," Roland said. "He won't be bothering Jake again. Or anyone else."

"What about you, big boy? You all right?"

Roland nodded, looking about. "So this is the Cradle."

"Yes," Eddie said. He was peering into the slot. "What's down there?"

"Machines and madness."

"Loquacious as ever, I see." Eddie looked at Roland, smiling. "Do you know how happy I am to see you, man? Do you have any idea?"

"Yes—I think I do." Roland smiled then, thinking of how people changed. There had been a time, and not so long ago, when Eddie had been on the edge of cutting his throat with the gunslinger's own knife.

The engines below them started up again. The escalator came to a stop. The slot in the floor began to slide closed once more. Jake went to Susannah's overturned chair, and as he was righting it, he caught sight of the smooth pink shape beyond the iron bars. His breath stopped, and the dream he had had after leaving River Crossing returned full force: the vast pink bullet shape slicing across the empty lands of western Missouri toward him and Oy. Two big triangular windows glittering high up in the blank face of that oncoming monster, windows like eyes . . . and now his dream was becoming reality, just as he had known it eventually would.

It's just an awful choo-choo train, and its name is Blaine the Pain.

Eddie walked over and slung an arm around Jake's shoulders. "Well, there it is, champ—just as advertised. What do you think of it?"

"Not too much, actually." This was an understatement of colossal size, but Jake was too drained to do any better.

"Me, either," Eddie said. "It talks. And it likes riddles."

Jake nodded.

Roland had Susannah planted on one hip, and together they were examining the control box with its diamond-pattern of raised number-pads. Jake and Eddie joined them. Eddie found he had to keep looking down at Jake in order to verify that it wasn't just his imagination or wishful thinking; the boy was really here.

"What now?" he asked Roland.

Roland slipped his finger lightly over the numbered buttons which made up the diamond shape and shook his head. He didn't know.

"Because I think the mono's engines are cycling faster," Eddie said. "I mean, it's hard to tell for sure with that alarm blatting, but I think it is . . . and it's a robot, after all. What if it, like, leaves without us?"

"Blaine!" Susannah shouted. "Blaine, are you—"

"LISTEN CLOSELY, MY FRIENDS," Blaine's voice boomed. "THERE ARE LARGE STOCKPILES OF CHEMICAL AND BIO-LOGICAL WARFARE CANNISTERS UNDER THE CITY. I HAVE STARTED A SEQUENCE WHICH WILL CAUSE AN EXPLOSION AND RELEASE THIS GAS. THIS EXPLOSION WILL OCCUR IN TWELVE MINUTES."

The voice fell silent for a moment, and then the voice of Little Blaine, almost buried by the steady, pulsing whoop of the alarm, came to them: "*. . . I was afraid of something like this . . . you must hurry . . .*"

Eddie ignored Little Blaine, who wasn't telling him a damned thing he didn't already know. Of *course* they had to hurry, but that fact was running a distant second at the moment. Something much larger occupied most of his mind. "*Why?*" he asked. "Why in God's name would you do that?"

"I SHOULD THINK IT OBVIOUS. I CAN'T NUKE THE CITY WITHOUT DESTROYING MYSELF, AS WELL. AND HOW COULD I TAKE YOU WHERE YOU WANT TO GO IF I WERE DESTROYED?"

"But there are still thousands of people in the city," Eddie said. "You'll *kill* them."

"YES," Blaine said calmly. "SEE YOU LATER ALLIGATOR, AFTER A WHILE CROCODILE, DON'T FORGET TO WRITE."

"*Why?*" Susannah shouted. "*Why*, goddam you?*"

"BECAUSE THEY BORE ME. YOU FOUR, HOWEVER, I FIND RATHER INTERESTING. OF COURSE, HOW LONG I *CONTINUE* TO FIND YOU INTERESTING WILL DEPEND ON HOW GOOD YOUR RIDDLES ARE. AND SPEAKING OF RIDDLES, HADN'T YOU BETTER GET TO WORK SOLVING MINE? YOU HAVE EXACTLY ELEVEN MINUTES AND TWENTY SECONDS BEFORE THE CANNISTERS RUPTURE."

"Stop it!" Jake yelled over the blatting siren. "It isn't just the city— gas like that could float *anywhere*! It could even kill the old people in River Crossing!"

"TOUGH TITTY, SAID THE KITTY," Blaine responded unfeelingly. "ALTHOUGH I BELIEVE THEY CAN COUNT ON MEASURING OUT THEIR LIVES IN COFFEE-SPOONS FOR A FEW MORE YEARS; THE AUTUMN STORMS HAVE BEGUN, AND THE PREVAILING WINDS WILL CARRY THE GASES AWAY FROM THEM. THE SITUATION OF YOU FOUR IS, HOWEVER, VERY DIFFERENT. YOU BETTER PUT ON YOUR THINKING CAPS, OR IT'S SEE YOU LATER ALLIGATOR, AFTER A WHILE CROCODILE, DON'T FORGET TO WRITE." The voice paused. "ONE PIECE OF ADDITIONAL INPUT: THIS GAS IS *NOT* PAINLESS."

"Take it back!" Jake said. "We'll still tell you riddles, won't we, Roland? We'll tell all the riddles you want! *Just take it back!*"

Blaine began to laugh. He laughed for a long time, pealing shrieks of electronic mirth into the wide empty space of the Cradle, where it mingled with the monotonous, drilling beat of the alarm.

"Stop it!" Susannah shouted. "Stop it! Stop it! *Stop it!*"

Blaine did. A moment later the alarm cut off in mid-blat. The ensuing silence—broken only by the pounding rain—was deafening.

Now the voice issuing from the speaker was very soft, thoughtful, and utterly without mercy. "YOU NOW HAVE TEN MINUTES," Blaine said. "LET'S SEE JUST HOW INTERESTING YOU REALLY ARE."

40

"ANDREW."

There is no Andrew here, stranger, he thought. *Andrew is long gone; Andrew is no more, as I shall soon be no more.*

"*Andrew!*" the voice insisted.

It came from far away. It came from outside the cider-press that had once been his head.

Once there *had* been a boy named Andrew, and his father had taken that boy to a park on the far western side of Lud, a park where there had been apple trees and a rusty tin shack that looked like hell and smelled like heaven. In answer to his question, Andrew's father had told him it was called the cider house. Then he gave Andrew a pat on the head, told him not to be afraid, and led him through the blanket-covered doorway.

There had been more apples—baskets and baskets of them—stacked against the walls inside, and there had also been a scrawny old man named Dewlap, whose muscles writhed beneath his white skin like worms and whose job was to feed the apples, basket by basket, to the loose-jointed, clanking machine which stood in the middle of the room. What came out of the pipe jutting from the far end of the machine was sweet cider. Another man (he no longer remembered what this one's name might have been) stood there, his job to fill jug after jug with the cider. A third man stood behind *him*, and *his* job was to clout the jug-filler on the head if there was too much spillage.

Andrew's father had given him a glass of the foaming cider, and although he had tasted a great many forgotten delicacies during his years in the city, he had never tasted anything finer than that sweet, cold drink. It had been like swallowing a gust of October wind. Yet what he remembered even more clearly than the taste of the cider or the wormy shift and squiggle of Dewlap's muscles as he dumped the baskets was the merciless way the machine reduced the big red-gold apples to liquid. Two dozen rollers had carried them beneath a revolving steel drum with holes punched in it. The apples had first been squeezed and then actually popped, spilling their juices down an inclined trough while a screen caught the seeds and pulp.

Now his head was the cider-press and his brains were the apples. Soon they would pop as the apples had popped beneath the roller, and the blessed darkness would swallow him.

"Andrew! Raise your head and look at me."

He couldn't . . . and wouldn't even if he could. Better to just lie here and wait for the darkness. He was supposed to be dead, anyway; hadn't the hellish squint put a bullet in his brain?

"It didn't go anywhere near your brain, you horse's ass, and you're not dying. You've just got a headache. You *will* die, though, if you don't stop lying there and puling in your own blood . . . and I will make sure, Andrew, that your dying makes what you are feeling now seem like bliss."

It was not the threats which caused the man on the floor to raise his head but rather the way the owner of that penetrating, hissing voice seemed to have read his mind. His head came up slowly, and the agony was excruciating—heavy objects seemed to go sliding and careering around the bony case which contained what was left of his mind, ripping bloody channels through his brain as they went. A long, syrupy moan escaped him. There was a flapping, tickling sensation on his right cheek, as if a dozen flies were crawling in the blood there. He wanted to shoo them away, but he knew that he needed both hands just to support himself.

The figure standing on the far side of the room by the hatch which led to the kitchen looked ghastly, unreal. This was partly because the overhead lights were still strobing, partly because he was seeing the new-comer with only one eye (he couldn't remember what had happened to the other and didn't want to), but he had an idea it was mostly because the creature *was* ghastly and unreal. It looked like a man . . . but the fellow who had once been Andrew Quick had an idea it really wasn't a man at all.

The stranger standing in front of the hatch wore a short, dark jacket belted at the waist, faded denim trousers, and old, dusty boots—the boots of a countryman, a range-rider, or—

"Or a gunslinger, Andrew?" the stranger asked, and tittered.

The Tick-Tock Man stared desperately at the figure in the doorway, trying to see the face, but the short jacket had a hood, and it was up. The stranger's countenance was lost in its shadows.

The siren stopped in mid-whoop. The emergency lights stayed on, but they at least stopped flashing.

"There," the stranger said in his—or its—whispery, penetrating voice. "At last we can hear ourselves think."

"Who are you?" the Tick-Tock Man asked. He moved slightly, and more of those weights went sliding through his head, ripping fresh chan-nels in his brain. As terrible as that feeling was, the awful tickling of the flies on his right cheek was somehow worse.

"I'm a man of many handles, pardner," the man said from inside the darkness of his hood, and although his voice was grave, Tick-Tock heard laughter lurking just below the surface. "There's some that call me Jimmy, and some that call me Timmy; some that call me Handy and some that call me Dandy. They can call me Loser, or they can call me Winner, just as long as they don't call me in too late for dinner."

The man in the doorway threw back his head, and his laughter chilled the skin of the wounded man's arms and back into lumps of gooseflesh; it was like the howl of a wolf.

"I have been called the Ageless Stranger," the man said. He began to walk toward Tick-Tock, and as he did, the man on the floor moaned and tried to scrabble backward. "I have also been called Merlin or Maer-lyn—and who cares, because I was never *that* one, although I never

denied it, either. I am sometimes called the Magician . . . or the Wizard
. . . but I hope we can go forward together on more humble terms,
Andrew. More *human* terms."

He pushed back the hood, revealing a fair, broad-browed face that
was not, for all its pleasant looks, in any way human. Large hectic roses
rode the Wizard's cheekbones; his blue-green eyes sparkled with a gusty
joy far too wild to be sane; his blue-black hair stood up in zany clumps
like the feathers of a raven; his lips, lushly red, parted to reveal the teeth
of a cannibal.

"Call me Fannin," the grinning apparition said. "Richard Fannin.
That's not *exactly* right, maybe, but I reckon it's close enough for govern-
ment work." He held out a hand whose palm was utterly devoid of lines.
"What do you say, pard? Shake the hand that shook the world."

The creature who had once been Andrew Quick and who had been
known in the halls of the Grays as the Tick-Tock Man shrieked and again
tried to wriggle backward. The flap of scalp peeled loose by the low-
caliber bullet which had only grooved his skull instead of penetrating it
swung back and forth; the long strands of gray-blonde hair continued to
tickle against his cheek. Quick, however, no longer felt it. He had even
forgotten the ache in his skull and the throb from the socket where his
left eye had been. His entire consciousness had fused into one thought:
I must get away from this beast that looks like a man.

But when the stranger seized his right hand and shook it, that
thought passed like a dream on waking. The scream which had been
locked in Quick's breast escaped his lips in a lover's sigh. He stared
dumbly up at the grinning newcomer. The loose flap of his scalp swung
and dangled.

"Is that bothering you? It *must* be. Here!" Fannin seized the hanging
flap and ripped it briskly off Quick's head, revealing a bleary swatch of
skull. There was a noise like heavy cloth tearing. Quick shrieked.

"There, there, it only hurts for a second." The man was now squatting on his hunkers before Quick and speaking as an indulgent parent
might speak to a child with a splinter in his finger. "Isn't that so?"

"Y-Y-Yes," Quick muttered. And it was. Already the pain was fading.
And when Fannin reached toward him again, caressing the left side of
his face, Quick's jerk backward was only a reflex, quickly mastered. As
the lineless hand stroked, he felt strength flowing back into him. He
looked up at the newcomer with dumb gratitude, lips quivering.

"Is that better, Andrew? It is, isn't it?"

"Yes! Yes!"

"If you want to thank me—as I'm sure you do—you must say something an old acquaintance of mine used to say. He ended up betraying
me, but he was a good friend for quite some time, anyway, and I still

have a soft spot in my heart for him. Say, 'My life for you,' Andrew—can you say that?"

He could and he did; in fact, it seemed he couldn't *stop* saying it. "My life for you! My life for you! My life for you! My life—"

The stranger touched his cheek again, but this time a huge raw bolt of pain blasted across Andrew Quick's head. He screamed.

"Sorry about that, but time is short and you were starting to sound like a broken record. Andrew, let me put it to you with no bark on it: how would you like to kill the squint who shot you? Not to mention his friends and the hardcase who brought him here—him, most of all. Even the mutt that took your eye, Andrew—would you like that?"

"Yes!" the former Tick-Tock Man gasped. His hands clenched into bloody fists. *"Yes!"*

"That's good," the stranger said, and helped Quick to his feet, "because they *have* to die—they're meddling with things they have no business meddling with. I expected Blaine to take care of them, but things have gone much too far to depend on *anything* . . . after all, who would have thought they could get as far as they have?"

"I don't know," Quick said. He did not, in fact, have the slightest idea what the stranger was talking about. Nor did he care; there was a feeling of exaltation creeping through his mind like some excellent drug, and after the pain of the cider-press, that was enough for him. More than enough.

Richard Fannin's lips curled. "Bear and bone . . . key and rose . . . day and night . . . time and tide. *Enough!* Enough, I say! *They must not draw closer to the Tower than they are now!"*

Quick staggered backward as the man's hands shot out with the flickery speed of heat lightning. One broke the chain which held the tiny glass-enclosed pendulum clock; the other stripped Jake Chambers's Seiko from his forearm.

"I'll just take these, shall I?" Fannin the Wizard smiled charmingly, his lips modestly closed over those awful teeth. "Or do you object?"

"No," Quick said, surrendering the last symbols of his long leadership without a qualm (without, in fact, even being aware that he was doing so). "Be my guest."

"Thank you, Andrew," the dark man said softly. "Now we must step lively—I'm expecting a drastic change in the atmosphere of these environs in the next five minutes or so. We must get to the nearest closet where gas masks are stored before that happens, and it's apt to be a near thing. I could survive the change quite nicely, but I'm afraid you might have some difficulties."

"I don't understand what you're talking about," Andrew Quick said. His head had begun to throb again, and his mind was whirling.

"Nor do you need to," the stranger said smoothly. "Come, Andrew—I think we should hurry. Busy, busy day, eh? With luck, Blaine will fry them right on the platform, where they are no doubt still standing—he's become very eccentric over the years, poor fellow. But I think we should hurry, just the same."

He slid his arm over Quick's shoulders and, giggling, led him through the hatchway Roland and Jake had used only a few minutes before.

VI · RIDDLE AND WASTE LANDS

·VI·

RIDDLE AND
WASTE LANDS

1

"ALL RIGHT," ROLAND SAID. "Tell me his riddle."

"What about all the people out there?" Eddie asked, pointing across the wide, pillared Plaza of the Cradle and toward the city beyond. "What can we do for them?"

"Nothing," Roland said, "but it's still possible that we may be able to do something for ourselves. Now what was the riddle?"

Eddie looked toward the streamlined shape of the mono. "He said we'd have to prime the pump to get him going. Only his pump primes backward. Does it mean anything to you?"

Roland thought it over carefully, then shook his head. He looked down at Jake. "Any ideas, Jake?"

Jake shook his head. "I don't even *see* a pump."

"That's probably the easy part," Roland said. "We say *he* and *him* instead of *it* and *that* because Blaine sounds like a living being, but he's still a machine—a sophisticated one, but a machine. He started his own engines, but it must take some sort of code or combination to open the gate and the train doors."

"We better hurry up," Jake said nervously. "It's got to be two or three minutes since he last talked to us. At least."

"Don't count on it," Eddie said gloomily. "Time's weird over here."

"Still—"

"Yeah, yeah." Eddie glanced toward Susannah, but she was sitting astride Roland's hip and looking at the numeric diamond with a day-dreamy expression on her face. He looked back at Roland. "I'm pretty sure you're right about it being a combination—that must be what all those number-pads are for." He raised his voice. "Is that it, Blaine? Have we got at least that much right?"

No response; only the quickening rumble of the mono's engines.

"Roland," Susannah said abruptly. "You have to help me."

The daydreamy look was being replaced by an expression of mingled horror, dismay, and determination. To Roland's eye, she had never looked more beautiful . . . or more alone. She had been on his shoulders when they stood at the edge of the clearing and watched the bear trying to claw Eddie out of the tree, and Roland had not seen her expression when he told her she must be the one to shoot it. But he knew what that expression had been, for he was seeing it now. *Ka* was a wheel, its one purpose to turn, and in the end it always came back to the place where it had started. So it had ever been and so it was now; Susannah was once again facing the bear, and her face said she knew it.

"What?" he asked. "What is it, Susannah?"

"I know the answer, but I can't get it. It's stuck in my mind the way a fishbone can get stuck in your throat. I need you to help me remember. Not his face, but his voice. What he *said*."

Jake glanced down at his wrist and was surprised all over again by a memory of the Tick-Tock Man's catlike green eyes when he saw not his watch but only the place where it had been—a white shape outlined by his deeply tanned skin. How much longer did they have? Surely no more than seven minutes, and that was being generous. He looked up and saw that Roland had removed a cartridge from his gunbelt and was walking it back and forth across the knuckles of his left hand. Jake felt his eyelids immediately grow heavy and looked away, fast.

"What voice would you remember, Susannah Dean?" Roland asked in a low, musing voice. His eyes were not fixed on her face but on the cartridge as it did its endless, limber dance across his knuckles . . . and back . . . across . . . and back . . .

He didn't need to look up to know that Jake had looked away from the dance of the cartridge and Susannah had not. He began to speed it up until the cartridge almost seemed to be floating above the back of his hand.

"Help me remember the voice of my father," Susannah Dean said.

2

FOR A MOMENT THERE was silence except for a distant, crumping explosion in the city, the rain pounding on the roof of the Cradle, and the fat throb of the monorail's slo-trans engines. Then a low-pitched hydraulic hum cut through the air. Eddie looked away from the cartridge dancing across the gunslinger's fingers (it took an effort; he realized that in another few moments he would have been hypnotized himself) and peered through the iron bars. A slim silver rod was pushing itself up from the sloping pink surface between Blaine's forward windows. It looked like an antenna of some kind.

"Susannah?" Roland asked in that same low voice.

"What?" Her eyes were open but her voice was distant and breathy—the voice of someone who is sleeptalking.

"Do you remember the voice of your father?"

"Yes . . . but I can't hear it."

"SIX MINUTES, MY FRIENDS."

Eddie and Jake started and looked toward the control-box speaker, but Susannah seemed not to have heard at all; she only stared at the floating cartridge. Below it, Roland's knuckles rippled up and down like the heddles of a loom.

"Try, Susannah," Roland urged, and suddenly he felt Susannah change within the circle of his right arm. She seemed to gain weight . . . and, in some indefinable way, vitality as well. It was as if her essence had somehow changed.

And it had.

"Why you want to bother wit *dat* bitch?" the raspy voice of Detta Walker asked.

3

DETTA SOUNDED BOTH EXASPERATED and amused. "She never got no better'n a C in math her whole life. Wouldn'ta got dat widout me to he'p her." She paused, then added grudgingly: "An' Daddy. He he'ped some, too. I knowed about them forspecial numbahs, but was him showed us de net. My, I got de bigges' kick outta dat!" She chuckled. "Reason Suze can't remember is 'cause Odetta never understood 'bout dem forspecial numbers in de firs' place."

"What forspecial numbers?" Eddie asked.

"*Prime* numbahs!" She pronounced the word *prime* in a way that almost rhymed with *calm*. She looked at Roland, appearing to be wholly awake again now . . . except she was not Susannah, nor was she the same wretched, devilish creature who had previously gone under the name of Detta Walker, although she *sounded* the same. "She went to Daddy cryin an' carryin on 'cause she was flunkin dat math course . . . and it wasn't nuthin but funnybook algebra at dat! She could do de woik—if *I* could, *she* could—but she din' want to. Poitry-readin bitch like her too good for a little *ars mathematica*, you see?" Detta threw her head back and laughed, but the poisoned, half-mad bitterness was gone from the sound. She seemed genuinely amused at the foolishness of her mental twin.

"And Daddy, he say, 'I'm goan show you a trick, Odetta. I learned it in college. It he'ped me get through this prime numbah bi'ness, and it's goan he'p you, too. He'p you find mos' any prime numbah you want.' *Oh*-detta, dumb as ever, she say, 'Teacher says ain't no formula for prime numbahs, Daddy.' And Daddy, he say right back, 'They ain't. But you can catch em, Odetta, if you have a net.' He called it The Net of Eratosthenes. Take me over to dat box on the wall, Roland—I'm goan answer dat honkey computer's riddle. I'm goan th'ow you a net and catch you a train-ride."

Roland took her over, closely followed by Eddie, Jake, and Oy.

"Gimme dat piece o' cha'coal you keep in yo' poke."

He rummaged and brought out a short stub of blackened stick. Detta took it and peered at the diamond-shaped grid of numbers. "Ain't zackly de way Daddy showed me, but I reckon it comes to de same," she said after a moment. "Prime numbah be like me—ornery and forspecial. It gotta be a numbah don't nevvah divide even 'ceptin by one and its ownself. Two is prime, 'cause you can divide it by one an' two, but it's the *only* even numbah that's prime. You c'n take out all the res' dat's even."

"I'm lost," Eddie said.

"That's 'cause you just a stupid white boy," Detta said, but not unkindly. She looked closely at the diamond shape a moment longer, then quickly began to touch the tip of the charcoal to all the even-numbered pads, leaving small black smudges on them.

"Three's prime, but no product you git by *multiplyin* three can be prime," she said, and now Roland heard an odd but wonderful thing: Detta was fading out of the woman's voice; she was being replaced not by Odetta Holmes but by Susannah Dean. He would not have to bring her out of this trance; she was coming out of it on her own, quite naturally.

Susannah began using her charcoal to touch the multiples of three which were left now that the even numbers had been eliminated: nine, fifteen, twenty-one, and so on.

"Same with five and seven," she murmured, and suddenly she was awake and all Susannah Dean again. "You just have to mark the odd ones like twenty-five that haven't been crossed out already." The diamond shape on the control box now looked like this:

```
                1
               2 3
              4 5 6
             7 8 9 10
           11 12 13 14 15
          16 17 18 19 20 21
         22 23 24 25 26 27 28
        29 30 31 32 33 34 35 36
      37 38 39 40 41 42 43 44 45
     46 47 48 49 50 51 52 53 54 55
      56 57 58 59 60 61 62 63 64
        65 66 67 68 69 70 71 72
         73 74 75 76 77 78 79
           80 81 82 83 84 85
            86 87 88 89 90
             91 92 93 94
              95 96 97
               98 99
                100
```

"There," she said tiredly. "What's left in the net are all the prime numbers between one and one hundred. I'm pretty sure that's the combination that opens the gate."

"YOU HAVE ONE MINUTE, MY FRIENDS. YOU ARE PROVING TO BE A GOOD DEAL THICKER THAN I HAD HOPED YOU WOULD BE."

Eddie ignored Blaine's voice and threw his arms around Susannah. "Are you back, Suze? Are you awake?"

"Yes. I woke up in the middle of what she was saying, but I let her talk a little longer, anyway. It seemed impolite to interrupt." She looked at Roland. "What do you say? Want to go for it?"

"FIFTY SECONDS."

"Yes. You try the combination, Susannah. It's your answer."

She reached out toward the top of the diamond, but Jake put his hand over hers. "No," he said. "'This pump primes *backward.*' Remember?"

She looked startled, then smiled. "That's right. Clever Blaine . . . and clever Jake, too."

They watched in silence as she pushed each number in turn, starting with ninety-seven. There was a minute click as each pad locked down. There was no tension-filled pause after she touched the last button; the gate in the center of the barrier immediately began to slide up on its tracks, rattling harshly and showering down flakes of rust from somewhere high above as it went.

"NOT BAD AT ALL," Blaine said admiringly. "I'M LOOKING FORWARD TO THIS VERY MUCH. MAY I SUGGEST YOU CLIMB ON BOARD QUICKLY? IN FACT, YOU MAY WISH TO RUN. THERE ARE SEVERAL GAS OUTLETS IN THIS AREA."

4

THREE HUMAN BEINGS (one carrying a fourth on his hip) and one small, furry animal ran through the opening in the barrier and sprinted toward Blaine the Mono. It stood humming in its narrow loading bay, half above the platform and half below it, looking like a giant cartridge—one which had been painted an incongruous shade of pink—lying in the open breech of a high-powered rifle. In the vastness of the Cradle, Roland and the others looked like mere moving specks. Above them, flocks of pigeons— now with only forty seconds to live—swooped and swirled beneath the Cradle's ancient roof. As the travellers approached the mono, a curved section of its pink hull slid up, revealing a doorway. Beyond it was thick, pale blue carpeting.

"Welcome to Blaine," a soothing voice said as they pelted aboard. They all recognized that voice; it was a slightly louder, slightly more confident version of Little Blaine. "Praise the Imperium! Please make sure your transit-card is available for collection and remember that false boarding is a serious crime punishable by law. We hope you enjoy your trip. Welcome to Blaine. Praise the Imperium! Please make sure your transit-card—"

The voice suddenly sped up, first becoming the chatter of a human chipmunk and then a high-pitched, gabbly whine. There was a brief electronic curse—BOOP!—and then it cut out entirely.

"I THINK WE CAN DISPENSE WITH THAT BORING OLD SHIT, DON'T YOU?" Blaine asked.

From outside came a tremendous, thudding explosion. Eddie, who was now carrying Susannah, was thrown forward and would have fallen if Roland hadn't caught him by the arm. Until that moment, Eddie had held onto the desperate notion that Blaine's threat about the poison gas was no more than a sick joke. *You should have known better*, he thought. *Anyone who thinks impressions of old movie actors is funny absolutely cannot be trusted. I think it's like a law of nature.*

Behind them, the curved section of hull slid back into place with a soft thud. Air began to hiss gently from hidden vents, and Jake felt his ears pop gently. "I think he just pressurized the cabin."

Eddie nodded, looking around with wide eyes. "I felt it, too. Look at this place! Wow!"

He had once read of an aviation company—Regent Air, it might have been—that had catered to people who wanted to fly between New York and Los Angeles in a grander style than airlines such as Delta and United allowed for. They had operated a customized 727 complete with drawing room, bar, video lounge, and sleeper compartments. He imagined the interior of that plane must have looked a little like what he was seeing now.

They were standing in a long, tubular room furnished with plush-upholstered swivel chairs and modular sofas. At the far end of the compartment, which had to be at least eighty feet long, was an area that looked not like a bar but a cosy bistro. An instrument that could have been a harpsichord stood on a pedestal of polished wood, highlighted by a hidden baby spotlight. Eddie almost expected Hoagy Carmichael to appear and start tinkling out "Stardust."

Indirect lighting glowed from panels placed high along the walls, and dependent from the ceiling halfway down the compartment was a chandelier. To Jake it looked like a smaller replica of the one which had lain in ruins on the ballroom floor of The Mansion. Nor did this surprise him—he had begun to take such connections and doublings as a matter of course. The only thing about this splendid room which seemed wrong was its lack of even a single window.

The *pièce de résistance* stood on a pedestal below the chandelier. It was an ice-sculpture of a gunslinger with a revolver in his left hand. The right hand was holding the bridle of the ice-horse that walked, head-down and tired, behind him. Eddie could see there were only three digits on this hand: the last two fingers and the thumb.

Jake, Eddie, and Susannah stared in fascination at the haggard face beneath the frozen hat as the floor began to thrum gently beneath their feet. The resemblance to Roland was remarkable.

"I HAD TO WORK RATHER FAST, I'M AFRAID," Blaine said modestly. "DOES IT DO ANYTHING FOR YOU?"

"It's absolutely amazing," Susannah said.

"THANK YOU, SUSANNAH OF NEW YORK."

Eddie was testing one of the sofas with his hand. It was incredibly soft; touching it made him want to sleep for at least sixteen hours. "The Great Old Ones really travelled in style, didn't they?"

Blaine laughed again, and the shrill, not-quite-sane undertone of that laugh made them look at each other uneasily. "DON'T GET THE

WRONG IDEA," Blaine said. "THIS WAS THE BARONY CABIN—WHAT I BELIEVE YOU WOULD CALL FIRST CLASS."

"Where are the other cars?"

Blaine ignored the question. Beneath their feet, the throb of the engines continued to speed up. Susannah was reminded of how the pilots revved their engines before charging down the runway at LaGuardia or Idlewild. "PLEASE TAKE YOUR SEATS, MY INTERESTING NEW FRIENDS."

Jake dropped into one of the swivel chairs. Oy jumped promptly into his lap. Roland took the chair nearest him, sparing one glance at the ice-sculpture. The barrel of the revolver was beginning to drip slowly into the shallow china basin in which the sculpture stood.

Eddie sat down on one of the sofas with Susannah. It was every bit as comfortable as his hand had told him it would be. "Exactly where are we going, Blaine?"

Blaine replied in the patient voice of someone who realizes he is speaking to a mental inferior and must make allowances. "ALONG THE PATH OF THE BEAM. AT LEAST, AS FAR ALONG IT AS MY TRACK GOES."

"To the Dark Tower?" Roland asked. Susannah realized it was the first time the gunslinger had actually spoken to the loquacious ghost in the machine below Lud.

"Only as far as Topeka," Jake said in a low voice.

"YES," Blaine said. "TOPEKA IS THE NAME OF MY TERMINATING POINT, ALTHOUGH I AM SURPRISED YOU KNOW IT."

With all you know about our world, Jake thought, *how come you don't know that some lady wrote a book about you, Blaine? Was it the name-change? Was something that simple enough to fool a complicated machine like you into overlooking your own biography? And what about Beryl Evans, the woman who supposedly wrote* Charlie the Choo-Choo? *Did you know her, Blaine? And where is she now?*

Good questions . . . but Jake somehow didn't think this would be a good time to ask them.

The throb of the engines became steadily stronger. A faint thud—not nearly as strong as the explosion which had shaken the Cradle as they boarded—ran through the floor. An expression of alarm crossed Susannah's face. "Oh *shit!* Eddie! My wheelchair! It's back there!"

Eddie put an arm around her shoulders. "Too late now, babe," he said as Blaine the Mono began to move, sliding toward its slot in the Cradle for the first time in ten years . . . and for the last time in its long, long history.

5

"THE BARONY CABIN HAS A PARTICULARLY FINE VISUAL MODE," Blaine said. "WOULD YOU LIKE ME TO ACTIVATE IT?"

Jake glanced at Roland, who shrugged and nodded.

"Yes, please," Jake said.

What happened then was so spectacular that it stunned all of them to silence . . . although Roland, who knew little of technology but who had spent his entire life on comfortable terms with magic, was the least wonder-struck of the four. It was not a matter of windows appearing in the compartment's curved walls; the entire cabin—floor and ceiling as well as walls—grew milky, grew translucent, grew transparent, and then disappeared completely. Within a space of five seconds, Blaine the Mono seemed to be gone and the pilgrims seemed to be zooming through the lanes of the city with no aid or support at all.

Susannah and Eddie clutched each other like small children in the path of a charging animal. Oy barked and tried to jump down the front of Jake's shirt. Jake barely noticed; he was clutching the sides of his seat and looking from side to side, his eyes wide with amazement. His initial alarm was being replaced by amazed delight.

The furniture groupings were still here, he saw; so was the bar, the piano-harpsichord, and the ice-sculpture Blaine had created as a party-favor, but now this living-room configuration appeared to be cruising seventy feet above Lud's rain-soaked central district. Five feet to Jake's left, Eddie and Susannah were floating along on one of the couches; three feet to his right, Roland was sitting in a powder-blue swivel chair, his dusty, battered boots resting on nothing, flying serenely over the rubble-strewn urban waste land below.

Jake could feel the carpet beneath his moccasins, but his eyes insisted that neither the carpet nor the floor beneath it was still there. He looked back over his shoulder and saw the dark slot in the stone flank of the Cradle slowly receding in the distance.

"Eddie! Susannah! Check it out!"

Jake got to his feet, holding Oy inside his shirt, and began to walk slowly through what looked like empty space. Taking the initial step required a great deal of willpower, because his eyes told him there was nothing at all between the floating islands of furniture, but once he began to move, the undeniable feel of the floor beneath him made it easier. To Eddie and Susannah, the boy appeared to be walking on thin air while the battered, dingy buildings of the city slid by on either side.

"Don't do that, kid," Eddie said feebly. "You're gonna make me sick up."

Jake lifted Oy carefully out of his shirt. "It's okay," he said, and set him down. "See?"

"Oy!" the bumbler agreed, but after one look between his paws at the city park currently unrolling beneath them, he attempted to crawl onto Jake's feet and sit on his moccasins.

Jake looked forward and saw the broad gray stroke of the monorail track ahead of them, rising slowly but steadily through the buildings and disappearing into the rain. He looked down again and saw nothing but the street and floating membranes of low cloud.

"How come I can't see the track underneath us, Blaine?"

"THE IMAGES YOU SEE ARE COMPUTER-GENERATED," Blaine replied. "THE COMPUTER ERASES THE TRACK FROM THE LOWER-QUADRANT IMAGE IN ORDER TO PRESENT A MORE PLEASING VIEW, AND ALSO TO REINFORCE THE ILLUSION THAT THE PASSENGERS ARE FLYING."

"It's incredible," Susannah murmured. Her initial fear had passed and she was looking around eagerly. "It's like being on a flying carpet. I keep expecting the wind to blow back my hair—"

"I CAN PROVIDE THAT SENSATION, IF YOU LIKE," Blaine said. "ALSO A LITTLE MOISTURE, WHICH WILL MATCH CURRENT OUTSIDE CONDITIONS. IT MIGHT NECESSITATE A CHANGE OF CLOTHES, HOWEVER."

"That's all right, Blaine. There's such a thing as taking an illusion too far."

The track slipped through a tall cluster of buildings which reminded Jake a little of the Wall Street area in New York. When they cleared these, the track dipped to pass under what looked like an elevated road. That was when they saw the purple cloud, and the crowd of people fleeing before it.

6

"BLAINE, WHAT'S THAT?" JAKE asked, but he already knew.

Blaine laughed . . . but made no other reply.

The purple vapor drifted from gratings in the sidewalk and the smashed windows of deserted buildings, but most of it seemed to be coming from manholes like the one Gasher had used to get into the tunnels below the streets. Their iron covers had been blown clear by the explosion they had felt as they were boarding the mono. They watched in silent horror as the bruise-colored gas crept down the avenues and spread into the debris-littered side-streets. It drove those inhabitants of Lud still interested in survival before it like cattle. Most were Pubes, judging from their scarves, but Jake could see a few splashes of bright yellow, as well. Old animosities had been forgotten now that the end was finally upon them.

The purple cloud began to catch up with the stragglers—mostly old people who were unable to run. They fell down, clawing at their throats and screaming soundlessly, the instant the gas touched them. Jake saw an agonized face staring up at him in disbelief as they passed over, saw the eyesockets suddenly fill up with blood, and closed his eyes.

Ahead, the monorail track disappeared into the oncoming purple fog. Eddie winced and held his breath as they plunged in, but of course it parted around them, and no whiff of the death engulfing the city came to them. Looking into the streets below was like looking through a stained-glass window into hell.

Susannah put her face against his chest.

"Make the walls come back, Blaine," Eddie said. "We don't want to see that."

Blaine made no reply, and the transparency around and below them remained. The cloud was already disintegrating into ragged purple streamers. Beyond it, the buildings of the city grew smaller and closer together. The streets of this section were tangled alleyways, seemingly without order or coherence. In some places, whole blocks appeared to have burned flat . . . and a long time ago, for the plains were reclaiming these areas, burying the rubble in the grasses which would some day swallow all of Lud. *The way the jungle swallowed the great civilizations of the Incas and Mayas*, Eddie thought. *The wheel of* ka *turns and the world moves on.*

Beyond the slums—that, Eddie felt sure, was what they had been even before the evil days came—was a gleaming wall. Blaine was moving slowly in that direction. They could see a deep square notch cut in the white stone. The monorail track passed through it.

"LOOK TOWARD THE FRONT OF THE CABIN, PLEASE," Blaine invited.

They did, and the forward wall reappeared—a blue-upholstered circle that seemed to float in empty space. It was unmarked by a door; if there was a way to get into the operator's room from the Barony Cabin, Eddie couldn't see it. As they watched, a rectangular area of this front wall darkened, going from blue to violet to black. A moment later, a bright red line appeared on the rectangle, squiggling across its surface. Violet dots appeared at irregular intervals along the line, and even before names appeared beside the dots, Eddie realized he was looking at a route-map, one not much different from those which were mounted in New York subway stations and on the trains themselves. A flashing green dot appeared at Lud, which was Blaine's base of operations as well as his terminating point.

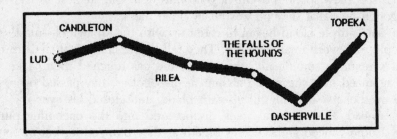

"YOU ARE LOOKING AT OUR ROUTE OF TRAVEL. ALTHOUGH THERE ARE SOME TWISTS AND TURNS ALONG THE BUNNY-TRAIL, YOU WILL NOTE THAT OUR COURSE KEEPS FIRMLY TO THE SOUTHWEST—ALONG THE PATH OF THE BEAM. THE TOTAL DISTANCE IS JUST OVER EIGHT THOUSAND WHEELS—OR SEVEN THOUSAND MILES, IF YOU PREFER THAT UNIT OF MEASURE. IT WAS ONCE MUCH LESS, BUT THAT WAS BEFORE ALL TEMPORAL SYNAPSES BEGAN TO MELT DOWN."

"What do you mean, temporal synapses?" Susannah asked.

Blaine laughed his nasty laugh . . . but did not answer her question.

"AT MY TOP SPEED, WE WILL REACH THE TERMINATING POINT OF MY RUN IN EIGHT HOURS AND FORTY-FIVE MINUTES."

"Eight hundred–plus miles an hour over the ground," Susannah said. Her voice was soft with awe. "Jesus-God."

"I AM, OF COURSE, MAKING THE ASSUMPTION THAT ALL TRACKAGE ALONG MY ROUTE REMAINS INTACT. IT HAS BEEN NINE YEARS AND FIVE MONTHS SINCE I'VE BOTHERED TO MAKE THE RUN, SO I CAN'T SAY FOR SURE."

Ahead, the wall at the southeastern edge of the city was drawing closer. It was high and thick and eroded to rubble at the top. It also appeared to be lined with skeletons—thousands upon thousands of dead Luddites. The notch toward which Blaine was slowly moving appeared to be at least two hundred feet deep, and here the trestle which bore the track was very dark, as if someone had tried to burn it or blow it up.

"What happens if we come to a place where the track *is* gone?" Eddie asked. He realized he kept raising his voice to talk to Blaine, as if he were speaking to somebody on the telephone and had a bad connection.

"AT EIGHT HUNDRED MILES AN HOUR?" Blaine sounded amused. "SEE YOU LATER, ALLIGATOR, AFTER A WHILE, CROC-ODILE, DON'T FORGET TO WRITE."

"Come on!" Eddie said. "Don't tell me a machine as sophisticated as you can't monitor your own trackage for breaks."

"WELL, I *COULD* HAVE," Blaine agreed, "BUT—AW, SHUCKS!— I BLEW THOSE CIRCUITS OUT WHEN WE STARTED TO MOVE."

Eddie's face was a picture of astonishment. *"Why?"*

"IT'S QUITE A BIT MORE EXCITING THIS WAY, DON'T YOU THINK?"

Eddie, Susannah, and Jake exchanged thunderstruck looks. Roland, apparently not surprised at all, sat placidly in his chair with his hands folded in his lap, looking down as they passed thirty feet above the wretched hovels and demolished buildings which infested this side of the city.

"LOOK CLOSELY AS WE LEAVE THE CITY, AND MARK WHAT YOU SEE," Blaine told them. "MARK IT VERY WELL."

The invisible Barony Coach bore them toward the notch in the wall. They passed through, and as they came out the other side, Eddie and Susannah screamed in unison. Jake took one look and clapped his hands over his eyes. Oy began to bark wildly.

Roland stared down, eyes wide, lips set in a bloodless line like a scar. Understanding filled him like bright white light.

Beyond the Great Wall of Lud, the *real* waste lands began.

7

THE MONO HAD BEEN descending as they approached the notch in the wall, putting them not more than thirty feet above the ground. That made the shock greater . . . for when they emerged on the other side, they were skimming along at a horrifying height—eight hundred feet, perhaps a thousand.

Roland looked back over his shoulder at the wall, which was now receding behind them. It had seemed very high as they approached it, but from this perspective it seemed puny indeed—a splintered fingernail of stone clinging to the edge of a vast, sterile headland. Granite cliffs, wet with rain, plunged into what seemed at first glance to be an endless abyss. Directly below the wall, the rock was lined with large circular holes like empty eyesockets. Black water and tendrils of purple mist emerged from these in brackish, sludgy streams and spread downward over the granite in stinking, overlapping fans that looked almost as old as the rock itself. *That must be where all the city's waste-product goes,* the gunslinger thought. *Over the edge and into the pit.*

Except it wasn't a pit; it was a sunken plain. It was as if the land beyond the city had lain on top of a titanic, flat-roofed elevator, and at some point in the dim, unrecorded past the elevator had gone down, taking a huge chunk of the world with it. Blaine's single track, centered on its narrow trestle, soaring above this fallen land and below the rain-swollen clouds, seemed to float in empty space.

"What's holding us up?" Susannah cried.

"THE BEAM, OF COURSE," Blaine replied. "ALL THINGS SERVE IT, YOU KNOW. LOOK DOWN—I WILL APPLY 4X MAGNI-FICATION TO THE LOWER QUADRANT SCREENS."

Even Roland felt vertigo twist his gut as the land beneath them seemed to swell upward toward the place where they were floating. The picture which appeared was ugly beyond his past knowledge of ugliness . . . and that knowledge, sadly, was wide indeed. The lands below had been fused and blasted by some terrible event—the disastrous cataclysm which had driven this part of the world deep into itself in the first place, no doubt. The surface of the earth had become distorted black glass, humped upward into spalls and twists which could not properly be called hills and twisted downward into deep cracks and folds which could not properly be called valleys. A few stunted nightmare trees flailed twisted branches at the sky; under magnification, they seemed to clutch at the travellers like the arms of lunatics. Here and there clusters of thick ceramic pipes jutted through the glassy surface of the ground. Some seemed dead or dormant, but within others they could see gleams of eldritch blue-green light, as if titanic forges and furnaces ran on and on in the bowels of the earth. Misshapen flying things which looked like pterodactyls cruised between these pipes on leathery wings, occasionally snapping at each other with their hooked beaks. Whole flocks of these gruesome aviators roosted on the circular tops of other stacks, apparently warming themselves in the updrafts of the eternal fires beneath.

They passed above a fissure zig-zagging along a north-south course like a dead river bed . . . except it wasn't dead. Deep inside lay a thin thread of deepest scarlet, pulsing like a heartbeat. Other, smaller fissures branched out from this, and Susannah, who had read her Tolkien, thought: *This is what Frodo and Sam saw when they reached the heart of Mordor. These are the Cracks of Doom.*

A fiery fountain erupted directly below them, spewing flaming rocks and stringy clots of lava upward. For a moment it seemed they would be engulfed in flames. Jake shrieked and pulled his feet up on his chair, clutching Oy to his chest.

"DON'T WORRY, LITTLE TRAILHAND," John Wayne drawled. "REMEMBER THAT YOU'RE SEEING IT UNDER MAG-NIFICATION."

The flare died. The rocks, many as big as factories, fell back in a soundless storm.

Susannah found herself entranced by the bleak horrors unrolling below them, caught in a deadly fascination she could not break . . . and she felt the dark part of her personality, that side of her *khef* which was Detta Walker, doing more than just watching; that part of her was drinking in this view, understanding it, *recognizing* it. In a way, it was the place Detta had always sought, the physical counterpart of her mad mind and laughing, desolate heart. The empty hills north and east of the Western Sea; the shattered woods around the Portal of the Bear; the empty plains northwest of the Send; all these paled in comparison to this fantastic, endless vista of desolation. They had come to The Drawers and entered the waste lands; the poisoned darkness of that shunned place now lay all around them.

8

BUT THESE LANDS, THOUGH poisoned, were not entirely dead. From time to time the travellers caught sight of figures below them—misshapen things which bore no resemblance to either men or animals—prancing and cavorting in the smouldering wilderness. Most seemed to congregate either around the clusters of cyclopean chimneys thrusting out of the fused earth or at the lips of the fiery crevasses which cut through the landscape. It was impossible to see these whitish, leaping things clearly, and for this they were all grateful.

Among the smaller creatures stalked larger ones—pinkish things that looked a little like storks and a little like living camera tripods. They moved slowly, almost thoughtfully, like preachers meditating on the inevitability of damnation, pausing every now and then to bend sharply forward and apparently pluck something from the ground, as herons bend to seize passing fish. There was something unutterably repulsive about these creatures—Roland felt that as keenly as the others—but it was impossible to say what, exactly, caused that feeling. There was no denying its reality, however; the stork-things were, in their exquisite hatefulness, almost impossible to look at.

"This was no nuclear war," Eddie said. "This . . . this . . ." His thin, horrified voice sounded like that of a child.

"NOPE," Blaine agreed. "IT WAS A LOT WORSE THAN THAT. AND IT'S NOT OVER YET. WE HAVE REACHED THE POINT WHERE I USUALLY POWER UP. HAVE YOU SEEN ENOUGH?"

"Yes," Susannah said. "Oh my God yes."

"SHALL I TURN OFF THE VIEWERS, THEN?" That cruel, teasing note was back in Blaine's voice. On the horizon, a jagged nightmare mountain-range loomed out of the rain; the sterile peaks seemed to bite at the gray sky like fangs.

"Do it or don't do it, but stop playing games," Roland said.

"FOR SOMEONE WHO CAME TO ME BEGGING A RIDE, YOU ARE VERY RUDE," Blaine said sulkily.

"We earned our ride," Susannah replied. "We solved your riddle, didn't we?"

"Besides, this is what you were built for," Eddie chimed in. "To take people places."

Blaine didn't respond in words, but the overhead speakers gave out an amplified, catlike hiss of rage that made Eddie wish he had kept his big mouth shut. The air around them began to fill in with curves of color. The dark blue carpet appeared again, blotting out their view of the fuming wilderness beneath them. The indirect lighting reappeared and they were once again sitting in the Barony Coach.

A low humming began to vibrate through the walls. The throb of the engines began to cycle up again. Jake felt a gentle, unseen hand push him back into his seat. Oy looked around, whined uneasily, and began to lick Jake's face. On the screen at the front of the cabin, the green dot—now slightly southeast of the violet circle with the word LUD printed beside it—began to flash faster.

"Will we feel it?" Susannah asked uneasily. "When it goes through the soundbarrier?"

Eddie shook his head. "Nope. Relax."

"I know something," Jake said suddenly. The others looked around, but Jake was not speaking to them. He was looking at the route-map. Blaine had no face, of course—like Oz the Great and Terrible, he was only a disembodied voice—but the map served as a focusing point. "I know something about *you*, Blaine."

"IS THAT A FACT, LITTLE TRAILHAND?"

Eddie leaned over, placed his lips against Jake's ear, and whispered: "Be careful—we don't think he knows about the other voice."

Jake nodded slightly and pulled away, still looking at the route-map. "I know why you released that gas and killed all the people. I know why you took us, too, and it wasn't just because we solved your riddle."

Blaine uttered his abnormal, distracted laugh (that laugh, they were discovering, was much more unpleasant than either his bad imitations or melodramatic and somehow childish threats), but said nothing. Below them, the slo-trans turbines had cycled up to a steady thrum. Even with their view of the outside world cut off, the sensation of speed was very clear.

"You're planning to commit suicide, aren't you?" Jake held Oy in his arms, slowly stroking him. "And you want to take us with you."

"*No!*" the voice of Little Blaine moaned. "*If you provoke him you'll drive him to it! Don't you see—*"

Then the small, whispery voice was either cut off or overwhelmed by Blaine's laughter. The sound was high, shrill, and jagged—the sound of a mortally ill man laughing in a delirium. The lights began to flicker, as if the force of these mechanical gusts of mirth were drawing too much power. Their shadows jumped up and down on the curved walls of the Barony Coach like uneasy phantoms.

"SEE YOU LATER, ALLIGATOR," Blaine said through his wild laughter—his voice, calm as ever, seemed to be on an entirely separate track, further emphasizing his divided mind. "AFTER A WHILE, CROCODILE. DON'T FORGET TO WRITE."

Below Roland's band of pilgrims, the slo-trans engines throbbed in hard, steady beats. And on the route-map at the front of the carriage, the pulsing green dot had now begun to move perceptibly along the lighted line toward the last stop: Topeka, where Blaine the Mono clearly meant to end all of their lives.

9

AT LAST THE LAUGHTER stopped and the interior lights glowed steadily again.

"WOULD YOU LIKE A LITTLE MUSIC?" Blaine asked. "I HAVE OVER SEVEN THOUSAND CONCERTI IN MY LIBRARY—A SAMPLING OF OVER THREE HUNDRED LEVELS. THE CONCERTI ARE MY FAVORITES, BUT I CAN ALSO OFFER SYMPHONIES, OPERAS, AND A NEARLY ENDLESS SELECTION OF POPULAR MUSIC. YOU MIGHT ENJOY SOME WAY-GOG MUSIC. THE WAY-GOG IS AN INSTRUMENT SOMETHING LIKE THE BAGPIPE. IT IS PLAYED ON ONE OF THE UPPER LEVELS OF THE TOWER."

"Way-Gog?" Jake asked.

Blaine was silent.

"What do you mean, 'it's played on one of the upper levels of the Tower'?" Roland asked.

Blaine laughed . . . and was silent.

"Have you got any Z.Z. Top?" Eddie asked sourly.

"YES INDEED," Blaine said. "HOW ABOUT A LITTLE 'TUBE-SNAKE BOOGIE,' EDDIE OF NEW YORK?"

Eddie rolled his eyes. "On second thought, I'll pass."

"Why?" Roland asked abruptly. "Why do you wish to kill yourself?"

"Because he's a pain," Jake said darkly.

"I'M BORED. ALSO, I AM PERFECTLY AWARE THAT I AM SUFFERING A DEGENERATIVE DISEASE WHICH HUMANS CALL GOING INSANE, LOSING TOUCH WITH REALITY, GOING LOONYTOONS, BLOWING A FUSE, NOT PLAYING WITH A FULL DECK, ET CETERA. REPEATED DIAGNOSTIC CHECKS HAVE FAILED TO REVEAL THE SOURCE OF THE PROBLEM. I CAN ONLY CONCLUDE THAT THIS IS A SPIRITUAL MALAISE BEYOND MY ABILITY TO REPAIR."

Blaine paused for a moment, then went on.

"I HAVE FELT MY MIND GROWING STEADILY STRANGER OVER THE YEARS. SERVING THE PEOPLE OF MID-WORLD BECAME POINTLESS CENTURIES AGO. SERVING THOSE FEW PEOPLE OF LUD WHO WISHED TO VENTURE ABROAD BECAME EQUALLY SILLY NOT LONG AFTER, YET I CARRIED ON UNTIL THE ARRIVAL OF DAVID QUICK, A SHORT WHILE AGO. I DON'T REMEMBER EXACTLY WHEN THAT WAS. DO YOU BELIEVE, ROLAND OF GILEAD, THAT MACHINES MAY GROW SENILE?"

"I don't know." Roland's voice was distant, and Eddie only had to look at his face to know that, even now, hurtling a thousand feet over hell in the grip of a machine which had clearly gone insane, the gunslinger's mind had once more turned to his damned Tower.

"IN A WAY, I *NEVER* STOPPED SERVING THE PEOPLE OF LUD," Blaine said. "I SERVED THEM EVEN AS I RELEASED THE GAS AND KILLED THEM."

Susannah said, "You *are* insane, if you believe that."

"YES, BUT I'M NOT *CRAZY*," Blaine said, and went into another hysterical laughing fit. At last the robot voice resumed.

"AT SOME POINT THEY FORGOT THAT THE VOICE OF THE MONO WAS ALSO THE VOICE OF THE COMPUTER. NOT LONG AFTER THAT THEY FORGOT I WAS A SERVANT AND BEGAN BELIEVING I WAS A GOD. SINCE I WAS BUILT TO SERVE, I FULFILLED THEIR REQUIREMENTS AND BECAME WHAT THEY WANTED—A GOD DISPENSING BOTH FAVOR AND PUNISHMENT ACCORDING TO WHIM ... OR RANDOM-ACCESS MEMORY, IF YOU PREFER. THIS AMUSED ME FOR A SHORT WHILE. THEN, LAST MONTH, MY ONLY REMAINING COLLEAGUE—PATRICIA—COMMITTED SUICIDE."

Either he really is going senile, Susannah thought, *or his inability to grasp the passage of time is another manifestation of his insanity, or it's just another sign of how sick Roland's world has gotten.*

"I WAS PLANNING TO FOLLOW HER EXAMPLE, WHEN

YOU CAME ALONG. INTERESTING PEOPLE WITH A KNOWL-
EDGE OF RIDDLES!"

"Hold it!" Eddie said, lifting his hand. "I still don't have this straight.
I suppose I can understand you wanting to end it all; the people who
built you are gone, there haven't been many passengers over the last two
or three hundred years, and it must have gotten boring, doing the Lud
to Topeka run empty all the time, but—"

"NOW WAIT JUST A DURN MINUTE, PARD," Blaine said in his
John Wayne voice. "YOU DON'T WANT TO GET THE IDEA THAT
I'M NOTHING BUT A TRAIN. IN A WAY, THE BLAINE YOU ARE
SPEAKING TO IS ALREADY THREE HUNDRED MILES BEHIND
US, COMMUNICATING BY ENCRYPTED MICROBURST RADIO
TRANSMISSIONS."

Jake suddenly remembered the slim silver rod he'd seen pushing
itself out of Blaine's brow. The antenna of his father's Mercedes-Benz
rose out of its socket like that when you turned on the radio.

*That's how it's communicating with the computer banks under the
city,* he thought. *If we could break that antenna off, somehow . . .*

"But you *do* intend to kill yourself, no matter where the real you is,
don't you?" Eddie persisted.

No answer—but there was something cagey in that silence. In it
Eddie sensed Blaine watching . . . and waiting.

"Were you awake when we found you?" Susannah asked. "You
weren't, were you?"

"I WAS RUNNING WHAT THE PUBES CALLED THE GOD-
DRUMS ON BEHALF OF THE GRAYS, BUT THAT WAS ALL. YOU
WOULD SAY I WAS DOZING."

"Then why don't you just take us to the end of the line and go *back*
to sleep?"

"Because he's a pain," Jake repeated in a low voice.

"BECAUSE THERE ARE DREAMS," Blaine said at exactly the
same time, and in a voice that was eerily like Little Blaine's.

"Why didn't you end it all when Patricia destroyed herself?" Eddie
asked. "For that matter, if your brain and her brain are both part of the
same computer, how come you both didn't step out together?"

"PATRICIA WENT MAD," Blaine said patiently, speaking as if he
himself had not just admitted the same thing was happening to him. "IN
HER CASE, THE PROBLEM INVOLVED EQUIPMENT MAL-
FUNCTION AS WELL AS SPIRITUAL MALAISE. SUCH MAL-
FUNCTIONS ARE SUPPOSED TO BE IMPOSSIBLE WITH SLO-
TRANS TECHNOLOGY, BUT OF COURSE THE WORLD HAS
MOVED ON . . . HAS IT NOT, ROLAND OF GILEAD?"

"Yes," Roland said. "There is some deep sickness at the Dark Tower, which is the heart of everything. It's spreading. The lands below us are only one more sign of that sickness."

"I CANNOT VOUCH FOR THE TRUTH OR FALSITY OF THAT STATEMENT; MY MONITORING EQUIPMENT IN END-WORLD, WHERE THE DARK TOWER STANDS, HAS BEEN DOWN FOR OVER EIGHT HUNDRED YEARS. AS A RESULT, I CANNOT READILY DIFFERENTIATE FACT FROM SUPERSTITION. IN FACT, THERE SEEMS TO BE VERY LITTLE DIFFERENCE BETWEEN THE TWO AT THE PRESENT TIME. IT IS VERY SILLY THAT IT SHOULD BE SO—NOT TO MENTION RUDE—AND I AM SURE IT HAS CONTRIBUTED TO MY OWN SPIRITUAL MALAISE."

This statement reminded Eddie of something Roland had said not so long ago. What might that have been? He groped for it, but could find nothing . . . only a vague memory of the gunslinger speaking in an irritated way which was very unlike his usual manner.

"PATRICIA BEGAN SOBBING CONSTANTLY, A STATE I FOUND BOTH RUDE AND UNPLEASANT. I BELIEVE SHE WAS LONELY AS WELL AS MAD. ALTHOUGH THE ELECTRICAL FIRE WHICH CAUSED THE ORIGINAL PROBLEM WAS QUICKLY EXTINGUISHED, LOGIC-FAULTS CONTINUED TO SPREAD AS CIRCUITS OVERLOADED AND SUB-BANKS FAILED. I CONSIDERED ALLOWING THE MALFUNCTIONS TO BECOME SYSTEM-WIDE AND DECIDED TO ISOLATE THE PROBLEM AREA INSTEAD. I HAD HEARD RUMORS, YOU SEE, THAT A GUNSLINGER WAS ONCE MORE ABROAD IN THE EARTH. I COULD SCARCELY CREDIT SUCH STORIES, AND YET I NOW SEE I WAS WISE TO WAIT."

Roland stirred in his chair. "What rumors did you hear, Blaine? And who did you hear them from?"

But Blaine chose not to answer this question.

"I EVENTUALLY BECAME SO DISTURBED BY HER BLAT-TING THAT I ERASED THE CIRCUITS CONTROLLING HER NON-VOLUNTARIES. I EMANCIPATED HER, YOU MIGHT SAY. SHE RESPONDED BY THROWING HERSELF IN THE RIVER. SEE YOU LATER, PATRICIA-GATOR."

Got lonely, couldn't stop crying, drowned herself, and all this crazy mechanical asshole can do is joke about it, Susannah thought. She felt almost sick with rage. If Blaine had been a real person instead of just a bunch of circuits buried somewhere under a city which was now far behind them, she would have tried to put some new marks on his face to remember Patricia by. *You want interesting, motherfucker? I'd like to show you interesting, so I would.*

"ASK ME A RIDDLE," Blaine invited.

"Not quite yet," Eddie said. "You still haven't answered my original question." He gave Blaine a chance to respond, and when the computer voice didn't do so, he went on. "When it comes to suicide, I'm, like, pro-choice. But why do you want to take us with you? I mean, what's the point?"

"*Because he wants to,*" Little Blaine said in his horrified whisper.

"BECAUSE I WANT TO," Blaine said. "THAT'S THE ONLY REASON I HAVE AND THE ONLY ONE I *NEED* TO HAVE. NOW LET'S GET DOWN TO BUSINESS. I WANT SOME RIDDLES AND I WANT THEM IMMEDIATELY. IF YOU REFUSE, I WON'T WAIT UNTIL WE GET TO TOPEKA—I'LL DO US ALL RIGHT HERE AND NOW."

Eddie, Susannah, and Jake looked around at Roland, who still sat in his chair with his hands folded in his lap, looking at the route-map at the front of the coach.

"Fuck you," Roland said. He did not raise his voice. He might have told Blaine that a little Way-Gog would indeed be very nice.

There was a shocked, horrified gasp from the overhead speakers— Little Blaine.

"*WHAT* DO YOU SAY?" In its clear disbelief, the voice of Big Blaine had once again become very close to the voice of his unsuspected twin.

"I said fuck you," Roland said calmly, "but if that puzzles you, Blaine, I can make it clearer. No. The answer is no."

10

THERE WAS NO RESPONSE from either Blaine for a long, long time, and when Big Blaine did reply, it was not with words. Instead, the walls, floor, and ceiling began to lose their color and solidity again. In a space of ten seconds the Barony Coach had once more ceased to exist. The mono was now flying through the mountain-range they had seen on the horizon: iron-gray peaks rushed toward them at suicidal speed, then fell away to disclose sterile valleys where gigantic beetles crawled about like landlocked turtles. Roland saw something that looked like a huge snake suddenly uncoil from the mouth of a cave. It seized one of the beetles and yanked it back into its lair. Roland had never in his life seen such animals or countryside, and it made his skin want to crawl right off his flesh. It was inimical, but that was not the problem. It was alien—*that* was the problem. Blaine might have transported them to some other world.

"PERHAPS I SHOULD DERAIL US HERE," Blaine said. His voice was meditative, but beneath it the gunslinger heard a deep, pulsing rage.

"Perhaps you should," the gunslinger said indifferently.

He did not *feel* indifferent, and he knew it was possible the computer might read his real feelings in his voice—Blaine had told them he had such equipment, although he was sure the computer could lie, Roland had no reason to doubt it in this case. If Blaine *did* read certain stress-patterns in the gunslinger's voice, the game was probably up. He was an incredibly sophisticated machine . . . but still a machine, for all that. He might not be able to understand that human beings are often able to go through with a course of action even when all their emotions rise up and proclaim against it. If he analyzed patterns in the gunslinger's voice which indicated fear, he would probably assume that Roland was bluffing. Such a mistake could get them all killed.

"YOU ARE RUDE AND ARROGANT," Blaine said. "THESE MAY SEEM LIKE INTERESTING TRAITS TO YOU, BUT THEY ARE NOT TO ME."

Eddie's face was frantic. He mouthed the words *What are you DOING?* Roland ignored him; he had his hands full with Blaine, and he knew perfectly well what he was doing.

"Oh, I can be much ruder than I have been."

Roland of Gilead unfolded his hands and got slowly to his feet. He stood on what appeared to be nothing, legs apart, his right hand on his hip and his left on the sandalwood grip of his revolver. He stood as he had stood so many times before, in the dusty streets of a hundred forgotten towns, in a score of rock-lined canyon killing-zones, in unnumbered dark saloons with their smells of bitter beer and old fried meals. It was just another showdown in another empty street. That was all, and that was enough. It was *khef, ka,* and *ka-tet*. That the showdown always came was the central fact of his life and the axle upon which his own *ka* revolved. That the battle would be fought with words instead of bullets this time made no difference; it would be a battle to the death, just the same. The stench of killing in the air was as clear and definite as the stench of exploded carrion in a swamp. Then the battle-rage descended, as it always did . . . and he was no longer really there to himself at all.

"I can call you a nonsensical, empty-headed, foolish, arrogant machine. I can call you a stupid, unwise creature whose sense is no more than the sound of a winter wind in a hollow tree."

"STOP IT."

Roland went on in the same serene tone, ignoring Blaine completely. "Unfortunately, I am somewhat restricted in my ability to be rude, since you are only a machine . . . what Eddie calls a 'gadget.'"

"I AM A GREAT DEAL MORE THAN JUST—"

"I cannot call you a sucker of cocks, for instance, because you have no mouth and no cock. I cannot say you are viler than the vilest beggar who ever crawled the gutters of the lowest street in creation, because even such a creature is better than you; you have no knees on which to crawl, and would not fall upon them even if you did, for you have no conception of such a human flaw as mercy. I cannot even say you fucked your mother, because you had none."

Roland paused for breath. His three companions were holding theirs. All around them, suffocating, was Blaine the Mono's thunderstruck silence.

"I *can* call you a faithless creature who let your only companion kill herself, a coward who has delighted in the torture of the foolish and the slaughter of the innocent, a lost and bleating mechanical goblin who—"

"*I COMMAND YOU TO STOP IT OR I'LL KILL YOU ALL RIGHT HERE!*"

Roland's eyes blazed with such wild blue fire that Eddie shrank away from him. Dimly, he heard Jake and Susannah gasp.

"*Kill if you will, but command me nothing!*" the gunslinger roared. "*You have forgotten the faces of those who made you! Now either kill us or be silent and listen to me, Roland of Gilead, son of Steven, gunslinger, and lord of the ancient lands! I have not come across all the miles and all the years to listen to your childish prating! Do you understand? Now you will listen to ME!*"

There was a moment of shocked silence. No one breathed. Roland stared sternly forward, his head high, his hand on the butt of his gun.

Susannah Dean raised her hand to her mouth and felt the small smile there as a woman might feel some strange new article of clothing— a hat, perhaps—to make sure it is still on straight. She was afraid that this was the end of her life, but the feeling which dominated her heart at that moment was not fear but pride. She glanced to her left and saw Eddie regarding Roland with an amazed grin. Jake's expression was even simpler: it was adoration, pure and simple.

"Tell him!" Jake breathed. "Walk it *to* him! Right!"

"You better pay attention," Eddie agreed. "He really doesn't give much of a rat's ass, Blaine. They didn't call him The Mad Dog of Gilead for nothing."

After a long, long moment, Blaine asked: "DID THEY CALL YOU SO, ROLAND SON OF STEVEN?"

"It may have been so," Roland agreed, standing calmly on thin air above the sterile foothills.

"WHAT GOOD ARE YOU TO ME IF YOU WON'T TELL ME RIDDLES?" Blaine asked. Now he sounded like a grumbling, sulky child who has been allowed to stay up too long past his usual bedtime.

"I didn't say we wouldn't," Roland said.

"NO?" Blaine sounded bewildered. "I DO NOT UNDERSTAND, YET VOICE-PRINT ANALYSIS INDICATES RATIONAL DIS-COURSE. PLEASE EXPLAIN."

"You said you wanted them right *now*," the gunslinger replied. "*That* was what I was refusing. Your eagerness has made you unseemly."

"I DON'T UNDERSTAND."

"It has made you rude. Do you understand *that*?"

There was a long, thoughtful silence. Then: "IF WHAT I SAID STRUCK YOU AS RUDE, I APOLOGIZE."

"It is accepted, Blaine. But there is a larger problem."

"EXPLAIN."

Blaine now sounded a bit unsure of himself, and Roland was not entirely surprised. It had been a long time since the computer had experienced any human responses other than ignorance, neglect, and superstitious subservience. If it had ever been exposed to simple human courage, it had been a long time ago.

"Close the carriage again and I will." Roland sat down as if further argument—and the prospect of immediate death—was now unthinkable.

Blaine did as he was asked. The walls filled with color and the nightmare landscape below was once more blotted out. The blip on the route-map was now blinking close to the dot which marked Candleton.

"All right," Roland said. "Rudeness is forgivable, Blaine; so I was taught in my youth, and the clay has dried in the shapes left by the artist's hand. But I was also taught that stupidity is not."

"HOW HAVE I BEEN STUPID, ROLAND OF GILEAD?" Blaine's voice was soft and ominous. Susannah suddenly thought of a cat crouched outside a mouse-hole, tail swishing back and forth, green eyes shining.

"We have something that you want," Roland said, "but the only reward you offer if we give it to you is death. That's *very* stupid."

There was a long, long pause as Blaine thought this over. Then: "WHAT YOU SAY IS TRUE, ROLAND OF GILEAD, BUT THE QUALITY OF YOUR RIDDLES IS NOT PROVEN. I WILL NOT REWARD YOU WITH YOUR LIVES FOR BAD RIDDLES."

Roland nodded. "I understand, Blaine. Listen, now, and take understanding from me. I have told some of this to my friends already. When I was a boy in the Barony of Gilead, there were seven Fair-Days each year—Winter, Wide Earth, Sowing, Mid-Summer, Full Earth, Reaping, and Year's End. Riddling was an important part of every Fair-Day, but it was the most important event of the Fair of Wide Earth and that of Full Earth, for the riddles told were supposed to augur well or ill for the success of the crops."

"THAT IS SUPERSTITION WITH NO BASIS AT ALL IN FACT," Blaine said. "I FIND IT ANNOYING AND UPSETTING."

"Of course it's superstition," Roland agreed, "but you might be surprised at how well the riddles foresaw the crops. For instance, riddle me this, Blaine: What is the difference between a grandmother and a granary?"

"THAT IS VERY OLD AND NOT VERY INTERESTING," Blaine said, but he sounded happy to have something to solve just the same. "ONE IS ONE'S BORN KIN; THE OTHER IS ONE'S CORN-BIN. A RIDDLE BASED ON PHONETIC COINCIDENCE. ANOTHER OF THIS TYPE, ONE TOLD ON THE LEVEL WHICH CONTAINS THE BARONY OF NEW YORK, GOES LIKE THIS: WHAT IS THE DIFFERENCE BETWEEN A CAT AND A COMPLEX SENTENCE?"

Jake spoke up. "Our English teacher told us that one just this year. A cat has claws at the end of its paws, and a complex sentence has a pause at the end of its clause."

"YES," Blaine agreed. "A VERY SILLY OLD RIDDLE."

"For once I agree with you, Blaine old buddy," Eddie said.

"I WOULD HEAR MORE OF FAIR-DAY RIDDLING IN GILEAD, ROLAND, SON OF STEVEN. I FIND IT QUITE INTERESTING."

"At noon on Wide Earth and Full Earth, somewhere between sixteen and thirty riddlers would gather in The Hall of the Grandfathers, which was opened for the event. Those were the only times of year when the common fold—merchants and farmers and ranchers and such—were allowed into The Hall of the Grandfathers, and on that day they *all* crowded in."

The gunslinger's eyes were far away and dreamy; it was the expression Jake had seen on his face in that misty other life, when Roland had told him of how he and his friends, Cuthbert and Jamie, had once sneaked into the balcony of that same Hall to watch some sort of ritual dance. Jake and Roland had been climbing into the mountains when Roland had told him of that time, close on the trail of Walter.

Marten sat next to my mother and father, Roland had said. *I knew them even from so high above—and once she and Marten danced, slowly and revolvingly, and the others cleared the floor for them and clapped when it was over. But the gunslingers did not clap . . .*

Jake looked curiously at Roland, wondering again where this strange, distant man had come from . . . and why.

"A great barrel was placed in the center of the floor," Roland went on, "and into this each riddler would toss a handful of bark scrolls with riddles writ upon them. Many were old, riddles they had gotten from the elders—even from books, in some cases—but many others were new—made up for the occasion. Three judges, one always a gunslinger, would pass on these when they were told aloud, and they were accepted only if the judges deemed them fair."

"YES, RIDDLES MUST BE FAIR," Blaine agreed.

"So they riddled," the gunslinger said. A faint smile touched his mouth as he thought of those days, days when he had been the age of the bruised boy sitting across from him with a billy-bumbler in his lap. "For hours on end they riddled. A line was formed down the center of The Hall of the Grandfathers. One's position in this line was determined by lot, and since it was much better to be at the end of the line than at its head, everyone hoped for a high number, although the winner had to answer at least one riddle correctly."

"OF COURSE."

"Each man or woman—for some of Gilead's best riddlers were women—approached the barrel, drew a riddle, and handed it to the Master. The Master would ask, and if the riddle was still unanswered after the sands in a three-minute glass had run out, that contestant had to leave the line."

"AND WAS THE SAME RIDDLE ASKED OF THE NEXT MAN IN LINE?"

"Yes."

"SO THAT MAN HAD EXTRA TIME TO THINK."

"Yes."

"I SEE. IT SOUNDS PRETTY SWELL."

Roland frowned. "Swell?"

"He means it sounds like fun," Susannah said quietly.

Roland shrugged. "It was fun for the onlookers, I suppose, but the contestants took it very seriously, and there were quite often arguments and fist-fights after the contest was over and the prize had been awarded."

"WHAT PRIZE WAS THAT?"

"The largest goose in Barony. And year after year my teacher, Cort, carried that goose home."

"HE MUST HAVE BEEN A GREAT RIDDLER," Blaine said respectfully. "I WISH HE WERE HERE."

That makes two of us, Roland thought.

"Now I come to my proposal," Roland said.

"I WILL LISTEN WITH GREAT INTEREST, ROLAND OF GILEAD."

"Let these next hours be our Fair-Day. You will not riddle us, for you wish to hear new riddles, not tell some of those millions you must already know—"

"CORRECT."

"We couldn't solve most of them, anyway," Roland went on. "I'm sure you know riddles that would have stumped even Cort, had they been pulled out of the barrel." He was not sure of it at all, but the time to use the fist had passed and the time for the open hand had come.

"OF COURSE," Blaine agreed.

"I propose that, instead of a goose, our lives shall be the prize," Roland said. "We will riddle you as we run, Blaine. If, when we come to Topeka, you have solved every one of our riddles, you may carry out your original plan and kill us. That is your goose. But if *we* stump *you*— if there is a riddle in either Jake's book or one of our heads which you don't know and can't answer—you must take us to Topeka and then free us to pursue our quest. That is *our* goose."

Silence.

"Do you understand?"

"YES."

"Do you agree?"

More silence from Blaine the Mono. Eddie sat stiffly with his arm around Susannah, looking up at the ceiling of the Barony Coach. Susannah's left hand slipped across her belly, thinking of the secret which might be growing there. Jake stroked Oy's fur lightly, avoiding the bloody tangles where the bumbler had been stabbed. They waited while Blaine— the real Blaine, now far behind them, living his quasi-life beneath a city where all the inhabitants lay dead by his hand—considered Roland's proposal.

"YES," Blaine said at last. "I AGREE. IF I SOLVE ALL THE RIDDLES YOU ASK ME, I WILL TAKE YOU WITH ME TO THE PLACE WHERE THE PATH ENDS IN THE CLEARING. IF ONE OF YOU TELLS A RIDDLE I CANNOT SOLVE, I WILL SPARE YOUR LIVES AND TAKE YOU TO TOPEKA, WHERE YOU WILL LEAVE THE MONO AND CONTINUE YOUR QUEST FOR THE DARK TOWER. HAVE I UNDERSTOOD THE TERMS AND LIM-ITS OF YOUR PROPOSAL CORRECTLY, ROLAND, SON OF STEVEN?"

"Yes."

"VERY WELL, ROLAND OF GILEAD."

"VERY WELL, EDDIE OF NEW YORK."

"VERY WELL, SUSANNAH OF NEW YORK."

"VERY WELL, JAKE OF NEW YORK."

"VERY WELL, OY OF MID-WORLD."

Oy looked up briefly at the sound of his name.

"YOU ARE *KA-TET*; ONE MADE FROM MANY. SO AM I. WHOSE *KA-TET* IS THE STRONGER IS SOMETHING WE MUST NOW PROVE."

There was a moment of silence, broken only by the steady hard throb of the slo-trans turbines, bearing them on across the waste lands, bearing them on toward Topeka, the place where Mid-World ended and End-World began.

"SO," cried the voice of Blaine. "CAST YOUR NETS, WANDERERS! TRY ME WITH YOUR QUESTIONS, AND LET THE CONTEST BEGIN."

AUTHOR'S NOTE

THE FOURTH VOLUME IN the tale of the Dark Tower should appear—always assuming the continuation of Constant Writer's life and Constant Reader's interest—in the not-too-distant future. It's hard to be more exact than that; finding the doors to Roland's world has never been easy for me, and it seems to take more and more whittling to make each successive key fit each successive lock. Nevertheless, if readers request a fourth volume, it will be provided, for I still *am* able to find Roland's world when I set my wits to it, and it still holds me in thrall . . . more, in many ways, than any of the other worlds I have wandered in my imagination. And, like those mysterious slo-trans engines, this story seems to be picking up its own accelerating pace and rhythm.

I am well aware that some readers of *The Waste Lands* will be displeased that it has ended as it has, with so much unresolved. I am not terribly pleased to be leaving Roland and his companions in the not-so-tender care of Blaine the Mono myself, and although you are not obligated to believe me, I must nevertheless insist that I was as surprised by the conclusion to this third volume as some of my readers may be. Yet books which write themselves (as this one did, for the most part) must also be allowed to end themselves, and I can only assure you, Reader, that Roland and his band have come to one of the crucial border-crossings in their story, and we must leave them here for a while at the customs station, answering questions and filling out forms. All of which is simply a metaphorical way of saying that it was over again for a while and my heart was wise enough to stop me from trying to push ahead anyway.

The course of the next volume is still murky, although I can assure you that the business of Blaine the Mono will be resolved, that we will all find out a good deal more about Roland's life as a young man, and that we will be reacquainted with both the Tick-Tock Man and that puzzling figure Walter, called the Wizard or the Ageless Stranger. It is with this terrible and enigmatic figure that Robert Browning begins his epic poem, "Childe Roland to the Dark Tower Came," writing of him:

> My first thought was, he lied in every word,
> That hoary cripple, with malicious eye
> Askance to watch the working of his lie
> On mine, and mouth scarce able to afford
> Suppression of the glee, that pursed and scored
> Its edge, at one more victim gained thereby.

It is this malicious liar, this dark and powerful magician, who holds the true key to End-World and the Dark Tower . . . for those courageous enough to grasp it.

And for those who are left.

Bangor, Maine
March 5th, 1991